P9-CCO-745

ALSO BY FANNIE FLAGG

Daisy Fay and the Miracle Man
(originally published as *Coming Attractions*)

Fried Green Tomatoes at the Whistle Stop Cafe

Fannie Flagg's Original Whistle Stop Cafe Cookbook

Welcome to the World, Baby Girl!

STANDING IN THE RAINBOW

STANDING IN THE RAINBOW

A NOVEL

Fannie Flagg

RANDOM HOUSE
NEW YORK

 Published in the United States by Random House, Inc., New York, and simultaneously in Canada by Random House of Canada Limited, Toronto.

ISBN 0-679-42615-9
Printed in the United States of America
Book design by Victoria Wong

For Eudora Welty and Willie Morris

STANDING IN THE RAINBOW

To the Public at Large:

As a character in this book I can tell you that everything in it really did happen, so I can highly recommend it without any qualms whatsoever. Although I am not the main character in this book, I will tell you this much: I own my own house, keep it clean, and I pay my taxes. I've never been to jail and I am most probably older than you are unless you have one foot in the grave and in that case, Hello, friend.

I do not claim to be a professional critic but I like a book with a beginning, a middle, and an end and hopefully a plot and a few laughs in between. I hate a book that jumps around. Also I can promise you, this is not one of those personal tell-alls that will bore you to death by talking about how wonderful somebody is now, how bad they used to be but then got saved and now they are wonderful again. And as of this morning I have not gone addlebrained like my neighbor Mrs. Whatley, who thinks her grandson Travis is still working in the tire department over at Sears instead of where he really is and will be for the next five years unless he gets off for good behavior. But I am not one to carry gossip. I cannot afford to in my business. Believe it or not, I still work for a living although I sometimes wonder why because with all the taxes I pay I could just as well stay home and collect my benefits and do just as good but when I don't fix hair for a few days my fingers get all itchy. Besides I have to go in and try to make sure my daughter does not ruin another customer's hair (a few hairs fall out and they want to sue) or burn the place down again. Also I need the money. I am still paying on my car that Dwayne Jr. wrecked, not once but twice in six months.

I cannot depend on my children but that's another story. Enough said. You get the picture. I have a lot of nervous energy but I am not perky. There is nothing worse than a perky old person. It is not natural. Although I am not a main character, being in a book has made me stop and think. So before I get myself out of the way and let you start, I will say this: people's lives are sure ruled by a lot of what-ifs, aren't they? For example, on a personal note . . . what if I had died giving birth to Dwayne Jr. (not an unpleasant thought, considering recent events)? I would not even be here, but more important to the story you are about to read, what if Dorothy Smith had never met the Oatman Family Gospel Singers? What if Betty Raye Oatman had never even met Hamm Sparks? What if Hamm Sparks had not met up with foul play? Oh, I could go on and on but I won't. I hate when somebody tells me how something ends. And a word to the wise: don't be like me and skip to the last page. I have ruined many a book doing just that. As I said before, I am only included in the story every once in a while but after you finish, I'll bet you dollars to doughnuts you will wonder how I have managed to wind up as good-natured as I have.

Sincerely,
Mrs. Tot Whooten

P.S. Don't ever marry a man that drinks.

THE BEGINNING

THE PLACE:
SOUTHERN MISSOURI

THE TIME: THE 1940s

THE MOOD: HOPEFUL

Elmwood Springs

Almost everyone in town that had an extra room took in a boarder. There were no apartment buildings or hotels as of yet. The Howard Johnson was built a few years later but in the meantime bachelors needed to be looked after and single women certainly had to have a respectable place to live. Most people considered it their Christian duty to take them in whether they needed the few extra dollars a week or not, and some of the boarders stayed on for years. Mr. Pruiet, a bachelor from Kentucky with long thin feet, boarded with the Haygoods so long that they eventually forgot he was not family. Whenever they moved, he moved. When he finally did die at seventy-eight, he was buried in the Haygood family plot with a headstone that read:

The homes on First Avenue North were located within walking distance of town and school and were where most of the town's boarders lived.

At present the Smith family's boarder is Jimmy Head, the short-order cook at the Trolley Car Diner; the Robinsons next door have Beatrice Woods, the Little Blind Songbird; the Whatleys up the street have Miss Tuttle, the high school English teacher. Ernest Koonitz, the school's band director and tuba soloist, boards with Miss Alma, who, as luck would have it, has a hearing problem. But soon the Smith family will take in a new boarder who will set in action a chain of events that should eventually wind up in the pages of history books. Of course they won't know it at the time, especially their ten-year-old son, Bobby. He is at the moment downtown standing outside the barbershop with his friend Monroe Newberry, staring at the revolving red and white stripes on the electric barber's pole. The game is to stare at it until they are cross-eyed, which seemed to them to be some sort of grand achievement. As far as amusements go, it is on a par with holding your breath until you pass out or dropping from a rope into the freezing swimming hole outside of town named the Blue Devil, so cold that even on a hot day when you hit the water the first shock jolts you to your eyeballs, stops your heart, and makes you see stars before your eyes. By the time you come out your body is so numb you can't feel where your legs are and your lips have turned blue, hence the name. But boys, being the insane creatures they are, cannot wait to come crawling out covered with goose bumps and do it all over again.

These were some of the activities that thrilled Bobby to the core. However, for Bobby just life itself was exciting. And really at that time and that place what red-blooded American boy would not wake up every morning jumping for joy and ready to go? He was living smack-dab in the middle of the greatest country in the world—some said the greatest country that ever was or ever would be. We had just beaten the Germans and the Japanese in a fair fight. We had saved Europe and everyone liked us that year, even the French. Our girls were the prettiest, our boys the handsomest, our soldiers the bravest, and our flag the most beautiful. That year it seemed like everyone in the world wanted to be an American. People from all over the world were having a fit trying to come here. And who could blame them? We had John Wayne, Betty Grable, Mickey Mouse, Roy Rogers, Superman, Dagwood and Blondie, the Andrews Sisters, and Captain Marvel. Buck Rogers and Red Ryder, BB guns, the Hardy Boys, G-men, Miss America, cotton candy. Plus Charlie McCarthy and Edgar Bergen, Amos 'n' Andy, Fibber McGee and Molly, and *anybody* could grow up and become the president of the United States.

Bobby even felt sorry for anyone who was not lucky enough to have been born here. After all, we had invented everything in the world that really mattered. Hot dogs, hamburgers, roller coasters, roller skates, ice-cream cones, electricity, milk shakes, the jitterbug, baseball, football, basketball, barbecue, cap pistols, hot-fudge sundaes, and banana splits. We had Coca-Cola, chocolate-covered peanuts, jukeboxes, Oxydol, Ivory Snow, oleomargarine, and the atomic bomb!

We were bigger, better, richer, and stronger than anybody but we still played by the rules and were always good sports. We even reached out and helped pick up and dust off Japan and Germany after we had beaten them . . . and if that wasn't being a good sport, what was? Bobby's own state of Missouri had given the world Mark Twain, Walt Disney, Ginger Rogers, and the great St. Louis World's Fair, and aboard the battleship *Missouri* the Japanese had surrendered to General Douglas MacArthur. Not only that, Bobby's Cub Scout troop (Bobwhite Patrol) had personally gone all over town collecting old rubber tires, scrap paper, and aluminum pots and pans. That had helped win the war. And if that wasn't enough to make a boy proud, the president of the entire United States, Mr. Harry S. Truman, was a true-blue dyed-in-the-wool Missourian, and St. Louis had won the World Series. Even the trees stood a little straighter this year, or so it seemed to Bobby.

He had a mother, a father, and a grandmother and had never known anyone who had died. He had seen only photographs in store windows of the boys who had been killed in the war. He and his best friend, Monroe, were now official blood brothers, an act so solemn that neither one spoke on the way home. His big sister, Anna Lee, a pretty blue-eyed blond girl, was quite popular with all the older boys, who would sometimes hang around the house and play catch or throw the football with him. Sometimes he was able to make a quarter off the guys just to leave them alone on the front porch with Anna Lee. In 1946 a quarter meant popcorn, candy, a movie, a cartoon, and a serial, plus a trip to the projection booth to visit Snooky, who read Mickey Spillane books. And after the movie he could go next door to the Trolley Car Diner, where Jimmy, their boarder, would fry him a burger if he was not too busy.

Or he might stop by the drugstore on the corner and read a few of the newest comic books. His father was the pharmacist so he was allowed to look at them for free as long as he did not wrinkle or spill any food on them. Thelma and Bertha Ann, the girls who worked behind the soda fountain, thought he was cute and might slip him a cherry Coke or, if he was lucky, a root-beer float. Downtown Elmwood Springs was only one long block so there was never any danger of getting lost, and the year-round weather couldn't have been more perfect if he had ordered it off a menu. Each October a nice big round orange harvest moon appeared just in time for Halloween. Thanksgiving Day was always crisp and cool enough to go outside and play tag after a big turkey dinner and snow fell once or twice a year, just when he needed a day off from school.

And then came spring, with crickets, frogs, and little green leaves on the trees again, followed by summer, sleeping out on the screened porch, fishing, hot bright sunny days at Cascade Plunge, the town's swimming pool, and so far every Fourth of July, after all the firecrackers, whirligigs, and sparklers were gone, lightning bugs and large iridescent blue-and-green June bugs showed up in time to make the night last a little longer.

On hot muggy August afternoons, just when you thought you would die of the heat, clouds would begin to gather and distant thunder boomed so deep you would feel it in your chest. Suddenly a cool breeze would come from out of nowhere and turn the sky a dark gunmetal gray, so dark that all the streetlights in town got confused and started coming on. Seconds later an honest-to-God Missouri gully washer would come crashing down hard and fast and then without warning pick up and run to the next town, leaving behind enough cool water to fill the gutters so Bobby could run out and feel it rushing over his bare feet.

Although Mr. Bobby Smith had only been on this earth for a very short time and at present occupied only four feet eight inches of it, he was already a man of considerable property. Most of which he kept in his room on the floor, on the walls, on the bed, under the bed, hanging from the ceiling, or anywhere there was an empty space. As the decorators would say, he was going in for that casual, devil-may-care, cluttered look that his mother had the nerve to say looked like a Salvation Army junk store. It was only an average-sized bedroom with a small closet, but to Bobby, it was his personal and private magical kingdom full of priceless treasures. A place where he was the master of all he surveyed, rich as a sultan. Although in truth there was nothing in the room that a sultan or anybody else, for that matter, would want unless they were in the market for a box of painted turtles or an assortment of rocks, a flattened-out penny he and Monroe had put on the streetcar tracks, or a life-sized cardboard stand-up of Sunset Carson, his favorite cowboy, that Snooky had given him from the Elmwood Theater. Or maybe two silver dollars or an artificial yellow fish eye he had found behind the VFW or a small glass jeep that once had candy in it, for about five seconds. Among his possessions that year was a homemade slingshot, a bag of marbles, one little Orphan Annie decoder pin, one glow-in-the-dark ring, one compass, one Erector set, three yo-yos, a model airplane, a boy's hairbrush with a decal of the Lone Ranger on it (a birthday present from Monroe that Monroe's mother had bought), a cardboard Firestone filling station complete with pumps, a bookshelf full of ten-cent Terry and the Pirates, Joe Palooka, and Red Ryder books. Under the bed were several Spider Man, Porky the Pig, Little Audrey, and Casper the Friendly Ghost comic books, plus an L&N train set, his plastic braided Indian bracelet a girl gave him that he thought he had lost, and one white rubber handlebar cover from an old bicycle.

But Bobby's world was not limited to just what he could see or touch or to the space inside the four walls of his bedroom. He had traveled a million miles in the L&N train under his bed, ridden up treacherous mountains through long black tunnels over raging rivers, and in the little plane hanging from the ceiling he had flown around the world, often over Amazon jungles teeming with alligators. Even the streetlight on the corner provided Bobby with a wonderful show. As he was lying in bed on breezy summer evenings, watching the shadows made by the leaves of the poplar tree dancing on the side of the house next door, they soon became palm trees, swaying back and forth in the warm trade winds of the nearest tropical island. Some nights he could hear the faint strains of Hawaiian music and see rows of hula girls dancing right above the Robinsons' bedroom window. So enthralled was Bobby with this image that he had sent off for a ukulele. Nobody was more disappointed. He had expected it to play a song when strummed but it had not. The sound it made was a far cry from music, Hawaiian or otherwise, so he quickly moved on to the harmonica and was convinced he was really playing a song when he wasn't. So great was his imagination that when he rode a broomstick handle around the backyard he could see the dust and hear the sound of the thundering hoofs as he galloped across the dry western desert. That year he went to sleep each night with his eyes full of cowboys and Indians and his head filled with voices. "Tom Mix and the Ralston Straight Shooters are on the air!" "From out of the West comes America's fighting cowboy!" "Quaker Oats . . . delicious, nutritious, makes you ambitious!" "You bet 'um, Red Ryder." "I'm back in the saddle again." "Well, I'll be a lop-eared kangaroo if it isn't roundup time." "Me Tonto, you Kemo Sabe." And his favorite, "Hi-yo, Silver, away!"

An outside observer might think his life was just about perfect. However, to be fair, there were two distinctive and troublesome drawbacks to being Bobby Smith. One was his appearance. He was a nice-enough-looking boy with brown eyes and brown hair. His teeth were straight. His ears stuck out slightly but nothing out of the ordinary. One problem was that his mouth turned up a bit at both corners, making him look like he knew a secret and was pleased about it. This expression caused his mother and his teachers to ask constantly, "What are you up to?" even when he wasn't up to anything. No matter how much he professed his innocence, they always replied, "Don't lie to me, Bobby Smith, I can tell you're up to something by the look on your face."

The other drawback was his parents. Everybody knew who they were and would tell on him the minute he did something wrong. His father, the town's only pharmacist, a Mason, a Rotarian, an Elk, and a senior elder at the First Methodist Church, was just naturally on a first-name basis with the entire town. But to make matters even worse, his mother was a local radio personality known as Neighbor Dorothy, who five days a week broadcast her show from their living room. And each year she would send her listening audience Christmas cards with the family's picture on them, so that people for miles around knew who he was and what he looked like, and sometimes when a guest did not show up his mother would grab Bobby and make him be the guest and ask him all kinds of questions as if he were a complete stranger. On holidays his mother would put him on the radio to recite some stupid poem. And to add insult to injury, his personal and private business was often discussed on his mother's radio show and everything he did, good or bad, was talked about for all the world to hear.

His only consolation was that this was a cross both the Smith children had to bear. This was of little consolation to Anna Lee. Last year his sister had gotten hysterical when their mother happened to mention that Anna Lee did not have a date as of yet for the prom because she was holding out, hoping the boy she thought looked just like Glenn Ford—her major movie-star crush at the time—would ask her. Dorothy had always shared things about her family with her audience before but when Anna Lee heard that piece of information going out over the airwaves she ran through the house screaming as if someone had shot her and flung herself on the bed sobbing, "Oh, Mother, how could you? You've ruined my life. I'll never get another date as long as I live. I might as well just kill myself." She stayed in bed wailing with a cold cloth on her head for two days while her mother, who felt terrible about it, tried to make it up to her by bringing her homemade peach ice cream and promising never to mention her name over the air again.

At the time Bobby thought it was pretty funny but Bobby was not yet at the sensitive stage where what other people thought about you was a matter of life and death. So for the moment, other than not being able to get away with much, he didn't have a care in the world and, like most ten-year-old boys, believed that something wonderful was always just about to happen.

Neighbor Dorothy

In the late 1920s and early 1930s, as more and more electric lines were strung down county roads to the farmhouses, the long, lonely days of isolated farmwives living far away from their nearest neighbors were suddenly filled with warm and friendly voices. They were the voices of other women coming into their homes via the radio. As early as 1924, women all over the Midwest known as "radio homemakers" began broadcasting, supplying the wives with new recipes, tips for raising children, household hints, gardening advice, local news, and entertainment, but most important, a daily visit from a good friend. Every day listeners in Iowa heard over KMA in Shenandoah *Kitchen-Klatter* with Leanna Driftmiller or *Down a Country Lane* with Evelyn Birkby. Those who tuned to WNAX in Yankton, South Dakota, heard Wynn Speece, "the Neighbor Lady." Also broadcasting were Adella Shoemaker, Ida Bailey Allen, Bernice Currier, Alma Kitchell, Edith Hansen, and others.

One such radio homemaker was Bobby's mother, Mrs. Dorothy Smith, who broadcast from her home in Elmwood Springs, Missouri, between 9:30 and 10:00 A.M. over local radio station WDOT, number 66 on your dial. She was certainly qualified for the job. Besides loving to talk she had gone to Boston to study and had come home two years later armed with a degree in home economics and child care and with her eye on Robert (Doc) Smith, who had recently graduated from the University of Tennessee's School of Pharmacy. Six months later they were walking down the aisle of the First Methodist Church, anxious to settle down and start a family. By the end of the war, she had been broadcasting since 1936 and over the years became known to her many listeners as, simply, "Neighbor Dorothy." Every day, Nalon Klegg, the male announcer from the main station in Poplar Springs, would introduce her with the phrase "And now here she is from that little white house just around the corner from wherever you are, your neighbor and mine, the lady with the smile in her voice, Neighbor Dorothy . . . with Mother Smith on the organ." Her mother-in-law would then break into a rousing rendition of the show's theme, "On the Sunny Side of the Street."

This theme song was not chosen by accident. When Doc bought the house in 1934, he knew his wife would love to have plants blooming in every window, in and among all the little blue-glass violins she collected, so he made sure the new house really *was* on the sunny side of the street. Neighbor Dorothy was a pleasingly plump woman with a sweet smile on her face, a face that eventually graced the cover of her cookbooks and billboards all over the Midwest. Most people, seeing her picture or listening to her calm and friendly, always cheerful radio voice, might never have guessed she had ever had a worry or a problem in her entire life. What most people did not know and she never talked about was their first child, a four-year-old little blond boy named Michael. Dorothy had thought it was just another childhood fever or maybe a cold coming on, certainly nothing serious. But by midmorning he had started going into convulsions. He died quite suddenly and with little warning. One day he was laughing and alive and the next day he was gone.

The doctors said it had been an unusually virulent bacterial infection that had hit him overnight and by five-thirty that afternoon he was dead. They never found out exactly what it was or why he had gotten it but by the time they reached the hospital the infection had already spread and settled in his lungs. No one can ever really be prepared for the death of a loved one but losing a child is surely the worst pain a human being will ever have to bear.

It struck them so suddenly and so hard that Doc's mother, a widow, moved into the house to take care of them. After a while Doc went back to work but Dorothy was still unable to do anything except sit in the little boy's room and stare at the bed.

She wouldn't eat no matter how Mother Smith tried and she couldn't sleep unless she took one of the pills Doc got for her. Though the doctors repeatedly told her there was nothing anybody could have done, she never really believed it. She questioned it over and over in her mind. She asked herself a hundred whys and what-ifs and she couldn't find one answer that made any sense. At that time Doc was little or no help. If anything, she resented the way he had seemingly just gone on with his life as if nothing had happened. He wouldn't even talk about it with her and when she tried he just walked out of the room. She was young and did not know that men deal with grief in different ways. Doc, who was also young, was mistakenly trying to hold himself together to be strong for her. She did not know that he often drove outside of town, parked the car, and sat and sobbed.

The loss of their child was a wound that would not heal, something they would never really get over. But, after a year or so, they were both able to make it through the days.

It was at this time that Dorothy first began to bake. It helped her, somehow, to keep busy. There were days when she baked as many as five or ten cakes. Pretty soon everybody in town started carrying forks in their pockets or pocketbooks because if you passed her house, you would be offered a piece of cake. Soon she was overrun with cakes and needed desperately to get rid of them so when she said, "Please come in and have a piece of cake," you knew she meant it. Gerta Nordstrom, her friend who owned the bakery, said her cake business dropped in half because Dorothy was giving so many away. Pretty soon Dorothy began supplying the Nordstroms and became well known for her baking. The year her recipe for a six-layer surprise upside-down pineapple cake took second place in the Pillsbury Bake-Off contest she was invited to be a guest on a radio show in Poplar Bluff. In the midst of the interview she just happened to mention that she always used Golden Flake Lite-as-a-Feather Flour. When Golden Flake Flour sales doubled overnight, they offered her a show of her own. Soon the large radio tower with the red light on the top went up in the backyard and she was "on the air." Later, after Anna Lee was born, she and Doc began to be their old selves again, although the little blond boy was not forgotten. Life went on pretty much as usual until, one day when Dorothy was forty-three, long after either one of them had given it a thought, life changed again. The doctor informed her that she was not, as she had suspected, going through the change of life but was pregnant. And seemingly out of a clear blue sky, along came Bobby, who turned out to be a real change-of-life baby in every sense of the word.

The Water Tower

Maybe it's because they are still short and close to the ground or maybe their senses have not yet been dulled by the years but to children days seem longer, smells stronger, colors brighter, noises louder, fun more fun. Bobby was no exception. He viewed the world each day through brand-new eyes, almost vibrating with excitement. If you could have plugged him into the wall he would have lit up like a 500-watt bulb. This was all very well and wonderful for him but for his family it was like living with a sixty-eight-pound puppy running in and out of the house all day. And this day, as usual, he and Monroe were up to something they shouldn't be.

They had walked almost a mile outside of town, to the water tower that had ELMWOOD SPRINGS written on it in huge black letters, with the express intention of climbing all the way to the top. An idea that if his mother knew anything about would have caused her to have a heart attack or worse. Years before, a high school senior had fallen off and killed himself. But when you're young facts do not concern you. You are convinced that nothing will ever happen to you. Besides, he and Monroe had double-dog-dared each other to climb it, so there was no turning back.

Secretly both of them were a little nervous. Scared that they might chicken out at the last minute. But overriding any fear of being called a sissy by the other was the lure of being able to brag to everyone they knew, except their parents, that they had climbed it. And just to make sure that everybody would know for certain they really had done it, Bobby had come up with a plan.

That morning he had gone over to Warren's Hardware and bought a large ball of heavy string. Monroe had a pocketful of red balloons that they were going to blow up and tie to the top of the tower to prove to any nonbelievers that they had been there. But when they finally arrived at the base of the tower and looked up, what had appeared from a distance to be just a round silver ball hanging up in the sky now seemed as big as a football field. It was so high it hurt their necks to look up at it. People said that from the top if you turned around in a circle you could see six states and on a clear day you could see all the way to Iowa . . . at least that's what they said. Bobby and Monroe hemmed and hawed and kicked the ground a little and discussed the balloon plan.

"Do you think we should blow them up before we go?" asked Monroe, stalling for time.

"No. Don't you remember what we said? If we blow them up first, somebody might see them while we're climbing up."

"Oh, that's right."

"When we get to the top, we blow them up and tie them to the side, then get down as fast as we can."

Monroe, a chunky, carrot-topped boy with pinkish skin, suddenly looked a little pale. He glanced back up at the top. "Who's gonna go first?"

Bobby thought about it for a minute but made no move. Then Monroe said, "This was your idea. I think you should get to go first."

"No, it's O.K., you can go first if you want to. I don't care."

"No, fair is fair. You're the one who thought it up—you go."

Monroe had him there, so Bobby could not very well back down now. "O.K., if you're scared, I'll go first if you want me to."

"I'm not scared, it was just your idea, that's all."

"Then you go first if you want to."

Monroe looked back up at the top. That settled it. "I don't want to."

Bobby assumed a nonchalant attitude. "All right, I'll go first, but remember—Macky Warren said the trick is not to look down until you get up there."

"O.K."

"All right then, let's go." Bobby took a deep breath and put his foot on the first rung of the ladder and started up the long, thin steel stairs that led to the top. As they both soon found out, it was a long and steep climb. What they had not counted on was how hot the sun would be the higher they got or how hard it was to hold on to the slippery rails with sweaty hands, not to mention the wind that almost blew them off the ladder. After what seemed an hour of climbing, they finally made it, both of them out of breath, dripping wet with perspiration, hot, and thirsty. When they stepped off the ladder onto the small, round corrugated-steel platform at the very top, their legs were so shaky from the climb that they had to sit down and rest. Monroe's face was now about as bright red as the balloons in his pocket.

After a while they mustered the strength and the courage to stand up and look over the side. The first thing Monroe said when he looked over was: "Whoa! . . . We must be ten thousand hundred feet up in the air . . . higher than an airplane or the Empire State Building even!"

They weren't, of course, but you sure could have fooled them. Bobby and Monroe had never seen the world from anything higher than a tree or the top of a garage. They could see for miles around, and when Monroe spotted a cornfield way off in the distance he was positive he had seen all the way up to Iowa.

Bobby was so overwhelmed at the sight he was speechless. He stood there stunned. He had not known what the world would look like from this far up. He had thought maybe it would look round, like the world globe in his father's den, but to his surprise it was all flat! Nothing before him but big flat brown and green squares as far as the eye could see. It looked just like a map! But when Monroe spotted their town off to the right and pointed it out, Bobby was in for the second shock of his young life. "Look," Monroe said, "there's the church and the school—see it?"

Bobby's mouth hung open in total disbelief. Elmwood Springs, which an hour ago had seemed to him to be such an enormous place, was now nothing more than a block of buildings, houses, and streets no bigger than an inch, just stuck sitting out there in the middle of nowhere. He could see where downtown was, the church on one end and the Masonic Hall on the other. The small black specks walking back and forth were no bigger than ants, and the cars looked like Matchbox toys; the buildings were the same size as the ones in a Monopoly set.

Monroe said, "Look, there's your house . . . see the radio tower in the backyard?"

Bobby peered over to where Monroe was pointing. It was his house all right. He could see the red light on top of the radio tower and if he squinted he could just make out a black speck moving around in the backyard, hanging clothes on a clothesline. Then it struck him: that speck was his mother! At once another thought hit him, scaring him half to death. What if he were at home right now and out in the yard and somebody else was up here looking down at him? Then *he* would be no bigger than an ant. No, half an ant . . . no bigger than a flea! From up here he would no longer be the huge center of his huge universe, the apple of his parents' eyes; from up here he would be nothing and nobody special, just another black dot. Suddenly he broke out in a cold sweat.

"I've got to go home, my mother's calling me," he said. He started back down, leaving a startled Monroe calling after him: "Wait. You can't go . . . we haven't done the balloons yet. Wait!"

But Bobby did not hear him. All he could hear was the sound of his own heart pounding in his ears and his only thought was to get on the ground as fast as he could. He had to get back home, where he was the right size.

But Monroe, who had been deserted, abandoned, was not going to leave. He was determined. If he had climbed all the way to the top, people were going to know about it. The heck with Bobby Smith; he would just blow up the balloons himself. As he pulled one out of his pocket and started to blow, he suddenly remembered. He ran to the side and yelled down the ladder. "Bobby, wait, stop, you've got the string! Throw me the string!" But it was too late. Bobby was more than halfway down the ladder.

Sometime later Bobby hit the front door of his house running and didn't stop until he got to his room and onto his own bed. When Anna Lee, who was out on the porch, saw the look on his face as he went by, she figured someone was chasing him. She got up to look and see if it was Luther Griggs, the big bully who was always beating Bobby up any chance he got, but Luther was nowhere in sight.

Poor Monroe had stayed up on the tower for at least another forty-five minutes, trying as hard as he could to attach one of those red balloons to the side of the railing, but they all flew off.

But for Bobby the day had been far more than just the failure of the balloon caper. It was the first time he had seen his life from a distance or from anywhere, for that matter, except from the center of his own giant universe. Could it really be possible that he was nothing but just another small dot among a bunch of other small dots? He had always thought he was something different, something special. Now he was thrown for a complete loop.

Raggedy Ann

That night Bobby was especially sweet and after dinner, when they were all out on the porch, he went over to his mother in the swing, lay down with his head in his mother's lap, and went to sleep, something he had not done since he was six. It was an extraordinarily warm evening and the entire family, including Jimmy and Dorothy's red-and-white cocker spaniel, Princess Mary Margaret, all sat out trying to catch a little night breeze. It was a quiet night and they were enjoying the sound of the crickets and the soft squeak of the swing. Dorothy looked down at Bobby. He was now in such a deep sleep that when she crossed her legs with his head in her lap he did not awaken. She smoothed his hair back off his forehead. "He must have been up to something today because he's dead to the world tonight."

Anna Lee said, "I thought Luther Griggs was after him again. He ran in the door this afternoon going about a hundred miles an hour."

His mother sighed. "I'm worried that the Griggs boy is really going to hurt him one of these days. He's already a head taller than Bobby."

Doc knocked the ashes out of his pipe against the side of the porch. "Oh, I wouldn't worry too much. He'll have to catch him first. Bobby may be little but he's fast."

Dorothy thought about it and was somewhat reassured. "Well, that's true. The other day, by the time I got my switch he was out the door and so far out in the field all I could see was the top of his head."

Anna Lee, who, now a teenager, had recently started referring to her brother as "that child," made an observation. "That child is certainly a lot of trouble, isn't he, Mother?"

"Yes, but he can be sweet when he wants to. He's just at that age, I suppose."

"Was I ever like that?" asked Anna Lee.

"No. You were just a little angel—wasn't she, Mother?"

Mother Smith agreed. "Absolutely. You were the best-behaved little girl. I used to take you everywhere with me and all I had to do was to put you down with one of your little dolls and you'd sit there and play and I never heard a peep out of you."

"You loved your dolls," Dorothy said. "That big Raggedy Ann was your favorite; you used to take it everywhere."

They sat there in the quiet listening to the crickets for a few more minutes. Then Dorothy turned to Anna Lee. "What ever happened to your Raggedy Ann doll?"

"Bobby knocked its head off."

"Oh."

Just then Tot Whooten, a frazzled-looking woman, walked by on the sidewalk headed somewhere in a hurry. She did not stop but waved her hand in the air and called out over her shoulder, "Momma's left her purse at the picture show again and I've got to get there before they close."

Mother Smith shook her head. "Poor Tot, that's the second time this week."

Dorothy agreed. "Poor Tot."

A few minutes later, Tot came walking by again, this time with her mother's huge black purse on her arm. Mother Smith called, "I see you got it."

"Yes, thank heavens Snooky found it and was waiting for me. Good night."

They all said, "Good night." Mother Smith added, "Tell your mother I said hello."

"O.K."

And after she was out of earshot Dorothy said "Poor Tot" again. Several other people walked by on their way home from the movie and waved. After a moment, Dorothy said, "I wish Bobby hadn't done that to Raggedy Ann. I was hoping you could give it to your little girl someday.

You just loved that doll. You even took it to first grade with you." She looked at her daughter with a sad, wistful expression in her eyes. "It seems like only yesterday when I was taking you to your first day of school."

"Didn't I just walk?" Anna Lee said. "It's only two blocks."

"No. I took you the first day but you weren't afraid. You seemed happy to go really, you and Raggedy Ann. I stood there and watched you go up the steps and when you got to the top you turned and gave me a little wave and went on in. And oh, it nearly broke my heart, I was losing my little girl. I stood there on the street just crying my eyes out for all the world to see."

Anna Lee said, "You *did*?"

Doc nodded. "Oh yes," he said and relit his pipe, shook the match out, and put it in the ashtray by his chair. "Your mother came down to the drugstore practically hysterical. You would have thought she had just put you on a freighter headed for China."

This was the first time Anna Lee had heard this story. "Were you that upset when Bobby went off to the first grade?"

Dorothy looked down at her sleeping son for a moment. "No. I hate to say it but I think I was actually relieved. The day before he had ruined all six cakes I had baked for the church sale, ran his finger around the bottom of each one and ate the icing. So, no, I was glad to let somebody else have him for a while. But little boys are different. When you get married and have one of your own, you'll see for yourself."

Anna Lee shook her head. "Not me. I'm not having any boys. I'm only going to have girls."

Mother Smith laughed. "That's not something you can control, honey. You may want little girls but wishing doesn't make it so."

"Then I'm not ever getting married."

Mother Smith smiled. "That's what we all say until Mr. Right comes waltzing in the door. Isn't that right, Dorothy?"

"It was for me. I told everyone I was going to New York to go on the stage and become the next Sarah Bernhardt. Then your father asked me to the Christmas dance and there went my Broadway career plans out the window." Dorothy moved a little in the swing, and Bobby's head moved with her. "Now my other leg has gone to sleep. I don't know what he has in his head but it weighs a ton."

"Rocks probably," said Anna Lee.

Jimmy stood up, yawned, and stretched. "Well, folks, I guess it's about that time. See y'all tomorrow."

"Good night, Jimmy."

Dorothy looked at Doc. "You better come over here, Mr. Right, and take your son to bed. I need to get on in and work on the show before it gets too late. It's almost ten o'clock."

Doc put his pipe down and walked over and picked Bobby up and put him over his shoulder. "Should I put his pajamas on?"

"No, just let him sleep in his clothes. It won't hurt him."

Doc said, "Good night, all." As he got to the screen door he turned to Dorothy and said, "Good night, Miss Bernhardt."

Doc Smith

Doc was much older than the other fathers of Bobby's friends and it worried him because he could not roughhouse or play football with his son like they could, but as far as Bobby was concerned there were plenty of things he did with his father that more than made up for it. Doc, it seems, had been a good baseball player in his youth and was still an avid baseball fan and so was Bobby. They listened to all the games on the radio together and studied the players' statistics. With Doc's vast knowledge of baseball he taught Bobby to appreciate the finer and more subtle elements of the game. And though Doc was never much of a hunter, he did love to fish and from the time Bobby could walk he always took him along. Doc would come into his room at about 3:30 in the morning, long before it was light, and wake him. Bobby would get up and dress and they would both quietly slip out the front door so the Robinsons' chickens would not wake up the neighborhood. Doc would start the 1938 Dodge with the bad muffler as quietly as possible and drive in the dark through the back roads until they came to the river. It was on these mornings that his father would let him have a sip of coffee from the thermos he had brought, preceded with "All right, just a sip, but don't tell your mother." This little ritual made Bobby feel as if he and his father were partners in a grand conspiracy. Even though the coffee always tasted bitter and horrible, he endured it without making a face. It was a man thing. Sometimes they would go with Glenn Warren and his son, Macky, but he liked it best when it was just him and his father. He loved having his father introduce him to the other men at the camp as his son. He could tell they all respected his father and it made him feel proud. He also enjoyed going to Old Man Johnson's fishing camp, where they rented their boat. The ramshackle wooden cabin was filled with rods and tackle. Mounted fish of all kinds and sizes hung on every inch of the wall. Also alongside the fish hung a 1945 calendar with a picture of a pretty girl in short shorts fly-fishing in a stream that Bobby thought was exotic. They always bought their live bait out of the cooler plus two cold drinks, crackers and tins of sardines and Vienna sausages for their lunch, and were usually out on the water just as the sun was coming up. Bobby's job was to row the boat back up into the deep shady places, where the big fat trout and catfish liked to hide, while his father cast his line as close to the bank as possible. The crackers Mr. Johnson sold were stale and the drinks warm by noon but it didn't matter. Anything tastes good when you are hungry. Some days they would catch a huge string of fish, sometimes just three or four. One day the fishing had been so bad that his father bought some trout from Old Man Johnson to take home. That night Bobby went into such long and elaborate detail about how each trout was caught and how hard it fought that his mother began to suspect something. But Bobby didn't really care how many fish they caught; he just loved being alone with his dad. A few years before, his father had casually laid out a handful of baseball tickets on the kitchen table and asked, "Son, would you like to go to the World Series with me?" Miracle of all miracles, their team, the St. Louis Browns, was playing the St. Louis Cardinals that year and everybody in the state of Missouri was trying to get tickets. As it turned out, a friend of Doc's from pharmaceutical school just happened to be Luke Sewell, the St. Louis Browns' manager's brother-in-law, and Doc had been able to get tickets from him. Doc brought in a replacement to work for him at the drugstore and Dorothy packed their bags. On October 3, the two of them got on a train headed up to St. Louis with tickets for all six games if it lasted that long and they hoped it would. What a town. What a trip. Just him and his dad staying at a real hotel, eating out at restaurants just like two grown-ups. A Yellow Cab ride to the huge Rexall drugstore in downtown St. Louis to visit his father's friend and back. He had his picture made under the big steel Gateway Arch, and got a brand-new Browns baseball cap. Each day they took a streetcar from downtown to North

Grand Avenue, all the way out to Sportsman's Park. Going and coming it was always filled with the aroma of Old Spice shaving lotion and cigarette smoke and packed full of loud, exuberant men and boys of all ages headed to and from the game. The sight of the ballpark that first day—the crowds—the noise—the smells—the crack of the bat—the green grass—the hot dogs—the peanuts—that sip of Pabst Blue Ribbon beer! It was all too much. Bobby was so excited he was dizzy. Their team won the first game 2 to 1, which gave them hope, but went on to lose the series as expected. Still, they had been there cheering them on anyway. It had been a wonderful time for both of them. Although the poor St. Louis Browns were never to play in a World Series again, at least Bobby did not come home empty-handed. He was the proud owner of a real, genuine World Series baseball, a foul ball his father had managed to catch, autographed by none other than the National League's MVP of the year, shortstop Marty Marion. Bobby and his dad stood in line for about two hours to get the autograph but it was worth the wait. When they got home Bobby showed it to everybody. He was quite the big man around town for a few days, or at least until everyone had seen it several times. As for Doc, he came home happy and rested, a rest he had much needed.

On the surface, being a small-town druggist did not seem like such a hard job, certainly not a hazardous or a grueling profession. But it had its own hidden stresses that few knew about. His was a multifaceted job of many duties. Not only did he have to stand and listen with great patience to everybody in town who seemed compelled to tell him in long, drawn-out detail all about each and every little pain or complaint they had, but people also brought him birds with broken wings to fix, kids with cuts and scrapes, smashed fingers, and sprained ankles to bandage, and a variety of colds, upset stomachs, sore throats, cat scratches, dog bites, black eyes, and poison ivy rashes to ask about. All this he was glad to do but for Doc, as Elmwood Springs' only pharmacist, it meant that he was also privy to private information and secrets he sometimes wished he didn't have to know. With his knowledge of medicine he often knew exactly what was wrong with people by what the doctor had prescribed.

He was painfully aware, for example, that his best friend had a bad heart condition by the strength of the medicine and by the frequency it was to be taken but he never mentioned it. He also knew that Poor Tot

Whooten had been given a prescription for Antabuse and she was secretly slipping it into the coffee of her husband, James Dwayne, every morning to try to get him to stop drinking. He knew which soldier had come home from the war having contracted syphilis, what lady was taking pills for bad nerves, which men were being treated for impotence, and those women who were having female trouble, as well as who did not want any more children and who did. All this he kept to himself. It was especially hard when his own family was involved. The day his father's prescription for morphine was called in he knew his dad was dying, long before his father did.

But if his job was sometimes complex, Doc's life at home was a pleasant escape. And it certainly was never dull. Just last week a complete stranger had wandered in and had dinner with them.

Because the Greyhound Bus stopped in front of their house, people were always sitting around on the porch or in the living room. This combined with the number of Neighbor Dorothy's fans that dropped by all day caused the man to make an honest mistake. When he saw everyone going in and out and the radio call letters written on the front window, he naturally assumed the place was a restaurant called WDOT and decided to stop by later and have a bite to eat before driving on to Poplar Bluff. At around 5:30 he parked his car, strolled in, and sat down in the living room with Doc and Jimmy, who were reading the paper, and asked, "What time is dinner served?" Doc did not know who he was but pleasantly told him, "In about thirty minutes." Then the man asked where the men's room was and went down the hall and came back, sat down, and picked up a magazine and waited. As far as Doc knew, he could have been one of Dorothy's sponsors come to town. When Dorothy called out that dinner was on the table the man got up and went in. Nobody asked him who he was, all thinking he was a friend of someone else's, and Neighbor Dorothy quietly put out another place setting. He thoroughly enjoyed the pot roast and mashed potatoes and happily chatted away all through dinner, entertaining everyone with his tales of life as a professional poultry inspector for the state of Missouri. And how people always kidded him about being a poultry inspector with Fowler for a last name. He amazed them with how many different breeds of chickens were in the world. After finishing his second piece of coconut cake, he pushed himself back from the table and announced, "Well, folks, I better get on the road before it gets too late," and dug into his pocket and asked Dorothy how much he owed.

A surprised Dorothy said, "Why, you don't owe a thing, Mr. Fowler—we were just happy to have you. I hope you'll be sure to drop in and see us again anytime you are passing through."

That night Mr. Charlie Fowler left town thinking that Elmwood Springs was the friendliest place he had ever been. He *did* come back often and they were always glad to see him.

An Ordinary Day

On an ordinary weekday Jimmy Head, the Smiths' boarder, is usually the first person awake. He gets up around 4:30, goes out to the kitchen, puts on the coffee, drinks a cup, then heads out the door before five. The only other lights on in town are at Nordstrom's bakery, which opens at 7:30, but Jimmy has a big breakfast crowd and has to get the Trolley Car Diner ready to go by 6:00. Doc and Mother Smith are also early risers and usually come into the kitchen and have a cup of coffee together around 5:30. Dorothy is up and dressed by 6:30, comes in, and starts her day by putting a batch of radio cookies in the oven for her guests and then feeds Princess Mary Margaret and her two yellow canary birds, Dumpling and Moe. If it is summer Bobby is up by 7:00 and Anna Lee tends to float into the kitchen around 8:00 or 8:30. She needs her beauty sleep. Doc is down at the drugstore by 7:30, which opens at 8:00.

The milkman, the iceman, and the bread man have already been there by 9:20 and Beatrice, the Little Blind Songbird, who sings on the show every day, has come over from next door. She and Mother Smith, who accompanies her on the small organ, go on into the living room to run through Beatrice's song. Dorothy and Princess Mary Margaret arrive for the broadcast around 9:25.

Princess Mary Margaret greets anyone else who is in the living room to see the show with a wagging tail and often jumps up and sits in someone's lap during the show. Or if she is not in the mood she gets into her basket under Dorothy's desk (many have remarked how the dog is much better trained than Bobby). Then Dorothy says hello to her guests and welcomes her live audience, usually people waiting to catch the bus or ladies from women's clubs. Dorothy sits down and runs over the format and her commercials for a last-minute check and looks out the window so she can give her radio audience the very latest weather update. At 9:30 on the dot the red light on the organ blinks, the on-air signal, and Mother Smith hits the first strains of the theme song, the show begins . . . and everyone in town and thereabouts is usually tuned in.

Today, fifteen miles outside of town Mrs. Elner Shimfissle, a large-boned farm woman with a plain but pleasant face, dipped her hand into a blue-and-white speckled pan filled with Purina feed and threw it to the chickens in her yard. The chickens, mostly Rhode Island Reds, ran every which way with their heads down close to the ground, trying their best to beat all the other chickens to each grain. She wore a new green-checked apron over her somewhat faded floral-print dress and comfortable old-lady white tie-up shoes.

She shielded her eyes from the sun and looked far out into the fields and saw her husband plowing behind the reins of their two black mules and called out, "Whoo hoo, Will!" The small man in the large straw hat stopped and waved back and then continued plowing. After she emptied the pan she walked over to the water pump and rinsed it out and hung it on a nail on the side of the house by the big tin washtub. She looked up at the sun again, wiped her hands on her apron, and guessed that it was getting to be about that time and went on back in the house. She had been up since four A.M. and had already done the milking, gathered the eggs, gotten her husband's breakfast, scrubbed the kitchen floor, done some washing, hung it up on the line, put a pair of overalls to soaking, killed a fryer, and put up sixteen jars of fig preserves. She figured she could afford to sit down and relax awhile and went over and poured herself a cup of coffee and got her pencil and pad ready to take down the receipts. She turned on the radio—it was always set on WDOT, the only station that comes in clear this far out—and heard *The Neighbor Dorothy Show,* the same program that she had been listening to for the past sixteen years.

It was the only show other than *Gospel Time, U.S.A.,* the farm report, and the *Grand Ole Opry* that Mrs. Shimfissle listened to on a regular basis. And this morning Neighbor Dorothy started the show as she always did with a cheery, "Good morning, everybody, it's a pretty day over here in Elmwood Springs and I hope it's just as pretty where you are. We've got so many wonderful things to tell you about on the show this morning . . . so many special guests . . . that I can hardly contain myself. And sitting right here in the living room with me is somebody I know you are going to want to hear from. Mr. Milo Shipp, who has traveled all the way from New York City to tell us about his brand-new book, *Hilltop in the Rain,* and we can't wait to hear about that. And also we want to welcome our in-studio visitors.

"We have six ladies from the Claire De Lune Garden Club with us and they are headed all the way up to St. Louis for the big flower show later this morning"—Mother Smith played a few strains of "Meet Me in St. Louis"—"and I know you all are going to have a big time up there. We have a good show for you today. Along with our regulars, Nurse Ruby Robinson and Beatrice, the Little Blind Songbird, who will be singing . . . what? 'I'm in Love with the Man in the Moon' . . . and also on our musical menu this morning the Goodnight sisters have promised to drop by later to sing a song in honor of our out-of-town guest, entitled 'My Sweetheart Went Down with the Ship.' They say it's a sad song but it was the only one they could find with *ship* in the title.

"But before we get to our interview I want to say a big hello to one of my brand-new sponsors, Verna Clapp's original strained baby food, and we'll be talking a lot more about that a little later in the program. First, just in case you're wondering what you are hearing, it's not your radio. Poor Tot's fox terrier got out again and that noise is coming from a box of twelve of the cutest puppies you have ever seen—don't you think so, Mr. Shipp? He says he does."—Mother Smith played a bar or two of "How Much Is That Doggie in the Window" and Dorothy laughed.—"Well, they are absolutely free and all Tot wants is to find good homes for them. She says there are five boys and seven girls but not to hold her to it. We know who the mother is but she says she has no idea about the father. As far as I can tell from the look of them, I think the honors will go to that Airedale up the street, so come on by and get yourself one.

"Also, before I forget I wanted to mention how pleased we are with all the responses we are getting from all of you for the dessert cookbook. Mrs. Frances Cleverdon of Arden, Oklahoma, writes:

> "Dear Neighbor Dorothy,
>
> "I think your idea for a dessert cookbook is a good one and will gladly contribute my favorite in the line of a Nesselrode pudding.

"Thank you, Frances. And I see we have a few items on our swap-and-shop segment this morning. Mrs. Irene Neff of Elkton writes to ask if there is anyone with a pair of size nine men's maroon felt house shoes with a black embroidered Indian on them and is willing to swap four tea towels for both or just the left one. Also Mrs. Claudia Graham of Blue Springs is looking for a Lady Esther face-powder box. She just wants the box not the powder, and will swap an Evening in Paris perfume bottle. But before we get to our interview and our songs, we have a winner in our What's the Funniest Thing That Ever Happened to You Contest and here it is." Mother Smith played a fanfare.

> "Dear Neighbor Dorothy,
>
> "One day I scrubbed and scrubbed my kitchen sink but it would not come clean. It was then my daughter came in and asked why I was sprinkling Parmesan cheese in the sink. My husband took me for glasses the next day.
>
> "Signed, Mrs. Mina Fleet of Mount Sterling, Kentucky.

"So, congratulations! You have just won a five-pound sack of Golden Flake Flour, the flour that makes biscuits that make all your family say 'yummy.' And I know just how you feel, Mina; I am headed for spectacles myself. Now, what else did I have to pass along this morning? Oh, here it is. James Whooten has finished with the Whatleys' house and is available. He says you get the paint, I need the work, so call. What else did I have? What? Oh, Mother Smith said I forgot to give out the question of the week. I'm sorry, girls, Monday is such a busy day—I guess I'm a little rattled, so many exciting things happening. Now, where's the question? I know I had it."

The phone in the hall suddenly started ringing.

"Here it is, I found it. The question is, 'What is your favorite cooking utensil and why?' Didn't we have that one before, Mother Smith? She says no, so I guess we didn't. And whoever is calling me on the phone is going to have to ring me back in thirty minutes because I'm on the air. Call back after ten." The phone stopped ringing. "Pardon me a second, girls." Dorothy put her hand over the microphone. "Bobby! Put that back in the kitchen where you found it right now!"

Just then a large man walked up on the front porch, leaned through the living room window, and handed Dorothy a note, which she took and promptly read over the air. "Merle says in case it rains on Saturday, the Elks Club fish fry will be held over at the American Legion Hall across the street. All right. Thank you, Merle, but let's just hope it doesn't rain. Now, coming up next is our interview with our famous author all the way from New York City, who will be telling us all 'bout his new book and I know you're going to enjoy hearing what he has to say."

Dorothy reached over and pulled a piece of paper she had Scotch-taped to the side of the sack of Golden Flake Pancake Mix sitting on her desk so she would not forget it. "And speaking of books, here's a fun fact for you, Mr. Shipp. Did you know that a Mrs. Patricia Lennon of St. Paul, Minnesota, while going through her attic, found a library book that had been overdue for twenty-eight years? Her library fee came to over three thousand dollars. The title of the book? *How to Improve Your Memory*—so make sure you get your books back on time. But before we get to Mr. Shipp, let me ask you this: did you ever long for a trip south of the border, down Mexico way?" Neighbor Dorothy signaled to Mother Smith, who immediately played a little of the Mexican hat dance. "The people at Niblets say down with drabness and up with flavor. That's right, viva Niblets brand Mexicorn! The whole-kernel corn mixed with red and green peppers. Now you too can have a real Mexican fiesta right in your own kitchen and have your whole family shouting *Olé!*"

Meanwhile Milo Shipp, author, a thin man in a bow tie, sat in a wooden chair stunned, with a cookie in one hand and a large cocker spaniel on his lap, while a young boy grinding an eggbeater ran in and out of the room. Eight people carrying suitcases had just gotten up and left to catch a Greyhound bus that had pulled up and honked, and a puppy that disproved the old adage "all puppies are cute" had escaped the cardboard box and was now busy chewing on his shoelaces.

Several small children all under the age of six who were attending nursery school on the back porch continued to wander in to get cookies and pet the puppies, while two teenage girls kept sneaking around the corner to catch a glimpse of him and giggle. In a few minutes a pair of middle-aged women dressed alike, named Ada and Bess Goodnight, came in and proceeded to sing in perfect harmony a terrible song about the sinking of the *Titanic,* nodding and smiling and waving at him the whole time. As he sat there dazed, trying to nod back and fake a smile, he wondered what in the world had he gotten himself into and what the hell had his publishers been thinking of by sending him into this madhouse. He had made the long trip all the way across the country to the middle of nowhere because they had assured him in glowing terms that this Neighbor Dorothy woman sold more books on her show than anyone else in the Midwest. But now, looking at this unimpressive round little housewife sitting behind a desk covered with stacks of paper, potted plants, and a goldfish bowl sitting on the base of a green ceramic cat, he found it all hard to believe.

Twenty-nine minutes, one interview, and three recipes later, Dorothy looked up and said, "Oh . . . I see by that old mean clock on the wall . . . it's time to go. It's always so pleasant to sit and visit with you every morning, share a cup of coffee. You make our days so happy. And when I go and look in our basket to see all the mail you send me I feel as rich as a millionaire, so until we see you again you'll be missed and do come back tomorrow, won't you? This is Neighbor Dorothy and Mother Smith from our house to yours, saying have a good day."

Back out at the farm Elner Shimfissle stood up and went over and turned off the radio and threw what was left of her coffee in the sink. She wished that Neighbor Dorothy had been giving away kittens instead of puppies. Will said the next time she had some they would go into town and get one. Elner added the cake recipe to the rest and also jotted down the name of the man's book. She was not much of a reader but that sounded like a good one. She then went on about her day a little happier, feeling as if she had just had a nice visit with a good friend.

As for Mr. Shipp, he had no idea how lucky he was that Neighbor Dorothy had agreed to have him on the show. Her vast listening audience, which now covered a radius of five states or more, knew she never recommended a book she didn't really like. And they could be pretty sure that if Neighbor Dorothy liked it, by and large they would too.

Three weeks later Mr. Shipp found himself in his publisher's office amid the "I told you so"s of the publicity staff, having to admit that the trip to the Midwest had not been a fool's errand, as he had so loudly proclaimed upon his return to the big city. Much to his surprise, *Hilltop in the Rain* had suddenly popped up to the number three spot on the *New York Times* bestseller list, a place he had never been before in his life. But he was just one of the many who had been and would be surprised over the years at what this woman could do.

The Goodnights

While Mr. Milo Shipp might have thought Dorothy's friends the Goodnight sisters, who sang and did expressive gestures in unison, were a bit odd, everybody else in town had known them all their lives and saw nothing strange about them.

Of course, when they were first born their arrival had caused quite a stir. Twins were rare and everybody for miles around had come to look at them. Their mother, Hazel Goodnight, postmistress at the time, had them on display in the back room of the post office until they were five.

Although Hazel always referred to them as identical twins and dressed them as such, they were not. Ada, the eldest by a minute and a half, was larger by a dress size and always ten pounds heavier than Bess but to please their mother they continued to dress alike. They even kept their hair in the same short hairdo, permed in tight little brown curls, and always went to the beauty shop on the same day. Both were good-natured and friendly and known as the town's cutups. If you asked one a question, the other might answer and they were so close they often finished each other's sentences.

The only time they had ever been separated for any length of time was Bess's one-week honeymoon and during the war. After Pearl Harbor was hit, Ada, always the bolder of the two, took the attack personally and surprised everyone the next day by packing her bags, vowing to help "smash those Japs flat" in any way she could.

A vow most people in town believed. She had led the women's softball team to the state championship in '36. Because Ada used to date Vern Suttle, a crop duster, she had some knowledge of planes and eventually wound up in the WASP flight training program at Avenger Field in Sweetwater, Texas. It was a tough program and many washed out. Ada had to put in many long and grueling hours but when she wrote home she said she had only two complaints about Sweetwater. Too few men. Too many bugs.

When Ada had joined up, her sister Bess had jumped into the war effort on the home front. Not only did she take over running the Western Union office downtown, she became a Red Cross volunteer and helped serve food down at the train station whenever she could. Shortly after the war started Neighbor Dorothy organized a women's committee to make sure that every troop train passing through Elmwood Springs was met at the station with hot coffee, doughnuts, sandwiches, and homemade cake. Most of the soldiers were just scared young boys trying to be brave but just the same they wrote their names and addresses on pieces of paper and threw them out the train windows, hoping to get some girl to write to them. At the end of the war Elmwood Springs prided itself on the fact that not one boy who had thrown his name and address out the window had ever gone without an answer. During the war the girls spent hours every night answering letters. Every morning, right after they had applied their bright red lipstick for the day, the younger women sealed their letters with a big red kiss. Hundreds of boxes of homemade cookies, cakes, candy, and knitted socks were sent overseas. Bobby and Monroe's job was to run all over town and collect all the letters and get them down to the post office so they could go out in the first mail. Macky Warren, a cute sandy-haired boy who was too young to enlist, was not happy about his girlfriend, Norma, writing to so many soldiers but he didn't say so. It would not have been patriotic to be jealous of fighting men. The soldiers who wrote back and said they had no girlfriend of their own asked for photos. As a result Anna Lee, Norma, Patsy Marie, and others had their pictures carried into battles halfway around the world and looked at several times a day by boys they had never met. During those years some of the soldiers without much family developed lasting friendships with their pen pals in Elmwood Springs. But not *all* were pretty young girls. Bess Goodnight was thirty and married; she had eighteen soldiers she wrote to. She even sent all of her boys a pinup photo of Rita

Hayworth and had signed each one love and kisses from Bess Goodnight. After the war several of the boys came to town to visit her. They wanted to meet Bess, whose letters had meant so much and had helped them feel connected to home. As all wars do, it brought many people together who might never have met. For instance, in 1943, after she had gotten her wings, Ada Goodnight, while visiting New York City on a weekend pass, was to have a brush with greatness and with a real Hollywood star. And if it had not been for a complete stranger the incident could have gone unnoticed.

That night Ada and a bunch of gals in her squadron went out on the town and wound up at a famous place where a man asked Ada to dance.

And as she was to tell the tale later: "Honey, I danced the rumba at the El Morocco nightclub with a movie star and didn't even know it. This cute little short fellow came up and asked me to dance and when I stood up he grabbed me by the waist and off we went in a tizzy fit. I was jerked this way and that, back and forth all over that dance floor, and when I finally got back to my seat and caught my breath—so help me, Hannah—this man at the next table leans over and says to me, 'Young lady, you may not know it but you have just danced the rumba with Mr. George Raft!' And, oh, did I feel the fool. Not only did I not recognize George Raft, I didn't even know I had danced the rumba!"

Ada was to have many more exciting and dangerous experiences after that. One of her squadron's assignments was to fly over an artillery field dragging long white silk targets behind them so our soldiers could practice tracking and shooting down enemy planes. And some were not such good shots as yet and would occasionally miss the target and hit the plane. Ada wrote Bess that her tail had been hit so many times that it looked like Swiss cheese.

Back at home, although life may not have been as glamorous or nearly as dangerous as it was for Ada, the whole town was focused on winning the war. Neighbor Dorothy had adjusted all her radio recipes, leaving out or reducing the amount of the items that were rationed, sugar and fat, butter and meat. Victory gardens were planted in every yard and Doc Smith was the town's air-raid warden. They staged several blackouts and did well, although few really worried that the Japanese or the Germans would go out of their way to attack Elmwood Springs. But even without the threat of being bombed, the war years, as they did everywhere, brought heartbreak and change. In 1942 the entire senior football team at the Elmwood Springs high school had enlisted the day after graduation and some did not come back. The Nordstroms, who owned the bakery, lost their boy Gene in Iwo Jima in '44 and several farm boys living on the outskirts of town did not come back as well. Some of the older girls and women who had left town and gone to the larger cities to take factory jobs returned with different attitudes and ambitions than they'd had before they'd left. Ada Goodnight told her sister that if she could fly a plane there was no limit to what women could do—and proved it. She brought her new husband home and proudly introduced him all over town as her "war bride" and soon owned and ran her own flying school. Soldiers who returned seemed more serious than they had when they'd left. But even people who stayed home during the war had grown up a little faster than they should have, including Anna Lee.

At an age when she should have been concerned with nothing more than going to dances, wearing pretty clothes, and having fun, she received a letter.

October 24, 1945
Yorkshire, England

Dear Miss Smith,

I regret to report that your friend Pfc. Harry Crawford, United States Army, passed away in hospital this morning resulting from wounds received.

Although I did not know him long I can tell you he was a lovely boy and displayed bravery and courage right up to the very end.

If it is any consolation do know your letters and your photo cheered him greatly during his last days. As I was the one who read them to him, I felt I might take the liberty to write and return your letters and photo, along with my deepest sympathies for your loss.

Respectfully,
Glyniss Neale, R.N.
Veterans Hospital

That afternoon her mother tried to console her but there was little she could do except sit and listen as Anna Lee sobbed. "Oh, Mother, I'm so ashamed, I didn't even answer his last letter. I thought now that the war was over it didn't matter if I didn't write so much. . . . Now it's too late. . . . I feel so bad. I wish I could die."

It was shortly after that day that Anna Lee solemnly announced to her family that she had made a decision never to marry and to dedicate her entire life to the nursing profession. Her mother said, "Well, that's wonderful, honey, but let's wait until you finish high school and then see how you feel."

Dorothy certainly would not mind. As their next-door neighbor Nurse Ruby Robinson always said, "Nursing is a good steady profession." But Dorothy was not convinced Anna Lee would stick to her decision. Last year Anna Lee had announced to the family that she planned to become a professional ice skater and travel around the world. An odd ambition for a girl who had never been near an ice-skating rink in her life, but as Mother Smith quietly pointed out, Anna Lee might have seen one too many Sonja Henie movies.

The Songbird

After the war the town's population had remained much the same, except for the addition of Ada Goodnight's new husband and the Nordstroms' daughter-in-law, Marion, and their new grandbaby, who had come to live with them. Beatrice Woods, known professionally to her radio fans as the Little Blind Songbird, first moved to Elmwood Springs in the spring of 1945. Although she was Ruby and John Robinson's official boarder and paid rent, she was a distant relative of Ruby's. How she came to board with them that year turned out to be a stroke of good luck for everyone involved. As Dorothy said, "Everybody was in the right place at the right time."

The right place in this case being the funeral of Mrs. Lillian Sprott, who was Ruby's oldest sister. Ruby and her husband, John, had traveled to Franklin, Tennessee, for the occasion. Beatrice Woods, who was Lillian's niece by marriage, had been asked to sing at the funeral. At the time Beatrice and her father lived on a small farm outside of town.

Blind from birth, Beatrice had passed all nineteen years of her life so far pretty much limited to the house. Her little Philco radio was her only window to the world. Except for church on Sundays or a rare outing, she spent most of her days alone listening and had learned to sing just about every song she heard.

From the moment she sang her first song in church, her reputation quickly started to spread around the county. People came from miles around to hear the blind girl who sang like an angel. One Sunday, a visiting preacher, moved to tears by the beautiful sound of her high, lilting, almost ethereal voice, said it was as pure and clear as a songbird at dawn. From then on she was known as the Little Blind Songbird of Tennessee.

On the day of Lillian Sprott's funeral, when the preacher signaled it was time, Beatrice's father led the girl in a white dress up the aisle and put her in a chair and placed her zither in her lap. She sang the old hymn "Someone's Waiting for Me Up There" and ended the service with "There'll Be Peace in the Valley."

After she finished there was not a dry eye in the house. One woman who had not particularly cared for the dear departed remarked that old Lillian had most certainly been sung into heaven that day, whether she deserved to be or not. John Robinson told Ruby they should get Beatrice to sing on *The Neighbor Dorothy Show*. Dorothy was always looking for talent. That afternoon her father asked Beatrice if she wanted to go. She immediately said yes and two days later she went on the radio and sang "Always." A guest artist on *The Neighbor Dorothy Show* was certainly not an unusual occurrence. Throughout the years Dorothy had featured many singers. Only the week before, twelve-year-old Ian Barnard, billed as Windsor's Wonder Boy of Song and Dance, had come all the way from Canada and had caused quite a stir singing and tapping to the tune "If You Knew Susie." But never before had there been such an overwhelming response to a single performance as there was to Beatrice Woods's first appearance. Calls and letters came pouring in, everyone wanting to hear more from the "Little Blind Songbird of Tennessee." And on the next appearance, when Beatrice sang "Old Shep," a song about a dog, everyone who had ever had a dog that died, or even one that might, broke down and sobbed, including Neighbor Dorothy, who had to leave the room and when she came back was barely able to sign off the air. Down at the hardware store, fifteen-year-old Macky Warren, who was helping his daddy, heard it and cried so hard over his dog Tess he made himself sick and had to go home. She was such a hit that Neighbor Dorothy asked her to appear on the show every week and the Golden Flake Lite-as-a-Feather Flour company agreed to pay her room and board if she would. Her father drove her back over to Elmwood Springs, this time with her clothes and her radio. As it turned out, Beatrice knew the words to hundreds of songs and could sing anything—hymns, popular songs, gospel, country, you name it. Pretty soon she received so many requests she was appearing on the show every day. Since she was now living in Missouri she dropped the "of Tennessee" from her title and just went by the "Little Blind Songbird." She did not have far to go every day since Ruby and John lived right next door. Doc ran a clothesline from one back door to the other so she could hold on to it and find her way back and forth between the two houses without any trouble. This worked out fine unless it rained. Then she was told to wait on the back porch until someone came over to get her.

The Secret

Bobby would be the first one to discover Beatrice's secret. One rainy morning Dorothy looked out the window in the kitchen and saw that it was not letting up and told Bobby he better go get Beatrice. He had just finished his breakfast, said O.K., and started for the door when his mother stopped him.

"Bobby, take the umbrella."

Bobby moaned. He did not mind going to get Beatrice—he liked her—but he did mind having to take the umbrella. Muttering to himself, he went to the hall closet and rummaged around behind the heavy winter coats his mother had hanging there and pulled out the large black umbrella he despised with a passion. The huge multispoked creature had tortured him for years. Besides being almost as big as he was, it had a mind of its own and was mean and ornery. One spoke was always off and by the time he wrestled it to the ground three or four more had popped off. Then there was the problem of maneuvering it out the back door without falling down the stairs. Mother Smith said never to open an umbrella in the house because it was bad luck but if he stood outside on the back steps he would be drenched before he could get it open, so what was the point.

He dragged the dreaded monster to the back door, pushed with all his might, and the thing popped into place but as usual one spoke on the left side flipped up. He decided not to even fool with it and he banged and pulled himself and the umbrella out the door and down the steps.

Beatrice was dressed and waiting. She had on her yellow raincoat and rain hat and galoshes, which Nurse Ruby always insisted she wear just to walk from one house to the other. Beatrice greeted him before he opened the screen door.

"Hi, Bobby," she said, knowing it was him by the way he ran up the steps.

They walked arm in arm, chatting.

"What are you going to sing today, Beatrice?"

"Oh, I don't know yet. . . . What do you think?"

Bobby thought about it as he guided her around a big puddle.

"What about 'Cool Cool Water'?" Bobby's musical tastes always led him to suggest cowboy songs first. "Or maybe 'April Showers'?"

Beatrice nodded. "Those are two good ones."

Mother Smith was waiting for them on the other end and opened the door. "This is a humdinger, isn't it? Come on in and let me get those wet things off of you." Beatrice loved going to the Smith house every morning. It was a treat for her, with the aroma of warm, freshly baked cookies and the sounds of people running in and out and busloads of fans dropping by to visit. It was a far cry from the quiet rooms where she spent most of her time.

The Robinson house, given Nurse Ruby's fear of germs and considering her personal credo, "I never met a germ I couldn't kill," always had the slight smell of Lysol disinfectant lingering in the air. After the show Beatrice usually stayed for lunch and went home around one. That day the rain continued in a constant downpour and Bobby was summoned from the attic, where he had been busy mowing down an army of clay soldiers with a tank made out of a large matchbox. When they stepped out Dorothy's back door, Beatrice heard Bobby grunting and struggling with the umbrella and whispered, "Bobby, let's not even use that thing. Let's just go without it."

Bobby's eyes lit up. "You don't care if you get wet?"

"No. Don't you think a walk in the rain would be fun?"

"Yeah!"

She took her rain hat off and put it in her pocket. "Let's go!"

About ten minutes later Bobby and Beatrice were having the time of their lives, running up and down the sidewalk in their bare feet, stomping in every puddle Bobby could find. They were headed up to the end of the block again when Ruby Robinson, who had just come in from work, looked out the window and saw them. She ran out on the front porch and hollered for them to come in this very minute. Hers was clearly a medical concern; she took the responsibility of her boarder's health very seriously.

They were both soaking wet and by the time they came up the front stairs, Ruby was in a fit. "Well, I've heard of people who didn't have enough sense to come in out of the rain but this is the first time I've seen it with my own eyes. And to think, Bobby Smith, that you of all people would lead a poor little blind girl around in a downpour."

Beatrice defended Bobby. "It's not his fault. I'm the one who wanted to walk in the rain."

Nurse Ruby looked at Bobby, dripping all over her rug. After she moved him off the rug onto some newspapers, she said somewhat skeptically, "Well . . . whoever's idea it was, if you die of double pneumonia it's not going to matter. Both of you ought to be ashamed, putting your health at risk for such foolishness. I'll be surprised if you live out the week."

Despite her dire predictions, neither one got sick, not a cold or a sniffle, a disappointment to Nurse Ruby, who took their temperature daily for a week. After the seventh day, unable to detect the slightest symptom, she relented. As she held the thermometer up to the light and it read 98.6 again she said, "Well, all I can say is that you both were just lucky this time, that's all."

Later that day she said to Dorothy, "Imagine if that girl had come down with pneumonia and died while she was living under the roof of a registered nurse, what would people think? After all, I have the responsibility for the health of this entire community and I take that seriously."

Neighbor Dorothy said, "I know you do and everybody appreciates it but—"

She continued. "Beatrice takes this whole episode lightly but I have a medical reputation to uphold. How could I go on giving out medical advice on the radio if my very own boarder had died right out from under me, I ask you that?"

Dorothy tried to be sympathetic and tactful at the same time. "Ruby, I know you worry about her and that's very sweet of you but don't you think she needs just a little bit of fun every once in a while?"

Nurse Ruby puffed up and slung one side of her blue cape over her shoulder. "Fun? Well, Dorothy, if you call putting your health at risk fun, then no, I don't."

There was no getting around Ruby, but what she did not know would not hurt her, was Bobby and Beatrice's way of thinking. From that day forward Beatrice was taken on many secret excursions that Nurse Ruby knew nothing about. Including one wild ride in a wheelbarrow, a trip out to Blue Springs on the back of one of Anna Lee's boyfriend's motorcycles, a gallop on the back of an old mule that Monroe had borrowed and brought over, and a slide down a hill in the snow on a flattened cardboard box.

They had only been caught once when some busybody happened to mention to Ruby, "Oh, by the way, I saw your boarder Beatrice out at the state fair riding that big roller coaster and she and Bobby Smith were screaming their heads off."

This information was serious enough to cause Ruby to put on not only her official nurse's cap but her cape as well and immediately march over to the Smith house to tell his mother. And even Dorothy was a little alarmed at the thought of a blind girl on a roller coaster. "What if she had fallen out and broken her neck?" she said afterward to Bobby. Bobby just thanked his lucky stars that someone had not told Nurse Ruby about the other rides he and Beatrice had gone on that night, including the Loop the Loop, the Thunderbolt, the Whip, the Wild Mouse, the Caterpillar, and the bumper cars. Especially the bumper cars. They both could have gotten hurt the way he drove. With Beatrice at his side, going as fast as the car would go, he had whizzed around the track like a madman, with blue electrical sparks flying overhead, crashing into everybody he could. And in turn Monroe, a speed demon in his own right, had shown them no mercy and banged them back and forth with a vengeance. Not to mention the time Luther Griggs bashed them from behind so hard that they both were almost knocked out of their car. But bumps and all, Beatrice had loved every minute of it. At the end of the ride she exclaimed, "Oh, Bobby, let's do it again!" and they had. Two more times, as a matter of fact.

That was the summer Bobby found out her secret. Something that most people just looking at this sweet, serene, almost ethereal person would never have guessed in a million years. Beatrice Woods had a wild streak. She longed for romance and adventure. And more than anything in this world, she loved to ride.

Anna Lee

Bobby's sister and her two best friends, Norma and Patsy Marie, were growing up together. Norma was a pretty brunette girl whose father ran the only bank in town. Patsy Marie's parents, Merle and Verbena, owned and operated the Blue Ribbon Cleaners. Patsy Marie made the best grades of the three but was not a beauty. As her aunt put it, "She had old-maid schoolteacher written all over her from the time she was six," but she was sweet. All three were nice girls and if they had a fault it might have been that at present they were right in the middle of their movie-star phase.

Every time the feature at the Elmwood Theater changed they were there in the twelfth row center. Each had a different movie actor they adored. Anna Lee's major heartthrob this month was Dana Andrews. She filled piles of scrapbooks with pictures of him cut out of movie magazines. Patsy Marie's current crush was Alan Ladd, whom she had just seen in *The Blue Dahlia.* But Norma's movie star du jour was a puzzlement to both the other girls. She chose a lesser-known actor named William Bendix. They asked her why him; he wasn't even good-looking. "Well, that's the point," she said. "*Somebody's* got to like him."

However, as the school year grew closer to the end they concentrated on the upcoming high school prom and movie stars took a backseat. Norma would be going with Macky, of course, and Patsy Marie would go with her cousin, as usual. Anna Lee was the only one who had not committed to any of the boys who had asked her so far. The really overriding question was what they were going to wear. All the girls in high school, no matter who they were, wanted store-bought prom dresses. Wearing a "homemade" prom dress would be akin to sprouting a big red *H* on your forehead. Although Neighbor Dorothy had a degree, made her own patterns, and was one of the best dressmakers in the state, she knew that nothing would do but to let Anna Lee go down to Morgan Brothers department store with the rest of them and buy her dress off the rack. It would cost about three times as much as it would for her to make it, but her daughter had to have a store-bought dress or die of humiliation. At least that's what she said.

One of the other lures of buying a dress at Morgan Brothers department store was the saleslady, Mrs. Marion Nordstrom, who was in charge of the Better Dresses Department. If Mrs. Nordstrom helped you pick out your dress, then you had arrived. All the girls in Anna Lee's group thought she was one of the most exquisite creatures who had ever lived. Tall and aloof, always impeccably dressed in the latest fashions, she was their ideal. A war widow, she had come all the way from San Francisco, California, and the wardrobe she had brought with her was the constant topic of all the high school girls. "She never wears the same thing twice," they declared in admiration. After school Anna Lee and Patsy Marie would stroll into the store and pretend to shop just to see what she had on that day.

Anna Lee even copied the way she wore her hair piled high up on her head. The hairdo, Dorothy suggested, might be a little mature for a girl who still wore bobby socks and penny loafers but Anna Lee thought it was the last word in sophistication. The only concern Dorothy ever had about Anna Lee was that she might be getting a little spoiled. In every school there is always one girl that all the boys are crazy about and from first grade on Anna Lee had been that girl.

The only male who seemed to be oblivious to her charms was Bobby, who could not wait to torment her every chance he got. And she in turn could not wait to run and tattle on him for every little thing he did and because she was older everybody always believed her side of the story. Consequently, Bobby was not at all happy about the fact that Anna Lee had arrived on earth six years before he had. A fact that she never let him forget. He hated it when the family sat around and told stories about things that had happened before he was born. He would ask over and over, "But where was I?" His mother would answer, "You weren't here yet," at which point his sister would always sigh and say, "Those were the good old days. I was still an only child," or something equally obnoxious. Not only did it irritate him that he had not arrived sooner; it completely baffled him.

No matter how hard he tried, Bobby could just not seem to comprehend the world without him. Where had he been? What had he been doing? One afternoon, confined to the house because Luther Griggs was floating around the neighborhood waiting to beat him up again, he took the opportunity to follow his mother around the kitchen, asking her the same old questions.

"But if I wasn't here, where was I?"

"You weren't born yet," she said, slicing potatoes.

"But where was I *before* I was born?"

"You were just a twinkle in your daddy's eye, as they say. Could you hand me the butter?"

"When I was born was I already me or did I just come here and then I was me?"

"You were always you."

He handed her the butter plate. "Would I still have been me if I had been born in China—or would I be a Chinaman?"

"Oh, Bobby, I wish you wouldn't ask me all these silly questions. All I know is that you are a part of Daddy and me and you are who you're supposed to be."

"Yeah, but what if you hadn't married Daddy, then what would have happened?"

"I don't know," she said as she greased a glass casserole dish with the stick of butter. "I can only tell you that you were born at the exact time and place you were supposed to be, and besides I wished for you."

"You did?" said a surprised Bobby. "Like on a wishbone or something?"

"Something like that."

"What did you say when you wished?"

"I said, I want a little boy with brown eyes and brown hair that looked just like you, and here you are. So, you see, you're a wish come true. What do you think about that?"

"Wow." Bobby stood there for a minute thinking it over. Then he said, "How do you know you didn't get the wrong boy?"

"Because don't forget, there is somebody up there that knows better than you and I."

Dorothy went over and turned the oven on and pulled the cheese out of the icebox as Bobby trailed behind her. "Yeah, but what if He got mixed up and made a mistake? What if I was born in the wrong year or the wrong country even . . . ?"

"He doesn't make mistakes."

"But what if He did?"

"He doesn't."

"Yeah, but suppose He *did,* then what would happen?"

Dorothy placed the casserole dish in the oven. She stood at the sink to wash her hands with Bobby right behind her, waiting. After she dried her hands she turned around and looked at him. "Well, Bobby, is there somewhere else you would rather be than here with us?"

Bobby immediately said, "No . . . I was just wondering, that's all," and tried to look as innocent as possible, pretending to suddenly remember that he had to water his daddy's bed of fishing worms in the backyard.

He had not been entirely truthful with his mother. Sometimes at night he would secretly fantasize that one day someone would knock on their door and say, "We are here for the boy." Then his parents would come and get him and tell him who he *really* was. He was really the rightful prince of England and they had just been keeping him until he was twelve. Then he would ride through the streets of cheering people and as he passed by they would bow and whisper, "It's the young prince." All his teachers at school would curtsy and bow. As he went by his house his parents and grandmother would all be gathered together on the front porch and would bow, too. He would quickly motion for them to stand up and Anna Lee would run to the carriage and grovel at his feet in tears. "I'm sorry for everything I ever did to you, Your Majesty. I didn't know who you really were. Forgive me, forgive me." "You are . . . forgiven," he would say with a sweep of his hand. He would be a gracious, forgiving ruler for all the people except for Luther Griggs. He would have him arrested and dragged through the streets in chains, crying and begging for mercy but to no avail. Ah, the pure joy of it all.

Then there were other times when he daydreamed he was really the son of Roy Rogers and Dale Evans who had been kidnapped at birth but found at last. There would be another parade down Main Street, only this time he would be riding on the back of Trigger with Roy tipping his big cowboy hat to all as they rode by. Dale and Gabby Hayes would be riding beside them smiling and waving to the cheering crowds. He would go to live with Roy and Dale on the Double R Bar Ranch and bring his Elmwood Springs family with him. His days would be spent riding the range for bad guys, nights sitting around the campfire listening to the Sons of the Pioneers sing cowboy songs, and they would all live happily ever after. *"Happy trails to you . . . until we meet again."*

But for the time being, at least, he was just plain Bobby Smith. And unfortunately for Anna Lee, he was, as she always suspected, up to something.

Bobby knew of only one sure way to get even with his sister for telling his mother he had been out at Blue Springs, a betrayal that had caused him to get grounded and miss seeing *Pals of the Saddle* and *Wild Horse Roundup* the following Saturday. He and Monroe had been plotting and planning for weeks. "It" was to happen the night of the prom.

His mother and Grandmother Smith were chaperones and Doc always kept the drugstore open late on prom night so the kids could come in afterward and eat ice cream. Jimmy would be off playing Friday night poker with his buddies at the VFW. Bobby and Monroe had the house entirely to themselves, so they could put their plan in action without anyone seeing them.

After the deed was done they went back to Bobby's room and waited. Anna Lee was the last one home and floated in on a pink cloud at around 12:29, only one minute away from her 12:30 curfew, still glowing from her romantic evening. She had danced all night under silver paper stars and blue and white crepe-paper banners that hung from the ceiling of the gymnasium with her date Billy Nobblitt, a Van Johnson look-alike, or so she thought. She dreamily undressed, still hearing the strains of "It Had to Be You" and "Polka Dots and Moonbeams" playing over and over in her head.

When she had put on her nightgown and brushed her teeth, she carefully placed her gardenia corsage in a glass of water and put it on her dresser. She crawled into bed tired and happy, a feeling of bliss that lasted about one second.

She immediately shot out of bed screaming, "Snakes, snakes," over and over at the top of her lungs. She ran to her parents' room, threw their door open, and screamed, "Help . . . I've been snakebit!" and fainted dead away in a heap.

After Doc and Dorothy had tended to Anna Lee and had gotten her revived and somewhat calmed down, and after Mother Smith, out in the hall in her hair net and clutching her robe, had announced, "If there are reptiles in the house, I'm not staying," peace reigned briefly. Mother Smith would not go back to bed until Doc went over to Anna Lee's room to check. But it was no nightmare. Anna Lee's bed was crawling with about a hundred slimy, squirming red worms straight from his own worm bed in the backyard. He'd guessed correctly.

"I don't know why she has to make such a big deal out of it. They're just harmless little worms," said Bobby as he was being pulled out from under the bed by his father. And to make matters worse, the minute Doc had opened the door, Monroe, his true-blue blood brother, had jumped out the window and run all the way home in his Hopalong Cassidy pajamas, leaving Bobby to face the music alone.

Anna Lee was furious at Bobby and said that as far as she was concerned, he did not exist anymore. She made it a point to ignore him. She did not speak to Bobby for quite a while, until one day she forgot she wasn't speaking to him and asked him to bring her some milk from the kitchen.

He reacted by laughing and pointing at her, saying, "Ha, ha, I thought you weren't speaking to me. Go get it yourself" and ran off the porch and down the street. A disgusted Anna Lee got up and went to the kitchen and opened the icebox and asked her mother, "What I don't understand is why you had to have another child. Why didn't you just stop with me?" Dorothy smiled. "Well, honey, we thought we had." Anna Lee turned and looked at her mother in surprise; this was the first she had heard of this. "What happened?"

"I guess the Good Lord just decided to send us another little angel down from heaven."

"I may be sick," said Anna Lee and left the room.

Mother Smith came in. "What's the matter with her?"

Dorothy laughed. "She wanted to know why we had to have Bobby."

"What did you tell her?"

"I blamed it all on the Good Lord."

"Well, that's as good an excuse as any. According to the Presbyterians, everything in life is preordained, or at least that's what Norma's mother says."

"Ida? How would she know, she's a Methodist."

"Not anymore. As of last week she claims she's a Presbyterian."

"What?"

"Oh yes . . . right in the middle of the bridge tournament she announced it."

Dorothy, amazed, cracked three eggs in a tan bowl with a blue stripe and stirred. "But there's not a Presbyterian church within a hundred miles around here. Why would she want to be a Presbyterian all of a sudden?"

Mother Smith poured herself a glass of iced tea. "I suppose it's all part of her plan to move up in the world."

Dorothy was baffled. "Well . . . I just don't know what to say. . . . There's a lemon in the icebox. I just hope she'll be happy."

Mother Smith reached into the icebox. "I do, too, but I don't think anything can make her really happy unless, of course, Norma marries a Rockafella and she can at last take her rightful place in society."

High Society

What Mother Smith said was true. If there was such a thing as high society in Elmwood Springs, Norma's mother aspired to be it. After all, Ida Jenkins's husband, Herbert, was the town banker and as such Ida felt she had a certain position to uphold and it was her civic duty to set the standards of genteel behavior. To light the way. Set an example. She was in charge of all the refinements of life and in her relentless pursuit to bring culture and beauty to the community she nearly drove Norma and her father crazy.

Even though she was living in a small town in the middle of nowhere, she subscribed to all the latest women's magazines to keep abreast of the times. In the late thirties she took to spelling the word *modern* "moderne" and referring to their house as a "bungalow," her clothes as "frocks." She used the word "intriguing" as much as possible, had her hair styled just like Ina Claire, the Broadway star, and she never cried when she could weep or have "wept."

Too, Ida was a club woman from tip to top. She was the grande dame of the National Federated Women's Club of Missouri and had spearheaded the local Garden Club, Bridge Club, the Wednesday Night Supper Club, the Book Club, and the Downtown Theatrical Club and was never seen on the street without a hat and white gloves. She never served a meal in her home without having an individual nut cup at each place setting and a clean white tablecloth. "Only heathens eat off a plain table," she said.

On Norma's sixteenth birthday she had given her a copy of the new and enlarged edition of Emily Post's book on etiquette, in which she had inscribed:

> If everyone would read this we would certainly be spared a lot of unpleasantness in this world.
>
> Happy Birthday
Love,
Mother

Ida was even on a first-name basis with the author and often wondered out loud, "I wonder how Emily would handle this?" Or she would sometimes preface her remarks with, "Emily says . . ." Ida's life goal and, she assumed, all of America's was to bring enlightenment not only to Elmwood Springs but to the entire world until even in the farthest igloo at the North Pole and the wilds of the deepest darkest jungles in Borneo people everywhere would know that the fork belongs on the left and that fresh flowers on a table supply a delightful treat for the eye, that a clean house is a happy house, and come to embrace the fact that raising one's voice in anger is rude and uncalled for on any occasion.

Ida always said, "Remember, Norma, in America a person of quality and class is not judged by aristocracy of birth but by his or her behavior." Norma figured that by that standard her mother must have thought she was the duchess of Kent by now.

Norma loved her mother but, as Norma said to Anna Lee, "You try living with her twenty-four hours a day. You just don't know how lucky you are to have your mother and not mine." In fact, Norma spent the night at Anna Lee's as often as possible, as did Monroe. The house was always full of people and fun things to do and the food was delicious. And most important, over at Neighbor Dorothy's house you could actually sit on the living room furniture, something Ida never let Norma or her father do. In Ida's house the living room was only shown to people as they passed by and was called the formal room. It was so formal that nobody had been in it since she had decorated it eighteen years before.

◆ ◆ ◆

On one of the numerous occasions when Norma was spending the weekend over at Anna Lee's house, she helped Anna Lee pull a good one on Bobby and Monroe. One Saturday afternoon, Bobby and Monroe were in the parlor with the blinds and shades drawn, sitting in the dark eating peanut-butter-and-banana sandwiches and listening to their favorite scary detective shows on the radio. They had just heard *Yours Truly, Johnny Dollar, Boston Blackie,* and *The Whistler* and now a new show was just starting.

First strange and weird chords played on an organ, then a voice came through:

WOMAN: There he goes into . . . that drugstore. He's stepping on the scales.

(*Sound: Clink of a coin.*)

WOMAN: Weight, two hundred and thirty-seven pounds.

(*Sound: Card dropping.*)

WOMAN: Fortune. *Danger!*

Organ: (*Stinnnng!*)

WOMAN: Whooo is it?

MAN: The Fat Man!!!

As promised, this week's program was chock-full of suspense and mystery. Near the end both boys were literally sitting on the edge of their seats. Just as the strange man in the raincoat was being followed down a wet, dead-end street, with the sound of footsteps following behind him, growing louder and louder . . . click click . . . footsteps . . . closer and closer . . . louder and louder . . . nowhere to run . . . nowhere to hide . . . just at the very moment when the terrified man, his heart pounding, turned to face his fiendish killer, suddenly two figures wearing hideous rubber masks popped up from behind the couch with green flashlights shining under their chins, shouting *BAAA! BAAA!*

It scared them so badly that both boys shot straight up in the air and screamed like two little girls. They almost knocked each other down trying to get out of the room, falling over the coffee table and chairs while they scrambled for the door and ran down the hall.

Norma's boyfriend, Macky, had rigged the flashlights with green bulbs and the masks had come from last Halloween. The girls had been hiding behind the couch all afternoon, just waiting for the right moment. When Anna Lee gave the signal, all the waiting had been worth it.

The Winner

Neighbor Dorothy started with a great big "Good morning, everybody! Well, I could hardly wait to get on the air this morning because as Gabriel Heatter says, 'Ah, there's good news tonight!' or in our case, today, and we are just tickled pink and chomping at the bit to tell you about it. But first let me ask you this: does your soap powder make you sneeze?

"Mrs. Squatzie Kittrel of Silver Springs, Maryland, says, 'Rinso washes my clothes fast in rich soapy suds and it's so easy on my hands and on wash days it does not make me sneeze like all the others.' So remember, Rinso white, Rinso bright, the only granulated soap that is ninety-eight percent free of sneezy soap dust. And also, are you looking for checked, striped, or polka-dot material for that bedroom den or kitchen window? If so, Fred Morgan of Morgan Brothers says come on in and he's also got a big bolt of dotted Swiss material he's going to discount by the yard, so if you have been thinking about making curtains, this is the time.

"And now to the *big* news of the day . . ." Dorothy picked up the letter with the good news and beamed with pride. "You know, usually we don't like to blow our own horn but we are all so excited we can hardly contain ourselves, so we just had to tell you about it." Mother Smith played a fanfare on the organ. "Yesterday it was announced that Doc has won the Rexall Pharmacist of the Year Award for proficiency in dispensing drugs for the second year in a row. And he's to receive it in person at this year's Southeastern Pharmaceutical Convention in Memphis and I plan to be right there to see him get it. So if you are listening at the drugstore, Doc, we are mighty proud of you."

Down at the Rexall, Thelma and Bertha Ann, the two gals in the pink-and-white uniforms who worked behind the soda fountain, had the radio sitting on the shelf behind them. Thelma was washing a glass banana-split dish and Bertha Ann was making the egg salad for the lunch crowd when they heard the news. They both stopped what they were doing and whistled and clapped and yelled to the back, "Yeah! Whoopee! Great going, Doc. Congratulations! Our hero!" Doc, who had just finished filling a prescription, handed a customer a bottle of paregoric for her baby who was teething. When she asked Doc what had happened, he said, embarrassed, "Oh nothing, those two are just acting crazy. You know how they are . . . just silly." He continued, "Now you don't need much, just a few drops in a glass of water, and that should do the trick."

After she left Doc walked over to the soda fountain shaking his finger in mock anger. "You girls, what am I going to do with you two?"

They laughed. Bertha Ann said, "That's what you get for not telling us."

He sat down on a stool. "I guess I'm just going to have to put a muzzle on that wife of mine."

But he was secretly pleased. "Fix me a lemon ice-cream soda, will you, Bertha, and fix something for yourselves. Now that the cat's out of the bag we might as well celebrate."

Meanwhile, back on the show Dorothy made another announcement. "The other winner today of our What Is the Biggest Surprise You Ever Had Contest was sent to us by Mrs. Sally Sockwell of Hot Springs, Arkansas. She writes, 'Last year I lost the diamond out of my ring and I was so despondent because my husband, now deceased, had bought it for me when we were first married and now both were gone forever. So you can imagine my joy and surprise three weeks later when, frying an egg, I noticed something shiny in the white part and lo and behold it was my lost diamond. One of my hens must have pecked it out when I was collecting eggs. The Lord works in mysterious ways.' Yes, he does, Mrs. Sockwell, and thank heavens you weren't making an omelette or you might never have seen it.

"And speaking of missing objects, Leona Whatley called in and said that someone must have sold her sweater and purse at the school rummage sale. She says she put them down on a table for just a second and when she turned around they were missing. So whoever bought a blue woman's beaded sweater and a black purse with a small box of Kleenex that had not been opened inside please call Leona, as she would like to buy them back. We have a lot more coming up on the show this morning. Beatrice is going to be singing one of your favorites, 'I'm Forever Blowing Bubbles.' And yes, unfortunately, it's that time of year again. Next Saturday down at the Elmwood Theater they are having the annual Bazooka Bubble Gum Bubble Blowing Contest . . . well that's a mouthful . . . so mothers, get ready. I know Bobby is about to drive us insane over at our house—*pop, pop, pop, chew, chew, chew,* night and day. Also don't forget every Wednesday night is dish night at the Elmwood Theater, so go on down . . . and let's see . . . do we have anything else I'm forgetting, Mother?"

Mother Smith played a few strains of the funeral march and pointed to a jar on the desk. "Oh, that's right, thank you, Mother Smith. Last week we told you about a new instant coffee but we will have to take it off our list of recommendations, and I am just as sorry as I can be about it but it's just not up to snuff, as they say, is it, Mother Smith? She says no and made a face but as I say to all my sponsors, Keep trying because we are behind you one hundred percent.

"And remember our motto: If at first you don't succeed, try again."

Unfortunately for Bobby, his mother's motto was one he was to hear from her firsthand the very next week, when he dragged in the door having lost the Bazooka Bubble Gum Bubble Blowing Contest for the second year in a row. It didn't help him feel much better. He had practiced long and hard until his jaws were sore but he came in sixth. Rats, he thought. Everybody in the family is always winning something but me.

The Boy Who Cried Wolf

Doc was home for lunch and Dorothy stood by the kitchen table waiting for an opinion about the new hat she had just bought for their upcoming trip to Memphis. He studied the object perched on her head for a long moment and then said, "Oh, I don't know, Dorothy. As far as hats go, I've seen worse."

"Well, thanks a lot," she said.

Mother Smith jumped in and offered, "I like it," and gave her son a dirty look.

Dorothy blinked hopefully. "Really?"

"Oh, yes, it's very stylish. Don't ask him. He doesn't know anything about hats."

Doc readily agreed. "That's right. Don't ask me. I can't tell one from the other."

"Honestly," said Dorothy, "I don't know why I go to so much trouble if you don't know the difference. I could just stick a pot on my head for all you care."

When she left the room Mother Smith said, "Now you've done it."

Doc shrugged. "Well, they all *do* look alike, only this one looks like a pancake with some fruit and a dead bird on top." Beatrice Woods, who was sitting at the table, laughed. Doc leaned over and spoke under his breath. "Count yourself lucky you can't see it. You wouldn't know whether to shoot it or eat it."

After Doc had gone back to the drugstore they all sat around the table talking about the upcoming trip. Dorothy sighed. "I just wish I could lose ten pounds before I go."

Mother Smith said, "I just wish I was eighteen again and knew what I know now."

Dorothy said, "What would you do differently?"

"Oh," she said, "I'd marry the same man and have a child, of course, but I would have waited awhile before I did it . . . maybe been a bachelor girl like Ann Sheridan or a career woman and had my own secretary, smoked cigars, and used bad language."

Dorothy and Beatrice laughed and Dorothy said, "Beatrice, if you could have any wish come true, what would it be?"

Beatrice, whose favorite radio show was the *Armchair Traveler,* thought for a moment. "I would wish I could get in a car and drive all over the world and never stop."

Dorothy reached over and touched her hand. "Would you, honey?"

"Oh yes," she said. "Wouldn't that be fun?"

"It sure would," said Mother Smith and quickly changed the subject. She could see that Dorothy was about to get emotional. What was doubly heartbreaking about Beatrice was that even though being blind had limited her life, she did not have an ounce of self-pity and they had to be sure she never heard any in their voices. And it was especially hard when the thing she wished for could never come true.

A week later, the old adage about the boy who cried wolf once too often came true for Bobby when he woke up and claimed he couldn't go to school that day because he had broken out all over in big red spots. Dorothy knew this was the day of a big math test that he had probably not studied for. Last year at this time he had claimed his leg was broken. The year before it was appendicitis. So she sent Anna Lee to his room for the third time with a simple message. "Mother says if you're not up and dressed and out the door in five minutes you'll wish you had spots."

"But I do!" Bobby protested. "Come here and look at all these big red spots all over me and I feel sick. . . . Come and look." He pulled up his pajama top for her to see. "Look at these spots, they're getting redder by the minute, and I feel sick and I think I have a temperature, feel my head." But Anna Lee ignored him and said as she left, "Stay in bed—I don't care, I hope you do get a whipping." Bobby got up, mumbling and grumbling to himself, and put on his clothes and went to the kitchen to find his mother, who promptly handed him a banana. "Here, eat that on the way to school."

"But, Mother—" he said.

"I don't want to hear it, Bobby. Now you go on before you're late." He mumbled some more under his breath and stomped down the hall and out the door, slamming it behind him.

At about 2:00 that afternoon Bobby's teacher called.

"Dorothy, I just wanted you to know that I had to take Bobby down to the sick room because he was all broken out in red spots. Ruby says he's come down with measles and needs to be quarantined."

Dorothy was alarmed. "Oh, no. Tell Ruby I'm on my way to get him right now, and thank you for calling."

Dorothy could not have felt any worse and Bobby played the part to the hilt. "I told you I was sick, Mother," he said in a thin voice and by the time Anna Lee got home from rehearsal, at 5:30, Bobby was propped up in his bed like a king, his every whim catered to. His bed was covered with loads of new comic books his father had brought home for him from the drugstore. He had already been served ice cream, two Cokes, and a 7UP, and his mother stood by ready to do his slightest bidding. When Anna Lee walked into the room, Dorothy looked at her daughter with stricken eyes. "Your brother has the measles—the poor little thing really *was* sick." Bobby lay back and smiled weakly for her benefit and waited for Anna Lee to apologize. But instead of an apology she looked at him in horror and said, "Measles!" and ran out of the room to scrub her hands and face.

She was terrified of contracting a pimple, much less the measles. She had a performance to do. She was president of the Drama Club this year and was in the upcoming school play. It wasn't until Nurse Ruby assured Anna Lee that she could not catch the measles twice that she consented to go anywhere near him. Even then she wore gloves and a scarf over her face. She could not afford to take any chances. Not only was she in the school play, she was the lead!

Mother Smith, Jailbird

Unlike her son, Doc, who was easygoing, Mother Smith was a thin feisty little woman who had been quite a beauty when she was younger. Born in Independence, Missouri, right down the street from Bess Wallace, who eventually married Harry S. Truman. He and Mother Smith had once played the "Missouri Waltz" together on the twin pianos, and she often remarked about the president, "I met him on his way to greatness."

Mother Smith had always been a free-spirited woman, long before it was fashionable; she said you could not be born and raised in a town called Independence and not have it affect you. And it must be true: she had been one of the state's early suffragettes and in 1898 she, along with a group of her college girlfriends, had marched on Washington to fight for votes for women and had been arrested for disturbing the peace. This is a story Bobby and Anna Lee loved to hear over and over. "They sure threw us in the old hoosegow that day," she would say, then laugh and add, "Your grandmother may be a jailbird but we finally got the vote!" And although she was already in her forties at the time, she had been the first woman in town to get her hair bobbed. She had also visited a speakeasy in Kansas City, gotten a little tipsy on a teacup full of bootleg gin, and had played a jazz tune on the piano. But since she played organ for the First Methodist Church she did not spread that one around.

Mother Smith had small, dainty feet and was proud of them and liked to show them off. She owned over thirty pairs of shoes. And if Bobby got his curiosity from her, then surely Anna Lee had inherited her love of shoes. Just last week Anna Lee had gone downtown on Bargain Day and had spotted a pair of black-and-white saddle oxfords in the window of Morgan Brothers department store she was dying to have. But of course of all the shoes in the window those were the only ones not on sale. She had already spent her entire allowance buying her prom dress and was broke. For the next week, she was busy racking her brain trying to figure out how she could earn the money and living in fear someone else would buy them before she could. Every day she would go down and stare at them but she was having no luck until a few days before Doc and Dorothy were to leave for the convention in Memphis and Mother Smith suddenly had to go back to Independence to look after her sister, who had fallen and broken her hip. Even though Bobby's measles were practically over, Dorothy did not feel she should leave town with him still sick. She was still a little nervous about either of her children being ill, but to everyone's surprise Anna Lee immediately volunteered to stay home the entire weekend and baby-sit Bobby and look after Princess Mary Margaret for the price of the shoes, if she could get it in advance. Nurse Ruby said she would come over and check on him every day, and Jimmy assured her he would look after both Anna Lee and Bobby, too. So with much coaxing from everyone Dorothy decided to go after all.

For the next three days Bobby knew that Anna Lee was his captive slave. He spent them propped up in bed, listening to the radio, reading comic books, and barking orders for Cokes, root beers, ginger ale, ice cream, and anything else he could think of, while poor Princess Mary Margaret, a worrier from birth, wandered from room to room looking for Dorothy, clearly wondering where in the world she had gone and if she was ever coming back.

Doc and Dorothy had arrived at the Peabody Hotel in Memphis for the pharmaceutical convention on Friday night and the next day they were having a lovely time visiting with all their friends, unaware of the disaster in the making behind the scenes. In room 367, just down the hall, Norvel Float, the entertainment chairman for the big awards banquet, was fit to be tied. He had just been informed by telegram that the singing duo Willy and Buck, also known professionally as the How-Do-You-Do Boys, whom he had personally booked eight months ago for that night, had gotten into a fistfight over some woman in Shreveport, Louisiana. Buck had broken Willy's nose and run off to Chicago with the woman. Needless to say, they had canceled at the last minute and Norvel Float was left holding the bag with 723 pharmacists who would have no after-dinner entertainment. He immediately got on the phone and frantically called every booking agent in the area. But they had nothing. Not a single tap dancer, singer, comic, or even accordion player was available for that night. He even tried to get Tommy Troupe, the man who did bird-calls and was terrible at it, but was informed that Tommy had died a month ago. As a last-ditch effort Float took a chance and called one of the local radio stations, WRCC, located upstairs on the eighteenth floor of the hotel. The man there was not encouraging. He said all they had to offer was a traveling gospel group that had appeared on their station that morning at 6:00 A.M. and was still in town. Norvel hired them immediately over the telephone, no questions asked, sight unseen. The man on the phone hesitated a moment and then asked, "Are you *sure* you want them? They're kind of raw."

"Listen, mister," said Norvel. "I'm desperate. At this point, I'll take anything I can get. Just have them here by nine-thirty." He hung up a happy man. He had no idea what or whom he had just booked; he was just relieved to have something that could carry a tune.

The banquet that night was a splendid affair. Doc and Dorothy and all the other druggists and their wives were decked out in their finest formal attire. When Doc went up to receive his award, amid much applause, he looked so handsome and distinguished in his tux with his silver hair glistening in the spotlight that after he came back to the table Dorothy whispered to him, "I'm married to the best-looking man here."

He laughed and whispered back, "You're just saying that because you're stuck with me." Later, after all the other awards had been given out, the emcee for the evening came out and read what Norvel Float had hastily jotted down on a service napkin backstage:

"I hope you all enjoyed your dinner and congratulations to all the winners. And now, on with the show. Tonight we are lucky enough to have with us, all the way from Sand Mountain, Alabama, the famous Oatman Family Gospel Singers . . . and here they are, straight from their successful appearance on WRCC's *Yellow Label Table Syrup Gospel Hour* to sing some of your good old southern gospel favorites."

At this point the curtain opened, revealing the five Oatmans, a mother and father, two boys, and a girl. The mother, seated at the piano, a two-hundred-pound woman with white skin, her jet-black hair in a bun, without makeup, and wearing a homemade lavender dress, suddenly and without warning attacked the unsuspecting piano and took off from there, one chubby hand banging out the rhythm while the other banged out something else. The small upright seemed to be jumping up and down, fighting for its life, as she pumped away at the foot pedals. And again without warning the large older man, the two younger men, all in matching suits, and the young girl who had been standing motionless sang out at the top of their lungs, "HAVE YOU HEARD THE GOOD NEWS?"

There was not a person in the room that could not *help* but hear the good news. Minnie Oatman would see to that. Hers was the strongest voice in the group, a deep whiskey tenor so powerful it was said she could knock the paint off the back wall when she really let go. Those that did not care for her voice simply said she was loud. Over the next half hour the group ripped right on through "Glory, Glory, Clear the Road," "Every Time I Feel the Spirit," "Mansion on the Hill," "Tell Mother I'll Be There," "Some Glad Day," and "When I Reach That City." As they sang away, the pharmacists and their wives, particularly those from New York, Boston, and Philadelphia, sat in the audience, stunned, while most of the southerners nodded and smiled and tapped their feet. But the Oatman clan seemed completely oblivious to the audience one way or the other and continued on with rousing renditions of "Hang On, It Won't Be Long Now," "What a Day That Will Be," "I'm Climbing Higher and Higher," and ended with a song that Minnie proudly informed them she had just written that very morning while sitting in the hotel coffee shop having breakfast. She said, "It's called 'Can't Wait to Get to Heaven' . . . hope you like it," and threw her head back and proceeded to sing out with full-throated joy.

> I'll climb up those crystal stairs
> And run down that ivory hall
> Right up to that throne of gold
> Because I know Sweet King Jesus
> Will be waiting for me there.

Oh I'll know Him when I see Him
I'd know Him anywhere.
His wounds have turned to rubies.
Where thorns once did dwell
Diamonds now sparkle in his hair.

Can't wait to get to Heaven
Oh I'll be so happy there
To leave all this pain and sorrow.
All my struggles will be lifted
No more earthly burdens to bare.

Can't wait to run up those crystal stairs
And down that ivory hall
Can't wait to shout . . . *Hallelujah!*
At last my trials are over
'Cause Sweet King Jesus will be there!

When she hit the final E-flat at the end of the song and held it, many people in the room heard the ice in their glasses crack. Some singers sing at the top of a note, some at the bottom, but Minnie Oatman had perfect pitch and always hit the note dead center with the accuracy of a silver bullet. More than a few in the audience still had a ringing in their ears long after the curtain closed.

The Oatmans Are Coming

It had been a lively show, to say the least. When it was over Doc commented to the man next to him, "I'll say this for them: I never saw folks look more forward to dying in all my life." But Dorothy had *thoroughly* enjoyed the show. She had heard gospel music before but she had certainly never heard it sung like this. What the Oatmans may have lacked in polish and style they certainly made up for in enthusiasm. She and Doc were not particularly fans of gospel but she knew that a lot of her listening audience out on the farms loved it. While most of the other banquet attendees began stumbling out of the room in a daze, headed for the bar, not really sure what they had seen and heard, Dorothy headed backstage to find the Oatmans and compliment them on their performance.

When she finally found her way backstage they were still packing up their sound equipment. She walked over and introduced herself to Minnie Oatman and told her how she had so enjoyed their singing and said if they were ever in the vicinity of Elmwood Springs, Missouri, she would love to have them on her radio show. Minnie, who had worked up quite a sweat, was dabbing her face with a big white handkerchief. She said, "Well, bless your heart," then turned and called out, "Ferris, ain't we doing a revival somewhere in Missouri this year . . . or is it Arkansas? Look it up in the book. This nice lady wants us on her radio show." She apologized to Dorothy. "We hit so many places, honey, I can't keep up."

Ferris Oatman, who weighed a hundred pounds more than his wife, struggled to pull a long thin black book from his inside coat pocket. After he looked through it he said, "We're booked at the Highway 78 Church of Christ outside of Ash Hill, Missouri, first week in July." Minnie turned to Dorothy. "Is that anywheres near you, honey?"

Dorothy said, "Yes, I know Ash Hill; it's not that far away from us. I'll be happy to have somebody come and pick you up—and bring you back. Where will you be staying?"

Minnie laughed. "Oh Lord, honey, we never know till we get there. We stay with whoever can put us up. The church usually finds us a place. There's six of us including Floyd—he's out in the car waiting, he don't work banquets, just churches and revivals, so if you know of a family willing to put one or two of us up for a week, let us know. You don't happen to have an extra bed or sofa, do you?"

Dorothy was put on the spot because the woman had just agreed to appear on her radio show. She glanced over at the young girl in the group, who looked to be about fifteen or sixteen, and said, "Ahh . . . well, as a matter of fact, Mrs. Oatman, we have a girl just about your daughter's age and I'm sure she would be just tickled pink to have her stay with us."

Minnie looked up to the ceiling and sang out, "PRAISE JESUS!" and looked back at Dorothy and said, "I tell you, Mrs. Smith, the Lord just drops good people right in our path every day." She sang out again in a loud voice, "THANK YOU, SWEET JESUS!" Dorothy was a little taken aback at this display and quickly added, "But now, Mrs. Oatman, just so you know, we're not members of the Church of Christ and I don't know if that matters but—"

Minnie waved her hand and dismissed the idea.

"Oh honey, that don't matter a whit just as long as you're Christian and don't drink alcohol or smoke or gamble." Before Dorothy could say anything one way or another Minnie yelled, "Ferris, we already got one placed in Ash Hill," and then turned back to Dorothy. "That's real kind of you, and of all of us, she's the leastest trouble, hardly eats a thing, you won't even know she's there." She waved the long white handkerchief at her daughter. "Betty Raye, come over here. This nice lady wants you to stay with her when we're over there in Missouri." Betty Raye, a pale thin girl with light brown hair and brown eyes, wearing a lavender dress exactly like her mother's, came over somewhat reluctantly.

Dorothy smiled at her. "Hello, Betty Raye. We're looking forward to having you with us. We have a daughter about your age and I know she's going to be very happy you are coming."

Minnie nudged Betty Raye. "Tell the lady thank you." The girl blushed and said something but she spoke so softly Dorothy could not hear what she said.

Later, after Dorothy returned to the table and realized what she had just done, she said to Doc, "Anna Lee is going to *kill* me."

Dinner on the Ground

The Oatman family was just one of the many white gospel groups traveling all over the South and Midwest that year. Groups like the Spear Family, the Happy Goodman Family, the Statesmen, the Harmony Boys, the Weatherfords, the LeFevres, the Dixie Four, the Tennessee Valley Boys, and the Melody Masters made their living by traveling and appearing at small churches, singing conventions, revivals, all-day sings, and dinner-on-the-ground events. The roots of what was now called southern gospel music had actually started in New England in the 1700s, when early colonists brought hymnbooks from the Old World. Gospel was the dominant musical style in America for a long time and was very popular at churches and camp meetings all over the country. However, after the Civil War the style of singing known as Sacred Harp or shape-note music lost its popularity in the North but was kept alive in the rural churches of the Deep South. In 1910 a man named James D. Vaughan published his first songbook, *Gospel Chimes.* To promote it he sent out the Vaughan Quartet, the first all-male southern gospel group in America. Eventually, he started the Vaughan School of Music in Lawrenceburg, Tennessee. Soon other schools opened, and by the 1930s southern gospel groups featuring men and women and children were springing up everywhere and crisscrossing the South, Midwest, and as far north as Iowa. The more successful gospel groups began to appear and thereby advertise over the radio and were able to promote a good crowd at their appearances.

But in 1946 radio appearances were a fairly new thing for the Oatmans. Ferris and his brothers, Floyd and Le Roy, had all been raised on a hardscrabble dirt farm in northern Alabama by strict Pentecostal parents. Because of his upbringing Ferris believed that just listening to the radio, much less singing and preaching over it, was a sin. As Minnie put it, "Ferris is bad to think the devil is behind everything." However, in 1945, after seeing how the other groups were attracting so many people to their appearances by using broadcasts to tell people where they would "be at," he prayed about it. A week later he said, "Minnie, the Lord spoke to me and said he wants us to go on the radio," and so it was settled.

Minnie Varner, the fourth child of an Assembly of God preacher, was born outside of Shiloh, Georgia. The Varners were a musical family and Minnie was playing piano in church by age nine. She met Ferris Oatman when she was twelve and he was twenty-four. She had been at an all-day sing and dinner on the ground playing for the Harmonettes, an all-girl gospel group from Birmingham. That day Minnie saw Ferris, with all that black curly hair, she fell in love. Ferris must have felt the same. That night he told his brother Le Roy, "I just met my wife today." Two years later, when she was fourteen, she ran off with him, ignoring the warnings of her parents and older brothers about marrying into a traveling gospel group. They said if she did she would be living in the back of a car hawking songbooks out of the trunk all her life. So far they had been right. But Ferris Oatman, who had worked picking cotton to send himself through the Stamps-Baxter School of Gospel Music in Dallas, felt he had a real calling. From the age of six all he ever wanted to be in life was a gospel quartet man. All Minnie wanted from age twelve was to be his wife and so she joined the group and went on the road.

After the two boys, Bervin and Vernon, and later Betty Raye were born, Minnie's parents bought them a small, two-bedroom house a few miles from where she was raised. They wanted the children to have a home base but they were hardly there long enough to do anything but wash and iron all their clothes and take off again. It was a hard life. During the Depression they lost Ferris's brother, Le Roy, their bass singer, who ran off to join a hillbilly band. Aside from the few dollars they made selling songbooks, they performed for free-will offerings, which could range anywhere from five dollars to ten dollars a night, depending on the size of the congregation. Money was scarce. Minnie said the only consolations were knowing they were doing the Lord's work, and the food. Most of the churches were in the country and there was always plenty to eat. In the homes where they stayed and at the numerous dinner-on-the-ground all-day singing events, even during the Depression, they were well fed. Fried chicken, ham, pork chops, fried catfish, fresh vegetables, sweet potatoes, mashed potatoes, biscuits and gravy, cornbread, fresh buttermilk, honey, jellies and jam, homemade bread, cakes, pies, and cobblers. They ate so much rich food it began to look like a lot of the gospel singers had been picked out by the pound. One man in Louisiana who had been an eyewitness to a car wreck outside of Shreveport involving a well-known gospel group remarked, "Why, they must have pulled out two thousand pounds of gospel singers in that one car alone. Of course the advantage of all that padding was that not one of them had been hurt." The disadvantage was, as Minnie put it, "Gospel singing is good for the soul but bad on the gallbladder." In the Oatman family only Betty Raye was thin and they couldn't understand it. But there were many things about Betty Raye they did not understand.

Home Again

Dorothy and Doc got back from the convention late Sunday night and Monday at 9:30 she was back on the air as usual. She opened the show with a "Good morning, everybody, I hope it's a beautiful day where you are but I'm mad at the weather over here—it's an old gray drizzly day. But rain or shine I am glad to be home again and especially to be back with all my radio friends. Our trip to Memphis was wonderful and we saw quite a few sights. Not only was there a family of ducks living in our hotel lobby, right across the street there was a hot dog stand that was open twenty-four hours a day. I said to Doc I couldn't imagine anyone wanting a hot dog in the middle of the night but I guess they do. Anyhow, Memphis is lovely but . . ." Mother Smith played a few bars of "There's No Place Like Home" and Dorothy laughed. "That's right, Mother Smith, and by the way, we are so glad to have Mother Smith back with us this morning and she reports that her sister Helen is doing well and is on the mend, as we say . . . and we send out our special good wishes to her this morning and to all our precious little shut-ins everywhere. And speaking of special, I have an exciting announcement for all of you gospel fans coming up later, but first . . .

"Let me ask you this: can you make biscuits that make your family say 'yummy'? If not, I want you to get yourself a bag of Golden Flake Lite-as-a-Feather Flour, guaranteed to make your entire family say 'yummy.' And before I read the winning letter of our How I Met My

Husband Contest, I need to say a great big hello and thank-you to our radio homemaker friend Evelyn Birkby, whose show *Down a Country Lane* is heard on KMA all the way up in Shenandoah, Iowa, for the sour-cream raisin pie recipe she has sent along. And let's see what else do I have. . . . Oh, Fred Morgan called and says he just got in a new shipment of brand-new Philco console radios, so come on down. I hate to say it, but I'm so old I can remember homemade radios, crystal sets made out of oatmeal containers and an old cigar box. What? Mother Smith says she remembers when we didn't have radio at all. Well, I'm glad we are living now instead of then because I love visiting with all my radio neighbors by way of the airwaves but how it works don't ask me. With so many of us on the air at the same time, why radio shows don't crash into one another up in the sky is still a mystery. I often wonder if a show disappears into thin air after it is heard or if it just keeps on floating around up there, but if you know don't tell me—I'm sure it would just scare me to death.

"Beatrice is here and has a song for all my Kentucky listeners, 'Starlight on the Blue Grass,' but first to our contest winner. Mrs. Boots Carroll of Enid, Oklahoma, writes,

> "Dear Neighbor Dorothy,
>
> "I met my husband at Alcatraz. No, he was not a criminal he was a prison guard. My church group was on a tour and when he saw me and I caught his eye, he followed us back to the tour bus and found out where we were staying and called me that night for a date. Although he was a guard he was handsome in his uniform and we have four grown children.

"Well, Mrs. Carroll, you win the prize hands down, so look for your certificate for a free five-pound bag of Golden Flake Flour." After Beatrice sang and Dorothy did a few more commercials, she made her announcement. "You know I'm always looking for good entertainment for you and while Doc and I were in Memphis I was lucky enough to see and hear a wonderful singing group, the Oatman family, and they will be here live on our show next month. I'll keep you posted on the exact date for all of you out there who love gospel music. Be sure to tune in, because you are in for a big treat."

Some of Neighbor Dorothy's audience in the towns may not have been aware of the Oatmans, but many others out in the country were happy to know they were coming. Particularly Norma's Aunt Elner Shimfissel, who had heard them on *Gospel Time, U.S.A.* She was just beginning to lose the hearing in her right ear and loved a group that sang loud.

After the show, as Dorothy was in Anna Lee's room admiring her new saddle oxfords and hearing all about how impossible Bobby had been while they were gone, Dorothy tried to find a way to gently drop the news about the houseguest that was coming next month. She pretended to be preoccupied with fluffing the curtains. She started off with a casual "And oh, by the way . . ." but it did not work.

"A Church of Christ gospel singer?" Anna Lee screamed. "In my room for an entire week? I can't believe it!"

"Now, sweetheart, I'm sure you will like her when you meet her. She seemed very nice," said Dorothy hopefully.

Anna Lee wailed and fell back on her bed in agony. "Oh, Mother, how could you do this without even asking me?"

"Well, it just sort of happened. Mrs. Oatman asked me if we had an extra bed . . . and you weren't there to ask. . . . I thought you wouldn't mind. She's about your age and, besides, you might enjoy meeting someone a little different."

"Different! Mother, those people don't even go to the movies or dance or wear makeup or anything!"

Dorothy remembered what they had looked like and had to confess, "Well, probably not. But that's their religion, so we'll just have to respect the fact. You can give up going to the movies or a dance for just one week, can't you?"

Anna Lee looked at her mother in horror. "Why do I have to give it up? I'm a Methodist."

"I just don't think it would be very nice to do something that she couldn't do."

"How am I supposed to entertain her if she can't do anything?"

"You can introduce her to some of your friends. I'm sure you can find a lot of things to do."

"Name one."

"Well, take her to the swimming pool or . . . maybe we can plan a little party for her in the backyard. Take her on a picnic."

"What else?"

"Oh, I don't know, Anna Lee, I'm sure you'll come up with a lot of things to entertain your guest while she's here."

"She's not *my* guest—I'm just the one who's going to be stuck with her night and day. What if she goes through all my things?"

"Don't be silly. She's not going to go through your things. She's a very sweet girl and I'm sure it will all work out just fine and it's not going to kill you to be nice to someone for one week. We'll talk about this later. Right now I've got to go and get supper started."

Dorothy was almost out the door when Anna Lee added, "All right, but if she shows up here wearing some tacky homemade dress I'm not taking her anywhere. She can just stay home."

Anna Lee had not really meant it but that last statement stopped Dorothy cold.

Her mother rarely got upset with her but Anna Lee knew in an instant she had gone too far. Dorothy turned around and looked at her for a long moment. "Anna Lee, don't tell me that I have raised a daughter who has turned out to be a snob. If I thought for one minute that you would ever be unkind to anyone, much less some poor girl who is probably looking forward to coming here and meeting you, it would just break my heart. I told that girl you would be happy to have her here but I guess I was wrong."

Anna Lee immediately felt terribly ashamed of herself. "I'm sorry, Mother, I didn't mean it."

Dorothy stood there thinking about what to do, then said, "I'll get in touch with Mrs. Oatman tonight and tell her they will have to make other plans. . . ."

"No, *don't* . . . I'm sorry, Mother."

But Dorothy turned and left the room. Anna Lee ran after her mother, pleading, "No! Please don't. Mother, please!"

"I'm not having that girl come where she's not wanted."

"But I want her to come. I promise I'll do anything she wants. Please let her come! I'll kill myself if you don't let her come." With that she collapsed on the floor in full-blown teenage-girl hysteria. "Please! Please! She can have my entire room, she can wear all my clothes, I'll sleep with Grandma. I'll entertain her night and day, I promise, please don't call!"

Dorothy had seen these histrionics before and was not convinced. "All right, Anna Lee, get up. I won't call today. But I'm not promising anything. Let's just see how you feel about it tomorrow."

From that day forward Anna Lee made it a point at dinner to mention that she was so looking forward to Betty Raye's visit and just couldn't wait for Betty Raye to get there.

Although it was not quite true, Anna Lee would rather walk through fire than ever disappoint her mother again.

The Reluctant Houseguest

A month later, at about four o'clock in the afternoon, a dusty old four-door green Packard, packed full of people, songbooks, and clothes, with sound equipment piled up on the top and on the running boards, drove up to the Smith house. A hand-painted sign on the back read THE OATMAN FAMILY—TRAVELING FOR JESUS.

Dorothy called out from the living room, "Anna Lee, Bobby, Betty Raye is here." All day Anna Lee had practiced smiling and looking happy for the arrival but when the beat-up car pulled up she secretly hoped nobody would see it.

The car door opened and three people stumbled out, and just as Anna Lee had feared the girl was wearing a light blue homemade dress with some sort of ugly green zigzag piping around the neck and sleeves. One of the Oatman boys untied a small brown cardboard suitcase from the running board and handed it to her and got back in the car.

Minnie was in the front seat by the window waving her handkerchief. "Here she is, Mrs. Smith," she said, then looked up at the house and exclaimed, "Oh, just look at what a pretty place you got. Look at all them nice shrubs and your pretty little flower beds—this is probably the nicest house she's ever stayed at."

Dorothy thanked her. "Won't you and your family come in and have a cold drink or a sandwich? I've made cookies for you."

"Oh no, honey, we can't, we just drove all the way from Oklahoma packed in here like sardines and my legs is all swelled up so bad I need to get where we're going. Besides, if we was to all get out now, no telling when we'd get everybody back in. The boys is bad to wander off whenever we stop . . . but we will take us a sack of them cookies if they're handy."

"Of course," Dorothy said. "Anna Lee, you and Bobby run in and put some wax paper around the cookies and wrap up the sandwiches." Minnie motioned for Dorothy to step over to the car and whispered, "Mrs. Smith, like I say, she won't eat much. . . . The only trouble you might run into is that she's a-liable to sit in a corner and not talk but don't take it personal. She's just real timid like and I don't know why or where she gets it from. Lord knows none of the other Oatmans is one whit timid. We've been praying she'll get a healing . . . but no luck so far."

After they got the cookies and the sandwiches, Minnie said, "I'll bring your plate back in the morning. We'll be here at nine sharp for your show, so don't you worry," and they drove off, leaving Betty Raye standing alone on the sidewalk.

A little too brightly Anna Lee said, "Hi, I'm Anna Lee, welcome."

Dorothy pulled him over and said, "And this is Bobby."

Bobby said, "Hello."

Betty Raye looked down at the sidewalk and nodded. There was an awkward moment when they all just stood there but Dorothy jumped in with "Come on in and let's get you settled. Bobby, take her suitcase." Bobby, who had been fascinated, staring at her odd dress, said, "Oh . . . O.K.," and took it from her, immediately asking, "Hey, is this made out of cardboard?"

Dorothy shot him a look. "I was just wondering," he said.

Betty Raye, who was used to staying with strangers wherever she went, seemed resigned to the situation and followed behind them, waiting to be told where to go. She said nothing until she was taken to Anna Lee's room. Dorothy opened the door and announced, "And this will be your room while you're here."

The large sunny room with the big white-lace canopy bed and the floral wallpaper looked like something out of a magazine. Anna Lee and Dorothy had worked all morning to get it ready. Dorothy had washed and starched the curtains to make the room as nice and as cheerful as possible for her arrival. They all waited for her to go on in first, but Betty Raye did not move from the doorway. Then she looked up at Dorothy, almost cringing, and asked in an apologetic voice, "Mrs. Smith, do you have anywhere else I could stay?"

Dorothy was completely taken aback. This was the last thing in the world they had expected to hear. "Oh," she said. "Don't you like this room? Is there anything wrong?"

"No, ma'am."

Dorothy was at a loss. All she could come up with was "Oh dear."

Bobby jumped in with a bad idea. "Hey, you can stay in my room if you want to. I've got all kinds of stuff in there."

"No, Bobby, she's not staying in your room. I'm just trying to think of where else you might like. We can take a look around if you like."

Betty Raye cringed again and almost whispered a scared little "Would you mind?"

Thoroughly flustered, Dorothy said, "No of course not, you're our guest. We want you to be happy."

As the three of them followed behind Betty Raye like a small parade all over the house from room to room, Dorothy glanced over at her daughter and threw her hands up and shook her head, as if to say silently, "I don't know what she's doing, do you?" But Anna Lee was suddenly enjoying this strange turn of events and did not respond. Instead, she just looked up in the air and innocently batted her eyes with an attitude that translated as "Don't look at me, you're the one who invited her." And at that moment Dorothy could have pinched her head off.

Betty Raye had almost gone through the entire house when she opened the door to the little sewing room off the sunporch. She looked in and pointed to the daybed that was against the wall, covered with old scraps of material and patterns. "Can I stay here?"

Dorothy, crushed, said, "Why yes, I suppose you can . . . but it's just a little hole in the wall no bigger than a closet. There's not even a place to hang your clothes. Wouldn't you really feel better having a nice big bedroom with your own bathroom?"

But Betty Raye said, "No, ma'am, this will be fine."

Dorothy tried to be cheerful. "Well, all right, we want you to be happy while you are here. Anna Lee, help me get all this stuff off the bed, and let's fold up the ironing board."

That night at dinner Betty Raye hardly ate a thing. She spoke only when spoken to and even that was minimal.

Doc had just gotten home in time for dinner and tried to chat with her. He asked pleasantly, "So, Betty Raye, how do you like your room?"

Bobby piped up. "She didn't like it. She's sleeping in the sewing room."

Doc looked at Dorothy. "Why is she sleeping in the sewing room? I thought she was going to stay in Anna Lee's." There was a pause you could have driven a truck through as Dorothy tried to come up with a tactful answer. But Bobby, oblivious to the awkwardness of the moment, noticed that their visitor did not have much of an appetite and took this opportunity to inquire, "If she doesn't want her dessert, can I have it?"

After dinner, without saying a word, Betty Raye went to the kitchen and stood by the sink, ready to help wash dishes. When Dorothy realized what she was doing she said, "Oh no, dear, you are a guest. You run on and enjoy yourself. Mother Smith and I will take care of this." Betty Raye seemed surprised but went straight to her room and closed the door. When Anna Lee, who had been dragging games out of the closet so they could play, came in and asked where she was, Dorothy said, "I'm not sure but I think she's already gone to bed."

"But it's only seven o'clock."

"Maybe she's tired from her trip, honey," Dorothy said.

"Well," said Anna Lee, "I guess we won't be playing Monopoly, will we?"

Later, before Dorothy had joined them on the front porch, Mother Smith confided to Doc, "She's an odd little person, isn't she?"

Is It Any Wonder?

That first night Mother Smith had thought Betty Raye was odd, but the next morning, after having encountered the *entire* Oatman clan in all its glory, including mystery man Uncle Floyd Oatman, complete with his Scripture-quoting ventriloquist's dummy named Chester, who wore a cowboy hat and proceeded to sing "Jesus Put a Yodel in My Heart," she changed her mind. Once she had seen the rest of the Oatman family, she quickly realized that Betty Raye was the best of the lot.

After they left and Betty Raye went back to her room, Mother Smith whispered to Dorothy, "Good God, no wonder she's a little peculiar. Who can blame her?"

At exactly 9:15 they had all piled out of the car and banged into the house like an invading army, and had eaten every one of the six dozen cookies in the entrance hall in less than ten seconds. During their segment on the show Minnie took over Mother Smith's organ and almost pumped it to death. After the group had done three songs, Chester the dummy announced in his high squeaky voice, "Don't forget, folks, starting tonight we're all gonna be at the Highway 78 Church of Christ annual dinner on the ground and tent revival all week—there's gonna be a whole lot of good singing . . . good eats . . . and soul saving, so come on out!" And then they all piled back in the car and left. The rest of the living room audience that day had thoroughly enjoyed their singing, particularly Beatrice Woods, the Little Blind Songbird, who had loved every song they sang and had clapped her hands in delight when Chester the dummy had yodeled. Mother Smith, not quite so enthralled, was glad to get her organ back in one piece. The fact that Betty Raye wore homemade clothes or was a gospel singer didn't make a bit of difference to Bobby. He was delighted to have another person in the house.

It gave him someone new to show off in front of. The second morning he waited until he saw Betty Raye go into the kitchen for breakfast. Just as she sat down at the table with Dorothy and Mother Smith, they heard a strange eerie whistle coming from down the hall. Then, wearing his father's long overcoat with the collar turned up over his ears and a big gray felt hat pulled down over his eyes, Bobby appeared in the doorway and in an odd voice announced to the room, *"I am the Whistler and I know many things, for I walk by night. I know many strange tales hidden in the hearts of men and women who have stepped into the shadows. Yes . . . I know the nameless terrors of which they do not speak!"* And then he disappeared as suddenly as he had appeared, laughing maniacally all the way down the hall.

Betty Raye had been somewhat startled by this odd behavior but everyone else at the table just kept eating. The only thing Dorothy said, as she buttered a piece of toast, was "If he would spend as much time with his schoolwork as he does listening to his radio shows he'd be a genius." Betty Raye glanced out the window and saw a woman in sunglasses holding on to a clothesline coming across the backyard and up the back steps as a frazzled woman in pin curls wearing a hairnet ran in the front door to the kitchen and asked, "Have you seen Momma?"

Dorothy looked alarmed. "No, she hasn't been here. Is she missing again?"

"Yes . . . I turned my back for five seconds and off she goes. If you see her, grab her."

After the woman left Mother Smith said, "Poor Tot, that's the second time this week."

Dorothy shook her head. "Poor Tot."

Mother Smith turned to speak to Betty Raye, but she had disappeared, leaving most of her breakfast uneaten. A second later they heard the lock on her door click shut. The two women looked at each other in surprise.

"Well," said Mother Smith.

"Well," said Dorothy. "I don't know what to think, do you?"

"No."

Anna Lee came in for breakfast. "Is she up yet?"

"Yes, been here and gone. You missed her."

Betty Raye never came back out of her room until it was time to go to the revival and then she slipped out the front door without anyone hearing her and stood on the sidewalk and waited to be picked up by the family. Later, when Dorothy knocked on her door and there was no answer, she went into the room to see if Betty Raye was all right but she was gone. She didn't mean to pry but she could not help but notice that the dress Betty Raye had arrived in was on the bed and the open suitcase on the floor was empty. Dear God, she thought, that little girl only has two dresses to her name.

Her first impulse was to run downtown and buy her an entire new wardrobe. That night she talked it over with Doc. Throughout the years they had both quietly supplied people with clothes and food or sent them money anonymously when they needed it. But Betty Raye was a different situation. She was a guest in their home. How could they do it without seeming to regard her as a charity case and maybe take a chance on hurting her feelings?

It was a dilemma that tugged on Dorothy's heart every time she saw her in the same threadbare dress, day after day.

The Revival

Ever since the Oatmans had come to town and appeared on *The Neighbor Dorothy Show*, Anna Lee, Norma, and Patsy Marie were just dying with curiosity about the revival and having a fit to get out there and see it. All three girls had been raised in town and had never really wanted to go to one, until now. Dorothy, however, was immediately suspicious about their sudden interest in tent revivals.

"Now, Anna Lee, I don't want you girls going out there and making fun of those people . . . do you hear me?"

"Mother!" said Anna Lee, shocked at the idea. "Why would you think something like that?"

"Because I know how silly the three of you can act."

Finally, Anna Lee was able to convince her mother to let her go but Ida, Norma's mother, was adamantly against it. "I will not have you going out there to that thing. There's no telling what sort of people will come crawling out of the backwoods and start babbling in tongues. . . . Besides, we're Presbyterians—we don't believe in that sort of primitive carrying on." But Norma told her mother that she was spending the night with Patsy Marie and went anyway.

On the second night of the revival Norma got her boyfriend, Macky, to drive them out to the country. They started around six but before they left town Norma made Macky go into the Trolley Car Diner and get them all hamburgers to go. She pointed to the flyer with the map that advertised TENT REVIVAL AND DINNER ON THE GROUND. "I'm not eating anything off the ground; if I got sick my mother would know exactly where I'd been." As they turned off Highway 78 and onto a dirt road they saw crude signs pointing the way that said THE WAGES OF SIN IS DEATH, ARE YOU SAVED? PREPARE TO MEET YOUR MAKER, and GOD TAKES ALL CALLS PERSONALLY—HE HAS NO SECETARY. Patsy Marie observed, "They misspelled *secretary*." About forty-five minutes later, when they got close to the spot called Brown's Pasture, behind the Highway 78 Church of Christ, they could see a large round tan tent with red and white triangle banners hanging from the ropes, way off in the distance. The sides of the road were lined with cars and trucks and tractors already and they had to park about a half mile away. The place was teeming with people, all carrying plates and baskets. When they finally got closer to the tent, they saw long tables and benches set up everywhere, laden with food the families had brought to share. Norma was surprised to see that "dinner on the ground" did not literally mean on the ground but dinner on tables covered with tablecloths made out of newspapers. When the others saw the piles of fried chicken, homemade macaroni and cheese, plates full of fresh corn on the cob and watermelon, they were sorry they had listened to Norma and had only hamburgers to eat. Norma defended herself as they walked, saying, "Well, how was I to know—it didn't *say* dinner on the table!"

By the time they got inside the big tent, most of the wooden folding chairs were already taken and they had to sit toward the back, which is where Norma wanted to sit anyway. The ground was covered with sawdust and it smelled like the circus, with almost a circus excitement as well. Instead of acting serious like they were in church, children were allowed to run up and down the aisles and make all the noise they wanted. It was a festive atmosphere with a feeling of anticipation. Anticipation of what, the Elmwood Springs girls did not know yet. The place was packed with people they had never seen before: Pentecostal; Church of Christers; hard-shell, foot-washing Primitive Baptists; you name it, all come together for a good time.

The men were in clean overalls and the women all had on the same kind of homemade dresses that Minnie and Betty Raye wore. It was a hot night and the ladies, most with their hair done up in buns at the back of the neck, sat there fanning themselves with cardboard fans, a picture of the Last Supper on them, which the church had provided, and chatted happily with one another. The round stage in the middle of the tent was bare except for a piano and sound system and one artificial fern in a stand-up basket. While they waited for things to start Anna Lee, Patsy Marie, and Norma sat around punching one another and giggling as Macky pointed out an old lady dipping snuff and spitting it back out in a tin can she had brought with her. Just then a large, big-boned, sweet-looking lady and a small man in overalls walked past. Norma looked up and immediately dropped to the floor and hid under a chair.

Macky looked at her. "What are you doing, Goofy?"

Norma whispered, "It's my Aunt Elner! If she sees me she'll tell Mother." Norma, who at the time was wearing dark sunglasses and a scarf, was to spend the entire evening bobbing and weaving behind the people in front of her, terrified that her aunt might somehow turn around and pick her out of a crowd of seven hundred. But Norma's chance of her Aunt Elner seeing her that night was to be the least of her worries.

At exactly 7:00 P.M. the Highway 78 Church of Christ preacher came out. In a few moments, after a lengthy prayer, he introduced the Oatman Family Gospel Singers and they filed onstage to thunderous applause.

Patsy Marie nudged Anna Lee. "Which one is Betty Raye?"

"The skinny one."

Patsy Marie noticed that she was also the only one of the Oatmans that did not have thick coal-black hair and commented, "She doesn't look a thing like the rest of them, does she?"

Norma said under her breath to Macky, "Who would want to?" In a few minutes, after the Oatmans got the evening started with a rousing, foot-stomping, hand-clapping rendition of "Give Me That Old-Time Religion," they continued on with "Are You Washed in the Blood," "Tell Mother I'll Be There," "I'll Meet You by the River," "I Believe in the Man in the Sky," and just when they had the audience shouting and rocking in their seats, the visiting preacher and revival leader, the Reverend Stockton Briggle, straight out of Del Rio, Texas, came running down the aisle, jumped up on the stage, and with Bible in hand danced and shouted, "I feel the spirit moving tonight!" He proceeded to put on a show the likes of which the four of them had never seen. Reverend Briggle had been saved by the famous evangelist Billy Sunday and was determined to return the favor. He hopped on one foot, then the other, and warned those in the audience who had not been saved about the eternal fires of hell. He raved on about fighting the devil for souls, yelling, "I'll fight him with a shovel . . . I'll fight him with an ax . . . I'll fight in the morning . . . I'll fight him in the night!" He got himself so worked up he was red in the face. He was so upset and agitated over the devil that he started to spit every time he shouted and the people in the front row were dodging back and forth. Macky thought this one of the funniest things he had ever seen and suddenly laughed out loud and then tried to pretend he was coughing. Anna Lee and Norma lost control and got the giggles so bad they almost choked. But Reverend Briggle did not let up until several women jumped to their feet and started dancing and shouting in an unknown tongue. Soon the sinners in the crowd began to sweat and squirm in their seats and after about an hour of ranting and getting everybody all worked up and scared to death about going to hell he finally called out for all the unsaved to come forward, confess their sins to the Almighty God, and be saved from eternal damnation. About three hundred people jumped up, some who always got up to get saved over and over, others for the first time, all headed up the aisle toward the altar, amid shouts of "Praise Jesus" and "Hallelujah!" One man down at the end of their row jumped up and did a dance right there like he had just stuck his finger in a light socket.

Norma and Macky and Anna Lee had been so busy watching him they didn't notice that their friend had suddenly gotten up and started marching down the aisle with the crowd, headed for the altar. When she looked over and saw her Norma screamed, "Oh my God, Macky, there goes Patsy Marie—grab her!" But it was too late; she was already halfway to the front. An hour later, after they had pulled a dazed Patsy Marie out of the tent and were heading home, she tried to explain. "I was just sitting there and before I knew it I was up out of my seat and going down the aisle. It was like someone had picked me up and was putting one foot in front of the other, and I couldn't stop myself." She said, "After that I don't remember a thing, so I must have been saved."

Anna Lee, who was fascinated and somewhat in awe, asked, "What's it like to be saved, Patsy Marie? Do you feel any different?"

Patsy Marie thought it over for a moment and then answered sincerely, "I don't know . . . but my headache's gone."

Macky laughed but Norma did not find Patsy Marie's recent experience with salvation even slightly amusing. "It's not funny, Macky." But then she said to Patsy Marie, "If you go crazy and start babbling away in some strange tongue, I swear I'll never speak to you again."

Alarmed at that thought, Anna Lee looked more closely at her friend. "Do you feel like you want to babble in the unknown tongue, Patsy Marie?"

Patsy Marie gave the question serious thought. "No, I don't think so . . . not yet, anyway."

Norma rolled her eyes. "Oh, great . . . now we are going to have to watch her like a hawk night and day. This is your fault, Macky."

Macky said, "Me? What did I do?"

"If you had grabbed her when I told you to, she wouldn't have gone up there in the first place."

"Norma, I couldn't . . . she was already way up the aisle. Why didn't you go after her? You were the closest."

"And have Aunt Elner tell my mother she saw me? Do you want me grounded for the rest of my natural life? You know Mother—she would have a fit if she knew Aunt Elner had been to a Church of Christ revival, much less her own daughter."

The Party

The next afternoon, on the way over to the Coke party Anna Lee was having for Betty Raye, Norma got Patsy Marie to make a solemn promise that if she felt in the least bit strange or as if she might start speaking in the unknown tongue she was to leave at once. "If we want to be cheerleaders next year, we can't afford for you to have a relapse and get all religious." Then, more considerately, she asked, "How is your headache today?"

Poor Patsy Marie, who had been stared at by Norma for the past twenty-four hours, said, "I think it's back."

This was good news to Norma. Perhaps Patsy Marie was unsaved.

The party was to be held in the little clubroom over at Cascade Plunge. Anna Lee had warned her friends in advance that Betty Raye's religion did not allow dancing and so that was out. They all squawked but they showed up anyway. The party was supposed to take place from three to five but the family who drove Betty Raye out to the revival every night came and picked her up at four. It was just as well. They had all been on their best behavior but the minute Betty Raye left, they ran to the jukebox and the jitterbugging began.

When Anna Lee came home her mother was in the kitchen having a meeting with the local chapter of the Red Cross, discussing the upcoming annual drill. Anna Lee was returning some plates she had borrowed.

Dorothy, who had been anxious all afternoon, asked, "How did the party go?"

Anna Lee made a face and motioned for her mother to come out on the back porch. Dorothy excused herself and closed the door. Anna Lee whispered, "Oh, Mother, it was just awful. Everybody tried their best to be nice but all she did was stand over in a corner and shake."

"Oh no."

"She dropped an entire plate of food all over herself. I felt so sorry for her, I didn't know what to do. All the boys tried to talk to her but she just doesn't know how to act. Do you think there's something wrong with her, that she's retarded or something?"

"No . . . of course not. She's probably not used to going to parties, that's all." But secretly Dorothy was concerned and wondered.

The next afternoon, after Betty Raye had been picked up, Anna Lee said, "I think she just hates me."

"She doesn't hate you, honey," Dorothy said.

"Well, she sure doesn't like me much. I invited her to come to my room so we could talk and try to get to know each other better but all she did was sit there and act like I was holding her prisoner or something." Anna Lee was sincerely baffled. "I don't understand it, Mother, everybody else likes me. . . . I was voted the most popular junior . . . and every time she sees Bobby she turns around and goes the other way."

Mother Smith laughed and said, "That I can understand."

"And poor Jimmy," Anna Lee continued. "The other day, when he came in the kitchen and said hello, she backed all the way into the pantry and hid behind the door until he left."

"It's like living with a little mouse in the house, isn't it?" Mother Smith mused. "I hear her late at night scurrying into the bathroom, washing out her little things; then she scurries back to her room. She tiptoes around almost like she's apologizing for living, scared to make a sound. I think she would mash herself into the wall and just disappear if she could."

"I know," said Dorothy, "it just breaks my heart. But all we can do is keep trying to make her feel at home and be as sweet to her as possible."

For the rest of the week Mother Smith and Anna Lee tried their best to make conversation the few times they saw her, but without much luck. At the end of her visit, Dorothy and Princess Mary Margaret seemed to be the only ones Betty Raye might have felt somewhat at ease with.

She never came out of her room when the radio show was going on. But a few times in the afternoon, if no one else was around, she would quietly slip into the kitchen and sit in the corner, petting the dog and watching Dorothy cook. Dorothy wanted to chat, but did not push her to talk and just let her be. But on Betty Raye's last morning there, Dorothy felt she just had to say something, and she went into the little sewing room and sat down on the bed.

"Sweetie, come over here and sit and talk to me for a minute, will you?"

Betty Raye sat down. Dorothy took her hand and looked her in the eyes. "I know it's none of my business but I'm worried about you. You know, you really mustn't be so timid and afraid around people. We all like you very much but if you won't talk to us, we don't know if you like us."

Betty Raye's cheeks turned red and she looked down at her lap. Dorothy continued: "I know it's probably just because you are shy—and believe it or not, when I was your age I felt the same way. But, sweetheart, for your own good you need to understand that you are a perfectly lovely girl and people will always want to be your friend if you let them." Dorothy patted her hand. "I know you can do it . . . will you promise me to at least try?"

Betty Raye nodded, big tears welling up in her eyes.

Good-bye

When the Oatmans came to pick up Betty Raye, the Smiths all walked out to the car with her. Minnie leaned out the window and said to Dorothy, "I hope she weren't no trouble to you, Mrs. Smith."

"Not at all—we loved having her."

"I told you she wouldn't eat much."

"Mrs. Oatman," Dorothy said, "could I trouble you to come inside for just a minute? I have something for you."

Minnie said, "Sure," and turned to her husband. "Turn the motor off, Ferris, you're burning up the gas."

When they were inside the kitchen, she could see that Dorothy had prepared a huge basket of sandwiches and cookies for them to take on their trip.

"Well, ain't this nice of you. We sure loved them other cookies you give us, we just enjoyed them to the highest."

Dorothy closed the door and said, "The truth is, Mrs. Oatman, I wanted to get a chance to talk to you privately. Could we sit for just a second?"

"Sure, honey." Minnie sat down at the table. "And, by the way, thank you for letting us advertise over the radio. We never had so many people to show up . . . they had to bring in a hundred more chairs and benches to fit them all in."

"You are certainly more than welcome."

"And thanks again for taking my little girl in."

"That's what I wanted to talk to you about, Mrs. Oatman. . . . I know this is none of my business, but are you aware that Betty Raye shakes?"

Minnie nodded. "Oh yes. She been doing that for I don't know how long, ever since she was five or six, I guess." She glanced up at the kitchen window and exclaimed, "Oh, look at your pretty little curtains and all them plants in them little glass fiddles in the window . . . I swear I've never seen nothing like that before."

"Do you know why she shakes, Mrs. Oatman?"

"Call me Minnie, honey. No, I haven't an idea in the world what makes her to do it. Maybe she's just too thin for her own good. She's got all them delicate little bones just like a bird." She laughed and held up her arm. "She sure don't take after me. Look, even my wrists are fat. Momma says when your wrists is fat then you know you're fat."

"Mrs. Oatman . . . Minnie . . . I know you know best, but considering she's so shy I just wonder if all this traveling from place to place could have something to do with it."

"You know, you might be right, Mrs. Smith." Minnie leaned forward and lowered her voice as she confided to Dorothy, "It pains me to say this but I don't think gospel singing is in her blood. It just don't come natural to her. We have to just about drag her onstage and even then she won't sing out and I can't understand it for the life of me. She's got gospel singing on both sides of the family, the boys couldn't wait to jump on the stage, but Betty Raye . . ." She shook her head sadly. "She was always real different and it's been hard on all of us, especially her."

"Yes, I can imagine."

Minnie sighed. "Mrs. Smith, I know she don't like traveling and I know she hates singing but what can I do?" Just then Ferris blew the horn and Minnie got up. "Well, I better go. We got to be in Humboldt, Tennessee, for an all-night sing by seven but I sure appreciate you putting her up and all the nice food you made for us."

As they walked to the car Dorothy said, "We'd be happy to have her back anytime, Mrs. Oatman." She looked in the car to say good-bye, but Betty Raye was already lost in the crowd in the backseat. Anna Lee and Bobby and Mother Smith all stood and waved good-bye as they drove away.

Mother Smith said, "Lord, those country people love to travel in a pack, don't they."

As the car turned the corner, Dorothy felt a wave of sadness and had to fight back tears. There was something about Betty Raye that touched her. She had given Betty Raye their address and asked her to write but she wondered if she would ever see her or hear from her again. When they were out of sight, Dorothy put her arm around Anna Lee. "You were very sweet to her, and I appreciate it."

Bobby piped up behind them. "I was sweet to her. I gave her one of my best rocks."

"Did you?" said Dorothy and put her other arm around Bobby, which is what he wanted in the first place. They walked back to the house together. Bobby added, "Yeah, and it was probably worth a hundred dollars, too, or maybe even more!"

Anna Lee asked her mother, "Do you think she had a good time while she was here or did she just hate it?"

"I don't know, honey," Dorothy said. "I hope she enjoyed herself. But I really don't know."

What They Didn't Know

Four hours later and a hundred and seventy-eight miles from Elmwood Springs, the Oatmans were crossing over the Tennessee River. Betty Raye was mashed between her older brothers, Bervin and Vernon, who were hitting at each other, and as usual everyone in the car was talking at the same time. Minnie was fussing at Ferris because he had not stopped at the last gas station so she could go to the bathroom. Chester the dummy was out of his box, yammering away at Ferris and complaining because Floyd had also wanted to stop at the gas station and get himself a cold Dr Pepper. But Ferris, who was determined to drive straight through without stopping, ignored them and started singing his favorite hymn, "Oh for a Thousand Tongues." Betty Raye sat in the back with her eyes closed, holding on to the small rock Bobby had given her, and tried to shut the noise out all the way to Humboldt.

What the Smith family did not know and she had been unable to tell them was that theirs was the nicest house she had ever stayed in. Compared with the hundreds of sofa pads on the floor and the lumpy beds she had shared with as many as four or five children, to her the little sewing room had been as grand as the Mansion on a Hill her mother was always singing about. The reason she had not wanted Anna Lee's room was not because she did not like it. It was the most beautiful bedroom she had ever seen, in fact, much too nice for her. The real problem was its size. She would have been scared to stay in such a big room. She was used to staying in the small homes around the various country churches where they usually sang. If the Smiths thought she ran to her room every time she got a chance because she had not liked them, they were wrong. It was just the first time in her life she had ever been able to go in a room and shut the door and be completely alone—the first time she could remember not being surrounded by family and by strangers. If they had wondered what she had been doing in her room, they might have been surprised to know that she had done absolutely nothing but sit quietly for hours at a time. And as far as not liking Anna Lee, nothing could have been further from the truth. She thought Anna Lee was wonderful and was in awe of her and her friends. If she had not talked much it was only because she could not think of anything to say. She had liked everyone she met, particularly Dorothy, who had been so nice to her. On that last morning it had taken all her strength just to keep herself from begging them to let her stay. She had only been in Elmwood Springs for one week but it had been the best week of her life.

But by this time next week the Oatmans would be headed to Fayetteville, North Carolina, for another revival and dinner on the ground, and Elmwood Springs would be farther and farther away.

Stargazing

The Friday after Betty Raye left, Bobby's Cub Scout troop was supposed to have gone on a field trip to the Indian mounds outside of town to look for arrowheads. The trip was canceled because of rain. But Bobby did not mind. He loved to go sit on the porch on warm rainy days and listen to the sounds of the cars swishing up and down the wet streets. Everything was green and lush and wet. He daydreamed all afternoon until about four o'clock, when the sun came back out as bright as ever. But the rain had left the air fresh and cleared away some of the mugginess of August. This was Monroe's turn to spend the night with him, and after dinner, as usual, they all started to wander out onto the porch. Mother Smith walked over to the edge and looked up at the sky and announced, "I'm going out and look at the stars. Anybody want to come with me?" Bobby and Monroe said they would go and all three headed out to the backyard. Mother Smith sat in a wooden chair and Bobby and Monroe lay on the lawn beside her to enjoy the show. "It's so clear tonight," Mother Smith said. "Have you ever seen so many pretty stars? Look, there's the Big Dipper and Venus. I'll bet we see a shooting star before the night's over."

Bobby loved to be with Mother Smith like this, watching for shooting stars and asking her questions.

"Grandma, what was the world like when you were little? Was everything real different?"

"Well, it was a different time."

"Did people look different than we do?"

"No, people looked pretty much the same but we didn't have a lot of things you do today. Don't forget, that was way back in the eighteen hundreds."

"During the Civil War?" asked Monroe, wide-eyed.

"Not that far back. But I can remember my father talking about it and when I was little we had this sword hung over the mantelpiece."

"A sword?" said Bobby. "A real one?"

"Oh yes. He was a Confederate soldier during the war."

"Did he kill people with it?"

"Oh, I doubt it. I think it was mostly for show."

"Do you still have it?"

"No, that was years ago. I think my brother took it or maybe it got lost."

Bobby said, "But he was a real soldier though, wasn't he?"

"Absolutely, and so was your Great-grandfather Smith on your daddy's daddy's side, but he fought for the Union. Both from the same town. But that's how it was back then."

Bobby was amazed. He could not imagine that his grandmother had been alive so long ago. "Were there stars back then?"

She laughed. "Yes, honey, when I was your age I saw the same stars and moon that are up there now. Nature doesn't change, just people. New ones are born every year but the stars and the moon stay the same. We just didn't have cars or movies or radios or electricity yet."

"What was that like?"

"Very quiet."

Monroe made a face. "That must have been terrible."

"Yeah," Bobby agreed. "You must have been bored."

"Not really. We had other things. We had books and we played games and sang and went to parties. You know, you don't miss what you don't know."

"What did you want to be when you grew up, Grandma?"

Mother Smith smiled. "Believe it or not, at one time I thought I'd like to be a famous scientist like Madame Curie, maybe find a cure for some terrible disease."

"Why didn't you?"

"My father could only afford to send one child to college, so Brother was the one to go and there went my dreams of being the next Madame Curie."

Bobby said, "Tell us about where you went on your honeymoon and that hotel."

"Bobby, you've heard that story a hundred times."

"I don't care, Monroe hasn't heard it. Tell it again."

"I haven't heard it," said Monroe.

"Well . . . after your grandfather and I were married we got on the train and rode it all the way to North Carolina for our honeymoon. He wouldn't tell me where we were going. He wanted it to be a surprise and all he would tell me was that it was a famous hotel overlooking the most beautiful lake in the world. I'll never forget that first night we were there. After dinner we walked out on this wide veranda overlooking the lake and they had all these pretty different-colored little paper Chinese lanterns strung all from one end to the other. Then, around eight o'clock, as soon as it got really dark, everybody in the hotel came out on the porch and said, 'Look out on the lake.' "

On cue Bobby asked, "Then what happened?"

"Well, all of a sudden this huge sign made up of a thousand golden light bulbs lit up that said HOTEL LUMINAIRE right out in the middle of the lake."

"Whoa!" said Monroe.

"Then we all went down and got into canoes and rowed all the way out to the sign. I don't know which was a prettier sight, looking back at the hotel and seeing all those little green and red and yellow Chinese lanterns glowing in the dark or paddling right through the words HOTEL LUMINAIRE reflected in the water. It was a magical night, I can tell you that."

"Now tell him about going to Coney Island."

"I will. So . . . from there we went to New York City but it was so hot that every day we would ride the trolley way out to the ocean to Coney Island and walk around and see all the sights."

Bobby punched Monroe. "Just wait till you hear the next part."

"And we went to this big amusement park called Dreamland, so big that they had an entire little town in there, called Midget City. You could go in and nobody lived there except hundreds of tiny midgets."

"Whoa!" said Monroe.

"They had their own little houses and stores and their own little midget mayor and tiny midget policeman. When we went through we met the nicest little married midget couple who had two normal-sized children that lived in New Jersey."

"Oh, wow," said Monroe, impressed out of his mind. "I'd give anything to see a town full of midgets."

"It was a sight I'll never forget."

"What else do you remember in olden times that was great like that, Grandma?"

"Well, let's see. I remember at the turn of the century, January the first, 1900—that was a big event."

"What happened?"

"Oh, there were parties everywhere and at midnight of 1899 everybody in Independence went out in the street and rang bells and blew whistles and set off firecrackers and stayed up all night ringing in the next century. We thought the twentieth century was going to be the best one, but not more than fourteen years after that World War One started, so there went that dream out the window."

After a moment Mother Smith said, "Well, boys, it's getting late, so I'm going to leave you two to the stars and head on in."

"Good night, Grandma."

"Good night, Mrs. Smith."

After she had gone Monroe said, "I guess she's the oldest person I know."

"Yeah," agreed Bobby. "Just think, she's a whole century old. . . ."

They lay there staring up at the stars. Bobby asked, "I wonder what it's going to be like when it gets to be the year 2000?"

"I don't know but I'll bet everybody will be riding around in their own spaceships, going back and forth to Mars."

"How old are we gonna be in the year 2000?"

Monroe sat up and counted on his fingers. He looked at Bobby incredulously. "We're going to be sixty-four years old!"

Bobby sat up. He could not believe it. "Nooo!"

"We probably won't even be alive, we'll be so old."

The prospect of being as old as the men who sat around the barbershop all day was a sobering thought. After a while Bobby said, "Monroe, let's make a pact. If we're both alive in the year 2000, no matter where we are, we will call each other up and say, Hooray, we made it, O.K.?"

"O.K., shake."

They shook hands and lay back down. They both wondered where they would be and what they would look like but they could not even imagine it. To them the distance from this night, August the ninth, 1946, all the way to the year 2000 seemed as far away as Elmwood Springs was to the moon.

They stayed out in the yard and kept looking to see a falling star until Dorothy called to them and said they had to come in.

Time Flies

Other than Mr. Peanut coming to town and the Elmwood Theater showing four Gene Autry movies in one day and Bobby getting stuck in the arm at Monroe's birthday party while playing Pin the Tail on the Donkey, nothing else exciting happened and before they knew it September came rolling around again.

But as much as Bobby hated summer ending and shopping for school clothes with his mother, because she made him try on everything, there was something exciting about starting back to school. He loved the smell of new books and going to the five-and-dime and getting school supplies. Brand-new pencil boxes, notebooks, and big thick rubber erasers, and a new satchel. The boys in town had gone to the barbershop and gotten a haircut for the first day of school, the girls had tight new curly permanents and new dresses, and everybody had brand-new shoes.

The school had been slicked up as well. The wooden floors had been waxed to a high shine, the lunchroom polished and scrubbed. Even the teachers, rested from their summer vacations, looked optimistic and eager, ready to inspire the tender young minds that would be in their care for the next nine months. Fresh new chalk, new shiny maps on the walls, the white round globes hanging from the ceilings, beaming with bright new bulbs. The entire building vibrated with enthusiasm and anticipation of the best year yet. Everyone was happy to see each other—almost everybody—and ready to begin anew with high hopes.

This euphoria lasted about three days and by the end of September it was the same old drudgery as it had been the year before. Bobby was still the shortest boy in class and Luther Griggs still threatened to beat him up every day.

Christmas came and went and Bobby got a new maroon-and-white Schwinn bicycle and a silver-colored cowboy holster with the multicolored artificial gems and a Dick Tracy cap pistol. Plus lots of socks and underwear he did not want. He had been hoping for a genuine Jungle Jim pith helmet.

Besides Bobby getting underwear and socks, the other bad news was that on Wednesday, January 3, dish night at the Elmwood Theater, the movie that was supposed to come in on the Greyhound bus had not come in. Consequently, Snooky had to show the backup movie he kept in the booth for this sort of emergency. But that night most people left after all the dishes were given away. After all, just how many times can you sit through *Lassie Come Home*?

January and February were both fairly mild but March came roaring in. The first Monday of the month started off looking like it might be a nice day but by eight o'clock in the morning things had changed drastically and in a hurry. Dorothy hardly had time to run around and get all her windows shut before the storm hit. By the time the show went on the air, several houses had lost part of their roofs, the awning at the A & P grocery store had been ripped, and Poor Tot Whooten had just called, all upset because part of Merle and Verbena's roof had blown through her dining room window and had broken all that was left of her good dishes.

Mother Smith opened the show with a few strains of "Stormy Weather" and Dorothy ran in and sat down and said, "That's right, Mother Smith, it is stormy weather, as stormy as can be over here, and looking out my window I can tell you everything is a big mess. I just hope everything is all right where you are. It was so bad I was worried we were going to get knocked right off the air, so I am glad we are on." She stopped for a moment. "At least I think we are. Bobby, run next door and see if we are still on. But in the meantime I'll just keep talking until he tells me we are not on the air. Oh, what a day: one minute the sun is shining and the next rain is blowing up and down the street every which a way. I didn't even have time to get my clothes off the line."

The day had turned so dark that Doc called and said they had to put the lights on at the drugstore just to see. Bobby came running in and slammed the door and shouted, "You're on!" Dorothy said, "Oh good. Bobby says we're still on the air . . . so after the thing hit there wasn't a thing to do but wait it out. We all watched it from the bay window in the dining room and I must say we enjoyed it, even though we did see Doc's pajamas fly by. Storms always manage to hit us on a wash day, don't they? Mrs. Whatley over behind us just brought a couple of Doc's shirts back but we lost everything else. Everybody in town has been calling, saying they have somebody else's clothes. Mr. Henderson said a pair of ladies' drawers had wrapped themselves around his weather vane but I don't know who would have the nerve to claim them. What? Bobby says we have all kinds of clothes hanging off the radio tower, so if you're missing some come over and look, they might be here. Oh, I am so discombobulated this morning I can't find my format or anything."

She picked up her potted plant and put it down again. "For all of those of you at home, just thank your lucky stars you can't see me through the radio. I look just like an old frump this morning and, believe it or not, I am still in my robe. Between the storm and so many calls the time just got away from me. And today of all days. The very day when we are announcing our brand-new sponsor, the Cecil Figgs Mortuaries and Floral Designs for all your floral and funeral needs, and here I sit with no face on, in my hair net, and still in my robe. And I do apologize, Mr. Figgs, and I promise to do better tomorrow."

Dorothy looked at Bobby sitting in the front row with Beatrice, happily chomping away on a radio cookie, and suddenly realized something. "Excuse me a minute, girls," she said and put her hand over the microphone. "What are you doing out of school, young man?"

"I had to go get Beatrice," he said.

"That was very sweet of you but I think we can get along without you the rest of the morning.

"Sorry, everyone. I have a boy here who needs to be at school, so if anybody's listening in the teachers' lounge, he will be right there . . . and call me if he's not." A moment later the audience heard the front door slam.

"Rats," said Bobby, stomping off to school.

Dorothy, who was still searching for her format, announced, "And now here's Beatrice to sing for us on this rainy old day, 'Let a Smile Be Your Umbrella' followed by 'Painting the Clouds with Sunshine,' and maybe by then I'll find what I'm looking for."

The rest of the year went by with no more major upsets or dramas and was fairly uneventful until Saturday, June the first at 4:16 in the afternoon, when something major did happen.

Life Changes

Bobby had been down at the drugstore since early that morning, working in the stockroom unloading boxes and stacking them in a pile outside the back door in the alley. He received an allowance of fifty cents a week but he wanted to earn extra money so he could send off for the Charles Atlas bodybuilding course. He and Monroe had vowed to become muscle men before they went back to school next September. Considering that he weighed sixty-eight pounds soaking wet and had arms like sticks, it was an ambitious goal. He had whipped through boxes of red-and-white straws, paper napkins, boxes of shampoo, cough medicine, baby powder, aspirin, Band-Aids, and Whitman's Samplers in record time. He was in a hurry. Today was the day the swimming pool opened for the season.

Doc paid him his fifty cents and yelled after him as he ran out the back door, "Be careful, son, don't hit your head on the diving board." Doc heard a faint "Yes, sir" as Bobby ran as fast as he could down the block, heading for home. Neighbor Dorothy had just told her radio listeners that, unlike other prune juices on the market, Sunsweet prune juice was guaranteed by *Good Housekeeping* to have the same laxative potency in every glassful when he came flying through the screen door, slamming it behind him, *wham,* on the way to his room. Neighbor Dorothy informed her listeners, "As you might have guessed, that was Bobby," and went on to announce that a Mrs. Aline Staggers of Arden, Oklahoma, was interested in locating a recipe for old-fashioned strawberry-and-rhubarb pie. "So if you have a good one, send it on in." At that moment Bobby came crashing down the hall carrying his bathing suit in one hand but before he hit the front door his mother said, "Hold it, young man!" and stopped him in his tracks. "Since you are making so much racket, why don't you come in here and tell everybody where it is you are going in such a hurry."

Bobby poked his head in the room and shouted, "Cascade Plunge opens today!"

Neighbor Dorothy said, "Oh, I see. . . . Well, everybody, I guess we can say that summer is officially here. Bobby has just informed me that the pool is open." Mother Smith hit a few happy chords of "By the Sea, by the Sea, by the Beautiful Sea" while Bobby stood there, chomping at the bit to be released. His mother said, "Well, go on but for heaven's sake, don't hit your head on the diving board!" Everybody at home heard a faint voice disappearing into the background saying "O.K." and the slam of the door.

Bobby knew the shortcut to everywhere in town through the back alleys and was at the pool in two minutes flat. As he had whizzed by their houses, the ladies listening to Neighbor Dorothy heard all about the saga of how last year he had been showing off for some girl and had cracked his head on the diving board and had knocked himself out cold and had to have three stitches. Most people would have learned their lesson and not gone near the pool, but not him.

Bobby loved the water. His mother did not know it but he had already been swimming out at the Blue Devil several times. That was fun but not like Cascade Plunge. To him there was something wonderful about the certain smell of chlorine on hot, wet cement, and swimming underwater in that clear, aqua pool water streaked with wavy strips of white sunlight—something about the quiet under there, the whole world above muffled and far away. And then, too, there were girls at the pool. He wanted to show off for a girl in his class, not the same one he liked last year, a new one. She was a tap dancer, and when Bobby, who Dorothy had to practically drag to the Dixie Cahill dance recital, saw her solo to "Tiptoe Through the Tulips with Me," he thought she was as cute as a pair of new yellow shoes.

Bobby ran up to the big cement building with blue sky and white clouds painted over the sign that said CASCADE PLUNGE and dug in his jeans for a dime and got his locker key and ran on in, practically pulling all his clothes off before he reached the men's changing room. He was in such a hurry that he almost tripped on his bright orange swim trunks. He quickly locked his locker and ran out from the shadowy dressing area into the shining white sunlight. There it was. At last he had reached that oasis of shimmering crystal-clear water he had been dreaming about all winter, and the sight of it almost took his breath away. It looked like a big lake, sparkling like a thousand diamonds in the sun, surrounded by a sea of hot white concrete. Oh, it was all too much. He was far too excited to wait another minute and he ran and flung himself into the pool. He swam underwater for a while and came up right beside Monroe and they immediately began to splash water at each other while all the girls around them who didn't want to get their hair wet screamed. Let the fun begin!

At about 4:30 that afternoon when Bobby had not come home yet, Dorothy said to Anna Lee, who was in her bedroom with Patsy Marie working on their movie-star scrapbooks, "Anna Lee, I'm worried about Bobby. He's been down at that pool six hours. Would you and Patsy Marie take a walk over there and tell him to come home, he's had enough for one day." Anna Lee groaned as if her mother had just told her that she had to build an Egyptian pyramid by hand. "Oh, Mother, do I have to?"

"Yes, I'm worried he might have cracked his head again."

"But, Mother, if he wants to knock himself silly on that diving board, I can't stop him."

"Please, for my sake."

Anna Lee sighed monumentally and got up. "Come on, Patsy Marie, let's go. But I don't know why you let him go down there in the first place. All he does is swim around underwater all day, pinching people and acting like a jerk." What she said was largely true. At the moment Bobby and Monroe were swimming around underwater, pestering everyone they could. The best fun was to dive down and swim between unsuspecting people's legs and scare them to death. Bobby was having a grand time. The pool was jam-packed with potential victims. He had just gone between one pair of legs when he suddenly saw another pair nearby and swam over and went for them. He thought this was hilarious until he realized a second too late that the pair of legs he was now swimming under belonged to none other than Luther Griggs. *Big* mistake!

Bobby swam as fast and as far away from him as he could but not far enough. Just as Bobby emerged at the surface, gasping for air, Luther was right behind him and rolled over on his back and kicked him as hard as he could and caught him right between his shoulder blades.

Bobby did not know what hit him. The powerful kick knocked the wind out of him and sent him flying toward the deep end of the pool. Luther swam away, laughing his head off, but Bobby did not come back up. Having seen Bobby drift around underwater all day, nobody paid much attention to him, even the lifeguard, who had his hands full with a pool crammed with excited kids.

It wasn't until some minutes later that Macky Warren, who was standing around talking to Norma, looked over and noticed that Bobby was floating around on top of the water, facedown. He was not moving. Macky ran over to the side of the pool and reached in and jerked him up by his hair and pulled him out. Bobby was unconscious and had already started turning blue. A few minutes later, when Anna Lee and Patsy came strolling into the pool area, they noticed a group of people gathered around, looking at something on the side of the pool. Anna Lee wondered what it was but did not think much about it until she got closer and realized it was a person on the ground. Norma blurted out, "Oh, Anna Lee, I think he's dead!"

Anna Lee walked over, still not knowing who it was. Suddenly everyone moved aside. When she looked down and saw Bobby's lifeless body lying on the cement she almost fainted. The lifeguard was gasping, counting out loud, giving him artificial respiration, desperately trying to get him to breathe. Unable to move, Anna Lee screamed over and over, "That's my brother!" In that minute before Bobby finally started to cough and spit up water, the thousands of irritating things he had ever done were forgotten. All Anna Lee wanted was for him to be alive.

When Bobby finally did come to and opened his eyes, he looked up and when he saw so many people peering down at him it scared him to death. He didn't know where he was or what he was doing on the ground. When his eyes began to focus a little better, he suddenly recognized his sister's face, as she knelt down beside him. He was so happy to see her that he threw his arms around her neck and wouldn't let go.

Still in a state of shock, not really understanding what had happened, Bobby began to shiver and to cry. Anna Lee held him and said, "It's all right, you're all right, Bobby, I'm here." Even when the lifeguard picked him up and carried him into the poolhouse and laid him down on the couch he would not let go of her hand. They covered him with a blanket and rubbed him all over to get his circulation back. After a while he sat up and had a Coke. He was a bit shaken by the ordeal but apparently none too worse for the wear. When he felt well enough Anna Lee got his clothes out of the locker and helped him dress and they walked home together, his arm around her waist, her arm around his shoulder. As they got closer to the house they saw their mother out standing on the sidewalk.

"I've been worried to death," she said. "I was just about to go down there and find you. What were you doing all this time?"

Anna Lee squeezed his hand and said, "Nothing. I was just fooling around talking to some people, that's all. It's my fault."

The next day Bobby decided it was in his own best interest and a matter of personal safety not to go back to the pool anytime soon. Particularly as long as Luther Griggs was still lurking around. So he stayed in his room and read comic books.

At about 12:30 that afternoon, Monroe came running through the side yard and knocked frantically on Bobby's window, his eyes wide open as if he had just seen a Martian. "Let me in," he said. Bobby opened the window all the way and Monroe climbed across the sill flush with excitement. "Whoa . . . wait till you hear what just happened to Luther!"

"What?"

Monroe put his hands on his head, walked around the room, and exclaimed, "Fantastic! . . . It was fantastic. . . . You should have seen her. *Wham,* a right cross right on the chin and then *bang,* she let him have it again with a left hook and another right. Oh, she was great." Monroe danced around the room demonstrating the fight. *"Wham . . . bam!"*

"Who?" asked Bobby.

"Anna Lee!"

Bobby couldn't believe it. "My *sister* Anna Lee?"

"Yeah."

"You're kidding."

"No, I'm not, I saw it. She came down to the pool a little while ago looking for him and she went over and jerked him up by his shirt and told him to pick on somebody his own size. Then she hauled off and knocked him flat on his back. When she got him on the ground she just about kicked the stuffing out of him. He was crying and everything. It was great. You should have seen it."

"Anna Lee?"

"Yeah, and she told him if he ever bothered you again she'd get Billy Nobblitt on him."

"My sister?"

Monroe flopped back on the bed. "Boy, are you lucky. I wish I had a sister like that."

"He really cried?" Bobby smiled.

"Oh, yeah, she had him begging for mercy."

That night at dinner Bobby looked across the table at his sister with new eyes, filled with awe and admiration. Although nothing was said, their relationship began to change after that day. Gradually, the thought of how wonderful it would have been to be an only child slowly faded away, and they finally quit tattletelling on each other every chance they got. They even began to share their own little secrets. It had only been a slight adjustment but it was to make all the difference in the world. As Dorothy remarked later, "It's so pleasant not to have the children at each other's throats night and day. I wonder what happened?"

Although Dorothy was relieved she no longer had to worry about her own children killing each other, from time to time she still worried about Betty Raye Oatman. She had never received a letter from her. Often, she wondered if the girl was all right. She even called the minister out at the Highway 78 Church of Christ, but he had no idea where the Oatmans were.

Betty Raye did not find the envelope that Neighbor Dorothy had slipped into the side of her suitcase until a few days after she had left Elmwood Springs. Inside was fifty dollars in cash and a short handwritten note.

> Sweetheart,
>
> Take this and buy yourself a little something special or just save it for a rainy day if you want. Please don't forget us and come see us again.
>
> Your friends,
> Doc and Dorothy Smith
>
> P.S. Drop me a note and let me know how you are doing from time to time, will you?

◆ ◆ ◆

Betty Raye wanted to write but did not know what to say. But Dorothy need not have worried about Betty Raye ever forgetting them. Although she was being jerked from town to town, she often thought about her time in Elmwood Springs. On the road, she had only been able to go to school periodically and missed more days than she attended. She longed to be in one place, go to one school. She wished she could be like Anna Lee, have the same friends from year to year, and live in the same house. Often at night as they drove through small towns she would see the families on the porches or see them inside having dinner and it would remind her of her time with the Smiths. As unhappy as she was, she never told her mother. Minnie had her own problems.

The Prodigal Son

For the Oatman family the summer had been extremely busy. Since May they had been from Nebraska to Arkansas, Oklahoma, Michigan, Louisiana, West Virginia, Kansas, and back again. After an all-night sing in Spartanburg, South Carolina, they finally had a day off from traveling. Ferris was staying at a farmhouse with Bervin and Vernon and Betty Raye was at another house staying with a family of seven. Minnie had spent the night with the Pike family, who were local gospel singers of some note. The next morning she was sitting outside in the backyard, visiting with Mrs. Opal Pike, whose husband was already at work. Besides being a gospel singer he was also a distant relative of the Pike's Mentholated Salve family and handled all sales in the Carolinas. The two women were drinking iced tea and discussing the problems and pitfalls of being gospel wives. Minnie said, "It's not always easy having everyone looking up to you."

"No," agreed Mrs. Pike.

"You know, Ferris has not always been the good strict Christian he is today. Most people don't know but he's had years of on-and-off bouts of drinking and running around, getting saved and then slipping back."

"You don't mean it?" said Mrs. Pike.

"Yes. But praise be to God, as of six weeks ago this Tuesday, he's permanently saved and a new man, and what a blessing. A redheaded faith healer from Mississippi cured him of the arthritis and saved his soul at the same meeting."

"You don't mean it," Mrs. Pike said again as she slapped a mosquito on her arm into oblivion.

Minnie nodded. "Up until that time he had been struggling with a serious crisis of faith. He'd been studying for his Church of Christ ministership certificate through the mail for about three months when he came in one morning after sitting up all night out in the car with his Bible and he just looked terrible. I said, 'Ferris, what's the matter?' And he looked at me and said, 'Sit down, Minnie, I have something to tell you.' He said, 'Honey, I want you to know I have struggled and prayed a thousand hours over this thing but no help has come.' Then he took my hand and held it and said, 'We've got a serious problem. I might have to give up the ministry.' Well, I got all shaken up inside when I heard that because up to this point it had been his whole life. And I said, 'Ferris, what is it, is it another woman?' And he said, 'No, honey, it's the prodigal son.' He said, 'As hard as I've tried to come to terms with it and be in agreement with the Word, I can't.' He'd lost his faith over a parable. He said, 'If a man can go out and raise hell and spend all his money and live in sin and then comes back home and his father throws his arms around him and says welcome home, come on in, and acts like nothing happened, how does that make his other sons feel, the ones that stayed home and worked the farm, saved their money, and lived a Christian life? Why, it would make them feel like all those years of trying to be good didn't mean a thing to their daddy. They might as well have gone out and had a good time themselves.' He said, 'Don't you see, Minnie? Why should a man try and be good if in the end it don't matter one way or the other to your daddy? Why be good if, like the prodigal son, you can do anything you want and get away with it?'

"Well, what could I say? I said, 'Ferris, I see your point. You can't very well sing and preach something you don't see the point of yourself, it wouldn't be right.' But we had to go on because we was booked and I just kept praying the whole time. Then a few months later we was singing out at a big tent revival and camp meeting in Pelham, Alabama, and I'll never forget that night. There wasn't a star in the sky and it was as black as Egypt outside and Ferris is out wandering around and pretty soon he drifts over to this Harper woman's tent. Now, mind you, he's seen some of the best preachers and evangelists there is and was pretty much immune to any of them but he wasn't in there no more than twenty minutes till she came off that stage and grabbed ahold of him and said something to him and he's been saved ever since."

"Thank the Lord," said Mrs. Pike.

"The Lord and the Harper woman. Now, I don't know what it was she said but it must have been good because he hadn't had a pain in his knee since. No wonder she's got a big following. They say up in Atlanta people come to see her in ambulances and go home on the streetcar. You go to one of those healing meetings and you're gonna be cured of what ails you. We went one night up in Detroit and people was being healed left and right of back trouble, blindness, bunions, goiters, liver problems, ringworm, you name it. One woman came in with a crooked index finger and by the time the service was over it was as straight as a stick."

"You don't mean it!"

"I do. Honey, she turned around and pointed it right at me!"

Minnie stared off in the backyard. "I just hope Ferris will stay saved for a while, leastways till I get the boys raised. Both is at that age where they's starting to act up, and between them and having to watch Uncle Floyd like a hawk night and day I'm wore out."

The Princess Mary Margaret Fund

Not only did Dorothy care about people she thought needed help but she also had a soft spot for animals and everybody for miles around knew it. On July first she started her broadcast with yet another abandoned kitten in her lap that had been left at her back door the night before. After she opened the show and had done her first commercial she announced, "By the way, the noise you are hearing is not a motorboat. It is the sweetest little cat I have here, just purring away, and he is in need of a home. He is just a little orange angel and would make a wonderful companion for somebody out there, I just know it, so if anybody can take him, please give us a call."

Norma's Aunt Elner, a regular listener who almost never missed Dorothy's show, had a soft spot as well.

The following morning Mother Smith started off the show with a rousing rendition of "Happy Days Are Here Again." "That's right, Mother, it is a happy day over here and I can start the show with good news. I have gone into my own personal voting booth and voted Elner Shimfissle for the Good Neighbor of the Year Award. After the show yesterday she called us and said that she would take the little cat and yesterday afternoon she and her husband, Will, came to pick him up. So our little orange orphan has a nice home on a farm. This is the fifth cat she has taken this year, so thank you, Elner. She said she didn't have an orange one and has always wanted one. So it's turned out fine for everybody . . . and she has named the cat Sonny. . . . So good luck to Sonny in his new home.

"People are just wonderful, aren't they? And now, to celebrate our big day . . ." Mother Smith played a touch of "Happy Birthday" on the organ. "Yes . . . it's our precious Princess Mary Margaret's birthday . . . and she thanks all of you out there in her fan club for her birthday cards . . . and we'll tell you more about that later. But first, I just want to remind you that each and every donation you are so kind to send in to the Princess Mary Margaret Fund goes to help pay for the care of our little animals that need our help. I am happy to report that last year we found loving homes for over five hundred little dogs and cats, plus a box of painted turtles that had been abandoned and three rabbits. Plus funding for a Seeing Eye dog for our own Beatrice Woods.

"The dog came last week and is a beautiful golden retriever named Honey, and if you could only see Beatrice and Honey walking up and down the streets, you would know what a wonderful cause your money went to. How can we ever thank you enough?

"I also wish you all could see Princess Mary Margaret in her basket with all of her new birthday toys. Our girl is twelve years old today. It's so hard to believe that when Doc brought her to me she was no bigger than my hand . . . wasn't she, Mother Smith? And now she's as big and fat as I am. I guess that comes from both of us eating too much ice cream. Here's a card I want to share with you . . . it says,

> "Happy Birthday to Princess Mary Margaret.
> I hope you have a happy day. Keep up the good work.
> Mother, Bess, and Margaret send their best wishes.
> President Harry S. Truman"

Mother Smith played "Hail to the Chief" on the organ. Neighbor Dorothy laughed and continued, "After the show Princess Mary Margaret is going to get her special birthday hot dog from Jimmy at the Trolley Car Diner, then she's going to go across the street to the shoe hospital and visit with her friend Bottle Top. Poor Princess Mary Margaret, she gets so excited—she loves that cat. I don't know why, he doesn't care a thing in the world about her. But love is blind, as they say. . . ."

More Changes

The phone rang about two o'clock in the morning and Doc figured it was just another call from someone who needed something in the middle of the night. He often had to get up out of bed at all hours and go down and open up the drugstore for mothers who needed paregoric or cough medicine for sick children, or else it would be Tot Whooten on the phone calling to have Doc go find her mother, who had wandered off, or else help her get James off the lawn and into the house before the sun came up. But it was neither. It was Olla Warren telling him that his best friend, Glenn, who ran the hardware store, had just had a heart attack.

He hung up and was dressed and over at their house in less than five minutes and Dorothy was right behind him. When they arrived young Dr. Halling was already there and an ambulance was on the way. The next few days were touch-and-go but Glenn finally came home from the hospital with a warning to take it easy for the next few months. So his son, Macky, would have to run the hardware store for him until he got back on his feet. Bobby sort of hero-worshiped Macky, especially since he had pulled him out of the pool and saved his life. But he was someone all the younger boys looked up to. He was not only a movie usher but a top football and baseball player. Some said he was so good at shortstop he could play professional ball if he wanted. Bobby felt bad about

Macky's father being sick and Macky having to work all summer but he did not know what to do or say.

Several nights later Doc was sitting in the parlor reading the paper when Bobby came in. He went over and spun the world globe sitting on the desk a few times, picked up a pipe out of Doc's pipe holder, looked at it and put it back, and then he said, "Daddy, I need to talk to you." By the seriousness of his tone, Doc was prepared for the worst and wondered what trouble he had gotten himself into now.

"You know that baseball we got at the World Series?" Bobby said.

"Yes."

"Well, I know you caught it and all but would you be mad at me if I was to loan it to Macky Warren for a while? I was over at the hardware store today. And I remembered he sure liked that ball when I showed it to him . . . I could tell by the way he looked at it. What do you think?"

"It's your ball, son, and if that's what you want to do, it's fine with me."

Bobby said, "I've been thinking about it—I'm not sure yet if I will or not. I just wanted to see if it would be all right if I did."

"I see."

Doc didn't say anything more but he was secretly pleased. It looked as if despite all of Bobby's antics and craziness, underneath it all he was turning out to be a really nice guy.

Although some things about Bobby changed for the better, some remained the same. This morning he was standing in the hall causing trouble as usual.

Neighbor Dorothy was on the air and informed her listening audience, "If you are wondering what that noise is, it's not your receiver—it's Bobby with that bat, the ball paddle . . . bat . . . bat . . . bat . . . he's about to drive us all batty over here.

"Bobby, I want you out of this house with that thing right now!

"Would the person who invented that bat, the ball paddle, let me know who they are? Bat, bat, bat, night and day, just when he was getting over his yearly bubble-gum-blowing phase. So, if any of you out there don't have a little boy and want one, call me. . . ."

Having been thrown out of his own home and tired of batting the ball, Bobby was bored and restless. So far, this had not been the best of summers. Besides almost drowning, he had just lost the Bazooka Bubble Gum Bubble Blowing Contest for the third year in a row, Monroe was out of town visiting his grandparents for a month, it was hot, and he had nothing to do. He went downtown and floated around, had a free lime freeze at the drugstore, read a few comic books, and went over and hung around the barbershop for a while until mean Old Man Henderson came in. Everyone knew he poisoned cats and hated children, so Bobby left in a hurry. Then he decided to go up and hang out with Snooky at the projection booth at the movie theater. It was a weekday, so the movie was not playing anything he wanted to see but he liked visiting with Snooky, who sometimes let him rewind the film. As soon as he walked through the glass doors and into the lobby he began to feel better. No matter how hot it was outside, inside the theater it was always cool and he loved the smell and the sounds of the huge glass popcorn machine grinding and popping all day. He went over and bought himself a large red-and-white-striped bag of buttered popcorn and a box of Milk Duds and a Coke for himself and one for Snooky. If you have money, why not spend it? Bobby had three jobs and his pockets were so full of change and new tubes of BBs that his pants kept slipping down. Other than working for his father, he had a paper route and cut grass but he longed for the day he would turn sixteen and be able to apply for the job of movie usher. He couldn't wait to get his own brass-buttoned uniform with a cap and be assigned his very own long silver flashlight with the red plastic on the end. It was something to look forward to but that was years away. He needed something more immediate and Snooky gave it to him. His eyes lit up when Snooky said, "I hear some people from St. Louis are coming here and are fixing to open up a brand-new fancy restaurant."

"Really?" Bobby ran out of the booth and ran up and down the street asking everybody all about it. It turned out to be true!

The A & P grocery store was moving across the street to a bigger space, where the Goodyear tire store used to be before they moved into the back of Western Auto. He was excited. The pending opening would be quite an event for Bobby. As far as he could remember, since the day he was born this would be the first time anything in town had ever changed.

Every day he went down and watched the grocery store being turned into a restaurant. He saw tables and chairs and all sorts of kitchen equipment and steam tables being moved in the back door. He watched them change the tan-and-white awning to a pink-and-white one and hung little half curtains in the windows. The whole town was dying to know what kind of a restaurant was coming but that was the big mystery. People guessed at what it might be, but they all had to wait for the night of the grand opening and what a surprise it turned out to be.

In the middle of the night workmen came in and attached a long sign, still covered in brown wrapping paper, to the front of the building. It was not to be taken off until the grand opening. Finally the big moment arrived. At exactly 8:30 the paper was removed, and everybody standing downtown that night waiting, including Bobby and the entire family, applauded when they saw the sign plugged in for the first time. A pink neon sign is something . . . but a pink neon sign the shape of a pig that runs in a circle and blinks on and off set everyone wild. Oh the wonder of it! The downright cuteness of it! A little fat pink pig with that little curly tail that circled around and around over a sign that read

Three Little Pigs Cafeteria
Good Food in a Hurry

was a sight that caused people to practically knock the door down trying to get in. Even if there had been no pink neon pig, just the word *cafeteria* was enough to stir up everyone for miles around. They had all heard of a café, a diner, even a sandwich shop but an eating establishment called a cafeteria sounded so modern, so up to date and fashionable . . . urbane even. Bobby thought the whole idea of sliding your own brown plastic tray down a long line of clear glass cases filled with every kind of food you could think of, and all you had to do was point at what you wanted, was paradise. They had *every*thing: Jell-O squares with shredded carrots and green grapes inside, vegetables, meat, fish, rolls, corn sticks, and any kind of beverage or dessert you could want. They even offered foreign food, Italian spaghetti and Chinese chicken chow mein. What next, everyone wondered?

Several women in town, after seeing all the varieties of food available, vowed they would never fix dinner at home again and three or four didn't.

Ida Jenkins, Norma's mother, was so impressed that she dropped the word *cafeteria* in every sentence she could.

Of course, it took a while for people to get used to it and realize that they had to watch what the kids chose. The first night Bobby picked out three desserts and two bowls of mashed potatoes and gravy. And when Poor Tot took her mother up there for dinner, her mother put sixteen corn sticks and four iced teas on her tray. Tot tried to put a few back but her mother kicked and yelled so, she had to take her home.

But other than that and a few people dropping their trays before they got to their tables, it was a very welcome addition to the town. Inside and out. Now added to the orange-and-white neon sign that ran around the marquee of the movie theater, the bright green neon of the Victor the Florist sign, and the blue-and-white neon of the Blue Ribbon Cleaners and the Rexall drugstore was the big-pink-neon-pig-running-in-a-circle sign.

Main Street was suddenly ablaze with color. Looking at it from the Smiths' front porch was wonderful. The whole street glowed in the night and looked as bright and as cheerful as a Ferris wheel.

September Again?

Monroe had been home from his grandparents' for only a week when, much to Bobby's regret, September came rolling around again and, as it must, school started. But for his sister, this year was a completely different story. Anna Lee was now a senior in high school, with all the rights and privileges the name implies. Seniors were a special breed apart. Unlike the rest of the students, who were still having to slug through the long boring days, every minute of their school year was filled with football games, excitement, pep rallies, dances, romances, and anticipation. They don't know it yet but for many it would be the happiest year of their lives.

But Bobby was still in sixth grade. Right now all he had to look forward to was Halloween and scaring mean Old Man Henderson.

Several weeks into October, Dorothy opened her Monday morning broadcast with "Good morning, everybody. Oh, did you all see that beautiful harvest moon last night? I just love it this time of year, when, as Mr. James Whitcomb Riley says, the frost is on the pumpkin . . . and I have some good news this morning. Elmwood Springs finally won a football game, thanks to young Mr. Macky Warren kicking the ball and saving the day. In fact, making the day. So hooray for us. Anna Lee and her crowd are having their own wiener and marshmallow roast out at the lake this Friday and Doc and I are chaperones, so if I can get through this month without gaining twenty pounds I'll be lucky. Later on, Beatrice, our Little Blind Songbird, will be singing 'In the Shadow of the Whispering Pines' for you, but meanwhile a seasonal message from Dr. Orr, our dentist here in Elmwood Springs. He writes, 'October is the month for candied apples, taffy apples, and parties where bobbing for apples is often featured. I strongly advise denture wearers to abstain from these foods and activities.' Thank you, Dr. Orr, for that reminder. Of course, we all remember last year when Poor Tot Whooten lost a perfectly good front tooth eating a candied apple at the state fair. Personally I would just as soon take a bite out of the dining room table than to eat one of those things. And what else do I have?

"Oh, here it is. Doc said to remind you that all the money collected at the Lions Club Haunted House this year is going to the Crippled Children's hospital, so be sure to come by. But he says all the people with bad hearts should stay home, so it sounds like it's going to be another scary one. You can be sure I won't be going in. I'll just give my nickel at the door and go on home, thank you. Last year Bobby drug me through that thing and it nearly scared me to death. Things jumping out at you from every which way but for those of you who enjoy having the wits scared out of you, take it from me, the Lions do a good job at it. Mother Smith says she will be in the haunted house this year but she won't say doing what."

On October thirty-first at 5:30, Bobby, dressed as Abraham Lincoln, was standing around in his black suit and the two-foot-tall black stovepipe hat Jimmy had made him out of cardboard. He was busy eating big orange-colored marshmallow peanuts from a bowl on the entrance hall table when his mother came out of the kitchen and caught him. "Bobby, stop that! That's not for you. That's for my trick-or-treaters."

He looked at her indignantly. "But I *am* a trick-or-treater."

"You know what I mean." She glanced down in the other bowl on the table and he took off in a shot. She would really be mad when she saw he had bitten all the white tips off the candy corn. He was right. He heard a loud "BOBBY!" but he was out the back door, on his way over to Monroe's with a sack. Inside the sack were two large pieces of cardboard shaped like gorilla feet, or what he thought looked like gorilla feet, which he had cut out of the side of a box. Doc should have known something was up when Monroe had started coming into the drugstore every other day buying large economy-size containers of baby powder.

◆ ◆ ◆

Around midnight, as soon as they knew Old Man Henderson was in bed, Monroe and Bobby did what they had been planning for weeks, then ran home to Monroe's house, where Bobby was to spend the night. The next morning Old Man Henderson was in for a shock—and got one. His entire front porch was completely covered in white powder, smooth except for the paw prints of a few cats and the enormous footprints of what must have been a giant monster. Old Man Henderson never did figure out just what had walked across his front porch that night—but for the next few months he kept his shotgun by the door in case it came back.

Christmas came and went with a hundred more socks, endless underwear, again not one genuine Jungle Jim pith helmet, but there was snow on December twenty-eighth. That was something, at least. On New Year's Eve, James Whooten got drunk and fell down the back stairs of the VFW hall and broke both his elbows and lost his job as a house painter. To make ends meet Tot had to start doing shampoos and sets in her kitchen. "Poor Tot, now she has to support the entire family," they all said, and everyone went to her to get their hair done, even if they did not need it. Tot had been to beauty school before she married and figured it was the only thing she was good at. Unfortunately, she was wrong. Mother Smith and a number of gray-haired ladies had come home from their appointment with bright purple hair, but none complained, and they went back anyway. It was a small price to pay to help out a friend.

After an unusually cold February and March, spring finally decided to come back again and all of April and May were busy months at the Smith house. As the time drew near for Anna Lee's graduation, there was constant shopping for clothes to wear to dances and parties and the senior prom. Among the seniors themselves there was the drama of wondering who would be voted what in the "Who's Who" section of the senior yearbook, the hysteria when the school rings arrived and they had a blue stone instead of the red one they'd ordered and it had to be sent back. Norma and Macky were voted "Cutest Couple," Patsy Marie tied with Mary Esther Lockett for "Smartest Girl," and Anna Lee was "Class Beauty." Dixie Cahill had her spring tap and twirl recital and the high school graduation went off without a hitch. Dorothy and Doc gave Anna

Lee a Lady Bulova watch, Mother Smith and Jimmy both gave her money, and Bobby, following a suggestion from his mother, bought her a bottle of White Shoulders perfume with his paper route money. The last day of school came and, as always, Bobby was eternally grateful. But for Anna Lee, after all the excitement and fun of graduation had died down and she had time to think, she started the summer in a somewhat sad and melancholy mood. It dawned on her that her life as she had known it for the past twelve years would never be the same.

On the other hand, Bobby worried that his life would always be the same.

The first warm Sunday after school let out, while everyone else was at church, Bobby rode his bicycle out to the water tower with his pockets stuffed with red balloons and string, determined that today would be the time he would climb all the way to the top and do the deed. Ever since the time he had climbed it with Monroe, he had been living with a terrible secret that even Monroe did not know. Nobody knew. He was scared to go back up. Not only that: now he was scared of being scared. He had ridden out there at least a dozen times determined to climb it, and each time he had failed. But today, he vowed, would be different. Today he would just go right to the top.

But it wasn't. It was just like all the other times. He stood at the bottom, trying with all his might to muster the courage to go back up, but no matter how hard he tried he just could not do it. The minute he put one foot on the ladder his heart would start to pound and he'd break out in a cold sweat and could not go any farther. After trying for more than an hour, he gave up and rode back home, defeated and humiliated again. He began to fear the one thing in the world that terrified boys the most. He was afraid that down deep he was a coward. Maybe Luther Griggs was right: maybe he was a sissy.

After each defeat he worried that people would be able to tell just by looking at him. But the farther away from the tower he got, the better he felt. When he got back to town and rode past the barbershop and the theater and saw people he knew, his defeat began to fade a little. Dixie Cahill came out of the drugstore and waved at him. He waved back. He began to feel more relieved. People were not looking at him funny. Nobody knew. Next time, he vowed. He would do it next time. Besides, he could not really be a coward; he had too much to do. He had to fly planes, sail the ocean, and ride in rodeos, save girls, beat up bullies. He had to pitch winning games and make touchdowns, round up cattle and command spaceships to Mars. By the time he reached home he had convinced himself that it could not possibly be true: he was not a coward.

But not quite persuasively enough, because a few nights later he had the same old dream. The one where he was climbing up the tower and the rungs of the ladder started to drop off one by one and he fell. Each time he would wake up with a start just before he hit the ground.

He started to hate that water tower.

The Salesman

July turned out to be hot and dry that year and by ten o'clock in the morning it was already boiling hot, without a cloud in the sky. That day the young man in the black Plymouth was driving about fifteen miles outside of town when he spotted a small cloud of dust moving way off in a distant field. As he got closer and slowed down he saw that the dust cloud was exactly what he'd suspected. A lone man in overalls and a straw hat was plowing behind a two-mule team. The young man glanced at his watch. He had time. He turned around and parked on the side of the road.

He figured he might as well try and do a little business. He looked at the mailbox on the post and read the name printed in white paint on the side.

He got out and climbed over the fence and headed out toward the man plowing. When the farmer looked up and saw him coming, he stopped his mules. "Whoa. Whoa."

The younger man knew to immediately put a big smile on his face and wave to let him know he was friendly and not from the government or the bank. He took no chances; from his past experience he knew that, depending on their situation, farmers would sometimes call the dogs on them or shoot at them. As he got closer he called out, "Mr. Shimfissle?"

The farmer nodded. "Yes, sir," he said slowly and waited to see what the caller wanted.

As he reached the farmer he said, "How are you doing today? It's a hot one, ain't it?" and took a business card out of his shirt pocket and handed it to him. He then walked over and patted one of the mules on the hindquarters. "Hey, boy . . . you're a big son of a gun, ain't you," he said while the farmer read his card. It introduced him as a salesman for the Allis-Chalmers tractor company. The farmer was not surprised. This was not the first tractor salesman who had stopped by trying to sell him something and he wouldn't be the last but to be cordial he asked, "What can I do for you today?"

"Not a thing. I was passing by on my way to Elmwood Springs when I saw you out here and I wondered if it would be all right if I was to walk along with you for a bit?"

The farmer, who was not interested in buying a tractor, knew what was coming but said, "Nope, come right ahead if you want to."

"Thanks, I sure appreciate it," the salesman said, and sat down and quickly took off his shoes and socks and rolled up his pants legs. As they walked along, he said, "To tell you the truth, Mr. Shimfissle, I haven't seen one of these old plows since I was a kid. I spent many a day behind one of these things. My daddy had about twenty-five acres outside of Knoxville but we lost all of it to the TVA—it's all under water now."

Shimfissle shook his head in sympathy. He knew what losing your land meant to a farmer. After they had walked and plowed for a while and after they had discussed the price of corn, the weather, and the best time to plant which crop, the salesman said, "Do you think I could try my hand at it for a minute . . . just to see if I remember how?"

The farmer stopped the team again with a "Whoa" and handed him the reins. "Here you go. But don't be afraid to prod them a bit. They can be as stubborn as hell."

The salesman took the reins and stepped behind the yoke, gave a whistle, a few clucks, and after a small tap on their backsides, off they went just as lively as they had been at 5:30 that morning. They even picked up their pace as he talked to them like old friends.

Shimfissle was impressed. This was not your ordinary, run-of-the-mill tractor salesman that didn't know a cornrow from a teakettle. This boy was a farmer. After about ten minutes the younger man slowed them down and stopped. "I sure do thank you, Mr. Shimfissle. It felt so good to get hold of one of these things again I hate to quit."

"I hate to have you quit. I was enjoying the rest. Anytime you get the urge to plow, come on back."

"Yessir, thank you, I will. You've got yourself a couple of fine mules. You just don't see them much anymore . . . everybody's in a hurry, everybody wants to speed up nowadays."

The farmer took the reins back. "Well, enjoyed talking to you."

"Same here." The salesman had to slap some dust off himself. "I'm a mess, ain't I? You wouldn't have a place where I could wash up a bit, would you? I've got a date with a lady in town and I better not show up looking like this."

"Sure, go on in the house and tell the wife I sent you. She'll fix you up."

"Much obliged." He picked up his shoes and socks and headed toward the white farmhouse. Will Shimfissle continued on, somehow sorry that the Allis-Chalmers man had not even tried to sell him a tractor.

In fact, he had not even mentioned it once. For that very reason, Will made a note to himself: if he ever was in the market for a tractor, this is the guy he would buy it from.

When the salesman reached the house he stamped off as much dust as he could, then knocked on the back door. He could hear the radio being turned off and a few seconds later a large woman in a cotton housedress came to the door.

"Mrs. Shimfissle, I'm sorry to bother you but your husband sent me up here to see if I could borrow a little soap and water. I got myself all dirty out there in the fields talking to your husband."

She opened the screen door. "Well sure, honey, come on in and I'll get you some soap and a rag."

"No, ma'am, I better not come in, I'll get your kitchen dirty."

"Well, then wait a minute," she said and came back with a washcloth and a bar of homemade lye soap and a small pan. "When you're finished come in and I'll give you a glass of iced tea—you must be scorched."

He went to the pump outside the kitchen and stuck his head under and washed his face and hands and rinsed off his feet. After he put his shoes and socks back on he pulled a black Ace comb out of his pocket and ran it through his hair. He knocked on the door again. "Ma'am, here's your pan back."

She opened the screen door and saw a neat, nice, almost new-looking young man in a white shirt. "Come on in. Can I fix you a sandwich?"

He stepped in and took the iced tea. "No, ma'am, thank you but this is all I need. I'm fixing to go on a lunch date as soon as I get to town. She says we are going to go to something called a cafeteria."

"Oh lucky you, my sisters Ida and Gerta tell me it's quite the place. I haven't been there yet but I'm going one of these days, whenever I can talk Will into dressing up. He won't get dressed up unless it's for a funeral, so I guess I'll have to wait till somebody dies to get a meal there. Ida says they've got a pink pig running in a circle, so be sure and see that."

"Yes, ma'am, I will." He handed her the empty glass and was about to leave when it occurred to him that as long as he was here it wouldn't hurt if he fished around in his pocket for another card. "Mrs. Shimfissle, I'm thinking of running for a political office someday. I don't know for what yet but let me give you my card." He went through all his pockets but was unsuccessful. "I can't find one . . . but anyway, if you ever see the name Hamm Sparks on a ballot, I sure would appreciate your vote. Can you remember that?"

"Your first name's Ham? Like a Christmas ham? Like the meat ham?"

"Yes, ma'am, only it's spelled with two *m*'s."

She repeated it. "Hamm. . . . Well, it's unusual but easier to remember than Billy or John, I'll say that for it."

"Yes, ma'am, it's my mother's family name. She was a Hamm before she married."

"You don't say. My mother was a Nuckle with an *N* before she married, and my daddy was a Knott with a *K* out of Pennsylvania. . . . They said the people that got invites to the Nuckle-Knott nuptials thought it was pretty funny."

He laughed. "I guess so."

She said, "It's a good thing they didn't have a boy and called him Nuckle. That would have made a name, wouldn't it . . . Nuckle Knott. But then," she mused, "we went to school with a boy with the first name of Lard, only it was spelled Laird but they called him Crisco all his life anyway. I don't think he ever married, or leastways I never heard if he did. He used to sell buttons."

Hamm opened the door to escape. He knew from past experience that these farm women were starved for company and would talk for hours to a total stranger. "Well, thanks for everything, Mrs. Shimfissle," he said as he hurried out the door and down the back steps. She followed him and opened the door. "Hey, wait a minute—I forgot your last name."

He turned around and called out, "Sparks, ma'am, Hamm Sparks."

"Sparks? Like electrical sparks?"

"Yes, ma'am," he said, as he waved over his shoulder and ran for the car.

Aunt Elner Saves the Day

After the salesman left Elner called her sister Gerta Nordstrom and told her she had just met a man named Hamm. Gerta laughed and said, "Next you'll be telling me you met a woman named Egg." There were three Knott sisters, Elner, Gerta, and the youngest, Norma's mother, Ida. Despite the fact that everyone in town knew all three had been raised on a midwestern farm, sometime after she had married Herbert Jenkins, Ida suddenly started dropping little hints here and there that she was descended from a fine old southern family who had fallen on bad times. By 1948 she had alluded to her aristocratic forebears so often that she began to believe it. This delusion about her background had started nine years ago, after she had seen the movie *Gone with the Wind* a dozen times at the Elmwood Theater. She was convinced she recognized Tara and therefore must have lived there in a previous incarnation. It never occurred to her that "Tara" was only a movie set or that her recently acquired southern accent was only a poor imitation of an English girl doing a poor imitation of a southern accent. The only real southerner in town was a seventy-eight-year-old widow lady named Mrs. Mary Frances Samples, born in Huntsville, Alabama. She too had been adversely affected by the movie. As if losing the War Between the States was not bad enough, she had been completely devastated when it was announced that Tallulah Bankhead, a true daughter of the South and a fellow Alabamian, had not been cast as Scarlett O'Hara. Mary Frances

Samples vowed never to see another movie as long as she lived. She said her only consolation was that "at least the role did not go to a Yankee girl."

Mrs. Samples aside, Ida was bound and determined that her daughter, Norma, was going off to college in the Deep South. It might be too late for Ida to fulfill her rightful destiny as a daughter of the Confederacy, but she secretly envisioned herself in her later years visiting Norma and sitting on the veranda of her large plantation home in Virginia, being waited on hand and foot. A vision Norma did not share. All she ever wanted to do was marry Macky Warren and settle down in Elmwood Springs and start a family. Norma and Macky had been girlfriend and boyfriend since the seventh grade. And on the night of the senior prom, when he gave her an engagement ring, nobody was surprised. But Ida was at once adamantly against it. In fact would not hear of it. "I like Macky," she said, "but no daughter of mine is marrying a little small-town hardware-store owner's son."

"I will, too!" said Norma.

"Over my dead body," said Ida. "Besides, you are not marrying anybody until you finish college."

Norma looked to her father for help but he had not stood up to his wife in years. Doomed! For a while Norma and Macky became the local Romeo and Juliet. Everybody took sides. Ida on one side and everybody else on the other.

Living so far out in the country, Norma's Aunt Elner had not been aware of the tragedy of her niece and her boyfriend until one afternoon when the two drove out to see her. Norma was miserable and teary and Macky just sat stoically, trying to be brave. "Aunt Elner, if she makes me go to that stupid college and leave Macky here alone, I swear I'll just kill myself. She's going to make us waste four years of our lives because of some whim."

Macky looked at Norma. "I'd go with her if I could but I can't with my daddy being so sick—I've got to stay here and help him run the store." Then he looked over at Elner and asked earnestly, "Mrs. Shimfissle, what would you think if we were to elope? Would you be willing to come with us?"

Elner was taken aback at this request. "Oh no, Macky, you don't want to do that. Just give it a little while longer, I'm sure she'll come around."

"What if she doesn't?" asked Norma.

"I believe she will. But let's just hold our horses and wait and then we'll figure out what to do from there."

After they left, Elner stood in the yard and smiled and waved goodbye until they were out of sight. Then she went inside and picked up the phone.

"Ida, this is your sister. Now, what's all this mess about you not letting Norma marry the Warren boy?"

"I didn't say she couldn't marry him, Elner. I just said not now."

"Why not now?"

"Because I want her to go to college first, where she will get an education and at least have a chance to meet boys from the nicer families. I know she doesn't think so now but in the long run I know she will be happier and better off if she at least dates a boy from her own kind . . . maybe someone from a fine old southern family with a similar—"

Elner, not letting her finish, snapped, "Oh, Ida Mae, give it up. You are not from some fine old southern family. Your grandfather was a German pig farmer from Pennsylvania and everybody knows it. Up to now, Gerta and I have always babied you and let you carry on with all your silly little airs because we thought it was cute but I can't stand by and see you ruin Norma's life over your foolishness, so you just stop all this nonsense right now." Then she hung up.

Ida stood with phone in hand and her mouth open. Elner, the oldest sister, had practically raised her when their mother died and had rarely if ever spoken harshly to her in her life. Still, Elner said later, "I hated to do it, but drastic times calls for drastic measures."

The next day Elner was way back in the yard picking butter beans when she heard the phone ringing. Whoever was calling would not hang up, so she figured she better get it in case someone was dead. When she picked it up an excited young Norma was on the other end.

"Aunt Elner?"

"Hey."

"You are not going to believe what happened. Mother said I could marry Macky and not have to go off to school."

Aunt Elner pretended to be surprised. "Well, I'll be . . . What did she say?"

"She told me that if I wanted to ruin my life and destroy my chances of happiness forever that I had her permission—isn't that great?!"

"Oh, honey, I just couldn't be happier for you," she said while emptying the butter beans from her apron into a bowl. "I told you she'd come around."

"You did. Anyhow, we're going down to the church this afternoon and set up the date."

"Good. Best to move fast before she changes her mind. You tell little Macky I'm glad it worked out." A little while later, after Elner had her beans cooking on the stove, the phone rang again. This time it was Macky. "Mrs. Shimfissle, I just called to thank you. I know you must have done something to get Norma's mother to change her mind."

"No no, honey, she has her own mind. She did that all by herself."

"Just the same, if you had not said something, and I know you did, it's no telling what that crazy woman might have done to break us up."

"I'm just glad it's all going to work out. . . . And, honey . . . I know Ida's caused you and Norma a lot of trouble but try not to be too hard on her. With all of her faults, I don't think she means to hurt people. She's just desperate to be somebody she's not and doesn't know how to go about it."

"I'll try," Macky said, "but it won't be easy."

"Good, because don't forget: for better or for worse, she's your mother-in-law now." There was a long silence on the other end before Macky said good-bye.

Elner turned to her cat Sonny and said, "Uh-oh, I may have just killed that marriage with my big mouth."

But she hadn't. The wedding went off. Ida somehow managed to pull herself together, at least until the honeymoon, but hope springs eternal. On the off chance that Macky should suddenly become wealthy in the hardware business, for one of her wedding presents she gave Norma the book *How to Handle Household Servants and Staff* by Vivian Clipp.

Progress

She was in her kitchen doing a last-minute check of the show when she heard Mother Smith call out, "Dorothy!" She looked up and it was 9:28. Dorothy rushed down the hall with the papers and with Princess Mary Margaret running behind her, barking frantically. "Here I am!" she said as she ran through the door at the last minute. She waved at the sizable audience in the room. "Hello, sorry I'm late," she said as she sat down just as the red light came on and the theme music started.

"Good morning, everybody. . . . It's another beautiful day over here and I hope it's just as nice where you are . . . but first, before I say another word, if you are wondering why I sound a little funny this morning, I want you to know that I have not been in the kitchen hitting on the cooking sherry." Mother Smith played one bar of "How Dry I Am." Dorothy laughed. "The reason I sound this way is I was up at Dr. Orr's this morning and got a filling and the Novocain has not worn off yet and so, with that disclaimer, on with the show.

"Independence Day is just around the corner, so hurray and three cheers for the red, white, and blue. Glenn Warren down at the VFW post says that all the food they will be serving on the Fourth of July will be red, white, and blue—red beets, mashed potatoes, white-meat chicken only, blueberry pie with vanilla ice cream. Let's just hope the watermelons cooperate this year and turn bright red, too. Also don't forget that the Pony Man will be in town next Wednesday, so if you want to have your child's picture made, he will be over in the vacant lot behind the church from twelve to four."

Dorothy smiled at her audience. "And we are happy to have some visitors with us this morning. Mrs. Ida Jenkins is here with seven of her out-of-town Garden Club members, who are visiting all the way from Joplin. Welcome, ladies. As you all know, Ida is the mother of our precious little newlywed, Norma Warren. And being a mother myself, I hope you won't mind me bragging a little on my own. We are so happy for Anna Lee, who has just been accepted at the Chicago School of Nursing, which is our own Nurse Ruby Robinson's alma mater and I know she is as proud of Anna Lee as we are. How fast time goes by . . . it seems like only yesterday that Norma and Anna Lee were getting ready for their first dance recital. It seems like the whole world is changing right before my eyes. Doc just informed me last night that two new business establishments are going up outside of town. One is a drive-in Tastee-Freez that is going to be built in the shape of an igloo, complete with a polar bear on top. The other is an overnight motor court called the Wigwam Village, made out of individual cement wigwams. As if that's not enough excitement, there is a rumor that a new Howard Johnson's motel is in our near future. At the rate Elmwood Springs is growing, pretty soon we won't even be able to recognize our own town!

"And speaking of growth, I want to remind all of you in the Raymore and Harrisonville area that Cecil Figgs Mortuaries and Floral Designs has just opened two new branches close to you . . . open twenty-four hours a day for your convenience. And remember, Cecil Figgs is my only sponsor that really does not *want* your business but is always there when you need him. . . .

"Now here's Beatrice Woods to sing a song that is certainly apropos for us this morning, 'There'll Be Some Changes Made.' " Two and a half minutes after doing her Golden Flake Pancake Mix commercial and giving out a recipe for green tomato pickle relish, Dorothy glanced up at the wall and said, "Oh dear, I see by that mean old clock that it's time to go. I had some births and deaths to announce but births and deaths will just have to wait until Monday. So until then, this is Neighbor Dorothy with Mother Smith on the organ saying we loved visiting with you this morning, so come back and visit with us again, won't you? And remember, you're always welcome at 5348 First Avenue North."

As she had said, Dorothy was glad, of course, that Anna Lee had decided to become a nurse, but at the same time she was not happy thinking about her going so far away from home. Lately, she would sometimes sit and stare at Anna Lee, her eyes filled with tears. To think that she would soon be losing her little girl.

Gospel Grows

Not only was Elmwood Springs changing, the whole country seemed to be taking a giant leap forward. More and more people were buying their own homes. New radio stations were being built everywhere. Thousands of radios, cars, washing machines, refrigerators, and stoves were being sold every day. More roads were being paved, and new inventions put on the market faster than you could shake a stick at them. Electric dishwashers, electric can openers, electric everything—all you had to do was push a button. By 1960, they said, they would even have robots that would do all your housework. According to Dorothy, if things continued at this pace, housewives would soon be on Easy Street.

But nothing was changing faster than gospel music. During the war years, with so many rural people migrating from the country to the large cities to work in factories, it had suddenly found its way out of the small backwoods country churches of the South and Midwest. People's addresses may have changed from Alabama and Georgia to Detroit or Chicago but not their taste in music. They wanted to hear what they were used to and gospel was popping up on radio stations everywhere, gaining a brand-new audience in the North, and the crowds of fans soon outgrew the small church and school auditoriums and moved into the large auditoriums of the big cities and ballparks. New songs were being written by the hundreds. Even *Time* magazine acknowledged the existence of a growing and lucrative "Gospel Tin Pan Alley." Southern gospel was now being heard all over the country and even as far away as Canada and some of the groups were getting more famous by the day.

The better-known groups had their radio shows and recording and publishing companies and traveled to personal appearances in big black limousines. But not the Oatmans. They traveled in the same old beat-up car and still mostly sang in country churches and at all-night sings. Ever since he had been saved again, Ferris believed that this new popularity was causing gospel music to drift further away from the church and dangerously close to show business. He felt the devil was slipping hip-wiggling and bebop rhythms into gospel, tempting groups and luring good Christians away from the Lord with the idea of making a fast buck. He preached to anyone who would listen that singing gospel not church related was sinful. After losing his own brother Le Roy to the lure of honky-tonk and hillbilly music, he was frightened that his boys Bervin and Vernon might be tempted to run off as well, so he would allow the family to sing on radio shows that featured only gospel.

One was a fifteen-minute broadcast the Blackwood Brothers did twice a day over station KMA in Shenandoah, Iowa. Their pianist, Cat Freeman, was an old friend of Ferris's. Cat and his sister Vestal Goodman (now singing with the Happy Goodmans) had all grown up together in northern Alabama and had picked cotton together as kids, so it was a happy reunion. As it turned out, it was also a reunion between Dorothy Smith and the Oatman family. Dorothy was up in Iowa that weekend to visit with her friend and fellow radio homemaker Evelyn Birkby and to participate in the big home-demonstration show at the Mayfair Auditorium in Shenandoah.

Dorothy had just given her "Decorating Cakes for All Occasions" talk and was backstage watching Adella Shoemaker speak and demonstrate how to choose wallpaper when someone handed her a note.

> Dear Mrs. Smith,
>
> I seen a poster at KMA that you are here and so are we. I would love to talk with you after the show if you got the time.
>
> Minnie Oatman

Dorothy quickly wrote on the bottom, *Wonderful! Meet me at the stage door when it is over. Dorothy,* and gave it back to the lady to deliver.

Dorothy would be more than happy to see Minnie Oatman and

hoped that Betty Raye would be with her. She had thought about Betty Raye so many times and wondered how she was. But after the show, it was Minnie alone who met her at the stage door.

The two women walked across the street to a little café and sat in a booth that Minnie had trouble squeezing into. After catching up on all the places the Oatmans had been, Dorothy asked what she had wanted to ask from the beginning. "And how is Betty Raye?"

A look of concern suddenly crossed Minnie's face. She hesitated a moment and then confessed, "Not so good. . . . To be honest with you, Mrs. Smith, that's what I wanted to talk to you about. She don't know I'm here but you and your family was so sweet to her and with you having your own daughter and all, I thought maybe you could give me some advice, because I don't mind telling you I am just worried to tears over her."

"Oh dear. Is there anything wrong with her?"

"Not as of *yet* but I am having a terrible time right now. Both the boys is on the verge of a rebellious streak, and Floyd is gone more woman crazy than ever, and Ferris ain't in his right mind."

Dorothy was alarmed. "What's the matter with him?"

"Oh, every once in a while he gets saved again and goes off the deep end with the spirit but this last time was the worst he's been. I tell you, Mrs. Smith, right now he's about one step up from snake handling and I have to keep my eye on him every minute to keep him from falling back. You know all his people from Sand Mountain is like that. Three of them is dead from snakebites right now." She heaved a sigh. "And I don't have no one to blame but myself. My momma warned me about marrying a Sand Mountain man but nothing would do till I got Ferris Oatman, so I have made my bed and I've got to lump it. But I can't look after him and the whole family too. And Betty Raye is now getting of an age to where all the boys is wanting to date her. I'm afraid when I'm not looking one of them little hip-wiggling hot-lipped gospel boys that's always hanging around at them all-night sings is liable to go behind my back and run off with her."

"I see. How does she feel about it?"

"As of yet she don't pay them no never mind. She ain't interested in anything but sitting in a corner and reading. She's ruined her eyes so bad we had to get her glasses but she hates traveling from place to place so bad I'm afraid she'll marry one of them just to get herself off the road."

"Do you really think so?"

"If she's anything like *me* at that age she will and we don't have the money to hire another singer to take her place, so I'm just at the bottom of my rope with worry."

"Yes, I can understand your concern." Dorothy's face showed her own concern.

Minnie then leaned over and confided to her: "Mrs. Smith, I know I'm not a very smart person. I've had little or none education. And don't get me wrong, I love 'em to death, but Ferris and the boys and, God knows, Floyd is not the brightest of men. This life is all right for folks like us but Betty Raye's different. She's smarter than the rest of us. She thinks I don't notice but I see her reading her books, wanting to learn things. I tried my best to keep her in school over at my sister's but they was too many kids in that house and it made her nervous. But, Mrs. Smith, if I don't do something soon she's gonna wind up just like me and stay dumb all her life."

An idea suddenly occurred to Dorothy about a possible replacement for Betty Raye, but she decided not to say anything specific yet. Dorothy sat back. "Minnie, I don't know if this will work out or not but will you call me at home next week?"

Minnie said she would, and squeezed her way back out of the booth. They parted with Minnie promising to call as soon as they landed somewhere that had a phone.

The next day Dorothy was on her way back to Elmwood Springs, and the Oatman family left Iowa early in the morning, headed straight down to Nashville, Tennessee, known as the Belt Buckle of the Bible Belt, to appear on Wally Fowler's all-night sing at the Ryman Auditorium. Minnie prayed all the way there that Ferris would not roam around backstage and preach at all the other gospel groups about going commercial and that Floyd would not start chasing after the Carter sisters again.

The last time they had sung with the Carter family Chester, the dummy, had made a suggestion to June she did not like and she'd ripped his wig off. It had cost them twenty-eight dollars to replace it.

All the way back home Dorothy was torn. She wanted to help Betty Raye but she would also hate to lose another girl she cared about. But she also knew that same someone longed to travel.

Oh well, she rationalized, it couldn't do any harm to ask. The first day she was at home she and Beatrice were sitting in the kitchen when she broached the subject.

"Guess who I ran into up in Iowa?"

"I don't know."

"Do you remember the Oatmans?"

Beatrice smiled and petted her Seeing Eye dog, Honey. "Oh yes."

"And Betty Raye?"

She nodded "Yes . . . the girl who stayed here. How is she?"

Dorothy cleared her throat. "Not well, it seems. She's not doing well at all."

"Oh, that's too bad."

"Yes. Her mother tells me that she is not really that happy traveling. She would like to stop for a while and maybe go back to school."

"Really?"

"Yes, her mother said she would like for Betty Raye to have a chance to at least finish high school." Beatrice nodded but said nothing. "But," Dorothy continued, "it doesn't look like that is going to happen." She paused.

"Why not?" asked Beatrice.

Dorothy had hoped she would ask. "Well, in order for her to stop singing they would have to find someone to replace her in the group."

"Oh," said Beatrice. She began to pet Honey's head a little faster. "Really?"

Dorothy stirred two more teaspoons of sugar into her coffee to give Beatrice time to think. "Of course, it would mean a great *deal* of traveling for someone . . . always going from one place to another . . ."

"Really?"

"Oh yes. I didn't say anything to Minnie . . . but you wouldn't be interested in anything like that, would you?"

Beatrice immediately stood up. "Oh, Dorothy, do you think they would take me? Do you think they ever would? I know all the songs and I can learn the harmonies—"

"Well, Minnie *is* calling me in a few days and if you want I can certainly ask her. But now, I don't think it would pay much."

"I don't care about that. And if they're worried about me being blind, tell them about Honey. Tell them we get around fine. I can do almost anything. I would not be a burden. Tell them I'd sing for free."

They were both on pins and needles until Minnie called, as promised. Dorothy told her that Beatrice would be available to go on the road in Betty Raye's place if they wanted her. Minnie said she would talk it over with Ferris and call back.

An hour went by and finally the phone rang again. "Mrs. Smith, you tell that girl if she is willing to put up with us we would just love to have her. Hold on, I'm gonna put Betty Raye on the line."

While she was waiting Dorothy called out to Beatrice, who was in the kitchen waiting to hear. "They want you, honey." Then Betty Raye came on.

"Hello?"

"Betty Raye . . . has your mother told you everything?"

"Yes, ma'am."

"Is this all right with you? You know, we really want you to come."

There was a long pause. "Mrs. Smith, you just don't *know* how much I want to be there."

This was almost the first complete sentence Dorothy had ever heard Betty Raye say in all the time she had known her.

As worried as Dorothy had been about doing the wrong thing, at that moment she knew that she had done the right thing.

Minnie got back on. "Tell Beatrice we'll be over to get her in a few weeks. I swear, just when you think there is no answer the Good Lord sends you an angel. God bless you for a saint, Mrs. Smith. You don't know what a burden has been lifted from my heart."

Dorothy hung up and went to the kitchen but Beatrice was gone. She was already next door in her room, starting to pack.

The Exchange

Ferris Oatman was not at all happy about losing Betty Raye and breaking up the family but for the first time in their marriage Minnie had put her rather large foot down.

"Ferris, my baby wants to get off the road and go to school and that's what she's gonna do."

"Over my dead body," he said.

"If that's what it takes, then so be it but she's going."

Ferris saw the look in her eye and decided not to push it and two weeks later the Oatmans made a swing down into Missouri on their way to Arkansas to drop off Betty Raye and pick up Beatrice Woods and her dog. When they drove up Minnie rolled down the window and said, "Mrs. Smith, I don't even have time to get out and hug your neck, we are already running late; we have to be at an all-night sing in Little Rock by eight, but I'll be praying for you all the way there." The back door opened and Betty Raye got out and Beatrice and Honey got in.

Uncle Floyd was in the front seat with Ferris and Minnie and as soon as they pulled out Chester, the Scripture-quoting dummy, turned around and looked at her and his eyebrows shot up and down and he said, "Whoo, whoo—well, hello there, good looking."

Beatrice answered right away, "Well, hello there yourself!"

Mother Smith, Dorothy, Bobby, Anna Lee, and Nurse Ruby Robinson all stood and waved good-bye, moist-eyed. But Beatrice Woods never looked back. She would not have, even if she *could* have seen them. She was too busy concentrating on what was ahead. At last she was out on the road, headed for the wild blue yonder and beyond. Ya-hoo!

Betty Raye had not changed much from the last time they had seen her. She had grown a little taller and wore glasses now. Someone else had obviously picked them out for her. The frames were a bad combination of black plastic and metal rims and were not at all flattering on a teenager. As they walked into the house, Dorothy vowed to herself that the first thing she was going to do was get the poor girl a new pair of glasses.

Even though they would miss Beatrice, everybody was glad that Betty Raye was coming back to stay with them. Especially Anna Lee. She had been sad and moody all summer. Besides being worried about going away in the fall and leaving her family, she was feeling a little abandoned by her two best friends, and for the first time in her life she was lonely. Patsy Marie had started working full-time for her father down at the cleaners and Norma had gotten married. And no matter how much she and Norma vowed that nothing would ever change between them, it had. It was not like the old days, when she could call her night and day and had her to go places with anytime she wanted. Norma was now a married woman and things were different. It was nobody's fault. Anna Lee still had all the boys in town buzzing around her as usual, but still she was lonesome for a girlfriend to do things with.

And there were other considerations.

On the first night, Anna Lee went into Betty Raye's room and sat down on the bed and watched her unpack. She said, sincerely, "You just don't know how grateful I am that you are here. I felt so guilty about going off so far away from Mother and leaving her all alone with just Bobby, I almost backed out of going. But now with you here I know she won't be so lonesome and worry about me so much."

Betty Raye was still shy around Anna Lee and mumbled, "Thank you."

Anna Lee went on. "You know, if you think about it, it's almost like you're a younger sister staying behind, isn't it." She sighed. "I wish I *had* had a sister. Mother depends so much on me that it's hard . . . and as long as we are going to be like sisters, I wish you'd think about staying in my room when I leave. It would mean a lot to me if you did."

"Really?"

"Oh, yes, and I know it would make Mother very happy. She feels funny about you being in this little dinky room. Oh, not that it's not nice or anything," she added quickly, "it's just that if you stay in my room it will be like you really are my sister." Betty Raye unpacked still another homemade dress. "You know, Betty Raye, I'll bet you and I are the same size. I've got a whole closetful of clothes. I'm not taking most of them, so they will be just hanging there, and you can wear anything you want. I was going to give them away. If you don't mind hand-me-downs. They're perfectly good."

Betty Raye, who had worn hand-me-downs all her life, said, "No, I don't mind."

During the next few weeks Anna Lee spent a lot of time with Betty Raye and she made her try on all the clothes in her closet. One day Anna Lee just came right out and asked what she had wanted to ask all along. "Would you let me fool with your hair a little bit?"

By the time Anna Lee had finished "fooling with" Betty Raye's hair, she had also put a little lipstick and rouge on her. "There, don't you look better?"

Betty Raye looked in the mirror but could not see a thing without her glasses, and said yes anyway. The next thing Anna Lee did was to paint Betty Raye's nails bright red. Betty Raye was still too shy to say anything. But who could refuse Anna Lee anything in her pink angora sweater and pink pearls? Betty Raye was putty in her hands.

Every day Anna Lee took her shopping downtown, an event that lasted for hours. Anna Lee was busy shopping at Morgan Brothers department store for her new college wardrobe and she tried on every hat, every pair of shoes, every suit or dress—some twice—before she would decide what she wanted.

Dorothy was happy that Anna Lee and Betty Raye were spending so much time together but after a while she began to be a little concerned for Betty Raye. She told Mother Smith, "She is dragging that poor girl around town like she was that Raggedy Ann doll she used to have." And she was.

One afternoon Anna Lee said to Betty Raye, "I know you are real religious and all that but would it be a sin for you to go to the movies? Ginger Rogers is from Missouri and I'm just dying to see *Kitty Foyle* again. It wouldn't hurt you to go just once, would it?"

Betty Raye thought for a moment. "I don't know. I've never been."

When Dorothy found out, she said, "Now, Anna Lee, I don't want you to be pushing Betty Raye into doing things she might not want to do." Anna Lee, who was busy at the moment braiding Betty Raye's thin brown hair into pigtails, said innocently, "I'm not, Mother. She wants to go, don't you?"

Betty Raye, sitting at Anna Lee's dressing table, said, "Yes, ma'am." The next night Anna Lee took her to see *Kitty Foyle* and she loved it.

That Friday Dorothy drove the two girls over to Poplar Bluff to get Betty Raye some new glasses. When they got home Dorothy said to Mother Smith, "You should have come with us—you would have gotten the biggest kick out of Anna Lee. You would have thought she was Betty Raye's mother, the way she was carrying on."

Mother Smith said, "Did she get a new pair?"

"Finally," said Dorothy, sitting down on the sofa. "They should be here next week. Anna Lee picked them out. Blue plastic with sort of wings on the end. It's not the pair *I* would have picked but that's the pair Anna Lee wanted and that's what she got. Betty Raye is the sweetest girl; she just sat there and let Anna Lee stick every pair of glasses they had in the store on her and she never said a word."

It was true, Anna Lee was enjoying her newfound project, pushing and pulling at poor Betty Raye, trying to make her into a version of herself. If she had had another few weeks she might have even taught Betty Raye to jitterbug. But the day finally came when she had to leave for nursing school. That night the whole family went down to the train station to see her off. On the way over, Dorothy talked too much and tried her best to be brave, but at the last minute, when Anna Lee, looking so smart and grown up in her brown hound's-tooth suit and hat to match, climbed on the train and turned around and waved, she could no longer control herself. She put her hand over her mouth to hide a sob and watched the train pull away and she broke down completely. Doc put his arm around her. "Come on, now," he said, "it's not for that long. She'll be back at Christmas."

"I know," Dorothy said, "but she just looked so little on that great big train," and she almost broke down again. She knew she was being silly but she couldn't help it. It hurt just as much to see her daughter go off as it had on her first day of school twelve years before.

Bobby was also sad to see Anna Lee go but he didn't know what to say, so he said, "That was a dumb hat she had on." When they got home

Dorothy went to bed, Bobby went to his room and listened to the radio, and Mother Smith helped Betty Raye quietly move her things into Anna Lee's room as she had promised. Hanging up Betty Raye's dresses in the closet, Mother Smith said, "Betty Raye, you just don't know what a godsend you are to Dorothy right now. If you weren't here, I'd hate to think what she would do. She lost one child and I know how it hurts her to lose another, even if it is just for a short time."

Doc and Jimmy sat out on the porch and did not say much. But after a long silence Doc finally offered, "I just wish Dorothy wouldn't act like it was the end of the world. She'll be back at Christmas, for heaven's sake." He then looked at Jimmy and shook his head. "Women . . . the way they carry on, you'd think a few months was ten years."

"Yeah, they get pretty upset over things, don't they?"

Both men sat there in the dark and smoked, trying to pretend that they were above such silly emotions as missing Anna Lee. But they weren't.

Anna Lee had been on the train about two hours when she found the envelope Doc had sneaked into her purse without telling Dorothy. Inside was a brand-new shiny nickel and a short note.

> If for any reason you don't like it up there, call me and I'll come and get you.
>
> Daddy

Doc did not know it but Jimmy had already slipped a twenty-dollar bill into her coat pocket before she'd left. "A little spending money," he had said.

Glory, Glory, Clear the Road

The other set of parents that had to deal with being separated from their daughter that year was Minnie and Ferris Oatman. From the moment they had driven away and left her behind in Elmwood Springs they had been kept busy, rehearsing songs quietly with Beatrice all the way to Little Rock, and had been traveling ever since. They both missed Betty Raye terribly. Ferris worried that without his daily preaching and Bible readings she might wander off from the Lord and fall prey to the wicked ways of the world. Minnie, on the other hand, was more concerned that Betty Raye fit into her new life and try to be happy. Before she left she told Betty Raye not to pay too much attention to her daddy's strict Pentecostal ideas. She said this in private.

Ferris would have a fit if he knew she was now wearing lipstick and had gone to a Ginger Rogers movie. But as Minnie said to Betty Raye on the phone, "Baby, what your daddy don't know ain't gonna hurt him one whit."

Their lives had been changing almost as fast as Betty Raye's, ever since that first night when they arrived in Little Rock for the all-night sing. By the time they got to the auditorium all the other groups were already there, dressed and ready. It was going to be a big night. The Spears, the Happy Goodmans, the Lester-Stamps Quartet, the John Daniels Quartet, the Melody Masters, the Dixie Boys, the Sunny South Quartet—groups from all over the country were backstage visiting before the show, happy to see one another again and catch up on heart attacks and gallbladder operations since they were last together. Also, they compared notes on who was having trouble with the IRS, a constant problem with gospel groups, who, it seems, were always being harassed by the tax people over income taxes.

It was only a half hour before the show started, so Minnie and Beatrice went straight to the dressing room while the boys got ready in the men's dressing room downstairs. Floyd was in charge of the Oatman sound system and was busy getting it out of the car and ready to set up. The halls were buzzing with excitement, as they always were, and the auditorium was filling with hundreds of people. This all-star affair had the Oatmans in high cotton, as Minnie said. It was not a good night to break in a new member of the group. But it could not be helped. They had taken time to get Betty Raye to Elmwood Springs at least a few weeks before school started and they needed the money. Seventy-five dollars for an all-night sing was the highest they had ever been offered. They were to go on third, after the Dixie Boys. When the time came, Minnie led Beatrice and Honey to the wings and as Beatrice heard all the noise and excitement going on backstage as well as onstage she grabbed Minnie's arm and squeezed. Minnie patted her hand. "Don't be scared, darling, I'm right here with you."

Beatrice said, "Oh, Minnie, I'm not scared—I just can't wait to get out there."

After the Dixie Boys had finished their last number, "Many Thrills and Joys Ago," the audience continued to fill up, a lot of people arriving late because they knew the really good groups did not come out until after intermission. When Hovie Lister came out to announce the Oatmans, a few hundred were still wandering around looking for good seats.

A few looked up when the Oatmans walked out and were surprised to see a dog coming onstage with a little woman in a white dress wearing sunglasses. What was going on, they wondered. Minnie sat down, stared straight ahead like she always did, started tapping her foot, and when the spirit hit her, off she went into their first number, "Glory, Glory, Clear the Road." Then something unexpected happened that surprised even the Oatmans. The sound coming out of the loudspeakers and wafting high across the auditorium was one they had never heard before.

Minnie knew at *once* they had something special. So did everyone else. Suddenly, the people in the audience that had been moving around shopping for seats stopped and sat down. Soon all the dressing rooms emptied as the other groups backstage started to gather in the wings to listen.

Beatrice singing alone was something. Minnie alone was something. Betty Raye's voice had been soft and sweet but Beatrice's clear and powerful soprano blended perfectly with Minnie's equally powerful tenor. This sound, combined with Ferris's deep bass and the two boys' alto voices, was a sensation and set the audience wild. They stood up and clapped and cheered after each number. By the time they had finished their last song, "Sweeter as the Days Go By," their appearance fee had gone up from $75 to $150, and they would never sing before the intermission again.

As one of the Dixie Boys remarked later, "Them Oatmans got themselves a gold mine in that little blind woman." While Betty Raye was being given a new look and a new life, the Oatmans were getting a brand-new sound.

The only person who had not been totally amazed at this phenomenon was Minnie. As she always said and believed with all her heart, "God never shuts up one door till He slings open another!"

Jimmy and the Trolley Car Diner

After Anna Lee left for college, Dorothy was uneasy for a few days, until she received her phone call. Her mother knew she was all right and had arrived safely. Soon Dorothy was back to her old self again, happy to be busy with all the many details of getting Betty Raye enrolled in Elmwood Springs High School, making sure she had all the books and supplies she needed. They had had her tested a few weeks before and, to everyone's surprise, she scored high enough to be entered as a senior. It really was going to be like having Anna Lee back. They would be going through another senior year all over again, with so many wonderful things to look forward to.

But poor Bobby was getting ready to slug through another year of the sixth grade. It had been quietly decided between his parents and his teacher, Miss Henderson, that since his grades last year had been so bad, particularly in math and English grammar, it would be best to hold him back a grade now and not let him get so far behind in the future that he would never catch up. Between having to repeat the grade and not being able to climb the water tower again this summer, Bobby was not very happy. Now the only thing he had to look forward to before the holidays came around again was a double feature each Saturday at the Elmwood Springs Theater and then over to the Trolley Car Diner afterward. That was something, at least.

The Trolley Car Diner was a small, round, white building with glass bricks along the side. After the movie, Bobby loved to sit on a stool at the counter in the front window and eat chili dogs, drink an Orange Crush, and watch the rest of the world go by. Jimmy would watch him sitting there swinging his feet and hitting the wall each time. This meant a lot more work for Jimmy, cleaning the scuff marks, but he never said a word. He got a big charge out of Bobby with all his tall tales and was always glad to see him come in. Being a boarder with the Smiths for so long, he'd begun to think of them as his family. He had long since given up hope of starting a family of his own. Although his limp was not very noticeable to other people, he was embarrassed about it and it prevented him from ever asking a girl out for a date, much less asking one to marry him.

He had joined the navy at sixteen and was twenty-five when the Second World War began. But for him the war ended the same day it had started. Sunday morning, December 7, 1941, he had been aboard the battleship *Arizona.* After that he spent years in and out of veterans hospitals, learning to walk again, but no one ever heard him complain. He had been luckier than most of his shipmates. He had just lost a leg; they had lost their lives. Jimmy had a steady and simple life that consisted of going to the diner every day, a week's vacation once a year, which he spent up in St. Louis visiting some of his buddies at the V.A. hospital, and poker on Friday night at the VFW. He did not really need to work, with all the disability pay he got from the government, but the thought of not working never occurred to him.

When Betty Raye had first come to the house to live she had been shy but she'd liked him right away. He was not loud like the men in her family. She always felt anxious around most people, afraid they were waiting for her to say something, but not Jimmy. He was quiet and sweet and easy to be around. And he liked her as well. Dorothy could tell by the little changes in his behavior. Ever since Betty Raye arrived he'd started wearing a clean white shirt to dinner every night. She also noticed that Jimmy often waited until Betty Raye left the porch, ashamed to get up in front of her. But Dorothy never said a word. Betty Raye did not know Jimmy had a wooden leg but if she had, it would not have mattered. She of all people knew what it was like to be different from the rest of the world around them.

They did not realize it but both were handicapped and afraid of life, only in different ways.

The Return of Ida Jenkins

As much as poor Bobby dreaded repeating a grade, Norma dreaded her mother's next visit even more. On September 21, Ida had returned from her museum tour in Washington and her National Federated Women's Club meeting in Baltimore, and that afternoon was walking through her daughter's new little house, offering a running commentary.

"I'm not sure about those curtains, Norma."

"What's the matter with them?"

Ida did not go into specifics. "I just wish you would have let your father and me hire a professional decorator like we wanted to." She glanced around the room. "And *where* is your silver tea set?"

"In the closet."

Ida looked at her daughter in disbelief. "Norma, you *display* your tea set, it should be out so people can see it. A tea set is the earmark of a gracious home."

"Mother, I don't have enough room to display a teacup, much less an entire tea set I'm never going to use."

Ida sat down in the kitchen and took her gloves off. "I don't know why you and Macky insisted on buying this place; it's no bigger than a matchbox . . . and how you expect to entertain with no guest bathroom is beyond me."

Norma poured her mother a cup of coffee. "I don't expect to entertain and it's all Macky and I could afford."

Ida gave her a look. "I won't say it but you know how I feel. We offered to buy you a bigger place."

"Yes, Mother. How was your trip?"

"Wonderful . . . we heard the most enlightened talks from the most interesting women in all fields. Oh, I wish you would join the club, then you could have gone with me."

The fact that Norma would not join any of her clubs was a constant source of pain for Ida. Norma said, "Mother, please don't start up on that again," and brought her some cream.

"All right, all right, that's not what I came here to talk to you about anyway." Ida looked at the small, plain white cream pitcher her daughter had put on the table. "Norma, where is the pretty pitcher with the hand-painted flowers that Gerta and Lodor bought you?"

"I broke it," she lied.

"Well, don't tell Gerta—tell her you're saving it for special occasions."

Ida suddenly noticed something different about the way Norma looked. "What in the world happened to your hair? Why is it all fuzzy like that?"

"Tot Whooten."

"Say no more."

Norma sat down at the table. "What was it that you wanted to talk to me about?"

"What?"

"You said you wanted to talk to me about something?"

"Oh yes. Now, Norma, I want you to know that I have thought about this a great deal. Now that you are grown and married, it's time we had a woman-to-woman talk. After all, you're my daughter and you should benefit from what little wisdom I have gained over the years. After many years of careful observation, I have come to a conclusion." Norma waited while Ida paused for effect as she always did when she was stating one of her ten thousand conclusions. "Norma, *women* are simply going to have to take over this world and that's all there is to it. All men want to do is start wars and show off in front of each other." She leaned over and looked out the window to make sure that no man was around to hear. "I am beginning to think that most of them don't get past age twelve—not your daddy, of course, thank God; he is a sensible and adult man but if I hadn't been around, who knows? Men are just like gardens. You have to tend to them every day or they just can go to seed. It's a sad fact that I have had to learn the hard way. Men without women to guide them lose all their training."

Norma looked somewhat skeptical.

"Norma, it's the *truth.* Look at what happened in the American West. Now *that* is how men act if you let them, never bathing, always shooting Indians and buffaloes and one another, drinking and gambling and I don't know what all. It wasn't until decent, respectable women went west that they straightened up and started behaving themselves. And don't forget—it's the *men* that stir up all the mischief in this world. Let me ask you this . . . if women were in charge of everything, do you think we would have so many fatherless little orphans in this world? You know, the male lion even eats his young if the mother is not careful."

"Mother, what do lions have to do with anything?"

"It proves my point. Norma, you have to watch them every minute or they will revert back to jungle ways."

"Oh, Mother, Daddy is not like that."

"I know he isn't now—not when he's with us—but I hate to disillusion you, my girl: no matter how well-bred they may be or how nice they may act in polite society, you put a group of men alone in a cabin for a week and if you think they bother to use their napkins or set the table or even have the courtesy to shave, you are sadly mistaken. Now, I'm not saying they can help it, all I am saying is that in order for this world to keep on progressing the women have got to run things. The trick is to do it without them knowing it."

After her mother left she dialed the hardware store. When he picked up she said, "Macky, will you promise me one thing?"

"What?"

"If I ever start acting like my mother, will you just take out a gun and shoot me?"

The Shy Senior

When Betty Raye had started her senior year at Elmwood Springs as the new girl in school, she had naturally attracted a lot of attention. Also having been a gospel singer, she had been quite an oddity for the first couple of weeks but after the initial curiosity about her had worn off she'd more or less faded into the background. It would have been difficult for anybody entering into a class where most of the students had been together since the first grade to fit in but it was doubly hard for Betty Raye. She certainly did not stand out in a crowd and the boys her age were most definitely *not* interested in this thin, rather plain girl wearing blue plastic glasses. Some of the girls tried their best to bring her into the conversation at lunch or invite her to the drugstore for a soda, but she was so shy she never said much of anything. After a while they gave up. They figured she did not have much of a personality or was probably some sort of religious nut. They did not dislike her—they just stopped trying to get to know her. So Betty Raye did not go anywhere except to school and back and sometimes to a movie with the family but that was really fine with her. She was happy just to come home and Dorothy was glad to have her. In fact, she was a big help. Dorothy received hundreds of letters a week and Betty Raye helped her sort them out and put her recipe letters in one pile, her requests and announcements in another. Betty Raye also helped Bobby, only Dorothy did not know about that. Sometimes when he could not figure out his math or

English problems he would sneak over to her room and she would do them for him. Mother Smith, who loved to play cards, was teaching Betty Raye how to play and was amazed at how quickly she learned. After a few days a pleased Mother Smith confided to Dorothy, "That girl is a natural-born card sharp. I wouldn't be surprised if she was playing bridge by the end of the week."

Everything seemed to be going along smoothly until one day in early November.

Dorothy was at the A & P picking out some russet potatoes when Pauline Tuttle, the high school English teacher, a tall woman without much of a chin, came in the door. She spotted Dorothy and came right over and asked in a loud voice, "Well, how is our Anna Lee doing? Have you heard from her?"

"She's just fine, Pauline. She says she's doing so well and apparently loves it up there."

"I knew she would. I always said if anyone succeeds in this world, it will be Anna Lee Smith."

"I'll tell her you asked about her."

"Of all the students I have had she was one of my smartest girls—straight *A*'s and so pretty."

"Thank you, I appreciate that. And how is my little boarder Betty Raye doing?"

Pauline suddenly frowned and picked up a paper sack. "I was going to call you and talk to you about that, Dorothy. I'm afraid we have a *serious* problem."

Dorothy was alarmed. "What is it?"

"She does well with her paperwork but it's in classroom participation where she falls down. She never raises her hand and when I do call on her she just mumbles and says she doesn't know the answer." Pauline picked up a potato and looked at it. "When I know full well she does. She just will *not* speak up. I hate to be the bearer of bad news, Dorothy, but the girl has absolutely no verbal skills whatsoever!" She then threw a large red tomato in her bag to emphasize the point. "The few times I did call on her to recite I thought she was going to faint dead away, so I just don't call on her anymore."

"Oh dear, that's not good," said Dorothy.

"No, it is not good."

Miss Tuttle threw an onion in the same sack. "That little girl is never going to amount to anything in this world if she does not learn to assert herself and she most certainly will not be making the grades she should be making."

"We knew she was a little timid."

"Dangerously so, and if we don't nip this in the bud right here and now, her entire future may be at stake. She may be left behind forever."

Now Dorothy was truly alarmed. "Oh dear. What can we do?"

"I was thinking she should join the Drama Club as soon as possible. Maybe Miss Hatcher can do something with her, teach her to express herself, speak up, speak out. It may be her only hope." She picked up a head of lettuce, weighed it in her hand, and put it back down. "It's so hard to fix dinner for just one. You can't buy a half a head of lettuce. You're lucky you have a big family to cook for. If you want me to talk to Betty Raye, I will."

"No, thank you. No, let me see what I can do first. Well, nice to see you, Pauline."

As she walked away Miss Tuttle called out, "Tell Anna Lee to drop me a line when she has time."

Dorothy worried all the way home. This was a problem she had never come up against before. Certainly not with her own two children. With Bobby the exact opposite was true. His teachers had a problem trying to get him to stop talking and concentrate on his paperwork, which was always messy and misspelled, if he managed not to lose it and turn it in at all. But right now she was concerned about Betty Raye. She hated for her not to do as well as she could be doing. Pauline seemed to think it was an emergency. Maybe Pauline was right; maybe Dorothy needed to say something today, before it was too late and she was lost forever.

That afternoon in the kitchen, when Betty Raye was busy mashing potatoes, she decided to broach the subject. "So, honey, how are you doing at school?"

"Fine."

"Are you having any problems?"

"No, ma'am."

"How are you doing making friends?"

"Fine."

"I don't know if you know this or not, but a good way to make friends is through extracurricular activities. I was the president of the Homemakers Club in high school and I really enjoyed that."

Betty Raye smiled.

Dorothy continued on. "You know, I ran into Pauline Tuttle today and we were talking about you, and she, well, both of us were saying we thought that it might be a good idea if you were to join a club of some kind. We thought maybe you might want to think about joining the Drama Club. I know Anna Lee had lots of fun being in all the plays." She spoke brightly, but at the mere mention of the words *Drama Club* Betty Raye actually turned pale right before her eyes. She turned to Dorothy with a stricken look on her face. "Oh, Mrs. Smith, I just couldn't."

Dorothy suddenly realized what a terrible idea this had been and immediately felt sorry for even bringing it up. She put her arm around Betty Raye. "No, of course you don't. I'm so sorry. How stupid can I be. . . . you've been pushed up on stage all your life, haven't you?"

"Yes, ma'am," said Betty Raye, close to tears, "and I just hated it."

"I know you did, I don't know what I was thinking of. And you don't ever have to do another thing you don't want to."

"Will she be mad?"

"Of course not. It was just a stupid suggestion. Don't you worry about a thing. I'll just tell Pauline that we don't want to join any old Drama Club or anything else, right?"

"Yes, ma'am."

After Dorothy had finished making the meatloaf and got it in the oven, she sat down at the table to string the green beans. She smiled at Betty Raye, who was busy rinsing out a bowl in the sink, and she thought to herself, Who cares if Pauline Tuttle doesn't call on her in class? So what if she doesn't set the world on fire? Not everybody has to be Mr. or Mrs. Personality. What difference does it make if she gets a *B* or a *C* instead of an A? She's perfectly happy the way she is and she certainly is a big help in the kitchen, quiet and good-natured. She'll probably make someone a wonderful wife. Betty Raye might not be a beauty like Anna Lee but she can already cook better than Anna Lee. For better or worse, men like a quiet girl who can cook.

Then she thought: A good thing Anna Lee is pretty, because she sure cannot cook. When Betty Raye sat down at the table, she smiled at her warmly and asked her favorite question. "Honey, if you could have one wish come true, what would you wish for?"

Betty Raye picked up a handful of string beans and thought about it and then answered. "A house."

"A house?" Dorothy was surprised. "What kind of a house?"

"Oh, just a little one with maybe a little dog."

"What about a husband? Don't you want a nice husband to buy it for you?"

"No, ma'am. After I graduate I'm going to get a job and buy it for myself. I don't think boys like me very much."

Dorothy looked at her with a twinkle in her eye. "I know a certain somebody who works at the Trolley Car Diner who thinks you're pretty wonderful. . . ."

Just then Bobby came mincing into the kitchen wearing a pair of red wax lips.

Dorothy looked at him. "Young man, why are you not in your room doing your homework like you're supposed to be?"

Bobby minced right back out again.

But later, when Dorothy came down the hall to check on him, she found him hanging by his fingers from the doorframe like a bat. She said, "Bobby, do you want to spend the rest of your life in the sixth grade? Get in there and get to work." Bobby dropped back down to the floor and went to his desk. His mother had made her point.

The next Friday Betty Raye came home from school looking somehow pleased. She handed Dorothy a small, yellow membership card that said BETTY RAYE OATMAN, ELMWOOD SPRINGS HIGH SCHOOL LIBRARY CLUB.

"Well, good for you! I'm so proud of you I don't know what to do!" She knew this had not been easy for Betty Raye. "This calls for a celebration." Dorothy got up and walked through the house, calling out, "Mother Smith, Bobby, get your coats on. We are all going up to the drugstore for sundaes!" Within five minutes all were seated on stools at the soda fountain ordering hot fudge sundaes, except Bobby, ever the opportunist, who ordered a double banana split.

Turkey Time

Ever since Beatrice had left town to join the Oatman family, the two Goodnight twin sisters, Bess and Ada, had stepped in to help Dorothy. On special occasions they would come over and sing on the show and today was such an occasion.

Right before she went on air, Dorothy looked out the window and checked for her daily weather report and was pleased. "Good morning, everybody. It's another pretty fall day over here in Elmwood Springs and I hope you are having the same. I know this is a busy time, everyone getting ready for Thanksgiving and the holidays, and we're so glad you were able to find a few minutes to spend with us. I don't know about you, but I for one will be glad when this week is over. Bobby is about to drive us all crazy trying to memorize the poem 'The Song of Hiawatha' by Friday. If I hear 'By the shore of Gitche Gumee, by the shining Big-Sea-Water' one more time I am going to scream. Poor Betty Raye has been helping him and that girl must have the patience of Job. So far everyone in the house knows it by heart except Bobby.

"Well, tomorrow is November the fourth, the big day when we are all going to the polls to vote." Mother Smith played the opening of "You're a Grand Old Flag." "That's right, Mother, democracy in action. We got a call this morning from Ida Jenkins, who is head of the local women's political caucus, and Ida says to remind all you ladies out there to be sure to get out and vote, don't just leave it up to the men. And

Mother Smith agrees—don't forget, our own Mother Smith was a suffragette and fought for the vote for us, and we are mighty proud of her, too. And later on in the program Ada and Bess Goodnight have promised to drop by and sing 'Bongo Bongo Bongo, I Don't Want to Leave the Congo' for us . . . although I don't know what that has to do with Election Day. . . . I wonder if this is a mistake. . . . No? Mother Smith says that's what they are singing." Dorothy picked up a piece of paper. "And let's see. Oh . . . and I have an announcement from the chamber of commerce. They have a request to change the name of the Miss Turkey Contest to the Miss Thanksgiving Contest, so if you agree go down to the drugstore tomorrow and vote on that as well. Harry Johnston at the A and P says to tell all you gals he's got a special Thanksgiving offer on Del Monte early garden peas—buy one can, get one—and he says he's got lots of turkeys all ready dressed and ready for roasting. . . .

"Now, let me ask you this: have you ever been shocked when changing your fuses? If so, here's something that you need to get yourself right away. It is safe and as easy as changing a light bulb. Use Royal Crystal fuses with the shockproof glass top. Ask for Royal Crystal fuses and also Royal cord sets and Christmas lights. Those are available down at Warren's Hardware. Speaking of the Warrens, yesterday Mother and I paid a visit to our little newlywed Norma Warren, who gave us a tour of her kitchen. She has a brand-new Formica dinette set and you never saw anything so bright and cheery in your life. She said they come in all colors, yellow, aqua, or green, but Norma's set is cherry red." Mother Smith ran through "Life Is Just a Bowl of Cherries." "That's right, she says it's so easy to keep clean, just give it a swipe with a wet cloth. Everyone says this is the furniture of the future and I believe them! Once Norma gets her new red-and-white linoleum down, her kitchen is going to be the showplace of the Midwest!"

Don't Sit Down!

Macky and Norma had only been married for a little under four months but Norma was thoroughly enjoying her new role as wife and homemaker. She was so pleased with the way their little house was coming along, particularly her new kitchen, which she kept as spotless and polished as Macky kept their new Nash Rambler. Their first Christmas as a married couple was coming up in a few weeks and Norma made a momentous decision. After talking it over with Macky, she called her mother with the exciting news.

"Hello," Ida said.

"Mother, guess what? This year I want everybody to come to our house for Christmas dinner!"

"Who's everybody?"

"You, Daddy . . . the Warrens, Aunt Gerta, Uncle Lodor, Aunt Elner, and Uncle Will. The whole family, won't that be fun?"

Ida weighed her words carefully. "That's very sweet of you, dear, but I don't think you have thought this through."

"Yes, I have."

"Norma, how are you going to serve dinner for that many people? You don't have a buffet table."

"Easy, it doesn't have to be all that formal. I'll just put everything out on the counter in the kitchen and everybody can get their plates and come in and serve themselves sort of casual like. Macky said he could set up card tables in the living room and we can throw sheets over them."

There were not enough words in the English language to describe just how much Ida Jenkins did *not* want to eat a meal off a card table covered with a sheet but she sensed how much it meant to Norma. She held on to the telephone table for support and said, "Fine dear, if that's what you want to do, I'm sure it will be lovely."

After everybody Norma had invited to Christmas dinner said they would come, it suddenly occurred to her that she had never cooked for more than two people. Cooking for ten might not be as easy as it sounded and she wanted it to be perfect. She called Neighbor Dorothy, who then helped her plan her menu, right down to the last morsel. To make sure there would be no mistakes, she wrote out a list of exactly what time she was to put things in the oven, exactly what time they were to come out, when to start the potatoes, how long to cook the roast beef, how many minutes to cook the gravy, and when to heat up the four cans of English peas and when to warm the rolls.

Norma spent almost the entire next week in the kitchen, rehearsing everything she was to do. One day she spent making sure all her timers worked, with everything in the right place, ready to go. She had decided to empty the peas into a covered dish on Christmas Eve and throw the cans away. It was cheating, she knew, but she also knew what her mother would say if she by any chance saw the cans. She had heard it a hundred times. "Norma, only hoboes and derelicts eat out of a can." Macky came in and watched her setting timers, walking back and forth from the oven to the counter to the refrigerator with her list, pretending to carry things and talking to herself. She looked so intense he felt sorry for her and asked, "Can I do anything to help?"

She looked at him. "Yes—keep everybody out of the kitchen, especially Mother. I'm going to be nervous enough as it is without having her in here staring at me and getting in my way. Just keep them entertained until I come out and say, 'Dinner's ready, come and get it.' "

"Dinner's ready, come and get it?"

"I might not say those exact words, I may say 'Time to eat' or something like that but when I do, have everybody get up, get their plate off the table, and come on in—but not before that."

"O.K."

"Just pray I don't burn anything or drop something."

"What if you do? It's not the end of the world, it's just a dinner."

"Just a dinner?" She looked at him in utter disbelief. "Just a dinner? Is that what you think after I have gone to all this trouble so we can have our first Christmas in our own home?"

"No, that's not what I mean. I mean, so what if you do mess it up, nobody cares."

"Nobody *cares*?"

Macky realized he was digging a hole for himself and tried to get out. "But you won't mess it up. Everything will turn out just great."

"Well, that's easy for you to say. You try cooking for ten people."

Saturday, a full week before the dinner was to take place, Norma cleaned the house from top to bottom. When Macky came home that afternoon she met him at the door with a scrub brush. "Macky, do not sit on the sofa or the chairs, or walk on the rug, and try not to use the bathroom."

Still a newlywed, Macky was learning the hard way that when Norma was nervous about something, it was best not to try and reason with her.

Christmas Window

December twenty-first was an especially busy day. Dorothy baked fifteen dozen gingerbread men to have at the house for the holidays, Bobby was pulling down all the Christmas decorations from the closets, and Betty Raye and Mother Smith were making gumdrop trees out of toothpicks for the dining room table. At about five-thirty Doc walked in the door carrying a huge peppermint candy cane, his cheeks a little flushed from the cold and the two paper cups of pretty potent eggnog he had just drunk. Before coming home he had joined Ed and the gang down at the barbershop for a little pre-Christmas cheer, as he did every year, and he was in every sense in high spirits. In a few days Anna Lee would be home for Christmas and tonight they were going downtown to pick out their tree.

He went in the kitchen and handed Dorothy the candy cane, saying, "Ho, ho, ho." She laughed and said, "Ho, ho, ho, yourself." After dinner Dorothy made Bobby put on his leather cap with the flaps and the whole family, including Betty Raye and Jimmy, walked down to the vacant lot behind the church. The Civitan Club had run a string of white lights around the area and was holding its annual Christmas tree sale. The cold air was filled with the scent of pine, and the old familiar smells of Christmas put Doc in even higher spirits. Gene Autry was singing "Rudolph, the Red-Nosed Reindeer" on the small radio Merle had on in the shed as Doc walked around looking for just the right tree. He stopped and picked up several and shook them and continued walking up and down the aisles. "What do you think, Dorothy, should we get a big one or a little one?"

Bobby said, "Let's get a big one."

"What do you think, Mother Smith?" asked Dorothy.

"Oh, I think since Anna Lee is coming home it would be nice to have a big one this year."

They all continued to walk through the lot looking at all the different kinds of trees. Some were flocked in odd colors this year. At one point Doc heard Mother Smith talking to Dorothy over in the next row. "Why would anyone in their right mind want a pink Christmas tree?"

"Oh, I suppose it's modern. Maybe some people want a change," said Dorothy.

"Well, there's modern and there's ugly, if you ask me."

The search went on, as Doc backed up and scrutinized each tree that might be a likely candidate. Nothing had caught his eye so far, until he spied a large blue spruce still wrapped in rope lying on the ground. He pulled it up and was examining it when Fred Haygood, one of the Civitans, asked Doc if he would like him to cut it loose for him. Doc said he would and after it was cut Fred shook it out and banged it up and down so Doc could get a better look at it. The tree was about eight feet tall and full and had a good shape. Doc said, "This is a nice one, don't you think?"

Fred offered his expert, considered opinion. "Yep, this would make you a pretty tree."

"What do you think, Jimmy?" Doc asked.

Jimmy nodded. "It looks good to me."

"How much?" asked Doc.

Fred called out to the shed, "Merle, how much for this blue spruce just came in?"

Merle called back, "Let him have it for a dollar fifty."

One more opinion poll and they all agreed and Doc said, "Have the boys bring it over and put it on the porch; we can get it in from there." They then headed down the street to Morgan Brothers department store to look at the Christmas display in the window. As they went past the barbershop a few of the men, including James Whooten, Tot's husband, were still inside and waved at them. While they walked they could hear music playing from the speakers outside the stores. Perry Como was singing "It's Beginning to Look a Lot Like Christmas" and it was. MERRY

CHRISTMAS was written across all the windows in red, white, and green. To Bobby it seemed that downtown had changed magically overnight. The two large glass bottles filled with red and blue colored water that had always been in the drugstore window before suddenly looked like two huge lighted Christmas balls. Tonight even the cement in front of the theater seemed to sparkle like tiny chips of silver tinsel. When they got down to the department store, there was already a crowd of people and children standing there enjoying the "Winter Wonderland" display, amazed by the hundreds of little mechanical figures all moving at the same time. Elves and Mr. and Mrs. Santa Claus, trains full of toys running up and down a white mountain and in and out of tunnels. Skiers in ski lifts moving up to the top of the mountain and skiing back down again. Reindeer with their heads bobbing, horses and buggies and tiny cars moved through the miniature village. Dogs wagging their tails, little figures of men, women, and children skating and twirling across a pond made out of a large round mirror surrounded by glittering snow and miniature green trees. There was an entire world going on inside the window. Bobby would have stayed there for hours with his face pressed to it if they had let him.

On the way back home they passed the Civitan lot again just in time to meet Norma and Macky Warren coming out with the pink Christmas tree. "Hi," Norma said cheerfully. "Look what we just got. Isn't it the cutest thing you have ever seen?"

Mother Smith was speechless for the moment but Dorothy jumped in. "Oh, it is. We were looking at it earlier this evening ourselves," she said, not telling a lie.

Norma said, "Please tell Anna Lee to call me when she gets home."

"We will."

After they had gone on, Mother Smith remarked, "I'd give a million dollars to see Ida Jenkins's face when she sees that thing in Norma's living room."

When they got home everyone was tired and went straight to bed and Bobby dreamed about the Christmas window all night. He was inside ice-skating on the mirror pond, twirling around and around, with the pretty little girl in the short red skirt and white skates, but in his dreams she looked a lot like Claudia Albetta, the little girl that sat in front of him in class.

◆ ◆ ◆

Three days before, Jimmy had wandered around Morgan Brothers department store looking for last-minute presents but had found that he was having trouble. A saleswoman watched him as he picked up one thing after another and put it back down. Finally, she went over to him. "Jimmy, why don't you tell me what you are looking for," she said. "Maybe I can help you."

"Well . . ."

"Who are you trying to buy something for?"

Jimmy was too embarrassed to tell her but did manage to say that he needed the help. "It's for a lady."

"I see. Well, how about a nice scarf?" she said. "A scarf is always nice. What color hair does she have?"

"Brown," he murmured as he followed her over to the scarf counter.

The Christmas Show

After school the next day, Betty Raye and Bobby started unwrapping the Christmas ornaments and Doc came home with three new strings of glass candle lights that bubbled. He thought bubbling ones would look nice with the blinking lights they already had.

When Jimmy came in, he and Doc hung on the front door the splendid fresh holly Christmas wreath that one of Dorothy's sponsors, Cecil Figgs, had sent. After dinner they all went into the living room and started to decorate—all except Mother Smith. It was her job to sit on the sofa and point out what was needed and where. By nine o'clock that night, cream-colored cardboard candleholders with blue lights were in every window, with strings of red cutout paper letters that said MERRY CHRISTMAS hung over all the doors, and the tree in the corner was covered with green and red satin balls, and shiny red and dark blue ones with white frosted strips around them. They finished it off with silver tinsel, strings of popcorn, and, on top, a cocker spaniel angel with wings, which one of Dorothy's listeners had sent her in honor of Princess Mary Margaret.

The next morning at 8:54 A.M. Dixie Cahill led all sixteen of her dance students in full costume and makeup down the stairs of the Dixie Cahill School of Tap and Twirl and out onto the sidewalk. She lined them up single file, blew her whistle, and marched them through town and over to *The Neighbor Dorothy Show* to make their annual Christmas appearance. Since they were all wearing bells on their tap shoes, they made quite a racket as they marched down the street. Ed the barber said they sounded like a herd of reindeer going by. A few minutes later they marched up the porch stairs and into Neighbor Dorothy's house and lined up in the back of the living room to wait until it was time for their number.

The house was packed with people. The handbell choir was lined up down the hall, waiting to go on after them, and Ernest Koonitz was smashed in a corner in the dining room ready to be called for his annual tuba solo. Neighbor Dorothy, in a wonderful mood, came down the hall wearing her green Christmas dress and a silver-bells corsage. It was a doubly festive day for her. She loved doing her Christmas show and Anna Lee was coming home today. After she greeted everyone, she squeezed through the crowd and stepped over children who were sitting on the floor; then she sat down, gathered her commercials, and the show started with a big "Good morning, everybody, and happy December twenty-third! We have so many wonderful surprises for you and so much fine entertainment on our show today I can hardly wait to get started.

"We are so excited over here in Elmwood Springs this morning. . . . We have our students here from the Dixie Cahill School of Tap and Twirl to do a wonderful tap number to 'Jingle Bells' and I know we are going to enjoy that. Also the handbell choir from the First Methodist Church is here to play 'It Came upon a Midnight Clear' for you. We have lots of bells this morning but I guess you can never have too many bells at Christmastime, can you. And Ernest Koonitz is here to do another solo entitled . . ." She paused. "Somebody stick your head in the dining room and ask him." Dixie called out the title and Dorothy relayed it to her listeners. "He's playing 'Joy to the World' but before we get to our entertainment I have another reminder for you. . . ." Mother Smith played a chord or two of "Santa Claus Is Coming to Town." "That's right, Mother Smith, Santa Claus *is* coming to town and he will be in the back of Morgan Brothers department store today and all day tomorrow, so be sure and go down and have your photograph made with him. I'm taking Princess Mary Margaret down right after the show to have her picture made with Santa and don't forget, all proceeds go to benefit the Salvation Army, who do so much good, not just at Christmas but all year long." Suddenly everybody in the audience started to laugh at something behind her and she turned around to see Mr. and Mrs. Santa Claus standing on the porch at the living room window and waving. Dorothy said, "Well, as I live and breathe, here are the Santa Clauses now."

She opened the window and Santa leaned in and said to Dorothy in a deep voice, "Merry Christmas, little girl!"

Dorothy had to laugh; she had not expected this surprise visit from Santa, especially one who sounded a lot like Bess Goodnight.

Ada and Bess, who had been up at the grammar school earlier this morning handing out presents, had stopped by the barbershop for a little Christmas cheer on the way home and were feeling no pain. As modern women of the world, they often joined the boys in a friendly drink or two and had brought Mother Smith, who also enjoyed a little nip now and then, a paper cup of eggnog.

Anna Lee arrived at the train station looking wonderful and full of news about all the new boyfriends she had. No surprise there. And of course Doc was happy to have the apple of his eye home, looking so beautiful on the platform, and so was everyone. Dorothy couldn't wait to get her home. She told Anna Lee that no matter how old or grown-up they were, she just did not sleep well unless both her children were home in their own beds and she knew they were safe and sound.

That night, by the time Dorothy finished up in the kitchen, Doc was already in bed. She cleaned her face with cold cream and turned off the light and got in beside him. After a moment, she said, "Doc, are you still awake?"

"Just barely."

"Hasn't this just been the loveliest day? Practically perfect?"

"Yes."

After another moment, she said, "Doc, ask me what I would wish for if I could only have one wish come true."

He did not have to ask.

"He would have been twenty-six this year, Doc."

He reached over and patted her hand. "I know, honey."

No matter how many years had passed since their first son, Michael, died, every holiday had always been tinged with a secret sadness. For the first ten years every Christmas morning the two of them had gone out to his grave and decorated it with a small tree and little toys, and every

Easter an Easter basket had been placed there. Every year on his birthday and on the anniversary of the day he died they missed him more. Rarely did a day go by when one or the other did not think to themselves *Michael would be six* or *twelve* or whatever the age he would be that year. Although they never discussed it with anyone, donations made in memory of Michael Smith had paid for beds and wallpaper for an entire wing of the Children's Hospital. Most of the money to buy a Seeing Eye dog for Beatrice Woods came from a large donation to the Princess Mary Margaret Fund in his name.

Now twenty-two years had gone by. Dorothy wondered what kind of man he would have been. What young girl would have loved him and maybe even married him by now? What would his children be like, and would they look like him? Although he had been gone for many years, a picture of him as a child was always alive in Dorothy's mind. She continued to see him standing there and waving at her, the little boy that did not live. She often thought about the bud that never bloomed, the egg that never hatched, and wondered what happened to them. Did they just disappear, never to exist, lost forever, or would they come back again some spring? For years she looked for her little boy in every small child she saw, looked for him in the eyes of every blond boy with blue eyes like his. But she never found him again.

Merry Christmas

On the morning of December twenty-fourth, Bobby could hardly wait for the night to come. Ever since Jimmy had become their boarder and lived with them, the Smiths had started to open their presents on Christmas Eve. Jimmy had to catch the 11:45 P.M. bus to Kansas City to spend Christmas Day visiting his friends at the veterans hospital. And it was a good thing, because by that time Bobby and Mother Smith, both too curious for their own good, had usually poked, shook, and rattled their presents almost to death and the gifts might not have lasted until Christmas morning. Still, it was a long wait. Once Dorothy had seen a newsreel of Joan Crawford, her favorite movie star, and her children gathered around a piano singing carols on Christmas Eve, they had to do the same thing. Now, every year after dinner she made them all go in and gather around the organ and sing. Bobby hated the custom with a passion. As far as he was concerned, it just delayed the real meaning of Christmas: presents. At around 9:30 that night, when they finally sat down to open them, the phone rang. Dorothy said, before picking up the phone, "Wait a minute . . . let me see who this is. . . . Don't open anything yet." Oh, rats! thought Bobby, who was just about to tear into the big box with his name on it.

They could hear Dorothy saying to someone on the phone, "Oh no . . . oh, you poor thing. . . . Oh . . . well, bless your heart. . . . Yes . . . I'm sure he will. . . . Oh, you poor dear." She came back in and looked at

Doc. "That was Poor Tot. Her mother stole all the presents she had wrapped and hid them in the backyard and now she can't find them and she wondered if you would go down and open up the drugstore for her so she could get a few things for the kids to have in the morning. I told her you would."

"All right," said Doc and got up to get his coat. "You all go ahead and open the presents. I'll be back in a little while."

Dorothy said, "We will do no such thing. We are not going to open anything until you get back."

Bobby asked his mother, "Can't we open just one?"

"No, Bobby, put that back down."

Mother Smith sighed. "Poor Tot, to have to work all day and then to have to put up with that crazy mother of hers and try to raise those two children at the same time. I don't know how she puts up with it all myself."

"I don't either, and to make matters worse," Dorothy said, "James fell into the tree and broke everything again."

When Doc got downtown he went in and turned on the lights in the drugstore and Poor Tot came in right behind him wearing her aqua chenille robe and house shoes, looking as frazzled as she had the last time this had happened. They went through and picked out a Sparkle Plenty doll and some hair barrettes for Darlene, who was seven, and a few stuffed toys for Dwayne Jr., who was two and a half. As they walked around looking, she picked up a little plastic see-through purse and said, "I just don't know what to do next, Doc, scream or jump off a building. James is spending my money faster than I can make it. I'm fixing hair all day, and he's out all night drinking it up."

Doc told her what he had been telling her for years. "Honey, what you need to do is throw the bum out."

Tot looked up at him and said what she always said. "I know I should but if I don't take care of things, who will? God knows nobody else is going to put up with him."

After Tot left, with profuse thanks, Doc had to wait on several other people who'd come in and wanted to get things as well. But he did not charge them. Everything was free on Christmas Eve, he said.

It was an hour later by the time he could get home. *Finally,* Bobby was able to rip open the big box from his parents. Inside was a great record player, and his grandmother gave him the two records he wanted most, *Mule Train* and *Ghost Riders in the Sky.*

And underwear.

He received money from Jimmy, a Rover Boy book from Betty Raye, and Anna Lee surprised him with a genuine Jungle Jim pith helmet.

Dorothy got a robe, a cameo, and new curtains, Doc a new pipe and pajamas and slippers and, from Bobby, a fishing-tackle box. Mother Smith's presents were handkerchiefs, perfume, and a beautiful new boxed set of playing cards. Jimmy got his yearly twelve cartons of Camel cigarettes and, from Bobby, a toenail clipper. The girls got perfume, clothes, and cash money, toenail clippers from Bobby, and Dorothy had bought them both scrapbooks. Minnie and Ferris Oatman, who were doing a Christmas-week gospel sing in North Carolina, sent Betty Raye a white leather Bible with her name embossed in gold on the front. And she unwrapped a lovely silk scarf that had her name on the name tag but not the name of who it was from. Later they all went out on the porch and waited for the bus with Jimmy and at 11:45 it pulled up in front and he got on.

As usual, Dorothy was the last one up and when she finished doing a few final things in the kitchen she went into the living room to turn off all the Christmas lights. She stood there for a moment and looked at them glowing, blinking, and bubbling in the dark and they looked so pretty she decided to leave them on all night.

Uncle Floyd Has a Fit

Two days after Christmas, Dorothy was on the air when the phone rang. Betty Raye, walking by, picked up and to her surprise it was her mother. Minnie Oatman was on the other end, calling long-distance from the office of the Talladega, Alabama, Primitive Baptist Church and she was hysterical.

"Oh, Betty Raye, honey, something terrible has happened, brace yourself for bad news."

"Momma, what is it?"

"Honey," Minnie sobbed, "we lost Chester last night. Chester's gone and your Uncle Floyd is locked hisself in the men's room, blaspheming the Lord, and he won't come out."

"What men's room?" said Betty Raye.

"Over at the seafood place. One minute we was happy without a care in the world eating fried shrimp and the next thing we knowed Floyd was running around the parking lot, screaming like a banshee. In the time it took to eat twelve fried shrimp Chester had been snatched right out of his little suitcase in broad daylight and was gonded . . . kidnapped just like the Lindberger baby. And the next thing we knowed Floyd run in the men's room and locked the door and threatened to drown hisself. We all tried to pry him out, Beatrice and everybody there, but he won't budge. The boys tried to get in the window to him but he throwed water on them and wouldn't let them in. We had to leave him at the restaurant and come over here to do our show last night. Floyd's still holed up over there and your daddy is besides hisself. We've got bookings all this week."

"Oh, Momma, what are you going to do?"

"We've got the highway police looking for him right now. If we don't find Chester your uncle is liable to *never* come out of that bathroom." Then she wailed, "Poor little Chester, who would steal a poor little dummy? I got to go, your daddy's waiting. . . . Pray for us, baby," she said and hung up.

Later, Minnie and Ferris went over and formed an emergency prayer circle at the restaurant while an eight-point missing-person bulletin was being released across the state. *Missing: One ventriloquist's dummy known professionally as Chester the Scripture-quoting dummy. Blond wig, blue eyes, and freckles. Last seen in a car parked in the parking lot of Wentzel's Sea Food on Highway 21 wearing a cowboy suit and small cowboy hat.*

Ferris was convinced that Chester's disappearance was the work of the devil, while some of the hard core of the congregation wondered if he had been taken up in the Rapture. Bervin, Vernon, and Beatrice did not know what to make of it but Minnie just kept praying and holding on to her faith that he would come back. Floyd stayed in the men's room at Wentzel's Sea Food Restaurant for seventy-two hours until finally Chester was returned safe and sound.

As it turned out, it had all been a harmless prank. Another gospel group passing by saw the Oatman car and, knowing how much Floyd loved that dummy, one of them had snuck in the back and grabbed it. Chester had ridden all the way to Marianna, Florida, where they bought him a child's ticket on the Greyhound bus and sent him back.

That night in Loxley, Alabama, Chester returned to the stage and sang "Riding the Range for Jesus" and "When It's Roundup Time Up Yonder."

"Thank the Lord he's back with us," said a much-relieved Minnie to Dorothy on the phone. "I just knowed He wasn't gonna desert us in our time of need. . . . I tell you, Dorothy, when I saw little Chester come off that bus, oh, it touched my heart so. It was just like the Bible says . . . once't he was lost but now he's been found. . . ."

Later that night Dorothy confided to Mother Smith, "She may be loud and she may mangle the English language to a fare-thee-well, but I'll tell you the truth—if I ever really needed someone to pray for me, or someone I loved, Minnie Oatman would be the first person I would call."

February, the Month of Love

As it turned out, the Three Little Pigs cafeteria not only brought more good food to town, it brought romance as well. The new owners from St. Louis had a daughter who was now in the sixth grade with Bobby. Her Italian father and her Greek mother had produced a dark-eyed, olive-skinned beauty named Claudia Albetta, who soon had all the boys acting silly. In a town that was made up of mostly Swedish and Norwegian and Irish stock she was an exotic creature, as glamorous as Yvonne De Carlo and Dorothy Lamour rolled into one. By February, Bobby was a goner as well. They should have guessed something was up by his recent change in behavior. For one thing, he was using a lot of Wildroot Cream Oil on his hair, and he had put a brand-new shiny dime in his penny loafers.

When Dorothy came home from the grocery store she was surprised to see Bobby still sitting in the kitchen, the table littered with a pack of penny valentines he had bought at the dime store.

"Haven't you picked one out yet?"

"No," he said, pushing them around. "These are all too silly. It has to be just right."

"And, may I ask who this valentine is going to—or is it private?"

"Claudia Albetta," he told her but added quickly, "It's not my idea to send some stupid card. Miss Henderson made us all pick a name out of a hat—she wants to make sure everybody in class gets a valentine."

"Weren't you lucky to get the name of a girl you like."

"I didn't," Bobby admitted. "I swapped Monroe my Boy Scout knife and an Indian bracelet for it. He kind of likes her, too."

"Oh, I see." She sat down beside him. "Well, you have a big selection here." She looked through the cards and picked up one. "Here is a picture of a kitten with a basket of hearts—that's a nice one, don't you think?"

Bobby looked at it again. "I want it to be more serious than that."

"Ahh . . . I see." She shuffled through the cards and picked up one with a cupid, looked at it, and put it back down. "No, you don't want that; what we need is something in the middle, a cross between an adult valentine and a child's valentine. Not silly . . . but not too mushy." She chose another card. "Well . . . let's see, no, you don't want that either. All right, here's one. . . . Look, it just has a nice simple heart on it and a nice simple message. *You Are My Ideal Valentine . . . Be Mine.*"

Bobby took it from her and studied it. "Do you really think this is a good one?"

"Oh yes, very tasteful, understated but to the point."

"Are you sure?"

"Oh yes."

Bobby seemed pleased and took his pen and wrote across the bottom. *Guess Who.* His mother looked at what he had signed. "Do you mean to tell me that you have gone through all this agony and you're not even going to sign your name?"

Bobby was horrified. "I don't want her to know it's from me! Besides, we're not supposed to sign our names."

"Well, how about giving her a hint, just a little one? That would be O.K., wouldn't it?"

"What kind of hint?"

"I don't know. Maybe you could narrow it down for her just a tad."

"Like what?"

"You could say, From your admirer, the boy with the brown hair."

"Oh, Mother, that's stupid."

"No, it's not. Think about it. Wouldn't you hate it if a girl liked you and never let you know? You have to have courage about this. . . . Remember, you have to take a chance on romance."

"What if she throws up or something?"

"Oh, for heaven's sake, Bobby, I can't believe with all the noise you make that now suddenly you've gone shy and retiring. What's happened to you?"

Bobby sat and thought about it for a long time. Then, mustering up all his courage, he even went a step beyond, threw caution to the wind, and signed, *From the boy in the third row with the brown hair and brown eyes.*

The next morning Dorothy told her listeners, "If you are standing up, sit down, because I never thought I'd live to see the day that Bobby Smith actually got up, combed his hair without me having to send him back to his room. Oh, isn't love grand . . . and I do speak from experience. For years now I have been wanting a Sweetheart Swing in the backyard. I don't know how many times I have said to Doc, Wouldn't the spot right under the crab apple tree be just perfect for a little Sweetheart Swing so we could sit out here and look out over the fields and watch the sun go down? If you can believe it, yesterday morning after the show, I looked out in the backyard and there was Glenn and Macky Warren putting up a brand-new Sweetheart Swing. Glenn said, 'Doc sent us over and said to tell you Happy Valentine's Day.' So young people don't have a monopoly on love." Mother Smith played a few bars of "Don't Sit Under the Apple Tree with Anyone Else but Me." Neighbor Dorothy chuckled. "That's right, Mother Smith . . . he better not sit under the apple or any tree with anybody else but me . . . or I'll have to bean him. Are you listening, Doc?"

Bobby fidgeted in his seat all day, waiting for the valentine party to start, when finally Miss Henderson brought out the cookies and handed out all the valentines. When she called Claudia Albetta's name, Bobby pretended to be looking around the room but he watched her as she sat down and opened the envelope. She then turned around and smiled and gave the sweetest little wave.

Bobby smiled and waved back but she did not see him. She was smiling at the boy who sat three seats behind him, a boy that Bobby forgot had brown hair and brown eyes as well. Rats.

When he came home Dorothy met him at the front door. "Well?" she said.

"I told you it was a stupid idea. Now she likes Eugene Whatley."

"Oh, dear," said Dorothy.

When their friend Mr. Charlie Fowler, the poultry inspector, arrived at the house for dinner that night the first thing he asked was how Anna Lee was doing at school.

"Just wonderful," Dorothy told him, "loving every minute of it, she says."

"And how is young Robert?"

Dorothy shook her head. "I'm afraid young Robert is having romance problems, compounded by a slight case of mistaken identity."

Claudia Albetta was not the only one that year to make a similar mistake. When Betty Raye found the unsigned valentine that had been slipped under her door that morning she had seen Bobby in the kitchen the other day and assumed it was from him. Bobby wondered why she had kissed him for no reason. Other than the box of candy from Doc and Dorothy, it was the only valentine she got that year.

Another Graduate

The time between February and May seemed to fly by for everyone except Bobby. To him, three months felt like ten years and by the end of the school year he was like a wild animal ready to be let out of his cage. Dorothy did manage to get him into his good suit and a bow tie for Betty Raye's high school graduation. Dorothy wanted to be sure that everybody made a big fuss over her that day. The entire family was there, including friends like Monroe, who came along to help. They all yelled and applauded loudly when her name was announced and Jimmy even whistled. Dorothy was worried about her not being as popular as some of the other students and since the Oatmans could not be there, Dorothy wanted her to feel like she was not alone and know she had people who cared about her. After the graduation exercises were over, they were all standing around congratulating her when two girls walked up and asked Betty Raye if she was going to the party over at Cascade Plunge. "I don't think so," Betty Raye said, and before she'd thought it out Dorothy said, "Oh Betty Raye, you don't want to miss your senior party. Why don't you go—I'll bet you'd have a lot of fun."

"Yeah," said one girl, "you don't have to have a date. You can go with us if you want to."

"I'll take you if you want me to," Bobby said.

The girls did not wait for an answer. "If you change your mind, call us." All the way home Dorothy had to bite her tongue to keep from saying anything more but she managed. She had promised Betty Raye that she would never have to do anything she did not want to, but she still hated the idea that Betty Raye was not going tonight. She had not gone to the senior prom, either. One boy had asked her but she'd told him she could not dance, so he'd asked someone else. On prom night she'd stayed home and worked on her scrapbook. She had not seemed to mind but all night Dorothy had felt just terrible about it—and now the girl was missing the big senior party as well.

Later, everybody else was out on the porch and Mother Smith and Dorothy were sitting in the kitchen drinking coffee. Dorothy said, "I feel so sorry for her I just don't know what to do."

"Why, did she say something about her parents not being here today?"

Dorothy shook her head, "No . . . it's not that. She never says anything about that. It's just when I went in her room earlier she was sitting all by herself working on her scrapbook while everybody else is out having fun."

"Maybe she enjoys working on her scrapbook."

"Do you know what she puts in it? Pictures of houses that she cuts out of magazines."

"Houses . . . why houses?"

"Because she says that's what she wants more than anything else."

"Movie stars I can understand but houses, that's a new one. What kind of houses?"

"Just little houses. She must have over a hundred pictures pasted in there."

"Is that why you feel sorry for her?"

"No, it's not that. It's just that I get the feeling she's always sad about something. Not on the surface but deep down inside of her and I don't know what it is." Dorothy looked away and her eyes filled with tears. "But sometimes when I look at her she looks just like a little lost dog, wandering around all alone in the world, and it breaks my heart."

Mother Smith reached in her pocket and handed her a Kleenex.

"Sorry," said Dorothy, "I didn't mean to get so upset."

"That's all right, love. You're just too tenderhearted where that girl is concerned. I think Betty Raye is happy here."

Dorothy wiped her eyes. "Really?"

"Yes. I think she's much happier with us than she was with that family of hers."

"Do you think so?"

"Definitely."

"Well, maybe I'm wrong," she said and blew her nose, adding, "I hope so."

Another Case of Mistaken Identity

Dorothy had not been wrong. Betty Raye was sad. And she had felt lost all of her life but she did not know why. She also felt guilty for not being like the rest of the Oatmans and the Varners and for being such a disappointment to them—for not being outgoing and a good singer like the rest of them were. She loved her family but there were times when she felt as if she had just been dropped down from another planet into a group of strangers. There was no good reason why she felt that way, no good reason why she had always felt so different from all the others. But for as long as she could remember, she'd felt set apart.

Betty Raye did not know it but there was a perfectly good reason she felt so different from the rest of the Oatmans and the Varners. She *was* different. In fact, she was not even remotely related to them. They were strangers. But nobody knew it. Even Minnie Oatman believed she had given birth to her seventeen years ago, but she had not. The real truth about the matter was stranger than fiction.

In the last month of her pregnancy, Minnie and Ferris and the boys were living in Sand Mountain with Ferris's mother and daddy and when it was time for the baby to be born they all piled in the car and drove down to Birmingham and checked her into the Hillman Hospital. On November 9, 1931, three babies were born not more than thirty minutes apart. A little boy named Jesse Bates, a little girl named Carolina Lee Sizemore, and Betty Raye Oatman all saw the light of day on the same night. It was unusually busy on the fourth floor and it didn't help matters much that the entire Oatman and Varner clans all descended on the maternity ward like an invading army, including Floyd and his dummy Chester. Ferris Oatman's brother Le Roy was still singing with the gospel group at the time and he called a bunch of his hillbilly musician friends in Birmingham who sang on the Country Boy Eddie radio show and invited them to the hospital for a party. And so, combined with the normal everyday chaos of a big-city maternity ward, there was now a hillbilly band playing in the waiting room, the two Oatman boys and all their cousins running and yelling up and down the hall. Besides this commotion, plus being excited at seeing real live hillbilly stars such as Country Boy Eddie and his sidekick Butter Bean in person, was it any wonder that nurse Ethylene Buck was all atwitter that night? She had been nervous to begin with, as this was only her second week working in the maternity ward. And to make matters worse, she had just been handed three babies at once and she had to weigh and clean up and get them ready to go and see their mothers. Not only that—now there was a man standing at the window with a dummy shooting his eyebrows up and down at her, saying "Whoo, whoo, whoo." Chester banged his wooden head against the window, trying to get her attention. Which, unfortunately, he did. Nurse Buck became so flustered that she put the Sizemores' baby's name bracelet on the Oatman baby and the Oatmans' baby name bracelet on the Sizemore baby.

When Mrs. Kathrine Sizemore, the lovely young blond wife of a prominent Montgomery attorney, was handed her baby, she was surprised to see that her hair was so dark. Just as Minnie had been surprised that her baby had such light hair. She had immediately remarked to Ferris, "She's a pale little thing, ain't she. And just look at them tiny little ears!"

If anyone had known about the error Nurse Buck had committed that night, it certainly would have explained why, eighteen years later, a plump large-boned girl with coal black hair and short arms was desperately trying to stuff herself into a white evening gown to prepare for her debut at the Montgomery Country Club. Of course her parents adored her but secretly they wondered why, when her mother had been so tall and slim and graceful, each time Carolina practiced her debutante curtsy to the floor she always fell over on her side in a lump. Just as the Oatmans wondered why Betty Raye had been unable to carry a tune. But what has been done cannot be undone. Fate is fate, and while Carolina was getting ready to be presented to Montgomery society as one of the city's leading debutantes, Betty Raye, who should have been there, was miles away applying for a job as a vegetable girl at the Three Little Pigs cafeteria.

Betty Raye had wanted to get a job after graduation but she was not equipped to do anything that required intimate dealings with the public or being outgoing in any way. The job at the cafeteria seemed just right for her. All she had to do was stand there and dish out portions of whatever vegetable the customers pointed to. She did not have to talk a lot, so she was very happy she got the job. Now her world consisted of offering beans, okra, creamed corn, black-eyed peas, or whatever was on the menu that day and going home. Not knowing she might have been a debutante, she was perfectly content being a vegetable girl. And who knows—she might even work her way up to the desserts someday.

Anna Lee stayed in Chicago that summer to do her student nursing and after the valentine fiasco Bobby gave up on girls forever. When he was not at the swimming pool he spent most of his time reading Zane Grey cowboy novels, which Betty Raye brought home from the library for him. He was so caught up in reading about the romance of the Old West that by June he had finished them all, from *The Riders of the Purple Sage* to *The Thundering Herd,* and he took great comfort that most real cowboys did not even have girlfriends.

The Lady Bowlers

When the car full of women pulled up in front of the house and tooted the horn, Dorothy called out, "Sweetie, your bowling team is here." In a few seconds Betty Raye came out dressed and ready to go and said good-bye to all as she ran down the stairs. Everybody was out on the porch eating ice cream, including Monroe, and Bobby waved at the car and said, "Good luck tonight."

"Thank you," they said and drove away.

As they turned the corner Doc stood up and walked over and tapped his pipe on the side of the house. "I'm glad they asked her to join. She needs to get out once in a while."

Jimmy nodded. "Yeah. I think it's been good for her."

Dorothy got up to take her bowl back in the kitchen and agreed. "I do too. I just hated seeing her sit at home every night, a young girl like that."

"I just wish some nice boy in town would ask her out," Mother Smith said, "somebody her own age."

Jimmy grunted. "There's nobody around here worth going out with, if you ask me."

Monroe, sporting a new crew cut, his red hair shooting out of his head like wires, said, "I'd take her out . . . if she'd pay for everything," and thought it was the funniest thing anyone had ever said, punching Bobby in the ribs.

Bobby punched him back. "She wouldn't go out with you, you cootie head."

Jimmy said to Doc, "See what I mean?"

He did not say so, but Jimmy often thought that if he had been younger and had not lost his leg, things would be a lot different. He wondered why the boys who had fallen all over Anna Lee, who would not give most of them the time of day, never paid the least bit of attention to Betty Raye. He was pretty well disgusted with the whole lot of them. When Jimmy had slipped the valentine under her door, he had said to himself, If the local Romeos are so dumb that they cannot see what a fine girl she is, then, by God, he would see to it that the day would not go by without her knowing there was at least one person in town who thought the world of her. Not while he was around at least.

Jimmy was also right about one thing: the bowling team had been good for Betty Raye. A few months before, when Ada and Bess Goodnight had come marching into the house to lobby for her to join the Elmwood Springs ladies bowling team, Dorothy and Mother Smith had encouraged her. And despite her initial reluctance, Bess and Ada could be very persuasive. Ada, the larger of the two, had once worked in the WASP recruiting office and knew just what to say. In the end Betty Raye could not say no. According to Ada it would have been, at the least, unpatriotic, un-American, and letting down the entire female sex if she did not join.

Although Betty Raye was a last-minute replacement and had never bowled or played any sport before, to her surprise, unlike the other Oatmans, she seemed to be a natural athlete. She was graceful and coordinated and after a few lessons from Doc turned out to be a pretty decent bowler. Ada and Bess and their younger sister, Irene, who they called Goodnight Irene, were good too. But *nobody* was better than Tot Whooten. Just the mention of her name struck fear in the hearts of all the other teams. She was known throughout the county as "Terrible Tot, the left-handed bowler from hell." Tonight they were driving all the way over to the huge new bowling alley in East Prairie. Tot's next-door neighbor Verbena was staying with Darlene and Dwayne Jr. and watching her mother so Tot could go. The county championship was at stake.

Hours later it was down to the wire at the bowling alley. The Elmwood Springs Bombers had matched New Madrid's Wildcats strike for strike, game for game. But the last Wildcat had missed her point and now there was a chance that victory would be theirs.

The atmosphere was tense. Goodnight Irene had just picked up her spare and if Tot could get this last strike and score the extra point, they would win. A hush came over the large, usually noisy, air-conditioned room. Tot, wearing brown slacks with her hair freshly permed for the occasion, stood up, all eyes upon her. She squinted at the pins, put out her cigarette, walked over, picked up the chalk bag, threw it down, hoisted her ball and lifted it high in front of her, concentrated on the spot with all her might, took a deep breath, and let her rip.

The moment the ball left her hand and spun down the alley toward the pins she knew what had happened. In the intensity of the moment and the pressure of knowing that this one throw could mean the championship, she had jammed her fingers into the holes so hard that her wedding ring went down the alley with the ball. Not only did she miss the strike and sprain her finger, but the entire team had to spend hours after the game searching for Tot's ring. They had searched almost four hundred bowling balls with a flashlight before Betty Raye spotted it. But once they had it, the ring would not come out for love nor money and Tot had to buy the bowling ball just to get her ring back.

Even that was no small task. The bull-necked owner of the bowling alley eyed Tot suspiciously. "And just how do I know this is your ring, lady?" Tot could not believe her ears. Hands on her hips, she looked him right in the face and said, "Well, mister, just how many people do you know that have JAMES AND TOT WOOTEN FOREVER written inside their wedding ring?" Betty Raye knew it was not funny but she broke up at Tot's remark and had to walk away while Tot stood there and went at it toe to toe with the owner. She was not going to leave without her ring, even if she had to wait all night, she said. Finally, he sold her the ball and she left in a huff, as the team trailed behind her, vowing never to bowl again. Nobody dared laugh on the drive back to town but they were all dying to.

When Betty Raye arrived home it was late. Dorothy, who could not really rest well until she knew everyone was in for the night, safe and sound, heard Betty Raye come in, laughing all the way to her bedroom. They must have won, she thought, and rolled over and went to sleep.

• • •

The next day Tot carried the bowling ball over to the hardware store, where Macky tried everything he knew to get the ring out, from every size screwdriver to hammer and pliers, but nothing would work. Finally he said, "Mrs. Whooten, I don't know what to tell you but this sucker's stuck for good."

She said, "Thank you anyway, Macky," and took her ball and went home.

True to her word, that ended the short but eventful career of Tot the Terrible, the left-handed bowler from hell. "Wouldn't you know it," she said later, "the only sport I was ever good at." But not only was her career as a bowler over, she lost almost two weeks of work.

"You cannot do pin curls with a sprained finger," she said.

The Contest

When Bobby called the drugstore, Bertha Ann answered the phone with "Rexall." Bobby said in a voice he thought sounded like a man's, "Do you have Prince Albert smoking tobacco in a can?"

"Yes, we do," she said.

"Well, you better let him out before he suffocates."

Bertha Ann heard Monroe laughing in the background before Bobby hung up.

They were clearly bored. Other than he and Monroe getting caught in his father's den going through his *National Geographic* magazines looking for pictures of native women with their tops off, and having three cavities filled by Dr. Orr, the summer was turning out to be uneventful. But fate can turn on a dime and fortunes change and one event can alter a child's life forever. Or if not forever, it can certainly change the way he views himself in the world, good or bad. For Bobby that day was here, although to others it might not seem special.

Jimmy got up as usual at 4:30, lit his first cigarette, made the coffee, put on his white shirt and pants and black leather bow tie, and was down at the Trolley Car Diner at 5:00. Jimmy didn't know it yet, but he would be the first one in the Smith household to find out what was happening that day. This morning he went about his business as usual. He had great pride in his diner and kept it spotless. Every morning the black-and-white tile floor was scrubbed sparkling clean. The silver chrome on the counters and on the base of all the round red leather stools was polished and kept as shiny as a new car in a showroom. He gave the doors and the light green cigarette machine on the wall a wipe-down as well. Next he cut the pies—chocolate, a sky-high lemon-meringue, apple—and a marble pound cake in slices and placed them on small white plates and put them in his display case. He chopped onions, put pickles in a small chrome container, and placed a handful of toothpicks with bright red and orange cellophane on the tops in a small thick glass. He then wiped down the grill and removed slices of cheese, plus eggs, bacon, hamburger patties, weenies, tomatoes, and lettuce from the icebox. He fried up a batch of bacon and got his potatoes for hash browns and sliced the tomatoes. Last, he cut open several loaves of Merita white bread and dozens of hamburger and hot dog buns and was ready to open.

Jimmy had learned to cook in the navy and was a short-order cook of the first order. He could fry eggs any way you wanted and make a grilled cheese sandwich to perfection, golden brown, just right with the cheese dripping down the sides of the crust, or make a bacon, lettuce, and tomato so good you wanted another one before you finished the first. At exactly one minute to six he put on a clean apron, his white paper hat with the red stripe, and opened the door for business. To his surprise, there stood Bobby.

"Hey. What are you doing downtown so early?"

Bobby said, "Couldn't sleep, so I figured I'd come on down and have a cup of coffee with you. You know, the bubble gum contest is today."

"Oh, that's right. Well, come on in."

Jimmy knew that Dorothy did not let him drink coffee but he figured a little bit wouldn't hurt him. Bobby climbed up on a stool and Jimmy put out a thick white cup and saucer and poured him a half cup. Bobby picked up the container and happily added four teaspoons of sugar.

"So what do you think your chances are, buddy?"

"I don't know. I came pretty close last year."

"Do you want something to eat?"

"No, I think I better not." He added another spoonful of sugar. "You know, the secret is breath control. I learned that the last time—I ran out of breath right at the end or I would have won."

"I see. So what's your plan of attack this year . . . your strategy?"

Bobby took a sip of his coffee. "I've been practicing every day and trying to build up my breath control, holding my head underwater in the tub. But other than that, I don't know what else to do. I was kind of hoping you might give me some last-minute advice."

"Have you practiced any yet this morning?"

"Not yet. I thought I'd get in a couple of hours before nine."

Jimmy opened a large can of chili and thought carefully before he spoke. "Well, here's my advice. Now, you can take it or leave it, but now, if I were you, I wouldn't practice at all this morning."

"Not at all?"

"I wouldn't. You can pretty much figure that everybody else will, right?"

"Yeah, I guess so."

"So if you walk in nice and rested you have an advantage. See what I mean?"

Bobby's eyes widened. "Yeah . . . I see!"

"You save up all your energy for the big push—when you need it. And when you're up there, concentrate. Remain calm and steady as she goes. Don't look right, don't look left, don't let yourself get rattled, just stay the course, nice and easy all the way."

Bobby listened intently. "Yeah. Don't get rattled . . . nice and easy."

"What's the prize on this thing?"

"Twenty-five free passes to the theater."

Jimmy was impressed or acted as if he was. "Hey, that's a pretty good deal." Just then two of Jimmy's breakfast regulars came in the door.

"Morning, boys," he said.

Bobby quickly finished his coffee and ran out the door. "Thanks, Jimmy."

"Good luck, buddy."

Bobby ran back home and made a big production of resting, lying in the middle of the living room floor so everybody had to ask him what he was doing lying in the middle of the floor. When Princess Mary Margaret would not stop barking and running around him in a circle, he complained to his mother that it was very important for him to rest and to come and get her. However, she took the dog's side and said, "You get up off that floor. You're upsetting her. She thinks there's something wrong with you!"

At exactly 9:00 A.M., a dozen boys, all at least two inches taller than Bobby, stood in a straight line on the stage of the Elmwood Springs Theater, each in various stages of nervous breakdowns. Ward McIntire, the man from the Bazooka bubble gum company, stood holding a glass bowl filled with gum all wrapped in shiny wax paper, each containing a shiny wax-paper cartoon inside. As he stood there, Bobby kept repeating over and over in his mind, *Don't get rattled . . . don't look right, don't look left,* but it was hard. Claudia Albetta was sitting in the front row with two of her girlfriends. Ever since Mr. Yo-Yo had come to town he had wanted to win a contest. Last month he had lost the Bat the Ball contest by only three bats but coming in second was not good enough. Following his mother's motto—If at first you don't succeed, try again—he had tried over and over but without success. Bobby was beginning to wonder if he was destined to always be second at everything for the rest of his life.

This morning he had gotten to the theater an hour early so he could be first in line. He knew the longer you held the gum in your hand and warmed it up, the softer it would get. He had been first in line until three minutes before they opened the doors, when Luther Griggs and three of his friends pushed in front of him, so he wound up fourth in line. There was some consolation, however, because when the man started walking down the line so everyone could pick out their gum, he started at the other end and after all that pushing and shoving, Griggs wound up being last. Bobby heard Monroe let out a big donkey *hee-haw* from the audience when it happened. After everyone had a piece, Mr. McIntire then walked back to the side of the stage where the microphone was and announced in a booming voice, "Gentlemen, unwrap your gum." Bobby's heart was pounding and his hands were sweaty as he struggled to unwrap the slickly sticky paper and get his gum out. He kept repeating to himself *Nice and easy . . . don't get rattled.* Soon the boys stood at attention with huge marshmallow-sized chunks of white powdery sugary hot pink bubble gum in their palms, waiting for the next signal from the man. Mr. McIntire looked at his stopwatch, then said, "Get ready . . . begin!" In unison twelve boys jammed the gum into their mouths and furiously began chewing it like it was something they were trying to kill. Bobby forced himself to remain calm. He knew that part of the secret of a good bubble is not to start blowing until all the gum has been chewed properly . . . not too soft . . . not too hard. . . . Timing was everything. *Wait, wait,* he repeated over and over in his head. *Don't get rattled, don't get rattled, wait, wait.* He could hear that some of the boys had already started blowing but he waited until the moment he felt it was just right. Bobby started to blow, slowly at first, then as the bubble grew larger he increased his breathing, deeper and deeper each time, until his shoulders were heaving up and down with each breath. All around him bubbles were popping one by one, up and down the line, but Bobby kept going until he was the only one left. But he didn't know it and just kept on going. He was alone on the stage, all alone looking at the world through the soft pink gauze of a now vast bubble that was growing still larger and larger. There was complete silence in the theater. The entire audience was holding its breath. *Will it ever pop?* But it kept growing until the bubble covered his entire face and head—and more. All the audience could see was an immense pink bubble with a boy's arms and legs below. It grew larger and larger until Bobby felt like he might float up in the air . . . out the door, over the buildings, and out into the world, never to return. Then it happened. He heard an amazingly soft slow pop and there he stood with bubble gum covering his entire face, including his ears and the top of his head.

"The winner!" screamed Ward McIntire and the audience was on its feet applauding. What glory. What a triumph. Five minutes later Bobby ran into the Trolley Car Diner with gum still sticking to his eyelashes and ears, waving his free-pass book in the air, yelling, "JIMMY . . . I WON. . . . I DIDN'T GET RATTLED. I WON!" But before Jimmy had a chance to congratulate him he had run out the door, headed for the drugstore to tell his father. When he got home his mother had to use kerosene to get all the gum out of his hair, and he used up all twenty-five passes in less than a week taking everybody to the movies but he didn't care. He had blown the biggest bubble in the history of the contest, people said. Maybe the biggest in the entire state. From that day on he felt special.

Winning that contest meant he had been chosen to become a man of destiny after all.

Success

As Bobby found out, sometimes in life you just get lucky and hit the right combination. After years of trying, one day you press the lever of the slot machine and all three cherries line up in the right order and you've hit the jackpot. Such was the case the day Beatrice Woods joined the Oatman Family Gospel Singers.

They had only been together for a few months when a producer from Hallelujah Records heard them sing in Atlanta. After they cut their first album, things started to happen. When *Can't Wait to Get to Heaven* climbed to the top of the gospel charts, offers started coming in from everywhere. *The Singing News* soon wrote that they were becoming the hottest new group of the year.

Soon their second album, *Once I Was Lost but Praise the Lord Now I'm Found,* named after a song Minnie had written inspired by Chester's disappearance, shot to the top of the charts as well. This combined with their appearance on the Arthur Godfrey show and they suddenly became the number one gospel group in the country. To Beatrice's delight, this sudden popularity meant traveling to almost every state in the Union and within six months they had even sung in the White House. By the end of 1949 they were booked fifty-two weeks out of the year and had their own big silver bus with THE OATMAN FAMILY GOSPEL SINGERS written in big, bold, black letters on both sides.

Although this meant she did not see the family very often, Betty

Raye was very happy for their success and equally happy that she was not involved in any of it. As far as she was concerned, her life was perfect. Quiet and peaceful. She did not have to be onstage performing every night and have to pack up and drive somewhere else for the next one. She got to sleep in the same bed in the same town week after glorious week. She had a nice little job she liked, all the books she could read, and went bowling once a week. For the first time in her life she was able to do the same old thing day after day and she loved it. At last she was beginning to feel as if she really belonged somewhere. She wanted it to go on forever. But one day Hamm Sparks walked in the door.

Hamm Sparks was an ordinary young man in most respects—smoke a little, dance a little, drink a little, flirt a little. Ordinary except for the one thing. Ambition. When the Ink Spots sang "I Don't Want to Set the World on Fire" the lyrics failed to apply to him. Not that other young men were without ambition but Hamm Sparks burned with it. If he had been a car it would have been racing on all sixteen cylinders and running hot. So hot you got the feeling he could explode at any minute.

But unlike some men, who were sick and driven with ambition, he'd never felt better in his life. Hamm thrived on it like it was mothers' milk. Some would say later that he even glowed in the dark with it. And he had a plan, a goal in life, and at the moment it involved going to college on the G.I. Bill, waiting on tables in the dorm six hours a day, and selling Allis-Chalmers tractors on the weekends and during summers to help support his mother and two younger sisters. Work was something he was not afraid of or resented. He had been working since he was ten years old. Work for him was just a means to an end. In America, no matter how poor you started out or where you came from, you could go as high as you wanted if you were willing to work for it. Hamm thought this was about as good a deal as you could get. It gave him hope for a bright and shining future and he was on his way. He did not know exactly where yet—he would figure that out later; all he knew was that he was in a hurry. He had to make up for lost time. He ate fast, talked fast, walked fast, and hardly ever slept. He shook hands, patted backs, and never missed an opportunity to introduce himself to everyone he ran across. What brought him to Elmwood Springs that one particular day was Bess Goodnight. In 1942 he had passed through town on a train headed to Fort Leonard Wood and, like a lot of the other soldiers, had thrown his name out the window, hoping to get someone to write to him. Bess Goodnight wrote to him throughout the war. Like so many of Bess's wartime pen pals, Hamm came to visit her whenever he was near enough to make it over to Elmwood Springs. He got a big kick out of Bess and loved to take her out to the cafeteria for lunch. Hamm loved the idea of good food in a hurry but this Saturday, while going through the line, he slowed a bit when he noticed the pretty girl in the glasses standing behind the steam table waiting for him to tell her what vegetables he wanted. Usually he passed right by the vegetables, on to the desserts, but today he stopped. This girl stood with a spoon in one hand and a small brown plastic bowl in the other, waiting for his order. He looked down at the steam table at the choices.

"Ah . . . let's see, I'll have some potatoes and how about some macaroni and cheese?"

He pointed to something green in one of the containers. "Are those turnip greens?"

"No, sir, collard greens."

"All right, good. Give me some of those then."

He would have ordered more but the line behind him was backing up and he had to move on. Even before they got to the table and had emptied their trays Hamm asked Bess about the girl with the glasses dishing out the vegetables.

Bess glanced over and said, "Oh, that's Betty Raye, Dorothy's little boarder. Ever hear of the Oatman family?"

"Yeah," he said. "I hear them on the radio."

"Well, that's their daughter; she used to sing with them but she quit."

Hamm glanced back over at Betty Raye, even more impressed.

"Well, I'll be. She's not married yet?"

"No."

"Is she going with somebody?"

"Not that I know of."

"Do you reckon she'd go out with me?"

Bess laughed. "You sure don't waste any time, do you, boy?"

During the next four weekends Hamm never drove so far or ate so many vegetables in his life. Going to the cafeteria was the only way he could get to see her. Every Saturday when he came down the line Betty Raye was horrified and embarrassed at all the attention and commotion he would cause. She asked him to please stop holding up the line but each time he said, "I will, just as soon as you say yes." One Saturday, after he had been down the line for the fourth time, he pleaded with her. "Come on now, Betty Raye, you've just got to go out with me. If I eat one more bowl of those collards I'm liable to turn green. You don't want that on your conscience, do you?" At that moment Mr. Albetta came out of the double doors of the kitchen and glared at him and Hamm moved on, while the girls giggled. But he would not give up. Late that afternoon, when Betty Raye came home, there he was sitting on the front porch, chatting away with Mother Smith and Bess Goodnight. Mother Smith was clearly charmed and smiled and said, "Betty Raye, this nice young man tells me he is a friend of yours." Hamm grinned from ear to ear. "I brought Bess with me to vouch for my upstanding character."

Bess laughed. "I don't know how upstanding he is but I wish you'd go out with him for my sake, because he's about to pester me to death over it."

Well, what could she do? Hamm was a force hard to resist.

The First Date

Monday was Betty Raye's day off and Hamm was to pick her up in the early afternoon and take her to Poplar Bluff for dinner. She was nervous about going all that way with him but she did not have much say in the matter. Dorothy and Mother Smith were so excited she was going on a date that they called Tot and set up an appointment for her that morning to get her hair shampooed and set. It was the last thing she wanted but she went. They picked out her outfit and at the last minute Dorothy ran in with a string of pearls for her to wear. And so at four o'clock, Betty Raye in a pair of Anna Lee's high heels and with a head full of fluffed-up frizz and Hamm wearing a borrowed suit, off they went.

Betty Raye had never been on a real date. The whole idea of it made her feel very uncomfortable. She had no idea how she was supposed to act and the entire time they were driving over to Poplar Bluff she wished this date would hurry up and be over so she could go back home. They made quite a pair. She did not know it but he had not been on many dates himself. He had been too busy working and had not had the money to take many girls out. He'd had to sell a few of his books just to get the money to pay for tonight.

All through dinner she did not talk much. Luckily she did not have to; he talked enough for both of them. This was the first time Hamm had seen her in anything but a white uniform and cap and he was impressed.

She wasn't exactly pretty in a conventional way but there was something so sweet and shy about her that as the night wore on, the prettier she became.

On the drive back Betty Raye was even more nervous than before. She hardly heard a word he said. She worried all the way home that he might try to kiss her or something but he did not. He did not have much of a chance. When they reached the front door she shook his hand and said, "Well, good night," and was in the house with the door closed and back in her room before he could do anything. Dorothy and Mother Smith were in the kitchen when she came in, the two of them dying to know all the details, but they would have to wait till the morning.

"Well," said Dorothy as she entered the kitchen, dressed for work. "Did you have a nice time last night?"

Betty Raye said, "Yes. It was fine."

But that was all she volunteered. Mother Smith picked up the ball. "So do you think you'll be seeing him again?"

Betty Raye looked surprised at the question. "No, I don't think so." As far as she was concerned, she had gone out with him once. Why would she want to do it again? Dates were too hard. She just wanted to serve vegetables and be left alone. After she left Dorothy said, "Too bad. I was hoping things would have worked out."

"Me too." Mother Smith sighed. "But when there's nothing there, there's nothing there and you can't do a thing about it."

However, no two people interpret the same event the same way. The following Saturday morning Hamm walked into the drugstore and nodded at Bertha Ann and Thelma, said, "Hello, girls," went straight back to the pharmacy, stuck his hand over the counter, and shook Doc's hand. "Sir, my name is Hamm Sparks and I just wanted to ask you if it would be all right with you if I married Betty Raye."

Doc, who had heard about this character but had never met him, was a little thrown. "I don't know. I suppose it depends on her. What does she say?"

"I haven't asked her yet but I can assure you that you won't have to worry. I have a fairly good job now and as soon as I finish college I intend to do even better in the future. I'm thinking about going into public service and people tell me I have a pretty good shot at it."

"I see," said Doc.

Hamm said, "Yessir, and I sure would appreciate if you would put in a good word for me," and handed him his card. " 'Bye, ladies," he said on the way out.

"Who was that little banty rooster?" Bertha Ann asked.

Doc laughed. "Betty Raye's boyfriend. Or so he thinks."

Thelma was surprised. "Your Betty Raye?"

"That's what he says."

Bertha Ann said, "Well, whoever he is, he sure is a cute little thing. Doc, you tell Betty Raye for me she better watch out or I'm liable to steal him."

Thelma, still amazed that Betty Raye even had a boyfriend, said, "Well, I guess it's true what they say."

"What?" asked Bertha Ann.

"Still waters run deep."

"I could have told you that," Bertha Ann said. "It's those quiet ones you have to watch out for."

Doc did not mention the young man's visit to Dorothy, Betty Raye, or Mother Smith. Where women were concerned, when the subject was romance he had learned that it was best to stay out of it and let them deal with it on their own, so he wisely kept his mouth shut and let nature take its course.

The Boyfriend

As it turned out, Doc was glad he had not said anything. After the first date Betty Raye heard no more from Hamm.

After a month went by Betty Raye had more or less forgotten about Hamm Sparks but that thought had never occurred to him. It had not taken him long to make up his mind. He had known after that first date that he wanted to marry her, so why wait? He was almost twenty-seven, in a hurry to get married and get started on his career, so the next day he got busy making plans for both of them. The first thing he had to do was get the money. The next day he talked the district manager of Allis-Chalmers into letting him sell in three more areas. It took him almost a month, working nights and all weekend, but he finally earned enough money to make a down payment, plus a little left over. The next Friday Hamm put on his brand-new blue suit from Sears and drove over to Elmwood Springs with the box in his pocket. He had not bothered to inform Betty Raye he was coming because he wanted to surprise her.

He walked up the steps to the house and knocked. Dorothy came to see who was there.

"Hello, Mrs. Smith, is Betty Raye here?"

"Well, hello, Hamm." Dorothy opened the door. "Yes, she is. Come on in. We are just sitting down for supper; why don't you come in and join us."

"Thank you, I think I will, if it's all right."

"Of course it is, all I have to do is set a plate. You just go on in the dining room and sit down." She called down the hall as she went to the kitchen, "Betty Raye, everybody, Hamm is here."

When Doc looked up and saw the new blue suit coming in the door, he thought to himself, Uh-oh, here comes trouble. Hamm walked into the dining room and said, "Hi, everybody," pulled out a chair, and sat down across from Betty Raye. Everybody said hello but Jimmy just nodded. He was not sure about this guy. A little too pushy for his taste. Hamm soon sat there eating and talking all about tractors, farmers, Allis-Chalmers, and anything else that came to mind, including a joke he had just heard. Bobby thought he was funny and liked him right away but Betty Raye was confused. She did not know whether she was glad to see him again or not. She liked him O.K., she guessed, but he made her so nervous the way he talked so fast and moved so fast that she didn't know what to think. She was embarrassed that he had just shown up like that but it had not seemed to bother anyone else. Mother Smith and Doc and Dorothy chatted away as if nothing was out of the ordinary.

After dinner Betty Raye picked up a few plates and started for the kitchen, relieved to get away for a while. He had grinned at her all through dinner and she had felt herself blushing every time he caught her eye. But Dorothy said, "Betty Raye, you put those down and go out on the porch and visit with your young man. He's come all this way to see you. Mother Smith and I will do the dishes tonight." Betty Raye had no choice but to go. When Doc and Bobby got up to go out on the porch with them, Dorothy gave Doc a funny look.

"Don't you and Bobby have a ball game to listen to tonight?" she said in a high voice, blinking her eyes.

"What?" he said.

She fired him another look and he finally figured it out. "Oh, yeah. Bobby, come on with me, let's go listen to the ball game."

"What ball game? They don't have a game tonight," he said as his father led him away by the back of his neck to the parlor. Jimmy excused himself and headed out the back door to the VFW for his poker night with his buddies and Betty Raye found herself on the way to the porch, wondering how someone she did not even know at all well had suddenly become her young man.

• • •

They sat on the porch and after a few minutes Hamm reached in his pocket and handed her the little box. "Open it," he said.

She asked, "What is it?"

"Open it. I bought you a ring."

She was puzzled. "Why?"

"Because I want you to marry me."

First she was not quite sure what she had heard. Hamm may have had this in mind for a month but for her this had come out of the blue. "What?" she said again.

"Will you marry me?"

"Me?"

"Yes, you. What do you say?"

By this time she was so flustered she didn't know what to do, so she handed the box back and said, "Oh, thank you for asking but I don't think I want to get married. I hope I haven't hurt your feelings or anything but I can't. I have a job, I'm sorry," she said. "I have to go in but thank you anyway." And she stumbled into the screen door and said, "Oh, excuse me," to the door and went in, leaving him sitting in the swing.

This was not exactly how Hamm had envisioned the evening turning out.

But it was only one night.

Hamm did not give up. Every free moment he had he came over to see her. He would show up at the cafeteria and go down the line singing out, "Aw, come on, honey, say you will, I'm coming back every night until you say yes." He even started to show up at the bowling alley. Ada and Bess Goodnight, pulling for him, told him where they would be and all the women on the team liked him and encouraged Betty Raye to let him drive her home, which she did.

This went on for weeks. Doc said, "I'd hate to have that boy chasing after me. Hell, at this point I'll marry him and he hasn't even asked me."

Weeks of this kind of intense attention and flattery is hard to resist, even to someone who does not want to get married. But Betty Raye did not have much choice in the matter. Hamm was like a small tornado and she got caught up in the whirlwind and, like most women, was at first curious and then dazzled by him.

That night he had parked the car in front of the house. "Now, Betty Raye, you can't go in until I get just one little kiss. Just one. You don't want to break my heart, do you?"

After one and then more than one, she walked onto the porch and into the house in a daze and said to Dorothy, "I think I might be engaged."

After Betty Raye had gone to her room Mother Smith spoke to Dorothy. "Now, personally, you know, I like him, but I worry that that boy has just come in here and swept her right off her feet."

Dorothy suddenly looked concerned. "Oh, dear. You think so?"

"Oh, not that way. It's just I don't know if he's given her enough time. They've only known one another for a few months. What do you think, Doc?"

"She must like him; she said yes. But he certainly seems to be in one hell of a hurry, I'll grant you that."

Meet the Folks

The next thing Betty Raye knew Hamm had tracked down the Oatmans, who were performing in Charlotte, North Carolina, and the two of them along with Ada and Bess Goodnight as chaperones drove all night to get her parents' blessing. The Oatmans did not go on until after the first intermission and the Elmwood Springs contingent managed to get to the auditorium in time. Betty Raye had not seen them perform since she'd left and since they had become such a success. She was surprised at how much the act had changed. Her mother and Beatrice still wore no makeup but they did have matching dresses with rhinestone trimming. The boys and Ferris had on shiny suits with plaid cummerbunds. They started their part of the show with the spotlight on Minnie, who held a microphone in her hand. As the group in the background hummed, she began to speak. "I am but a poor woman. I have no precious jewels, no silver or gold, I own no earthly mansions nor wealth in this world. My father is but a poor man. . . . I've had many burdens to bear . . . cried many a bitter tear. . . . There were times I wondered how I could go on. . . . But one day a tattered and torn old woman knocked on my door and saw me there in my deep despair. . . . And with eyes filled with joy she said, 'Oh, daughter, have you not heard the Gospel? Do you not know the good news? Your Father in heaven has given you more than the millionaire's child. More than the queen on a throne. Open your eyes, daughter, and behold the gifts and precious jewels He has laid out before you. He's given you diamonds that sparkle in the sky, rubies in the redbirds' wings, and sapphires in the deep blue sea. Priceless emeralds lay stretched before you in the green grass; there's silver in the mountain streams and gold in the sunsets of every day. You are clothed in His love and your home is a mansion in the sky. There's no depression in heaven, no hunger, sorrow, or pain, no dirty dishes to wash, meals to cook, or wood to chop.' Oh, brothers and sisters, I ask you, is it any wonder why I just can't wait to get to heaven!" The stage suddenly lit up with dozens of colored lights and they launched into their big hit.

The audience as usual went wild and stood clapping and cheering. After the show was over, Hamm and Betty Raye had to fight their way through the hundreds of fans wanting their albums signed to get to the family so she could introduce him.

Later, Minnie took Betty Raye on their new bus and shut the door so they could be alone. She sat her down and said, "You know, all I want in this world is for my little girl to be happy."

"I know that, Momma."

"Now, he seems like a fine young Christian man and I only have one question for you."

"Yes, ma'am?"

Minnie took her hand and looked her right in the eyes. "Do you love him, honey?"

This was a question Betty Raye had hardly had time to think about. What had seemed to be important up to now was how he felt and how much he loved her. She turned and looked out the window at Hamm, who was standing outside in the middle of a group, talking away, smiling and shaking hands. She could not hear what he was saying, but seeing him down there so small, all alone in the crowd, not knowing anybody and trying so hard to give her family a good impression, touched her so that suddenly a tremendous wave of affection for him swept over her. It was at that moment when she felt her heart go right out to him. She looked at Minnie and answered, to her own surprise, "Yes, Mother. Very much."

Minnie squeezed her hand, then pushed something that made a hissing sound, and the bus doors flew open and she called out down the stairs in a loud voice "PRAISE THE LORD, FERRIS, OUR BABY IS GETTING MARRIED!"

Soon, after much hugging good-bye, the big silver Oatman bus pulled out, headed for an all-night sing in Birmingham. Minnie hung out the window, tearfully waving her large white handkerchief, and Chester the dummy hung out another one, making eyes at the couple until they were out of sight.

When they came back, they told everybody the news. They were going to drive up to Poplar Bluff and be married by a justice of the peace the very next day. Jimmy was the only one who was not quite sold on the idea but if that was what Betty Raye wanted, then he was not going to say anything. However, later that night, when he and Hamm were on the porch smoking, he said quietly, "I hope you are going to treat that girl right now that you got her."

Hamm said, "Oh I will. I know how lucky I am."

Jimmy flicked his cigarette off the side of the porch. "Good, 'cause I'd hate to have to kill you."

Hamm laughed and started to say something but Jimmy had already gone in.

The next morning Hamm picked her up at the house and the entire bowling team, including ex-member Tot, came over and stood in the yard to say good-bye, and off the engaged pair went, amid tears and good wishes.

"Name the first one Bess even if it is a boy!" Bess called out as they drove away.

"We didn't even have time to buy her a decent trousseau," said Dorothy. "I just hope she won't have any regrets down the line. He hardly gave her time to pack, let alone shop for a trousseau."

That afternoon, standing in front of the justice of the peace, when Betty Raye said, "I do," she meant it. She had no idea how this all had happened or why but the new Mrs. Hamm Sparks found that she was hopelessly in love with her new husband.

Two weeks later Dorothy walked into the house with a big smile on her face and handed Mother Smith the postcard from the Blue Haven Motor Court outside Centralia, Missouri.

Dorothy said, "I know we both had our doubts for a moment but it looks like everything is going to work out." Written on the back of the card was:

Dear Smith family,

I am so happy! Thank you for everything.

Love,
Betty Raye

Congratulations

It seemed as if the summer was to be a lucky one for everybody. On the morning of August twentieth Dorothy came fluttering down the hall, like a great butterfly. She was elated over the news she had just received and she could hardly wait to get on the air and tell all her listeners. The red light went on just as she sat down.

"Good morning, everybody. It's a beautiful day over here in Elmwood Springs and I hope it's just as pretty where you are. You know, over the years I have announced so many weddings, births, deaths, engagements, and what all and I never thought I'd live to see the day when I would have a wedding so close to home." Mother Smith played two bars of "Here Comes the Bride." "That's right, Mother, last night Anna Lee called home and told us all the good news. It's official. She's engaged to that nice boy I've been telling you about . . . so . . . I, too, am going to be the mother of the bride. We are so excited for our girl. She and William will be married next June, right after she finishes her nurse's training, and we are glad of that, of course. And also, this morning in the believe-it-or-not category, I am not the only mother in Elmwood Springs that has good news today." Mother Smith hit a few cords of "My Blue Heaven." "Right, Mother . . . and baby makes three. Ida Jenkins called right before the show went on this morning and informed me that she expects to be a grandmother before the year is up, so congratulations to her daughter, Norma, and husband Macky.

"Oh, we have all sorts of good things planned for you today but first—did you know that nine out of ten screen stars use Lux soap? 'I'm a Lux girl,' says beautiful movie star Linda Darnell. So if you want clear, glamorous skin tomorrow, use Lux today. And we have a good-neighbor item to pass along. Mrs. Ellen Nadel of Booker, Missouri, writes in and asks if anyone has a copy of the last chapter of Vera Caspary's serial murder *The Murder in the Stork Club,* which was carried in *Collier's* last month. She says her subscription has run out and she wants to see how it ends. So let us know if you do. And now, here are the Goodnight twins, joined by sister Irene, to sing a song expressing exactly how I feel this morning, 'I'm Sitting on Top of the World.' "

And as if Bobby's having become the Bubble Gum King and the news of Anna Lee's engagement were not enough good news for one year, something else wonderful was about to happen. On a beautiful Sunday morning, one week after Bobby was to enter the seventh grade, Old Man Henderson went out in his yard with his pair of World War I binoculars. He had spotted something odd a few minutes before.

When he focused them he mumbled to himself, "Some gol-darned fool has gone and tied red balloons all over the top of the water tower."

THE FIFTIES

Cowboy Bob

The next time Mr. Charlie Fowler, the poultry inspector, came to town, he was surprised to see that "young Robert" had grown almost five inches and his voice was already starting to change. If he kept growing at that rate, they said, he might get to be taller than his father by next year. Two weeks after Bobby's fifteenth birthday, the letter he had been waiting for from the national office of the Boy Scouts of America in Irving, Texas, arrived. He ripped it open and was elated to read:

Dear Robert,

Congratulations! You are an Eagle Scout. With the completion of the requirements you have mastered many skills and made the Scout Oath and Law a part of your life. Our prayers are with you and your future successes.

Sincerely,
Bruce Thompson
Chief Scout Executive

Both he and Monroe had made Eagle Scout, and the following summer they took the train all the way across the country to the big Boy Scout Jamboree in Santa Ynez, California. This would be the first time either of them had ever been out of Missouri and, for Monroe, his first trip out of Elmwood Springs. When they crossed into Oklahoma and Texas and into New Mexico and Arizona, they might as well have been on the moon. As they stared out the window at the western landscape they could not believe their eyes. It was hard to even imagine it was all real. They were both in awe of the vast landscape that stretched as far as they could see. Neither one had any idea how big the county was. All Monroe could say as they passed by the Painted Desert, Indian reservations, herds of buffalo, and saw their first western sunset, was "Whoa!" He repeated the word a lot all the way to California and also when he first saw the huge Alisal Ranch, where the Boy Scouts were staying. It was a real working ranch and they met a genuine bowlegged cowboy, who showed them where they would be sleeping. In a real bunkhouse, as it turned out. That night, after they'd walked back from the first Boy Scout ceremony, the dark blue sky was spangled with stars so close you could almost touch them. And they had thought the stars in Elmwood Springs were bright. Even though it was summer, the night was cold and Jake, the hired hand, made a fire in the big stone fireplace. What a day. They had met boys from all over the world who had also never seen a ranch before but none was more impressed than Bobby.

Later, when everyone else went to bed, he was too excited to sleep. He lay there watching the reflections of the orange and black flames dancing on the ceiling and listened to the sound of coyotes from a distant hill and he felt as if he had just stepped into a Zane Grey novel. As he fought to stay awake his mind began to wander . . . and dream.

> The boy's father walked into his room with a letter in his hand and a solemn look on his face.
>
> "Son, we never told you this before today . . . but you have an uncle out West who has just died and left you his entire ranch. Running a five-hundred-thousand-acre spread is a big responsibility but I know you can handle it."
>
> The young stranger rode up to the Double R Ranch house and thought to himself, as he surveyed the thousand head of cattle mooing gently in the meadow and the cowpokes that stood around warily eyeing the slow but steady approach of the new young owner, "Yes . . . you may be a tenderfoot today, Bob Smith, but tomorrow . . ."
>
> Just then the daughter of the ranch foreman, a shy, pretty

girl, suddenly appeared on the vine-shaded veranda. "Howdy, ma'am," he said as he swung down from his horse. "And what is your name?"

"Margarita," she replied, her dark eyes flashing. . . .

This was a trip he would never forget.

The Baby Boom

The fifties brought many profound changes both at home in Elmwood Springs and all over America. Everywhere you looked, hundreds of TV antennas seemed to pop up overnight, until every house on every block had one. Names like Philco, Sylvania, Motorola, Uncle Miltie, and Howdy Doody were now part of the language. But television sets and performers were not the only things multiplying. Babies were being born by the thousands every minute of the night and day.

Norma and Macky Warren now had a little girl named Linda, and Anna Lee had a child on the way, and this morning Dorothy had yet another birth to announce. On April 7 Dorothy came down the hall as usual, greeted her guests, and the show started. "Good morning, everybody . . . it's another pretty day over here. Mother Smith as usual says hello and is feeling good today. Flash, as Walter Winchell would say. Attention, Mr. and Mrs. America and all the ships at sea. Last night our little friend Betty Raye over in Sedalia, Missouri, gave birth to a seven-pound little Hamm Sparks, Junior . . . So a great big welcome to the world, baby boy! I know your parents are proud. It seems like only yesterday we were waving good-bye to your mother. Oh, how time flies. We have a lot of fun things lined up for you today. Our two special guests, Ruth and Dawn, the Bohemian harpists, are here all the way from Gaylord, Missouri, and they will be doing their famous rendition of 'Sing Gypsy Sing' for us.

"But before we start the show, we have one more little cat that needs a home and I'll tell you he's the sweetest thing, just wants to sit in your lap all day and love on you. Dr. Stump says he's in good health and he will do his male operation for free. . . . We really need to make sure that all our animals have their male and female operations . . . there are just too many precious dogs and cats out there with no home. I look at Princess Mary Margaret and it almost breaks my heart to think she could be out in the world all alone without a family and I'm sure you feel the same way.

"Also we do want to thank Mrs. Lettie Nevior of Willow Creek who sent Princess Mary Margaret the loveliest little coat with her name embroidered right on it. And Mrs. Nevior, how I admire your tiny little stitches. You are just an artist, that's all I can say, just an artist."

Bess Goodnight, who worked at the Western Union office, walked up on the porch and handed Dorothy something that had just come in over the wire. "I thought you might want to see this," she said.

"Thank you, Bess," Dorothy said as she quickly scanned the news item. "A fanfare, if you please, Mother Smith. An announcement has just come in and I am happy to report that our own wonderful sponsor, Mr. Cecil Figgs of Cecil Figgs Mortuaries and Floral Designs, has just been named Missouri Businessman of the Year for the second time in a row. So another great big congratulations to you! We always love it when our advertisers do well."

The Funeral King

If there was ever a business that proved advertising paid off, it was Cecil Figgs Mortuaries and Floral Designs. What had started out as one small, pink concrete-block building was now thirty-six large, white-columned affairs designed to resemble Tara in *Gone with the Wind* scattered across the state, two in Kansas City alone. By now Cecil Figgs was the biggest name in the funeral and floral business. He was advertised statewide, on the radio, on billboards, on bus stop benches, in newspapers and the Yellow Pages. Everywhere you looked or listened you would see or hear about Cecil Figgs. "Open twenty-four hours a day to better serve you and will arrange pickup at any location. We treat your loved ones as one of our own." Of course, he advertised layaway plans. After Cecil had been named Businessman of the Year for the second time, Helen Reid, a woman with the local newspaper, who was assigned to do a story on him, arranged an interview with his two aunts, who still lived in the small town of Eudora, Missouri, where he'd been born. Mrs. Mozelle Hemmit was sitting in her parlor recalling his childhood for the reporter. "Cecil always loved a funeral. From the time he was six years old, you bring him a dead cat and you had yourself a funeral. Flowers, music, and headstone to boot." His other elderly aunt, Mrs. Ethel Moss, agreed. "It's true. Whenever most boys were off playing ball he'd be down at Shims' Mortuary in his little blue suit attending somebody's funeral. It didn't matter whether he knew the family or not. Did it, Mozelle?"

"No," she agreed. "He just liked mingling with the crowd and sympathizing with the grieving relatives. By the time he was twelve Mr. Shims had already put him to work overseeing the visitors book and handing out fans. Remember, Ethel?"

Ethel nodded. "That's right and he made good money too and I'll tell you this, if there is such a thing as a born mortician, he's it. Cecil just loves the public, dead or alive, and he always did."

"And," said Mozelle, "he was just a natural florist right from the get go. Cecil was always a whiz with flowers, wasn't he, Ethel?"

"Oh yes, that boy could whip up an arrangement out of what most people threw away . . . and creative! Remember that spray of wheat and corn shucks he arranged for old Nannie Dotts's casket? He's just a miracle worker when it comes to arranging. You hand him five dandelions and a handful of weeds and by the time he gets done, you've got yourself a dining room table centerpiece."

"I remember when he first started out," Mozelle said. "He bought Mr. Shims's place. He was a one-man band as far as the funeral business. He did the flowers, embalmed the departed, greeted the mourners, sang the hymns, and preached the sermon . . . and if that wasn't enough, he drove the hearse. Now, if that's not service, I don't know what is. But he's come a long way from those days. I know Ursa is proud of him. He's been a good son. How many boys that age would bring their mother to live with them and be so sweet? He takes her everywhere, buys her anything she wants. Hired a maid for her and treats her like a queen. She doesn't have to lift a finger."

Mozelle shook her head, puzzled. "A sweet boy like that but he never married and I don't know why. He was always real popular. Wasn't he, Ethel?"

"He was. Cecil was the band major in high school and in all the school plays."

The reporter asked, "Did he have a high school sweetheart?"

Mozelle said, "Well . . . there was that one girl, remember? That he went around with for a while. We thought maybe something would happen but when I asked Ursa about it she said that girl was a Christian Scientist and it never would have worked out. But he has lots of friends. He's very active in the Young Men's Christian Association and he directs the Miss Missouri contest every year and runs the Little Theater group up there in Kansas City."

"And directs sacred-music festivals," Ethel added. "And don't forget his church work. He's choir director over at the big Methodist church. So with all his theater and music friends, I'm sure he never has time to be lonesome. He's made a lot of friends in the gospel world. There's not a gospel-singing family in a six-state area that's not a customer. When one of them dies he's the first one they call to come and officiate."

Ethel nodded. "They're always falling out with massive strokes and heart attacks and things. Cecil said he has to special-order the caskets and keep a few in stock just for them."

Mozelle said, "That gospel crowd alone keeps him busy night and day."

The reporter addressed the next question to both of them. "What would you say is the secret of his success?"

They both thought about it and Mozelle spoke first. "I would say that it's his love of pageantry and knowing people. He told me one time, he said, 'Aunt Mo'—Mo, that's what he calls me—he said, 'Aunt Mo, people need a little help to cry over their departed.' He said most people try to hold it in when they should let go and get it over with. And believe me, with his theater background he knows exactly how to tug at your heartstrings . . . with music and lighting and all. He really knows how to pull it out of you."

"That's true. I'll guarantee you will not go to one of Cecil's funerals and not wind up crying along with the rest of them. I know. He did Old Lady Brock's funeral and by the time we were halfway into the service he had me carrying on like she was my own mother. By the time he's done you come out feeling like a dishrag—but you feel good too, don't you?"

"You do," said the other aunt. "And with him it's not just a business. I've never been to one of his services that he didn't get all emotional himself. Every time, no matter who the departed is, he sits in the back and has himself a good cry. I think he enjoys his work as much as the customers do. And he is not afraid to spend money. He hires only the best cosmeticians and hair people."

"That's right. I've yet to go to one of his funerals where the family didn't say that the deceased looked better dead than when they were alive."

The reporter thanked them and went home and wrote her story. She was tempted to headline the piece "Better Dead Than Alive" but thought better of it and used "Funeral King Kind to His Mother" instead.

Ferris's Funeral

True enough, when Ferris Oatman died suddenly in 1952 of a massive stroke, Cecil Figgs was the first one called. Although it was seventy-five miles from Ferris's hometown, Cecil decided the service was to be held at the old Boutwell Auditorium in Birmingham, where the Oatmans had sung at so many sacred-music festivals. On the day of the funeral every gospel group in America showed up to pay their respects. Everyone said it was one of the biggest the gospel world had seen, by far. Besides all the Oatmans and the Varners and the devoted fans, and the gospel groups by the hundreds, so many buses rolled in that they did not have room to park them all. Even the mayor and the governor himself showed up.

Ferris's large white casket was covered in a spray of white carnations with black musical notes shaped out of little black pipe stems that Cecil had personally designed. As a tribute, Beatrice Woods, backed up by a stage full of twenty-six gospel groups, sang "There Will Be Peace in the Valley." By the time it was over, Minnie was so torn apart she had to be put in a wheelchair and rolled out of the auditorium. It was a fine funeral, just the kind that Cecil Figgs loved. Big and showy. Everything had gone well except for Ferris's brother Le Roy. He had been so riddled with guilt over leaving the group and joining up with the hillbilly band that he showed up drunk and kept yelling all through the service for Ferris to forgive him. Betty Raye was the only member of the family that would speak to him that day.

Hamm had driven Betty Raye over to Birmingham for her father's funeral and he used this opportunity to shake hands and introduce himself to as many people as he could. Before the service started, while working the crowd, Hamm had watched the governor out of the corner of his eye. He had never been this close to a real governor, a man of such power and importance. He noticed with fascination how everyone clambered around him, how all the men on his staff jumped when he said jump, and how the entire auditorium hung on his every word as he delivered his short eulogy.

Before the day was over and they went back home, two momentous things had happened.

1. Hamm had discovered exactly what office he wanted to run for.
2. Hamm had met Cecil Figgs.

Emmett Crimpler

Beatrice Woods had been the first to call Dorothy and tell her what had happened to Minnie. Dorothy immediately got on the phone and called Betty Raye, who had taken the baby and gone over to be by her mother's side.

Dorothy said, "Honey, I just heard. Is there anything you need or anything Doc and I can do to help?"

"Oh, thank you," Betty Raye said, "but I just don't know what anybody can do now. I'm so worried about her—she won't see the doctor, and it's been almost three weeks since she's eaten a thing."

"Oh, dear. Well, keep me posted and just know we are all sending you our love."

After Ferris's funeral Minnie had said to the boys and Uncle Floyd, "Take me home." They'd put her on the bus and drove her, Minnie crying all the way. When she got to the little house in Sand Mountain, she announced, after the boys helped her get in bed, "I can't go on without Ferris. I've come home to die."

The entire family was so upset that they called in her personal preacher, the Reverend W. W. Nails, and prayed over her. But it did no good. "It's no use, Reverend Nails," she said weakly. "Yea . . . though I have oft walked through the valley of the shadow of death, due to high blood pressure, diabetes, inflammatory arthritis, and gout, I always prayed myself out the other side. But now I don't want to come out the other side. I'm just gonna lay here reading Scriptures until I go."

The Reverend W. W. Nails came out of the bedroom and reported, "That woman has gone sick to the soul with grief and nothing can help her now except a miracle."

Everyone pleaded with her. Betty Raye cried and begged her to at least eat a cracker. But she would not. The house was flooded with flowers and letters from fans, although nothing helped. Chester the dummy came in and pleaded his little wooden heart out. "Oh, Momma Oatman," he said, "get up, we need you. What will happen to the Oatman family without you?"

"Little Chester," she said, "honey, I lost the will to sing when we lost your Uncle Ferris. . . . You take care of Floyd and be a good boy."

Floyd could not take it and ran out of the room and locked himself in the bathroom again.

Bervin and Vernon came in, not knowing what to say. She took their hands and said, "Boys, music is left my heart. You and the rest is going to have to be brave and go on without me."

There was great speculation in the entire gospel world. Articles appeared in the *Singing News* wondering if the death of Ferris meant the end of the Oatmans. Someone even called and asked if their bus was for sale.

But help was on the way in a six-foot five-inch package called Crimpler. A few days later a green Studebaker drove up to the house and he got out.

Vernon saw him first and exclaimed, "It's Emmett Crimpler!" The boys threw the door of her bedroom open and said, "Somebody's here to see you, Momma." Minnie was so weak at this point she could barely sit up. Emmett walked in and stood at the end of her bed and, not saying a word, he opened his mouth and sang to her "Sweeter as the Days Go By" in the most beautiful bass voice she had ever heard. After he finished he said, "Minnie, if you can hear me, I've come to tell you that I'm available to sing with you if you want me."

Minnie sat up a little more in the bed. Emmett Crimpler was considered, along with J. D. Sumner and James (Big Chief) Wetherington, as one of the great basses in gospel music. He told Minnie he had had a dream where Ferris had come to him and told him to leave the group he was with and to go over and take his place.

After an hour she said to Bervin, "Run down to the drive-in and get me an order of fries and a ham-and-cheese sandwich."

Emmett did not mention that he had wanted to leave the Harmony Boys for over a year but it did not matter. His arrival had been a miracle, said Reverend Nails.

Minnie had lost over thirty-five pounds—and the Oatmans were on the road once more!

A Man of the People

Hamm Sparks was not, as noted, particularly good-looking, not very tall, only about five foot nine, and of average build. He had brown hair, dark brown eyes, but he had something more. He had charm and was naturally seductive and he did not even know it. There is a certain kind of appeal about people who know *exactly* what they want and let you know up front what you can do to help them get it and what you can expect in return.

But the most seductive thing about Hamm, which made his overt, raw ambition oddly charming, was that, unlike most ambitious men, he meant what he said. There was not a covert or phony bone in his body. He believed that everyone was his friend and that he was his or her friend. He believed that he was the person to speak for them, to fight for the average person, and for those who were being pushed around. And he was a man looking for a fight. Dukes up, ready to take on the world. He was nice but tough and single-minded and came from a long line of proud people.

When the Tennessee Valley Authority had wanted to take over the family's land and build a dam to supply electricity for the entire region, his father had fought them as hard and as long as he could. But to no avail. In the end the TVA flooded the entire area and nothing of theirs was left. They even dug up his ancestors who had fought and died in the Civil War and moved them to another place. Unlike most of the others in Norris, Tennessee, who had made the best of a bad situation and had gone to work for them, his father had refused to accept a government job or to live in the company town they had created. He had moved his family around and had spent his remaining years painting the roofs of barns all over the South with SEE ROCK CITY. It was a rough job and paid little money and eventually killed him at age forty-one but by God he had not caved in to the federal government. And as far as his son was concerned, he died a hero. His father had told him over and over, "Son, if the federal government can steal one man's land and get away with it, democracy is in danger of failing. Once they sacrifice one for the so-called good of many, you've got socialism. Now, if they had asked me for my land, I might have given it up. I'm not dumb enough not to realize that electricity was a good thing but when they just come in and don't give me a choice—that's what wars are fought over. That's why I fought, to be able to be free from government. To own my own land. That's all we had. And the bastards took it away from us and don't ever forget it." This one event had changed his father and his family's life forever. It had forged Hamm into a fierce defender of individual rights. His own and everybody else's. In this one respect he was like a horse with blinders and could see neither left nor right. Now that the Depression and the war were over, he thought that Roosevelt's handout programs should be stopped. He had no sympathy for anyone who would not work if they could. He knew firsthand what a toll a handout exacts from the spirit and dignity of a man. The only time he had ever taken anything from the federal government was one terrible day after his father had died. His mother was sick and he had walked all the way to Knoxville to get help. Although they had not signed up for it, the woman at the welfare office had begrudgingly handed him a sack with navy beans, a piece of a side of beef, a few potatoes, flour, and sugar in it. He had taken it and cried all the way home, thinking about how his father would have felt. But they were just about starving to death so they ate it. Afterward he had gone outside and vomited it back up. Sick with shame. That day he'd vowed never to take another thing from the government as long as he lived.

He went to work the next day at age thirteen and saved enough money to buy a used twenty-two rifle and every day before and after school he hunted and brought home meat for the table. In summer he fished and planted vegetables, swapped catfish and turnips for eggs, sugar, and cornmeal. Swapped rabbits, deer, and squirrels for money to buy shoes and clothes for his sisters. It was understandable why Hamm was to grow up hard-pressed to understand why any man that could would not work. To have little patience with men who would not fight and die for what they believed. Just like his father and grandfather before him, within a few hours after Pearl Harbor he had joined the army as a foot soldier. Hamm's total belief that he was put here on this earth for a purpose and would certainly not die made him the perfect soldier and leader of ground troops. His expert ability with a gun and his lack of fear caused him to do things that another man would not have. In war, if you want to live, these feats are rewarded with medals and offers of advancement. But even then, between battles, some in the deepest jungles of the Pacific, he considered his future. When the army tapped him for officers training, he declined. He knew that after the war, just by sheer numbers, a lot more enlisted men would be voting than officers. He made a lot of good and loyal friends while he was in the army. When he returned home he worked part-time and almost finished college, but after he and Betty Raye married he dropped out and went to work full-time, trying to save a little more money for a house. But in 1952 the urge to go into politics was too great, so he quit his job at the Allis-Chalmers tractor company and ran for Pettis County commissioner of agriculture.

Even though it was just a county election, their rented house was in constant upheaval. Phones ringing, people in and out, and after he won, Betty Raye made him promise not to do that to her again. He held that office for a year and did a good job. But he was anxious to move on. What Hamm wanted next was to run for the office of state commissioner of agriculture. All Betty Raye wanted was for them to buy a small home of their own and have some security. At the moment they did not have anything but a two-year-old baby and the use of a car the county had provided and now they were about to lose that. The county job had paid very little and they'd had to move from one rental to another. But Hamm was not thinking about a house or security. He was thinking about his future. He knew that if he could just win this one election it would get his foot in the door of statewide politics. All those years of selling tractors and shaking hands had to add up to something. But he would be running against a strong incumbent. He needed campaign money and a car. He tried to get a bank loan but the bank turned him down. He knew only one person who might be able to lend him the money. He hated to do it but he called his old army buddy Rodney Tillman. Rodney had been a top Pontiac showroom salesman before the war and now owned a few used-car lots outside of Sedalia. When Hamm got him on the phone, Rodney listened a few minutes without comment, then said, "How much do you need, Hambo? If I haven't got it, I'll get it."

Hamm said, "I think I can do it with five hundred."

"I'll get you six."

Hamm said, "I'll pay you back."

"I know you will."

"I'll never forget this, buddy," said Hamm.

"Don't worry about it. You just go out and win the damn thing."

Once again they moved and again Betty Raye's home life was turned upside down. As soon as he announced, the house was filled with men coming and going, day and night. When she went to bed there were men in her living room. She slept, got up, got dressed, got the baby changed, and by breakfast there were already four or five men sitting at the kitchen table, filling up the place with cigar smoke. She hardly ever saw Hamm alone. If he was not traveling, he was always with his pack of cronies. The house was in a constant mess and she spent most of her time cleaning up after them. There was only one bathroom, so all day long men were traipsing through her bedroom. And if she went into the bathroom she could never be sure that some man would not walk in on her. She tried her best but when she woke up with a strange man she had never seen before walking through her bedroom, that was the last straw. Hamm never understood why she was so upset. It did not bother him at all to have people around him twenty-four hours a day. In fact, he thrived on it. It seemed to energize him. This constant and relentless lack of privacy, however, was making a nervous wreck out of Betty Raye. She could not even find a place to sit down and cry by herself. Six long months later, it was all over: between the radio ads, the posters, and Hamm stumping all over the farm areas, he'd won. He was now state commissioner of agriculture.

Betty Raye was so glad when it was final. At last she could have her husband all to herself and they could get back to a normal life again.

Hamm and Rodney

The phone rang in the office of the Tillman and Reid used-car lot and Rodney Tillman picked it up. "Hello?"

A man's voice said, "Hey, sport, what are you doing?"

It was his friend Hamm Sparks. Rodney said, "Right now I'm sitting here trying to figure out if I should kill my ex-brother-in-law or not."

Hamm laughed. "What's he done now?"

"We got the best looking little forty-nine Chevy in here and he went out and started fooling around with the odometer after I told him not to and the damned idiot just put an extra two hundred miles on the thing."

"Why don't you just run it back the other way like you always do?"

"I would if I could, Hambo," he said, glaring at his ex-brother-in-law, who'd just passed by, "but the damned thing's stuck. What are you doing?"

"I'm gonna be working in your area today. Why don't you come take a ride with me this afternoon, keep me company."

Rodney looked through the glass window at the lot, full of dusty cars and empty of customers. "Might as well."

As they rode out to the farms Hamm was checking on that day, Rodney pulled his pint out of his back pocket and took a swig. "I tell you, son, some days I wish I had just stayed and married that little Japanese gal; this alimony is about to kill me. You sure lucked out with Betty Raye. Now, that's a sweet woman."

"Yes, she is," said Hamm.

While he stopped at the farms on his list, Rodney sat in the car scrunched up in the front seat and watched Hamm trudging out in the fields, walking around in barnyards and pigsties, talking to each farmer, patting them on the back, saying whatever agriculture people say to each other, and swigged from his pint. After about the fifth farm Rodney asked, "How many more places do you have to go to today?"

"Just six more."

"Well, can we stop somewhere? I need to eat something."

"Oh sure, there's a place right up the road."

Right up the road turned out to be twenty-three miles.

As they came out of the small roadside filling station and country store with sausage biscuits, cheese crackers, and Cokes, Hamm headed back to the car.

"Can we eat outside?" Rodney said. "I hate to say it, buddy, but you're beginning to smell like a barnyard. God knows what you've been stepping in, and those hog-snout marks on your pants ain't all that appetizing, either."

Hamm looked down at his pants and laughed. "Yeah, I see what you mean. Sorry, it's just part of the job."

They walked over to a wooden bench set up beside a creek behind the store and sat down. Rodney handed Hamm his Coke. "Drink some of this for me, will you." Hamm took a swig and handed it back and Rodney filled it back up to the top with whiskey, took a drink, and said, "Now, that's a Coke. So, Hambo, is this what you do every day? Stomp around in barnyards?"

"Just about."

Rodney examined the sausage biscuit in his hand with skepticism but bit into it anyway. "Why you ever wanted this job in the first place is a mystery to me. I know you aren't making any money."

Hamm agreed, "No, it's sure not the money. But somebody has to give these folks a hand, trying to scratch out a living with nothing but these little piecrust roads between them and the market. Most of them are just hanging on by a thread as it is." Hamm bit into a cheese cracker with peanut butter in the middle and said, "When it rains, they can't get out and the government won't fix the roads. They throw money at the big cities and build fancy buildings and all those overpasses and underpasses and in the meantime the small farmer is getting ignored. I'll tell you . . . it makes me mad to see good, hardworking, tax-paying people being kicked around like that. I watched my daddy get kicked around like that, so I know how it feels. . . . But I can't do much. Just give them a little encouragement."

"Well, that's life, Hambo. The rich get richer and the poor get poorer, bless their pea-pickin' little hearts. The only difference between you and me and the rich is they've got money and we don't."

Hamm said, "Naw, Rodney, I don't think it's just the money—they are different from us. I was around a few of those rich people once and found that out myself."

"When was this?"

"After the war, when I was in school, I met a few of those rich college boys while I was waiting tables. I used to joke around with them every once in a while. I wasn't friends with them or nothing like that, but this one kid from Minneapolis must have thought I was unique or something and invited me to go home with him one weekend."

"Wait a minute. You? Unique?"

Hamm smiled. "Yeah, well, they thought I had a funny accent and I laid it on a bit, you know, played the hayseed for them. So anyhow, I go home with him and we pull up to this big, huge three-story deal where he lives. I never saw anything like that in my life, the whole damn backyard is a lake."

"What lake was it?"

"It was *their* lake. I'm telling you, these people were rich, and the kid tells me it's their summerhouse. I said, Where do you live in the winter, Buckingham damn Palace? Anyhow, I never felt so out of place in my life. That family of his was nothing but a bunch of cold fish. I don't even think they liked each other and they treated me like I was something that just dropped out of a tree. And I'll tell you something: after that weekend, I'd take any one of those farmers over them any day of the week. I don't want a thing they have. They can keep all their big houses, the servants, the cars, I don't need them." Then his voice trailed off. He looked down at the little stream with a faraway look in his eyes and said quietly, "But they did have this boat. One day his old man took us all out on the lake in it and oh, man alive, that was the prettiest thing you ever saw . . . all white, with shiny wood inside." He shook his head. "To tell you the truth, sport, I'd cut off my right arm for a boat like that."

Rodney suddenly felt sorry for him. He tried to cheer him up. "You know what you need, Hambo? You need to come up to St. Louis with me, play a little poker, we've got some good games up there, and fool around a little. Have some fun for a change, what do you say?"

"Wish I could but I just don't have the time to spare," Hamm said, getting up to leave.

"Well, you know what I always say . . . if you can't get anywhere in this world, you might as well have fun while you aren't getting there."

Up in a Tree

After Aunt Elner lost her husband, Will, she had wanted to stay on the farm but Norma was worried about her living out in the country all by herself and insisted she move to town. She wanted her close so she could keep an eye on her and she was not going to rest until she did. So Aunt Elner sold the farm and Norma and Macky found her a house a couple of blocks from them. It was a small house, with a bedroom, kitchen, living room, and a nice front porch; but the thing Aunt Elner liked right away was the big fig tree in the backyard. She brought a few of her favorite chickens and her cat Sonny and moved in, but Norma still checked on her day and night. Aunt Elner said, "You'd think two blocks was twenty miles the way you carry on. I might as well have stayed out on the farm."

"Yes, but at least I know we can get to you in a few minutes if anything happens."

"Honey, if I die here or out on the farm, getting to me faster is not going to make much difference."

"Maybe not to you but I'll feel better knowing you're not lying around in the yard dead, with the chickens pecking at you."

Aunt Elner laughed. "It would not bother me. I've eaten enough of them in my day." Aunt Elner liked to tease her but promised her she would take good care of herself. Even though Elner said and meant it, she was still capable of upsetting Norma from time to time. Just this morning there had been a incident, and Norma was still going on and on about it. "You shouldn't even be climbing stairs at your age, much less a ten-foot ladder. I have never been so close to fainting in my life. I came out into the yard and looked up and there you were just hanging in the top of the tree."

"I wasn't hanging, I was sitting."

"Well, sitting or hanging, what if I had not come over? You've *got* to be more careful. What if I'd found you dead on the ground?"

"Oh, Norma, I've picked fruit all my life and I'm not dead yet. Besides, it's that Griggs dog's fault. He's the one that knocked the ladder down chasing after poor Sonny. Go fuss at him."

"I don't care whose fault it was, promise me you will not get on that ladder again. Let Macky do it or call next door and get Merle."

"All right."

"You are not as young as you used to be, you know."

Later that night, Aunt Elner called. "Norma, let me ask you this."

"What?"

"Who *is* younger than they used to be? I don't know anybody; even those that get face-lifts are still just as old as they were. Even if you went into a different time zone you'd still be the same age, wouldn't you?"

Norma had to admit she was right but added, "That's not the point; the point is you need to be more careful."

"The point is that Griggs dog ought to stay out of my yard and quit chasing my cat."

"Aunt Elner."

"I know, a promise is a promise."

But a new day is a new day. The next morning around ten, when Linda was at school, the phone rang. Norma picked up.

"Norma? I have a question for you," said Aunt Elner.

"Hold on, let me turn off my beans."

"What kind of beans are you making?"

"String beans. I just threw in a handful so Macky would have something green with his lunch. Why?"

"I just wondered. . . . What's he getting?"

"Salmon croquettes, sliced tomatoes, corn, and string beans."

"What kind of bread?"

"Cornbread. I had a few slices left over. Why?"

"Just wondered."

"Did you have a question for me?"

"Yes, I did."

"What was it?"

"Wait a minute . . . let me think."

"What was it about?"

"I know. Norma, do I have any insurance?"

"What kind of insurance?"

"Any kind."

"Uncle Will had his Mason's policy, I think. Why?"

"Well, some lady came to the door and wanted to know and I didn't know what to tell her so I told her she'd have to ask you."

"What woman?"

"Some woman. I don't know who she was . . . she left her card. Do you want me to go and get it?"

"Yes."

There was a loud clack when Aunt Elner put the phone down on the table. A few minutes later she came back on the line.

"Her name is June Garza. Do you know her?"

"No, what company is she with?"

"Aetna . . . Insurance . . . so I told her that my niece and her husband handle all that for me."

"Good, what did she say?"

"She said she wanted to know where you lived so she could ask you about it."

"Good Lord, you didn't tell her, did you?"

"Well, I had to. She asked me."

"How long ago . . . ?"

"Just a little while ago—"

"Oh Lord . . ."

"She's real nice. She has on a green suit and—"

"Aunt Elner, let me call you back."

"Okay . . . I just wanted you to be on the lookout."

"I'll call you back." Norma put down the phone and ran into the living room and looked up and down the street and shut the front door and closed her blinds and pulled the curtains. She went back to the kitchen and closed those blinds and she hid down under the wall phone, reached up, and dialed Macky's number. When he picked up she whispered, "Macky . . . when you come home, don't come in the front door, come up the alley and come in the back. And knock three times so I'll know it's you."

"What?"

"Aunt Elner gave some insurance woman our address and she's headed over here . . . and I don't want to have to deal with her."

"You don't have to deal with her—just go to the door and tell her you don't need any insurance."

"I'm not going to be rude to her, for God's sake."

"That's not being rude."

"You can't just say no, until you let them go through their sales things. You don't know why that poor woman is having to work . . . she might have children to support. You might be able to break her heart but I can't—"

"Norma, you are not going to break her heart. She's an insurance salesman."

"She's probably married to some alcoholic and . . . shhh." There was a knock at the front door. "Oh my God, she's here . . . be quiet!" She pulled the phone into the pantry and hid.

"Norma, just go to the door and tell her thank you very much but we don't need any insurance. If you don't go now, she'll just come back. You don't want to get her hopes up . . . that's even worse. You have to learn to say no. You don't have to be rude. Go on now, get it over with."

The woman at the door continued to knock. She was not going away.

"Oh, Macky, I could just kill you."

Norma put the phone down, stood there for a moment, screwed her courage to the wall, took a deep breath, and headed for the door.

About forty-five minutes later the bell over the hardware store door rang and a lady of about forty, wearing a green suit and carrying a brown attaché case walked in. She approached Macky with a pleasant smile. "Mr. Warren?"

Macky said, "Yes, ma'am, what can I do for you?"

"Mr. Warren, I'm June Garza from Aetna Insurance and your wife said that you might be interested in hearing about our new three-and-one policy . . . and I wondered if now might be a convenient time?" The phone rang. "I can come back after lunch if you like. . . ."

Macky was caught. "Uh, well . . . excuse me, Mrs. Garza . . . let me get that." He picked up the phone. Norma was on the other end.

"Macky, is she there yet?"

Macky smiled back at Mrs. Garza. "That's right."

"Now, before you get mad at me, I just wanted you to know her husband is a diabetic and lost his left leg and is probably going to lose the other one somewhere down the line."

"Yes, well, thank you very much."

Norma continued. "And her mother-in-law has had three strokes and is on very expensive high-blood-pressure medicine. And one of the reasons she has to work today is because they didn't have insurance."

"All righty, anything else?" He pretended to be writing down a list of things.

"I know you're mad at me . . . but—"

Macky tried to sound pleasant. "That's correct."

"Don't take it out on her. Just come on home and take a gun and kill me, shoot me in the head, put me out of my misery."

"Thank you, I'll be sure and do that. Good-bye, Mrs. Mud."

Macky wound up buying two home-owner policies, one for them and one for Aunt Elner.

Small-Town Living, February 1953

If a stranger walked down the street past the barbershop in Elmwood Springs on Saturday afternoon and glanced in, he would see a group of middle-aged, gray-haired men sitting around chewing the fat. But if you were one of the men inside you would see six friends you had grown up with, not old men. Doc didn't see the wrinkles on Glenn Warren's face or notice that his neck had turned red and sagged with age or the wide girth straining his suspenders to the breaking point. He saw a skinny boy of seven with lively eyes. They were fixed in one another's eyes as the boys they used to be. When Doc looked at sixty-eight-year-old Merle he saw the blond boy of ten he used to go swimming with. And to all of them, the balding man in the short sleeves with the little potbelly was still the boy who scored the winning touchdown that won the county championship. There wasn't a secret among them. They knew one another's families as well as they knew one another. Their wives, now plump gray matrons in comfortable shoes, they still saw as the pretty dimpled girls of eight or twelve that they had once had crushes on. Since they'd all grown up together, they'd never had to wonder who they were; it was clearly reflected in each other's eyes. They never questioned friendship; it was just there, like it had been when they were children. They had all been at one another's weddings. They'd shared in all the sadness and happiness of one another's lives. It would never occur to them to be lonely. They would never know what it was like to be without friends. They would never have to wander from town to town, looking for a place to be; they had always had a place to come home to, a place where they belonged and where they were welcome. None of these men would ever be rich but they would never be cold or go hungry or be without a friend. They knew if one died the others would quietly step in and their children would be raised and their wives would be cared for; it was unspoken. They had a bond. Small-town people usually take these things for granted. As a certain young man named Bobby Smith was to find out for himself that year.

On January 3 Dwight D. Eisenhower was sworn in as the president of the United States and Tot Whooten was not happy about it. She said, "Just my luck. The first time I take the trouble to vote and my man loses." On January 21, Neighbor Dorothy and Mother Smith traveled all the way up to Kansas City to welcome Harry and Bess Truman back home to Missouri. They stood in the crowd at the station along with ten thousand other people and waited for the train. It was an hour late but they were there as Harry and Bess arrived and the American Legion Band played the "Missouri Waltz." It was hard to realize that Harry would no longer be in the White House but, as they say, time marches on. Yet, even though other things in the world may have changed, *The Neighbor Dorothy Show* remained the same. She still had her same loyal audience, who would no more think of missing her show than not having their first cup of coffee in the morning.

February 19 was a cold, wet, windy day in Elmwood Springs. Dorothy had just finished her last Golden Flake Flour commercial and was rather circumspect and subdued. As the show was ending she said, "You know, so many of you have written in over the years and asked me what is the best thing to do for a blue mood . . . and asked if I have ever been in a blue mood, and yes, you can be sure I have. I can only tell what helps me and that is baking. I can't tell you how many cakes I have baked over the years, how many cups of flour I have sifted, how many cake pans I have greased, all because there is something about baking a cake that gets me out of a mood, and so I'll just pass that on for what it's worth. Speaking of that, you all know I've been a little blue lately, missing my children, but I feel so much better today and I'd like to share a letter with you we got from Bobby yesterday . . .

"Dear Mother,

"Since you gave out my address over the radio, you would not believe how many cards and letters and other good stuff has come my way. Please thank them all for me and the rest of the guys. A lot of these guys don't get mail and they are getting a big kick out of reading mine and helping me eat all the cookies, fudge, and cakes that have made it all the way to Korea. Most of the guys in my company are from big cities. I guess it took sending me all the way over here to really appreciate my hometown. So love to Dad and slam the screen door for me will you, so your listeners won't be too lonesome for me.

"Love, your son,
"Pfc. Bobby Smith

"And I also want to thank you. You all have been so sweet to write and send him things. You know I don't like to get sentimental but I will say this: we all know he was a handful and I think of all the times I yelled at him to sit still, to stop running, not to slam the door, but today I'd give a million dollars if I could hear him slam that door or see a cake where he had run a finger around the bottom. Oh, if we could only stop time and speaking of time . . . I can see by the old clock on the wall that it's time to go. I can't wait until tomorrow, when we can visit with each other again . . . you mean so much to us . . . each and every one of you. This is Neighbor Dorothy with Mother Smith on the organ . . . saying . . . have a nice day."

To Dorothy's great disappointment, the very day Bobby had turned eighteen Monroe had driven him over to Poplar Bluff and he had joined the army and left school. It had come as a surprise to everyone but there was nothing they could do. The night before he left Jimmy had come into Bobby's room and handed him his watch. "I want you to wear this for me while you're gone. I'd be going if I could."

Bobby was touched and put it on. "Thanks, Jimmy, I'll take good care of it."

"Well, I won't get a chance to see you in the morning, so good luck to you over there, buddy."

"He's just going to training camp," said Doc to Dorothy, trying not to make a big deal out of it, but the next day when he looked up and saw the 10:45 bus drive by the drugstore with his son on it, he wondered if he would ever see him again.

As soon as he finished dispensing Mrs. Whatley's thyroid pills, he stepped out in the back alley for a moment and leaned against the building. The sun was shining and he could hear the high school band practicing over at the football field just as if it were another ordinary fall day.

Winter Wonderland, March 1953

From the time Bobby had arrived in Korea he'd felt as if he were trapped inside of the big display he used to see in the window at the Morgan Brothers department store every Christmas. Only in this winter wonderland the things moving around were ugly, brown, grinding tanks, men with machine guns, and medics carrying stretchers full of wounded, dead, or dying soldiers. Bloodstains littered the white snow, as did an arm or blown-off leg, as well as bodies that lay twenty feet away. Trees that had been shot into nothing except shattered sticks were lying on the ground. He vowed that if he ever got out of there alive he never wanted to see snow again.

But with each hour that passed the chances of him getting out of there alive grew less likely. His company was surrounded on all sides.

It had happened overnight. They heard the North Korean tanks to the south and more moving in from the north. As it was, there were only fourteen men left. They had lost all communications a few days ago and were huddled together in a round ditch that they had dug last night. They were supposed to have been relieved a week ago by another company but they had been pushed back so far behind the lines, they couldn't be sure they would be found. In the frantic scramble they had lost most of their K rations and had no idea where they were or how far away the other Americans were.

Everything was cold and white. They couldn't see more than a foot in front of them. When it wasn't snowing, a white misty ground fog came in. It was such a strange, surreal war, as if it were being fought in cotton. The sound of machine-gun fire was all around them, soft and muffled, but still they knew it was deadly. So strange to be so terrified with the whole world gone soft and white or to be covered with sweat in the middle of a snowstorm. They could occasionally hear voices calling out in the distance, to them or to one another, they didn't know. Most of these men, including Bobby, had grown up in movie theaters watching World War II movies, and the shrill, high-pitched, Oriental language that sounded just like Japanese struck a twelve-year-old's fear in their hearts. But this was no movie. And their sergeant was not John Wayne. He was a twenty-two-year-old kid from Akron, Ohio, who had just gotten married a year ago. Soon they had run out of everything, food, ammunition, and any options. They could not signal where they were or they would be ambushed. They were trapped. Dead if they moved, dead if they didn't.

Then, at about one o'clock that afternoon, Bobby suddenly said to the man beside him, "The hell with this. I'm going to go and find them." He handed the man his gun and crawled over the top of the ditch and disappeared. He knew he could not stand up without getting his head shot off, so he crawled. As he slowly inched forward in the snow he suddenly remembered something Jimmy had told him at the Trolley Car Diner years ago, right before the bubble gum contest: "Don't look to your right. Don't look to your left. Concentrate. Remain calm, stay the course." He kept repeating it over and over in his mind. Thinking about that day, thinking about the bubble he blew, thinking about the applause. . . . *Don't get rattled. Concentrate. Nice and easy all the way.*

While he continued to move forward inch by inch, moving for his life and the life of the other men on the line, thousands of miles away in Elmwood Springs, the high school senior class was busy with such benign matters as who to vote for in "Who's Who," what color stone they wanted in the senior ring, and who they were going to ask to the prom. That afternoon his best friend, Monroe, would be sitting in the drugstore drinking cherry Cokes with his girlfriend, Peggy, and asking Doc if he had heard from him.

Twenty-eight hours later he had crawled within six feet of a dead body and twenty feet past a North Korean machine-gun nest, where three soldiers were sleeping. But he never saw any of them. After he made it up the hill, he stood up and ran and fell and ran again until someone heard him yelling at the top of his lungs, "Hi-yo, Silver, away!" The Americans, nervous and quick to shoot at anything that moved, knew at once that this was no Korean and came out and found him. He was half out of his mind and had no idea why he had been yelling, but it saved his life.

By the time he was able to lead that company to his outfit, six of the men had already frozen to death but they were able to save the rest. He refused a medal and never told anyone what he had done. As he explained to the major, "There was nothing brave about it. I was just too scared to stay there and die."

A Close Call

Bobby came out of the army happy to be home but a very different man from the one who had left. He was quiet and introspective and seemed to have lost his old zest for life. Although his parents did not say anything, they were worried. He did not seem to have any desire to date or go out with his old friends. While he was gone Monroe had married Peggy and was working for her father down at the tire store. They had gone fishing and bowling a few times but he mostly just sat around the house or went down to the diner and talked to Jimmy.

After a few months Dorothy became very concerned. She began to wonder if he would ever go back to being his old self or be able to find a girl he liked. She thought if he just found a nice girl and fell in love, maybe it would help him. She did not know it, but her son had fallen hopelessly in love and he was not over it yet. Maybe it was because he had seen too many movies, but Bobby had always been wildly imaginative and full of idealistic visions of knights in shining armor, damsels in distress, and living happily ever after. He had had his little crushes on girls for years but when he was seventeen he had fallen so completely and painfully head over heels in love that it had almost killed him. It had consumed him like a raging fire. She had been the first thing on his mind when he awoke and the last thing he thought about before he went to sleep and dreamed about her. It had not been just an infatuation. This was a real overwhelming passion, an obsession, and he had been almost sick with it. So in love with her that at times it hurt to breathe. When she'd smiled at him or spoke to him in the most casual way, he had lived off of it for a week. He was a gangly, awkward, pimply-faced boy and she was a grown, mature woman of twenty-eight. He could not tell anyone, not even Monroe, about how he felt, so he suffered in silence. He was sent flying into the heights of ecstasy and thrown down into the depths of hell by her slightest move, sometimes in the same day.

Miss Anne Hatcher, the drama teacher with the beautiful voice and soft brown eyes . . . Miss Anne Hatcher, who had broken his heart when at the start of his junior year she became engaged to Hugh Sparrow, the high school civics teacher. Sparrow was an older widower with two children. Bobby had been a movie usher that year and they had come to the theater a couple of times and he had walked the two of them down the aisle to their seats. He hated the way the paunchy, balding man had walked in front of her and it almost made him sick to his stomach when he saw him put his arm around the back of her seat like he owned her. He hated his guts. It was clear to him that Sparrow had no idea how wonderful she was. How special. He could not possibly love and appreciate her like Bobby did. All Sparrow wanted was a mother for his children. Bobby fantasized about going over to her house, declaring his love, and asking her to marry him. He fantasized about challenging the civics teacher to a duel and killing him. But he did neither. Instead, the day he was eighteen he joined the army. Anything other than being around for their wedding. He had thought about her all through the war. And now that he was home, what had been a raging, burning love was a dull ache in the pit of his stomach whenever he saw her or heard someone speak her name.

He had come back not feeling much enthusiasm about anything. He was feeling the same way he used to feel when he and Monroe would stumble out of the Elmwood Theater each Saturday, bleary-eyed from sitting through four hours of movies and cartoons. Compared to the Technicolor images they had just seen, the world outside the theater had always looked so gray and dingy. Real life had no beautiful background music, and all the people in town had seemed so dull and bland.

It seemed as if all the magic had gone out of the world and he was bored and restless.

But then one night, Monroe and his wife, Peggy, took Bobby with them to the Polar Bear Tastee-Freez drive-in and Wanda Ricketts, wearing a short skirt with fringe, skated up to the car and took their order and suddenly a light came back into Bobby's eyes. "Who's that?" he asked as she skated away. Peggy told him the Ricketts family had moved to town a few years ago and added, "I hear she's a little fast."

"Really?" said Bobby, his curiosity piqued even further. As it turned out, Wanda was quite the little femme fatale of the Elmwood Springs high school set. A few boys already had WANDA tattooed on their arms, including the Dockrill boy, who was going to be a preacher.

She had been dating three or four different boys in town but they were no match for Bobby, who had grown into a good-looking young man. Pretty soon he and Miss Wanda Ricketts were a hot-and-heavy item and his old enthusiasm started coming back, along with his imagination. As usual, Bobby started to romanticize Wanda and to see things that were not there. He spent a dazzled two months convinced she looked exactly like Marilyn Monroe, which could not have been further from the truth. Other than their dyed blond hair and being female, the similarity ended. When he brought her home for dinner the first time, after she had stuck her chewing gum on the side of her plate, she announced, "Me and my family are big wrestling fans. Me and Momma think Gorgeous George is cute enough to eat. Momma says he can put his shoes under her bed anytime."

"Oh, really?" said Dorothy pleasantly, but secretly horrified. Doc and Mother Smith had just stared at their plates but Bobby, oblivious to the sudden lull in the dinner conversation, continued to stare at her with a goofy look on his face. Needless to say, Dorothy had not been favorably impressed with Wanda, but she never said a word against her.

One day Bobby was down at the Trolley Car Diner going on and on about how beautiful Wanda was and asked Jimmy what he thought about the idea of them getting married. Jimmy had not said anything before but since he had been asked he said, "Frankly, I think it would be the biggest mistake you ever made. Your parents aren't going to say anything but I don't want to see you mess up your entire life just because some little carhop has you all whipped around and not thinking straight. If that girl were to come up pregnant, you're stuck with her. Think about what you're doing, buddy, before it's too late."

Just then Ed the barber came in for a chili dog and sat down. Before Jimmy went over he said quietly, "I'm telling you, that girl is not for you. You can do better than that."

Bobby felt like someone had just thrown cold water in his face. But Jimmy was right, of course. The rose-colored glasses started clearing up a little and he started noticing Wanda's black roots and how she began to look less and less like Marilyn Monroe. He suddenly took a closer look at the Ricketts family, the mother, an older version of Wanda with wrinkles and the same dyed blond hair and penciled-in eyebrows, who at fifty still wore short shorts and a halter top; the father, with the dirty fingernails and the collection of *Over Sexteen* magazines he kept trying to show Bobby; and the rest of the strangely misshapen Ricketts brothers and sisters . . . and the spell was broken. The thought of spending the holidays with the Rickettses for the rest of his life finally did the trick. Earlier, Mother Smith had offered her opinion of the entire Ricketts family to Dorothy quite succinctly. "Common, honey, just plain common." But when Bobby told his mother he had broken up with Wanda she did not ask why. All she said was, "Well, I'm sure you know best, dear."

When he asked Monroe what he thought he said, "I'm glad to hear it. Peggy and I hadn't wanted to say anything but that girl was as dumb as a post."

Several months later, Wanda, clearly not heartbroken over breaking up with Bobby, ran off and married the twenty-five-year-old manager of the Polar Bear drive-in.

Two weeks later, the next time Macky saw Bobby at the barbershop he said, "Had yourself a kind of a close call there, didn't you?"

It was a small town.

Tot Whooten Strikes Again

The Friday after Macky had run into Bobby, he was busy searching through his stock for a fifteen-foot extension cord for Old Man Henderson when the phone rang. He said, "Let me get this," and went back and picked up. "Hardware."

It was Norma on the other end. "Macky."

"Hi, honey. Can I call you back? I've got a customer."

"I'll hold on."

"Okay."

He put the phone down and returned to the old man standing in the aisle pulling out all the cords, trying to read the packages.

Macky said, "Are you sure you need fifteen feet?"

The old man said, "Yeah or I might use twenty. . . . Do you have that?"

"What's it for?"

"I want to put my television set out on the porch so I can see the ball game."

"Don't you have a plug on the porch?"

"Well, if I did I wouldn't need an extension cord, would I?"

Macky searched through the cords. "Here's a twenty-five."

Mr. Henderson scowled at him. "How much more is it by the foot?"

"Don't worry. I'll just charge you for a fifteen-foot. I thought I had them in stock but I guess I sold them."

"Well, I guess I'd rather it be too long than too short."

"Do you think St. Louis has a chance this year?" asked Macky.

"They might . . . if everybody else was to suddenly drop dead."

Macky pulled out a paper bag.

"I don't need a sack," Mr. Henderson said.

"All right, well, you have a good day now."

The old man slammed the door shut too hard and the bell on the door rang in Macky's ears. Macky started putting the cords back up on the hooks, trying to figure out just how old Old Man Henderson was. He had been a friend of his grandfather's, so that would make him at least in his early eighties. Then Macky remembered that Norma was holding on. He went back and took the phone.

"Honey, are you still there?"

"Yes . . . I am."

"I'm sorry. What's up?"

Norma sounded extremely controlled. After a pregnant pause she said, "I just had my hair done."

Macky sat down on the stool behind the counter. Today was her appointment with Tot Whooten. He knew what was coming.

"Do not say one word to me, Macky, I do not want to hear one word about my hair. If you're going to come home and say anything, just don't come home."

"I'm not going to say anything. What did she do this time?"

"I'm upset enough as it is without you saying something."

"Norma! I haven't said a word. I haven't even *seen* you."

"Well, I want you to promise me . . . give me your word . . . you won't say anything or I'm just going to check into the Howard Johnson's motel, and that's all there is to it."

"All right, Norma, calm down."

"I mean it now."

"I won't say a word."

"I am putting your lunch on the table . . . and I am just going to stay in the bedroom if you're going to make some smart remark."

"*Norma,* I won't say anything, O.K.? Just give me a hint. What did you have done?"

There was a long silence. "We tried something new."

"And?"

There was a longer silence. "It didn't work out."

Macky rolled his eyes. "Oh God."

"See! There you go. I knew it, just don't come home if you're going to have that attitude—"

"I don't have an attitude. I just said, Oh God, that's all."

"Yes . . . but it's *how* you said it. I know you're sitting there rolling your eyes, so if you *do* come home, I do not want you to even look at my hair."

"Norma, where am I supposed to look? Your face is attached to your head. Do you want me to talk to your knees?"

"See, there you go again. You just can't resist trying to be funny. I have had a serious hair mishap and I need your support. I don't need you to make me feel worse than I do!"

"All right. I'm sorry but at least tell me what you two were *trying* to do."

"A body wave."

"A body wave?"

"Yes, like a permanent only lighter. It was supposed to be a light body wave. . . ."

"What happened?"

"We don't know, all we know is it wasn't light."

"Well, honey, don't worry about it. It will grow out . . . it did the last time. . . ."

"It doesn't have to grow out," she said.

"Why?"

"Because if you must know, if it's *so* important to you to know . . . she cut it off."

"Oh Jesus."

"See! I can't tell you a thing without you having a negative attitude—you ask me to tell you, then you say something smart."

"O.K., O.K. . . . I'm sorry. But anyway, I'll bet it looks great." He held off. "How short is it?"

There was no answer on the other end.

"It can't be all that short, can it?"

"It's short."

"How short?"

"It's an Italian boy cut."

"What?"

"It's called an Italian boy cut."

"Oh Jesus . . ."

"That's it! Get your own lunch. I'm going to the motel."

"Oh, for God's sake, Norma, you're not going to any motel. I'll be home in a little while."

Macky had been home for ten minutes but Norma would not come out of the bedroom. Finally, after much coaxing, she stood in the doorway. He looked at her but did not react.

"*Well,* don't you have anything to say? I know you're just dying to say something—get it over with, just go ahead."

"Well . . . it's short all right."

Norma burst into tears. "I'm ruined . . . I look awful . . . it's horrible . . . I just want to die. I was supposed to look like Audrey Hepburn. . . . It looked cute in the picture."

"Oh, honey, honey, stop it. It looks cute."

"No, it doesn't. You're just saying that to make me feel better."

"No, I'm not. . . . It's cute. Really."

Later that night, just before Norma was about to fall asleep, Macky turned over and said, "Honey, I just wanted you to know one thing. . . ."

"What."

"You are the sexiest Italian boy I ever slept with."

There was a pause. Then Norma patted his hand. "Muchos gracias, senior."

Miss Henderson

Bobby had finished his high school equivalency test in the army and he had been home about four months when he finally decided that he would go to college after all and try to get a degree in something. In what he did not know. At one time Doc had hoped he would follow in his footsteps and become a pharmacist but, considering how bad Bobby was at math and chemistry, that was obviously out. He guessed maybe he would take business administration but he still was not sure about it. A week before he was to leave he was out on the porch thinking about it when he looked up and saw old Miss Henderson, his sixth-grade teacher, home from her summer vacation, slowly coming up the front steps of the house. "Hello, Robert," she said, a little winded. "Your mother told me you were home."

He jumped up, surprisingly happy to see her. "Hello, Miss Henderson, how are you?" he said and pulled out a chair for her to sit down.

"Just fine," she said, sitting down. She said, "You're headed off to college, is that right?"

"Yes, ma'am, Missouri State."

She started to rummage around in her purse, looking for something. "I wanted to stop by before you left and give you a little present I had for you. I had hoped to give it to you when you graduated from high school but you had already left for the army so I thought I'd bring it to you now."

She handed Bobby a slightly frayed package that had clearly been wrapped for a long time. Bobby was thoroughly surprised. "Thank you, Miss Henderson." As he was unwrapping it, she said, "You know, Bobby, you may not have known it, but you were always one of my favorite pupils."

"Me?" he said. "You're kidding."

Inside was a beautiful leather miniature map of the world with a written note attached that said *Yours for the taking. Good luck in all you do. Miss Henderson.*

Bobby was overwhelmed. "I don't know what to say, Miss Henderson, except thank you."

"You're welcome."

"You know, Miss Henderson, I always thought I must have been the dumbest one in your class."

She smiled. "Well, you may not have made the best grades and you were not the easiest boy to keep quiet, but you had that one thing most of the others didn't—you had a curious mind. And a curious mind is what we teachers look for."

Bobby, who had been caught so off guard, suddenly remembered his manners. "Oh, sorry, Miss Henderson—can I get you some iced tea or anything to drink?"

"No, I can't stay. But your mother also tells me you are struggling a little trying to decide what you are going to major in, is that right?"

"Yes, ma'am. I just hope I don't flunk out."

She nodded. "Having had you as my student for two years and knowing you as well as I do, all I can advise is for you to be sure to study something that you really like, Bobby, a subject that can hold your interest—and if you do, I know you will do just fine."

"Thank you, Miss Henderson," he said as she walked back down the stairs, "and thank you for the map."

He thought about what she said, but he was interested in everything in the world and it was still hard to pin down to one thing. He still had not made up his mind until he arrived on campus and reread all the options available. Everyone was surprised when he called home and announced what he had chosen. The only person who was not surprised at the news when she heard it was Miss Henderson. As far as she was concerned, American history was perfect for Bobby.

However, in the romance department, many times when a person does not know what is bad for them, they often do not know what is good for them, either. Bobby started dating Lois Scott, an English major, in his sophomore year after more or less playing the field. He had met her through a friend and, as it turned out, she was from Poplar Bluff and they had a lot of friends in common. Her mother had even been to his house to see his mother's radio show and had exchanged letters with her. On their first date Lois took him out on the tennis court and beat the socks off him. She was smart, attractive, had a great sense of humor, beautiful red hair, and *most* important, she was crazy about him.

The Christmas holidays of 1955 came rolling around and on the morning of December 23 a proud Macky Warren stood outside the hardware store and waved at his daughter, Linda, as she marched by with Dixie Cahill and sixteen other little girls in costumes, all wearing jingle bells, headed over to be on Dorothy's Christmas show. Norma and Aunt Elner were already sitting in the audience, waiting along with Ernest Koonitz and the handbell choir from the Methodist church. Ed, the barber, had already made up his first batch of eggnog and Bess and Ada Goodnight were dressed as Mr. and Mrs. Santa Claus and over at the grammar school giving out presents, as usual. There was a new tree at the house but it was decorated with the same old ornaments, and the lights they always had, the same cream-colored cardboard candles with the blue lights, were in every window. Anna Lee and her husband, William, who was now a practicing dermatologist in Seattle, Washington, and their little girls had already arrived to spend Christmas at home. The only thing different this year was that Bobby was bringing Lois Scott home for Christmas.

Outnumbered and Hog-Tied

Dorothy had taken to Lois in two seconds, in the mysterious way women do when they know the perfect daughter-in-law has just walked in the door. The next thing Bobby knew they were all chummy and were sharing little secrets with each other. And it was not only his mother; everybody liked her right away—Mother Smith, Anna Lee, and Doc. Jimmy even remarked, "Now, that's more like it." At the end of the visit they had all said that she was the perfect girl for him, and that they made a perfect couple. All this "perfect" talk began to irritate him and scare him at the same time.

He did not want to be the perfect couple. Bobby wanted a stormy, passionate relationship like the ones he had seen in the movies. It was because she was so perfect for him that he did not trust it. He also knew that once he made a commitment, Lois was not the kind of girl you could fool around with and he was beginning to suspect that his own mother would take her side against him. He felt like a big fish that had to have just a few more jumps out of the water before he was reeled in for good and he could feel everybody trying to pull him in. So he made a decision. One night before she went into the dorm, he said, trying to sound as casual as possible, "You know, Lois, I was thinking. Since we are both going home for the summer, I wonder if it might not be a good idea if we were to start seeing other people for a while. We can still go out but maybe if we take a little break it might give us a chance to find out how we really feel about each other."

She seemed perfectly calm to him.

"Fine, Bobby, if that's what you want to do."

He quickly added, "We don't have to, of course—it's just something to think about." As she got out of the car he said, "I'll call you tomorrow." Once inside the dorm, she, of course, cried all night. The next day he was handed a letter by one of Lois's sorority sisters, who glared at him with disgust. "Here," she said. "And I thought you were nice!" She marched off and he opened the envelope and read the short note inside.

Do not call me. Do not write me. I do not want to see you.

Lois

When he went home that summer and told his mother what had happened, she did not say anything but he could tell she was not pleased and for some reason seemed to blame him.

He called Anna Lee in Seattle to talk it over.

"I don't know what's the matter with Lois. She's acting crazy."

"What did you do to her?"

"Nothing. I just told her I thought we should think about seeing other people for a while."

"I see."

"I can't marry somebody just because Mother likes her."

"I know."

"I have to be the one to make the decision, this is my life."

"You're right, Bobby, you have to do what you think is the best for you."

"Anyhow, I need to get out of here for a while. Can I come out there and see you?"

"Of course you can. You know you are always welcome anytime, and stay as long as you like. The girls would love to see you, and so would William and I."

"Thanks, Anna Lee."

Bobby was in Seattle with Anna Lee for a month. He went out with a few girls Anna Lee and William had set him up with and they had been fun. One pretty nurse was a lot of fun. But he always went back to his sister's house feeling lonely and feeling like he had just cheated on Lois *and* his mother. One night around three A.M. he sat up in bed and broke out in a cold sweat. A thought had hit him like a ton of bricks. What if *Lois* had met someone else and he had lost her? He immediately went into a panic, jumped up, put his clothes on, and ran out the door to find a pay phone so he would not wake the entire house. He ran up the street; he had to get her back before it was too late. What had he been thinking of? By the time he found a phone his imagination had her already married with two children, even though it had only been a few months since he had seen her. He called her parents' house and was so relieved to hear her voice and know that at least she had not married anyone else yet and he still had a chance. She did not hang up on him and listened to what he said about what a fool he had been and how he wanted to get married right away, how sorry he was he had put her through anything, and how he had never been surer of anything in his life. But after he had poured his heart out, there was a definite coolness in her response. She informed him that now *she* was not really sure how she felt about him anymore and now *she* needed more time to think.

More panic. He ran back to Anna Lee's house, packed in the dark, left a note, and headed for Poplar Bluff. Now he had the drama and the conflict he had wanted but it was not like it was in the movies. This was terrible. He might lose her forever. When he thought he could not have her he wanted her more than life itself. She had a student-teaching job and two days later he was standing outside the school when she came out, hoping that just the sight of him would change her mind, but it did not. Of course she was more beautiful than he had ever remembered, more everything than he'd remembered, but it took him a long time to convince her that he was a changed man, that he was sure he would never doubt the way he felt about her again. He was shameless. He even had his mother call and plead his case. "Lois, it's Dorothy," she said. "I know you have to do what is best for you but if you care anything at all about this son of mine"—at this point she glared at Bobby, who was standing there—"although I don't know why you should after the way he has acted, you better come over here and take him off my hands because he's not going to be of any use to himself or anybody until you do."

Finally he got her back and after all that, just like a man, the night before his wedding he wondered if he was doing the right thing after all and was it too late to back out now, all the things you think right before you jump off a mountain. But his best man calmed him down with these few words of wisdom. "You stupid jackass," Monroe said. "She's the best thing that ever happened to you."

Yet the next day, after Mother Smith played "Here Comes the Bride" and Anna Lee and her three little girls started the wedding procession, he felt like he wanted to leap through a glass window and run. Then he saw Lois coming down the aisle. She looked at him and smiled and Bobby almost fainted when he realized that this beautiful woman was actually going to marry him.

Cecil Saves the Day

In 1956 Betty Raye had just had another little baby boy and was enjoying life as a wife and mother, even though they still lived in a rented house. Hamm was saving money to make a down payment on it and buy it. Everything was going along according to plan until, after serving only two years as state commissioner of agriculture, he found himself becoming angrier and more frustrated by the day with the way the small farmer was being ignored. He drove all the way to Jefferson City, the state capital, to have a meeting with the governor but was told, as usual, that something had come up and that he would have to reschedule. This was the fifth time this had happened. That day he walked over and stood outside the huge governor's mansion and stared at it. It's not all that big, he said to himself. That day he made up his mind. He was finally so fed up with not having any power to do anything that he decided to enter the Democratic primary for governor of the state of Missouri. Despite Betty Raye begging him not to.

It was not only Betty Raye who thought it a bad idea. *Everybody* tried to tell him he was a fool to think he could launch a gubernatorial campaign out of nowhere and with no money but he had made his mind up and he refused to listen. "Betty Raye," he said, "honey, if you just go along with me just this one time, I promise you if I lose I will get out of politics for good. But I can't give up without even trying." All she would have to do is just pose for one picture with him and the kids, and after that she would not have to be involved and would never have to appear in public. He would do the rest.

What could she do? She loved him. So Hamm Sparks entered the primaries with nothing more than a good reputation with farmers, a name that sounded vaguely familiar, and a willingness to work night and day if he had to. He was convinced he did not need flashy billboards or fancy campaign headquarters with a staff of political advisers and so-called experts. He said his headquarters would be the back roads and small towns across the state. All he had to do to get his platform across was look people in the eye and tell it to them like it was. Tell them they needed someone who would be on the side of the veteran, the workingman, and the small farmer. "Why, there are smart people all over this state who can make up their own minds and not be led into the polls like sheep by some big-city political machine. All I need to do is find them and explain how they're being taken advantage of by the big mules running the party in Kansas City." This sounded good but after running up and down the state for over a month in a field of twelve hopefuls, he was running dead last. Most people in the state had no idea who he was and he did not have a snowball's chance in hell of even making it through the primaries if he could not do something about that—and fast. He had already gone through their savings. He scrambled around and got some backing from a few friends but the kind of money he needed to get his name and platform out to the public was much more money than Rodney Tillman had. More than anyone he knew or had ever met . . . or so he thought.

Just four hundred miles away, in the six-room Kansas City apartment he shared with his mother, Cecil Figgs was preparing to go to work. He stood at his dressing table and carefully attached a small toupee to the front of his large round head and placed a fresh flower in his lapel and was ready to face the day. When he walked into his large, thickly carpeted office at the funeral home, he found a note from his assistant telling him that his first appointment of the day was going to be ten minutes late. He picked up the newspaper on his desk. Usually he just skipped straight through to the obituaries to check his ads but a picture of Sparks jumped out at him. He was listed as one of the remaining candidates running for governor. Cecil Figgs supposed Hamm would probably not remember meeting him four years ago at Ferris Oatman's funeral but Cecil had never forgotten the day he'd met Hamm Sparks. When the funeral had concluded, Hamm had walked up to him at the reception afterward and introduced himself as Betty Raye Oatman's husband, shaking his hand vigorously and telling him what a good job he had done. He then shoved a business card at him, patted him on the back, and said, "Mr. Figgs, if you're ever in the market for a good tractor or a combine, be sure and give me a call," and walked away.

Cecil had been dumbfounded. Was Hamm insane? He was the last person on earth that would ever be in the market for a tractor. Cecil could have been highly insulted and offended at such an outrageous assumption but there was something so genuinely earnest and sincere about the man that instead of tearing Hamm's card up, he put it in his pocket. For some unknown reason he had been very affected by the hunky little guy.

Although Cecil had been busy dealing with all the details, he had watched Hamm out of the corner of his eye, walking around the reception with nothing going for him but a bad blue suit, a two-dollar haircut, and sheer nerve, trying so hard to mingle with the governor and his staff. Hamm had more or less been ignored of course, but the little guy hung in there. That afternoon something unexpected happened to Cecil. He did not know what it was about Sparks but he found that he had developed a sort of odd affection for this complete stranger. He had felt sorry for him in a way and yet at the same time admired him. Maybe it was because he had noticed Hamm trying to hide the fact that the sleeves of his jacket were too short when he shook his hand or maybe it was that he reminded him of another young man he had known and liked years ago. Whatever it was, because of this strange attachment he had formed to Hamm Sparks, when he saw his picture in the paper, wearing the same bad suit with the same bad haircut, he felt compelled to look him up and try to help him if he could. And nobody needed more help at the moment.

Hamm had no real staff except for his old friends who stopped by every once in a while and Rodney Tillman. His campaign office at the moment was a small one-room storefront that used to be a lamp store before it went out of business. The amenities consisted of a desk, four metal folding chairs, and a phone, plus three old dusty lamps that had been left behind.

◆ ◆ ◆

Cecil picked up the phone and called Hamm to set up a meeting and was somewhat surprised that Hamm seemed to remember him. Cecil did not seem to understand that he was a man that very few people would forget meeting. How many men in Missouri wear purple flowers in their lapel and a bad hairpiece the color of root beer?

A few days later Cecil walked into the campaign office, looked around the messy, dingy room, and shook his head. The first thing he said to Hamm was "Oh, honey, you need a better place than this." Cecil cleaned off a chair, sat down, and said: "Listen, if you expect to stay in this thing, you are going to have to get a decent place to work out of and some better advertising. Now, I have a lot of money and if you are really *serious* about staying in this thing, I'm willing to back you."

Hamm could not believe his luck. This was the first time in his life anybody had ever offered him something before he even had to ask. He jumped up and came around the desk and shook Cecil's hand. "Mr. Figgs, I'm as serious as a boil on an old maid's behind and if you will help me I promise to fight as hard as I can. I'll work night and day."

"I'm sure you will," said Cecil. "Just figure out how much you need, let me know, and it's Cecil." Then he got up and started to leave. Hamm followed him to the door. "Hey, wait a minute. Don't you need to hear my platform?"

"Oh no, darling," Cecil said, dismissing him. "I don't know a thing about platforms. I'll just give you the money and leave the politics part up to you."

Thus began the most unlikely of friendships between the two men, one that nobody ever understood. They did not even understand it themselves.

When Rodney came sauntering into the office with a bottle of whiskey and two paper cups, as he did every afternoon, Hamm was sitting at his desk beaming from ear to ear.

"Hey, Hambo, what's up?"

"Rodney, I just got a serious backer with big money."

"Who?"

"Cecil Figgs, the Funeral King. You just missed him. He said he would pay for the whole campaign, give me whatever I needed. I'm writing out a list right now."

Rodney looked somewhat skeptical. He knew how much money it

would take. "Ol' buddy, I'm afraid somebody's been kidding you. Nobody's that rich."

But Cecil had not been kidding. He was that rich. Not only was he the Funeral King of Missouri, over the years he had quietly bought mortuaries in seven other states and branched out into wider areas as well. With the mortuary and floral business, combined with his 50 percent interest in the Perpetual Rest Custom Casket Company, he was a very wealthy man and he had no qualms about spending it. In his business he was reminded on an hourly basis that life was short and you cannot take it with you. He had no children to leave it to, so why not spend it and, in this case, take a chance on a dark horse? However, in this case there were also other motivations at play. There was something he wanted in return but he did not want to tip his hand yet.

As for Hamm, he was so excited he could hardly contain himself. All he really needed was a little advertising, a good hillbilly band, and a flatbed truck with good sound equipment and he would be on his way. He immediately phoned Betty Raye's uncle Le Roy Oatman over in Nashville, who had a hillbilly band called the Tennessee Plowboys and hired them. A week later Hamm Sparks, with a flatbed truck and Le Roy's group, renamed the Missouri Plowboys, said good-bye to Betty Raye and the kids and hit the road. They went everywhere, from VFW fish frys, Elks Club pancake breakfasts, and Kiwanis meetings to bingo games and even family reunions . . . anyplace where more than ten people gathered, Hamm was there.

Coleman and Barnes Public Relations handled all the advertising for the Cecil Figgs funeral homes, so when Cecil called Arthur Coleman, the ad man jumped on the phone immediately. Cecil was not only a good friend of his wife, Bipsey, but he was also one of his biggest and most lucrative accounts.

"Cecil, how are you?"

"Fine."

"What can I do for you?"

"Honey, I need you to do me a little favor."

"Sure, what do you need?"

"Could you take a look at someone for me on the Q.T. and tell me what you think?"

"Absolutely. Be glad to. Who is it?"

"His name is Hamm Sparks and he's running for governor. I'd like to help him if I can but I don't know a thing about politics."

"What is it that I'm looking for?"

"Just see if you think anything can be done to enhance his public image. You know about those things, I don't."

Arthur wrote the name down. "Hamm Sparks? Isn't he that hicky-looking guy with the bad hair?"

Cecil sighed. "Yes, that's him."

Good News, Bad News

Two weeks later Coleman called Cecil with his report.

"I checked out your man." He laughed. "You sure picked yourself one hell of a wingdinger there, Cecil, but he's colorful, I'll give him that."

"What do you think he should do?"

"Honestly? Not a thing."

"You don't think that maybe it would help if he got a suit that fits and maybe cleaned up his English just a little?"

"No. From a public-image point of view, I wouldn't mess with him a bit. This guy is all natural and if you try and fool with him at this point it will just confuse him."

"So you wouldn't suggest changing anything?"

"No. He has good instincts and he's doing just fine the way he is. And as far as the whole package, it's not bad—two kids, a nice little wife-and-mother type who doesn't get in the way . . . but now, Cecil, you *do* know that this guy doesn't stand a chance in hell against Wendell Hewitt, don't you?"

"Yes, but thank you anyway."

"Anytime. But I am curious. What made you decide to back this particular candidate?"

Cecil said sincerely, "I don't know, honey, I wish I could tell you. But I really don't know. Just a hunch I had, I guess."

◆ ◆ ◆

Wendell Hewitt, clearly the people's choice for governor, took the lead in the polls right from the first day of the race and kept it. He was a six-foot-two, affable, hard-drinking man with an eye for the ladies who was not only a good solid politician with a law background but an independent thinker. Most importantly, people liked him. However, the state Democratic higher-ups did not like him, and did not support him. They wanted a party man they could control and Wendell Hewitt was not it. As far as they were concerned, he was a loose cannon. Peter Wheeler, a wealthy, well-educated, rather effete insurance executive from Kansas City, was their man. But they had a problem. Their man was a bit stuffy and could never win against such a popular choice as Wendell. Behind closed doors, Earl Finley, the head of the party, agreed it would be best if Hewitt were to be out of the race altogether. A month later, by some miracle and a lot of money exchanging hands, their prayers were answered. A photograph of Wendell Hewitt leaving a motel room with someone other than his wife appeared in the *Kansas City Star* and was picked up by papers all over the state. Wendell and his staff assumed it had been the Republicans that had done him in but he took it like a good sport and did not whine about it or try to lie his way out of it. In his television address he said, "Due to recent events I have no choice but to withdraw from the governor's race because, ladies and gentlemen, if my opponents are going to continue to stoop so low and use beautiful young blondes as bait . . . I can tell you right now they are going to catch me every time."

With Wendell out of the race, Pete Wheeler was a shoe-in. Or so they thought.

To Earl Finley and the boys, Hamm Sparks was a man they had never considered as anything more than a joke, some pie-in-the-sky candidate thinking he could fiddle his way into the governor's mansion, running around the state with his half-baked, pseudo-cracker-barrel philosophy and hillbilly singers. But during the weeks they had been concentrating on getting rid of Wendell Hewitt and pushing Pete Wheeler forward, the Hamm Sparks dog-and-pony show had crisscrossed the state and hit every small town, farm community, creek bed, and railroad crossing with a vengeance.

Hamm more or less did the same speech everywhere he went but it seemed to hit a nerve with the farmers and with the people in the country towns he spoke to. As his numbers started to rise, Earl Finley started to wonder about him and sent out a man with a newsreel camera to see just what in the hell he was doing and saying. The man caught up with the Sparks campaign, such as it was, at a stop outside of Cooter, Missouri, close to the Tennessee-Arkansas border. What the big boys saw on film later was a shot of a dirt-road farm town where about seventy-five to eighty country people had all gathered around the back of a flatbed truck where Hamm stood speaking into a bad microphone. Every time he made a point or told a joke, someone in the crowd rang a cowbell. The audience seemed to be hanging on to every word he said. The men in overalls and John Deere caps, the women in cotton dresses and bonnets laughed and nodded and seemed to agree with what he was telling them.

"Now, folks," he said, "I'm not gonna get here and try to fool you with fancy language. First of all, I wouldn't know how, you have to be a lawyer to do that, and second of all, I think every American deserves the truth in plain English and I trust the people to know it when they hear it.

"Make no mistake, the big mules want your vote. Oh, they smile and grin at you and promise to love, honor, and obey. Trying to get you to the altar. But you should hear how they talk about you behind closed doors. . . . They think you're stupid. They think you'll fall for anything they tell you. They think they can just do anything they want up there and get away with it. It reminds me of when I was a boy growing up out in the country. My mother would open up the pantry and here would be all these mealy worms and moths eating away at our cornmeal and flour. And she would yell out, 'Daddy, we've got pests in the pantry.' Now, I've been up at the state capital for a few years and I've seen how that bunch up there is stealing the taxpayers blind, and folks, we've got pests in the state's pantry right now and if you elect me I'm gonna get rid of every one of them. I'll chop all that extra fat right off the budget and put that money back in the workingman's pocket, where it belongs, not to pay the salaries of folks in the governor's mansion to cook up lace-panty lamb chops and serve a lot of little sissy food on silver plates. Good old American hamburger is just fine with me.

"Now, I know my opponent, Mr. Peter Wheeler, claims his family goes way back. And that's fine. But I ask you, whose family don't? Oh, I may not have the poodle-dog pedigree behind me and I may not get invited to their little high-society pink-tea affairs. But I'd stack my momma and daddy and your mommas and your daddies right up there with the best of them. I know that bunch up in Kansas City, all dressed up in their furs and diamonds, driving in fancy cars to their million-dollar brick churches. But let me tell you this: a vote don't care if you're fat or skinny or if your socks don't match or if you smoke store-bought cigarettes or roll your own. A vote don't care if you listen to the Grand Ole Opry or sip your coffee out of a saucer. . . . Why, it don't even care if you're wearing silk drawers or flour-sack skivvies." By this time he had the audience laughing and cheering. "A vote is the best friend we have. A vote from my momma and yours that walks to a little ramshackle wooden church in the country counts just as much as the rich man's vote. Now, I hear some of you saying it don't matter if I vote or not, the whole thing is fixed anyway . . . and you're right, it is fixed. The man who gets the most votes wins—and I want your vote . . . I won't lie to you. I could have gone after support from some of these big-money interest groups and be doing a whole lot better but I didn't. Why? Because I don't want to be in debt to anybody but you. So I'm asking you to give me a little something today, it don't have to be much, just a little loan. What will I put up for collateral? Well, I don't have much. I don't own a house, my car's not paid for. You can't have my wife. But I'll tell you what you can have is my word. My word that if you send me up there as your governor, I'll work for you. And I want you to hold me to it. The only payback I want to have to make is to you people . . . and I'll pay it back, law by law, road by road, school by school, and electric pole by electric pole."

While the Missouri Plowboys played, the Finley men watched as every one of the farmers came up and put money in a big barrel that had HAMM'S PEST CONTROL written on the side and shook hands with him. When the lights went off and the projector shut down, Earl smiled. "This guy's an idiot. We can beat him at his own game."

The next day they hired for Pete Wheeler a huge Dixieland band to travel with him and brought in top entertainers from Hollywood and New York to appear at all his fund-raisers. At the big Kansas City "Peter Wheeler for Governor" dinner, they even flew big Kate Smith in from New York to open the evening by singing "God Bless America."

The New Dog-and-Pony Show

Now, with all the parties, money, and efforts going into the Peter Wheeler campaign, Hamm started to worry. The more he thought about the promise he'd made to Betty Raye to quit politics if he lost, the more desperate he became. After being gone for a week he came into the bedroom around 3:00 A.M. and tried to wake Betty Raye without waking the baby. "Sweetheart," he said, shaking her.

She opened her eyes. "Hey . . . what time is it?"

He sat down on the bed. "It's late. But I need to talk to you."

"Is anything wrong? Has anything happened?"

"No."

She sat up and switched on the light. "Are you hungry?"

"No. The boys and I stopped on the way home and got a bite."

She reached for her glasses and put them on and looked at him in the light. She could tell by the worried expression on his face that something was wrong. "What is it?"

He sighed. "Honey, you know I never wanted to bother you with any of this. And I wouldn't if I didn't have to, but I need your help."

He had never asked her for anything before except to marry him, so she knew it must be pretty serious. He looked so pitiful, she reached over and took his hand. He hesitated a moment and then said, "I hate to ask . . . but with all the big money being thrown at Peter Wheeler, I'm in trouble."

"What can I do?"

"Well," he said, "like I say, I hate to ask, but the boys were talking and they think that since your momma and the Oatmans have such a big following now, that if you were on the platform with me and let me introduce you to the audience it might help."

The baby in the other room suddenly started to cry. Betty Raye got up out of bed and Hamm followed her. "All you would have to do is just sit there, honey, you wouldn't have to sing or anything. And I'd get to be with you and the kids a lot more. . . . It would only be for a little while. . . ."

On April 6, Neighbor Dorothy reported to her listeners that the dessert cookbook had received an entry all the way from Lake Martin, Minnesota. "Mrs. Verna Pridgen writes, 'Dear Neighbor Dorothy, I am sending you a recipe for a layer cake, some have called it a Minnehaha cake but while it is similar to the Minnehaha cake it is even nicer. I live out here on the Minnesota prairie and we call it a prairie cake.' Thank you, Verna, but whatever it is called I can assure you it is a good one. And, let's see, I got a call from Tot Whooten and she said to tell all her customers that the beauty shop would be opened back up this Wednesday. As you all know, last week Tot had a faulty dryer blow up and had to have all her wiring redone and it's taken longer to fix than expected. Also, this morning I want to say how happy we were to see a picture of our little friend Betty Raye in the paper and to see how big Hamm Junior has grown. It seems like only yesterday when she was still in high school."

For the next two or three weeks of the campaign, they moved in a caravan made up of a large black platform truck loaded with sound equipment, wooden folding chairs, and HAMM SPARKS FOR GOVERNOR banners, followed by three cars: Le Roy and the Missouri Plowboys in one, Hamm and assorted cronies in another, and Betty Raye, Hamm Jr., and the baby in the last car. And for Betty Raye it was also the last place in the world she wanted to be but she could not seem to refuse Hamm anything. They traveled up and down the state from sunup to sundown, sometimes making six or seven stops in one day. This was a grueling schedule for the men, but with two children to take care of, by the end of a few weeks Betty Raye was exhausted. Still, Hamm kept his promise. All Betty Raye had to do was sit off to the side in a chair and smile and wave as he introduced her as not only his wife but also the daughter of Minnie Oatman, the great gospel star, and the announcement was met with strong applause.

She did all of this without complaining but a week later, when Hamm did his speech in Clark County, he pushed her over the edge. Right in the middle of it, out of a clear blue sky, he paused and said, "You know, folks, I have a soft spot in my heart for Clark County. My wife and I spent our honeymoon right up the road here." Then he looked over to where she was sitting and said, "So you might say that little Hamm Sparks, Junior, there got his start in Clark County." And if that was not bad enough, amid hoops and hollers and guffaws from the audience, he put his hand up and said, "That's all right, folks, I assure you the pleasure was all mine."

Betty Raye wanted to die right there on the spot.

She did not know if it was because she was so tired or because she had been so embarrassed but when she got back in the car she burst into tears. When Hamm finally came over, he was surprised to see she was upset.

"What's the matter?" he said, opening the door.

"Why did you say that?"

"Say what?"

"About our honeymoon . . . all those men laughing, looking at me funny—and it's not even true."

He chuckled and climbed in beside her. "Oh, come on, sweetheart. Don't be like that. Nobody was looking at you funny. It was just a little joke, that's all, made them feel good. People like to feel like where they live is special. Nobody was laughing at you, honey." He kissed her and put his arm around her. "Besides, if you think about it, it could have been true, couldn't it?"

The baby started to cry again. Hamm said, "Aw now, look, honey, you've got the baby all upset." He rolled down the window and called out, "Hamm Junior, come over here and give your mother a kiss and tell her to stop crying."

Hamm Jr., who at five was already turning into a charmer just like his daddy, crawled in over him and put his arms around her neck and gave her six big kisses. What could she do? She was outnumbered.

Because he had gotten such a big laugh in Clark County, Hamm continued to use the same line everywhere they went in the next few weeks. After a while Rayford Fusser, the bass fiddle player for the Missouri Plowboys, who was not too bright, turned and asked Le Roy: "How many honeymoons did this guy go on?"

The big newspapers, who were all against him, always referred to him with derogatory names, such as Hamm "Pests in the Pantry" Sparks, Hillbilly Hamm, or sometimes even Honeymoon Hamm, but not one compared with the names he was being called by Earl Finley's men when his numbers started to rise.

As Election Day grew closer, to counterattack Hamm's constant charges that Peter Wheeler was nothing but a rich man's son, a new slogan was added to his campaign ads. They began billing him as Pete Wheeler, "the little man's friend." But Hamm was smarter than they thought. He went on statewide television and made a statement right into the camera. "Folks, usually I try to remain friendly with my opponents but when Mr. Peter Wheeler says he is for the little man, I just have to take exception to that. Because, ladies and gentlemen, there's no such thing as a little man or a little woman in America. According to the Constitution we are all supposed to be equal. I may not be rich like old Pete, but being called a little man sort of hurt my feelings."

Hamm also announced that if elected he would ban all alcohol from the governor's mansion and not allow it to be served at any state function. This was a good move. He knew that would set well with the state's large Baptist and Pentecostal population. Hamm also knew they would always vote dry as long as they were able to stagger to the polls. It was smart politics to give the church something to get behind and vote against.

The Earl Finley crowd found out the hard way that Hamm was a scrapper. Everything they threw at him he threw right back. When a hastily staged photograph of Peter Wheeler sitting in a field of corn on a tractor appeared in all the papers, Hamm made the best of it. At his next press conference he said, "Old farmer Pete must have been surprised when he ripped up all his corn with that big number four wheat thresher he was sitting on."

On the morning of May 8 Cecil received a call from Coleman, at the advertising agency, who laughed and said, "Well, Cecil, where do I go and eat a little crow?"

Cecil said, "Oh, honey, I'm just as surprised as you are."

What it all boiled down to in the end was not so much that Hamm

Sparks won the primary but that more than a lot of people just did not warm up to Peter Wheeler. However, the next day a lot of people in the state woke up and said, "Who is Hamm Sparks?" Fortunately for Hamm, his Republican opponent in the election, incumbent Delbert K. Whisenknot, had a terrible voting record and the looks and personality of a hedgehog; but even still, beating him was no easy feat and the election was not a landslide by any means. Hedgehog or not, Delbert was at least a familiar hedgehog. Hamm and Delbert were neck and neck right down to the wire and Hamm won by only a narrow margin. In fact, he just barely squeaked in with a lot of last-minute help. In the rural counties the farmers backed him 100 percent, to the man. And late in the day, when it looked like he might lose, it was truly amazing how many goats, mules, bulls, and heifers showed up at the last minute to vote. One black-and-white sowbelly hog over in Sullivan County by the name of Buddy T. Bacon even voted twice. But this phenomenon was certainly no more amazing than the large number of deceased people around the state who suddenly rose from the dead and stuffed their names in the ballot boxes, voting for Hamm. And nobody knew more names of the dear departed than Cecil Figgs. It would not be an exaggeration to say that a lot of the polling places were loosely run. But none as loosely as the polling places set up in the Italian and Polish neighborhoods of St. Louis. One or two large fellows sitting outside the voting booth with a baseball bat more or less guaranteed a vote for Hamm.

The New Administration

Back in Elmwood Springs, Dorothy made it a policy never to discuss politics on her show or certainly never to brag about the important people she knew but she was so happy for Betty Raye she just had to say something. In early January 1957, after she announced the winner of the What Is Your Favorite Holiday and Why Contest, she said, "As some of you know, Mother Smith and Doc and I were lucky enough to be invited to the inauguration of our new governor and all I can say is we all can be mighty proud of the new first lady of Missouri. She looked as pretty as a picture in that stylish pink outfit and we all wish her just the very best of good luck!"

Jimmy had received an invitation as well but he decided that he would stay home and watch it on television with his buddies down at the VFW hall. And he was glad he did because it turned out to be the TV event of the year. The entire Oatman gang showed up, including Chester, dressed in formalwear for the occasion, and they all sat on the platform behind Betty Raye. During the ceremony Minnie kept waving her big white handkerchief at everyone in the crowd and the whole time Hamm was being sworn in Chester was in camera range, shooting his eyebrows up and down at people in the front row. It was a live show and somehow the wrong button got pushed and the audience at home heard the director in the booth screaming through the headsets, "Get that #$%&*@! dummy out of there!"

Other than that it went fine.

On the morning of November 5, to her secret horror, Betty Raye had awakened and been told she was now married to the governor of the state of Missouri. She was not alone in her shock. A lot of other people had also been horrified to wake up and realize that some unknown ex–agriculture commissioner was now their new governor. But on the first day of his administration Hamm did an admirable and also a smart thing. His first phone call was to Peter Wheeler, to offer him a position in his administration. Which Wheeler graciously declined, as Hamm knew he would. Next he called Wendell Hewitt, another man he had defeated in the primary, and asked him if he would consider the office of state attorney general. Hewitt said yes. It was a good move. Even though Wendell Hewitt had been caught in a motel with a blonde, he was still a popular man with the people.

The second thing he did was to save the taxpayers a lot of money. As part of his "Get Rid of the Pests in the Pantry" program, he announced he was eliminating all the paid staff at the governor's mansion and replacing all the cooks, maids, gardeners, and so on with inmates, trustees from the state prison, and from now on all the vegetables used at the state dinners would come from the garden he was putting in at the back of the mansion and all the eggs and milk from their own livestock.

And if anything could be said for Hamm, it was that he was loyal. His third order of business was to pay back all of those who had helped him. He brought in about twenty old friends and gave each of them an office. Everybody got something. Le Roy Oatman and the Missouri Plowboys were named "state musicians" and were hired to play for all the functions at the governor's mansion during his administration. Rodney Tillman was appointed his press secretary and Seymour Gravel, another old army buddy down on his luck, was named public safety director and was to serve as his personal bodyguard. These appointments came as a slight surprise but, more important, everyone wondered just how Cecil Figgs would fit into the new administration. They were curious. Figgs was not a politician. What could he possibly want from Hamm?

A few weeks later they found out. A very unhappy Rodney came into Wendell's office with the bad news. "He's just appointed Cecil 'chief of protocol of the state.' "

"What? There's no such thing as chief of protocol for the state of Missouri."

"There is now. He's giving him the office across the hall."

Wendell shook his head in disgust. "Jesus Christ . . . things are bad enough with all these bozos he's brought in that don't know what they're doing. Now we're going to have Cecil Figgs fluttering around here for the next four years."

In Kansas City Earl Finley sat in a room in the back of Democratic headquarters with ten other worried men, chewing on his cigar, his pig eyes darting back and forth.

"Well, boys," he said, "we now have a tractor salesman, an ex–gospel singer, and a fairy mortician, and a drunk sitting up in the governor's mansion. Now, just how in the hell are we going to get them out?"

The Real First Lady

People may have wondered why Cecil Figgs, who was so successful in the mortuary and floral business and certainly did not need the measly little pittance the office of chief of protocol paid, had accepted the post. But Cecil had a very good reason. After reaching the top of his profession, he had become increasingly restless and bored as the years went by. He no longer planned the smaller funerals, only the large and important ones, but they were few and far between. Cecil had a burning need to stage the big event. He loved those with music, special lighting, spectacular sets, and fancy costumes. He had been so bored that last year he had thrown a big funeral for Miss Lily Mae Caldwell, who had been dead for over ten years. She had founded the Miss Missouri Pageant, so he invited all the ex–Miss Missouris to come back for the huge memorial service to be held on the stage of the theater where all the Miss Missouris had been crowned. Most of the girls had not liked her very much, but they came anyway. They more or less had to. Cecil had arranged for the entire evening to be filmed and not to show up would have made you look bad. The memorial pageant was a grand affair. He'd hired Bert Parks to emcee and had filled the stage with an orchestra and twenty-four different church choirs from all over Kansas City, wearing specially designed blue velvet robes with a jeweled Miss Missouri crown embedded on the front. Ten of the ex–Miss Missouris performed their old talent numbers and all of the others dressed in evening gowns were called onstage one by one. After they had all arrived there, when Cecil gave the cue, twenty-five white doves were released as a huge portrait of Lily Mae Caldwell, lit up at the top of a long pair of glittering silver stairs, was revealed, and Karen Bo Bo, an ex–Miss Missouri, sang "I'll Build a Stairway to Paradise." That extravaganza had kept him busy for a while but after it was over he felt empty and hollow again. What Cecil wanted was a bigger venue and now, thanks to his investment in Hamm's campaign, he had the entire state to work with.

The first thing Cecil did as the new chief of protocol was to insist on changing the state troopers' uniforms. He came flying into the governor's mansion with his costume designer from the Little Theater and hundreds of sketches of the costumes the designer had done for *The Student Prince.* He explained to a room full of flabbergasted state senators, invited for a gala breakfast, who would have to pass the bill to get the funding, that he wanted to eliminate all the old gray-and-brown uniforms and create a new look, bright blue with red stripes and lots of gold buttons. Cecil got nowhere fast. At the end of the day he'd managed to get funding to create a special governor's Honor Guard uniform to trot out on state occasions. However, there were three stipulations in the bill: 1) No swords; 2) No plumes; 3) No white boots. Cecil was in a fit over that but at least he got his Honor Guard. The next week he had a slew of decorators descend on the mansion, laden with swatches and paint samples. Thanks to Hamm cutting the budget, the entire staff working in the governor's mansion were trustees brought in from the state penitentiary. The cooks down to a woman were all murderers, as well as the maids and yard workers, with a few thieves and one five-time bigamist thrown in for good measure. But no matter their checkered past, Cecil set out to make sure they were all in starched white uniforms, neat and clean at all times. One ice-pick murderess named Alberta Peets, who did not like to wear shoes when she cooked, was told by Cecil that she was no longer allowed to go barefoot around the mansion. This upset her very much and some said Cecil was living on borrowed time.

He did not seem to notice. He was too busy making sure that when out-of-town dignitaries came to visit they would not think they were in Dogpatch, USA. He was determined to see that Governor Hamm's administration was one that would move the state forward and he had a lot of moving to do. Most of the men who surrounded Governor Hamm still wore white socks and brown shoes. After about a month of Cecil

Figgs and his decorator friends running amok through the place, jerking down curtains, putting up new ones, and insisting that every male wear a fresh flower in his lapel, Rodney Tillman, at the behest of everyone, went into Hamm's office and complained about him.

But Hamm just dismissed it and said, "Oh let him have his fun—he earned it."

"But Hamm, he's upsetting the staff," said Rodney.

"Well, that's their problem. They're just going to have to learn to put up with him; he's not hurting anybody."

Rodney made no headway with Hamm. Whatever Hamm's reason for keeping Cecil around, he must have known what he was doing. Hamm was not going to stop Cecil from doing anything he wanted. It was clear Cecil had full run of the governor's mansion and there were no two ways about it. It also became clear that if you wanted the governor's ear, it was a good move to go through Cecil.

Of course, there were jokes. People snickered behind their backs that Cecil Figgs was really the first lady but Hamm didn't hear it and, besides, he was too busy to deal with that silly little gossip stuff. And Cecil was far too busy, as he said, "trying to bring a little couth into the governor's mansion." He did complain daily about Hamm's ban on alcohol. He said it had been an embarrassment to the state, offering only lemonade and grape Kool-Aid to the president and first lady of France when they visited. And even though he could be a holy terror and fly into a fit over the smallest detail, he was always kind to Betty Raye.

As far as Betty Raye was concerned, she was more than happy, even relieved, to let Cecil plan the parties and act as host or hostess and entertain the various guests who came to the mansion. She was grateful to have someone who knew how to do all the things that she had no idea how to do. Even though Hamm had promised her she would not have to get involved, she would do the few events Cecil said she should. Cecil understood how shy she was and would ask her to come to a function only if he thought it was absolutely necessary. "Darling," he would say, looking at her with his big eyes, "you really should come in just for a minute. It just wouldn't look right for the state if you didn't put in just a tiny appearance." She would go whenever he did ask and try her best but she always felt uncomfortable and was glad when Cecil gave her the nod that she could slip out.

Other than those few functions, she mostly remained pretty much in the background and tried her best just to stay out of everybody's way. It was not too hard being first lady. Not many people ever recognized her. When Cecil had taken her shopping to buy a dress for the inauguration, one woman had come up to her and asked "Miss, do you have this in a size fourteen?" And another had asked if she had anything in a black, off-the-shoulder evening gown. As a few unkind reporters had said in newspaper articles, she was not the most charismatic of first ladies. In fact, as only a few people had ever heard her, one said they even wondered if she *could* speak. The one thing she hated more than anything about being first lady was having to raise her children in the mansion. She felt as if they were living in a fish bowl. She was never alone, never had a moment to herself. The place was teeming with people night and day. She could not even go down to the kitchen for a drink of water without running into a tour group. And she could not leave or go anywhere without having a state trooper with her. But she did not complain. Hamm was happier than she had ever seen him. And, after all, it was only for four years. After this term was up, he promised her, he would go back to private life and buy them a home. For that, she could stand it for a few years.

Missouri Power and Light, 1959

In his first two years in office Hamm had proved to be more than just a greenhorn politician and stirred up one hornet's nest after another but he was determined to do what he had promised, especially to save the taxpayers money. He upset Earl Finley's sweetheart deals with the concrete and gravel companies and gave contracts to the lowest bidders, and he was particularly interested in utilities and finding out if they were efficient. He conducted surveys all over the state so he could learn where and how he could cut corners, and Elmwood Springs was high on the list.

A thin young man of about twenty, wearing a white short-sleeved shirt, brown slacks, a clip-on bow tie, and black shoes that looked like the kind mailmen wear, walked up the front steps and knocked on the door. No answer. He knocked again. He could see the old lady in the kitchen at the back of the house as she passed back and forth. She was ignoring him but he needed three more people for the survey, so he walked around and knocked on the back screen door.

The old lady looked up when she saw him. "Well, hey . . ."

"Ma'am, I knocked on your front door but you must not have heard me."

The old lady said, "Hold on, let me go and get my hearing aid." She came back in a moment. "What can I do for you? Are you selling something?"

"No, ma'am. I'm from—"

Before he could finish, she had opened the door. "Well, then, come on in. You're not a mass murderer, are you? I can't have any of those in my kitchen. I promised my niece, Norma, I wouldn't let any men in the house."

He stepped inside. "No ma'am, I'm conducting a—"

"Have a seat."

"Thank you. I am conducting a—"

"Do you want a piece of pound cake?"

"No, thank you, ma'am."

"Are you sure? I just made it."

"No, ma'am."

"Do you mind if I have a piece?" she asked, knife in hand. He stared at it.

"Oh no, ma'am, you go right ahead." He sat down and opened his large brown leather satchel.

The old lady went over and cut herself a slice and put it on a plate, opened a drawer, and took out a fork. "You sure? It looks pretty good this time. The last one I made was a mess. . . ." She looked at the papers he was putting out on the table. "Are you a schoolboy?"

"No, ma'am. I'm out of school. I'm conducting a survey for the Missouri Consumers Bureau for the Missouri Power and Light Company . . . and I'd like to ask you a few questions, if I may?"

Suddenly she perked up. "Is there a prize involved if I get the right answer?"

"No, ma'am, this is just an information survey. It's just for our records."

Somewhat disappointed, she sat down with her pound cake. "Oh well, go ahead. Fire away."

"Name?"

"First name Elner, middle name Jane, last name Shimfissle."

"Date of birth?"

"Well, I'd say sometime between 1850 and 1890, give or take a few years."

He put down *unknown.* "Miss, or Mrs.?"

"Mrs. Will Shimfissle, widowed in fifty-three."

"How many living in residence?"

She thought for a minute. "Five . . . a cat, me, and three mice."

He forced a small smile, erased the number 5 in front of *occupants* and wrote a 1.

"Occupation?"

She looked puzzled, as if she had not heard him. In a louder voice he leaned forward and said, "Mrs. Shimfissle, what is it that you do?"

After mulling it over for a long moment, Elner answered, "I just live, I guess, what else is there to do? Isn't that about what everybody does?"

"No, ma'am, I meant do you work outside of the home?"

"Oh, I see what you're getting at. . . . Well, I garden a little and take care of my laying hen out back. I used to do a lot more yardwork but my niece's husband, Macky, comes over every Saturday and cuts my grass and trims my hedges. Norma said she didn't want me to be fooling with anything sharp. Norma says a rubber hose is safe, so I do water the lawn when it needs it."

He wrote *unemployed.* "Do you own your home or rent?"

"I own it, bought and paid for. My husband, Will, said, 'Elner don't let anybody stick you with a mortgage after I'm gone,' so when I sold the farm, I just paid for it in cash and never had to fool with monthly payments. All I pay is my taxes."

"How many electrical appliances do you have in your home?"

The old woman brightened up. "Now, that's a good question. A good many of them. Let's see . . . all my lights, of course. My stove. My icebox. My toaster. My percolator. My radio, that's another. My—wait a minute, I have two iceboxes . . . the other one's on the back porch but it's not plugged in . . . does that count?"

"Not if you don't use it."

"But it works, at least it used to. I told Norma I don't really need it. I do a lot of canning and I have plenty of room in my new icebox, so I just keep my birdseed and things like that out there. I'm kind of thinking about giving it to some poor person down the line; that's probably what I should do. They'd be pretty happy to have it, don't you think?"

"Yes, ma'am." The young man, trying to move on, said, "All right now—"

"Wait a minute, I'm not through," she said. "My front-porch light, my vacuum cleaner, my fan, my air cooler. I put that on once in a while when I get—"

"Fine . . . what about gas?"

"What?"

"Gas appliances, do you have anything that uses gas?"

"Should I?"

"No . . . not really. So can we say that you prefer electric to gas?"

"I don't think we can say that. I don't rightly know. I don't have any gas things, only electric."

He wrote *yes.* "Mrs. Shimfissle, would you say that the amount of your monthly electric bill is, in your opinion, high, medium, or low?"

"That's a good one. Hmmm, I would say . . . just about right. To tell the truth, for what all you get for your money, it's a bargain. Now, don't hold me to it, but I would pay a lot more if they asked me to but don't put that down. I don't want them to raise my bill. That's just between you and me."

He checked off *low.* "So would you say you use your electrical appliances more than the average person?"

"As a matter of fact, I think electricity is just about the best value you can get for your money, other than having a baby or a heart operation. Did I say I had an electric heater in my bathroom?"

"No, ma'am, but—"

"Put that down. You know, sometimes I get to thinking about value . . . and you just wonder how people figure it, don't you."

"Ma'am?"

"How people figure the value of things. What things are worth, for instance. Do you know that an automobile costs more than it does to go to the hospital to have a baby? Now, who figured out that a car is worth more than a baby is what I want to know. My neighbor's husband, Merle, went all the way to Texas and had a doctor put him in a new heart valve so he wouldn't die, and it cost less than it does to buy a good house trailer. Now, have you ever heard of a house trailer saving a man's life?"

"No, ma'am but—"

"That's right, you haven't. I said, Verbena, what would you rather have, a new house trailer or your husband? You wouldn't even enjoy that trailer if your husband was dead, would you? And she had to admit I was right. I'd take a heart valve over a house trailer any day, wouldn't you?"

"Yes, ma'am. I just have a few more questions."

"But you're young yet, so you won't be needing a heart valve for a long time but when you do, think about this one. Think about how much money that heart valve, something that is no bigger than my thumb, costs and how big that house trailer is. No matter how you slice it . . . you may get something bigger but it won't keep your heart going. . . . So that brings me back to my point."

"Ma'am?"

"Electricity is the best value we have going and we can't even see it!"

He saw an opening and he took it. "So would you say in regards to your electric service that you are very satisfied, moderately satisfied, or not satisfied?"

"I would say that I'm extremely satisfied, satisfied-beyond-my-wildest-dreams satisfied. Back in 1928 my sister Gerta said, Just wait until you get electricity out there on the farm, and I remember the first time they ran it up to the house and I've loved it ever since. I don't know how we ever got along without it. You tell them down at the electric company that I think electricity is perfectly wonderful. Why, just think how much we depend on it and I'll tell you something else. After Jesus, I think that Thomas Edison is the second most important man that ever lived on this earth . . . bar none. And to think we don't even have a holiday named after him. They gave Saint Patrick his own day and what did he do but run out a bunch of snakes. Why, Thomas Edison lit up the world. If it hadn't been for him we'd all still be sitting here in the dark, with nothing but a candle, and we don't even celebrate his birthday. The Wizard of Menlo Park doesn't even get a holiday."

The young man started to push his papers back in his satchel. "Yes, ma'am, that's true."

"You're too young to remember but I remember the day he died, in thirty-one. Everybody put their lights out for one minute. But then after that they forgot all about him. But I don't forget him. Do you know what I do each year on Tom's birthday?"

"No, ma'am."

"I turn on everything I own, all my lights, my washing machine, my fans, my radio, my TV, and I let them play all day. And I say, Happy Birthday, Tom. Now, that is how highly I think of Mr. Thomas Edison."

"Well, thank you for your time, ma'am." He stood up, ready to leave.

"Let me ask you this . . . do they have a picture of Thomas Edison on the wall down at the Missouri Power and Light Company?"

"Not that I remember, ma'am."

"See what I mean? Here none of them would even have a job if it hadn't been for old Tom Edison and they don't even put his picture up."

"Yes, ma'am." He started inching toward the door.

"Am I all done? Is it over?"

"Yes, ma'am."

"Oh . . . well, how'd I do?"

"You did just fine."

"Above average?"

"I'd say above average."

She got up. "Wait a minute, let me give you some figs and plums before you go." She walked over and grabbed a wrinkled brown paper bag from a drawer and started to fill it with fresh fruit. "Now, I used this sack once, but it's clean, so don't you worry about germs and you don't need to wash these. I don't put any poison on them. I figure whatever bugs get to them first, they are welcome to them. Besides, they always leave me plenty . . . so much I can't even find enough people to give them away to and I hate to have them go bad, don't you? So I'm gonna put some extra ones in for your mother, O.K.?"

Dazed, he took the sack and headed for the door. "Thank you, ma'am."

"Well, that's just fine . . . and I wish you all the best of luck with your project. But tell them they ought to put Tom Edison's picture on the wall."

"Yes, ma'am, I certainly will." He was halfway down the back stairs when she came to the door. "Hey, I just thought of something I forgot . . . put down my electric blanket. Add that to my list, will you? And hey, you need to go over to Norma's house and give her the test. She has all kinds of appliances. She's two blocks over at 212 Second Avenue." Then she added, "But don't tell her I sent you. She's still mad about that insurance woman."

"Yes, ma'am," he said, but he was not going to interview anybody related to her. They all might be crazy.

Chris-Crossed

Except for wearing shoes and the flower boutonnieres, all the prison trustees were certainly glad to be living in the governor's mansion instead of jail and Cecil Figgs was as happy as a lark planning all the social events. But nobody on the governor's staff was having a better time than his old friend Rodney Tillman. Being in charge of the governor's public relations was quite a jump from used-car salesman, and he took full advantage of it. One afternoon Rodney came strolling into Hamm's office looking like the cat who ate the canary, sat down, and casually said, "Hey, Hambo, how would you like to have a boat?"

Hamm looked up from his papers. "A boat? What kind of a boat?"

"A big boat." He reached into his shirt pocket and threw a photograph of a brand-new thirty-five-foot Chris-Craft cabin cruiser on Hamm's desk. Hamm picked it up and looked at it and smiled.

"You know I've always wanted a boat. Why?"

Rodney leaned in and said, "Because, ol' buddy, I know a fellow that's just dying to give you one just like that."

"Give me one . . . what for?"

"He figured with all the stress you're under that you need a place where you can go and relax, get away from it all. This boat he's just dying to give you sleeps eight and can slip on down to Florida or the Bahamas for that matter, anytime you want to take a little trip."

"Who is this guy?"

"Just one of your big supporters . . . who wants to do something nice for you."

"What's the matter with you, Rodney? As long as I'm governor, you know I can't take any gifts from anybody."

"Well, hell, Hambo, I know that . . . but there's a lot of ways to skin a cat. Now, suppose he was to lock this boat up in a boathouse somewhere for you to borrow and take out for a ride anytime you wanted . . . that would be all right, wouldn't it?"

Hamm looked at him suspiciously. "Come on, Rodney, this sounds fishy."

"Now wait, hear me out on this. . . . Suppose he was to give me the key to this boathouse to keep it for you, until such time when you are no longer governor and *can* accept a gift from a friend." Rodney leaned back in the chair and crossed his hands behind his head. "In the meantime, why, you don't even know the name of the man who owns it. As far as you're concerned, I just borrowed it from a friend of a friend."

Hamm kept gazing at the picture of the boat. He had absolutely no intention of accepting it, but it was a beautiful boat, and for someone who had never made more than sixty-five dollars a week and could never hope to afford anything like this, it was tempting. He pushed the picture back across the desk. "Tell him thanks but I better not."

Rodney shrugged and said, "All right, I was just thinking how much fun it might be for your boys down the line. You do what you want to . . . but if it were me, I wouldn't be so quick to look a gift horse in the mouth like that. What's the point of being governor if you can't have fun?"

He walked out and left the picture lying on Hamm's desk. For a week Hamm kept taking that picture out of his desk drawer and looking at it. The second week he called Wendell Hewitt, the attorney general, into his office and said, "Listen, as governor would it be illegal for me to borrow a boat from somebody?"

Wendell said, "No, why?"

"I just wondered." On the fourth week Hamm decided it would not hurt to go down and just take a look at it. The friend of a friend had so hoped he would accept the gift, he had even gone so far as to have a name painted on the side for him. The moment Hamm saw *The Betty Raye* he was in love.

When Wendell, who had driven down with them that day, saw the name written on the side of the boat, he said, being no fool, "Don't tell me a thing, boys. I don't want to know. I'm just here for a boat ride."

Hamm did not know it but the friend of a friend was a Mr. Anthony Leo from St. Louis, and when the governor commuted his brother's scheduled execution to a life sentence he was grateful. All Hamm knew was that Rodney had come into the office that day and seemed very nervous until he had finished signing all his pardons. Wendell, who advised Hamm, agreed with Hamm's decision; after all, the man had not killed an innocent person; he had just shot some other mob hood.

Hamm said, "He probably did the state a favor."

They both had done Rodney a favor and did not know it; Rodney had a rather large gambling debt that had just been crossed off the books. But Hamm was no fool either. He never intended to accept a gift from anyone, never told anyone about *The Betty Raye* except a few people he could trust. But he did use it every chance he got.

One afternoon when he and Rodney were out cruising around the Missouri River, having a few drinks and smoking a few cigars, Hamm said, "You know, Rodney, I've been thinking, when my term is up, it sure would be nice if Betty Raye and the kids and I were to have a nice house we could move into right away and not have to wait. Sort of like a loan, and then, when I get settled and get a good job down the line, I can pay for it. What do you think?"

Rodney said, "Oh, I think that could be arranged."

"I don't think it would look too good for the ex-governor to have to go back to some little rented place, do you?"

"No, I agree with you there. What kind of a house do you think an ex-governor should live in?"

Hamm leaned back and thought about it. "I suppose it should be in a good neighborhood, for the kids, maybe something with a lot of red brick and a big porch, something along that line. Don't you think?"

"Yeah, that sounds about right. Let me do a little nosing around and see what I can come up with."

"And a car. Maybe one of those new DeSotos."

"No sweat," Rodney said. "What color?"

"Blue."

Blue was his favorite color. And after all, as Rodney had said, what is the point of being governor if you can't have a good time.

Rainbows and Cakes

Dorothy was very happy these days. Both her children were married to wonderful people, she already had three beautiful granddaughters, and Anna Lee had just called and told her she was expecting another baby. So she was particularly cheerful today.

"Good morning, everybody . . . I hope all of you out there are raring to go this morning, because you know what today is? Cakes, cakes, and more cakes is the rally cry of the Annual Golden Flake Cake Baking Contest and in its honor today Mother Smith is going to play a special song, 'If I Knew You Were Coming I'd Have Baked a Cake.' So ladies, and any of you men out there, make sure you have all your supplies at hand. Every second counts. Get ready. Get set . . . start your ovens! Let the bakeoff begin! Now, while all of you are waiting for your ovens to preheat, let me run the rules by you once more. Only one cake per contestant. As soon as you have your cake finished and frosted, get it over to the VFW hall as soon as possible for the judging.

"Good luck to one and all and for all you cake eaters out there, remember they all will go on sale after the judging, at around two this afternoon. All the proceeds are going to aid our policemen and firemen all over the state of Missouri. They do such a fine job all year 'round, so come over and buy a cake, and let them know how much we appreciate every one of them. We are so lucky this year to have such fine judges. All the way from Poplar Bluff, we have Mr. Jack Mann, president of Golden Flake Flour Company, also Mrs. Edith Cagle Pool, who is the author of the *Edith Cagle Pool Cakes for Every Occasion* cookbook and is listed in the *Who's Who in Home Economics,* and last but not least, yours truly, so come on by and see us . . . it's going to be a lot of fun.

"Wrens, robins, bluebirds, redbirds, hummingbirds, bobolinks, and finches have all been spotted so far this year by our bird-watcher, Emma Henson over in Walnut Shade, and Mrs. Joanne Ault of Woodlawn, Missouri, writes in and says . . .

> "Dear Neighbor Dorothy,
>
> "I read a good book and I would like to pass it on to your reading listeners. If they want to have a good laugh read *Cheaper by the Dozen* by Frank Gilbreth, Jr., and Ernestine Gilbreth Carey.

"All right . . . thank you for that. I only like to recommend books that are happy and cheerful. . . . I know there are sad things out in the world . . . but I just don't want to dwell on them. I guess I'm just like one of those ostriches; I just stick my head in the sand. I don't want to face the facts. All the scientists are determined to tell us what the moon is made of and what the stars are . . . and why there are rainbows . . . but I just don't want to know. When I wish on a star, I don't need to know what it's made out of—let the men figure it out—as for me, when a thing is beautiful, what does it matter why. I never get tired of looking at the moon. One night it is small and round as a shiny, ice-cold, white marble and the next it's a big soft yellow moon. How can we be bored when nature gives us so many wonders to look at. Which brings me to my next letter . . . it comes to us from Mrs. Anne Carter of Repton, Missouri. She writes . . .

> "Dear Neighbor Dorothy,
>
> "Have you ever wondered what is at the end of the rainbow? Well, I want to share with you what happened to us. Yesterday my family and I were driving out in the country and when a small rainstorm cleared, my son called our attention to a huge rainbow that had suddenly formed across the sky. The end of it seemed to be in the road up ahead of us. I drove as fast as I could to the spot and when we all got out of the car and looked at each other our skin

seemed to glow with iridescent colors of pink and blue and green. We could not believe our eyes. We were literally standing in the rainbow. If that is not a miracle, I don't know what is. God truly blessed my family and me that day and we will never forget it."

Mother Smith played a little of "Somewhere over the Rainbow." "Thank you for sharing that beautiful story with us, Mrs. Carter. . . . Now every time I see a rainbow I'll think of you and your family standing in the rainbow!

"Now I ask you. Isn't life wonderful?"

THE SIXTIES

The Chickens Coming Home to Roost

After Bobby graduated, he immediately got a teaching job at Franklin Pierce, a small college in Rindge, New Hampshire, and he and Lois were provided with a nice house on a lake. Although he made very little money, life was good for a while. They loved the college and the town but both of them, because they were from southern Missouri, were not used to the cold winters and the first year they nearly froze to death. Also, after his time in Korea, months of snow depressed him, and so Bobby started looking around for a warmer place. He had applied for jobs in Arizona and California but so far nothing had come through and in the meantime he and Lois were expecting their first child. As soon as they could, they came back to Missouri to visit. They spent a week with her parents and a week with Doc and Dorothy.

While they were in Elmwood Springs their old friend Mr. Charlie Fowler, the poultry inspector, called and said he wanted to stop by for dinner while they were there. It had been a few years and Bobby was glad to see him again. He had been at their wedding and had sent them a lovely gift. That night Dorothy made him his favorite, smothered pork chops and mashed potatoes, and after the first bite Fowler said the same thing he always did. "Dorothy, I'm not sure but I think these may be the best pork chops you ever made." After dinner, when the men headed out for a smoke, Fowler asked Bobby if he would take a little walk with him.

"Sure," said Bobby. They walked out in the backyard and sat down in the lawn chairs by the Sweetheart Swing and enjoyed the view. The sun was still pretty high in the sky. It had been an early spring that year and the apple tree was already full of pink-and-white flowers and the morning glories were already blooming and hanging off the old wooden fence and the garage. Ruby Robinson stuck her head out the window next door and said, "Tell your mother we have plenty of extra tomatoes over here if she needs any."

"Yes, ma'am, I sure will," he said.

Bobby sat there with Mr. Fowler and wondered why but figured he would find out sooner or later. After a while Fowler said, "That's a mighty fine little wife you have in there."

"Thank you, sir."

"I've been knowing you and your family for a long time now. Watched you and your sister grow up."

"Yes, sir."

Fowler cleared his throat. "You know, if I had married and had a son such as yourself just starting out in life, this is what I would say to him—but since I don't have one I'm going to tell it to you instead.

"Young Robert," he said, "we . . . you and I . . . have to stop pecking around in the barnyard of mediocrity and dare to fly with the eagles out into the world of big business. That's why a few years back I started buying up an interest in as many chicken farms as I could. I looked up and saw the handwriting on the wall, so to speak, and this is what it said. It said, Charlie . . . the poultry business is changing. It's no longer just an egg world out there. It's a fried-chicken-in-a-bucket-to-go world and you better jump in while the jumping's good." He leaned closer. "Now, son, this is strictly between you and me, but I just signed an exclusive contract with this fellow over in Kentucky for me to supply him with all his chickens. Now, don't get me wrong, I'm not making money yet, but I've got my eye on this fellow and the way business is booming I wouldn't be surprised if he doesn't open up another place real soon."

"Really?" said Bobby.

"Yep . . . and it all pans out with my theory about the future."

"What's your theory?"

"Quantity," he said emphatically. "Not quality. Fast, not friendly. That's the secret of making money nowadays, boy. This is the jet age. People want to eat on the move. How fast, how cheap, and how much do we get for our dollar, that's what folks are interested in today."

Bobby nodded and thought about it.

"Anyhow, young Robert, what I'm saying is this. I'm looking for a good man to work for me, somebody with personality, good P.R. skills such as my own, and I think that you fit that bill to a tee. Say the word and the job is yours."

Bobby was flattered by the offer but he did not know a thing about the poultry business. "I sure appreciate you considering me for the job, Mr. Fowler, but—"

Fowler did not let him finish his sentence. "Now, before you talk it over with your wife," he said as he pulled a small notebook out of his pocket, "I'm going to write down a figure as to what you can expect to earn the first year. And this is just to start, mind you." He jotted down a number and handed it to Bobby. "Of course, you would have to relocate but I think it is a chance worth taking and I give you my word, son, if *I* do well, *you* do well."

The number Fowler showed him was twice the salary he was making now.

The next morning when Monroe stopped by the house for coffee and Bobby showed him the figure, Monroe, true to form, said, "Whoa . . . that's some serious bucks." Bobby was torn. He hated to give up teaching but with a baby on the way and no new teaching offers, he and Lois talked. They decided to get out of the cold of New Hampshire and take a chance with Mr. Fowler.

The Missing Plate

Tot Whooten had never met Charlie Fowler but when Mother Smith was down at Tot's beauty shop having her hair dyed purple again she mentioned Bobby's new job. Tot said, "Well, for his sake I hope it works out. But no matter what you do in life there's a fifty-fifty chance that something will go wrong." She threw a teacup full of cream rinse on Mother Smith's head and added, "Of course, with me it's always been a ninety-nine percent chance that if something can go wrong, it will."

Tot must have had a premonition.

The following Monday Norma Warren had just returned from driving her eleven-year-old daughter, Linda, over to Poplar Bluff to spend the week with her grandmother, Ida Jenkins. Much to Norma's irritation, after her father had died her mother had picked up and moved there so she could be nearer to the Presbyterian church. "Now that I'm a widow," she said, "I need to be closer to my own kind." It hurt Norma to think her mother preferred the Presbyterians to her own family but she still had Aunt Elner, even though she was a handful. Today was Norma's at-home beauty day and she was right in the middle of giving herself her weekly Merle Norman facial when the phone rang again for the third time in an hour. She did not answer it but it would not stop ringing so she finally had to pick up.

"Hello, Aunt Elner," she said, as pleasantly as she could, trying not to ruin her facial, but this time it was not Aunt Elner again. It was Elner's neighbor Verbena calling from the cleaners.

"Norma, it's me. Have you heard what happened to poor Tot?"

"Oh God, what now?"

"You know Rochelle, his assistant, that heavyset gal who likes to have a snort or two with Dr. Orr?"

"Yes, what about her?"

"Well, I guess they lost poor Tot's upper plate over the weekend. Too much fooling around in the office."

"What do you mean they lost it?" she said, destroying her facial.

"Friday Dr. Orr pulled her teeth out and took an impression of her gums for a set of false teeth and told her to come back Monday and he would have her plate ready . . . and this morning she sneaks up there by the back alley—she said she would just die if anybody saw her without her teeth—so she goes in and sits down. She said she couldn't wait to get her new teeth. And then Dr. Orr walks in and she said she should have known something was wrong, she could smell the liquor on his breath, so anyhow he says, 'Open up,' and then he tries to put this upper plate in her mouth and it no more fits her than the man in the moon and *he* calls out, 'Dammit, Rochelle, this is not Tot's upper plate!' He says to her, 'Wait right here,' and then she hears all this yelling and cussing, so anyhow, about fifteen minutes later he comes back and says, 'Tot, I'm sorry, your teeth must have been thrown out by mistake. I'm going to have to take another impression and start over.' "

"Oh, no."

"Oh yes. So as you can imagine, Poor Tot was fit to be tied. She said it was no telling whose teeth he had put in her mouth. And not only that, this was the very week she was going to the new catfish place. You sure can't eat catfish without teeth, much less corn on the cob."

"No."

"And you know what the worst part is?"

"How could it possibly get worse?"

"I think James is slipping around on Tot with that Rochelle. That's what Merle said. He saw them out on the highway at that old Casa Loma Supper Club, and they were all over each other, kissing and carrying on."

"Oh no, poor Tot."

"I think it was sabotage, just plain sabotage. I think that girl just threw her teeth out for meanness so she could run around with James while Poor Tot has to stay home. But mind you, I didn't tell Tot that."

"Poor Tot."

"Isn't it the truth? If it's not one thing, it's another. And right after her mother set the house on fire and now this. It's a wonder she can even get up in the morning."

Norma went and cleaned her face and started again. She thought she better take care of her looks. She did not want Macky going out to the Casa Loma or someplace with some other woman.

The Pageant

Unfortunately, things had not turned out well for Betty Raye either. Hamm did not keep his word to her and in 1960 decided to run for another four years as governor. There went her dream of having her own home again. She had been heartbroken, but even she could see that his political career was like a train that could not be stopped. He was at the height of his popularity and he said not to run when he had all this momentum going would be such a terrible waste of all the time and energy he had put in. He pleaded with her, promised her that if he could have this one more term it would definitely be the end. "Anyway, honey," he said, "the state law says a governor *can't* serve three consecutive terms. So even if I wanted to I couldn't run again. What better guarantee can you have than that?"

As heartbroken as she was about having to stay on for another four years, she could see how much the people depended on him. He seemed to thrive on pressure and enjoy his every waking hour. And like it or not, she had to admit Hamm had turned out to be a wonderful governor and although she still longed to spend more time with him and live in a home of her own, there was a part of her that was very proud of him. As much as she missed him, she was pleased he was so happy.

Also the good news about Hamm's popularity was that in this election year his numbers were so high she and the two boys did not have to go on the campaign trail with him. There was almost no campaign, and as furious as it made him, Earl Finley had to sit and wait another four years until he could take back control of the state.

When Hamm won the election in a landslide, Cecil Figgs was of course delighted to have another four years and decided that it was time to put on a grand outdoor pageant celebrating the history of Missouri. It was to be a spectacular affair with a cast of hundreds, including an Indian pony to depict the first ride of the Pony Express in 1860 from St. Joseph to Sacramento. The pageant would re-create all the major events, starting from June 1812, when Missouri was first organized as a territory, and continuing up to modern-day Missouri.

They were rehearsing down at the big Shrine Auditorium and all day long Cecil had been losing his patience with State Trooper Ralph Childress, who, at six-four, could hardly be pushed around without something happening. Cecil was directing the governor's Honor Guard to march onto the stage in a straight line and to continue marching through a huge reproduction of the St. Louis Arch with a GATEWAY TO THE WEST banner at the very top. When they reached the front of the stage they were to turn, face the audience, salute and, in unison, put their hands behind their backs, and hold an at-ease stance—all on the count of ten that Cecil was snapping away with his fingers. "One more time," Cecil said, stomping his foot and clapping his hands at Trooper Childress. "Faster, *faster,* pick up your feet, you're too slow."

Finally the trooper, red-faced and ready to explode, stopped and said, "Listen, you little fairy, you snap your fingers at me one more time, I'm gonna rip them off and shove them up your fat ass."

Cecil stood and blinked at him, "What did you say?"

"You heard me."

Cecil frowned. "Don't you make me waste my valuable rehearsal time fooling with you. I am the director of this show and you are going to do it and you are going to do it right."

"Over my dead body," said Trooper Childress.

Cecil glanced at his watch. "Take a fifteen-minute break, people. I want you all back here onstage at exactly one-forty, ready to take it from the top." He then pointed at Trooper Childress and said, "And I want to see you downstairs right now, mister, let's go."

When they got downstairs to the large rehearsal hall, Cecil closed the door and said, "Take off that shirt. I'm not having you rip up a new shirt when we don't have time to order another one."

The trooper did so with glee, just itching to wipe up the floor with Cecil. The last thing Ralph Childress heard before Cecil hauled off and beat the living hell out of him was "I will not have a cast member setting a bad example."

Fifteen minutes later Cecil came back into the auditorium clapping his hands. "Let's go, people . . . right from the top." Behind him came Childress, limping slightly. A few minutes ago, he had been lying on the floor too exhausted to get back up, while Cecil had stood over him with his hands on his hips and asked, "Now, are you ready to get back to work or not?"

The trooper had been so surprised that he'd laughed and said, "Yeah, I guess so."

Cecil may have looked pudgy but he was as solid as a rock and as strong as a bull. He had been lifting dead bodies and caskets all his life. Although most of his military service had been spent arranging teas and bridge parties for the officers and their wives, he had been trained to defend himself. Nothing more was made of the incident but when the others asked Ralph what had happened he replied, "Aw, he's all right . . . just trying to do his job." In trooper language that must have meant a lot, because Cecil never had any more trouble with any of them and eventually they even came to like him. As a matter of fact, some came to him when they were having trouble with their wives or girlfriends and asked his advice. He seemed to understand women much better than they did.

And it was true in one important case. He had noticed Hamm and Betty Raye drifting further apart. After the pageant, he went into Hamm's office and closed the door. "You know I don't care what you do in your personal life but you need to start paying a little more attention to your wife."

Hamm, distracted, said, "What?"

"Betty Raye. She hasn't been anywhere with you in the last six months and that's not right."

"Oh yeah . . . yeah, I guess you're right. Maybe I should take her to dinner or something."

"It had better be something," Cecil said, "and soon."

Hamm said, "Yeah, I will as soon as I get a free night." But the free night never came. Betty Raye never said anything but she was lonesome. She really did not have any close friends in Jefferson City. Since it was the capital of the state, most people there were either in politics or married to someone who was. Betty Raye did not know a thing about politics except that it had taken her husband away, and she had nothing in common with the other wives, who seemed to love it. Alberta Peets, the ice-pick murderess, was her closest friend. She kept Betty Raye amused with stories of her many boyfriends, but when Alberta went home on a weekend furlough and the boys were off at camp, Betty Raye rattled around all by herself in the upstairs portion of the huge mansion.

One day in the middle of the afternoon, the phone rang at Neighbor Dorothy's house in Elmwood Springs. It was Betty Raye.

"Well, hello, honey, what a nice surprise."

"I didn't want anything," Betty Raye said. "I was just thinking about you and thought I'd call and say hello."

They chatted for quite a while. Betty Raye asked about everyone and wanted to know how Jimmy was doing and said to tell him hello. When Dorothy asked how she was enjoying being the first lady of the state, Betty Raye said, "Oh fine." She did not tell Dorothy but she often thought about them and her time in Elmwood Springs. And lately, there were times when she wished she had never left, but then one of her boys would run in looking for her and she'd be happy again.

The Dancing Storks

Luckily for Bobby and Lois, Charlie Fowler was a man of his word and as the company began to grow, so did Bobby's salary. Within a year after their son was born they were able to buy themselves a nice house and a new car. They found that they loved living in Kentucky and even brought Doc and Dorothy and Mother Smith and Jimmy over for the Kentucky Derby. Dorothy had just lost Princess Mary Margaret to old age and the trip did his mother good. It was especially wonderful when she met her new blond, blue-eyed grandson, Michael.

That year Poor Tot had lost her mother as well. Literally. While she was at work her mother had wandered off from the house and apparently had gotten into a car with strangers, who drove her all the way to Salt Lake City, where she wound up living in a Mormon home for the aged. By the time they found her she said she did not want to come home, but Tot still had to pay for her room and board each month.

On July 6, 1962, Macky and Norma Warren were celebrating a special day and early the next morning Norma called Aunt Elner, even before Elner had called, which was a first.

Aunt Elner wiped the flour off her hands on her apron and picked up. "Hello."

"Aunt Elner, it's Norma. Do you have your hearing aid on?"

"Yes."

"You are not going to believe what Macky got me for our anniversary. It is the cutest thing I have ever—"

"What did he get you?"

"Well, remember how mad I got at him last year when he gave me that stupid Rainbird sprinkler for the lawn?"

Aunt Elner laughed. "I remember. Poor little Macky."

Norma said, "Poor little Macky? Of course, I was upset. Can you blame me? Our thirteenth wedding anniversary and he buys me something for the lawn. He takes me outside, turns on the water, and says, 'Happy Anniversary.' I said, 'Macky Warren, after thirteen years of marriage I get a *sprinkler*?' And not only that, he got it out of his own hardware store. He didn't even shop for it. After I had driven all the way to Poplar Bluff and bought him all those cute boxer shorts, remember, with the little hearts on them, and baked him a cake. I could have killed him on the spot. Well, anyhow, this year he made up for it. Wait till you see what that crazy fool bought me. I'm looking at it right now."

"What is it?"

"It is the cutest thing you have ever seen. It is these two storks, at least I think they're storks—aren't they the birds with the long beaks? Anyway these two storks are all dressed up and are dancing. The male stork has on a tuxedo and the female is all dressed up in a green evening gown with a red headdress and they are dancing on this pedestal, and you turn it over and it's a music box. When you wind it up, it turns around in a circle and plays 'The Sheik of Araby' while they dance. I said to Macky, 'This is the cutest thing I have ever seen.' Listen, I'm going to wind it up for you."

Norma put it close to the phone while it played. Aunt Elner sat and listened. After about a minute Norma came back on the phone. "Can you hear that? Is that not the cutest thing you ever heard?"

Aunt Elner agreed. "Yes it is. I always loved that tune."

"Me too, I'm just tickled to death with it, and I said to Macky, 'This is more like it, this is much more romantic than a sprinkler.' Men, aren't they silly sometimes? He won't tell me where he got it, but it says on the bottom it was made in Czechoslovakia, so it must have cost him a fortune. He said he bought it for me to put on my knickknack shelf and I said, 'Macky, this is not an ordinary knickknack.' I've been thinking about where to put it and think I'm going to keep it in the living room on my end table. I mean, it certainly is a conversation piece. After all, how many homes could you go into and find storks dancing to 'The Sheik of Araby'?"

Aunt Elner said, "I've never seen it."

"No, as a matter of fact, I was surprised Macky had the good taste to pick it out all by himself. You know the kind of junk he usually gets. So I said to him, 'Macky, you can still surprise me. That must mean we have a good marriage.' He said, 'We must have, because you surprise me with something every day.' I said, 'Well good, I don't want you to get bored.' And he said he was anything but bored, wasn't that sweet?"

"Yes, it was. How did he like your present?"

"He loved it, but you know Macky—anything with a fish on it and he's happy."

Not every marriage was as happy as Macky and Norma's. Over the past few years things had started to change even more between Hamm and Betty Raye. It was not so much that they had stopped caring for each other; they had just slowly started drifting apart, until gradually, even before they were aware of it, he was living one life and she another.

Hers was a quiet life, trying to stay out of the spotlight, while it seemed he was always running toward it. His hours were so erratic—he only slept three or four hours a night—that they finally stopped sleeping together. He started to use the small room off the master bedroom so as not to disturb her and never came back. She had her two boys, whom she adored, and spent most of her time with them but still, being so in love with Hamm and not really having him was hard.

It was sometimes difficult to keep up a happy face all the time, particularly when her mother came to visit.

Minnie had just come from one such visit to the governor's mansion to see her daughter and her grandsons. Being that they had another few days off, she and Beatrice Woods had decided to have Floyd drive them down to Elmwood Springs for the day. Everyone was glad to see Beatrice again. She seemed very happy and still laughed at everything Chester the dummy said.

Why? No one knew. Ruby Robinson said if she could see him she wouldn't think he was so funny.

Like all mothers when they get together, the conversation usually revolves around the happiness and success of their children, and Minnie and Dorothy were no different. At this point Minnie could discuss success with authority. Her daughter was married to the governor and the Oatman Family Gospel Singers were doing so well they had just purchased another brand-new Silver Eagle custom-made Trailways bus and had a new hit album.

Minnie said, "With it all I'm so blessed and thankful to have the relationship with the Lord that I do. I look around me and people don't seem happy with all the money they've got. It's never enough. They always think they need more. And all you really need is the Lord. Money just don't do it, does it?"

Dorothy said, "Not in a lot of cases, I guess."

"I told Emmett Crimpler just the other day . . . I said, Emmett, just how many new suits do you need? You can only wear them one at a time. But every time we stop near a Sears, he's got to run in and buy him another one. He says it's 'cause he used to be so poor but I don't believe it."

"No?"

"No. He thinks all them new suits is gonna bring him happiness. But they ain't. You know, Dorothy, up to now I've had to scrimp for pennies every day of my life, trying to make ends meet. I've been poor as long as I've been alive and, you know, when you is poor, most won't give you the second time of day. Why, I can remember when I was nothing but a lil' ole barefoot child living in a little ole shack my daddy built us, setting on the top of a slump slab out in the country. Daddy worked from first light to last, picking out a few lumps of coal for us and the neighbors, *but* we was happy. Now that we've got money, I look at my boys and see they ain't happy. Bervin is chomping at the bit to run off and be the next Elvis and Vernon is on his third wife and is gone cold on the Lord." She sighed. "And Betty Raye . . . I just don't know what's the matter there. Here she has a cute little husband and two sweet boys but . . . Oh, she tried to put on a good face for me but a mother can tell when something's wrong.

"Something's wrong. I can't put my finger on it but the whole time we was there Hamm goes one way and she goes another. It don't seem right to me. Ferris and me was never apart a day or night from the first day we was married in 1931, by the Reverend W. W. Nails. He said, 'Who God is joined together let no man put asunder,' and I never forgot it . . . and I've got me a feeling that there's something asunder going on."

Vita Green

Harry S. Truman once said there were three things that could ruin a man: power, money, and women. Hamm already had power and the promise of money. And a woman was getting ready to walk in any day now.

Hamm was determined to be the best governor he could and he worked hard at it. He made sure he was informed about how people felt on every issue. Along with talking to as many people as he could, he also read every paper in the state before starting work each morning. Although he never paid much attention to the society pages, he did begin to notice something in the Kansas City papers. He kept seeing pictures of this one woman, always photographed at some party or function. He usually did not have much use for the rich or any interest in their silly activities but as the weeks went by he found himself starting to look for pictures of her in the paper and being disappointed when she was not there.

One morning he called Cecil into his office. "When you were in the funeral business in Kansas City, did you ever know a Mrs. Vita Green?"

"Know her?" Cecil said. "She was one of my best customers and still is. We do the flowers for all her parties."

"Is that so?"

"One year she gave a party for my theater group and we did her entire terrace in white roses. She has the whole top floor of the Highland Plaza apartment building, with a view from every room."

"Huh," said Hamm.

"You should see that place sometime. It is spectacular."

"I'd like to sometime. What does the husband do?"

"Just made a lot of money is all I know. She was divorced before I met her. Why?"

"No reason. I was just reading where this Mrs. Green was named head of some arts council and I was thinking that it might be a pretty good thing for the governor to get involved in."

Cecil looked surprised. "Really?"

"You're always bugging me about all that artsy stuff, aren't you? So I figure maybe I'll give it a try."

Cecil left the office, pleased that all his attempts to get Hamm interested in culture had finally paid off. Vita Green was one of the well-known cultural leaders in Kansas City and was admired by everyone, especially the men. She was a tall, striking woman of forty-three with shining black hair that she wore parted in the middle and pulled back in a bun at the nape of her neck. She was always dressed exquisitely but simply, usually in bright red, or emerald green to match her eyes, with one spectacular pin on her right shoulder. At first glance she could have been mistaken for Spanish or Greek aristocracy. Few who met her would have guessed that she was 100 percent black Irish. But in addition to being a pure pleasure to look at, she was smart, witty, and a man's woman in every way. She could converse on any subject and hold her own in any crowd. But when Mrs. Vita Green received the note from the governor asking if they could set up a meeting to discuss the state of the arts in Missouri, her first reaction was to laugh. Vita, along with the rest of her crowd, had always assumed Sparks was some country bumpkin straight from the agriculture department who would certainly never be interested in anything like the arts. She called her good friend Peter and said, "You are not going to believe who wants to have a meeting with me."

Peter Wheeler, whom Hamm had defeated six years ago and who had turned down Hamm's offer to join his administration, was a gentleman and as gracious as ever. "I think you should, Vita, and at least hear him out. You never know, and he may be trying to branch out a little."

She thought about what he had said and after a moment replied, "I suppose you're right, Peter—anything for art, as they say."

A few days later, a member of Hamm's staff called and informed her the governor was going to be in Kansas City for the day and asked if she would be available Wednesday morning between 8:30 and 9:00, before he did his speech at the Elks Club. Although it was an ungodly hour for her, she agreed to meet with him at the arts council building downtown. When she arrived that morning he was already in the president's office making phone calls. A nervous secretary said, "He says you are to go right in." His back was to the door and he was on the phone with his feet propped up on the windowsill. She stopped at the door but her perfume did not. It traveled on before her and wafted across the desk and caused him to turn around and hang up instantly. In that perfume were the possibilities of every kind of exotic evening, whether on the roof of her penthouse or on a moonlit beach in the tropics. All this before she said "Hello, I'm Vita Green."

When he saw the woman he had only seen in the black-and-white newspaper photographs standing there in living color, Hamm suddenly forgot every other pretty girl he had ever seen in his life—and as governor he saw quite a few, mostly blond beauty queens that had just won some contest or another. In his entire married life he had never thought of another woman in that way, but when Vita walked in, all thinking went out the door and slammed it shut. What stood before him now was the Rolls-Royce of womanhood. She was not a girl. She was a grown woman who, he could tell just by looking, was smarter and more powerful than he was by a mile and it excited him. He felt as if someone had just smacked him in the face with a million dollars. And as usual, it did not take him long to make up his mind.

What Vita Green now saw, jumping up and coming around the desk to shake her hand, was a stocky man about her height in low heels, not handsome in the way she was used to, certainly not sophisticated or well dressed. But when he grabbed her hand and held on to it as if he was afraid she would escape, she was somewhat taken by surprise by the energy and vitality and just the sheer *heat* of the man when he touched her. She was used to being admired by men but this one was different. On first meeting her, most men were overwhelmed and usually fumbled and stepped back away from her, trying to think of a clever thing to say. But, clearly, Hamm Sparks was not trying to think of clever things—or stepping back. There was nothing thought out or calculated about his approach. He said exactly what was on his mind at the moment, he looked at her with the unguarded genuine appreciation of a male for a female, and said, "Mrs. Green, what is it going to take for me to get you? Because I'm telling you right now, I'm gonna move heaven and hell to get it. You want me to jump through hoops for you? Just tell me how high and how many."

Now she was taken aback and, to her astonishment, she found this total candor to be refreshing and completely irresistible. She had to smile. At that moment someone started knocking on the door.

She said, "Why don't we start with dinner?"

Not letting go of her hand and looking right into her eyes, he said, "Mrs. Green, I can't wait that long. How about lunch?"

"It's Vita. Where would you like to go?"

"I don't care. You tell me where and when. . . ."

"How about the Downtown Club. Shall we say one o'clock?"

He nodded.

"Will we be discussing the arts, Governor Sparks?"

"It's Hamm, and I sincerely doubt it," he said.

She walked to the door and when she got there paused a moment and then turned around and looked back at him. "And by the way," she said, "I intend to be early."

"And I'll be there waiting."

All the way back to her apartment she had to laugh but the joke was on her. Of all the things she had expected to happen in her rather well planned life, a rube politician named Hamm Sparks was certainly the last person she would have guessed.

That night after dinner he told her he had decided to stay in town for a few more days.

"Really?" she said. "Don't you have a state to run?"

He looked at her. "Honey, I can do two things at once."

I'll just bet you can, she thought.

And this is how the relationship of Vita and Hamm began. There was no courting, no games, just raw physical attraction. They both had met their match and both felt as if they had unexpectedly stumbled upon something they had been searching for for years. There was no struggle for power, only the start of a powerful merger.

A Lot in Common

No one had been surprised when Mrs. Vita Green was named governor's adviser on the arts. People were not in the least bit suspicious when Hamm spent more and more time in Kansas City and left his wife at home. She rarely went anywhere with him anyway, so no one noticed. The fact that Vita and the governor were seen at some of the same events and parties did not cause eyebrows to raise; it seemed only natural. But then few knew that when the governor checked into his suite at the Muehlebach Hotel he walked in and walked right back out again, through the basement door, where Trooper Ralph Childress was waiting in the alley to take him over to Vita's apartment and would wait to take him back in the early morning.

Not only was Vita more wildly attracted to him than she had ever been to any man in her life, but she liked him. Hamm Sparks was exactly who he was, with no ego, no pretensions. He was an eager student. He wanted to learn, to improve himself. She had a lot to teach. Vita also recognized so much of herself in Hamm. They had a lot more in common than met the eye. Most people would not have guessed that Vita had ever worked a day in her life or that she had not been to the manner born. She had only heard about all of her rich cousins living in fine homes, going to the best schools, shopping in the finest stores. Her father, a likable man, had come from a nice, upper-middle-class family, attended a good college, but had been afflicted with an addiction to both gambling and drink. One by one, he'd lost every job he had been handed, until they wound up having to live off the small check that his embarrassed brothers sent them once a month, more to keep him away from them than from any real obligation. Growing up being thought of as the poor relations in a family takes its toll. Vita had seen her mother's eyes, which had once been blue and sparkling, turn dull and lifeless and her hair go white from the stress and strain of lace-curtain poverty. This, she decided, was not going to happen to her. She made a vow she would never depend on anyone. But on the bright side, for all their bad qualities, shame and humiliation had fueled the ambition that led her to where she was today.

Vita was a completely self-made woman. After finishing high school she had left Kansas City for Chicago and immediately got a job at Illinois By-Products, a company with about seven hundred employees. Over a period of three years she had worked her way up from the secretarial pool to one of five secretaries to private secretary to executive secretary. Two years later she was made personal assistant to the president of the company, with two secretaries of her own. The president and owner of the company, Robert Porter and his wife, Elsie, had no children of their own and they took an interest in the intelligent and ambitious young woman. They often invited her to join them at their home for dinner or at one of their clubs. Vita was a fast study. She quickly learned how to dress, how to use the right knife and fork. At night she studied art, music, and history. When she met the people the Porters introduced her to, she soon became a frequent guest in the beautiful residences along Lake Shore Drive. Vita felt that she was finally mingling with the kinds of people she should have been around all her life. The "by-products" of the company were a delightful little mixture of iron ore, copper, and steel, and with Mr. Porter's help, by the time she was twenty-eight she had already made a small fortune buying and selling World War II surplus scrap iron. Not a romantic product but when Mr. Porter died and left her even more stocks than she'd bought, *scrap* and *iron* became her two favorite words.

She had never married. There was no Mr. Green. When she had moved back to Kansas City, the creation of Mr. Green had been her own little private joke. She'd even named him after the color of money. There had been men, rich powerful men, but none she was willing to marry. She was already rich and very happy. She liked the life she led. She enjoyed coming into that spacious beige apartment, filled with her lovely things, sitting on top of the city where she had once been poor and unhappy. When she looked back on her life, she was grateful, in a way, and wondered if she would have enjoyed it quite as much if the money had been handed to her on a silver platter. She had worked for every dime she had. Granted, it had not been easy for a woman in business in a man's world but from where she sat now it had been worth it. She now had everything she wanted—including Hamm Sparks. There was something so wonderfully freeing about completely surrendering herself to him without reservation. It was those moments when she let go and allowed herself to flow and meld into him, that moment when she could no longer tell where she stopped and he began, that made her happier than she had been for a long time. This little fireplug lover of hers ate fast, walked fast, talked fast, and made love fast. She loved the way he was always ready, always full of energy and speed, like a car that could go from five miles an hour to seventy in less than five seconds. She could depend on him, count on never having to have a second thought wondering if he wanted her. Being with Hamm was like watching a starving man devour a huge meal and still manage to love every bite, no more, no less than the last time. And for a woman of a certain age, it was the kind of thing that kept a secret smile on her face and a hum in her body. But most of all she loved the way he was coming to trust her and depend on her.

Hamm had also found a person he could talk to, a woman who would not laugh at him or look down on where he had come from or think any of his ambitions were too much to try for. On the contrary, Vita had almost more ambition for him than he could have ever dreamed for himself. To his great surprise, he had discovered that Vita knew more about the working of politics inside and out than he did. For a while before her father fell apart completely, he had been involved in local politics and was one of old Boss Pendergast's men during the twenties and thirties, when Kansas City politics had been a hotbed of greed, graft, and good times. Until Pendergast went to jail. But during that time, although she was only twelve or thirteen years old, she had also learned where a lot of the bodies were buried, so to speak, due to her father's inability to keep his mouth shut when he had a snootful, which was often.

After she had been with Hamm a year, she decided to pay a visit to one of her father's old friends, Earl Finley. He had known Vita when she was a little girl and had always been very fond of her. He knew she had been a large donor to Peter Wheeler's campaign and he was very happy to see her after all these years, and catch up on old times. After a while, Vita steered the conversation around to Hamm. At the mention of his name, Earl practically bit the white plastic tip off his White Owl cigar. "Don't blame us for that, Vita, we tried our best to stop him. But the little redneck son of a bitch slipped right past us and now this stupid hayseed is thumbing his nose at us and won't listen to a word we say."

Vita said, "Earl, I think you may be wrong about Hamm. He might be stubborn but he's not stupid. I think he understands he can't fight you and the senate at the same time. Call off the dogs and quit blocking every move he makes and I'll give you my word he'll push a few things through you want."

He chewed on his cigar for a moment and blinked his eyes a few times, wondering what she meant. "Aw now, Vita, how can you be sure what that little maverick son of a bitch will do? He's never done anything we wanted him to yet."

She answered him with a smile that said everything.

He looked at her and said, "You don't mean it."

"Oh yes," she said. "You better believe I do."

Then, after a moment, he started to laugh from the bottom of his big gut until it came out and filled the room and shook the table where they were sitting. When he'd calmed down long enough to speak, he wiped his eyes with his pocket handkerchief with the *E.F.* embroidered on it and said, "Hell, Vita, let me see what I can do."

Suddenly Hamm's $150 million road-improvement bond, stalemated for almost three years, passed both houses, and Earl got a few little things he wanted. But not many; Vita made sure of that. As she wisely told Hamm, "Darling, there are some people in this world that are either at your throat or at your feet. Best to keep him at your feet."

Hamm Moves Up

At first Hamm had not wanted to meet many of Vita's friends or go to parties for the arts. He had resisted but Vita knew it would be good for him personally and politically.

"Look, Vita," he said, "I just wouldn't feel right around them."

"Why not? My friends are very nice. They give a lot of money. Why wouldn't you go?"

"Because I don't want to be around people always looking down their noses at me, thinking I'm dumb."

"Hamm, you are the governor of the state. Nobody is going to think you are dumb."

"It doesn't matter what I'm the governor of, I know what they think. I used to see that same bunch when I was in college, driving around campus in their fancy cars, joining their fancy fraternities. The only way I got in the doors of a fraternity house was as a waiter. I hated every one of those pompous, egg-sucking bastards. I wanted an education and a degree as bad as the next man, only I didn't have a rich daddy to pay my bills and I had to drop out. I never got a degree in anything except how to sell tractors. How could I talk to that crowd you run with?"

"Is that what's bothering you? You know just because someone has a degree does not make them smarter or more interesting. Hamm, look where you are, how smart you are about knowing what people want.

Most of those boys you knew in college would change places with you in a second."

"Do you think so?"

"Hamm, you don't need a degree to prove how smart you are."

He admitted something to her. "It's not just the degree, Vita. It's everything else. Those rich kids learned how to socialize with each other, how to act at parties. They had four years to do nothing but make friends and find out who they were. I envy them that; I've been working since I was thirteen years old. We never had any social life. . . . Oh hell, Vita, the truth is I'm scared. I'll say the wrong thing or use the wrong fork. I feel more comfortable being around Rodney and them. I know they're not gonna laugh at me. They don't know any better themselves."

She shook her head. "Honey, you are the hardest person to kick upstairs I ever met. But I am determined to do it."

Hamm continued to resist but Vita was persistent. He said he'd make a rare appearance now and then.

A month later Vita was at her apartment waiting for him. He came in looking very pleased. He sat down and loosened his tie and put his feet up on her coffee table. "Well, how did I do?"

"You were wonderful and everybody there adored you. People came up to me all night and told me how charming they thought the governor was and how handsome he was in person."

"Is that so?" he said, taking the drink she handed him.

"Yes. I was very proud of you."

"You didn't think I was too loud or anything?"

"No."

"I didn't look stupid in this monkey suit? People weren't laughing at me, were they?"

"Not a one."

"You know, Vita, I have to say I was a little surprised. Once you get to know him, that Pete Wheeler is a pretty regular guy, isn't he? I'm kinda sorry now I said all those things about him."

"I'm glad you liked him. He really is a fine person. So is his wife."

"Do you know what he said to me, Vita?"

"No, what?"

"He said that he envied me my ability to connect with people. He said he wished he had not been handed everything, could have been a workingman like me, and been given the chance to make good on his own, like I had." He looked at her in wonderment. "Can you imagine that—here I've been jealous of him and all the time he envied me."

She could have said I told you so but she enjoyed too much watching him discover things on his own.

Sometime later, Rodney, who rarely had anything to do except be on hand whenever Hamm wanted company, came strolling into the attorney general's office. Wendell Hewitt glanced up from the work on his desk and said, "Come in and close the door, I need to talk to you."

Rodney sat down. "What's up?"

"You know, we're the only two he'll listen to and he depends on us to tell him the truth and, frankly, I'm a little worried about him and I think we both should sit him down and talk to him."

"About what?"

"All this running back and forth to all those parties. I think he is beginning to enjoy this high life a little too much, all this getting written up in the society pages. If he's not careful, he's gonna get the people who voted for him riled up."

Rodney waved his hand and dismissed the idea. "Oh, don't worry about that. No matter how many new suits he gets or who he rubs shoulders with, they know underneath it all he's one of them."

"Do you think so?"

"Hell yes. Listen, those country people have some secret way of recognizing one another that you and I don't know anything about. And you can't fool them. They can smell a phony a mile away."

"Really?"

"Oh yeah—don't forget, I've known him for a long time. I've seen him with those people and first of all, he *is* one of them, and second, he likes them, he understands how they think, and what they want, and believe me, if he didn't like them, hell, love them even, they would know it. Right now they believe he'll stand up for them but, most importantly, *he* believes he will fight for them, even against us."

"Do you think he would?"

"You bet. He means all that stuff about how there are no little men. It's not just a come-on with him and it's just what they want to hear. He knows where they itch and how to scratch it. Now, you or I couldn't get away with it but they'll stick with him through thick and thin—and he knows not to go too far."

"You sure? I think he's mighty close myself."

"Naw . . . all those people have some invisible line. If you cross it, brother, watch out. They are done with you forever. But Hamm knows just where that line is. It's like a dog whistle that only other dogs can hear."

But despite Rodney's lack of concern, there were a few rumblings about Hamm and some people did start to notice he was changing. Several editorials and column mentions popped up here and there. Some said he was spending too much time with the elite and not looking after the ones who voted him into office. But as Rodney had said, Hamm knew just when to say what and just how to say it. In his last big television address to the state before he was to go to New York for the National Governors Convention he ended his remarks with a slight little chuckle.

"You know, folks, it seems you just can't please everybody. Some people complain that I've been hobnobbing with the rich too much lately and I agree, but let me ask you this. How am I supposed to keep my eye on them and make sure they're not stealing from you if I don't hobnob a little? Some say that I'm beginning to look like Lady Astor's pet goat with my new fluffed-up haircut and button-down collars. I don't like it any more than you do but now, I can't help what's in fashion; all I can do is make sure that nobody up there in New York is ever going to say that the governor of the great state of Missouri is a hick and he doesn't know how to dress. Not while I'm in office. Why, I'll wear a necklace with pearls if that's what it takes. And the way things are going, next year I just might be doing that."

The cameramen in the studio cracked up and so did most everybody listening and all was smooth again.

Electricity

Hamm Sparks was not the only one headed for New York that year. When she was four years old Norma Warren's cousin Dena Nordstrom had left town with her mother, Marion Nordstrom, and the Warrens had not seen her since. Dena was working in television in New York and was now a very successful TV journalist and Norma decided that it was time that she and Macky went up to New York and paid her a visit. After Dena's Grandmother Gerta died, Norma felt she needed to make sure that some family kept in touch with Dena. The morning they were to leave, Aunt Elner was in her kitchen frying some bacon when the phone rang. She picked up the phone, wondering who was calling this early.

"Hello."

"Aunt Elner, it's me, Norma."

Elner was surprised to hear her voice. "Are you there already? That was fast—"

"No, we're still at the airport—"

"Oh."

"Aunt Elner . . . do me a favor and go look out your bedroom window and see if you see any smoke."

"Wait a minute." Elner clanked the phone down on the telephone table. She came back in a moment. "No. No smoke."

"Are you sure? Did you look toward our house?"

"Yes."

"And there was no smoke?"

"No."

"Are you sure? Did you smell any smoke? Go take another look, will you?"

"Hold on."

After a silence, "Nope, the sky is as clear as a bell."

"You haven't heard any fire engines, have you?"

"Why?"

"Because I think I may have walked out and left the coffeepot on. I could just kill Macky. He rushed me, so now I can't remember whether I turned it off or not. I don't know why he thinks we have to get to the airport two and a half hours before the flight—we left in such a hurry, God knows if I remembered to do anything, much less turn off the coffeepot. I am a nervous wreck."

"I'm sure you did, honey. If I know you, you probably washed it before you left."

"All right, Macky! Aunt Elner, do me a favor. Call Verbena at work. She has a key to the back door. Ask her if she will come over there and see if I unplugged it and if I didn't, to unplug it."

"All right."

"I tried to call her at home but she had already left and I have to get on this plane in one minute; that's all I need is to have my house burn to the ground. . . . ALL RIGHT, MACKY. . . . He's yelling for me, so I have to go."

"Don't worry, I'll take care of it. You run on and don't worry about a thing. Just put your mind at ease. I've left my coffeepot on all day and night and I'm not burned up yet."

"Thanks, Aunt Elner. . . . All right, Macky. I've gotta run, I'll call you when I get there. 'Bye."

Aunt Elner put the phone down and went back in the kitchen. After she had finished her breakfast, she went into the living room and sat down at her telephone table and used the magnifying glass she kept by the phone book and looked in the Yellow Pages for the number to Blue Ribbon Cleaners. Then she dialed.

"Verbena, it's Elner. Norma just called from the airport about her coffeepot. . . . Yes, again. I tell you if it's not the coffeepot, it's the iron. Anyway, she said for me to call you, so I'm calling you. I've never seen a person so nervous about electricity in my life. Whenever there's a thunderstorm, she runs through the house like a chicken with her head cut off and unplugs everything, puts on her rubber shoes, and sits in the dark. Can you imagine? I guess she thinks lightning won't hit her if she's in rubber shoes. Somebody told her about that boy over in Poplar Bluff that got hit by lightning. You remember, Claire Hightower's nephew. He was that little sissy boy who was the tap dancer. Anyway, he was running home to his momma one day after his lesson and forgot to change his shoes and got hit by lightning, *bang,* right in the taps. Knocked him twenty feet in the air. It was in all the papers, but you know, Claire says he had curly hair after that. It used to be straight as a stick until he got hit. She says he never was the same afterward. He never did marry, so we just don't know what kind of damage it caused. Anyhow, when you get home tonight, go over there so I can tell her that her house hasn't burned down to the ground. We can say we checked. Well, you take care now."

At 5:28 Aunt Elner's phone rang.

"Hello."

"Elner, it wasn't on, it was washed out and in the dishwasher."

"What I figured."

"But it's a good thing I went over, because she had left the back door wide open and two of those old dogs that Macky feeds were flopped up on the sofa in the living room."

"Ohhh, well . . . I'm not gonna tell her that. She'll have a running fit."

"Oh, don't I know it."

"Was it that old chow?"

"Yes, and the other one . . . that . . . whatever it is . . ."

"It's a good thing you got them out."

"I just hope they didn't bring any fleas in, don't you? If they did, I'm not saying where they came from, are you?"

"No. I am prepared to lie like a rug."

After they got back from New York, Norma sat at the kitchen table and wrote out a list to give to Verbena and the fire department, instructing them what to do in case of fire. When Macky came home for lunch, she handed it to him.

"Would you take this down to the store and run off about twenty copies? Make sure they're dark enough to read."

"Sure. What is it?"

"It's a list for us to give to Verbena to hand to the firemen so they will know what to look for."

"What list?"

"In case we are out of town and there is a fire. I want to make sure they get everything that's important out first, before it's too late."

"Oh, for God's sake, Norma, the house is not going to burn down."

"Maybe not . . . but better safe than sorry. And you don't know, what if lightning strikes it or something. I just think it's better to be on the safe side and I need to go over this list with you, in case for some reason I'm not here and you are."

Norma sat down at the table with Macky. "Okay. Now, the very first thing, number one: go and get everything out of the bottom right dresser drawer. I've got all the birth certificates, our photographs, our marriage license, wedding pictures, our yearbooks, things like that, all our paper goods that can't be replaced."

"Norma, I'm sure we could get a copy of our yearbook."

"Maybe so, but how are you going to remember all the little cute things that everybody wrote? You won't remember that . . . you can't replace that. . . . And pictures of your family and mine, Linda's baby pictures, you can't replace those. Don't forget what happened to Poor Tot when her mother set the house on fire. They lost everything, photos, birth certificates—she didn't even have one picture of her family or anything. I don't want that to happen to us. . . . That's one thing I learned, you have to prioritize, be prepared for the worst."

"Why don't I just strap a fire extinguisher on your back so you can be ready at all times?"

"Oh, don't be silly."

"O.K., but Norma—on the off chance there is a fire—do you think the firemen are going to take time to read some list?"

Norma looked at Macky. "That's a very good point. They should have a copy of this in advance, so they can be familiar with it and not have to waste time to refer to it."

"I've got a better idea," Macky said. "Why don't we have them come over and practice while we're at it."

"Do they do things like that?"

"Norma, you are getting nuttier by the day. Let me see it."

Norma handed him the list.

"What's in the maroon hanging bag?"

"Your good coat, my good coat, my good hat, shoes . . . things like that. We don't want to wind up in rags, having to wear whatever we have on. Oh, and I put all the home movies in the bottom, you can't replace those. My jewelry, whatever I don't have on, my dancing storks, your Kennedy half-dollar, Linda's bronzed baby shoes, you don't want to lose those, do you? Can you think of anything I've missed?"

Macky ran down the list again. "I notice you didn't put down anything in my den."

"Well, what's in there that's worth anything, except a bunch of old dead fish on the wall? What would you want out of there anyway?"

"I have a few pictures . . . and a couple of books . . . and my baseball."

"Well, I don't think they'll have time to go in there, so whenever we leave, you just be sure and get what you want saved and put everything in the box under the bed. Here, as a matter of fact, I'm just not going to take a chance with Linda's twirling trophies. I'm going to bring them downstairs and pack them . . . the firemen may not have time to go all the way upstairs. Now is there anything else you can think of? Speak now or forever hold your peace. Remember, all the paper goods go first . . . letters, cards, newspaper clippings, our Wayne Newton photo, all our pictures, they're all gonna go in the first batch. So if you have anything like that, stick it in."

"Why do you want that stupid cuckoo clock on the list? It's a piece of junk."

"Well, it's *old.* And it was a wedding present. Put something down you want then."

Macky got up and walked around the house, looking for things. A few minutes later he came back with the baseball Bobby had given him signed by Marty Marion.

"Well, put it in the box under the bed then. I'm not going to waste their time having them look for some old baseball when too many other important things are at stake." She added it to the list and then said, "You know—I wonder how big a safety-deposit box is and are they fireproof?"

"Why?"

"Well . . . I think we'd be a lot better off when we left town if we just took everything we could down to the bank and put it in a safety-deposit box. Then I won't have to worry about human error. That way we would know for sure."

"What if the bank burned down?"

Norma looked at him. "Macky . . . *why* would you say something like that to me? Why would you want to put something like that in my head when you know how serious this is?"

"Oh, for God's sake, Norma. I was just kidding—the bank is not going to burn down. Neither is our house."

"All I'm trying to do is preserve our memories, protect our family history so that Linda and our grandchildren won't wind up without anything to look at after we are gone, and you make a joke out of it."

"Norma, I was kidding."

"I don't think you appreciate the things I try and do for this family. Children should have a sense of continuity, it's very important."

"Honey, first of all, we don't have any grandchildren."

"But we might someday."

"Even if we do, we can always have new pictures made if anything happens."

"I am aware of that, Macky—that's not the point. The point is, they would only see pictures of us when we were older and not when we were young . . . that's what I'm talking about. I want them to get to see a picture of me when I was young and still had a figure, not some old middle-aged woman."

"Oh, Norma, you're only thirty-five years old, just stop it. You are better looking now than you ever were." There was a pause. Macky saw his chance and he took it. "You look better today than the day I married you."

"Oh, you're just saying that."

"No, I'm not. I was looking at you the other night, when you had on that pink thing . . . you know?"

"My nightgown?"

"Yeah. I said to myself just the other night, Norma gets better-looking every day."

"Really?"

"Yes. You were a pretty girl but now you're . . . a . . . sexy, mature woman. Just like a ripe juicy plum ready to pick off the tree . . . just right . . ."

"I've had that old pink thing for years."

"Maybe so, but you look great in it."

"It's just an old nightgown I got over at Kmart."

"Well, you don't have a thing to worry about how you look now, that's all I can say. You're a good-looking old broad—and don't you forget it."

"It had a housecoat to match. I don't know why I never wear it. I don't even know if I still have it—I might have thrown it out or given it away by now."

After Macky left the house, Norma went into the bedroom and took out her pink Kmart nightgown and held it up to her and looked at herself in the mirror. She turned to the left and then to the right and smiled.

Ten minutes later the phone at the store rang. Macky picked up. "Warren's Hardware."

"Macky, let me ask you something, and tell me the truth."

"What?"

"You don't discuss me with other men, do you?"

"What?"

"You don't discuss what I look like in my nightgown with other men, do you?"

"Of course not."

"Because I would be horrified if you did—"

"Honey, I promise I don't discuss what you look like in anything with anybody, you know that."

"I would just die if I thought while I was talking to some man he was trying to imagine what I looked like in my nightgown."

"Norma, do you think I would take the chance of driving all the men in this town wild? I know better than that."

"That's not what I mean. I mean, oh, you know . . . I'd just feel funny if I thought somebody was looking at me funny."

"No. Your secret's safe with me."

"Good. I feel better. Guess what? I found that housecoat. I had put it up on the top shelf in that red box with those extra pillowcases we don't use, but guess what else?"

"What?"

"I can't wear it."

"Why?"

"It doesn't match anymore. It's a much darker pink than my nightgown, so it's not a matched set. I'm thinking about running out there and seeing if they still carry the same thing and that way I could just buy the gown if they would let me, they might not, but if they won't . . . I thought that maybe if I ran it through the washing machine every time I did a load, it would fade sooner or later. What do you think . . . should I do it?"

"Do what?"

"See if I can get a new nightgown. I thought since you like the way it looks on me, I should try and get a new one. If they still carry the same line; they keep changing things, I wish they wouldn't . . . don't you?"

"What?"

"Keep changing things. When you buy something you like, it's terrible to go there and they don't sell it anymore. That's something you should remember in your business. Don't discontinue things or change the make or brand."

"Okay, honey, I'll remember that."

"Macky, you're not going to be mad at me for going to Kmart, are you?"

"No."

"I'm not buying hardware. I might not be buying anything. If they have it I'll just get this one thing and then that's it, O.K.?"

"All right . . ."

"I'll take Aunt Elner with me . . . but we will just look, O.K.?"

"O.K."

"You won't think I'm a traitor, will you?"

"No, you go on and see about your nightgown."

"Macky, do you really still find me attractive after all these years or are you just kidding?"

"Do you want me to close the store and come home right now and prove it?"

"Macky Warren! You better stop that nasty talk. What if a customer should hear you?"

Macky laughed heartily, and Norma hung up the phone and smiled.

Maybe while she was there, she would see if it came in any other colors.

Near Miss

In all the time Vita and Hamm had been together there had only been one conversation that came close to being an argument. Early on, when the affair first started, Hamm went through a period where he talked about getting a divorce but she had quickly nipped that idea in the bud. "Absolutely not. You are not going to ruin your political future over me. Besides, I don't want to get married. I'm a grown woman and I want exactly what I've got. If this is some sort of guilt over me, forget it. You might as well know right now, I don't want children. I have no interest whatsoever in being a mother or a stepmother."

"But Vita," he said, "I do feel bad."

She took his face in her hands. "Darling, I know how you feel about me. You don't need to wreck your life to prove it. What you do at home is your business but what we have together is just between us. We are not hurting anyone. It's perfect the way it is."

Of course, Vita did not know it as yet but her affair with Hamm was hurting someone in ways that at this point were subtle.

Outwardly, to Betty Raye, Hamm seemed the same as he always was. He had always been on the move and never at home and when he was she seldom got to see him alone. She did not know it, but being with Vita had changed him and the way he looked at the world and Betty Raye. He still loved her—but differently from before. No matter what he might say, Hamm was caught up in the whirl of Vita's big-money and big-words crowd, still a little amazed and flattered to be suddenly socializing at black-tie affairs with people who would barely have spoken to him before. He seldom took Betty Raye along. First of all was her famous dislike of parties and social functions and second of all, she simply would not have fit in. The few places he did take her were for political purposes only and when they arrived he would immediately disappear into a circle of people dying to meet him. She usually wound up over in a corner, talking to one or two women who felt sorry for her or were curious about her, and then leave as soon as she could slip out and go home.

She tried to stay in touch with Hamm as much as she could, to be there when he needed her, but he never seemed to need her for anything. Over time Betty Raye felt herself slowly beginning to fade away, like a light starting to dim. She began to live in a world where she felt invisible.

Even the boys were slipping away. They were both getting to be much more like their father, aggressive and rowdy, and spent much of their time outside playing ball with the guards around the mansion. She did not know why but she began to feel like a stranger living in a house where everyone knew a secret but her.

Which was pretty much the truth. From the beginning, the inside circle knew about Hamm and Vita. Hamm had made it perfectly clear in a meeting with his staff right from the start.

"If Vita asks you for anything or needs anything, I want you to see that she has it, you understand? And if you want my opinion on an issue, ask Vita and she'll let you know."

Ralph and Lester, the two state troopers who usually picked her up, got the picture without having to be told. When they drove her somewhere to meet him they tipped their hats and called her Mrs. Green. There were no jokes, no sneers or attempts at familiarity. They knew who she was and what she was to the governor and it was not up to them to approve or disapprove. Vita did not complain or explain; she just was. The entire staff understood there were unspoken orders to make sure that Vita and the official first lady were never at the same function at the same time. And if, God forbid, for some reason they *were* to be at the same place, that they were *never* to be in the same room.

But accidents do happen. Peter Wheeler and his wife, Carole, were hosting a party at their home to celebrate the opening of the brand-new art museum in Kansas City. Many prominent artists from all over the world were flying in for the occasion and Cecil, ever vigilant about protocol, felt that if the first lady did not at least put in an appearance it would not look good. "Darling," he said, "just come for thirty minutes. Say hello, have your picture made, and I promise you can slip out anytime after that and one of the troopers will drive you home."

Betty Raye looked stricken. "Oh, Cecil, do I have to?"

"It would mean so much to the state if you would, and I know Hamm thinks you should be there with him to welcome everyone. This is no ordinary party. We don't want to disappoint him, do we?"

"No, I guess not," she said.

It was, in fact, a star-studded affair with over five hundred people mingling in every room of the magnificent Wheeler home. Betty Raye came in wearing the same beige cocktail dress she always wore, and as always, she felt like a piece of old vanilla fudge compared to the rest of the women in their vivid and colorful clothes and jewels. But true to her word, she posed for pictures and stood in the receiving line. She smiled and shook hands with each visitor and repeated what Cecil had told her to say, like a mynah bird. "Welcome to our state, we are so honored to have you." Finally, after about forty-five minutes, she made eye contact with Cecil. After she said her good-byes to the host and hostess, Cecil walked her out to the car and she was on her way home, early as usual, relieved as usual.

About ten minutes into the trip home Betty Raye took her earrings off and reached for her purse. But it was not there. She realized she must have left it at the party, in the upstairs powder room.

She would not have returned to the Wheelers' but her reading glasses were in the purse also and she needed them. The young state trooper who was filling in for Ralph Childress that night turned around and drove her back to the party. She slipped in and went upstairs and got her purse. As she was coming down the stairs, trying her best to be inconspicuous, she heard a woman's laugh that was so infectious she had to look and see where it was coming from. The woman, who had just joined the party, standing in the middle of a large crowd of men, laughed again and was clearly enjoying a story that was being told. Betty Raye could not help but stop and stare for a moment until Martha Ross, a woman she had met earlier, walked up and said in a loud voice, "Why, Mrs. Sparks, we all thought you had left!"

Betty Raye whispered and tried to head for the door, hoping not to be noticed by anyone else. "I did but I had to come back; I forgot my purse."

Martha followed her. "Oh, don't you just *hate* when you do that, I do it all the time." When Betty Raye reached the door, curiosity got the best of her and she said, "Mrs. Ross, who is that pretty lady over there?"

Mrs. Ross looked. "Why, that's Vita Green. Don't you know Vita?"

Betty Raye shook her head and Mrs. Ross looked at her in surprise. "She practically runs your husband's arts program. I can't believe you don't know Vita." She proceeded to grab Betty Raye by the arm and pull her across the foyer, calling out in an excited voice, "Vita! Look who I have here. . . . I can't believe you haven't met Mrs. Sparks yet."

An entire room full of laughing and chatting people suddenly went as silent as if they had all been struck dumb. Even the ice in the glasses stopped rattling. The men in Vita's group went visibly pale before her eyes.

Vita, who had her back turned to Betty Raye at the time, seemed to be the only person able to move and speak. She casually turned around, her expression unchanging, and with warmth and poise said, "Why no, Mrs. Sparks and I have somehow managed to miss one another until now."

Vita smiled and extended her hand and in a pleasant voice added, "Hello. I'm so pleased to finally meet you at last."

Betty Raye was dazzled by Vita's large diamond spray pin and her beauty in general but did manage to offer a faint "How do you do."

Vita smiled again. "It's so lovely to meet you, Mrs. Sparks. I hope we'll see each other again sometime."

"Thank you," said Betty Raye. As she made her way back out of the crowded room, Mrs. Ross, thinking she had just done a good deed, said, "That's nice, I am glad I was able to introduce you two."

As soon as Betty Raye got to the door and it closed behind her, an ice cube managed a weak little clink and gradually people began to move and within seconds, Vita, who had never blinked an eye, continued her conversation as if nothing momentous or so potentially dangerous as wife-meets-mistress had just happened.

• • •

On the drive back to the mansion Betty Raye thought about Mrs. Green. When they had met she had so gracefully and effortlessly moved her black cigarette holder from one hand to the other, with such elegance and style. She was like one of those movie stars that she and Anna Lee had seen at the Elmwood Theater. Betty Raye wondered if she should try to take up smoking. Vita, on the other hand, who had only seen Betty Raye in photographs, wondered how Hamm could have ever been attracted to this rather plain, nondescript person, a woman who, she was sure, was perfectly nice but had looked more like the help than a guest.

Hamm, who had been in another room at the time, had missed the entire event. Betty Raye had not said a word or seemed the least bit suspicious but Hamm was furious and promised Vita that it would not happen again. From that day forward, Betty Raye was never out of trooper Ralph Childress's sight for a moment.

Power

After Betty Raye and Vita had the near miss Cecil said to Hamm, "It's your life, honey, but you are not being very considerate of your wife and that's all I'm going to say." But Wendell Hewitt, the attorney general of the state, was worried about Hamm getting hurt politically. Wendell knew how fast that could happen firsthand. He had been caught with a blonde and ruined his own chances at being governor. But most of all, Wendell and Rodney had been used to being his only advisers and they resented Vita's influence over him. They tried to warn him how dangerous the situation was. But Vita never worried about what anybody said as far as Hamm was concerned. She knew she was the one he ran to when he was happy, sad, or scared or needed advice. She accepted who he was without question or judgment and he knew it. The night he gave his speech in front of seven thousand people at the state Democratic convention, he came back to her exhilarated, his eyes shining. He always ran a temperature about three degrees higher than most people but tonight he was burning up. "I tell you, Vita, that feeling, knowing all those people are listening to you and you can tell them anything, it scares the hell out of me how easily people are led." He looked at her, his eyes still glowing. "You know, sometimes I get so tired of having to fight Earl Finley and the rest of them for every little thing, running myself in the ground trying to push stuff through. I started asking myself why. Why was I doing it? What for? But tonight when I got up there in front of all those people, I knew that was the thing I'd been chasing after. He got up and paced the room. "I wish I could describe what it feels like to have thousands of people listening to your every word, how easy it is to please them, to get that applause and to hear them out there screaming for you. It's like being in control of one big ocean and you can calm it down or make it roar. God, Vita, it's not even people anymore, it's one big *thing* you want to control and once you've had a taste of it, you're hooked. It's like if you don't have it you will die, do you know what I mean? Somebody's handed you the baton and you can lead this rich, powerful orchestra. Does that make sense to you? I mean after that, leading a five-piece band means nothing, not after you've led that orchestra, thousands of people all playing the song just like you want them to."

Vita smiled at him and he stopped. "I've had too much to drink, I'm sorry."

"Don't be sorry. You don't ever have to hold back or be afraid to tell me anything, don't you know that? The more you tell me, the more I understand you. I love you, I'm on your side—remember that."

He sat down. "You must think I'm an idiot but I can't talk to the boys; hell, they wouldn't understand. You're the only person I can trust. Betty Raye's not interested in politics—the whole thing scares her. Oh, she tries but all she ever really wanted was a quiet, simple life and look what I drug her into. I try to leave her out of it as much as I can. She was put on display as a kid and she just hates it, me being governor.

"But God help me, Vita—I love it."

On the other hand, Betty Raye was counting the days when they would be out of the governor's mansion at last and into a real home they did not have to share with a hundred people. As per Hamm's instructions, Rodney had driven her past a brand-new red-brick house in a nice subdivision outside of town. And later when she walked into the governor's office Hamm did not look up but said, "Well, is that what you had in mind?"

"Oh Hamm, it's more than I could have ever hoped for."

Having been a used-car salesman, Rodney was able to figure out how to make deals in different ways and made an under-the-table, verbal agreement with a real estate agent to hold the house until Hamm left office.

Betty Raye would not miss being first lady but she would miss a few of the staff. Cecil, of course, and over the years she had grown quite fond of Alberta Peets, the ice-pick murderess, who besides cooking had helped her with the boys and was a great baby-sitter. When she said for them to go to bed, they did. They minded her much better than they ever had their mother or father.

But other than that she could hardly wait to pack up and get out of the governor's mansion for good.

Hamm tried to resign himself to the fact that he was going out of office but as the May primaries grew closer and closer, the more anxious and restless he became. While Betty Raye and Cecil shopped for furniture and dishes and silverware for the new house, Hamm complained and bellyached to anyone who would listen about the fact that a governor could not succeed himself for a third consecutive term. He even ranted and raved to a group of unsuspecting visiting Girl Scout leaders from Joplin.

"If I hadn't had to fight Earl Finley and the damn Republicans I might have done it but two terms is not enough time to get anything nailed down. I need at least four more years to finish what I started and now Earl is gonna bring in that idiot Carnie Boofer and wreck it all. . . ."

Betty Raye and Cecil were busy looking for rugs and drapes to match, but as the days went by Hamm became more irritable and could not sleep. The guys tried to cheer him up. Nothing seemed to work. Finally, one day Rodney said, "You need to get out of here for a while." So Wendell, Rodney, and Seymour drove him down to the secret boathouse and took *The Betty Raye* out for a cruise.

Usually the boat was where he loosened up and forgot about everything and enjoyed himself but not today. He did nothing but sit and stare at the water and try to think of what he could do. He turned to Wendell, who had his feet propped up on the side, drinking beer. "If we were to call the legislature into special session, what do you think our chances are of getting an amendment added to the constitution?"

Wendell knew what he was up to. "Hamm, there's no way in hell they are going to let you succeed yourself; it's a state law."

"But laws have been changed, haven't they?"

"Yeah, but you ain't gonna change this one. The Republicans won't vote for it and Earl is determined to bring in Carnie Boofer, so why don't you just relax and take it easy for the next four years. Then all you have to do is come back in and clean up the mess old Boofer makes. In the meantime, just sit on your boat, take a few trips, and enjoy yourself, boy."

Hamm had been offered jobs through Vita's friends but nothing that excited him. The next time he was at her apartment they sat on the couch and he tried to tell her what he was feeling. "It's not that I don't appreciate the offers, Vita, I do. I don't know how I'll be able to stand just being a nobody again. I'm gonna miss being out of that limelight now that I'm used to it."

"But, darling, you can run again in sixty-eight . . . it's only four years."

He looked at her almost desperately. "Vita, I don't think I can wait that long. I don't know how to explain it but it seems like I've been freezing all my life and it's the only place I feel warm, really warm. The thing is, once it gets ahold of you, you can't let go even if you wanted to. It's too late. Once you've been up there, there's nowhere else to go but down. That's where you live, the only place you feel alive, and you've got to fight to hold on. And what if I can't get back in? What if Carnie Boofer messes up so bad that the next time they elect a Republican? People forget about you once you're out of power. The truth is, Vita . . . I'm scared to let go."

A Drowning Man Is a Dangerous Man

Hamm was back in Jefferson City, sitting in his office having a few drinks with the guys, when Hamm Jr. ran in and asked for more quarters to put in the pinball machine in the basement and ran back out. When he left Hamm asked Wendell, "What's the age limit on running for governor?"

"Why?"

"If Hamm Junior was old enough, I'd run him."

Wendell grinned. "Damn, boy, next you'll be trying to run your wife."

Seymour Gravel said, "Yeah, Hamm, or how about your dog. He's pretty smart, a hell of a lot smarter than Carnie Boofer."

"But then who ain't?" Rodney added.

They all laughed except Hamm, who sat with a glazed expression, staring into space. Then he looked at Wendell. "Why not?"

"Why not what?"

"Run my wife."

"Oh, hell, Hamm, I was just kidding."

"Is there a law against it?"

"No, but you can't do that."

"Why not? Tell me one good reason. It would be almost the same as voting for me, wouldn't it?"

"Yes, but nobody is gonna vote for a woman even if she is your wife."

"Why not?"

Now Seymour asked Wendell: "Yeah, why not?"

An hour later, after going back and forth in a heated debate over why not, Hamm said, "Excuse me a minute, will you, boys?" and went in the other room to make a call.

Vita had invited people over for dinner and they were still in the living room having after-dinner drinks but her maid Bridget came in and said, "Mrs. Green, the archbishop is on the phone and said he needs to speak to you right away." Vita excused herself and took Hamm's call in her bedroom. When she heard what he was thinking she threw her head back and laughed with delight at his crazy idea. But he was more excited and enthusiastic about this than he had been about anything lately and was talking a mile a minute.

"Listen, Vita, it would be the same thing as me buying a house and putting it in somebody else's name. Wouldn't it? It would still be mine. I'd still be the governor . . . it would just be in a different name, that's all. . . . So what do you think?"

She was still laughing so hard she could not answer.

"I'm not joking, I'm serious."

"I know you are, Hamm."

"What do you think?"

"Well," she said, "it's a completely insane idea . . . but it would almost be worth it just to see the look on Earl's face when you announced it." She wiped the tears from her eyes. "Oh God, you've made me laugh so hard I've ruined my makeup."

"So, Vita—should I do it?"

"Why not," she said. "Go ahead and try. What do you have to lose? If nothing else, it will be fun to watch."

He came back into the office, sat down, and said, "I think we should do it."

After he got everyone to agree, Hamm pushed a button on the phone and said in a syrupy voice, "Betty Raye, could you come down here for a minute?"

They heard her answer over the speakerphone: "Hamm, I'm already in my nightgown."

"That's alright, honey, put your robe on and come on down the back stairs. I need to talk to you."

Rodney looked grim. "She ain't gonna go along with this, I can tell you that."

Hamm said, "Yes, she will. But now, you boys have got to help me out here, make her see how it's our only chance."

Betty Raye could not imagine what Hamm wanted with her at this hour or what he wanted, period, but she put on her robe and, wearing the big fuzzy pink bunny slippers that Ferris, her youngest boy, had given her for Christmas, went down the back stairs. When she opened the door she was startled to see a room full of men. She clutched at the neck of her robe. "Oh, I didn't know you had people here."

"That's all right, come on in, Betty Raye, and have a seat," said the spider to the fly.

As she reluctantly walked in she became even more uncomfortable. All the men in the room turned and stared at her as if they had never seen her before, including her husband.

"Is anything wrong?" she asked.

"No, not a thing, sweetheart. The boys and I just want to talk to you about a little something."

An hour later they were upstairs in the bedroom and Betty Raye was crying. "How could you do this? You gave me your word that this was the last time. Just four more years, you said."

"I know I did, honey, but you heard what the boys said. I've got to finish what I started. If I don't, Earl Finley will undo everything I did and those roads will never get built. I owe it to the folks that voted for me . . . and you running for me is our only chance, our only hope."

"Oh, but Hamm, the whole thing is ridiculous. I don't know anything about politics much less how to be a governor."

"You don't have to know anything. You wouldn't really be the governor, you'd just be standing in for me."

She went over to the dresser to get another Kleenex. "And that's another thing. I'm the mother of two children. I don't want to be involved in some scam, something that's illegal."

"But it is legal. Wendell told you it was."

"Maybe so. But it's totally dishonest. To pretend to be the governor when I'm not. What will people think?"

"Honey, it's not dishonest. People will know they're voting for me. And people will thank you. You know how high my ratings are. They would vote for me anyway if it were not for that stupid law. You're doing everybody a favor. Wendell told you that."

"Well then, why doesn't Wendell run?"

"Because. Honey—"

"I'll tell you why. Because everybody knows he's got good sense and I'm just an idiot you can push around. That's why."

"Oh now, Betty—"

"And what about my house? I've waited eight years . . . and you promised me, just four more years, you said."

He came over and sat down on the bed. "I know I did, sweetheart, and I'm just as sick about it as you are. But we have a duty to the people."

"But what about us? We're people. What about the boys? I wanted them to have a normal life for a change. They never see you. I never see you."

"But, honey, this *is* about the boys. And their future. I don't want them to have a daddy that failed. My name is all I have to leave them. I want to make sure for their sake the Hamm Sparks name is one they can be proud of. I owe it to them."

He could see she was now at least listening. He pulled out his big guns. "Betty Raye, I'm ashamed to tell you this but I haven't been completely honest with you. I was seriously thinking of running again in sixty-eight. But now I know it would be too late. If I don't hang in there now, while I still have a foothold, and fight now for everything good I did, all the work and sweat and sacrifice will be for nothing. And honest to God, Betty Raye, I don't think I could take it. You're the only hope I have. . . . Do you think I've enjoyed being away from you and the children so much? No. But if you stick with me one more time—"

"Hamm, don't. I've heard that before."

"I know you have. But—and I mean this—if you will do this, I will swear on my life, on my children's life, that I will never run for governor again. I'll swear it on the Bible in front of the Missouri Supreme Court if you want me to."

Another hour of Betty Raye crying, with Hamm pleading, went by and Betty Raye was beginning to weaken.

"Hamm, please don't make me do this. If you do, then you might as well get a gun and shoot me right now, because I'll just die if I have to get up there and make speeches."

"You won't have to do a thing—just stand up, introduce me, and sit down. That's all you have to do. Other than that, everything will be exactly the same as it always was. The only difference is this time you and

I will be together twenty-four hours a day. I'll be right by your side all the time; all you have to do is just be my silent partner. Why, if I was to take a regular job I'd be gone every day and we'd never see each other. Don't you see, honey, this way we can be close like we used to be. You'd like that, wouldn't you?"

"Yes, you know I would but—"

"It's just four little years and then I can leave knowing I've done the best job I could and we'd be done with politics forever."

She swallowed hard. "Are you sure it's the only way?"

"You heard what Wendell said. If you don't do it the whole state will suffer."

She teared up again. "But what about my house? I bought so many nice things . . . it was going to be so pretty. . . ."

"I'll tell you what. You can keep the house."

"Really?" she said.

"Sure. It will wait, it ain't gonna go anywhere. And you and Cecil can decorate to your heart's content. Then when the term is over, we will walk out this door and move right in. In the meantime you and the kids and I can go over and spend the night or the weekend anytime you want. Or you and I can go over by ourselves and leave the kids with Alberta. It can be sort of like our love nest. What do you say? Will you do this one last thing for me?"

She looked at him. "No speeches?"

"None."

"Do you swear?"

"I swear. On the Bible."

She moaned. "Oh, God, Hamm, I can't believe I'm letting you talk me into this. But if it's really for the good of the state . . ."

And so, at 2:34 A.M., the woman in pink fuzzy bunny slippers agreed to run for governor.

He looked at her, genuinely grateful. "Oh, thank you, honey, you won't regret it. I know I haven't been the best of husbands but from now on things will be different, you'll see. I promise." He kissed her and quickly jumped up and ran off to the office.

As she sat on the bed and blew her nose with a fresh Kleenex she wondered what she was in for now.

She sat there for a while and tried to think about what Hamm had said. Maybe he was right, maybe this would bring them closer together.

After all, it was the first time he had really needed her in eight years. Maybe it would not be so bad. She did get to keep the house and he had promised to swear on the Bible that this was the last time; he had never done that before. Maybe it could be like it used to be. She hoped so. Because for better or worse, she was still in love with her husband.

The Two-for-One Sale

Earl Finley called Vita, screaming at the top of his lungs. "That sorry son of a bitch promised me he would support Boofer. We had a deal and now he's harpooned me in the back. You tell that son of a bitch that I'll get him if it's the last thing I ever do."

"I'll tell him, Earl," Vita said.

"I could kill him with my bare hands."

"I know how you must feel. Believe me, I was shocked. Just shocked when I heard." Vita put the phone down, smiling. To hear a man who had done nothing all his life but pull one dirty deal after another so incensed and outraged that it had happened to him was highly amusing.

Minnie Oatman was in Pine Mountain, Georgia, at a Singing on the Mountain when she heard the news. She had just finished doing her new hit, "I Love to Tell the Story," when someone came running out onstage and handed her a note. She then threw her hands up in the air and called out to the boys, "PRAISE JESUS, YOUR SISTER IS GONNA BE GOVERNOR!"

When it was announced to the public that Hamm was running his wife, the news was met with mixed reactions. The people who were for him laughed and winked at each other, tickled that their man had pulled one over the big shots. The rest were furious. They felt Hamm was making a fool of himself and them. But for him or against him, the announcement caused a loud stir. This was news. So far in the entire history of the United States, there had only been two women governors and they both had been elected back in 1924. In a special election, Nellie Ross of Wyoming had succeeded her husband after he had died in office, and Miriam Ferguson of Texas had stepped in after her husband was impeached for misappropriating funds. In 1964 women in politics were still considered a novelty, as well as something of a joke. The Fergusons of Texas were laughingly called Ma and Pa Ferguson and when it was joked that Missouri now had a new Ma and Pa team, Hamm loved it. The national magazines had a field day, coming down and taking pictures of him in an apron and with a feather duster in his hand. And they all wanted to interview Betty Raye but everyone on staff was instructed, "For God's sake, whatever you do, keep her away from the press!"

Contrary to what Hamm had promised, Betty Raye was immediately picked and poked at by a slew of hairdressers and makeup artists and dress designers Cecil brought in to "improve her image," as he put it. Not that she had an image, as he also said. After endless hours of Betty Raye trying on dress after dress, "look" after "look," and standing there while Cecil and his friends argued back and forth, it was decided they would go with the Jackie Kennedy style, simple little knit suits and pillbox hats. But it turned out not to be a good look for someone with glasses. So the second thing Cecil did was to convince her that she simply must get contact lenses. "Darling, you have such beautiful eyes and you'll take a much better picture, trust me." What resulted was a disaster. At her first big press conference she stood beside Hamm, her hair in what was supposed to have been some hairdresser's version of a Jackie Kennedy flip and looking extremely uncomfortable, squinting and blinking her eyes in pain. Then right in the middle of Hamm's speech one lens popped out and Betty Raye panicked. "I've lost one!" she said and frantically started searching around the bustline of her dress to see if she could find it. A reporter turned to another and asked, "What did she lose?"

The second man said, "I don't know, buddy, but I'm afraid to ask."

What followed next were long days of running up and down every road in Missouri, packed in cars with trucks following behind carrying sound equipment, banners, folding chairs, a portable stage, and Le Roy Oatman and the Missouri Plowboys, who had been pulled back in for the occasion. Betty Raye would sit in the car and read until Seymour came to get her and escort her to the stage, where she would go to the microphone and say, "We are so pleased to be with you today and it is also my pleasure to introduce you to my number one adviser, my husband, your governor, Hamm Sparks," at which point she would sit down and Hamm would talk for the next forty-five minutes while she sat behind him, waiting to be taken back to the car and head to the next stop.

Hamm was attacked from all quarters. Carnie Boofer banged his fists. "This hoax Sparks is trying to pull on the voters of Missouri is an insult and an embarrassment to every woman in America." Editorials accused Hamm of using the state as a patsy and of trying to ride back in office by hanging on to his wife's skirttail. Everybody in the state and out had an opinion about the matter. Back in Elmwood Springs, the morning Dorothy heard she was running, even though she had a strict rule and never endorsed a political candidate on her show, she did say this: "It looks like our Betty Raye is running for governor and we just could not be happier. I don't know of a sweeter and nicer girl in the world."

But Doc and Jimmy were of a different opinion. One night the two of them were out on the porch when Doc said, "That girl shouldn't be dragged through all that mess. What is he thinking about?"

Jimmy said, "It's a hell of a mean trick to pull on a nice lady, that's for sure."

"He ought to be horsewhipped."

"Or something."

Jimmy did not say what he really wanted to do. He had hated Hamm Sparks with a passion ever since that Christmas four years ago when he had been visiting his buddies at the veterans hospital in Kansas City, where the name of Hamm Sparks had come up quite by accident. His friends had handed him a present and when he'd unwrapped the box there were twelve cartons of cigarettes inside. One of his friends said, "Don't thank us, thank the governor." Another said, "Yeah, he's over here all the time to see his lady friend. Since they took up, we get a lot of attention."

"He's a vet, so when he's in town he comes over and throws a few cartons of cigarettes our way. She's one of those society women, a looker, from her pictures in the paper—I guess he got tired of gospel singing. Yes, he's been showing up over here quite a bit. Can't say I blame him. I hear she's put a lot of money behind him—she and those people she runs with. . . ."

Jimmy nodded and lit one of his own cigarettes. "Is that so?" He was thinking, Why that no-good, sorry little son of a bitch.

He did not mention that he knew Hamm or Betty Raye. A boy in a wheelchair said, "Hey, I wouldn't kick a good-looking rich woman out of bed, would you? Hell, I wouldn't kick any woman out of bed, I don't care what she looks like."

They laughed and then the conversation changed. Most of the men were paraplegic and would never sleep with a woman again.

When Jimmy left the hospital and got to the Greyhound station to catch his bus back home, he tossed the cartons of cigarettes to an old fellow sitting outside the building. "Here, buddy. Merry Christmas." Jimmy loved to smoke but he'd be damned before he took anything from Hamm Sparks. It was all he could do to keep from going after him with a baseball bat.

Let's Go On with the Show

Of course, there were a few obstacles to overcome. A vote for Hamm Sparks was one thing but there were some men out there who would never vote for a woman even if she was just a surrogate candidate—stand-in or not, she was still a female. But the majority of the Democrats came through and Betty Raye won the primaries without a problem. Then came the Republicans to battle for the election in November. Their candidate was very careful not to attack Betty Raye and went after Hamm, but one of his top aides was overheard saying something snide about Betty Raye's backwoods gospel-singing beginnings and the newspapers printed it. It was just the thing Hamm had been waiting for. He jumped all over it. "My wife and I, unlike our honorable Republican opponent, are not ashamed of being God-fearing Christians. My wife is a humble woman but she is proud that she comes from a family with the rich traditions of the Oatman Family Gospel Singers. And I'm proud to be the son-in-law of such a fine woman as Minnie Oatman.

"I say to attack folks because of their religion is downright un-American and, if I may say so, not very gentlemanly. Frankly, I'm ashamed of him and surprised he would stoop so low as to take a swipe at my wife and her family." By the time Hamm got through dragging him over the coals, people had forgotten that it had not been the candidate who had said anything in the first place. During the campaign, although Hamm and Vita talked every day, Vita did not see as much of Hamm as she would have liked, but she was thoroughly enjoying the show and watching Hamm in action.

On the morning of November 5, almost everyone had their television sets on.

"Well, it's ladies' day in Missouri this morning," said a smiling Barbara Walters on the NBC *Today* show. The male cohost snorted slightly, then caught himself and changed the subject, but not before adding his congratulations to the new Governor Sparks.

Bobby and Anna Lee both sent her telegrams of congratulations, as did Doc and Dorothy and Mother Smith. The first Sunday after Betty Raye had won the election Dorothy ran into Pauline Tuttle, Betty Raye's old high school English teacher, at church. The very same Pauline Tuttle who, sixteen years ago at the A & P, had predicted that Betty Raye would never amount to anything. Dorothy did not want to rub it in but at the coffee-and-cake get-together in the parish hall afterward, she knew she shouldn't but she could not help saying just a little something as she passed by. "So, Pauline," she said, "what do you think about our girl up in Jefferson City?"

Pauline stood there holding her plate and looked at her with a helpless expression. "I just don't know what to say, Dorothy, I'm speechless. How that shy little girl could grow up and become the governor of the state is simply incomprehensible; frankly, the whole thing baffles me."

No more than it baffled Betty Raye. How she had let Hamm talk her into this charade was still a mystery to her but she had and now she was trapped. It was like being six months pregnant. She couldn't go back if she wanted to. She had no choice but to go forward.

And so on Inauguration Day, as much as she dreaded it, she went through the necessary motions of being sworn in and posing for the pictures and although her hands and her knees were shaking, she read the short speech they had written out.

"Ladies and gentlemen, it is with the utmost humility that I accept this office today. And with your support and the help of my husband and number one adviser, I promise to carry out my duties as your new governor to the very best of my abilities, so help me God."

Cecil then signaled the band to start up and she and Hamm walked down the avenue to the governor's mansion on the coldest day of the year. But the streets were lined with well-wishers and Hamm strutted beside her, smiling and waving at the crowd. Some said if you did not know better, the way he was carrying on you would have thought that he was the new governor. As they walked, even though the streets were lined with the cheering people, Betty felt lonely. Her mother was not there today because the Oatman family had an engagement they could not change. Dorothy and Doc were invited as well but Mother Smith was ill and they had to cancel at the last minute. When they arrived at the mansion, Betty Raye saw a familiar face at the top of the stairs waiting for her. "Welcome home, Governor Betty," said Alberta Peets, the ice-pick murderess. "I've already taken care of Governor Hamm's things and put them in his room and your things is all ironed and ready to go and so is the boys."

Betty Raye was never so glad to see anyone in her life. "Oh, thank you, Alberta."

"I'm glad to do it. You know it's not good for me to be idle. What do they say? Idle hands is the devil's workshop. Or something like that."

After she gave the boys their baths and got them ready for bed she came back in Betty Raye's room.

"I see that Figg man is here again."

"Cecil? Oh yes. Everybody's back, the same old people."

"Well, all I can say is he better be careful this time. My feet is worse than ever and he comes down in my kitchen and makes me wear them shoes again, no telling what I'm liable to do."

When Betty Raye was dressed and ready for the Governor's Ball, she sat down on the bed. "Alberta," she said, "I'd give a million dollars not to have to go tonight."

"Well, now that you're a governor too I'll bet they gonna have you do a lot of things you don't want to."

"I hope not."

Cecil Figgs knocked on the door. "Darling, I don't want to rush you but we need pictures before we go, so come on down as soon as you can. Do you need me to help you with anything?"

Betty Raye sighed and stood up. "No, I'm ready."

Cecil opened the door and said, "Oh you look wonderful." Then he noticed Alberta standing behind the door and added gaily, "Hello, Alberta, isn't it *exciting*. Here we are all back together again."

"Uh-huh," she said, looking at him out of the corner of her eyes. "Here we are again."

From the moment that they walked into the governor's mansion after Betty Raye's inauguration it was clear that nothing much had changed. Hamm immediately went to his office with his staff and they started setting up meetings and going over bills and laws that had not been passed during the last four years, figuring out ways to change them and still get what they wanted. However, Alberta's prediction was correct. From then on Betty Raye's days consisted of hours of standing around having her picture made with every beauty queen, FHA winner, Girl Scout, Boy Scout, Eagle Scout, Teacher of the Year, Businessman and -woman of the Year, and anyone to whom Cecil promised a picture with the governor, while Hamm and the boys sat in the other room working on state government. At the end of each day she sat with pen in hand and signed everything that Wendell put in front of her and then went upstairs to bed, alone as usual.

But life was not all bad. She spent most of her free time over at the new house, simply wandering around happily or outside doing a little gardening. And several months after the election, Neighbor Dorothy and Mother Smith, who was over her terrible flu, came up and visited for the day. She laughed when Dorothy gave her the chili dog Jimmy had wrapped in tinfoil to send her and she caught up with all the news about Bobby's new job and Anna Lee's new baby. They were surprised to see how big her two boys had grown. All in all it was a wonderful day.

Old Friends

Neighbor Dorothy never liked to brag, so after they had returned from visiting her friend the new governor of the state, close to the end of the show she simply told her listeners this:

"Over the weekend Mother Smith and I were lucky enough to have had a lovely visit with an old friend of ours and it was so good to see her. And this morning, before we run out of time and get too busy, I just want to take a moment to tell you how grateful Mother Smith and I are having all of you in our lives. We just don't know what we would have done all these years without all of our precious radio friends out there, who continue year after year to make our days so happy. And speaking of friends . . . one of our sweet listeners, Mrs. Hattie Smith of Bell Meade, Missouri, sent along this thought: 'When you plant seeds of kindness, you are sure to grow a crop of *good* friends.'

"Thank you, Hattie, and we have a winner in the spelling bee. The champion, thirteen-year-old Miss Ronnie Claire Edwards, her word *M-I-L-L-I-P-E-D-E.* Congratulations—you must be a genius in the making. We will watch your career with interest. I tell you I could no more spell some of those words than I could empty the ocean with a bucket.

"Oh, thank you, Mother Smith, she's looked it up in the dictionary. 'Millipede, an arthropod having a cylindrical body composed of from twenty to over one hundred segments, each with two pairs of legs.' Oh my. Now my question is, what's an arthropod? What? Oh that's right: Mother Smith says whatever it is, she doesn't want it crawling on her. I'm with you down to the rattle on that one, Mother.

"Watermelons, sweet corn, and tomatoes will be among the topics discussed at a Vegetable Field Day this Friday. It will feature the latest results of vegetable research, so be sure and attend. We have all sorts of fun things coming up, but first here's our big news of the day. I need a fanfare for this one, Mother Smith. Ada and Bess Goodnight have gone up to Kansas City and purchased themselves a brand-new Airstream trailer and now that they're both widows and have retired they say they are going to take off into the wild blue yonder and become tin-can tourists. They say they don't know where they are going to, or when they will be back, and they like it that way. Just think, they will have a different backyard every morning. Oh, I don't know what I would do if I looked out and saw my yard was different, but those two are just full of spunk and raring to go. Their first stop will be the Nite-O-Rest Trailer Court outside of Mill Grove. . . . So all of you out there, if you see a tomato-red Dodge that looks like a big tomato aspic pulling a trailer go by, it will be them, headed for the open road. So good luck to our girls, traveling in tin.

"Also in the good-news department this morning, yesterday I got a nice letter from my daughter-in-law, Lois, who tells me that Bobby has just been promoted to the new position of vice president in charge of operations of Fowler Poultry Enterprises, and for a boy who flunked the sixth grade and could not spell *monkey,* much less *millipede,* believe me, that is quite a feat!"

The Governors Convention

In 1966 Betty Raye was relieved to learn that there was another wife running for a governorship. Lurleen Wallace of Alabama had announced her candidacy. Betty Raye did not know anything about her but she prayed she would win so she would not have to be the lone woman governor in the United States anymore. It was not fun.

Early the next year, when Governor Betty Raye Sparks of Missouri received her invitation to the National Governors Convention in Washington, she said, "I'm not going to go up there with all those real governors, Hamm. I'd make a fool of myself."

"No, you won't honey, I'll be right there with you all the time." He patted her arm. "All you have to do is smile and be pleasant. I'll tell you how to vote on things." Cecil, who was looking forward to another week of shopping for the trip, said, batting his big eyes, "If you don't go, darling, it will look bad for the state."

Hamm arrived at the governors conference bright-eyed and bushy-tailed. This was his first trip to Washington as the husband of a governor and the press was particularly interested in him. Hamm played it up for all it was worth. Betty Raye, the only woman governor there, thought she would have physically mashed herself into a wall if she could. She was miserably unhappy but he showed up at all the governors' wives events—teas, ladies' luncheons, fashion shows—and charmed every woman there. He even won first prize at one of the many raffles, an original

Mr. John picture hat, and delighted the women by wearing it for the rest of the luncheon. Hamm's nature was naturally outgoing and spontaneous and if asked a question he would usually tell you exactly what he thought. To the reporters who had what they viewed as the dull job of covering all the governors' wives, Hamm was a welcome and a refreshing change. Political spouses in general were notorious for not saying anything more than "You'll have to ask my husband about that" or "I don't know, I leave all that up to my husband." Not Hamm.

And he didn't see the danger ahead. In his home state, this candor had been an asset. Here on a national level, it was a potential disaster waiting to happen and reporters began to circle around him, hoping to get a quote for a good story.

Vietnam was on everyone's mind and it was a dangerous and tricky issue for any politician. Hamm had been warned by Wendell to keep his mouth shut, but at a wives cocktail party, a nice-looking woman sidled up to him and, after complimenting him on his tie, asked, "What do you think about all these antiwar protesters that are popping up everywhere?"

Hamm did not have to stop and think. "They're a bunch of idiots. What they ought to be protesting is the government who's sitting on their butts and letting those little bastards get the best of us. . . . We have to either fish or cut bait. . . ."

"What do you mean?" she said.

"Stop playing patty-foot with those Vietcong and get it over with. There's a damn elephant standing in the living room and everybody's tippy-toeing around it."

The woman played dumb, as if she had no idea what he meant. "I'm not sure I follow you. What elephant?"

Hamm said, "The bomb, honey. We've got it; they don't. What's the point of having it if we don't use it? Truman had the right idea." He pointed out the window of the hotel at a group of protesters across the street. "All those little tweety hearts and dove types ought to shut up and let us stop the damn thing before it gets any worse; then we can bring our boys home and sling all those little turncoats out of the country and get on with it."

Afterward, he was sorry he had used curse words in front of the lady but that was how he felt and it was too late to take it back. Too late to realize that the lady was covering the event for the *Washington Times.* By the time they got back to Missouri the story had been carried all over the country and *Newsweek* had a drawing of him reaching in a bucket and throwing hippies like bait across the ocean. One editorial cartoon had his picture with a mushroom cloud rising from his head; another depicted him as a mad dog, foaming at the mouth, with Betty Raye trying to hold him back on a leash.

Even though Hamm had said what a lot of veterans thought, he took a lot of heat nationally and got into trouble in his own state for sounding like such a hothead. He lay low for a while.

A few weeks later, Rodney came in his office chuckling. "You made the big time, boy. I just got a call from Berkeley University out in California and they want you to come out and give them a speech."

Hamm looked up. "Really? When?"

Rodney dismissed it. "Don't worry, I told them you were unavailable."

"Why?"

"Why? I'm not going to let you go out there in the middle of that hotbed of loonies."

Wendell agreed. "Naw, you don't want to go there. It's too dangerous. Hell, there ain't nobody more violent than those peaceniks. They'd tear you apart if they could get near you."

Hamm said, "Now wait, let's think about this for a minute. That's a big famous university out there. It could mean more national press, couldn't it? It might make me look good to go and talk to them. Like I'm willing to see the other side of this thing . . . and if they're willing to listen to my side a little, I might even make a few points."

"No, you won't," said Wendell. "All they want to do is drag you out in front and shout you down. They won't listen to a damn thing you say."

Hamm knew they might be right but even so he was secretly flattered that he had been asked. Anything to do with a university or college intrigued him. Everybody, including Vita, told him it was a bad idea. In the end, he could not resist the challenge.

They flew out to San Francisco the day before his appearance, with Rodney, Wendell, and Seymour grumbling all the way. They checked into a hotel and Hamm did not sleep much that night. He had worked long and hard on his speech and had made an effort to be especially careful about his grammar and his accent. He wanted to be up to the task of speaking in such a distinguished place of higher learning. This was the first time in years he had been nervous before a speech. He asked Rodney four times if his suit was all right and changed his tie twice. They were picked up at nine and driven over the bridge to the campus, and as expected a lot of the students were out and waiting for him. As they drove past the crowd toward the back entrance of the auditorium, the students and others started yelling and banging on the car. For some reason, this did not phase Hamm. He was now calm and collected. But the others suddenly started to get jumpy. Seymour, his bodyguard, had insisted that Hamm wear a safety vest that morning and when he got a look at the protesters he was glad he had. "Damn," he said, "I fought Japs that weren't as mad as this bunch."

Seymour reached in his pocket and felt for his blackjack. "If we get out of here alive we'll be lucky."

The messages being waved in front of them varied from sign to sign. VIETNAM IS A RACIST WAR; HIROSHIMA HAMM; GO BACK TO THE BOONDOCKS, WARMONGER; WHITE TRASH, GO HOME; HEE-HAW HAMM; EAT DIRT, YOU STUPID REDNECK. But Hamm just smiled and waved at the crowd as if they were happy to see him, which infuriated them further. When they finally got inside the hall, the president of the university, a dry, colorless man with dandruff, greeted him coldly and when Hamm put out his hand, the man went out of his way not to shake it, afraid someone might take his picture. Once they got onstage, his charm-free introduction consisted of five words: "Ladies and gentlemen, Hamm Sparks."

From the start things did not look good. The mere mention of his name caused the audience to roar with disapproval. The president went down and sat in the front row with the other professors as Hamm walked to the podium with his speech in hand. "Thank you for that gracious introduction, Mr. President," he said, smiling, trying to make the best of a bad situation. "I am honored and privileged to have been invited to speak at your university today. I want you to know that nobody supports and admires education more than myself. I also bring all of you greetings from the people of the great state of Missouri." Suddenly, amid a growing chorus of catcalls and boos, six or seven tomatoes were thrown and one splattered by his foot.

Hamm glanced down at the front row, fully expecting the president to stand up and put a halt to this, but he did nothing; nor did any of the other professors who sat there, many with a slight smirk on their faces. It was at that moment he realized he was up there on his own. Hamm stood motionless for a moment while the melee continued and watched as the group of protesters from outside came into the hall and marched around chanting and waving their signs in what was obviously a well-planned demonstration against him.

They'd never had any intention of hearing his speech. He felt like a fool. Vita and the boys had been right. Rodney was in the wings and motioned him to come off the stage. He could have turned around and walked out but he did not. Instead, he got mad and he dug in his heels. Even though he knew no one could hear him above the chanting and foot stomping, he said:

"You may insult me but, by God, you are not going to insult the ex–governor of Missouri and I'll be damned if you're going to shout me down. You people asked me here for a speech and you're going to get one. I read all your little signs and you can call me a country bumpkin, a redneck hillbilly all you want. But at least at home we have manners enough not to invite somebody somewhere and then treat them like a dog. Right now I'm proud to be a redneck but I'm no bigot. When I say I'm for everybody in this country, I mean everybody, even all you hippies out there. I feel sorry for you because you don't know better." He looked down at the front row. "I'm for everybody except for these pea-headed, lily-livered college professors you got sitting down there who have been brainwashing you against your own country. Filling you full of subversive ideas . . . egging you on to burn your draft cards and letting you wear the American flag on your behinds." He pointed at the faculty. "No wonder you teach kids; if you tried to push all that anti-American propaganda on grown men you'd get the living tar kicked out of you. I have a message for you. If you don't like it here, I've got me a whole bunch of boys down at the VFW and over at the American Legion just itching to help you move to Russia. Those Russkies won't put up with your whining and bellyaching for one second. I believe in freedom and individual rights as well as the next man but *nobody* has the right to live here and do nothing but run us down."

Then he addressed the protesters, who were still marching and chanting at the top of their voices, "Hell no, we won't go," and "Hey hey, how many boys did you kill today?"

"All you people are just delighting the Communists, and when you spit on one soldier or one policeman, you spit on this nation. You're nothing but a bunch of scared little momma's boys who let the others do the fighting for them. A lot of them poor black boys you are so worried about—their mommas and daddies don't have the money to send them off dodging the draft. *You're* the bigots. And if the Communists ever do get over here, these same little pantywaist professors are going to look around for somebody to protect them and there ain't gonna be nobody here; you'll all be up in Canada.

"So chant all your little chants and wave all your little signs and have all your sit-ins but one day when you grow up you're going to be ashamed of yourselves. If you really want to help this country I suggest all you deadhead beatniks get a haircut, take a bath, and go over and pay a visit at the veterans hospital to those who fought so you *could* wave your little signs." He stopped for breath. The din was continuous. "When I got here today your president informed me I was not going to be presented the usual plaque of appreciation for coming because your so-called college board doesn't approve of me. Well, that's fine, because I don't approve of them. My staff did a little research and I found out that in the past few years you've had Fidel Castro, Nikita Khrushchev, and a member of the Black Panther Party up here and you couldn't wait to give a plaque to all three of these guys, avowed enemies of our government who would destroy your country if they got half a chance. So if that's who's getting the plaques of appreciation around here, then I appreciate not getting one."

He walked off to boos and jeers and catcalls and was rushed out to the car to find its tires slashed and orange paint poured all over it. When they finally made it off campus, riding on the hubcaps, Rodney turned around and gave the protesters the finger and laughed his head off. When Wendell asked him, "What's so damned funny?" he said, "They're so pig ignorant they don't even know this car belongs to them."

Hamm didn't laugh. He had given a speech that no one had heard. The audience had screamed and stomped their feet and booed the whole time. But later Hamm said that was all right; he had heard what he had said, and it made him feel better.

When they got back home, the verdict was unanimous. Even he had to admit that the Hamm Sparks appeal had not worked. Still, they thought that was to be the end of it. But a student reporter, anticipating that the speaker might be shouted down, had placed a small tape recorder on the podium that Hamm did not notice. It had recorded every word he said. Later, the student played the tape and typed it up, word for inflammatory word, and printed it in the university newspaper.

Somehow, having people read what he said in black and white was not something Hamm had counted on. Hamm had *assumed* that no one was listening. The reporter with the love beads had *assumed* that printing the speech would damage Hamm even further. However, in Akron, Ohio, the reporter's father, a World War II vet like Hamm, picked up the paper his son had wrapped his dirty clothes in when sending them home for his mother to wash. After he read the speech, the man said to himself, "Yeah, buddy." And sent mimeographed copies to all his friends, who sent them to their friends. Instead of the article doing damage to Hamm Sparks, as the reporter had hoped, his father stopped paying his college tuition, making him suddenly eligible for the draft. Love Beads had to hitchhike all the way to Canada.

Soon, copies of Hamm's speech were slowly but surely making the rounds of every VFW and American Legion hall. Police stations, firehouses, and union halls across the country stuck it up on their billboards and Hamm started to receive hundreds of letters of support and contributions from every state. A month later the headline in one major magazine read: HAMM VS. EGGHEADS: HAMM 10, EGGHEADS 0.

This set off a number of other articles. Soon, a spokesman from the NRA called and asked if they could name a gun after him, and when the sale of LOVE IT OR LEAVE IT bumper stickers almost doubled in a week, the printing company sent him a thank-you note with a nice donation.

People thought this sudden groundswell of support was what gave Hamm the misguided notion that he should run for president.

The day Hamm made his surprise announcement, Cecil Figgs was delighted, and went weak in the knees just thinking about all the wonderful parties and entertainments he could plan at the White House. Vita was more ambivalent. She would never stand in the way of anything he wanted, of course, but she was deeply uneasy about this decision. Politics was no longer just a bunch of men in a back room making deals. It was lethal business. People were getting killed. And Hamm already had a lot of political enemies. But for Hamm not to run would almost be the same thing as killing him.

Later that night she glanced down and beheld the sight of the de facto governor of the state and perhaps even the next president of the

United States asleep at her breast and thought to herself, "God help us all."

Hamm's unexpected and rash decision to run for president had caught everyone off guard, but no one more so than Betty Raye. He had not discussed anything with her. As usual, she had no idea he was going to do it until he did it. And almost overnight, it seemed, Hamm was off and running, starting to campaign all over the country, and she was really left in the lurch. Her number one "assistant" was no longer there. Before he left he promised a panicked Betty Raye she had nothing to worry about, that nothing would really change, they could handle everything over the phone. This worked for a while but as the days went by Hamm was becoming less interested in the state and more interested in lining up his campaign; in fact, he was becoming harder and harder to get in touch with.

When Hamm was out of the state, Wendell helped her as much as possible but more and more Hamm was dragging Wendell and the rest of the staff off with him, leaving her alone for days at a time. Consequently, Betty Raye wound up trying to run the state by herself, a job she'd never wanted, did not know how to do, and had not been trained for.

For the first time since she had been elected governor, Betty Raye was forced to start reading what she was to sign and even to make decisions by herself. Terrified that she would make a mistake, she stayed up until three and four o'clock in the morning, poring through books, trying desperately to learn as fast as possible how state government worked, while trying to deal with her two children as well. Hamm would call her from time to time and give her a pep talk, tell her he knew it was hard but that he had a duty and an obligation to the people of America to speak out on their behalf. This might be all well and good for America, she thought, but in the meantime she was left holding the bag, having to make decisions without any help. But she did the best she could. And a few people may have been surprised when their bond issue passed and was signed with the advice and recommendation she had received from Alberta Peets, who had been there and knew what she was talking about. She told Betty Raye she thought an appropriation of $15 million for the restoration of the Mabel Dodge Prison for Women was a fine idea.

Suddenly Betty Raye had to take a good hard look at what was really going on in the state. Paving roads and promoting business and building bridges was fine but she began to see a lot of little things that were wrong that Hamm had been too busy to be bothered with. She began to read all the letters addressed to the governor from women all across the state, letters that previously had always been answered by someone in Wendell's office. Betty Raye found herself being touched and deeply moved by the real problems she read about. Women whose husbands had either died or left them, with no way of making a living. Some had even had to give up their children. Old women who had worked all their lives and had wound up penniless and without a place to go. Hundreds of letters came pouring in, their writers hoping that because she was a woman she would understand, letters they would never have written to another politician.

Betty Raye had always signed papers and done everything from upstairs. But now there were so many to sign it was getting harder to do. One morning she walked into the governor's office, and for the first time sat down behind Hamm's desk and pushed a button she hoped was the right one.

Someone she did not know answered and said loudly, "Yes?"

Betty Raye jumped back.

"Yes," he said again.

She then leaned forward and asked in a small, apologetic voice, "Could you please bring me a list of all the state trade schools, if it's not too much trouble?"

"Who is this?" the voice said.

"It's the governor," she said, surprised to hear it herself.

There was a long pause and then the sound of sudden realization. "Oh. Oh . . . yes, ma'am, right away."

Betty Raye looked around the big room and waited. After a moment she picked up the nameplate on the desk that read GOVERNOR HAMM SPARKS, looked at it, then quietly opened a drawer and put it in and closed it.

Hamm was proud of all the trade schools he had opened but Betty Raye, who had never bothered to ask, discovered to her dismay that trade schools tended to be for males only. She also found out that the majority of the state scholarships offered were for boys. There were boys' clubs, mentor programs, sports scholarships, all for boys, and nothing for the girls. Young boys who got into trouble were sent to boys' farms and received help. Girls had few places to go.

That's not fair, she thought. Betty Raye knew she had no real political power but the day she walked into a decaying and crumbling rat-infested building that served as the state school for the deaf and blind was a turning point. These were the children of the poor whose parents had been unable to care for them at home. She saw for herself how badly those children needed a clean place to live and study and how terribly understaffed and underpaid the teachers were. The worst moment was when a blind girl came feeling her way through the crowd, thinking Betty Raye might be her mother, and, once beside her, kept pulling at her skirt, repeating, "Momma, Momma," over and over. Betty Raye was so shaken she could hardly make it to the car. She went home and sobbed. The little girl looked just like Beatrice Woods might have when she had been that age.

She did not know how she was going to do it but when Hamm came back for any length of time she was going to *insist* that if she was going to remain as the governor he was going to have to do something about these things.

For the first time in her life she was going to speak up.

The Gold Mine

Hamm called Vita from Detroit as excited as she had ever heard him. He had just come back to his hotel from speaking to over five thousand members of the teamsters union. "I can win this thing, Vita. For the first time, I really see I have to run. Walter told me he could deliver all of the union vote. He said I was just what the country needed, that people were tired of being pushed around."

"How did the speech go?"

"Great!"

Hamm had been campaigning nationally for just a few months but not only was he popular in the rural areas, as was expected, but to everyone's surprise he was already starting to draw huge crowds in Chicago, Newark, and Pittsburgh, and was gaining momentum every day. Hamm had hit a nerve or, as one columnist put it, he had tapped into a gold mine of unrest in the country and he was the only candidate who was "telling it like it is," saying publicly what they were thinking privately. Many people were upset at the way they thought the country was headed. They were angry at the way the federal government seemed to be forcing things on them they did not want. They worried that if someone did not stop it there was no telling where it would end. There was a growing concern in middle America that all the wealthy liberal eastern politicians, with their endless giveaway programs, were leading the nation down the road to socialism and bogging it down with needless bureaucracy.

Almost everyone was frustrated with the way the war was going and what they perceived to be a weakness on the part of the government to do anything to stop it. They were shocked at the lack of respect the protesters had for the American soldiers fighting in Vietnam, particularly those who had served in the Second World War and Korea. Ada Goodnight, who had been a pilot in the Second World War, said she would be happy to go to Vietnam right now if she could. To them war was war and a draft dodger was a traitor. There was racial unrest everywhere and uneasiness about the rise of crime, drugs, and gangs in the cities and how it was being handled. It seemed to numerous voters that, thanks to the growing power of the ACLU, criminals were beginning to have more rights than the victims. Preachers across the country were becoming alarmed about the young people's apathy and lack of morals. Some blamed television. Or as Reverend W. W. Nails put it, "The devil has three initials: ABC, NBC, and CBS. They love Lucy more than they do the Lord and they would rather leave it to Beaver than to Jesus." The average middle-class Americans who worked hard every day, who were not criminals, not on welfare, and had seldom complained, suddenly and collectively started showing signs of growing disillusionment, worried that with all the new social programs they were now going to have to carry the rich and the poor on their backs. They were tired of having to pay so much income and other taxes to support half the world while they struggled to make ends meet. They began to feel that no matter how hard they worked or how much they paid, it was never appreciated and it was never enough.

But most of all they were scared. They looked around and saw the bright and shining true-blue America they had known growing up beginning to tarnish, tear, and fall apart at the seams. Hamm Sparks knew exactly how to verbalize their fears and frustration for them. Unlike the rest of the potential candidates, he seemed to understand their point of view.

As Rodney said, Hamm knew where the public itched and just how to scratch it. And scratch it he did. He took full advantage of all the upset and unrest, told his audiences exactly what they wanted to hear. He got more people mad and upset, more frightened, and was gaining more support by the day. Soon Hamm came down with a full-blown case of Washington fever and started doing anything he thought could get him in the White House. He made deals with people he should not have, said things that were more and more outrageous. Vita told him to be careful. Betty Raye begged him to come home. But it was like trying to stop a moving train. He was not a bad man, just a recklessly ambitious man. Soon even the people around him began to worry and Wendell put it best. When a woman at the John Birch Society luncheon gushed that she thought Hamm was the only man who could save America, Wendell said, "That's fine if she believes it. But when Hamm starts believing it, we are in big trouble."

Genetic Flaw

Norma was over at the beauty shop for her weekly hair appointment and Macky was eating his lunch at the Trolley Car Diner, as he did every Friday. Sitting at the counter, a few of the other men were discussing politics and Hamm Sparks, as usual. Macky said, "The guy is dangerous. He's getting crazier by the minute. Right now he's got every lunatic-fringe group and hate group coming out of the woodwork. If somebody doesn't shut him up, he's going to drag us right back into McCarthyism and the next thing we know we're going to be dragged into a war with Russia."

"I read the other day that the Klan was backing him now," Ed said.

Merle, who was just a step away from being a part of the radical right wing, said, "He can't help who backs him. He came out in the newspaper and said he wasn't one of them."

Macky said, "He says that, I can guarantee it, but he's taking money from them right now and God knows who else."

"What do you think, Jimmy?" asked Ed. Jimmy, who had not said anything, said quietly, "I agree with Macky. He needs to shut up and quit putting his wife through all this mess."

Ed said, "Yeah, but how are you going to stop him? Like he says, it's a free country."

Monroe Newberry, who had come in from the tire store, added, "I was talking to Bobby on the phone the other day and he says all the big insurance companies up there are getting behind Hamm, but I don't know what his real chances are."

Merle said, "I don't care what the papers say, I think he has a good chance to win."

Jimmy took a swipe at the counter with his rag but said nothing else.

Two blocks away, at Tot Whooten's beauty shop, the conversation was definitely not about politics. Betsy Dockrill, who had just come out from under the dryer and was getting ready to be combed out, remarked, "They are having a sale on caper coats out at Montgomery Ward. I got two, they were so cheap."

Tot pulled Betsy's hair net off. "Well, I wish I had time to sit around the house in a caper coat. I don't even have time to shop for one, with my schedule. By the time I close this place up at night, all I want to do is go home and get off my feet."

"You need to take a day off once in a while."

"I would if I could." Tot cut her eyes in the direction of Darlene, her twenty-five-year-old daughter, who worked in the shop with her. Betsy got the implication. Darlene was not overly intelligent and could not be left alone in the shop without someone watching to make sure she wouldn't put the wrong thing on a customer's hair again. Tot's insurance was already sky-high.

Norma was sitting in the next chair, with her hair half rolled up, flipping through a magazine. She asked Tot, who was taking a drag off her cigarette, "Do you think Elizabeth Taylor is happy?"

Tot blew the smoke out. "She's sporting a diamond the size of a doorknob, why *wouldn't* she be?"

"I just wonder if all that fame and money and all those husbands have made her really happy."

"Well," Tot said, "if she's not, I'd like to switch places with her. I'd be downright delirious. She can keep the men; I just want the money and the ring. Between having to put up with Daddy and James, not to mention Dwayne Junior, I've done my time in hell, thank you."

"Oh Tot, you make it sound so terrible. I can't believe your life has been all bad. Weren't you ever happy?"

Tot took another drag on her Pall Mall and put it back in the black plastic ashtray. It was an interesting question, one she had never been asked before. She thought about it for a moment. "Well, let's see, there was the wedding. Other than Daddy getting drunk and passing out in the vestibule and me having to walk down the aisle by myself, that went fine, right up until we went outside the church and James got that piece of rice stuck in his ear. The honeymoon was ruined from the minute we got in the car because all he did was complain about the ringing in his ear. That ear drove him crazy for over two months. He was so dizzy all he did was lie down. It was so bad they had to operate on it three times looking for it, and we went into debt paying hospital bills."

Norma said, "I had forgotten about that."

Tot continued, "So I spent the first three months of my marriage being a nurse and then after he got drafted and went off to the army he came back home five years later a full-blown alcoholic, just like Daddy, who I'd married James to get away from. So I was happy from the time I said I do until we got outside the church and somebody threw rice in his ear. How long does it take to go from the altar down the aisle to outside the church, a minute? So you can say I was happy for a minute."

Norma felt terrible that she had even asked the question. "Poor Tot," she said. "I'm so sorry."

"Well, don't be, because it's my own fault. I did it to myself. I should have known when I had to give my own self away, it was a bad omen. I should have just turned around and gone home but everybody wants a wedding, I guess. Women are fools; they will marry anything that has a heartbeat just to have a man." She glanced over at Darlene again. "I'm still paying for her last fiasco, number three. And it's not just the women—Dwayne Junior has already got two girls pregnant that I'm having to pay child support to. Sometimes I wish both my kids had turned queer and saved the world a lot of trouble."

"Mother, I don't think that's funny."

"I know you don't but it's true." Tot looked at Betsy in the mirror. "From fifteen to twenty-five she managed to marry every half-wit in town and is dating number four."

Her daughter defended her latest fiasco: "He has a job, Mother."

Tot rolled her eyes. "Well, if collecting beer cans in the back of a truck is considered a profession, then I stand corrected." She changed the subject: "Darlene, run down the street and get me a tuna fish salad on whole wheat and a bag of chips. Do you want anything, Norma?"

"No thanks, I just had lunch. I've been up since five-thirty."

After Darlene left the shop, Tot shook her head. "Norma, just be glad you have a daughter with good sense. Darlene is about to drive me crazy. I tell you, from the day she flunked out of tap school it's been downhill ever since. I went in her house the other morning and she's sitting there at the table with a brick. I said, What are you doing and she said, I'm filing my nails. I spent a fortune sending her to beauty school and she's filing her nails with a brick. After the tenth grade she was flunking everything but fooling with her hair night and day so I shipped her off to beauty school. I figured she'd be good at it. But I was wrong. And I don't know where she got that thin fuzzy hair. She didn't get it from my side of the family. She got it from the Whootens. No telling what's in that gene pool, but it's the worst possible advertisement for the hair business. I swear, between her and James and Dwayne Junior I'm so worn out I can hardly get up in the morning."

Although she did not want people to know it, Tot had a heart of gold and would give you the shirt off her back if you needed it. That was the main reason she was so tired all the time. After working in the shop all day and on weekends she would pack up her kit and go over to all the older ladies' homes and fix their hair for them. Most were either sick or bedridden and could not pay but Tot did not care. She said as long as her fingers could move no lady she knew was going to do without her weekly shampoo and set.

And as much as she complained about Darlene and Dwayne Jr., she let them have just about anything they wanted and baby-sat her grandchildren anytime they asked, which, unfortunately, was often.

The Hunting Trip

Hamm had been campaigning for president for only a few months but already Hamm ("Tell It Like It Is") Sparks had become a big thorn in the side of a lot of people. Once more he was making powerful enemies in his own party, only this time on a national level. What had started out as a fly-by-night, grassroots campaign was suddenly not so funny and could no longer be dismissed. Besides, his poor English and backwoods manner were an embarrassment to the elite East Coast Harvard and Yale, pipe-and-tweed Democrats in Washington and elsewhere. They also believed that his radical, black-and-white, take-no-prisoners brand of politics was dangerous for them and for the country. The powers that be called him in and tried to reason with him, get him to step down for the good of the party, but Hamm was like a dog with a bone. He would not withdraw and if they threw him out they knew he might run on an independent ticket and take the votes with him anyway.

On December 31 Dorothy's first New Year's resolution was the same as last year:

1. Lose ten pounds.

On December 31 Minnie Oatman sat down at the small table on the big silver bus that was headed for a New Year's Day gospel sing in Bloomington, Illinois, and wrote out her same old resolution:

1. Lose fifty pounds.

Tot Whooten wrote out her yearly resolution, as she had for the past seven years, only this time she stuck it on the refrigerator:

1. Do not loan Darlene or Dwayne Jr. another dime.

But across the country a new resolution appeared on the top of a lot of people's lists that year:

1. Get rid of Hamm Sparks.

They did not write it down but they thought it.

He gained momentum every day. They knew Hamm could never have the numbers to win the election—he was too much of a wild card—but now even the Republicans were beginning to worry. To their utmost irritation, Hamm was quietly receiving thousands of dollars from a lot of big-money supporters that should have been going to their man. Both parties were afraid of his growing popularity. Despite the fact that all the newspapers, magazines, and national television network news shows were either ignoring him or ridiculing him, he gained on them every day. Something had to be done; if he continued on with this momentum he was going to upset the election for everyone.

Some of the people who supported Hamm financially did not want it known. And there were some people he was willing to take money from that *he* did not want known.

Rodney was contacted by Mr. Anthony Leo, the man who had given Hamm *The Betty Raye* eight years before, and was told there was a friend of his in New Orleans who might be willing to contribute a lot of money under the table. But he wanted to talk to Hamm about who he was considering running as vice president before he committed.

Hamm agreed to a meeting. Both he and the man felt that for privacy reasons it would be best for them to meet on the man's yacht in New Orleans. When the time was right, Hamm blocked out a weekend. Unfortunately, it was the same weekend he had promised Betty Raye he was going to come back to Jefferson City and spend with her. She had been so looking forward to it, not only because she missed him but also because she had so many questions to ask. That Friday morning, he called from Jackson, Mississippi, and informed her he would not be coming home because he and the boys had decided to go on a hunting trip instead. He said they would have to fly out of Jackson on Monday to another speech and he was not sure when he could get back. When Betty Raye hung up she was almost in tears.

Alberta Peets, who had been in the room, saw how upset Betty Raye was and went over and put her arm around her. "Them mens better stop treating you so mean while I'm around 'cause they liable to get me all riled up again. . . . They need to remember what happened to the last one who did that."

Wendell Hewitt and Seymour Gravel had called and told their wives the same thing. As far as Hamm and the boys were concerned, it was not too much of a lie. They were hunting for money. Since the press was dogging his every move and it was a tricky situation, the trip to New Orleans had to be very carefully coordinated. After much plotting and map studying, Rodney Tillman had come up with the plan. Since Hamm was already in Jackson for a speech, Rodney would go back to Missouri a few days before and pick up *The Betty Raye* and meet them near the Mississippi-Louisiana state line, at the boathouse of a relative of Mr. Leo's, and then take them on to New Orleans via the Mississippi River. In order for them to get to the boat without anyone seeing them, Cecil Figgs was to pick them up at the motel at four A.M. in an old hearse he would borrow from the back lot of one of his Kansas City mortuaries and drive them down to meet Rodney at the boat. Although it was uncomfortable, no one followed them or saw Hamm and Wendell crouched in the back with the curtains drawn. They stashed the hearse in the bushes about a half mile from the spot on the river where they were to meet *The Betty Raye* and walked the rest of the way. When they were all aboard they laughed all the way down the Mississippi, thinking how clever they had been.

Cecil had no idea what the meeting was about, nor did he care. He was just along for the ride. When they pulled into the dock in New Orleans and tied up beside the seventy-five-foot yacht where the meeting with Mr. Leo's friend was to take place, Cecil made plans of his own in the French Quarter. Besides, who cared about politics when there were so many pretty boys in the world and Mother was miles away and nobody at home knew where he was? What fun. He almost skipped off the boat. Oh joy!

HAMM SPARKS, FOUR OTHERS MISSING— FOUL PLAY SUSPECTED

By Tuesday morning every headline and radio and television in America screamed the same thing.

By Tuesday afternoon there were dozens of newsmen and television cameras on the front lawn of the governor's mansion, with hundreds more on the way. David Brinkley's lead on the NBC nightly news was one sentence: "Controversial presidential candidate Hamm Sparks, along with four other men, including the Missouri attorney general, seems to have literally disappeared over the weekend. The question is, Where did they go?"

It was a genuine mystery. The state police, the district attorney's office, the FBI had been called in and soon were all stumped. All they had been able to find out so far was that the last time any of the men had been seen was Friday night, and Monday morning none of them had showed up where they were supposed to be.

Hamm had been scheduled to address an auditorium full of six thousand AFL-CIO members in Grand Rapids and Cecil was to have taken his mother to the eye doctor that morning. Something was seriously wrong. The FBI questioned everyone for days. Seymour and Wendell's wives had been told the exact same story—their husbands were going on a hunting trip. Rodney's ex-wife knew nothing because they were not living together but she did mention to the press that Rodney owed her back alimony. The only odd thing was that Cecil had left his mother, Mrs. Ursa Figgs, a note saying he was on a business trip but would be back to take her to the eye doctor. He was the only one of the missing men who did not mention hunting. Being that he was not the hunting type, they could not be positive if he was with the other men or not, but because they'd all disappeared at the same time it could only be assumed. In the meantime, Betty Raye was walking around in a daze, trying her best to keep the two boys calm and keep them away from the press.

When Minnie first heard the news she left the Oatmans in Charlotte, North Carolina, and flew to her daughter's side. She was escorted through a herd of newsmen and when she got inside, a tearful Minnie rushed at Betty Raye, grabbed her, and said, "Oh, honey, it's just like when Chester was stole all over again. Now somebody's gone and snatched little Hamm away!"

Minnie immediately started to form prayer circles inside the mansion and out. The reporters, most of whom were from New York, suddenly found themselves kneeling on the lawn, holding hands with a fat woman, praying for Hamm's return. The Missouri National Guard was called in for an all-out search of the woods where Hamm and his staff usually went hunting or even could have gone. Day after day, an upset and increasingly terrified Betty Raye waited for news of her husband. Dorothy called and asked Betty Raye if there was anything she could do but there was nothing that anyone could do except find her husband.

Everyone, including Betty Raye, was at a loss as to what to do. It seemed inconceivable that five grown men could just disappear into thin air without leaving a trace. Jake Spurling, the FBI's number one missing-persons expert, was brought in from Washington and put on the case. All of Hamm's known enemies, of which there were many, were immediately questioned but as of yet none could be connected to the disappearance. The government offered a $500,000 reward for any information. In the meantime hundreds of people called radio and television stations, claiming to have spotted a flying saucer the weekend of their disappearance. One woman in Holt's Summit said she saw the men looking out the window of one as it took off from her cow pasture. Psychics from everywhere called in. One from London claimed that the men had stolen money and were now living in New Guinea with a Pygmy tribe. Another claimed they had been lost in the Bermuda Triangle. The entire country was in a state of pure shock, concerned and alarmed that a presidential candidate could just vanish from the face of the earth without leaving a trace or a clue.

Alberta Peets, who claimed to have premonitions, had gone home on a weekend furlough to see her mother the weekend the men disappeared and had told Betty Raye that Sunday night that she had had a cold chill to hit her. She said, "They need to look for them in Alaska."

A few days after the headlines hit, an extremely nervous Mr. Anthony Leo made a call from a phone booth to his friend in New Orleans. The friend claimed not to know what had happened to the men after the meeting and in turn asked Mr. Leo if he knew anything. Mr. Leo said no. After they hung up they both wondered if the other one was lying but did not say so. In those circles it was best not to.

People in Missouri were at a particular loss as to what to do or how to behave in a case like this. There had never been a case like this. They had no idea if they should fly the flag at half-staff or just lower it a little, since nobody really knew if the men were dead or not. Cecil Figgs was the only one who would have known what to do, but he was missing as well.

The only two people who had not seemed totally surprised Hamm and the others were missing were Earl Finley and Jimmy Head. Minutes after Earl had made the obligatory phone call to Betty Raye on behalf of the Democratic Party of Missouri to say how sorry he was to hear about the bad news, he was locked in a back room of a cheap hotel with several friends, trying his best to keep from smiling as he plotted his next move. Jimmy Head had been in Kansas City for a friend's funeral when the news hit but when he came back to Elmwood Springs all he said was, "I'm just surprised it didn't happen sooner. I feel bad for Betty Raye but she's a hell of a lot better off without him."

In time, it became painfully clear that they were not coming back. Betty Raye thanked her mother for coming but told her that she was fine and Alberta would look after her and Minnie should go back on the road. She was not fine but when she was not with her boys she just wanted to be alone and think, to try to come to terms with what was happening. No one ever dreams that the last moment, that last glance of someone, might really be the last. She could not sleep, or eat. Not knowing if he was dead or alive was torture, but in addition to grieving for her husband she had two children and an entire state to worry about.

A month later, after attending a rather strange and ambiguous memorial service for Hamm and the four men, it hit her that most likely Hamm was *not* coming back. And she wanted to die. Had it not been for her two boys, she might have. Hamm Jr., who had adored his father, was taking his loss particularly hard and he needed her.

As the widow of such a powerful man, Betty Raye had at least received the nation's sympathy and support but Vita Green had suffered through the entire thing alone and silent, waiting, like Betty Raye, for some word. But unlike Betty Raye, having a sense of how dangerous politics could be and how reckless Hamm had become, she had been halfway expecting something like this to happen. Expected or not, it was devastating for her.

Out of respect for his family, she did not attend the memorial service but stayed home and held her own very private wake. The people who knew about her relationship with Hamm tried to be helpful, but as Betty Raye had learned, nothing *could* help except, maybe, time.

Time and patience were two things that Jake Spurling had plenty of. An unattractive man with red pockmarked skin, Jake was as dedicated to solving missing-persons cases as most men were to their families.

Even though there had been a memorial service, none of the bodies had been found; as far as he was concerned, this case was far from over. Jake Spurling was one of the best criminal investigators in the country and he vowed he would never give up on the Hamm Sparks disappearance until he got to the bottom of it. And who had been behind it. Jake was known far and wide as a man who, once he had a case, was like a dog with a bone. He would root and dig for information no matter how long it took, or where he had to go to find it. To Jake this was *the* case of a lifetime.

Aunt Elner Goes Postal

Luther Griggs, the bully who used to beat up Bobby Smith, lived in a trailer park behind the post office and had a son as mean as his daddy had been at that age. Over the years Aunt Elner had had a series of orange cats that she always named Sonny. That morning Luther Griggs, Jr., had thrown a rock at Aunt Elner's present cat named Sonny and had hit him in the head.

At a quarter to twelve that night Aunt Elner called her niece with the news.

"Norma, I've killed the Griggs boy."

"What?"

"I've killed the Griggs boy, murdered him in cold blood. I didn't mean to but there you have it. Tell Macky to go on and call the police."

"Aunt Elner, what *are* you talking about?"

"I've killed him, poisoned him, he's probably lying over there dead and they're gonna trace the fudge back to me sooner or later, so I might as well give up and get it over with. I've tried to live a good life all these years and here I've wound up a cold-blooded killer."

"Aunt Elner, listen to me. You stay right where you are and don't do a thing, do you hear me?"

Norma went into the bedroom and shook him. "Macky, wake up!" He stirred a little. . . . "Macky, wake up. We have to go over to Aunt Elner's."

"What's the matter? Is she sick?"

"Get your clothes on . . . she says she killed the Griggs boy."

"What?"

"I don't know, Macky. She's hysterical. She said she poisoned him. Just get dressed before she calls the police."

Macky put his pants on over his pajamas, Norma grabbed her coat, and by the time they got there, Elner was out on the porch waiting for them, wringing her hands.

"I know I've disgraced the family," she said. "I don't know what caused me to do such a thing."

Macky led her back into the house. "Aunt Elner, just sit down and tell us what's going on."

Elner was distraught. "It's gonna be in all the papers; do you think they will handcuff me? Poor old Sonny has a hole in his head and now his owner is going to jail or maybe to the electric chair."

Macky said, "Aunt Elner, now, just calm down. What happened?"

"I must have gone insane. Maybe I can plead insanity—do you think so?"

"What did you do?"

"Well, I wanted to get back at him for hitting Sonny. I knew I couldn't catch him, so I tried to figure out a way to get him up on the porch and take a good whack at him. I made up some fudge to get him over here." She looked stricken. "Oh, I just should have stopped there. But I had a whole bunch of old chocolate Ex-Lax, so I just melted it up and threw it in."

"Is that all?"

"A little dab of Mennen's underarm deodorant."

"Just that?"

"No."

"What else?"

"A half cup of oven cleaner. Polident tooth powder . . . I sprinkled a little on the top . . . it looked kinda like sugar."

Norma couldn't contain herself. "Oh my God."

"Hold on, Norma," Macky said. He asked in a calm voice, "Is that all, Aunt Elner?"

Norma looked at him like he was crazy. "Is that all? . . . That's enough to kill an entire family right there!"

Aunt Elner said, "I never thought of that. Do you reckon he may have taken that candy home? I may have killed them all. They may all be laying up in the trailer park dead." She threw her hands up in the air. "Now I'm a mass murderer."

Macky said, "Aunt Elner, now slow down. Start from the beginning. Tell me everything that happened."

"I made the candy . . . and waited till I saw him skulking around in the backyard. Then I called him over and said, 'Come here, little boy, I've got some nice candy for you.' I just meant for him to have one bite and then I was gonna try and grab for him but before I had a chance to do anything he snatched most all of the candy off the plate and took off before I could get at him."

"When did this happen?"

"This morning."

Norma said, "Why did you wait so long to tell us?"

Aunt Elner shook her head. "I guess when you do a thing like that the criminal mind just takes over. I thought I might get away with it. I should have come clean from the start. And now I've killed the whole Griggs family."

"Oh my God," Norma said. "Shouldn't we call a good lawyer, Macky? Isn't that what you're supposed to do at a time like this?"

"We are not going to call anybody. I am sure he is fine."

"Macky, we can't guess about something like this. We're looking at a murder charge. You go over there right now and look at that boy. We may all have to go on the lam."

"For God's sake, all right, but this is stupid."

"Macky—promise me you won't come back until you have seen that boy walking and talking."

"All right, all right."

The door opened and Luther Griggs peered out first, and then opened the door wider, shotgun in hand. "What the hell do you want this time of night?"

"Are you all right?"

"Hell, yes. . . . Are you?"

"Can I come in? I need to talk to you."

As Macky stepped into the trailer, which stank of beer and cigarettes, he looked closely at Luther to see if he looked sick but Luther Griggs had never been a picture of health, so it was hard to tell.

"I'm sorry to come over this late but we might have a little problem. Is your boy home?"

"What's he supposed to have done now?"

"Nothing. It's just that he may have been given some bad candy and he might need to have a doctor look at him."

By this time Mrs. Griggs, in a ratty pink chenille robe with maroon flowers, had come into the room frowning. "What's he done now?"

"Nothing, Mrs. Griggs, I just need to see him for a moment. If you don't mind."

"What for?"

"It's a long story. But my aunt might have given him some bad fudge this morning and we just need to make sure he's all right."

She did not move but yelled, "Get in here this minute, you hear me . . . right now!" After a moment, Mrs. Griggs whipped around and flew into the bedroom. "I said get up! Now!"

Soon Mrs. Griggs reappeared, dragging the boy by the ears, with him kicking at her the whole time.

Macky said, "My aunt says you took a couple of handfuls of some candy she offered to you. . . . Is that right?"

"She's a damn liar . . . I never took no damn fudge," the boy said.

"She's not accusing you of stealing. She—"

"Well, she's a crazy damn old fool. I never took no candy."

Luther Griggs got all puffed up. "You heard my boy, he never took no damn candy. You calling my boy a liar?"

"No. I'm not. I just wanted to make sure he wasn't sick. The candy might not have been . . . uh, not made with the right ingredients." Macky looked closely at the little boy. "Are you sure you feel all right, son? That candy didn't make you sick?"

"I never took no candy."

"Well, all right then, as long as you are all right. But if you do feel sick, call me. . . . Here's my number." He wrote it down for them.

In truth, Luther Jr. had grabbed the candy but when he took one bite it was so bad he spit it out and threw the rest over the Whatleys' fence.

Macky walked in the door at Aunt Elner's and winked at Norma.

"Well, Aunt Elner, I've got bad news for you. They're still alive. Too bad. You might have gotten a medal from the town if you had wiped them all out."

Norma said, "I'm glad you can joke about it. We came very close to having Aunt Elner wind up in the state penitentiary. Wouldn't that have been nice for Linda, having her great-aunt sitting up on Death Row."

Macky laughed.

Norma looked at him. "Laugh if you want, Macky, but she would never have gotten into a decent sorority!"

The Meeting

It was some time after the memorial before Betty Raye could get up the nerve to do something she had wanted to do for a long time. She asked State Trooper Ralph Childress to let her out a half block away and when she reached the front of the building in Kansas City a uniformed doorman tipped his hat saying, "May I help you, ma'am?"

She fumbled around in her purse. "Uh, I'm here to see Mrs. Vita Green?"

"Yes, ma'am. Who shall I say is calling?"

Betty Raye, who was wearing a scarf and sunglasses, panicked. She had not realized she would be announced. She almost turned around and left but she figured she had come this far, she might as well come out with it. She said almost inaudibly, "Tell her it's Mrs. Sparks."

"Yes, ma'am." He pushed a button. "Mrs. Green, I have a Mrs. Sparks here to see you."

There was a pause.

He repeated the name "Mrs. Sparks" and there was another long interval. Betty Raye's heart was pounding so hard she wanted to run. After a moment, he hung up and said, "Go right in. Take the elevator up to fourteen, get off, and take a left up the stairs. Turn right and you will see 15A."

"Thank you," she said and got in the elevator and almost threw up.

Vita was caught a little off guard by this unexpected visit. Her first thought was to say that she was not home. But she might as well get this over with, so why not today? She had no idea why the woman was here but she guessed that whatever the reason, it was not going to be a pleasant one. She called out to her maid, who was in the kitchen. "Bridget, answer the door and tell the lady I'll be right out." She went to her bedroom to get some clothes on. After all this time it was still hard to even get up and get dressed.

When Betty Raye got off the elevator, she walked up the stairs. When she reached the door she pushed the buzzer to the apartment and the noise made her jump. After a moment the door opened and Bridget was prepared to say, as she had a hundred times, "Please come right in and have a seat. Mrs. Green will be with you shortly," but when she recognized Betty Raye from the pictures she had seen of her in the papers all she could do was to drop her mouth open and stare. Betty Raye was surprised as well; she had steeled herself, expecting Vita Green to be standing on the other side of the door. Finally she asked, "Is this Mrs. Green's apartment?"

Bridget managed a "Yes, ma'am."

"Is she in?"

"I'll go see."

She ran and threw open the bedroom door white as a ghost, her eyes wide with fright. "The archbishop's wife is here. She's at the door right now. What do you want me to do? Are you here?"

Vita was sitting at her dressing table, calmly putting on her lipstick. "It's all right, I'll handle it."

"I can tell her you just left town."

"No, but if you hear a gunshot call the police."

"Oh, Jesus, Mary, and Joseph," Bridget said.

Vita smiled and patted her hand. "Just kidding," she said but thought to herself, I hope, and walked out to greet Betty Raye, who was still standing at the door.

Vita was as smooth as silk and acted as if she were saying hello to just another acquaintance and not the wife of the man who had been the love of her life. "Governor Sparks, I'm sorry you had to wait but I was not dressed. Won't you come in?"

Betty Raye's knees were weak as she stepped into the living room. The entire apartment had a faint scent of Shalimar perfume, a familiar smell. Hamm always had the aroma on him.

"Have a seat, Governor. May I offer you coffee, tea?"

"Oh no, thank you. Just a glass of water, if you don't mind."

"Certainly. Bridget, would you please bring Governor Sparks a glass of water."

After they sat, Vita said, "I'm sure you know how sorry I am and all of us on the arts council are for your loss."

Betty Raye nodded. "Oh yes, and I appreciated your note and flowers."

There was an uncomfortable silence.

Betty looked around. "You have a beautiful apartment."

"Thank you." This was the first time the two women had seen each other since their brief meeting a few years ago, and Betty Raye found that she still felt like an awkward schoolgirl around Vita. Vita, now sitting across from her, wearing earrings made of two huge chunks of lime green crystal stones the same color as her eyes, was still one of the most glamorous women she had ever seen.

Vita was doing some observing of her own. She had seen plenty of pictures of Betty Raye, of course, and there were those few hurried seconds when they had met at the Wheeler party, but now that she had a chance to study her up close, it was a different thing. She saw a woman with nice enough features, nothing outstanding, but there was something about her eyes she had not noticed before. And she sat there wondering what it was. Her hands were long and graceful, her mouth generous in a way that saved a too thin face, but it was still her eyes that had caught Vita off guard again. She had not expected that.

When Bridget brought her a glass of water, Betty Raye took it and smiled and said, "Thank you."

Vita suddenly figured out what it was she saw in her eyes and where she had seen it before. Betty Raye's eyes had the same guileless look in them as a little female dog she had once had. There was a sweetness about them, mixed with sadness and something else, and all at once Vita realized that this woman was not going to shoot anybody. She was the one who was frightened. She told Bridget she could go and that she would call her if she needed her for anything else. The maid shot her an "Are you sure?" look and Vita nodded to reassure her.

They sat looking at each other. Finally Betty Raye spoke. "Mrs. Green, I thought I had a reason to come here but right now I can't remember what it was. I feel like a fool—all I've done, I'm afraid, is to embarrass myself. I thought you might need someone to talk to, someone who, well, I guess the thing I wondered about was if you were all right or if you needed anything. I know how fond you were of my husband and how fond he was of you . . .

how much he depended on you . . . for advice and things. You were not at the memorial service and I think I know why." At that point Betty Raye hiccuped. "Oh, I'm sorry. I thought how hard that must have been on you not to have—" She hiccuped again. "Well, that's great. I've got the hiccups."

Vita stood up and took her glass. "Here, let me get you some more water," she said and went in the kitchen while Betty Raye sat on her couch, hiccuping. When Vita handed her the water, Betty Raye said apologetically, "Thank you," took a big sip, and spilled water down the front of her dress. "Oh dear, this is not how I planned this to be. I wanted—" She hiccuped again. "I'm sorry. I just wanted to do what Hamm might have wanted someone to do."

Vita sat there and watched this woman fall totally apart right before her very eyes but there was nothing she could say. She *still* was not sure exactly how much she really knew. Betty Raye tried to continue. "I thought that I was being noble or something but now that I'm here I realize I came because I needed you to tell me some things." Then she burst into tears. "I think I need a friend and I don't know where to turn. Well, I better leave." She stood up. "I certainly did not mean to do this." When she reached the door she hiccuped again, said, "I'm so sorry," and went out and closed the door.

Vita sat there for a moment listening to Betty Raye hiccup down the hall, then got up and thought to herself, I'm probably going to regret this. She got to the elevator doors just as they opened and took Betty Raye by the arm. "Come back."

Betty Raye said, "No . . . I should just go and let you alone."

"I don't want you to go." Vita turned to the puzzled elevator operator standing there waiting and said, "She's not leaving."

Betty Raye said, "I'm *not*?"

"No, you're not, come on with me."

As Vita led her back up the stairs to the apartment, Betty Raye said, "I promise, I'm not really as dumb as I seem," and hiccuped again. When she got Betty Raye back inside Vita sat her down and handed her a glass of brandy. "Drink this."

Betty Raye took a drink and looked at Vita in horror. "What is that?"

"Brandy."

"Oh well, I thought I'd come here today because I wanted you to know if there was anything I could do for you and to tell you that you are welcome to see the boys anytime you want; I realize you must miss him terribly." She paused a moment, then said, "But I did have a question. Mrs. Green, I hate to ask you this, but I wondered: Do you have any idea what happened to him?"

"No, I don't, Mrs. Sparks. I wish I did. Believe me."

"Oh. I thought if anyone knew it would be you . . . "

Vita looked at her very carefully. "Did you know about your husband and me?"

"Oh yes."

"For how long?"

"From the beginning, I guess. Hamm was not the subtlest of men."

"And you never said anything?"

"No. But please don't think I'm a saint, I'm not. It nearly killed me. I cried over it, I prayed about it, but you can't make a person stop loving another person just by telling them to stop. If I had, he would have resented me the rest of his life. It was a problem with no solution or at least none I could think of. Oh, there was a time I thought about leaving him, and I should have, I guess. But I knew a divorce would have ruined his career, so I made the decision not to leave and I adjusted to it." She looked at the brandy glass. "I think this stuff has cured my hiccups. And of course I kidded myself that if I ran for governor for him he might have to depend on me. And I hoped that maybe one day he would get over you. But I think the real truth is I just didn't have the courage to leave. I'm not a very brave person, Mrs. Green, and the thought of having to go out on my own and raise the children alone . . ."

Betty Raye took another drink of the brandy and made another face. "But there *were* times when I did wonder what you thought of me or if you *ever* thought of me or if you were trying to get him to leave me. Of course, when I met you and saw how beautiful and smart you were, I could understand why he fell in love with you. I couldn't blame him, really. I mean, you were everything I wasn't. I even wondered if you hated me for *not* leaving him. . . . Did you?"

Vita got up and walked across the room to the bar and fixed herself a strong drink and after a moment said, "No, I didn't hate you. The truth is that I never thought about you."

"I see," said Betty Raye.

"Now that I think back, it wasn't so much that I didn't care, it was just that I couldn't *afford* to think about you. I suppose if any woman having an affair with a married man ever really stopped to think about the man's wife and what it was doing to her, she would not be able to keep doing it. I didn't even have the excuse that most have that the wife is terrible. I knew you weren't terrible but what I didn't know was just how well you did understand him."

She came back over and sat down. "I think there are some things I do need to tell you. First of all, I never wanted to marry him. I am not the wife type and, believe me, I never wanted children. It's *you* that should hate me. I'm the thief. I stole what should have been yours. I had the best of him and just gave you what was left over."

Betty Raye smiled a little. "Well, in a way I feel I got the best of him. I have the boys. But the truth is, as much as he loved you and loved me . . . the children even . . . none of us ever *really* had him. Politics was his real love. We all came second to that."

Vita acquiesced. "Maybe you're right."

Betty Raye knew she should leave. There was really nothing more to say. But for some reason she just sat there, unable to move. She kept looking at Vita as if she did have something more to say but she did not know what it was.

Vita wondered what was the matter with her, just sitting there looking so troubled. And then a thought occurred. She leaned over, took Betty Raye's hand, and looked her in the eyes. "Mrs. Sparks, do *you* need help?"

A relieved Betty Raye grabbed her hand and blurted out, "Oh God, yes, yes, I do. . . . I don't know what I am doing half the time or who to ask and without Hamm I'm scared to death. I know how smart you are and how much he depended on you. Oh, Mrs. Green, would you consider being my adviser?"

"First of all, it's Vita and I will be happy to help you in any way I can, Mrs. Sparks."

"Oh thank you, Vita—and it's Betty Raye, please."

They stood up and Vita walked her to the door. "So when would you like to get together again? Lunch tomorrow, say around one?"

"To tell you the truth, Vita, I don't think I can wait that long," Betty Raye said. "How about breakfast, say around eight?"

Vita laughed. "I'll be there." Vita did not usually like women but this one she liked. This little brown wren had more guts and heart than anyone had suspected. As they walked down the hall, Vita put her arm in Betty Raye's and said, "You know, Betty Raye, I think this might be the beginning of a beautiful relationship."

How Did You Meet Your Best Friend?

Neighbor Dorothy rushed down the hall calling out to Mother Smith, "I found it," and ran in and sat down at her desk just as the red light went on. "Good morning, everybody, I have so many things for you today. We have a winner in our How Did You Meet Your Best Friend Contest . . . but first let me tell you what I forgot to mention yesterday. Give me a little Indian music, please, Mother Smith. We got a letter from the Goodnight sisters all the way from Oklahoma . . . and they sent us a photograph. I wish you could see it, they both have on feather bonnets and are standing beside a real Indian. They write, 'Hello from the land of the redman. . . . We have just been adopted by Chief . . .' well, I can't make out the name . . . 'and we are now members of the Miami Indian tribe. . . . We are on our way to a powwow. Wish you were here. Ada and Bess Goodnight . . . *now* known as . . . Princess Laughing Bird and Little Thunder.' I tell you, those gals are fearless . . . no telling what they will be up to next. . . . But I can tell you what we are up to.

"Miss Virginia Mae Schmitt, our special guest all the way from Dale, Indiana, is here to sing a cute little novelty song for all you singles out there entitled 'I'm Living Alone, and I Like It.' But, before we get to our song, I want all you men listening to leave the room because I have a special announcement just for the ladies. Girls, make sure they are not listening . . . and Doc, I know you have the radio on down at the drugstore, so just turn it off for two minutes . . . and I mean it. Bertha Ann, go back behind the counter and make sure he does." At the Rexall, Bertha Ann looked to see where Doc was and reached behind her and turned the radio down. "Well . . . Father's Day is here again . . . and if you are anything like me, every year I wrack my brain trying to figure out just what to get Doc. Men . . . aren't they just the hardest creatures in the world to buy for? But this year I think I have come up with a good one that you might want to think about yourself. You know how Doc loves his tools, so this year we are giving him a gift certificate to Warren's Hardware store—so he can go pick out exactly what he wants. Just call Macky and he said he would be happy to make you out one for any amount."

After her guest had sung, Dorothy came back on. "Thank you, Virginia Mae. I'm sure all you single gals out there enjoyed that one. And now without further ado, on to our winning letter. Mrs. Joni Hartman of Bible Grove, Missouri, writes:

"Dear Neighbor Dorothy,

"We have a lot of squirrels here in Bible Grove and they are always dropping acorns out of the trees. One day I was watching as a stranger walked past my house when a squirrel dropped a large acorn out of the tree and hit her on the head. She fell down thinking somebody shot her. I went out and told her she had been hit in the head by an acorn. I invited her in and gave her an aspirin and found out she worked for the Internal Revenue Service—that was the reason she thought somebody had shot her. She quit her job right after that and now has a good job working in the dead-letter department in Washington, D.C., and we correspond regularly.

"Congratulations, Mrs. Hartman. When you hear about things like that . . . it just does your heart good. One day a squirrel drops an acorn and the next thing you know you have a new friend, not to mention a free five-pound bag of Golden Flake Flour.

"We just never know what to expect next in life, do we?"

The Unexpected

Betty Raye did not know it, but she had not become friends with Vita Green a moment too soon. She would need a good friend and all the strength and courage she had for what was about to happen next.

Earl Finley had quietly done his dirty work behind closed doors, made the right deals and promises to the right people of both parties. He waited, coiled like a snake, until what he deemed a respectable amount of time had passed and then struck swiftly. Almost overnight, it seemed, a motion for a recall was put before the Missouri house and senate, stating that since Betty Raye had been elected with the expectation and understanding that her husband would run the state, that expectation was no longer valid. Within twenty-four hours, the motion was passed declaring that Betty Raye's governorship was null and void and a new election was to take place to determine who would serve out her last two years in office.

And Carnie Boofer, who had been sitting in the wings waiting, was poised and ready to go. It was all done with the best of intentions, so everyone—or almost everyone—said. The motion had been passed to relieve a nice lady from an impossible situation so she could leave office and step down gracefully and with dignity. Betty Raye received a lovely letter from the Speaker of the House, thanking her for her valiant service for the past two years and stating that although she was no longer the legal governor, as a courtesy she and the boys would be allowed to remain living at the mansion until the election was over. They had even voted to allot her a lifetime pension of $10,000 a year.

Vita thought it was a lousy trick they had pulled but agreed that in the long run it was probably for the best. She did not tell Betty Raye this, but knowing Earl Finley as well as she did and how dangerous he could be, she understood his methods all too well. If he wanted someone out of office he would stop at nothing to see that it happened. Vita still had her suspicions about his involvement in Hamm's disappearance but so far all Jake Spurling and his men had come up with was that Finley and all his cohorts had an airtight alibi that weekend—but then, they always did.

It never occurred to anyone, not even Betty Raye, that she would not step down.

At first, after the surprise of the thing, there was a part of her that was actually relieved. Now she could leave before she might make some terrible mistake and disgrace herself and undo all of Hamm's good work. Now, finally, she could move into her own house. It was all furnished. She was almost beginning to feel grateful to them.

But a few days after she and Alberta Peets started packing up and getting ready to move, something slowly began to dawn on her. In essence, despite all the niceties, what had really taken place was that the state politicians, led by Earl Finley, had said, "Here's your hat, what's your hurry, and don't let the door hit you on your way out." She called Vita in Kansas City.

"Vita, I've been thinking. We don't know for sure who was responsible for getting rid of Hamm but if it was any of the same people who are trying to get rid of me, I don't think they should be able to get away with it. Do you? Not without a fight, at least for Hamm's sake, if nothing else."

Vita sat up and paid attention. "What can you do?"

"Well, if they say the last election was null and void, I'll run again, on my own."

"Do you know what you are up against?" Vita said.

"No, I don't."

"Well, I do. I know these people and they play rough."

"Vita, what more can they do other than kill me? I know I probably won't win. But I think I owe it to Hamm to at least *try,* don't you?"

Vita smiled. "It would be fun. To see Earl's face."

"Can you come back up here tomorrow, Vita, so we can talk some more about it?"

"I guess so. But just to talk. I'll be there for lunch."

There was a pause on the other end.

"Oh, *all right* . . . make it breakfast."

They say people two blocks away heard Earl Finley yelling when he heard the news.

Vita Green had called her good friend Peter Wheeler, whose wife had just died, and talked him into moving to Jefferson City to help her run Betty Raye's campaign. It was an interesting choice, considering Peter Wheeler had run against Hamm in his first governor's election and it was at a party at his home where Betty Raye and Vita first met.

Earl Finley vowed he was not going to take this sitting down. He had tried to get rid of Betty Raye in a nice, devious way but now he was taking off the gloves in an all-out assault. As head of the Missouri Democratic Party, he declared her candidacy invalid and refused to support her. This forced her to run as an independent.

Le Roy Oatman and the Missouri Plowboys geared up one more time. From the first, her polling numbers were so low they set a state record. As hard as she tried, she was still so shy that when she got up to speak everyone could see her knees shaking. And even when they hid her behind a larger podium, she frequently dropped her speeches to the floor. If there were men who would not vote for a woman even when she had Hamm behind her, almost *none* would vote for a woman without any man behind her. One editorial said, "It seems Mrs. Sparks, unlike the rest of the state, has forgotten that she was never considered anything more than a paper governor. One cannot help but suspect she is being used once more as a pawn and to what end is unknown. However, to prevent further embarrassment to herself, her children, and the memory of her late husband, Mrs. Sparks needs to step aside and go on about her real business, that of housewife and mother."

Carnie Boofer and the rest of the candidates ignored her at first but as time went by Carnie could not resist taking a swipe at her. In his first paid-for television address he ended up by saying, "As far as the little lady that is running, first of all, let me say that most of us respect our females and do not question their abilities but who of us here would feel right about letting our wives or daughters be subjected to the rough-and-tumble world of politics. This is a world where tough decisions have to be made every day. I am sure Mrs. Sparks is a lovely lady but having said that, I must point out the fact that an ex–gospel singer and one-time cafeteria worker with barely a high school education is sorely ill-equipped to run a state. Mrs. Sparks needs to be home, where she belongs, looking after her children and leave the business of politics to the men. After all, it was the men that fought for our independence in this country. There was no such thing as founding mothers, only founding fathers. There were no minutewomen, just minutemen. Betsy Ross stayed home and sewed the flag. I suggest that instead of politics, Mrs. Sparks take up knitting and I'll make a deal with her—if she won't run, I won't knit."

Boofer got a lot of laughs. But not from the women.

In fact, it made Neighbor Dorothy mad—mad as she ever got, which could better be described as highly irritated. After his speech, she turned to Mother Smith and said, "He makes me tired."

Mother Smith said, "He makes me more than that. If I had a gun, I'd shoot him."

For Dorothy, having read so many unkind things said about Betty Raye by the other candidates, the Carnie Boofer speech was the last straw. The next morning, after her "nine out of ten movie stars use Lux Soap" commercial, she broke with all convention and went out on a limb.

"You know, we never delve into controversy here on our show but darn it all and please excuse my French over the radio, but I just have to say something this morning. I, for one, am tired of some men, and you know who they are, going on and on about how a woman should not do anything more than stay in the home and take care of their family. Now, you know I am not against that. I am a homemaker myself. But these men have got to realize that times have changed." Mother Smith broke into a rousing rendition of "How You Gonna Keep 'Em Down on the Farm After They've Seen Paree." "That's right, Mother Smith, and the same holds true for the women. Men have got to realize that they did not win the war all by themselves, for heaven's sake. During the war we all worked in factories, ran the trains, drove the buses, joined the army, did everything the men did. Our own Ada Goodnight flew planes. But when it was over the men came home and wanted everything to go back to the way it was. We understood that, but once people find out they can do a thing and like to do things, it's not right to tell them they can't. We are supposed to be about playing fair in this country and that doesn't seem fair to me. And if you agree, I think we need to let them know how we feel, don't you? Well, enough of me ranting and raving on and on but like Mother Smith says, women fought too long and too hard to get the vote to be told they shouldn't vote for one of our own. Now, we don't believe in throwing brickbats at the other fellow but we can make a stand on Election Day, as far as I'm concerned. I don't think it's right to attack somebody just because she's a woman. As you all may know, we were lucky enough to have Betty Raye stay with us and let me tell you this—anybody that could get Bobby Smith to read thirty-four books in one summer can certainly run a state! And that's all I'll say on the subject."

That is all she *had* to say. In truth, not many women had been interested in politics until Neighbor Dorothy's call to arms, but the day after her broadcast letters began pouring into the Democratic headquarters, complaining about Carnie Boofer. The politicians had crossed the wrong bunch this time. They had hit a big, mad hornets' nest with a rock and shortly both the Democrats and the Republicans were running for their lives.

Since *The Neighbor Dorothy Show* was heard statewide, all the other candidates, including the Carnie Boofer supporters, immediately organized a call in protest to the offices of the Golden Flake Flour Company, asking them to take her off the air. But Jack Mann, president of the company, did what his eighty-two-year-old mother, Mrs. Suzanne Mann, owner and chairman of the board, told him to do, and that was nothing. She was sweetly reasonable. "You'll take Dorothy off the air over my dead body," she said.

Along with her thousands of other listeners, when Norma's mother, Ida Jenkins, heard Dorothy's show she puffed up like a white-breasted pouter pigeon and said, "Oh, woe to you, Mr. Carnie Boofer. You have crossed the wrong woman this time." As president of the Federated Women's Club of Missouri, past president of three garden clubs, and a top Presbyterian, Ida had a lot of clout and she knew how to use it. She alerted all the members of the women's clubs and garden clubs in the state to write in—and they did, by the sackful.

But perhaps the strongest message was a telegram sent to Missouri Democratic headquarters by one man, whose mother and whose wife, Bess, were faithful *Neighbor Dorothy Show* listeners. A man with, you might say, a lot of influence with the Democratic Party in the state—and beyond. The telegram simply said:

LET THE LITTLE LADY RUN!
HARRY S. TRUMAN

Earl Finley was in a fit. Not only was Truman on her side, but public sentiment was running higher and higher against them. As he paced the room he ranted at the top of his voice to the men at the table, who sat motionless. "Dammit to hell, they've got our asses in a sling. Why? I'll tell you why. You can't insult a widow with two kids on television, that's why. You can't touch her. If you don't let her run like a man, you're a no-good son of a bitch and if you do treat her like a man, you're a no-good son of a bitch. It's frigging emotional blackmail," he said, stopping to pound the table with his fist.

At the end of the day, they had no choice but to dump Carnie Boofer and let the little lady run.

The Rooster May Crow but It's the Hen That Lays the Egg

Even though Betty Raye was now running on the Democratic ticket again, the public-opinion pollsters' opinion was that she still had no hope of winning.

Vita had believed that. But when she saw what the response to Dorothy's show had been, it gave her an idea to do something that had never been done before in the history of the state or in the entire country, for that matter. They would forget trying to convince and beg the men to take her candidacy seriously and go after the women's vote. It was a slim chance but it was the only one they had. This approach had been an old trick of Hamm's. Vita would run Betty Raye as the underdog and the more she was attacked for being a woman, the better.

The big push was on and the newspapers and the other candidates pushed back, making the same mistake Carnie Boofer had. Some said she was unqualified.

One man said, "All she has to offer the state is a 'Kitchen Cabinet.' " Once the national press picked it up, as Vita had hoped they would, telegrams for Betty Raye started pouring in from everywhere.

GOOD LUCK. I AM PULLING FOR YOU. —MAMIE EISENHOWER

BEST OF LUCK. —PATTY, MAXENE, AND LAVERNE ANDREWS

WISHING YOU THE BEST. —MRS. LURLEEN WALLACE

BEHIND YOU IN EVERY WAY. —LADY BIRD JOHNSON

But the telegram that absolutely floored Betty Raye was from a Missouri woman, the first movie star she had ever seen, when Anna Lee had taken her to the Elmwood Theater to see *Kitty Foyle:*

GIVE THEM HELL, KID . . . GINGER ROGERS

Women started to listen and read what Betty Raye had to say about how if elected she would not only continue her late husband's policies but implement new ones of her own, of interest to them. She promised to introduce state laws forcing state monies to be spent on facilities for women and girls as well as the males. She talked about the inequities of the women's salaries compared with the men's, subjects that they had never heard another candidate speak about, and they liked what they heard. When Ada Goodnight and her sister Bess, who were now traveling around Arizona in their Airstream trailer, read that she was running all by herself and was being attacked, they turned around and headed home to help. Ada knew about the plight of women in a male-dominated world. In 1945, when the male soldiers started coming back home from Europe, she and all the other women pilots that had served as WASPs during the war were unceremoniously told to go home and never received a dime or even thanks from the government. When a WASP friend of hers had been killed flying a mission, the army had refused to pay to send the body back to the family. Ada was more than ready for a fight. When she got back she organized all her lady-pilot pals and they all went up in their counties all over the state and dropped thousands of leaflets, urging women to vote for Betty Raye. Bess organized the entire state's ladies' bowling-league teams to get out and roll for Betty Raye. Pretty soon the ladies' auxiliaries of the Elks, the Moose, and the Lions and members of the Eastern Star got behind her. The wives of the Allis-Chalmers tractor company took out a full-page ad in the farmers' weekly that went all over the state.

The women of Elmwood Springs jumped in and did their share. Aunt Elner donated fifteen jars of fig preserves to be raffled off at the VFW bingo game. Norma lobbied all the wives of the men in the Missouri Hardware Association, and Ruby Robinson, who was a bigwig in the Registered Nurses of Missouri organization, brought them in as well. They were easy. Having been pushed around by male doctors every day, they knew how it felt to be bullied by men. Dixie Cahill put on an outdoor show downtown called "Tapping for Dollars" that raised quite a bit, mostly to get them to stop tapping, as Ed the barber claimed. Even Poor Tot, who could not afford it, donated a day of beauty care to raise money. Mother Smith called an old college friend of hers, Juliette Low, the founder of the Girl Scouts, and got them on the march. Verbena did not have a lot of money but she did threaten to lock her husband, Merle, out of the house if he said one more word about how a female had no business in politics. That was something she could do at least and it did shut him up.

The widows of the men who had disappeared with Hamm, Mrs. Seymour Gravel and Mrs. Wendell Hewitt, and even the former Mrs. Rodney Tillman, went on the campaign trail to try to help Betty Raye, and Mrs. Ursa Figgs, mother of the late Cecil Figgs, despite being a lifelong Republican, donated a great deal of money to the cause. Money came in from hundreds of pancake suppers and bake sales and a lot of poor farm women just sent in their egg money, but it added up. The men were now threatened and really started to go after Betty Raye with the most vicious attacks yet.

Finally, Minnie Oatman had had enough. She went to the phone on the wall outside the dressing room in Columbus, Mississippi, and dialed.

"Elvis," she said. "It's Minnie Oatman."

"Oh, yes, ma'am," he said, happy to hear from her. "How are you?"

"Honey, my girl Betty Raye is running for governor of the state of Missouri and they is beating up on her pretty bad. I need you to make a personal appearance at one of her rallies. Could you do that for me?"

"Yes, ma'am. I'd be glad to, just tell me when and where you want me. I'll be there."

Elvis loved gospel. Although he made his money on rock and roll, it was still in his heart his favorite. Mrs. Gladys Presley, Elvis's mother, was Minnie's biggest fan and he'd grown up hearing the Oatman family and had gone to many of their all-night sings in Memphis when he was a boy. Minnie had always been nice to his mother and his daddy, Vernon. That went a long way with him. He would be there if he had to cancel something else to do it.

If one thing could be said about gospel people, it was that they were loyal, or, as Minnie put it, "When the chips is down, gospel people will stand behind you." Not only did Elvis, Jerry Lee Lewis, Johnny Cash, and the Carter sisters show up, but every other gospel group in the country came to Missouri at one time or another to help her out. And that went a long way with the voters. As did the hundreds of buckets of free fried chicken at every rally that Bobby Smith, who was now running the entire Fowler Poultry Enterprises, had donated to help out his friend. After all, if it had not been for Betty Raye he would never have gotten out of grammar school.

As her numbers started to rise in the polls, Vita began to worry a little more about Betty Raye's safety. There were bodyguards, of course, but Hamm had also had a bodyguard and it had not helped save him. But Vita need not have worried. Betty Raye had something Hamm did not: Alberta Peets. Alberta never left Betty Raye's side for an instant. There was not a man or a group of men alive that could get past her to Betty Raye and live to tell the tale.

As for Betty Raye herself, as time went by she became more confident and sure of herself. She was finally able to speak to groups of people without shaking or dropping her papers. It had happened during one of her campaign stops. Vita knew Betty Raye had turned a corner when, speaking in Clark County, she had remarked to the crowd, "You know, I have a special place in my heart for Clark County. My late husband and I spent our honeymoon a few miles down the road . . . so you might say that Hamm Junior got his start right here."

Hamm Jr., who was sitting behind her at the time, turned beet red, but she did receive 78 percent of the Clark County vote.

On the morning after the special election, Neighbor Dorothy did her show as usual and at the end, before she signed off, she said, without fanfare, "Well, congratulations to our brand-new governor. We always feel sorry for the other fellow that loses but, as they say, may the best man win. Only from now on we might have to change that old saying to 'May the best person win.' This is Neighbor Dorothy with Mother Smith on the organ saying have a nice day and remember . . . you make our days so happy, so do come back and see us again, won't you?"

THE SEVENTIES

A New Decade

In 1970, after a long illness, the Smith family lost Mother Smith. That same year, Bobby and Lois had another boy. The world in general had changed very little except that a man had walked on the moon and everyone in Elmwood Springs was elated that America had done it first. Aunt Elner had been the only one over at Macky and Norma's house that night at the moonwalk party who felt sad about it. When Linda asked her why she was not as excited as everybody else she said, "Oh, but I am. It's just that I can't help but feel sorry for that poor Neil Armstrong."

"Why would you feel sorry for him, Aunt Elner?"

"Because, honey," she said, "after you've been to the moon, where else is there to go?"

She had a point.

Linda Warren, Macky and Norma's daughter, was a pretty girl with reddish-blond hair and although Norma had tried to be different, she wound up saying and doing all the annoying things to Linda that her mother had when she had been a teenager. Her favorite complaint, when Linda did not do what she wanted, was "You're just like your daddy." However, there was some truth to the statement. Linda, a real daddy's girl, was much more like her father in likes and temperament. She loved baseball and fishing and was great at sports.

And despite all the nagging and pleading by Norma, she had refused to take the course in domestic science in school and much to her mother's horror, had taken shop instead. Linda told her mother that she would much rather learn how to make a birdhouse than bake a cake and, as usual, Macky agreed with her. "I don't know how you expect to raise a child and take care of a husband if you can't even boil an egg or make a bed!" said Norma.

When Betty Raye had been elected for her second term as governor, the first thing she had done was to appoint Vita Green as the state's first female lieutenant governor. So, unbeknownst to most people, Hamm's wife and mistress wound up pretty much running the state. They had the help of Peter Wheeler and other smart people who were brought into the administration. Betty Raye also named her old friend the former short-order cook to an office she had created, as adviser to the governor on disabled veterans' affairs. After the Trolley Car Diner closed, Jimmy moved to Jefferson City and did a good job helping her out with many things. Alberta Peets, what with the murder and all, could not serve officially but she did get an early pardon and stayed on as Betty Raye's private secretary. Earl Finley said he would not live to see the end of the Hamm Sparks era and he was right. He had a stroke in 1969.

But Betty Raye was not the only Oatman doing well. In 1970, the State Department put together a goodwill tour featuring a tribute to American music and the Oatman Family Gospel Singers were chosen to represent southern gospel. They traveled to sixteen countries and had a wonderful time, especially the night of the performance in London at the Royal Albert Hall.

Minnie was so excited to meet the Queen Mother that after she did the curtsy they had taught her, which on a three-hundred-pound woman was more of a dip, she clapped her hands in delight at the very sight of her. "Well, if you are not just the cutest thing in your little crown. I know we are not supposed to touch you but I could just hug your neck." The Queen Mother, fascinated with the large American woman in the red dress and rhinestone glasses with her hair piled up almost a foot high on her head, listened to her prattling on. "You know, you may not know it, but you and me has a lot in common. Your girl turned out to be a queen and mine is the governor of the state of Missouri. So we must have did something right, didn't we, honey?"

"Indeed we did, Mrs. Oatman," said the Queen Mother, smiling as she moved on to greet Rosemary Clooney.

◆ ◆ ◆

As to the ongoing mystery of what had happened to Hamm Sparks, Jake Spurling had far from given up. He had worked long and hard for the past three years and in January 1970 there was finally a break in the case.

When Jake received the call about the abandoned hearse down in Louisiana he ordered it and the entire area cordoned off. Some kids who had been down at the river playing found it in the woods. It was rusty and the upholstery was ripped with age. He had his men go over it from top to bottom. The hearse, an older model, was traced back to the Cecil Figgs Mortuaries car lot in Kansas City, where all the older models were kept. A check on it revealed that a hearse had gone missing sometime after Hamm and the men had disappeared. The man in charge of the lot at the time was located and questioned about why he had not reported it. He said those old hearses were stolen all the time by kids wanting to joyride, so he'd figured that was what had happened. Jake flew in to Louisiana and walked around the area but there was nothing there except an old falling-down boat dock.

Jake was curious about who it belonged to and had it traced. His ears pricked up when the name was found. The registered owner of the land and the boat dock in 1967 was Mr. Buddy Leo, uncle of Mr. Anthony Leo of Kansas City, Missouri. A man with definite ties to organized crime. It might turn out to be nothing at all but it was too much of a coincidence, as far as Jake was concerned. The boat dock had not been too far from Hamm's last known location in Jackson. Maybe he had come by boat. After a long search it was discovered that in May 1959, a brand-new thirty-five-foot Chris-Craft cabin cruiser had been purchased in Kansas City in the name of Mrs. Jeannie Micelli, sister of Mr. Anthony Leo. This might be the connection Jake was looking for. The abandoned hearse, the boat dock, and the missing men were all connected back to Kansas City.

Unfortunately, neither Mr. Leo was available for questioning. The uncle had died of old age and, as was often the case, Mr. Anthony Leo, although younger, was no longer alive and well. In 1968 he had accidentally stepped in front of five rapidly speeding bullets, which had proved to be fatal. When questioned, his sister, Mrs. Micelli, said she had never owned a boat. Which was probably true. These men were known to buy things they did not want traced by using other people's names.

When Jake questioned Betty Raye, she told him she remembered that Hamm had mentioned a few times that Rodney had a friend with a boat that they sometimes borrowed.

"Is that so?" said Jake.

"Yes. I think he took the boys with him a few times."

Hamm Jr. remembered it quite well.

Jake was pleased. Now we're getting somewhere, he thought.

The next thing was to find out what had happened to the boat.

Tot's Vacation

On April 21 Aunt Elner started the phone conversation, as she often did, without even saying hello first.

"Did you hear what happened to Poor Tot?"

Norma knew that whatever it was, it was not going to be good. "Don't even tell me."

Aunt Elner ignored her.

"You know, she's been miserable with that broken finger and so as long as she couldn't fix hair she let Dwayne Junior talk her into going to Florida with him and then that fish almost bit her right leg off—she's in the hospital right now, poor thing, and she was not even fishing at the time. Said she was downstairs in the galley of the boat minding her own business, not bothering a soul, just trying to fix herself a grilled-cheese sandwich, when the fish got her."

Norma sat down. "What fish?"

"I don't know but it was mad at having been jerked out of the water, I can tell you that."

"Who told you this?"

"Verbena, she just got off the phone with Tot this very second."

Norma said, "Aunt Elner, I'll call you right back," and dialed Verbena's number down at the cleaners to get the story firsthand. Verbena picked up: "Blue Ribbon."

"It's Norma."

"I was just calling you but your line was busy."

"Did you tell Aunt Elner that Tot was bitten by a fish?"

"No, I said she was stuck by a fish while making a grilled-cheese sandwich. I never said she was bitten."

"Why would she get stuck by a fish if she was downstairs cooking?"

"Because the fish just came down the stairs looking for her, I guess."

"But why?"

"Because she has the worst luck of anybody I know, that's why."

"How did it happen?"

"She was down in Florida on this fishing boat that Dwayne Junior and a friend of his had rented to try and cheer her up. That's what he said but he just wanted to go himself, if you ask me. Anyhow, after three hours of sitting upstairs in the hot sun, not catching a thing, she said, 'I'm hungry, I'm going down and fix myself a grilled-cheese sandwich. Does anybody else want one?' They said no and the next thing she knew, just as she was getting ready to flip her sandwich, this big fish came flying down the stairs. Dwayne had jerked it out of the water too hard and it flew right over his head and when it hit the deck it took a flying leap and came sailing down the stairs and stabbed Poor Tot in the thigh with its nose."

"Oh my God, it must have scared her to death."

"She said it was certainly a surprise to look down and see a strange fish sticking out of her leg. The captain packed her leg in ice and took her all the way to Pensacola to get the thing removed. She said she felt like a fool checking in with a fish sticking out of her leg but the captain said that they didn't dare pull it out on their own. It could cause too much damage."

"Damage to who?"

"The fish, I guess—Dwayne Junior is having it mounted as a souvenir of their trip."

"What kind of fish was it?"

Norma could hear Verbena shuffling papers. "I wrote it down. Here it is. It was identified as a needle-nosed houndfish. They took her picture for the paper."

"Is she all right?"

"Oh yes. Besides having six stitches and having to get shots."

"Can't she sue somebody?"

"Norma, who's she going to sue? She said the fishing-boat people won't cover it. They said it was an act of God. . . . So who can she sue, the Gulf of Mexico? Or the fish? No, she just got stuck in more ways than one, so she's coming home tomorrow. She didn't have but one day of vacation. If she was miserable when she left, you can imagine how she must feel now."

"Poor Tot."

The next day the citizens of Pensacola saw a picture of a Mrs. Whooten being wheeled into the emergency room under a caption that read WOMAN SPEARED BY FLYING FISH. People in Elmwood Springs tried not to bring it up but when they did, all Tot would say was "It's put me off tuna fish, I can tell you that."

To the Public at Large:

My recent experience has taught me an expensive lesson and I am passing it on as a warning. Do not ever call an ambulance if you can help it. Believe me, I could have gone to Europe twice for the money it cost me to ride no more than six blocks in one (it would have to be rush hour) but they did not take that fact into account. They were as nice as they could be and I was nice back, but at the time I didn't know I was being charged a small fortune, which I am still paying on, and now my insurance has gone sky-high as well. I only had a leg injury but they made me wear a collar on my neck and on the way to the hospital they gave me oxygen in my nose (that I did not need) and kept taking my blood pressure and temperature every two minutes. Not only that, they were training the boy that was taking it how to do it and I did not even get a discount. But that was not the worst of it. Once they get you to the emergency room, look out. Those emergency room doctors are expensive and they charge you by the second. I was X-rayed and CAT-scanned from stem to stern, pulled from one place to another the whole time almost freezing to death. They keep it as cold as ice in there. In my case I was sent to surgery to have the fish removed (you don't want to know what that set me back) and I was given a local anesthetic, so I was not able to walk out and they got to keep me overnight. If I were to tell you what they charged me for just the use of the bed, a couple of aspirins, and a tranquilizer, it would scare you to death. Don't be lulled into thinking that your insurance covers everything. It doesn't. My advice is this: if you can possibly walk, drive, call a cab, or take a bus to the emergency room, do it. Do not call 911 unless you are out cold.

A concerned citizen
Mrs. Tot Whooten

P.S. Watch out for flying fish.

Mother's Day

In the spring of 1970, among the radio shows that featured mostly teenage music, right after *Tops in Pops, The Neighbor Dorothy Show* could still be heard over station WDOT.

Except for the fact that Mother Smith was gone and Dorothy was almost all gray now, the show remained the same. Her voice was still as warm and friendly, a welcome relief from the blaring rock and roll that played the rest of the day and night.

"Good morning, everybody," said Neighbor Dorothy. "I don't know what's happening where you are but it seems everybody here has come down with a full-blown case of old-fashioned spring fever. And I can't blame them—this is such a pretty, warm April and I hope it is the same where you are. I've never seen so many jonquils popping up everywhere. And pretty soon Mother's Day will be upon us and if you're wondering what to get Mother this year, think about giving her a gift that sings. A canary of her very own for the parlor or kitchen, to start her day on a cheery note. I can recommend that from experience. I can't tell you how much joy my two precious birds, Dumpling and Moe, gave me over the years. Or if she already has a canary, you might think about getting her Rittenhouse door chimes and remember, Rittenhouse door chimes are always pleasant to the ear and a lovely way to say that company is at your door. And let's see what else . . . we received another postcard from our tin-can tourists . . . the Goodnight sisters . . . and I wish you could see this one.

They are both sitting on ostriches. It comes from the Corn Blough Ostrich farm in Kalamazoo—I tell you, those girls have no fear.

". . . If any of you folks are traveling in or around Lebanon, Missouri, and need a place to stay, don't forget Nelson's Dream Village Motor Court. . . . Stop in and see and hear the electrical and musical fountain. Spend a cool night in the Ozark Mountains on U.S. Highway Number 66 . . . the gateway to the South and the West. . . . Nelson's Dream Village—strictly modern, fireproof, individual bungalows where children stay free.

"And speaking of children. I got the sweetest letter from Bobby and Lois and I am happy to report that grandson Michael is now an Eagle Scout. I would have given anything to be there to see it. It's so hard to realize that both my children live so far away and no matter how old they get they are still our babies, aren't they? When I see Bobby now I can hardly believe that he runs such a big company. I know he is a grown man with children of his own but to me he's still my little Bobby and she is still my little girl Anna Lee, who, hold on to your hat, called me last night and reported that she might be getting ready to be a grandmother herself and make Doc and I great-grandparents." Dorothy laughed. "I told Doc I hope it happens because it will be the first time I've ever been great at anything.

"Later on in the program we will be having a talk from Gertrude Hazelette entitled 'The Superior Way to Crack Hickory Nuts' . . . but first let me ask you this: are there any more pack rats out there besides me? Every year when I do my spring cleaning I go up in the attic, determined to clean it out and throw out all that old stuff that does nothing but sit up there and collect dust and every time . . . I always wind up not throwing a thing away. . . . I sit there and so many pleasant memories come back with each and every thing I pick up. I know I should give all of it away, but I just don't have the heart. . . . Oh well . . . maybe next year . . ."

Empty Nest

Norma Warren was getting ready to have her daughter leave home for the first time and she was not at all happy about it. When their daughter, Linda, graduated from high school, she immediately went to work for AT&T. On career day the representatives had come to school trying to recruit women, in particular, for management training. They needed a quota of women now that the federal *and* the state governments were paying attention. Aunt Elner's niece by marriage, Mary Grace, had a good job at the telephone company in St. Louis and put in a good word for her. When Linda was chosen, Norma was disappointed. "I wish you'd think about going to college for at least two years, if nothing else. I wish I hadn't gotten married so young. I wish I had gone to college."

"I know, Mother, but think about the great opportunity this is. I'm going to be trained for a top job. Why waste four years in college when I can already be working and making good money?"

"But, honey, think of the fun you'll miss—the sororities, the dating, living in the dorm with all the other girls."

"People don't do all that anymore and I can have just as much fun making money. If you weigh all the options, Mother, it's really the most logical and practical thing to do."

"You're too young to be logical and practical. You must get that from your daddy. I was never practical or logical. Maybe I should have been more like you. I just got married and didn't learn a thing. If something happens to your daddy, I'll probably wind up as someone's maid or cook—that's all I know how to do. I don't have any skills but cooking and cleaning."

"Oh, Mother, you do too. Real cooking is a skill."

"No, it's not," Norma said. "Any old person can cook."

"I can't," said Linda.

"You never really tried. You know your daddy is going to be *very* upset that you're not going to college."

"No, he's not. He thinks it's a great idea."

"How do *you* know?"

"Because I went down to the store and showed him the letter."

"When?"

"This morning."

"Before you showed me?"

"Well, I wanted to see what he thought. And he said I should do it."

"Oh, I see, so as usual you and he have decided—I'm just out of the loop, I don't count."

"Oh, Mother . . ."

"Well, it's true. I don't know why you bother to tell me anything. I might as well be a knob on the door for all you two care. Why did you bother to ask me? You're going to do what your daddy says, you always do."

"Mother, you know that's not true. And if you're so dead set against it, I won't go."

"Sure, and if you don't go you'll never let me live it down. I was just hoping you would be a little closer to home, that's all, not too far away."

Linda said, "So that's what is really worrying you."

"Why shouldn't it? I'm a normal mother."

"But you don't have to worry. I'll be fine."

"Do you think I am going to let you go up to some big city full of gangs and white slavers and not worry?"

"Oh, Mother, there aren't any white slavers in San Francisco."

"You don't know. I look at television and I see things. Barbara Walters just had a piece about some Russian girls that mixed up with white slavers. It still goes on, don't kid yourself." Tears welled up in her eyes. "And here I thought you would be on some safe college campus for four years."

"Mother."

"I hope you carry a gun in your purse, that's all I can say. People are getting knocked in the head right and left. I hope you know I won't sleep for the next four years!"

An hour later Linda called Macky.

"Daddy, you're going to have to talk to Mother—she's having a fit about me getting knocked in the head or getting kidnapped by white slavers."

Macky said, "I figured as much. Has she said anything about earthquakes yet?"

"No, not yet, but I'm sure as soon as she has time to think, it will be next."

As expected, later that night Norma sat in the kitchen with Macky. "I just don't know what's wrong with those people at the telephone company. Expecting a young girl to go all the way to San Francisco all by herself."

"She's going to be with a whole *bunch* of people her age that will be in training with her."

Norma's eyes blinked wide open. "*San Francisco!* Oh my God, what about earthquakes!"

Macky got up and poured himself another cup of coffee. It was going to be a long night.

"I'm going to have a series of small strokes over this, I just know it."

"Norma, I wish you would just stop worrying over every damn thing. You are going to drive yourself crazy."

"I can't help it, I'm a worrier. My mother was a worrier and so am I. I was nervous as a child. I was nervous as a teenager. I've always been nervous. You knew I was nervous when you married me. I told you I was nervous."

"Yes, but I thought you would get over it after the first twenty years."

"You have never been nervous a minute in your life, so you don't know what it's like, so don't sit there and tell me to just get over it. You act as if it's something I want to do. I guess you think I wake up every morning and say, Oh boy, I just can't wait to be a nervous wreck all day and worry myself to death about everybody and just about jump out of my skin every time the phone rings, it's such fun. Honestly, Macky, I wish you would try and understand. You and Aunt Elner are just alike; neither one of you has a nerve in your body. I wish I could be like that but I can't. I guess it's just part of nature. Some animals are nervous and some aren't. I don't know why, but I am sure the Good Lord had his reasons. You can't change people's nature. You can't say to a bird, Be more like a cow."

"All right Norma, you've made your point."

"Or a lion to be like a monkey."

"O.K. Norma, all I was suggesting is that you might have more fun if you could relax more."

"Don't you think I know that? You think you're telling me something I don't know? I wish I could just let the house go to pot, let you and Aunt Elner and Linda do what you want. What if Linda wants to go off to a big city and live around killers and rapists, so what? You want to jump on and off roller coasters at your age, so what? Aunt Elner wants to leave her house wide open all night so anybody can come traipsing in and out and murder her in her bed, so what?"

"I know, but Norma, you're like Chicken Little, running around always thinking the sky's falling. Do you think that your worrying can prevent anything from happening? Whatever happens is supposed to happen and whatever doesn't, isn't."

Norma looked at him like she could kill him. "Well, thank you, Macky, that's a big help. I'll remember to tell you that the next time you are worried about something."

After Linda had left for San Francisco, Aunt Elner called Norma and said, "Norma, do you know what's the matter with you? You're an empty nester."

"What?"

"I read it in the *Reader's Digest* and I think you've got empty-nest syndrome. I think that's why you are so depressed and moping around. It says the symptoms are a feeling that your life is over, a feeling of uselessness. I see the signs as clear as day."

"What signs?"

"You can't fool me. Every time you come over here I know you're just itching to clean my house. What you need is a hobby. Listen, the *Reader's Digest* says, and I quote, are you listening?"

"Yes."

" 'The antidote to empty-nest syndrome is the following or a combination thereof. . . . Get up out of the house and make new friends, get new hobbies, donate your time to some civic cause, go on a second honeymoon with your husband.' "

"A second honeymoon? We never had the first one. Now I'm due two. Go on, what else?"

"Go out to eat at least once a week or take a dance class."

Norma had to admit that what Aunt Elner said was true. She had been feeling useless and she had been itching to clean Aunt Elner's house from top to bottom. But she did not want to take a dance class, or eat out once a week. There was no place to go now that the cafeteria had closed except Howard Johnson, and just how many fried clams can one eat? And she knew Macky would never shut down the hardware store to go on a second honeymoon. She supposed her only recourse was to search for a cause, but finding a cause in Elmwood Springs would not be easy. Everybody seemed to have what they wanted.

Tin-Can Tourists, 1974

Aunt Elner had been out in the yard dealing with a dog that was chasing her cat and had missed most of Neighbor Dorothy's show but she ran in and turned it on to try to catch the tail end of it anyway. This was Neighbor Dorothy's last week on the air and she did not want to miss one second of it.

"We received another postcard from our tin-can tourists, Ada and Bess Goodnight. Bess says their travels are over; they have settled down and plan to stay there forever. Their new home is the Ollie Trout Trailer Camp, located on Biscayne Boulevard at 107th Street, one and a half miles north of the Miami city limits. The postcard has a lovely picture and describes Ollie's as one of the finest automobile trailer tourist parks in the country, offering three hundred and fifty individual lots with a coconut palm on each corner. It sounds like heaven to me. The card is signed, 'Whoopee, come and see us. Ada and Bess Goodnight.'

"It seems like they just left yesterday and they have been gone for over nine years now. Well, I've caught you up on all the news, so I thought I'd take this time to talk about something that's been on my mind for a while. Last night Doc and I were sitting in the backyard watching the sun go down and the stars come out . . . and what a pretty sight . . . to see the first little star come twinkling on . . . the night was so warm and lovely and we sat there until they had all come out and I had a thought. I wondered how we would feel if we never had stars or the moon, just a dark sky and then, one night, they suddenly all appeared in the sky. We would all be in awe, I'm sure, and say, What a wondrous sight, but sometimes I get so busy I forget to look at the moon and the stars and appreciate how lucky we are to have them. We never appreciate the moon until he goes behind a dark cloud, do we. God gave us so many beautiful things to look at, and now that both my children are grown and gone, Doc and I spend a lot more time counting our blessings and we have had more than our share. I know that we were so lucky to have had Mother Smith with us for so many years. Both our children are happy and healthy and I have been blessed, too, with so many wonderful neighbors, my real neighbors and all my radio neighbors, who have been with me throughout the years. I often wonder what I did to deserve such a wonderful life. It's going to be hard not to come to the microphone every morning for our visit but you and I know that, unfortunately, time marches on and waits for no man, as they say, or even woman. I am sure that the new folks coming along will have a lot of exciting things to offer. It's been a long run . . . thirty-eight years of broadcasting is more than I could have ever hoped for.

"As most of you know, Doc is retiring this month and we are looking forward to doing some traveling and a lot of visiting. At the end of our lives we don't have much money and are not rich in material things, but as I sit and reread the letters you have sent me throughout the years I am wealthy as a millionaire and I hope you will still write to me every once in a while. I have been asked to stop by the studio in Poplar Bluff and chat with you from time to time, so you won't be rid of me altogether, but we still have a week to go, so I won't say good-bye. I'll just say until tomorrow, this is Neighbor Dorothy coming to you from 5348 First Avenue North in Elmwood Springs, Missouri. Where you are always welcome and have a nice day."

Elner got up from the table, sighing and wondering what in the world life would be like without *The Neighbor Dorothy Show.* She was not the only one. In a kitchen twenty miles outside of town, a farm woman went into the left drawer by the sink and pulled out a writing tablet and, after testing about six, finally found a ballpoint pen that still had ink in it. She sat down and started a letter.

Dear Neighbor Dorothy,

Just thought I'd drop you a line and tell you how much I'll miss hearing you on the radio every day. Listening to you was always such a comfort to me and I did not feel so alone way out here, so far from town. It would have been a lonely old life if it had not been for you and your family. At times I almost felt like Bobby and Anna Lee were mine as well. Lord, we have been through it all, haven't we? You have truly been a good neighbor.

Your friend,
Mrs. Vernon Boshell
Route 3

The End of an Era

Doc had been at the drugstore, training the young pharmacist who was taking his place, when the prescription was called in. The minute he saw who the heart medicine was for he went home. They never did travel. It was a warm autumn that year, so they spent some of the days sitting in the Sweetheart Swing out back and watching the sun go down.

On October 22, a tall, thin radio announcer walked into the booth, looked up at the clock, and waited. At exactly 9:30, instead of the *Tops in Pops* show, which usually aired after the news, a surprised listening audience heard: "Ladies and gentlemen, station WDOT is sad to report that a friend is dead. Last evening, Neighbor Dorothy passed away quietly in her home in Elmwood Springs. She is survived by her daughter, Anna Lee, and a son, Robert. We wish to extend our deepest sympathies to them and to the hundreds of radio listeners who came to know and love her over the years.

"The family requests that if you wish to remember her, in lieu of flowers, please send a donation to the Princess Mary Margaret Fund, in care of the Elmwood Springs Humane Society. In remembrance, we here at station WDOT will be off the air for one hour in silent tribute to a woman who will be missed by all.

"We would like to close with this thought. What is a life? The best and most noble life is one lived in such a way that it can be said of a person, as they pass on to the next life, that while she was here she brought love and joy and comfort to all she touched. Such was the life lived by the woman known to all simply as Neighbor Dorothy. Although her voice here on earth has been silenced, we would like to think that somewhere, in another place, people are just now turning on their radios and hearing her for the very first time. Good-bye, dear friend."

THE EIGHTIES

A Scare

For all the years and hours that Norma had spent worrying over every little thing, the moment that something really terrible did happen she was the one who was calm and was able to keep a clear head. She had not said a word to Macky or Aunt Elner. All they knew is that she had gone in for her yearly checkup. She did not tell them anything until two weeks later. That night after dinner, after she put the dishes in the dishwasher and turned off the kitchen light, she sat down by Macky in the family room.

"Macky, I'm sure it's nothing but they saw a little something on my mammogram that they didn't like and Dr. Halling wants to do a biopsy."

Macky felt the blood drain from his body. She went on.

"So, I'm going to go in on Wednesday. I should only be there for a day or so, but anyhow, I'm going to fix a few things and put them in the freezer for you so you can have them to eat while I'm gone."

Macky finally got his voice. "Jesus Christ, when did this happen?"

"A few days ago."

"A few days ago—why didn't you tell me?"

"Because there was no point for you to worry. The only reason I'm telling you now is because they might keep me overnight, depending on what they find, and I didn't want you to come home and wonder where I was."

"Have you told Aunt Elner or Linda? Is she coming home?"

"No. Like I said, there is no point to telling anybody anything until we know what it is and it's probably not anything at all."

"Why would you keep something like this from me? What is the matter with you?"

"Nothing is the matter, honey, I just didn't think you needed to worry, that's all."

"I'm your husband, for God's sake, you don't just say, Oh by the way, I think I might have cancer."

The minute he said it he was sorry. But Norma got up and came over, pushed his hair back off his forehead, and patted his shoulder. "Oh, honey, I don't have cancer."

"But you could have."

"The chances are rare, but even if I do, it's not the end of the world. He said we caught it early."

"Does he think it is?"

"No, he meant if, on the off chance that there is something, we caught it in time."

After they went to bed he could not sleep and got up at about three in the morning and walked out in the backyard and tears ran down his cheeks. Not so much because he was scared to death but because it was her bravery that had always touched him more than he could tell her.

The next few days were pure hell. He realized that if he lost her he would never forgive himself. He wanted more years with her, so he could wake up every day and look at her and appreciate who she was, what she was. She was his wife, his lover, the mother of his child, but most of all she was his best friend. Without her he would be more lost than he already was.

He sat in the waiting room of the hospital and while they were doing the biopsy on Norma he thought about *time,* the one thing that could not be stopped. As a child, time had seemed like a windup toy. It had seemed so long on those days he sat in school waiting for the bell to ring and so short when he was having fun. So long from Christmas Eve night to Christmas morning. Now, in just a few seconds, the doctor would tell them the results. In those few seconds his life would never again be the same—or they would have another chance.

Did the white-coated people in the lab know what they were looking at? Would they go to lunch and not know that whatever they found under the microscope would change lives forever? He wanted to yell at the entire hospital, *That's my wife, that's my entire life, our entire future you're looking at.* Here was a man who could not stand to have anyone else drive, hated to fly because he was not comfortable unless he was at the controls, and now he was helpless. Totally dependent on the hospital staff, who looked to him to be no more than teenagers. What had happened to the older, gray-haired nurses and doctors he had remembered the last time she was in the hospital, having their daughter, thirty-one years ago, and what the hell are they so happy about? Didn't they know how serious life and death was, for God's sake? That poor sweetheart could wake up with her breast gone and be told that it had spread everywhere and that she was dying. Why in the hell hadn't they found a cure for this thing yet?

What are we doing sending money all over the world, spending billions on the military budget and on making stupid movies and television shows? People are dying every day and we're just throwing money away. Why aren't they giving it to the scientists to find a cure? Something is wrong—cancer has been around too long; somebody must have a cure, they're just not letting anybody know. He had worked himself into a murderous rage when the doctor came down the hall.

"Mr. Warren, we just got the report from the lab and it's absolutely benign, so we're gonna close her on up. She should be out of recovery in a few hours." He spoke over his shoulder to another doctor that had just passed him in the hall. "Hey, Duke, can you get me two more tickets for the game tomorrow?"

Macky didn't hear Duke's response. He stood up and took a walk outside the hospital. Everything inside had been cold and sterile and now he was back out in the warm sunshine and he felt as if he could breathe again. He found himself smiling at the people he passed and at that moment he made a deal with himself. Anything that woman wants from now on, she gets.

Afterward, he had to remind himself of that deal he made that day outside the hospital. When he asked her the next year where she wanted to go for a vacation, she said, "Well, there is one place that I have been dying to go to, but I don't know if you will want to."

"Norma, I told you we will go anywhere you want."

"I've always wanted to go to Las Vegas and see Wayne Newton in concert."

He would have gone to the moon had she wanted.

Revitalize Downtown Elmwood Springs

Six months after they returned from Las Vegas, Norma finally found the civic cause she had been searching for. Somehow it seemed that after Neighbor Dorothy died, nobody ever came to town anymore. When she had her radio show, people came from miles around by the busloads, but now, with the new interstate, downtown was dying on the vine. At the next chamber of commerce meeting a brand-new committee to come up with solutions to revitalize downtown Elmwood Springs was formed and Norma was voted to head it. After walking downtown, clipboard in hand on a fact-finding tour, Norma reported her conclusion at the next meeting.

"We are too dull—what we *need* is a theme."

"A theme? What kind of a theme?" asked Leona.

"A theme, something to make us different, make us stand out, set us apart from other towns so people will want to come here. We just don't have any character; every building is just willy-nilly. We need to make an impression. When you drive in, what do you see? You see a sign that says *Welcome to Elmwood Springs* but we need more than that. We need to have one that offers an idea, a claim, something unique. *Home of the World's Largest Sweet Potato* or something. We need to give people something unusual, an attraction that will make them want to get off the interstate and stop."

They all fired at once:

"Can't we think of something like that to get us in the *Guinness Book of World Records*?"

"Like the world's largest cake. Or pie or pancake, even."

"What about a waffle, the world's biggest waffle?"

"But once you make it, it won't last—you have to offer them something to see that's still here."

"We need something that's indigenous."

"How about home of the largest squash ever grown? Don't you remember when Doc Smith grew that squash and sent it to the state fair?"

"How do you know it was the world's largest squash? It was the state's, but we don't know for sure if it was the world's."

"All right, we can say the state's largest squash—who's going to know anyway? Or care?"

"I think they took a picture of it. We could find out, we could display that."

"Well, I tell you what. I certainly wouldn't turn off the interstate to look at a squash, much less a picture of a squash," said Tot.

"What *do* we have a lot of?"

"Corn?"

"No, Iowa has corn. Idaho has the potato."

"Rhubarb? Does anyone else have rhubarb?" asked Verbena, biting into a doughnut. "We could get a whole bunch and plant it real quick."

"Why does it have to be a vegetable—why can't it be a meat or a pastry or a beverage?"

Norma said, "I still think a theme would be better and permanent, like having Main Street look different somehow. Maybe have it look like a street in a different country, you know, like that Danish town in California."

"What about this: we could have a town theme. All we would have to do is change everything into Swiss chalets and put bells on the cows and things. Call ourselves 'Little Switzerland' or something."

"What cows? We don't have any cows in town."

"All right, you come up with something."

"What about Hawaiian, I love that, everybody could wear muumuus and Dixie teaches the hula—maybe she could teach the whole town and we could give everybody a lei when they drove into town. Something like that."

◆ ◆ ◆

The next morning Norma drove around town trying to envision a theme that would, as the committee eventually had suggested, "more easily lend itself to fit the existing topography." There was not a body of water to speak of, unless you included the lake or the springs, so the Hawaiian idea was out. Nor was there a mountain within three hundred miles. Elmwood Springs was as flat as the world's largest pancake and inland.

Inland. She had a brainstorm. Why not capitalize on just that, Elmwood Springs right smack in the middle of the country. After all, they were not too far north, not too far south, east or west. And if you dropped New Mexico and Nevada, which you could because they were mostly desert, then Elmwood Springs was truly sitting right smack-dab in the middle of the country. Everybody said that if you climbed high enough you could see into Kentucky, Illinois, Indiana, Tennessee, Mississippi, Arkansas, and all the way down to Iowa.

And so it was voted on. George Crawford painted the sign and on May 22 the committee held the sign unveiling and applauded. There it was for all the world that passed by on the interstate:

NEXT EXIT ELMWOOD SPRINGS, MISSOURI,
VOTED THE MOST MIDDLE TOWN IN AMERICA

Not a single car turned off the road because of it, but the town felt better.

The Gospel World

One afternoon Mrs. Pike of Spartanburg, South Carolina, received a surprise visit from her old friend Minnie Oatman, who was passing through on her way to join the group for a sacred-music festival in Dadeville. Minnie was in the living room, holding forth about the state of her health and the state of the gospel music world. "You know, I was laid up for four months a while back."

"Yes, I heard you were," said Mrs. Pike with concern.

"But as soon as I got over my heart attack I get on a plane and go on up to Detroit to join the family and, honey, I did not get back a minute too soon. While I was laid up the boys and that fool Emmett went out and got themselves a manager. I look up and here they come, wearing them tight little pants and skinny little neckties and long sideburns and pencil-thin black mustaches with their hair all combed way up in slick pompadours on the top of their heads and the worst of it was *they* thought they looked good. I said, 'You boys is just one step away from show business and if your daddy could see you he'd roll over in his grave.' Oh, I was fit to be tied and I can't blame Beatrice, she can't see what they had on. Anyhow, I ran that manager off. But you know, I worry to death about how gospel has just gone commercial. I think it all started when the Oak Ridge Boys let their hair grow long and went country. And now lots of these boys have turned country trying to make a fast buck. I'm scared Vernon is gonna run off to Nashville for good and start popping those pep pills with the rest of them. Bervin got hisself a new wife and is threatening to run off and be an Amway salesman and if he does there won't be anybody left to sing tenor." She took a swig of her iced tea. "I had hoped to bring Betty Raye's two boys into the family group someday but that's not gonna work out. Neither one of them can carry a tune." She heaved a sigh and looked away, baffled. "I just don't understand it. Both of them tone-deaf, with me and Ferris for grandparents."

After her second term Betty Raye retired from politics altogether and spent most of her time doing just what she had wanted to do all her life. She stayed home and gardened. The only other thing she did besides an occasional visit with her boys was to serve on the board of the twelve Hamm Sparks schools for the deaf and the blind she had founded in her late husband's name. After Peter Wheeler's wife died he and Vita married and were traveling the world on cruise ships. Jimmy Head moved into Betty Raye's guest house out in the back and was very happy.

In 1984 Hamm Sparks, Jr., ran for governor and won. People say they heard Earl Finley turning over in his grave.

As far as the Hamm Sparks case, after tracking the boat back to Mr. Anthony Leo, Jake Spurling hit another brick wall. He could not find the boat. He and his men scoured the records of all missing boats found and every piece of a boat found from St. Louis to the Mississippi border and on out to the Gulf of Mexico but nothing showed up. And Jake was still not sure if the missing hearse or the missing boat had anything to do with the men's disappearance. All he knew was that Hamm had been in Jackson, Mississippi, one night and had vanished the next morning.

Every hunting and fishing camp in the area had been gone over with a fine-toothed comb and with a pack of bloodhounds. Nothing. Every fiber, bone, tooth, or hank of hair that had been recovered in the past seventeen years had been examined but nothing matched any of the men. So far this case was turning out to be the most baffling one he had ever run up against. If Jake Spurling had not been a pragmatic man and a forensic scientist who believed only in what he could see under a microscope, he might have started to wonder if they had really just disappeared into thin air like people said.

Monroe

Bobby had flown to New York for a round of business meetings. Fowler Poultry was in the process of merging with another, bigger company. On the third night, when he came back to his hotel he picked up at the desk the message Lois had left for him.

YOUR FRIEND MONROE NEWBERRY PASSED AWAY. FUNERAL IS WEDNESDAY AT 2. CALL ME AS SOON AS YOU GET THIS.

He went up to his room, sat down, and called her. Thank God for Lois. She had arranged everything with their travel agent and booked him on a flight from New York directly to Kansas City, where a rental car was reserved; he could drive to Elmwood Springs. After Bobby's mother had died, Doc had gone to Seattle to live with Anna Lee, and Bobby had not been back to Elmwood Springs since the day of his mother's funeral or seen Monroe for years. He had been so busy. But he and Monroe always called each other on their birthdays and at Christmas just to check in. They always planned to get together and do something but they had not. Both had always figured they had plenty of time. Now it was too late.

In Kansas City, his rental car was waiting and as he drove out onto the new superhighway he began to think about so many things he and Monroe had done together. Climbing the water tower, swimming at the Blue Devil, the train trip to the Boy Scout Jamboree, all the hundreds of times Monroe had spent the night at his house. The promise they'd made to one another that night, looking up at the stars with his grandmother, to call each other in the year 2000. Each had been best man at the other's wedding.

But time and distance had taken its toll. Bobby had moved up in the world. He had new friends. He and Lois had bought a home in Shaker Heights in Cleveland, where the corporate offices were now located, and had joined the country club. Monroe had stayed at home to manage his wife's father's tire store.

Bobby arrived at the church around 1:40 and said the appropriate words to Monroe's wife, Peggy, and a few other classmates. Then he walked over to the casket. He reached out and patted the body lying there, a body that was supposed to be Monroe but was only some cold, hard thing just taken out of a freezer. It startled him. Why was he so cold, had they put him in an icebox? What was lying there in a brown polyester suit and tie looked like a bad mannequin someone had made of Monroe as a joke. What was death anyway, some cruel magic trick pulled by the universe? One moment people are here and then somebody waves a cloth over them and in an instant they are gone.

What was once Monroe had disappeared. Where had he gone? Bobby wondered, just as he had as a child, what happened to the rabbit that the magician pulled out of the hat and made disappear—was Monroe hidden in a secret compartment somewhere waiting to come back?

He knew he should be feeling something more but he just felt numb, almost detached. And as he sat in the pew listening to the minister drone on and on, he realized that he had started to hum a little tune that for some unknown reason kept playing over and over in his head. A tune he had not sung in years. *Enjoy yourself, it's later than you think./Enjoy yourself while you're still in the pink.* He knew he should be paying attention to the service but he could not concentrate. When it was over, the women, as usual, handled everything well; they even seemed to know when to cry. And how to cry, what casserole to make, and where to bring it. All the men did was show up and line up as pallbearers and even then they had to be told what to do. As he carried the body he was still unable to comprehend that it was really Monroe in the box he was lifting. It couldn't be. He was only forty-nine years old. He was supposed to have had so many years left. Monroe had been walking down the aisle at the Wal-Mart garden and patio center, looking for a good crabgrass killer, and the next thing he was on the floor, dead of a massive heart attack. They say he never knew what hit him.

But Bobby wondered if Monroe had felt it coming, if he had had even a few seconds of wondering what this was. Was he dying? Was it all over? Had he been shocked to realize that this was it, the way it was going to be? Did he have a second to think about the last thing he said to his wife or his children? Did he think about what he had not done? Was he mad, was he scared? Had his life passed before his eyes, as they say it does? Or did it just go black? Is it like sleeping? Do you dream? Was Monroe somewhere watching him right now, pleased he had come after all these years—or did anything Bobby did today really matter?

If Monroe had known how short his life was to be, would he have done things differently? Would he have wasted so many days just fooling around his workshop or looking at baseball games? What would he have done, had he really known how fast life goes, like one train whizzing past another—a roaring noise, a vibration, and then gone as fast as it came.

After the graveside service, they went back to the house. Peggy had set up a little table with a candle on it, where she had put out some photographs. Bobby walked over and saw the one of Monroe sitting on a pony, the same pony he'd been on, and school pictures, Monroe's wedding picture, frames with his family's pictures of him holding a string of fish, Monroe getting heavier as the years went by but still that same, sweet, good-natured Monroe, who had gone along with every crazy thing Bobby had thought up. After a while, all the guys eventually went out on the back porch and stood around talking, trying to remember all the funny things over the years. That time when Monroe had shot his little toe off when he tripped over his hunting dog, the time he had been caught trying to steal Old Man Henderson's wheelbarrow, all the nutty times of their childhoods. One of the guys passed a bottle of Jim Beam whiskey around and they each took a drink. Most of them, including Bobby, had lost a parent but that was to be expected. This was different. This was the first friend of their own age who had died. This was too close for comfort.

Death did not scare Bobby; he had seen too much of it in Korea. What scared Bobby was the moment or even the few seconds when you might know you were dying and that everything was over. He had almost drowned once and had thought for a fleeting second that maybe it was his last moment on earth. But at the time he had been so young and after he had the devil scared out of him, he'd promptly forgotten it and continued to take stupid chances. The young can forget easily. As you get older, it becomes harder and harder to forget your own mortality. There are so many reminders. Little individual end of the worlds start to happen all around you. When your grandparents go, your parents are ahead of you, but when they go, you look around and realize you are next in line. Then one day you are actually talking about cemetery plots and insurance.

It was about five when the get-together was over. Before he left to go back to the airport, Bobby decided to take a walk around town. He had not been home since his mother's funeral all those years ago. As he walked down streets where he had once known every face he passed, there were now strangers who had no idea who he was. They thought this was their town. Streets and houses that he had once known as well as the back of his hand had all changed. He walked along his old paper route but there were strangers in the old Whatley house, strangers sitting on the porch where the Nordstroms used to live. He cut down a few alleys, which years ago had seemed twenty feet wide, and was surprised to see that they were just narrow little footpaths, lined with garbage cans. He had not remembered so much garbage. He walked by his old house. He and Anna Lee had sold it a few years ago and he was glad to see it looked just about the same, only so much smaller than he remembered. Everything was much smaller. Downtown was just a block long. It had seemed so much bigger, like an entire city, as he remembered it. He stopped in front of the window of the Morgan Brothers department store and wondered how they had managed to get a winter wonderland in that little window. The barber pole was gone. Almost every business on the street was closed for good, except for the hardware store and his dad's old drugstore. The glass doors to the old Elmwood Theater were chained shut, and a poster of the last movie shown there, in '68, was dusty inside the glass frame. He stood outside on the sidewalk and stared up at it. God, he thought, the hours he had spent inside, the theater filled with screaming children and squeaking seats being flipped up and down. The green tin light sconces up the sides of the walls, a place so dark you would be blind for a few minutes as your eyes adjusted, until you could make out those little white lights on the floor by each row of seats and you would head down the aisle, your feet carpeted by some wonderfully soft, multicolored maroon and pink and green stuff leading you deeper into the theater, closer and closer to the big screen, where life was exciting and full of a million possibilities and dreams. He walked over and peered inside the lobby but could not see much. He did not know if it was because of the Jim Beam but as he stood there he could almost hear the large glass machine popping corn. He could taste the salty, buttery taste of that popcorn in the greasy red-and-white-striped bags. And even though the diner had closed years ago, he could still remember the tangy taste of mustard and chili on the hot dogs, washed down with bottles of ice-cold Orange Crush. And as he went by the drugstore he could taste all the root-beer floats, lemon and strawberry sodas, the banana splits, and the steaming hot-fudge sundaes he had eaten over the years.

So many sounds and smells. He thought, I must be drunk. He walked back to his car and got in and sat there alone. It was fall and the leaves were just beginning to turn and a thousand new memories flooded his mind.

That time. That place. That feeling. What he would not give to get it, to find it again for a day or even an hour, but he knew it was as impossible as trying to catch smoke in your hand. How could anyone know, when he or she was living it, that they would someday look back with longing, that these would be the good old days? No one tells us, "This is the happiest you will ever be in your life." Why had he wasted so much of it dreaming about going to other places? For the first time, Bobby realized the thing he missed most in the world was gone forever and he sat there and cried like a baby. He wanted his childhood back. He wanted to go home, walk down the hall, and climb into his old bed, and wake up with his future laid out before him on a red carpet. He wanted to go back to when a day seemed to last an eternity and the field behind the house was a vast expanse that led to magic places and the swimming pool was as long and as wide as a lake. When your best friend was your blood brother and all the girls thought you were cute. He wondered whatever had become of the Bubble Gum King of 1949? That boy who was going to fly planes, jump freighters to the Orient, be a cowboy, and do so many wonderful things.

Nothing too terrible. He had just grown up.

Poor Tot

A bad childhood followed by a happy adulthood is one thing, and a good childhood followed by an unhappy adulthood is another. But for Tot Whooten, a miserable childhood had followed her like a black dog right into an equally miserable adulthood. She had been so busy she had not noticed until one day when she looked around and it seemed clear to her that life was not a constant struggle for other people. They seemed to actually enjoy it and look forward to the dawning of a new day.

It had suddenly become obvious to her that if you wake up every morning and it takes you almost an hour to talk yourself into just getting out of bed, something is wrong. Every morning for the past twenty-plus years she had been her own mental cheerleader, doing back flips and chanting, "Be happy you are alive, life is great, rah rah rah . . . sis boom bah! You will be dead soon enough, don't waste your life away, get up, get up, the sun is shining, the birds are singing, it's a new day," and so on. But this morning the cheerleader inside just sat down with her pom-poms and flopped back on the bed beside her, saying, "I'm exhausted . . . I give up, I can't do it anymore." She was like that Old Man River, tired of living, but feared of dying, and this morning she had realized that she could no longer jes' keep rolling along.

After a lifetime, day after day, of getting up and taking care of first her brothers and sisters, then her own children, a drunken husband, her parents, she was like the elephant, so exhausted from carrying such a heavy load that she just fell down and couldn't get up. Poor Tot knew that not only could she not go on but she did not *want* to go on. Each of her children had been such a disappointment, and she had not had one good holiday in her life. Every Christmas had been the same. James drunk as a coot by ten in the morning, passed out by noon, and Darlene and Dwayne Jr. constantly fighting over something. Darlene was on her fourth marriage and *her* daughter Tammie Louise seemed to be taking after her—only ten and already crazy about the boys with the motorcycles. The last time Tot had seen Dwayne Jr. he had come to visit and walked off with her good silver candlesticks to buy more dope with, she guessed, or to hand over to that skinny girlfriend of his, the one with the penciled-in black eyebrows who smoked one cigarette after another. Where he had found her was a mystery that she was afraid to solve.

And neither one of her children would listen to her. They both snapped, "Well, look who you married." Not that she hadn't tried with Darlene. She had sent her to the Dixie Cahill School of Tap and Twirl, but Dixie had sent her back home with a note.

Dear Tot,

Darlene does not know her right from her left and I am afraid she will never make a dancer. You work too hard for your money to waste it on any more lessons.

Sincerely,
Dixie

Then, after years of putting up with James and his drinking, and begging and pleading with him to quit, they found him one day passed out in the back of the garage, sick as a dog from one of his long binges. The doctor finally told him, "If you take one more drink it will kill you." After all the years of Tot threatening him, crying, that one sentence did it.

He sobered up and soon was holding down a good job and the next thing she knew he was sitting in the living room telling her about some woman he had met in A.A. He looked her right in the eye and said, "Tot, for the first time in my life I am really in love." There she sat, after having borne his two children, put up with his drinking for over thirty-two years, and he had the nerve to tell her he was in love for the first time in his life. At that moment it occurred to her why people are driven to murder and she made a mental note not to support the death penalty.

If she had had the strength, she would have killed him, but she was unable to move. So she sat and stared while he went on and on about how sometimes in this life people are lucky enough to find their true soul mate. How for the first time since he was a boy he was able to laugh again. How the world looked bright and new and shiny again. About how much he liked the new woman's children and that he felt he now had a chance to be a better father this time than he was the last time, now that he was sober, that is.

Then he finished off his dissertation on love and second chances. "I can't tell you how much better I feel now that I've been honest with you."

"Oh good. I'm so glad you feel better."

"My sponsor said that the sooner I told you, the better off we would both be."

"I'm glad he thought so," she said.

"So now that you know, what do you want to do about it?"

"What do I want to do about it?"

"Yes," he said and looked at his watch like he was late for an appointment.

"I want you to get up and call that woman and tell her that you are already married."

"Oh, now, Tot, be reasonable. Jackie Sue needs me and you don't."

Tot could not believe her ears. "*Jackie Sue Potts?* Who's been with every man in this town?"

"Tot, don't say anything you will regret. You don't know what a hard life she has had."

"*She's* had a hard life?"

"Tot, the past is the past. We all have to live in the present, one day at a time."

"I'll tell you one thing, One Day at a Time. I'll give you a divorce but on one condition. You take that woman and you get as far away from us as you can because I will not live in the same town and have to see her or you, do you hear me?"

Tot had felt like a complete fool. Not only was the girl younger than her daughter, but all this time she had been fixing Jackie Sue's hair. She had been doing it so Jackie Sue would look good for a date with Tot's own husband!

Of course James had not moved and soon she had to see him and Jackie Sue floating all over town, showing off their new baby. That morning she wondered why she had finally reached the end of her rope. Maybe it was because she was just so tired. So bone tired that at long last she could not hold on anymore. By seven o'clock that morning the phone started ringing. She knew it was Darlene, wanting to know if she could drop her children off at the house so she and that new husband of hers could go off to the stock-car races. But for the first time Tot did not pick up the phone. Several more times before noon the phone rang, and several more people wanting something were annoyed because she did not answer. She heard the phone, but even the sound of the ringing did not stir the slightest, smallest interest or need to answer. Tot wondered what had happened. What in her had finally broken. What had undone her at last so she could lie there as peaceful and as silent as a radio that had suddenly been unplugged. That was it, she thought, I am unplugged. Dead inside at last. No more currents running through me, forcing me to keep going, to turn on, to feel anything.

Was this permanent or was this just the vacation she had never had in her life? How long would she be off, she wondered, and she hoped it was forever. It was so peaceful, so soothing, so painless to be alive but not to feel. It was as if she had stepped out of her body and left the house, although the woman who used to be her was still there, empty, hollow.

Around three o'clock she decided to try to get up out of bed. She was almost afraid that if she moved that old self might jump back in but as she slowly got up and walked through the house she was so relieved. She could move and nothing of her old self came back. She was a ghost in her own home, floating around and observing life, but not being affected by it in any way. What a pleasant state! What a peaceful way to spend the days! What was it? she thought, as she wandered through the house, pulling down the shades, taking the phone off the hook, and sticking it in the closet. What *was* this new state? After a while she identified it. It was quite simple. She just didn't care. After a lifetime of caring, trying, struggling, looking for answers, today one had come. Today was the day that she simply did not care anymore about anything.

Let her kids get upset. *Let* the shop go to hell in a handbasket. *Let* the church committees wonder about why she wasn't there. *Let* the world go to hell, she no longer cared.

She made herself some Campbell's tomato soup, drank a Coke, ate some crackers and a piece of cheese, and went back to bed. The dishes were still on the table. She didn't care. She dreamed of that one day, that one afternoon when she was seven. It had been a warm day and her schoolmate had invited her to a birthday party and she had been allowed to go. For one afternoon in 1928 she had been allowed to go to a party alone. Not having to take her brother or sister, not having to do anything but attend a party. They had played games and eaten ice cream and afterward she had been allowed to run in the large meadow behind the girl's house and run without her mother yelling at her to be careful, without having to watch out for her brothers and sisters. She had been happy for a while, for one afternoon when she was seven.

She wondered what her life would have been like if she had not had that one hour that one day.

Tot's Flipped

Everybody in town was concerned about Tot Whooten. Norma was speaking to Aunt Elner on the phone about it. "I am just worried sick. I drove by and there was poor Tot out in the back of her house, wandering around in the fields all by herself like she didn't have a thing in the world to do. You know, she's quit the church and she told Darlene not to drop the kids by anymore. She's stopped going to Bingo altogether. Her yard is a mess and you know that's not right. She never let her yard get out of hand. She always kept her lawn cut and those hedges neat and trimmed. Why, you could set a place setting on her hedges and serve dinner on them. That's how right and neat she kept them."

"Why would you want to eat on a hedge?" asked Aunt Elner.

"That's not the point; I am afraid she's flipped. I always thought I would be the first one in town to flip out and it's turned out to be Poor Tot. Poor Tot, she has just gone around the bend. Just like her mother did."

Aunt Elner said, "I don't think so, Norma. I went over to see her the other day and she made perfect sense to me. She's tired, Norma, that's all that's the matter with her, and she'll either come around or she won't."

"Well, that's a comfort, Aunt Elner. What do we tell Darlene and Dwayne Junior—your mother is either going to get back to her old self or she isn't?"

"That's the truth, Norma. What else can you say?"

Norma thought about it. "I guess you're right. We can't do it for her, she's going to have to pull herself out of this one—all we can do is be there for her when and if she needs us. Isn't that right?"

"As far as I can see, that's the only thing we can do," said Aunt Elner.

But other people in town took a different view. Mrs. Mildred Noblitt, a thin woman with a tic in her right eye, marched over to Tot's house and banged on the door so long Tot finally had to open it and let her in. Tot was in her aqua chenille bathrobe with the pink flamingo on the back, and as Mrs. Noblitt marched in the house and sat down in the living room, she said, "Tot, are you aware that it is already ten o'clock and you are still in your robe?"

"Yes," said Tot.

"Tot, everybody is very concerned about you. You are just going to have to pull yourself up by the bootstraps and get back into life and put your phone back on the hook. You can't just sit around in your house all day with the shades down and your yard going to pot. What are people going to think?"

"I don't care."

"Well, you have to care what people think. Your yard has always been just lovely—you don't want it to just go wild, do you?"

"It can if it wants to," said Tot.

"Oh, Tot, now that's not like you, you know you're not like that."

"No, I don't. I haven't any idea of what I'm like."

"Well, I can tell you, you are a neat person. That's why we are all so worried about you; you're not being yourself."

"How do you know?" Tot said.

"Because you have been the example of grace under pressure, a figure to be admired. You don't want all of us to be disappointed, do you? We all look to you when anything bad happens, we always say, Yes, but look at what Poor Tot has had to put up with, and it always made us feel better . . . do better. If you fall apart, who can we look up to?"

Tot shrugged.

"All right, I'm going to tell you something that you don't know. Do you know what people call you? They call you a Christian martyr. If I've heard it once, I've heard it a thousand times: Poor Tot, she's just a Christian martyr. There now, doesn't that make you feel good to know how highly people regard you?"

Tot considered this for a moment. "Not really," she said.

"Well, the point is—. Oh, I don't know what the point is, except life is not worth living if you're not going to enjoy it."

Tot looked at her. "Bingo!"

"Listen, Tot, I just don't like the way you are sounding, and you've let all your ferns die. If you don't snap out of it, the next thing I know you'll be off on a killing spree."

A slight smile began to form on the right side of Tot's mouth, which made Mrs. Noblitt's tic act up.

Mrs. Noblitt stood erect. "All I can say is this, and then I am leaving." After searching around for a moment for something to say that might leave an impact, she said, "Pretty is as pretty does," and marched out the door.

Verbena was the next to take a shot at trying to help. "You know, Tot," she said, "whenever I get to feeling sorry for myself I always think of that poor little Frieda Pushnik."

"Who?"

"Frieda Pushnik, she was born without any arms or legs. I saw her in 1933 at the World's Fair in Chicago. They brought her out on a big red velvet pillow and here she was nothing more than just a stump with a head and she was just as cheerful and pleasant as can be. She just chatted away like a little magpie. She said she could thread a needle and told us all about how she had won a national award for penmanship. I bought an autographed photo of her that I still have today and she signed it right there before my very eyes. She held the pen between her chin and her shoulder and she signed it *Good luck, Frieda Pushnik.* I still have it. Whenever I get to feeling sorry for myself I take that picture out and look at it and it makes me feel ashamed to ever be upset over anything. I can tell you that with all her missing parts little Frieda Pushnik never felt sorry for herself. Never complained and she certainly had good reason to if anybody in this world did. Just imagine, Tot, if you had to be carried around on a pillow night and day, how would you feel?"

Tot answered truthfully, "Sounds good to me."

Verbena had failed. Because Tot was her closest neighbor she felt that she and she alone had a civic duty to single-handedly pull Tot back out of this malaise, or whatever it was, and two days later, after much soul-searching, she made the supreme sacrifice and slipped her prized, personally autographed photo of Frieda Pushnik under Tot's kitchen door. But even Frieda Pushnik's smiling face, with a ribbon in her hair, sitting on a velvet pillow, did not help poor Tot. She put the picture facedown under her one good set of silverware in the dining room and forgot about it.

Then, as these things sometimes happen, one Monday morning Tot woke up and looked out the window and watched Verbena out in the backyard hanging her laundry on the clothesline when all of a sudden what looked like a bumblebee flew up Verbena's dress. Verbena immediately dropped her basket and whooped and high-stepped around the yard, holding her dress up in the air as if she were dancing a jig, all the time hollering "Whooo! Whooo!"

After a moment, when the bee had finally found its way out of her skirt and flown away to safety, Verbena calmed down, regained her composure, and looked around to see if anyone had witnessed the event. Satisfied that nobody had seen her flying around her yard in broad daylight with her dress over her head, she went over and finished her task. But in the next house Tot was laughing so hard that tears ran down her cheeks and she had to put a pillow over her face to keep Verbena from hearing her. She had never laughed so hard in all her life and she couldn't stop. All alone in the bed, the minute she would start to quiet down, the vision of Verbena would reappear and she would be screaming with another fit of laughter. She laughed so hard and for so long that she could not get out of bed and finally went back to sleep, but the moment she opened her eyes she thought of Verbena doing the jig and had another laughing fit.

Later she had to get up to go to the bathroom and when she looked at herself in the mirror that started her laughing again. She laughed so hard all that day that her upper plate came loose, and even that made her laugh. The next day she woke up feeling sore all over but very calm and rested, and for the first time in months she felt like she might get up for good.

After all of Verbena's trying so hard to pep her up, Verbena never knew that a bee up her dress had finally done the trick. From that day forward, Verbena was convinced that it had been little Frieda Pushnik who had done the trick and Tot never told her any different.

Soon everyone in town knew Tot was going to recover from her terrible ordeal. For the first time in weeks she pulled up the shades in the living room, and week after week the shades came up room by room until one day Tot got dressed and went back to work with a new outlook on life. "Norma," she said, "I've been on the verge of a nervous breakdown all my life and now that I've had it, I feel a whole lot better."

Daughters

Macky and Norma's daughter, Linda, had married but continued to work to help put her husband through law school, a fact that irritated Macky to no end. "If he can't support a wife on his salary, then he shouldn't have gotten married," he said. However, at the time Norma thought it was a good idea for Linda not to quit her job. "I wish I had a job," Norma added wistfully.

Several months later, when the Pancake House opened, Norma applied for the job of hostess and, to her surprise, was hired but her mother, Ida, now an imposing dowager of seventy-five who wore six strands of pearls around her ample bosom and carried a black cane, talked her out of it. "Norma, for God's sake, how would it look to people? The daughter of the president of the National Federated Women's Club of Missouri being a hostess at a pancake house. If you will not think of your own social position, then think of mine!" And so Norma continued to be, as she put it, just a housewife. Her hopes of becoming a grandmother had been dashed when Linda had had a miscarriage in her third month. After the miscarriage, Linda and her husband had begun having problems. Linda had wanted to try again but he was against it until he finished school. Macky said it was because the husband was afraid he would lose his meal ticket but as Norma pointed out, he'd never liked him in the first place.

One afternoon a year later, when Macky walked in the door from work, Norma met him in the living room. "Linda called and said she is calling back at six because she wants to talk to both of us." They looked at each other wide-eyed. "What do you think?"

Macky said, "I hope it's what we think."

"Do you think it could be?" Norma asked.

"I'm hoping it is."

"Do you want anything to eat now or do you want to wait?"

Macky looked at his watch. "We only have forty-five minutes. Let's just wait."

"All right, but what are we going to do for forty-five minutes?"

"Should we call her?"

"No, she's on the road and said she had a meeting and would call us when she finished."

"I hope it's what I think it is," Macky said.

"I know you do, but you never know, and if it is what we think, don't offer any advice. Just say it's your decision and whatever you decide to do about it we will support you."

"Norma, I know how to talk to my own daughter. She knows how I feel."

"I know she knows how you feel. Especially about her husband—you certainly made that clear, nobody can accuse you of being subtle." Norma shook her head. "Making a complete spectacle of you. I've never been so embarrassed in my entire life."

"All right, Norma," said Macky.

"You could have at least said something in private and not waited till her wedding day to pull a stunt like that."

Macky got up and went into the den but Norma continued. "Imagine such a thing. It's part of the ceremony. Everyone knows when they say who *gives* this woman in marriage, you are supposed to say 'I do' and step back." Norma got up and started rearranging the pillows on the sofa. "But no, you had to say right out loud, 'I'm not giving her—I'm just loaning her.' "

"O.K., Norma," he said from the den.

"And then to glare at the groom like that . . . no wonder they're having trouble. I could hardly face his parents. They thought you were a drunk, or at least I hoped that's what they thought. I didn't want them to think you would do something like that sober. And then to have Aunt Elner laugh out loud like that, it's a wonder that our daughter even speaks to us."

Macky came back in. "Linda knows what I meant. I was not going to stand up anyplace, church or not, and say I'm giving my daughter away . . . like she was something that we had sitting around the house. And no matter what you and Linda think, I still say it was a rash decision."

"Macky, she had dated him on and off for six years, how rash can that be? You knew she was going to get married sometime, and then to sit there and carry on like that, everybody heard you. I was the mother of the bride, I was the one who was supposed to cry, not you."

"Norma, why are you dredging up all this old stuff?"

"Oh, I don't know, just nervous I guess. Do you want some crackers or something? I have some pimento cheese."

"No, I'll just wait until after she calls."

"But now, Macky, don't get your hopes up, we've had false alarms before."

"I'm not. I just hope it's good news, that's all."

They sat across from each other, waiting, and said nothing until the phone rang and then he got on the extension in the den and she picked up in the kitchen. After they hung up Macky came strolling into the kitchen all smiles but Norma was not smiling. "Well, I hope you're satisfied now."

"I am," he said, looking in the refrigerator for the pimento cheese.

Norma opened the cabinet where she kept the crackers. "Honestly, I never saw a man so happy his daughter was getting a divorce in all my life."

Dr. Robert Smith Tours

After Monroe's funeral something happened to Bobby. Going back home again had stirred up so many old memories. Being there had made him remember not so much who he was but all the things he had wanted to be. Yes, he had made good money, had enough in the bank, held good stocks, no complaints there. They had two homes, one in Cleveland and one in Florida. His children had gone to the best schools, he had worked hard, been a good provider, but now those old secret longings came creeping back. That boy who had watched the shadows of a fire dancing on the ceiling of the old bunkhouse and dreamed himself to sleep seemed to be waking up inside him again. He found he hated to put on a tie and sit in stuffy corporate offices in every stuffy corporate town. He found himself staring out windows more and more.

After three months of thinking about it, Bobby walked in the door one night and said, "Lois, what would you say if I told you I wanted to go back to school?" Lois said, without a moment's hesitation, "I would say do it!"

And so Mr. Robert Smith took an early retirement and went back to college and got his doctorate in history and his dissertation, *The American West: Dream and Reality,* was published and Dr. Robert Smith and his wife went on a lecture tour, and as Lois told their children, "Your father is having the time of his life."

Darling, We Are Growing Older

Macky was restless. He walked into the kitchen and sat down at the table across from Norma. "Norma, what do I look like?"

Norma glanced up from her Things to Do Today pad. "What do you mean, what do you look like? You look like yourself."

"No, I'm serious . . . what do I look like?"

"Macky, I don't have time to play some silly game. I'm trying to figure out how many sandwiches I need to order."

"It will only take a second. . . . Look at me . . . and tell me what you see."

Norma put her pencil down and studied him. "You look just like you always did, Macky, only older."

"How much older?"

"You look . . . oh, I don't know, Macky, you look the same to me as you always did. I don't know what you look like. Go look for yourself in the mirror."

"I want an objective view. I see myself every day."

"Well, I see you every day too. How am I supposed to know what you look like?"

"What if I was walking down the street and you saw me coming toward you, what would you say?"

"I'd say, There comes my husband, Macky Warren. What do you think I'd say? Here comes a perfect stranger?"

"Norma."

"Oh, all right. If I didn't know you and I saw you coming down the street, I'd say . . . Oh, I don't know, Macky, I'm no good at these silly games, you sound like Aunt Elner. Go look at a picture of yourself if you want to see what you look like, go look in the yearbook where we were voted Cutest Couple. That's what you look like now—older but still cute."

It was not the answer he was looking for.

"What's the matter? Don't you think a person can still look cute when they're older?"

"How old do I look?"

"Well . . . you look your age. You look like you're supposed to look, Macky. I don't know what you want me to say anymore. Macky, go ask somebody else. I've got to figure out if we should have potato chips or fruit salad. Just as soon as I decide on chips everybody will say they wanted fruit salad." She went back to her list but said to him as he got up to leave, "I've never heard of anything so crazy in my life."

After Macky left she thought about what he had said. He was obviously worried about getting old, but was he? How about her?

It was hard for her to tell, being with him day after day, year after year. They had never really been separated except for the night she'd stayed in the hospital when she had Linda and the three days she and Aunt Elner had spent in St. Louis visiting Aunt Elner's niece Mary Grace. But little things had started to happen. She found herself going sound to sleep sitting straight up in the chair at night when they were watching television. Macky would more often than not wake her up to go to bed. Her eyes were bad now; she had to wear her glasses almost all the time if she wanted to read or do any close work. Macky needed reading glasses but he was too stubborn to get them and picked hers up when he read the paper. He had stretched all her glasses.

Maybe he was right, maybe they were getting old. When he came back home she was standing in the bedroom in her panties and bra looking at herself in the full-length mirror. "Macky," she said, "does my body make me look fat?"

He would not have answered that question for all the tea in China.

THE NINETIES

Popsicle Toes

When Macky walked in the door Norma was waiting for him in the living room and said, "Macky, sit down." The look on her face told him she was about to tell him something terrible or wonderful, he never knew which. But he sat down.

"What is it?"

"I've been on the phone with Linda," she said.

"Yes, and?"

"And. She said she wants to have a baby, she says her biological clock is ticking."

"Uh-huh, has she met someone?"

Norma got up and started to rearrange the pillows on the sofa, just like she always did when she was nervous. "No, she hasn't met anyone but she has been calling different agencies."

Macky was alarmed. "Agencies? What the hell is she doing that for? There are plenty of men where she works."

Norma cleared her throat. "That's just it, she doesn't want a man; well, at least not in person. She wants the baby but not the husband . . . that's what she said."

"What?"

"Now, before you get mad at me, I did not say I thought it was a good idea but she has decided to go to a"—Norma weighed her words very carefully—"a place that specializes in that sort of thing. She's looking into one of those . . . you know . . . bank things."

"Banks?"

Norma was becoming impatient. "Oh, Macky, don't make me have to spell it out for you. She wants to get pregnant but she does not want to get married again. She's going to one of those places that deal in . . . frozen . . ." Norma struggled but no matter how hard she tried she could not bring herself to say the actual word. She glanced out the front window to see if anyone was in hearing distance, then spelled it out: "S-P-E-R-M."

"What?"

"Macky, have you never heard of artificial insemination? That's what she wants to get and she just wanted to let us know."

"Good God."

"You always said she could tell us anything—well, now she has. I just don't know what to say or what to think. She's your daughter. If you hadn't acted like you wanted a grandchild so much that other time, this might not have happened."

"Norma, she was pregnant—what was I supposed to say?"

"You acted like a grandchild was the only thing you'd ever wanted in your entire life, then when she had the miscarriage it made her feel even worse." Norma suddenly burst into tears and wailed, "I hope you're satisfied. You're about to have one with a Popsicle for a father!"

But after months of trying and many disappointments, Linda's attempt to become pregnant was not successful and she finally gave up. Macky and Norma assumed that was to be the end of it but when Macky came in from a fishing trip Norma met him at the back door and announced, "Well, I hope you like chop suey."

"What?"

"Your daughter called while you were gone. She is now on her way to China to pick up a foreigner baby."

"What?"

"She said she applied for a little girl a year ago. She said she didn't tell us before because she thought she would never hear from them but three days ago they called her and told her to come over and pick it up."

He stood there holding his string of fish with his mouth open. It was the last thing in the world he expected to hear.

"Congratulations, Macky, you are now the grandfather of a Communist who will probably grow up and murder us all in our beds." With that she left him standing in the kitchen and went back to bed in tears.

As upset and worried as they both were, the moment they saw the beautiful little button-eyed girl Linda had named Apple, they fell in love. Two years later Norma was out at the mall proudly wearing a sweatshirt with a picture of the little Chinese girl on it. Printed underneath was SOMEBODY SPECIAL CALLS ME GRANDMA.

Cecil Figgs, a.k.a. Ramón Navarro

When the body of the large, heavyset woman in the red wig had been picked up off the street and brought to the Cecil Figgs funeral parlor for embalming, they discovered that the lady on the table was no lady. Imagine their incredible surprise when they were told that the man in the bright green dress was none other than Mr. Cecil Figgs!

What a scandal. Thank heaven, Cecil's mother had not lived to see it. Jake Spurling immediately flew to New Orleans. But even he, with all his powers of deduction and all the resources of the F.B.I. behind him, could not figure out how Figgs had wound up living in New Orleans for the past twenty-something years as a Miss Anita "Boom Boom" De Thomas.

As hard as he tried, Jake could come up with nothing. The only human being who had really known what had happened to Hamm and the rest of the men was now dead, and even he had not known it all. Jake might have solved some of it but he had missed out on a very important clue years ago.

A piece of wood had washed up with the word AYE written on it. The river rescue authorities checked their logs, and a boat registered to a Mr. J. C. Patterson named *Aye Aye, Skipper* had been lost eighteen years ago. They assumed it was from the Patterson boat. But they were wrong. That piece of wood was from the only thing left intact of *The Betty Raye.*

• • •

When *The Betty Raye* had docked in New Orleans, Cecil had the name of a contact in Louisiana who would sell him formaldehyde by the ten gallons at a cut rate, so he figured that as long as he was there, he would have the man load *The Betty Raye* with eighty gallons, and Cecil would bring it back to Missouri.

Cecil did not know that the reason the man was selling the formaldehyde at such a good price was because it had been stolen from one of Cecil's own warehouses. While Hamm and the other men were off having their meeting, Cecil was in the French Quarter, and the boat was loaded not only with the formaldehyde but with fifty cases of cheap, tax-free bootleg rum from Cuba, which Rodney Tillman had arranged to take back to Missouri as well.

Later that night after the meeting, *The Betty Raye,* loaded to the gills with cheap booze and cut-rate formaldehyde, took off, headed back to the boathouse. They were playing cards en route and Seymour Gravel was chewing on his smelly cigar. "I'm out," he said and threw his cards down, complaining about his bad hand, and began looking for a match. It was a hot night and the rest of them were in the middle of a pretty intense poker game. Hamm said to Seymour, "If you're gonna smoke that thing, go sit in the back."

Seymour waddled back and sat down on a box and continued to search his pockets for a match. "Hey, Wendell—throw me your lighter for a minute."

Wendell, preoccupied with trying to decide whether or not to raise Hamm, reached in his shirt pocket and tossed his heavy silver Zippo with the marine insignia on it back to him. Seymour reached out but missed, and it sailed on past him. As it was turning over in midair, the top of the lighter flew open, and when it hit the side of one of the boxes, it landed right smack on its small wheel. As people often say when such a freak thing happens, "If you tried you would not be able to do it again in a million years." The spark from the lighter ignited the dry straw the liquor was packed in and started to spread like wildfire.

What none of the men knew was that a few months ago, the real owner of the boat, Mr. Anthony Leo, had acquired some stolen dynamite he was planning to use in the future to settle a business dispute. And he had it stashed in a secret compartment in the bottom of *The Betty Raye* for safekeeping.

The gallons of flammable formaldehyde, boxes of ninety-proof alcohol, and a cargo full of dynamite below proved to be not only illegal but a lethal combination. Two men who were out on the river in a rowboat fishing that night came in and said they had just seen a huge comet come hurtling down from the sky. They said it had shot across the horizon and had landed about a mile upriver. But they were wrong. What they had seen that night had not been a comet coming down. It had been Hamm Sparks, boat, and cronies going up!

The bad news: this spectacular event had certainly ended a remarkable political career. The good news: Hamm Sparks had always wanted to go as high in the world as he could—and he had. And as usual, the rest of the men had just been along for the ride.

But as it turned out, there was *one* man who had not been along that night.

Cecil Figgs had failed to show up at the time they were scheduled to leave and they had left without him, which was fine with him. He was having too much fun. He had left the car keys with Rodney, and Cecil figured he could always fly home.

He woke up in New Orleans two days later in a seedy hotel in the French Quarter with a bad hangover. His young companion was gone but had left a note.

Dear Ramón,

Thanks for the good time. Call me the next time you are in town.

Love,
Todd

Cecil always used the name Ramón Navarro when he was out of town. When Cecil suddenly realized it was Tuesday and that he had missed taking his mother to the eye doctor the day before, he felt sick with guilt. He would have to call her right away, but not before he had a cup of coffee. Cecil dressed and walked next door to eat breakfast and figure out what he would say to his mother, who was sure to be upset. Shortly before his first sip of coffee he picked up the *Times-Picayune* newspaper someone had left on the counter. When he saw the front page he almost fainted.

HAMM SPARKS, FOUR COMPANIONS PRESUMED DEAD

The article underneath the pictures of all five men, including him, said the police believed the missing men had most likely been murdered and as far as they could tell, it looked like the work of professionals. At the moment they were questioning several men in St. Louis with Chicago mob connections.

What little hair Cecil had stood up on the back of his head. He had no idea what had happened. After he got over the initial shock of the whole thing, his first instinct was to run and call his mother. But then he realized that if someone had been out to kill them and found out he was still alive, they might try it again. Desperately, he tried to figure out what to do next. While he sat before his cold coffee in a dilemma, pondering his future and perhaps his impending murder, it struck him like a bolt of lightning. Wait a minute, he thought. In the middle of this seeming tragedy there was another part of it he had just realized. He was, for all intents and purposes, dead, or at least everyone thought he was. For the first time in his life he was free. Free to be who and what he really was. He would no longer have to lead a double life, always looking over his shoulder, afraid of getting caught; always terrified he might upset his mother or disgrace the family. He'd have to die to do it. It would be a big price to pay but he figured it would be worth it.

In the end, the man Hamm and the boys had taken the meeting with in New Orleans said nothing. He could not afford to have his name involved in any scandal. Mr. Anthony Leo of St. Louis did wonder what had happened to the boat and his missing dynamite but he was certainly in no position to say anything and for years continued to wonder but kept his mouth shut. The man who'd sold Rodney the illegal Cuban rum said nothing and the man who'd sold Cecil the stolen formaldehyde certainly said nothing. And Cecil said nothing.

In fact, there was no Cecil. From that day forward, nobody but himself knew that Miss Anita "Boom Boom" De Thomas, gorgeous headliner at the famous My Oh My Club in New Orleans, Louisiana, was the sole survivor of the late Mr. Cecil Figgs of Missouri. Cecil had been given an opportunity that few people in this world ever get. He had been shown an open door that led to a new life and he had walked through it to the other side and there was no turning back. Mother Figgs and the entire Figgs clan were left a small fortune and the warm memory of a good son and he was going to have a good time the rest of his life. He had only one major and painful regret in leaving Cecil behind. It had just about killed him not to be able to plan the governor's funeral. It would have been the triumph of his career. Oh, well.

Time to Say Good-bye

Macky could read the handwriting on the wall. Long before he said anything to Norma, he knew he just could not compete as a small hardware store. Three different malls had sprung up, and now with the brand-new Home Improvement Center in one and Wal-Mart and Ace Hardware in the other, he had lost business. Most of his old customers had tried to stay with him but with so many new people moving in and the prices being so low, he was losing them one by one, and as he told his friend Merle, "Hell, I can't blame them, I'd shop out there myself." Selling out and retiring had been in the back of his mind but he had not had any serious thoughts about it until lately. But events tumbling upon one another had brought him to the moment when he actually sat down and talked with her about the prospects of selling their house.

Pretty soon Macky and Norma started sending off for brochures of retirement communities. From the pictures of the good-looking silver-haired men and women standing around having cocktails, playing golf, tennis, and swimming, it looked like fun. "Your home away from home, only better," they said.

As it turned out, the decision was made in less than forty-eight hours and it had nothing to do with anything that was planned. Verbena and Merle called in a fit. They had a nephew who was living in a gated community in Vero Beach and he had just found out that a house was coming up on the market in a few days and he'd called to see if they were interested. He said that it was one of the best retirement complexes down there and if somebody moved fast, before the realtors found out about it, they could buy it from the owner, a friend of his, and not have to pay the commission.

After Macky got off the phone he told Norma all about it. "But the bad news," he said, "is we have to make up our minds right away. Merle said there are people waiting in line to buy it if we don't."

Norma panicked. "Oh my God . . . do we have time to call Linda?"

"Yes, honey, go on."

After ten minutes Norma handed the phone to Macky.

"Daddy, what do you think?"

"It's up to your mother, whatever she thinks."

Norma threw up her hands. "You always do this."

"Well, Daddy, it sounds like a good deal to me. If you get there and don't like it, you can always turn around and sell it but it sounds like you have a chance to get a nice place at a good price. I think you would always be sorry if you didn't take advantage of it. Do you know anybody other than Verbena's nephew who lives in Vero Beach? Anybody you could ask?"

"No."

"Let me call around and I'll try and find out something." Twenty minutes later she called back. "Daddy, listen to this: Vero Beach, Florida, Indian River country home, home of famous Dodgertown, USA."

"What's that?"

"Daddy, it's where the L.A. Dodgers have their spring training. You and Mother can go and watch the Dodgers play."

The next afternoon Norma called Linda. "Well, honey, we did it. Your daddy and I have just bought a pig in a poke. He's told the man yes. I just hope to God we don't get down there and find out we're in the middle of a swamp."

"Great! Aren't you excited?"

"I don't know what to think, it all happened so fast. I just hope your daddy made the right decision."

After they packed up and sold everything, it was time, as Merle had said, to shake the dust off and see some new scenery. When Merle and Verbena had moved to Florida they had flown, but Macky decided to buy a

Minnie Winnie and see the country on the way down. He bought a captain's hat and hung a sign on the back that said THE CHUCKLEHEADS and the next day he put Norma, Aunt Elner, and Sonny Number Four in the back and took off. Macky was excited. He had remembered all the little charming, out-of-the-way cafés his family had stopped at the last time he went to Florida, in 1939. But as he soon found out, things had changed. For days all they saw were Burger Kings, Taco Bells, McDonald's, Jack in the Boxes, and Cracker Barrels. Norma said, "Macky, there are no more little places and Aunt Elner and I don't want to get ptomaine poisoning just so you can take a trip down Memory Lane." The one place he did find, Norma refused to go in. "Let's just go to the Cracker Barrel, where we know it's clean and the food is good." The road was not as he remembered either. It was nothing but a blur of huge trucks. There were almost no cars anymore. It seemed like the entire country was nothing but trucks following other trucks. Every town looked exactly like the last. Every gas station had the same mini-mart inside. It was hard to tell one state from another.

In Vero Beach, the man had said to look for a shopping center with a big Publix drugstore, but every shopping center they passed had a big Publix drugstore and Macky finally had to stop and ask directions. A man poked his head in and said, "Sure, go about five miles up past the Winn-Dixie and take a sharp left, right into Leisureville."

They found the sign with the arrow that said WELCOME TO LEISUREVILLE CENTRAL, FLORIDA'S FINEST GATED COMMUNITY but as they drove in they saw row after row of little mint-green, oleander-pink, or lavender stucco houses that, Aunt Elner noted, were the same color as those candy mints that Miss Alma used to keep in a glass bowl by the cashier.

As they drove in they did not see any vital, silver-haired, good-looking couples, as were shown on the brochure, standing around the pool, cocktail in hand, laughing and chatting with others of the same age with the look of "I've got the world by the tail." All they saw was a bunch of people who looked old to them but looked young to Aunt Elner.

They soon discovered that what had been advertised as Citrus View Patio Homes meant there was an orange grove across the street and a slab of concrete in the postage-stamp backyard. When they walked into their new home Norma was silent. The cottage-cheese ceilings were lower than expected and there were stains all over the mustard-gold shag rug, which did nothing to enhance the olive-green stove and refrigerator. The fact that the house had been closed up for three months and smelled like mildew did not help ease the initial shock. The walls were a dingy color described as champagne beige, popular in the fifties, as were the cheap aluminum sliding doors and windows throughout the house. Macky was already wondering how hard it would be to sell it when Norma surprised him, as she still could, by saying, "Oh, Macky, it's not so bad. I can whip this place into shape in no time." Sonny had no qualms about the shag rug and happily scratched away at it after depositing a welcome-to-your-new-home gift. They stayed in a motel until Macky could get the rug pulled up and have the walls repainted. Norma went to Sears and bought a new white refrigerator and stove and had Goodwill come and pick up the old green ones. Macky laid a new sheet of white linoleum on the floor in the kitchen and in the bathrooms. A week later, when the van carrying their furniture arrived from Missouri and everything was put in its place and the stucco house looked at least a little familiar, Macky sat down on his old chair from home and flipped up the leg rest and thought to himself, "Now what?"

The next week a new magazine came and he stared at it and asked Norma, "What the hell is AARP? It sounds like a dog throwing up."

Norma said, "It's a magazine from the American Association of Retired Persons. Everybody gets it after they hit fifty. It tells all about your senior citizen discounts."

Macky mumbled and went out to take a walk. What was going on? He was not ready to be a senior citizen—there seemed to be a national conspiracy to label anybody over the age of fifty-five a "senior" and move them on out of the mainstream. That's not how he remembered it when he was young; an old man was not old until at least seventy-five or eighty and even Old Man Henderson had still been doing his yard at ninety-three, for God's sake. Macky was still young; he had years left before he was old. Rest up for what, he wondered, to get ready to die? Take a short rest before you take the long one? Norma was sailing into the bay of senior citizenship with the wind to her back and with a smile on her face. But not him.

Macky wandered around the complex. Not only was he in a different state, he was in a different world and he was lost. Lost in Leisureville.

Seems Like Old Times

After a few months Norma had made a lot of new friends and Aunt Elner was as happy as a lark with all the bingo games they had down there. Sonny the cat was delighted to be living in a place with so much sand to dig in, but Norma was worried about Macky. As she said to Linda on the phone that very morning, "Your daddy is not adjusting to retirement."

Norma had been reading the volunteer-positions-for-seniors column to Macky, as she did every other day, and as usual he'd resisted her suggestions.

"Norma, I've told you, I am not going to stand around like some old senile fart and welcome people to Wal-Mart, for God's sake."

"I didn't say Wal-Mart. There are plenty of places that retired people go to work for . . . McDonald's . . . Burger King. Look, it says here you can even volunteer at the high school cafeteria or the library. They want seniors to set a good example to the young people. What's wrong with that? At home you used to do all kinds of things for the community."

"That was different."

"How can it be different?"

"It was my community; this isn't my community."

"It is now. Young people are just the same everywhere—don't you want to be a role model . . . be a good influence?"

He left the house and took a walk around the complex. It was only the end of November but some people had already put up their Christmas wreaths, brought with them from other parts of the country. The huge decorations, which might have looked fine on some door of a house in New Hampshire or Maine, looked bizarre in the glaring Florida sun, like an entire community had gone mad and decorated for Christmas in the middle of the summer. One pale orange house had put a fake snowman on the small front porch but had neglected to remove the pink plastic flamingo on the lawn. Macky knew by the calendar and by the ads that had already started on television that it was about to be Christmas but other than that, one day was no different from the next. All the earmarks of the season that he had gone by for the last sixty-two years were gone.

At home he knew when it was fall. He smelled it. He raked it up in the yard. He and Norma had a routine. At the end of September she collected all their summer clothes and put them away in the bottom drawers and moved the sweaters up to the top. All the winter coats were brought from the back bedroom closet and put in the coat closet. Summer shoes were replaced with winter shoes. He could count on a month or so of everything smelling slightly like mothballs. Then when May came around, back they went. But this year the clothes did not change. Everything was still seersucker and short-sleeved. They only had a few sweaters but that was mostly for air-conditioning, not weather. Macky had read somewhere that a person's ability to adjust was a sign of intelligence. So far he was failing the test. Not that he had not tried. In fact, at first he had been much more enthusiastic than Norma. But after the initial excitement, after he had done all the work on the new house, learned the neighborhood, and seen all the sights, it had slowly begun to dawn on him. Life as he had known it was all over. Life in a town where your family had lived for over a hundred years and everybody knew not only you but all your family was over. Here he was just another stranger. Just another transient. Nobody special. At home he had an identity. He was Macky Warren. Son of Olla and Glenn Warren. His father had owned and run the hardware store for fifty years, and then he had owned it and run it. For most of his life, whenever he had been anywhere where people did not know him and they had asked, as men do, *What line are you in?* he had been able to answer, *I have a little hardware store back home.* Now nobody ever asked what line he was in or what did he do. If they did ask, he had to answer by telling them what he used to do. What he used to be. Now what was he? Who was he? Just another displaced stranger trying to pretend that a get-together at the complex clubhouse was just like home only better.

Aunt Elner was making so many new friends her own age that she was loving Florida but Norma had problems with Macky. She came in after one of her flower-arranging classes and said, "Macky, I talked to my friend Ethel and she said that Arve went through the same thing and his doctor identified it as a male identity problem. And that what you need to do is to connect with your inner male."

"Oh good God, Norma, what did you tell her?"

"Nothing bad, I just said that you were depressed, having a hard time adjusting to being retired. It's not anything to be ashamed of, evidently a lot of men go through it. Anyhow, she talked it over with Arve and he went for help and she says it really helped him."

"Norma, Arve is an idiot. Do you really think that wearing gold chains and sticking a curly black wig on your head at seventy-five is adjusting? He's a joke."

"All right, so he may be a little silly but he's happy and isn't that the point, to be happy? Anyhow I'm not going to argue about Arve; the point is she gave me this brochure for you to look at." Macky took it and read where once a week, groups of men organized by Jon Avnet, Ph.D., gather to "reconnect with the warrior within, to drum, talk, weep, and tell their stories in a safe place."

He looked up at Norma and said nothing.

The Ant

Macky wandered over to Ocean Park, sat on a concrete bench, and stared out at the blue water. The world he had known was gone. Not only was he living in an alien place, but while he had been busy all these years making a living, someone had changed all the rules. For all he knew, he might as well have gone to sleep and awakened on the moon.

When he'd grown up, everybody had more or less agreed to a certain way of living. A certain standard. You didn't lie, you didn't cheat or steal, you honored your parents, your word was your bond. You didn't try to weasel your way out of things. You married the girl. You paid your bills. You took care of your children. You didn't cuss around girls. You didn't hit women. You played by the rules and it was expected that you would be a good sport if you lost. You kept your house, yard, and yourself clean.

Norma said you have to just swing with it and try not to let it bother you so much. He wished he could but somehow it seemed this new world was easier for the women to accept and adjust to. What bothered him and other men his age and older was that the things they had been willing to die for were no longer appreciated. Everything he had believed in was now the butt of jokes made by a bunch of smarty-assed late-night-TV so-called comedians making a salary you could support a small country with. All he heard was people saying how bad we were, how corrupt we had been, and how terrible white men were. He had not felt like a bad person. But just the fact that he was a white man of a certain age, a lot of people he did not know hated him. He had never knowingly been mean or unfair to another human being in his life. Now it seems he was the *oppressor,* responsible for every bad thing that had ever happened in the history of the world. War, slavery, racism, sexism—he was the enemy and all he had tried to do was live a good and decent life. History was being rewritten by the minute. All of his childhood heroes were now being viewed as villains, their lives judged in hindsight by the current fad of political correctness. Hell, now they were even taking *Huckleberry Finn* out of libraries, for God's sake. It was all too confusing.

You never saw people anymore, everything was self-service, everybody behind glass windows. And you could not get a real person on the phone. Everywhere you called, a recorded message connected you to another recorded message and then hung up on you. And everybody was mad and screaming about something. He did not know which was worse, the radical right or the radical left. It seemed nobody was in the middle anymore. We used to be on the right track and then we took a wrong turn but he did not know where. Was it the dope or television? Was it having too much that did it? He had tried to read what the experts thought but they did not know any more than he did. All he knew for sure was that after the '40s and '50s, when he had been raised, the world had flipped over like a giant pancake and everything was backward. When he was a kid everyone had wanted to be Tarzan; now they all want to be the natives. People were sticking rings in their noses—even pretty little girls were running around with green hair, their bodies pierced everywhere.

And nobody answered a direct question anymore with a simple yes or no. Everything was answered with some kind of rhetoric. And he knew far more than he wanted to know about perfect strangers. Things people used to be ashamed to talk about now sold books and got them on television. Murderers were being asked for their autographs and turned into celebrities. Football, basketball, and baseball players could beat up their wives, take drugs, go to jail, and still stay on the team and make millions. It didn't matter what kind of a person you were anymore. He remembered when a professional athlete was someone to look up to; now the sports page read more like a police blotter.

And never in a million years would he have dreamed that one day baseball players would be wearing earrings. Or that some girl would be singing on television in her brassiere. Life was all so different, with this one having two mommies and another one two daddies.

He did not know what to think anymore. The way it looked to him, the world was not getting better; it was getting worse. He sat there for about an hour and gazed out at the water, wondering where and when it was all going to end.

He leaned forward and rested his elbows on his knees and stared down at the sandy ground, as if looking for an answer. After a few minutes he noticed a tiny ant that walked underneath him, struggling to carry what looked like a large piece of potato chip. It was much too big for him to eat, but he was headed somewhere with it anyhow. He watched the ant as it kept going and banged into another concrete bench, went around it, crawling over rocks and other obstacles, determined to get back home with his treasure. It was much too big for him to carry but he did not seem to know it.

Macky sat there and watched the ant struggle along until it was out of sight and he smiled for the first time in weeks. "Who knows?" he thought. "If he keeps on going, the little son of a bitch might just make it."

Hey, Good Buddy

The next day Norma marched in the door and said, "I have made a decision. Since you won't go to any of the groups, I have taken the bull by the horns. Come out to the car and help me bring it in."

When they got to the car there it was, in a box that looked like the hide of a black-and-white cow. Norma had bought him a computer.

"Norma, I don't know how to use that thing."

"Neither do I but we are going to learn. I've signed us up for lessons over at Comp World. It can't be hard; they say now that even first graders can do it. Besides, Linda said if we got one we could E-mail each other."

"Norma, I'll help you set it up but I'm not going to any classes over at Comp World. You go if you like."

Five months later, after much cussing, he let Norma show him how to get on the Internet.

One day while she was gone, Macky was pleasantly surprised that after a few tries he was able to get into a chat room.

"Hey, any old guys out there remember the Hardy Boys?" Within two minutes Marvin from Beaver Falls, Pennsylvania, answered.

"Hey, good buddy, affirmative. I just found three old copies—*The Tower Treasure, The Missing Chums, The Clue of the Broken Blade.* Have two copies of *Missing Chums* would be happy to send on."

The next thing Norma knew she could not get him off the Internet. He was all over the map. He was even able to locate fly-fishing experts on the thing. What they had to discuss about the mayfly was a mystery to her but he chatted for hours with someone in Wyoming. And they seemed to know what the other meant. As for Macky, after he got the hang of it, he announced to Norma, "This is just like ham radio, only better."

Norma said, as usual, "See? I told you."

Life started to perk up a little more for Macky. His little granddaughter, Apple, started coming down for visits and he was able to teach her all the fine points of baseball. One beautiful Sunday the two of them went to the Dodgers game over at Dodgertown, USA, and had a wonderful time. The little girl did not know it, but one day years from now she would look back on that day and remember how the sun felt and the smell of the grass . . . all the hot dogs and peanuts her granddaddy bought her, the feel of his hand holding hers as they walked home, and she would smile.

All's Well That Ends Well

Take what happened to Betty Raye, for instance. Although she had started out poor in life and had been deprived of her rightful place in the world, the universe sometimes has a way of righting things. Her two boys were lucky in business and made a killing in real estate. Her Uncle Le Roy Oatman's guilt over leaving the gospel group and joining a hillbilly band finally paid off in a big way. In 1989, while on a three-day bender in Del Rio, Texas, he wrote a song about how fortune and fame don't mean a thing because, as the title says, "I Never Said Good-bye to Momma." Country-and-western star Clint Black recorded it and it became an overnight hit and had grown men sobbing in their beers for years. When Le Roy passed on, he left Betty Raye, the only one in the family who had been nice to him, millions of dollars in royalties that just keep on rolling in.

Then there was money from Hamm's life-insurance policy, which Vita helped her invest in several stocks. One was a pharmaceutical company that just happened to manufacture birth-control pills. When the sexual revolution hit in the seventies, she made $5 million on that one stock alone. But rich as she was, Betty Raye still lived happily in her red-brick house.

However, Le Roy was not the *only* Oatman to do well in the music world.

After a long dry period when southern gospel had been pushed into the background by a musical trend known as "contemporary Christian music," in 1992, the Oatman family was inducted into the Gospel Music Hall of Fame and, thanks to the Bill and Gloria Gaither Gospel Music television shows, they became more popular than ever. Minnie had diabetes, gout, emphysema, and two knee replacements and was on her fifth heart attack, but apparently nothing can kill her. The woman who just can't wait to get to heaven is going to have to wait a little longer. Right now she's doing four shows a week.

As for Beatrice Woods, the old saying that love is blind is just a metaphor but in her case love really was blind, literally, and it was a good thing. Floyd Oatman was not the best-looking of men, but in his heart he was as romantic as the next. His problem was he had little courage and was terrified to talk to women, but Chester was a ladies' man and had no fear. What poor Floyd was too shy to say to a woman, Chester, the Scripture-quoting dummy, said for him. He leered and whistled and flirted with every pretty woman he saw. But in 1969, with a little help from Beatrice, Floyd was finally able to find his own voice and speak for himself and to ask Beatrice to marry him without going through Chester.

Of course, Beatrice had no idea that he was not the most handsome man in America. He told her that he looked just like Clark Gable but having been blind from birth, she did not know what Clark Gable looked like, either. And later, with Beatrice's love and encouragement, Floyd, in an incredible leap of faith, threw Chester the dummy over the side of a bridge into the Pea River outside Elba, Alabama. He was free of Chester at last and was finally able to stand alone.

However, unbeknownst to Floyd, Chester was to make one final solo appearance. During the big Pea River flood, Chester the dummy washed up and floated through the town on his back and scared everybody half to death. The three firemen that risked their lives jumping into the river to retrieve the body of the poor little drowned boy were in for a surprise and took quite a bit of ribbing from the other men when they pulled him out. Chester spent the rest of his days hanging on the wall at the firehouse, until it burned down. Being made of wood, poor Chester the dummy finally bit the dust for good.

Beatrice and Floyd had one son. They did not name him Chester.

To the Public at Large:

It's Tot again, with a late update. Believe it or not, I have married again. I know it is a surprise; it was a surprise to me. He is a retiree from the poultry business with good benefits, a widower—i.e., no living wife or ex-wives, children, dog, or cat. Hoorah! He owns (totally paid for) a tan and brown Winnebago and he doesn't drink. He drove through here and stopped at the cemetery to see the graves of some friends of his, Doc and Dorothy Smith. I was out there pulling weeds off of Momma's grave and said, Who are you looking for? and the rest is history. I have sold my house and I gave the hair business to Darlene, lock, stock, and barrel. Dwayne Jr. is in the slammer again for selling drugs. Let the government have him. I never could do anything with him. My granddaughter, Tammie Louise, as predicted, has a baby on the way, which is one of the reasons we hit the road. I am not paying for raising any more kids. As I write this, Charlie and I are just outside Nashville headed on up to Minnesota to the Mall of America, where I plan to shop till I drop, then on down to Florida to Vero Beach, to visit Macky and Norma and Aunt Elner, where we may stay for good. The Goodnight sisters and Verbena and Merle have moved there and they say Bobby Smith and his wife, Lois, and Anna Lee and her husband come down and visit all the time, so it will be just like home only better. No Whootens. My health is still pretty good, considering what all I've had to put up with, and they say with all the advances in modern medicine that age sixty is now the new forty, so that makes me around fifty-one again!

Best wishes,
Mrs. Tot Whooten Fowler

P.S. I am happy for the first time in my life.

Epilogue

Robert Smith, given the fact that he had traveled all around the world and back lecturing on the Old West, had been asked to write a piece for Aunt Elner's favorite magazine, *Reader's Digest.* He wandered around the house for days thinking about the kings and queens, African chieftains, prime ministers and presidents of countries he had met; it was amazing how many people were still fascinated by cowboys and Indians. He had met so many interesting people that it was hard to just pick one. Then one day he chose his subject. He sat down and started on:

The Most Unforgettable Character I Ever Met
by
Dr. Robert Smith

Her name was Dorothy and she happened to be my mother. I guess a good place to start would be in 1946 in my hometown of Elmwood Springs, Missouri, a little place you have probably never heard of. . . .

Acknowledgments

The author wishes to thank the following people for their invaluable help with this book: Sam Vaughan and family, Wendy Weil, Bruce Hunter, Dennis Ambrose, Judy Sternlight, Carol Schneider, Todd Doughty, Sherry Huber, Lauren Krenzel, Trebbe Johnson, Bonnie Thompson, Susie Glickman, Joy Terry, Lois Scott, Cathy Calvert, and Sue Grafton for all her good advice. Special thanks to the Warren family of Birmingham, Alabama, and Jonni Hartman Rogers, my press agent and good friend for more years than either of us care to admit.

P9-BAW-097

ALSO BY M. SCOTT PECK, M.D.

THE ROAD LESS TRAVELED
A New Psychology of Love, Traditional Values and Spiritual Growth

PEOPLE OF THE LIE
The Hope for Healing Human Evil

WHAT RETURN CAN I MAKE?
Dimensions of the Christian Experience
(with Marilyn von Waldner and Patricia Kay)

THE DIFFERENT DRUM
Community-Making and Peace

A BED BY THE WINDOW
A Novel of Mystery and Redemption

THE FRIENDLY SNOWFLAKE
A Fable of Love, Faith and Family
(illustrated by Christopher Scott Peck)

A WORLD WAITING TO BE BORN
Rediscovering Civility

MEDITATIONS FROM THE ROAD
Daily Reflections from
The Road Less Traveled *and* The Different Drum

FURTHER ALONG
The Road Less Traveled

The Unending Journey Toward Spiritual Growth

THE EDITED LECTURES

M. SCOTT PECK, M.D.

SIMON & SCHUSTER

NEW YORK LONDON TORONTO SYDNEY TOKYO SINGAPORE

SIMON & SCHUSTER
Simon & Schuster Building
Rockefeller Center
1230 Avenue of the Americas
New York, New York 10020

Designed by Edith Fowler
Manufactured in the United States of America

10 9 8 7 6 5 4 3 2 1

Library of Congress Cataloging-in-Publication Data

Peck, M. Scott (Morgan Scott), date
Further along the road less traveled: the unending journey toward spiritual growth: the edited lectures/M. Scott Peck.
p. cm.
1. Self-actualization (Psychology)—Religious aspects—Christianity. 2. Maturation (Psychology)—Religious aspects—Christianity. 3. Interpersonal relations—Religious aspects—Christianity. 4. Spiritual life. I. Title.
BV4598.2.P43 1993
158'.1—dc20 93-31322 CIP
ISBN: 0-671-78159-6

A leatherbound signed first edition of this book has been published by The Easton Press.
Names and identifying characteristics of certain individuals portrayed in this book have been changed to protect their identities.
The author is grateful for permission to reprint excerpts from the following material:
Reverence for Life, *by Albert Schweitzer. Copyright © 1969 by Rhena Eckert-Schweitzer. Used by permission of HarperCollins Publishers, Inc.*
John of the Cross, Selected Writings, *ed. by Kieran Kavanaugh, O.C.D. Translated from the Spanish by Kieran Kavanaugh, O.C.D. © 1987 by Kieran Kavanaugh, O.C.D. Used by permission of Paulist Press.*
Evolution of Physics, *by Albert Einstein and Leopold Infeld. Copyright © 1938 by Albert Einstein and Leopold Infeld. Copyright renewed © 1966 by Albert Einstein and Leopold Infeld. Reprinted by permission of Simon & Schuster, Inc.*

TO

All who have been,
one way or another,
my "audience";
Thank you
for listening

Contents

Acknowledgments 11
Introduction 13

PART ONE
THE FIRST STEP: GROWING UP

ONE Consciousness and the Problem of Pain 17
TWO Blame and Forgiveness 29
THREE The Issue of Death and Meaning 47
FOUR The Taste for Mystery 69

PART TWO
THE NEXT STEP: KNOWING YOUR SELF

FIVE Self-Love versus Self-Esteem 87
SIX Mythology and Human Nature 100
SEVEN Spirituality and Human Nature 115
EIGHT Addiction: The Sacred Disease 135

PART THREE
THE ULTIMATE STEP: IN SEARCH OF A PERSONAL GOD

NINE	The Role of Religion in Spiritual Growth	153
TEN	Matter and Spirit	175
ELEVEN	New Age: Symboline or Diaboline?	194
TWELVE	Sexuality and Spirituality	219
	Epilogue: Psychiatry's Predicament	232

Acknowledgments

There are two ways to edit a collection of lectures: the easy way and the hard way.

The easy way is to simply transcribe audiotapes, correct the grammar, and print them, even though the result might appear to be a hodgepodge of unrelated subjects. The hard way is to try to take these disparate subjects and, weaving in new material, create an imaginative, unified, and easily readable whole.

Simon & Schuster and I elected this latter course, and I have spent countless hours meeting with my editors to reorganize and integrate my lectures, and to give them new material and answer their questions to fill in any gaps. I have also done extensive editing of the resulting manuscript to impart the flavor of my thinking. This book is very much my own creation, and I am pleased with it.

But it is also a co-creation and would simply not have been possible without the immense editorial assistance of Simon & Schuster. My several hundred hours spent on this project have been matched in triplicate by the staff of Simon & Schuster, including multiple typists, copy editors, and fact checkers. I am grateful to them all.

But I need to single out three people for special mention. One is Ursula Obst, who more than anyone else was responsible over the course of many months for the creative artistry of weaving a collection of assorted lectures into a coherent, very real book.

I also wish to express my gratitude to Burton Beals, who line edited Ursula's product in preparation for my own editing. Through his laborious efforts and many conversations with me, the whole has become, I believe, highly readable.

Finally, I would like to thank Fred Hills, my long-time editor at Simon & Schuster. The book was his idea. It has been his brainchild, and he has patiently shepherded it for two years, from start to finish. He was its instigator and coordinator and provider, and it simply could not have occurred without him.

Introduction

You may remember that *The Road Less Traveled* opened with the sentence "Life is difficult." And to that great truth, I will now add another translation:

Life is complex.

Each one of us must make his own path through life. There are no self-help manuals, no formulas, no easy answers. The right road for one is the wrong road for another. Nowhere in this book will you find it said: "Go this way," "Make a left turn here." The journey of life is not paved in blacktop; it is not brightly lit, and it has no road signs. It is a rocky path through the wilderness.

In this book, I will endeavor to put down some of the things I have learned in the past ten years which have eased my way as I groped through the wilderness. But if I tell you that when I lost my way, I found it again by following the moss growing on the north side of trees, I will almost certainly have to warn you that in the redwood forests there are many trees covered with moss on all sides.

I also caution you not to interpret the word "further" in the title or anything else in this book as suggesting that the road is linear—that you take one step after another in a

straightforward progression. Although "further" might sound as if I'm saying, "Here's where Scott Peck was, here's where Scott Peck is now, and if you are here, then this is where you will likely be next year," that is not what I intend to imply. That's not what the road is like. It is, rather, like a series of concentric circles expanding out from the core, and there is nothing simple or straightforward about it.

But we do not have to make the journey alone. We can ask help of the force in our lives that we recognize to be greater than we are. A force that we all see differently, but of whose presence most of us are aware. And as we make our way, we can help each other.

If this book aids you in any way, I hope, most of all, that it will assist you to think less simplistically. I hope you will abandon the urge to simplify everything, to look for formulas and easy answers, and begin to think multidimensionally, to glory in the mystery and paradoxes of life, not to be dismayed by the multitude of causes and consequences that are inherent in each experience—to appreciate the fact that life is complex.

PART ONE

The First Step: Growing Up

CHAPTER ONE

Consciousness and the Problem of Pain

All my life I used to wonder what I would become when I grew up. Then, about seven years ago, I realized that I never was going to grow up—that growing is an ever ongoing process. So I asked myself, "Well, Scotty, what is it that you've become thus far?" And as soon as I asked that question, I realized, to my absolute horror, that what I have become is an evangelist. An evangelist is the last thing on earth I ever thought I would become. And it's probably the last thing on earth you ever wanted to encounter.

The word "evangelist" carries the worst possible associations and probably brings to your mind the image of a manicured and coiffed preacher in a two-thousand-dollar suit, his gold-ringed fingers gripping a leatherette-covered Bible as he shouts at the top of his lungs: "Save me, Jee-sus!"

Fear not. I don't mean to suggest that I have become that kind of evangelist. I am using the word "evangelist" in its original sense—the bringer of good news. But I must warn you, I am also the bringer of bad news. I am an evangelist who brings good news and bad news.

If you are anything like me, you are into delaying gratification, so when you are asked, "Which do you want first, the good news or the bad news?" you answer, "Well, the bad news first, please." So let me get the bad news over with: I don't know anything.

It might seem odd that an evangelist, a "bringer of truth," would confess so readily that he doesn't know anything. But the real truth of the matter is that you don't know anything either. None of us does. We dwell in a profoundly mysterious universe.

Evangelists are also supposed to bring "glad tidings of comfort and joy." The other piece of bad news is that I am going to be talking about the journey through life, and in so doing I cannot avoid talking about pain. Pain is simply a part of being human and it has been so since the Garden of Eden.

The story of the Garden of Eden is, of course, a myth. But like other myths, it is an embodiment of truth. And among the many truthful things the myth of the Garden of Eden tells us is how we human beings evolved into consciousness.

When we ate the apple from the Tree of the Knowledge of Good and Evil, we became conscious, and having become conscious, we immediately became self-conscious. That was how God recognized that we had eaten the apple—we were suddenly modest and shy. So one of the things this myth tells us is that it is human to be shy.

I have had the opportunity, through my career as a psychiatrist and more recently as an author and lecturer, to meet a great number of wonderful, deep-thinking people, and I have never met such a person who was not basically shy. A few of them had not thought of themselves as shy, but as we talked about it, they came to realize that they were in fact shy. And the very few people I have met who were not shy were people who had been damaged in some way, who had lost some of their humanity.

It is human to be shy, and we became shy in the Garden of Eden when we became self-conscious. When this happened to us, we became conscious of ourselves as separate entities.

We lost that sense of oneness with nature, with the rest of the universe. And this loss of the sense of oneness with the rest of creation is symbolized by our banishment from Paradise.

GROWING UP PAINFULLY

When we were banished from Paradise, we were banished forever. We can never go back to Eden. If you remember the story, the way is barred by cherubims and a flaming sword.

We cannot go back. We can only go forward.

To go back to Eden would be like trying to return to our mother's womb, to infancy. Since we cannot go back to the womb or infancy, we must grow up. We can only go forward through the desert of life, making our way painfully over parched and barren ground into increasingly deeper levels of consciousness.

This is an extremely important truth because a great deal of human psychopathology, including the abuse of drugs, arises out of the attempt to get back to Eden. At cocktail parties we tend to need at least that one drink to help diminish our self-consciousness, to diminish our shyness. It works, right? And if we get just the right amount of alcohol or just the right amount of pot or coke or some combination thereof, for a few minutes or a few hours we may regain temporarily that lost sense of oneness with the universe. We may recapture that deliciously warm and fuzzy sense of being one with nature once again.

Of course, the feeling never lasts very long and the price usually isn't worth it. So the myth is true. We really cannot go back to Eden. We must go forward through the desert. But that journey is hard and consciousness often painful. And so most people stop their journey as quickly as they can. They find what looks like a safe place, burrow into the sand, and stay there rather than go forward through the painful desert, which is filled with cactuses and thorns and sharp rocks.

Even if most people have been taught at one time or another that "those things that hurt, instruct" (to borrow Benjamin Franklin's phrase), the education of the desert is so painful that they discontinue it as early as they can.

Senility is not just a biological disorder. It can also be a manifestation of a refusal to grow up, a psychological disorder preventable by anyone who embarks on a lifetime pattern of psychospiritual growth. Those who stop learning and growing early in their lives and stop changing and become fixed often lapse into what is sometimes called their "second childhood." They become whiny and demanding and self-centered. But this isn't because they have entered their second childhood. They have never left their first, and the veneer of adulthood is worn thin, revealing the emotional child that lurks underneath.

We psychotherapists know that most people who look like adults are actually emotional children walking around in adult's clothing. And we know this *not* because the people that come to us are more immature than most. On the contrary, those who come to psychotherapy with genuine intent to grow are those relative few who are called out of immaturity, who are no longer willing to tolerate their own childishness, although they may not yet see the way out. The rest of the population never manages to fully grow up, and perhaps it is for this reason that they hate so to talk about growing old.

Back in January of 1980, soon after I wrote *The Road Less Traveled,* which in many ways is a book about growing up, I was being driven around to a number of TV and radio stations on a promotional tour by a cabdriver in Washington, D.C. After the second or third station, he said, "Hey man, whatja doin'?"

So I told him that I was promoting a book, and he asked, "What's it about?"

I went into this intellectual bit about how it was an integration of psychiatry and religion. After about thirty seconds he commented, "Well, it sounds to me like it's about getting your shit together."

That man had the gift of discernment. So at the next TV talk show I went to, I asked if I could tell that story.

They said no. Thinking that they objected to the word "shit," I offered to say "stuff" instead. But they still said no.

People just don't want to talk about real maturation. It is too painful.

CONSTRUCTIVE SUFFERING

If I am willing to talk about pain, it does not mean I am some kind of masochist. On the contrary. I see absolutely no virtue whatsoever in unconstructive suffering. If I have a headache, the very first thing I do is go to the kitchen and get myself two superstrength, uncapsulized Tylenols. I see absolutely no virtue in an ordinary tension headache.

But there is such a thing as *constructive* suffering. And the difference between unconstructive suffering and constructive suffering is one of the most important things to learn in dealing with the pain of growing up. Unconstructive suffering, like headaches, is something you ought to get rid of. Constructive suffering you ought to bear and work through.

I prefer to use the terms "neurotic suffering" and "existential suffering," and here is an example of how I make that distinction. You may remember that about forty years ago, when Freud's theories first filtered down to the intelligentsia and were misinterpreted—as so often happens—there was a whole bunch of avant-garde parents who, having learned that guilt feelings could have something to do with neuroses, resolved that they were going to raise guilt-free children. What an awful thing to try to do to a child!

Our jails are filled with people who are there precisely because they do not have any guilt, or do not have enough guilt. We *need* a certain amount of guilt in order to exist in society. And that's what I call existential guilt.

I hasten to stress, however, that too much guilt, rather than enhancing our existence, impedes it. This is neurotic

guilt. It is like walking around a golf course with eighty-seven clubs in your bag instead of fourteen, which is the number needed to play optimal golf. It's just so much excess baggage, and you ought to get rid of it as quickly as possible. If that means going into psychotherapy, then you should do that. Neurotic guilt is unnecessary, and it only impedes your journey through the desert.

This is true not only of guilt, but also of other forms of emotional suffering, like anxiety, for example, which can be either existential or neurotic. And the trick is to determine which is which.

There is a very simple albeit brutal rule for dealing with the emotional pain and suffering of life. It's a three-step process.

First, whenever you are suffering emotionally, ask yourself: "Is my suffering—my anxiety or my guilt—existential or is it neurotic? Is this pain enhancing my existence or is it limiting it?" Now perhaps about ten percent of the time, you really won't be able to answer that question. But about ninety percent of the time, if you can think to ask it, the answer will be very clear. If, for example, you are anxious about filing your income taxes on time because you once got hit with a big late-payment penalty, I can assure you that the anxiety you feel is existential. It's appropriate. Go with your anxiety and file on time. On the other hand, if you determine that the suffering you are experiencing is neurotic and is impeding your existence, then the second step is to ask yourself: "How would I behave if I did not have this anxiety or guilt?"

And the third step is to behave that way. As Alcoholics Anonymous teaches: "Act as if," or "Fake it to make it."

The way I first came to learn about this rule was in dealing with my own shyness. It is human to be shy, but we can deal with it in ways that are either neurotic or existential. In the audience, listening to famous speakers, I sometimes felt there was a question I should ask them, some piece of information I wanted to know, or some comment I wanted to make

—in public, or even in private after the speech. But I would hold back because I was too shy and afraid of being rejected or of looking like a fool.

After a while, I finally came to ask myself: "Is this way of dealing with your shyness—which is holding you back from asking questions—enhancing your existence or is it limiting it?" As soon as I asked that, it was clear that it was limiting my existence. And then I said to myself: "Well, Scotty, how would you behave if you weren't so shy? How would you behave if you were the Queen of England or President of the United States?" The answer was clear that I would approach the speaker and have my say. So then I told myself: "Okay, then, go ahead and behave that way. Fake it to make it. Act as if you weren't shy."

I admit that is a scary thing to do, but this is where courage comes in. One of the things that never cease to amaze me is how relatively few people understand what courage is. Most people think that courage is the absence of fear. The absence of fear is not courage; the absence of fear is some kind of brain damage. Courage is the capacity to go ahead in spite of the fear, or in spite of the pain. When you do that, you will find that overcoming that fear will not only make you stronger but will be a big step forward toward maturity.

Just what is maturity? When I wrote *The Road Less Traveled,* although I described a number of immature people, I never gave a definition of maturity. But it seems to me what characterizes most immature people is that they sit around complaining that life doesn't meet their demands. As Richard Bach wrote in *Illusions,* "Argue for your limitations, and sure enough they are yours." But what characterizes those relative few who are fully mature is that they regard it as their responsibility—even as an opportunity—to meet life's demands.

CONSCIOUSNESS AND HEALING

To proceed very far through the desert, you must be willing to meet existential suffering and work it through. In order to do that, if you are like most of us, you need to change your attitude toward pain in one way or another. And here is some good news. The quickest way to change your attitude toward pain is to accept the fact that everything that happens to us has been designed for our spiritual growth.

Donald Nichol, the author of *Holiness,* refers to it in his introduction as a how-to book. He says if you're caught carrying around a book on the subject of holiness and people ask you what you are doing with it, you're likely to tell them, "Well, I'm simply interested in what authorities have to say about the subject." Actually, Nichol points out, there's absolutely no reason for you to purchase or borrow, much less carry around a book on the subject of holiness unless you want to be holy. And so he calls it a how-to book, about how to be holy. Approximately two thirds of the way through that book there's a wonderful sentence where Nichol says, "We cannot lose once we realize that everything that happens to us has been designed to teach us holiness."

Now what better news can there be than that we cannot lose, we are bound to win? We are guaranteed winners once we simply realize that everything that happens to us has been designed to teach us what we need to know on our journey.

The problem, however, is that this realization requires a complete shift in our attitude toward pain—and, I think, toward consciousness. Remember in the story of the Garden of Eden, we became conscious when we ate the apple from the Tree of the Knowledge of Good and Evil. Consciousness then became for us both the cause of our pain and the cause of our salvation, which is a word synonymous with healing.

Consciousness is the cause of our pain because, of

course, were we not conscious, we would not feel pain. One of the things that we do for people to spare them unconstructive, unnecessary suffering—physical suffering—is to give them anesthesia so that they can lose consciousness and not feel the pain.

But while consciousness is the whole cause of pain, it is also the cause of our salvation, because salvation is the process of becoming increasingly conscious. When we become increasingly conscious, we go further and further into the desert instead of burrowing into a hole like the people who choose not to grow up. And as we travel onward, we bear more and more pain—because of our very consciousness.

As I said above, the word *salvation* means "healing." It comes from the same word as *salve,* which you put on your skin in order to heal an area of irritation or infection. Salvation is the process of healing and the process of becoming whole. And health, wholeness, and holiness are all derived from the same root. They all mean virtually the same thing.

Even old atheist Sigmund Freud recognized the relationship between healing and consciousness when he said that the purpose of psychotherapy—healing of the psyche—was to make the unconscious conscious; that is, to increase consciousness. Carl Jung further helped us understand the unconscious, ascribing evil to our refusal to meet our shadow, or that part of our personality that we like to deny, that we like not to think about, not to be conscious of, that we're continually trying to sweep under the rug of consciousness and keep unconscious.

Note that Jung ascribed human evil not to the shadow itself but to the *refusal* to meet this shadow. And refusal is a very active term. Those people who are evil are not just passively unconscious or ignorant; they will go far out of their way to remain ignorant or unconscious; they will kill or start wars to do so.

I recognize, of course, that evil—like Love or God or Truth—is too large to submit to any single adequate defini-

tion. But one of the better definitions for evil is that it is "militant ignorance." Militant unconsciousness.

The Vietnam War is one of the best examples I know of this militant ignorance on a grand scale. When the evidence first began to accumulate in 1963 or 1964 that our policies in Indochina weren't working, our first response was to deny that anything was wrong. We said we just needed a couple more million dollars and a few more special forces. But then the evidence continued to accumulate—our policies clearly weren't working. So what happened then? We sent in more troops, the body count began to escalate, and incidents of brutality became commonplace. It was the time of My Lai. Then as the evidence continued to pour in, we continued to ignore it. Instead, we bombed Cambodia and started talking about peace with honor.

Even today, despite all that we now know, some Americans continue to think that we succeeded in bargaining our way out of Vietnam. We didn't bargain our way out of Vietnam—we were defeated. But somehow many still *refuse* to see this.

OASES IN THE DESERT

Consciousness brings more pain, but it also brings more joy. Because as you go further into the desert—if you go far enough—you will begin to discover little patches of green, little oases that you had never seen before. And if you go still further, you may even discover some streams of living water underneath the sand, or if you go still further, you may even be able to fulfill your own ultimate destiny.

Now if you doubt me, consider the example of a man who went on the journey far into the desert. He was the poet T. S. Eliot, who became famous early on in his career for writing poems of total aridity and despair. In the first, "The Love Song of J. Alfred Prufrock," which he published in 1917 at age twenty-nine, he wrote:

I grow old. . . . I grow old . . .
I shall wear the bottoms of my trousers rolled.

Shall I part my hair behind? Do I dare to eat a peach?
I shall wear white flannel trousers, and walk upon the
beach.
I have heard the mermaids singing, each to each.

I do not think that they will sing to me.

It is important to keep in mind that J. Alfred Prufrock of the poem lived—as did T. S. Eliot—in a world of high society, the ultimate civilized world, yet he lived in a spiritual wasteland. Not surprisingly then, five years later, Eliot published a poem called "The Waste Land." And in this poem, he actually focused on the desert. It is also a poem that has in it a great deal of aridity and despair, but for the first time in Eliot's poetry there are little patches of green, little hints of vegetation here and there, images of water, and of shadow under rocks.

Then in his late forties and early fifties, Eliot wrote poems like "Four Quartets," the first of which opens with references to a rose garden, birds calling and children laughing. And he went on to write some of the richest and most luxuriously verdant, and mystical poetry that has ever been written, and, indeed, he is reputed to have ended his life very joyfully.

There is much solace we could take from Eliot's example as we ourselves struggle along with our rocky path and our pain. We need some comfort on our journey, but one of the things we don't need is quick fixes. I have seen a lot of people who literally murder each other with quick fixes in the name of healing.

They do this for very self-centered reasons. For example, let's say that Rick is my friend and he is in pain. Because he is my friend, that causes me pain, but I don't like to feel pain. So what I'd like to do is to heal Rick as quickly as I possibly can to get rid of my pain. I'd like to give him some kind of easy answer like: "Oh, I'm sorry your mother died but don't

feel bad about it. She's gone to Heaven." Or: "Gee, I had that problem once and all you have to do is go running."

But more often than not, the most healing thing that we can do with someone who is in pain, rather than trying to get rid of that pain, is to sit there and be willing to share it. We have to learn to hear and to bear other people's pain. That is all part of becoming more conscious. And the more conscious we become, the more we see the games that other people play and their sins and manipulations, but we're also more conscious of their burdens and their sorrows.

As we grow spiritually, we can take on more and more of other people's pain, and then the most amazing thing happens. The more pain you are willing to take on, the more joy you will also begin to feel. And this is truly good news of what makes the journey ultimately so worthwhile.

CHAPTER TWO

Blame and Forgiveness

A big part of growing up is learning to forgive. We go through life blaming others for our pain. And blame always begins with anger.

Anger is a powerful emotion that originates in the brain. Throughout the human brain there are little collections of nerve cells called neural centers. And in that part of the brain which we call the midbrain, these centers are involved in the governance and in the production of emotions. Neurosurgeons have actually mapped out the locations of these centers. With a human being lying on an operating table under local anesthesia, they insert electrodes, or very fine needles, into the brain from the tip of which they can deliver a millivolt of current.

For instance, we have a euphoria center, and if neurosurgeons insert the needle in that area and deliver a millivolt of current, the patient lying on the table will say, "Oh wow! You doctors sure are wonderful and this is such a marvelous hospital. Do it again, will you?" This feeling of euphoria is very powerful, and the reason certain drugs like heroin are so habituating is that they may have a stimulating effect upon our euphoria center.

Studies have been done on rats in which neurosurgeons insert an electrode into a rat's euphoria center and allow the rat to stimulate itself by pressing a lever. As a result, the rat will be so busy pressing the lever that it will not eat and will starve to death. It will pleasure itself to death!

Not far away from the euphoria center, there is another center which governs a quite different emotion—the depression center. If neurosurgeons insert an electrode in that center and give it a millivolt of current, the patient lying on the table will say, "Oh God, everything looks gray, I feel horrible, I feel just awful. Please, please stop it." Similarly, there is an anger center. And if neurosurgeons stimulate that, they had better have the patient strapped down on the table.

These centers have been built into the human brain through millions of years of evolution, and they are there for a purpose. For example, if you somehow cut out the anger center in a child's brain so that she could not get angry, you would have a very passive child. But what do you think would happen to such a passive child when she got into kindergarten or first or second grade? She would be stomped on, she would be walked right over, she might even get killed. Anger serves a purpose; we need it for our very survival. It's not bad in itself.

The anger center in human beings works in exactly the same way as it does in other creatures. It is basically a territorial mechanism, firing off when any other creature impinges upon our territory. We are no different from a dog fighting another dog that wanders into its territory, except that for us human beings, our definitions of territory are much more complex. Not only do we have a geographical territory and become angry when someone comes uninvited onto our property and starts picking our flowers, but we also have a psychological territory, and we become angry whenever anyone criticizes us. We also have a theological or an ideological territory, and we tend to become angry whenever anyone criticizes our beliefs or casts aspersions upon our ideas.

Because our human territory is so complex and multifaceted, our anger center is firing off all the time, and often very inappropriately. To give you an idea of how inappropriately, sometimes it can fire off even when we invite people into our territory.

Back some twenty-five years ago when I went into analysis, I already had an interest in the relationship between psychology and spirituality, and knowing that Carl Jung had stressed this area, I went to great trouble to find a Jungian therapist. I went to see him, and I kept waiting for him to say something Jungian to me. The only problem was that he approached me like a Freudian, which, as I later learned, was exactly the way I needed to be treated.

After our introduction, this therapist didn't say a word for the next seven sessions. He made me do all the talking and I began to get more and more annoyed with him. Here I was paying him the vast sum (back then) of twenty-five dollars an hour, and he wasn't doing or saying anything to earn his money. Finally, during the ninth session as I was talking about how I felt about a particular matter, he actually said something. He said, "Well, I'm not quite sure I understand yet why you feel that way." And I snapped, "What do you mean you don't understand why I feel that way?" The first moment he challenged my psychological territory, I was furious at him, even though that was exactly what I was paying him to do, what I had invited him to do.

Because, as human beings, our anger center is firing off all the time, and often very inappropriately, we must learn a whole complex set of ways of dealing with anger. Sometimes we have to think, as I had to do in relation to my analyst, "My anger is silly and immature. It's my fault." Or sometimes we have to conclude, "This person did impinge upon my territory, but it was an accident and there's no reason to get angry about it." Or, "Well, he did violate my territory a little bit, but it's no big deal. It's not worth blowing up about." But every once in a while, after we think about it for a couple of days, we may discern that someone really did seriously violate our territory. Then it may be necessary to go to that person and say, "Listen, I've got a real bone to pick with you." And sometimes it might even be necessary to get angry immediately and blast that person right on the spot.

So there are at least five different ways to respond when our anger center fires off. We not only need to know those ways of responding, but we also have to learn which response is appropriate in any given situation. It is an extraordinarily complex task, and it is therefore no wonder that very few people learn how to deal well with their anger before they are into their thirties or forties, and many who never learn how to deal with it.

BLAME AND JUDGMENT

When we get angry and blame someone for making us angry, we are also making a judgment about that person—that he or she has sinned against us in some way.

Back when I was sixteen, I won my first and only speaking contest, on the topic "Judge not, and you will not be judged." Pontificating on Jesus' words, I said we shouldn't make any judgments of other people, and I won a can of tennis balls.

Today I no longer believe that it is possible to go through life without making judgments about other people. We have to make judgments about whom to marry or not marry, about when to intervene in the lives of our children or when not to intervene, whom to hire or whom to fire. Indeed, the quality of our life is determined precisely by the quality of our judgments.

I am not contradicting Jesus. First, His words are often misinterpreted. Jesus said, "Judge not, and you will not be judged"; He didn't say, "Never judge." But each time you judge, be prepared for judgment yourself. And second, He immediately went on to say, "Hypocrite! First take out the beam"—or two-by-four; he was a carpenter, remember—"out of your own eye, and then you will see clearly the mote"—or splinter—"in your brother's eye." In other words, Jesus said to judge yourself before you judge anyone else.

On this same subject Jesus also said, when confronting an angry crowd about to stone an adulterous woman, "Let that person who is without sin cast the first stone." Since all of us are sinners, does that mean we shouldn't cast any stones, that we shouldn't blame or judge anybody at all? In fact, no one threw a stone at the woman and Jesus then said to her: "Has no one condemned you? Then neither do I condemn you." Again he said to judge yourself before you judge others.

But despite the fact that we are all sinners, from time to time it is necessary that we cast a stone. It happens when we say to an employee, "This is the fourth year in a row that you have failed to meet your performance objectives, this is the sixth time that I have caught you lying, and I'm afraid I'm going to let you go. I'm going to have to fire you."

It is a terribly painful, brutal decision to fire someone. How do you know you are making the right judgment at the right time? How do you know you are right in blaming that person? The answer is, you don't. But you must always look at yourself first. Even though you might find that you have no choice but to fire that person, you may also find that there are many things you could have done—and did not do—that would have spared you that decision in the first place.

You need to ask yourself questions such as: "Was I concerned about this person and his problems? Did I confront him when I caught him in the first instance of lying or was that confrontation too difficult for me and I let it slide until the situation got unbearable?" If you answer such questions honestly, you may find that you will treat other employees differently, and you may be spared such a brutal judgment in the future.

THE AGONY OF NOT KNOWING

But how does one know exactly when the time has come for appropriate blame or judgment rather than self-criticism? When I first started public speaking, I didn't know whether it was the right thing to do. Was it really what God wanted me to do, or was I doing it out of an ego trip because I so enjoyed the roar of the crowd? I didn't know which and I agonized almost continually, looking for the answer. Finally, I got some help—and this reinforces my earlier point that everything that happens in life is there to aid our spiritual growth, and that we very much need each other in this regard. I had shared the agony I was going through with the person who sponsored my second speaking engagement. And about a month after that engagement, she sent me a poem she had written. She had not written it with me in mind, but the last lines of that poem were exactly what I needed to hear at the time:

> The Truth is that I want It,
> and the price I must pay
> is to ask the question again and again and again.

Reading the poem, I realized that I had been looking for some kind of revelation—a formula—from God, which would say: "Yes, Scotty, go speak for all time." Or: "No, Scotty, don't ever open your mouth." But there was no formula, no easy answer, and I knew that what I was going to have to do each time I was invited to speak, each year that I renegotiated my lecture schedule, was to ask the question again and again and again: "Hey, God, is this what You want me to be doing now?" All any of us can do whenever confronted with a painful decision is to ask the question each time and once again agonize over the answer.

For example, if you are a mother or a father of a sixteen-year-old daughter who confronts you with a request to stay

out until two a.m. on a particular Saturday night, what do you do? There are three ways that parents can respond. One is to say, "No, of course you can't. You know damn well your curfew is ten." Another way is to say, "Oh sure, dear, whatever you'd like." Those are what might be called right-wing and left-wing responses. But even though they are at opposite ends of the spectrum, there's something similar about them. They are shoot-from-the-hip, formulistic responses. They require no energy from the parents at all.

In my opinion what good parents would do is to ask themselves, "Should we or shouldn't we let her stay out until two a.m. this Saturday night?" And they will probably answer, "We don't know. It's true that her curfew is ten, but we set that when she was fourteen and there's probably no way that that's a realistic curfew anymore. On the other hand, at the party she's going to this Saturday night there's going to be alcohol and that's a little worrisome. But then, you know, she gets good grades in school, she does her homework, she's obviously got a sense of responsibility. Maybe we owe it to her to trust that sense of responsibility. On the other hand, the guy she's going out with looks to us like a total loser. Should we, or shouldn't we? Should we compromise? What's the right compromise? We don't know. Should it be midnight, should it be eleven, should it be one? We don't know."

Ultimately it does not matter so much what such parents decide. Because even though their daughter may not be terribly happy with the final decision, nonetheless she will know that she has been taken seriously, because her question has been taken seriously. And she will know that she is loved, because she is valuable enough for her parents to agonize over in their not knowing.

This is precisely why when I am asked, "Oh Dr. Peck, would you give me a formula so that I will know when it's the right time to blame and when it isn't the right time to blame?" I answer, "I cannot give you any such formula." Each in-

stance is different, each is unique, and each time, if you are seeking the truth, you have to ask the question. Should you do this you will likely come to the correct decision, but you will also have to put up with the pain of not knowing for sure you have done the right thing.

TRUTH AND WILL

I have just spoken of both truth and God. Their proximity is no accident, because when we are talking about truth, we are talking about a something higher than ourselves. We are talking about searching for and submitting ourselves to a "Higher Power."

Lest you be tempted to dismiss that as a primitive "religions" notion, let me point out that science is truth-submitted behavior. The scientific method is nothing more than a series of conventions and procedures that we have developed over the centuries in the interest of truth, in order to combat our very human tendency to want to deceive ourselves. And so science is submitted to a higher arbiter, a higher power—truth.

Mahatma Gandhi said: "Truth is God and God is Truth." I believe that God is also light and love, but certainly truth. Thus I propose that the pursuit of scientific knowledge, even if it doesn't answer all questions, is, in its place, very godly behavior—behavior that involves submission to a higher power.

The single greatest cause of inappropriate blaming is the combination of a strong will with the lack of submission to a higher power. A strong will is, I believe, the best asset that a human being can possess, not because it guarantees success or goodness, but because a weak will pretty much guarantees failure. It is strong-willed people who do well in psychotherapy, who have that mysterious will to grow. And so it is a great asset and a great blessing. But all blessings are potential

curses, all have their side effects. And the worst side effect of a strong will is a strong temper—anger.

The way I used to explain this to my patients was to tell them that having a weak will is like having a little donkey in your backyard. It can't hurt you very much; about the worst it can do is chomp on your tulips. But it can't help you that much either. Having a strong will, on the other hand, is like having a dozen Clydesdales in your backyard. Those horses are massive creatures and extremely strong, and if they are not properly trained, disciplined, and harnessed, they will knock your house down. On the other hand, if they are properly trained, disciplined, and harnessed, then with them you can literally move mountains.

But to what is the will to be harnessed? You cannot harness it to your own will because it thereby continues to remain unharnessed. Your will has to be harnessed to a power higher than yourself.

The distinction between the harnessed and the unharnessed will was beautifully drawn by Gerald May, in his book *Will and Spirit,* the first chapter of which is entitled "Willingness and Willfulness." Willfulness characterizes the unharnessed human will, whereas willingness identifies the strong will of a person who is willing to go where he or she is called or led by a higher power.

This distinction was also described poetically in that absolutely magnificent play *Equus.* The play is about a boy who has blinded six horses, and the psychiatrist treating him, Martin Dysart, who is going through a midlife spiritual crisis. At the end of the play, explaining how he has come through his crisis, Dysart says:

> ". . . I cannot call it ordained of God: I can't get that far. I will however pay it so much homage. There is now, in my mouth, this sharp chain. And it never comes out."

THE BLAMING GAME

It is no accident that people who commit the most evil in this world see no power higher than themselves. The evil are very strong-willed men and women. And because they are narcissistic, self-absorbed, and their will is supreme, they are the ones who are most into inappropriate and destructive blaming. They are the people who cannot—who will not—take the beam out of their own eye.

For most of us, if there is evidence around us that might point to our own sin and imperfection, if that evidence pushes us up against the wall, we usually come to recognize that something is wrong and we make some kind of self-correction. Those who do not I call "people of the lie" because one of their distinguishing characteristics is their ability to lie to themselves, as well as to others, and to insist on being ignorant of their own faults or wrongdoing. Their guiding motive is to feel good about themselves, at all costs, at all times, no matter what evidence there may be that points to their sin or imperfection. Rather than using it to make some kind of self-correction, they will instead—often at great expense of energy—set about trying to exterminate the evidence. They will use all the power at their disposal to impose their wills onto someone else in order to protect their own sick selves. And that is where most of their evil is committed, in that inappropriate extermination, that inappropriate blaming.

It is important to realize that blaming is fun. Anger is fun. Hatred is fun. And like any pleasurable activity, it is habit-forming—you get hooked on it.

Just how insidious this can be was brought home to me while reading some literature on demonic possession. I had come across several descriptions of the allegedly possessed person sitting in a corner, gnawing on his ankle. And this reminded me of some of the medieval paintings of Hell, in which you may see this same kind of figure—a damned person

gnawing on his ankle. This seemed to be a very strange and very uncomfortable position to get oneself into. It didn't make sense to me until I read a little book by Frederick Buechner entitled *Wishful Thinking: A Theological ABC.* Right in the beginning of that book, under *A,* Buechner lists Anger and compares it to gnawing on a bone. There's always a little more tendon, always a little more marrow, always just a little bit left, and you keep gnawing on it. The only problem, Buechner says, is that the bone you're gnawing on is you.

Blaming others becomes a habit. And you end up gnawing on that bone, over and over and over again as you remind yourself how someone has wronged you. For this reason perhaps the most common of all psychological games might be called the Blaming Game. The term "psychological game" was coined by the late, great psychiatrist Eric Berne in his book *Games People Play.* Berne was not writing about playful games, although there can be some analogies, since psychological games certainly may be fun of a sort. Rather, he defined a psychological game as a "repetitive interaction" between two or more parties with an "unspoken payoff." By repetitive interaction he meant something that is not only habituating but also stale, a kind of uncreative spinning of your wheels. By unspoken payoff he meant that there is something unsaid, something underneath the surface, underhanded, even something manipulative about psychological games.

The Blaming Game could also be called the "If It Weren't for You" Game. Most of us have played it. It is the most common of all marital games. For instance, Mary will say, "Well, I know I'm a nag, but that's because John has this emotional shell around him. I have to nag in order to get through to him. If it weren't for John's shell, I wouldn't be a nag." And John says, "Well, I know I have a shell around me, but that's because Mary's a nag. I have to have that shell in order to protect myself from her nagging. If it weren't for Mary's being a nag, I wouldn't have this shell."

So there is a kind of circular, repetitive quality to these games that is hard to interrupt. And in explaining how to stop a psychological game, Berne spoke one of the only two great truths I know that is not a paradox. He said that the only way to stop a game is to stop. That sounds simple, but in fact it is extremely difficult. Just how do you stop?

Remember what it's like to play Monopoly? You can be sitting there and saying, "You know, this is a really stupid game. We've been playing it for four hours now. It is really childish. I've got many better things I ought to be doing." But then you pass Go and say, "Give me my two hundred dollars."

No matter how much you might complain about it, as long as you keep collecting your two hundred dollars when you pass Go, the game goes on. And if it is a two-player game, it can go on forever unless one player gets up and says, "I'm not playing anymore."

The other player might then say, "But, Joe, you just passed Go. Here's your two hundred dollars."

"No, thanks, I'm not playing anymore."

"But, Joe, your two hundred dollars."

"Didn't you hear me? I'm not playing anymore."

The only way to stop a game is to stop.

Stopping the Blaming Game is called forgiveness. That is precisely what forgiveness is: the process of stopping, of ending, the Blaming Game. And it is tough.

THE REALITY OF EVIL

These days great numbers of people who are flocking to all types of New Age religions have somehow been seduced into believing that forgiveness is easy. Forgiveness is easy only when one becomes convinced that there really isn't such a thing as evil. And it just ain't so.

This misperception can lead people into certain traps, an example of which is found in a very popular New Age book

called *Love Is Letting Go of Fear,* by Gerald Jampolsky, a fellow psychiatrist. His book is about forgiveness, a terribly important topic, but my problem with it is that Jampolsky makes it sound easy. He makes the blanket statement that rather than making judgments about people, we should look for the good within them, look for God within them, and affirm them.

I am always leery of blanket ideas and concepts, because they tend to be simplistic and get people into trouble. I am reminded of the words of an ancient Sufi master: "When I say weep, I do not mean for you to weep always. And when I say don't weep, I don't mean for you to become a permanent buffoon." But unfortunately, a great many people in the New Age movement have come to believe that "affirm" means "always affirm." I do agree that ninety percent of the time that is exactly what you should do, but maybe ten percent of the time—when you are confronted with someone like Hitler—affirming is precisely the worst thing that you could do.

Make no mistake, forgiveness and affirmation are not the same thing. Affirmation is a way to avoid looking at evil. It is saying, "Well, yes, my stepfather molested me as a child, but that was just his human failing, part of his being damaged in childhood." Forgiveness on the other hand requires facing evil squarely. It is saying to your stepfather: "What you did was wrong, despite your reasons for it. You committed a crime against me. And I know that, but I still forgive you."

That is not easy by any stretch of the imagination. Real forgiveness is a tough, tough process, but it is an absolutely necessary one for your mental health.

CHEAP FORGIVENESS

A great many people suffer from the problem I have come to call "cheap forgiveness." They come for their first session with a therapist and say, "Well, I know that I didn't have the

greatest of childhoods, but my parents did the best they could and I've forgiven them." But as the therapist gets to know them, he finds that they have not forgiven their parents at all. They have simply convinced themselves that they have.

With such people, the first part of therapy consists of putting their parents on trial. And it is a lot of work. It requires briefs for the prosecution, and briefs for the defense, and then appeals and counterappeals, until a judgment is finally brought in. Because this process requires so much work, most people opt for cheap forgiveness. But it is only when a guilty verdict is brought in—"No, my parents did not do the best they could; they could have done better; they committed certain offenses against me"—that the work of real forgiveness can begin.

You cannot pardon someone for a crime he hasn't committed. Only after a guilty verdict can there be a pardon.

BLAME AND MASOCHISM

Many people who come for therapy suffer from masochism. And by masochism I do not mean that they get their sexual jollies out of physical pain, but simply that in some strange way they are chronically self-destructive. A typical example would be that of a man who is brilliant and competent and who rises rapidly in his field but then, at the age of twenty-six when he's about to become the company's youngest vice president, he does something absolutely outrageous, blows it, and is fired. Because he's so bright, he is immediately hired by another firm, rises up meteorically, and at twenty-eight, just as he's about to be promoted, he again does something outrageous, blows it, and gets fired. And after this happens for the third time, he may come to realize that he's following some kind of chronically self-destructive pattern, a masochistic pattern.

Another example might be that of a woman who is beau-

tiful and brilliant and charming and competent, but who keeps dating one loser after another. People who exhibit such chronically self-destructive patterns are often also victims of cheap forgiveness. You'll find them saying, "Oh, I didn't have the greatest of childhoods, but my parents did the best they could."

To explain why cheap forgiveness just won't do, and why real forgiveness is essential to escape from such self-destructive traps, let me first explain something about what underlies this masochism. And the best way I know to do this is to look at psychodynamics in children, because what may be seen as psychopathology—mental illness—in adults is often perfectly normal in children. Let's take four-year-old Johnny, who wants to make mud pies in the living room. And Mommy says, "No, Johnny, you can't do it."

But Johnny insists, "Yes I can."

So Mommy insists, "No, you can't!"

And Johnny stomps up the stairs crying, goes into his bedroom, slams the door behind him, and begins to sob. After five minutes, the sobs die down, but he stays in his room, and after another half hour goes by, his mother thinks she should do something to cheer him up. She knows the one thing that Johnny loves more than anything else in the world is chocolate ice cream cones. So she very lovingly makes him a chocolate ice cream cone and goes upstairs, to find Johnny still sulking in a corner of his room.

"Here, Johnny, I made you a chocolate ice cream cone," she says. And Johnny yells "Neah!" and smacks it out of her hand.

That's masochism. Johnny is being given the one thing he loves more than anything else in the world and he's throwing it away. Why? Obviously, the reason is that, at that particular point in time, Johnny happens to be more into hating his mother than he is into loving ice cream. And that is what masochism is. It is always disguised sadism. Disguised hatred. Disguised rage.

The self-destructive people who come to therapy are playing the Blaming Game. They are saying at some unconscious level, "Look how my parents [because it is usually about their parents] screwed me up!" If that is the bone they are gnawing on—and remember, they are always gnawing on themselves—it is their primary unconscious motive to show the world how those bastards screwed them up. If they are healthy and doing pretty well financially, if their marriages are working and their children are turning out golden, how can they say, "Look how they screwed me up!" They can't, can they? But, if that is their bone, the only way they can keep gnawing on it is by staying screwed up. And the only way they can change that is to forgive, truly forgive, their parents, and that is tough, tough work.

THE NECESSITY OF FORGIVENESS

One patient of mine, whose parents had put him through hell as a child and who was working through this, said to me: "You know, I could forgive them if I could go to them and tell them the ways they've hurt me and they would apologize. Or even if they would just listen. But if I did go and tell them how they'd hurt me, they'd say I was just making these things up. They'd refuse to even remember what they have done. I'm the one who has had all of the pain. They gave me all the pain. They haven't had any of it, but you're expecting *me* to forgive *them*?"

And I said, "Yes."

The reason is that it is necessary for healing. Painful though it is. I must explain to such patients that they are going to stay screwed up until they can forgive their parents, whether or not their parents apologize or even listen.

There are a couple of standard things that I used to hear from patients who were resisting the necessity of real forgiveness. A patient would ask me, "Why do we have to talk about

all this bad stuff? We're always talking about all the bad things my parents did, and that's really unfair to them. You know, they did some good things, too. This is unbalanced."

And I would say, "Obviously your parents did some good things. For one thing, you're alive, and you wouldn't even be alive unless they did something right. But the reason that we focus on the bad stuff is because of Sutton's law."

My patient would then look blankly at me. "Sutton's law?"

And I would say, "Yes, it's a law named after Willie Sutton, who was a famous bank robber. When Sutton was asked by a reporter why he robbed banks, he said, 'Because that's where the money is.' "

We psychotherapists focus on the bad stuff because that's where the payoff is—not only for us but for our patients—because that's where the wounds and scars are, because those are the areas that need healing.

Another even more primitive thing I used to hear people say when they first came into therapy was, "Why do we have to dredge up all this stuff from the past? Why not just forget it?"

The reason is that we cannot forget anything. We cannot truly forget. We can only truly forgive, although in order to avoid doing the hard work of forgiveness we often try to push the offense out of our minds.

With the caveat that sometimes people may invent false memories, through the psychological mechanism known as repression, it is possible to push a memory of something that happened to us out of consciousness. We cannot consciously remember it, but it doesn't go away when we do this. In fact, it becomes a ghost that haunts us and makes things worse than if we remembered it.

It is possible, for instance, for women who have been repeatedly sexually molested—week after week after week for a period of two or three years by their fathers or stepfathers—to actually forget that. They can't even remember that it ever

happened, because they have repressed it. But then these women end up in therapy, usually because the relationships they are trying to form with the men in their lives are abominable. That early experience, which they cannot remember, continues to haunt them.

And so I would tell my patients that we cannot really forget about anything. The best we can do is to come to terms with it, to such a degree that we can remember it without pain. Therefore, the first step in the safety of the therapeutic alliance is to remember the crimes that were committed. Then comes the anger. It must come, as must the trial and the naming of the crimes. But beyond a certain point, the longer you hold on to that anger, the longer you will continue to hurt yourself.

The process of forgiveness—indeed, the chief reason for forgiveness—is selfish. The reason to forgive others is *not* for their sake. They are not likely to know that they need to be forgiven. They're not likely to remember their offense. They are likely to say, "You just made it up." They may even be dead. The reason to forgive is for our own sake. For our own health. Because beyond that point needed for healing, if we hold on to our anger, we stop growing and our souls begin to shrivel.

CHAPTER THREE

The Issue of Death and Meaning

There is a poem entitled "Limited" by Carl Sandburg:

> I am riding on a limited express, one of the crack trains of the nation.
> Hurtling across the prairie into blue haze and dark air go fifteen all-steel coaches holding a thousand people.
> (All the coaches shall be scrap and rust and all the men and women laughing in the diners and sleepers shall pass to ashes.)
> I ask a man in the smoker where he is going and he answers: "Omaha."

This is—in case you haven't guessed it—a poem about death, a particularly succinct and incisive summary of our attitude toward this largely ignored subject, but one which I have been fascinated with for as long as I can remember. You could say I've had a romance with death since I was a teenager, which is not to imply that I've been suicidal. It was, rather, a reaction to the environment I was raised in. My

boyhood home was a place where superficialities were considered to be of the utmost importance. It was crucial in one's life to know which fork to use.

Some years ago there was a fad—preppie presents for Christmas. I bought one for my wife, an apron with a big mallard duck on it and above that, printed in big letters: BEFORE TRUTH THE RIGHT FORK. That is what my childhood was like. "Clothes maketh the man," my parents intoned on dozens of occasions. Disillusionment was bound to follow, because sooner or later it was inevitable that I would run across a well-dressed idiot.

So, at a relatively early age, perhaps out of a spirit of rebellion, I said to myself: "Forget the superficialities. What is it that's *really* important?" I began to develop a habit of looking beneath the surface of things, a habit that has stood me in good stead ever since. And when I asked what is most important about our human existence, the first answer that came to my mind was that it is limited. We are all going to die. That's when my romance with death began.

As an adult I've come to recognize that death may not be *the* most important thing about our existence, but it is perhaps the second most important thing. And part of growing up is recognizing the fact that we are all going to die. We are all going to turn to scrap and rust and ashes.

The knowledge that life is limited fills many of us with a sense of meaninglessness. Since we're going to be chopped down by the Grim Reaper like so much straw, what possible meaning could there be to our paltry human existence? Granted, we might live on for a while through our children, but as the generations pass in relatively short order, the memory of our very name will be lost.

You may recall the famous poem by Shelley, "Ozymandias," in which he describes the remains of a statue standing in the desert. On the pedestal is inscribed:

> "My name is Ozymandias, King of Kings:
> Look on my works, ye Mighty, and despair!"

Yet all that is left of the statue is the pedestal, two vast and trunkless legs of stone, and a shattered visage half buried in the sand—and no one can remember who the man was.

So even if you are among the very few who manage to leave their imprint upon human history, as the centuries roll on, even that imprint will be lost.

"Life's but a walking shadow," laments Shakespeare's Macbeth. "It is a tale told by an idiot, full of sound and fury, signifying nothing."

THE FEAR OF DEATH

Can that be right? That life signifies nothing—and even if it does, death wipes its meaning away? Is it all for naught?

I do not believe so. Death is the opposite of what we think. Death is not a taker-away but rather a giver of meaning.

More than anything else, my romance with death has given me a sense of the meaningfulness of this life. Death is a magnificent lover. If you are suffering from a sense of meaninglessness or ennui, there is nothing better I can suggest to you than that you strike up a serious relationship with the end of your existence. Like any great love, death is full of mystery and that's where much of the excitement comes from. Because as you struggle with the mystery of your death, you will discover the meaning of your life.

Of course, most people have very little taste for struggling with the idea of their death. They do not even want to think about it. They want to exclude it from their awareness, thereby limiting their consciousness. Thus, the title of Sandburg's poem, "Limited," not only refers to the train but carries a larger meaning. Life is limited and the man who says he is going to Omaha is limited in his awareness of his true destination: death.

But you will find that people who are not so limited—like many of the great writers and thinkers—sooner or later become fascinated with death. Albert Schweitzer wrote:

> We must all become familiar with the thought of death if we want to grow into really good people. We need not think of it every day or every hour. But when the path of life leads us to some vantage point where the scene around us fades away and we contemplate the distant view right to the end, let us not close our eyes. Let us pause for a moment, look at the distant view, and then carry on. Thinking about death in this way produces love for life. When we are familiar with death, we accept each week, each day, as a gift. Only if we are able thus to accept life—bit by bit—does it become precious.

That is not the usual view of death. In my practice of psychotherapy, I found that I had to push at least half of my patients to face the reality of their death. Indeed, their reluctance to do so seemed to be a part of their illness. They simultaneously found their life tedious and frightening. They failed to visit friends in the hospital, skipped over the obituary pages, forgot to write condolence letters. And at night they would wake up drenched in sweat, dreaming of drowning. Unless I could get them to break through these self-imposed limits to their consciousness, there could be no full healing. We cannot live with courage and confidence until we can have a relationship with our own death. Indeed, we cannot live fully unless there is something that we are willing to die for.

These limits on people's consciousness can sometimes be debilitating. Early in my practice, I was visited by a man who arrived in a state of panic some three days after his brother-in-law had committed suicide by shooting himself in the head with a pistol. This man was so terrified he couldn't even come to my office alone. He had to come with his wife holding his hand. He sat down and began rambling: "You know, my brother-in-law, he shot himself in the head. I mean he had this pistol, and I mean all it took was just this, I mean just an

ounce of pressure and he's dead now. I mean that was all it took. And if I had a gun, I mean I don't have a gun, but if I had a gun and I wanted to kill myself, I mean all it would take would just be—I mean I don't want to kill myself, but I mean —all it—just this much."

As I listened to him, it was clear that what had precipitated his panic was not grief over his brother-in-law's death, but rather that this event had put him in touch with his own mortality, and I told him so.

He instantly contradicted me. "Oh, I'm not afraid of dying!"

That's when his wife broke in, and she said, "Well, dear, maybe you ought to tell the doctor about the hearses and the funeral parlors."

He then proceeded to explain to me that he had a phobia about hearses and funeral parlors—indeed, to such a degree that every day walking to and from work, he would go three blocks out of his way—six blocks each day—just to avoid passing a funeral parlor. Also, whenever a hearse drove by, he had to turn away, or better yet, duck into a doorway, or even better, into a store.

"You really do have quite a fear of death," I said. But he continued to insist, "No, no, no, I'm not afraid of dying. It's just those damn hearses and funeral parlors that bother me."

Psychodynamically, phobias usually result from a mechanism called displacement. This man was so afraid of dying that he couldn't even face up to his fear of dying and displaced it onto funeral parlors and hearses.

Because I often use psychiatric patients as my examples, you may think they are more cowardly and frightened than most. Not so. Those who come to psychotherapy are the wisest and most courageous among us. Everyone has problems, but what they often do is to try to pretend that those problems don't exist, or they run away from those problems, or drink them down, or ignore them in some other way. It's only the wiser and braver among us who are willing to submit them-

selves to the difficult process of self-examination that happens in a psychotherapist's office.

The fact of the matter is that we live in a cowardly, death-denying culture. A psychiatrist colleague told me once that in her town, after one high school student died of leukemia and another died in an automobile crash, the juniors and seniors petitioned the principal to introduce an elective, noncredit course on death and dying. A minister even stepped forward and offered to organize the course and find the teachers for it for free, so it wouldn't cost anyone anything.

But any new course in that school system had to be approved by the school board, which immediately voted nine to one against it on the grounds that it was morbid. About thirty or forty people wrote letters to the newspaper protesting that decision, and one of the editors of the paper wrote an editorial on the subject. There was a sufficient hue and cry to force the school board to reconsider its decision. The board did that and once again voted nine to one against the course.

It was not coincidental, in my view, that, as my colleague recounted, everyone who wrote a letter to the newspaper, the editor who wrote the editorial, and the one member of the school board who voted for the course were all people who either were in therapy or had been in therapy. As I said, psychiatric patients are not more cowardly than most. They are more courageous.

CHOOSING WHEN TO DIE

In our death-denying culture, death is viewed as an accident, as something that strikes us down without any rhyme or reason, and without our having any kind of control over it whatsoever. It's a sad state of affairs because we are caught in a kind of vicious cycle. Because we are so afraid of death, we are afraid to get close enough to it to see that we have less to fear than we thought.

Our cultural vision of death as an accident without rhyme or reason is just plain wrong. Most of us will, in fact, *choose* when, where, or how we die. It may seem shocking, but it is true. Most of us—on some level, in some way—will make that choice. I am not talking about suicides or one-car accidents or other incidents that might be suicides. I am not talking about alcoholics who drink themselves to death, or emphysemics who continue to smoke. Nor am I even talking about any of the well-known psychosomatic disorders. I am talking about medical disorders like heart disease and cancer, and there is scientific evidence to support my contention.

About thirty years ago when open-heart surgery first began—and was much more dangerous than it is now—everyone got into the act. And it was discovered that the people who could best predict how someone would do as an open-heart surgery patient were not the heart surgeons, not the cardiologists, but the psychiatrists. In one such study psychiatrists interviewed patients prior to their surgeries and, based on their answers, divided them into high-, medium-, and low-risk groups. In the low-risk group they found the kind of man who, when asked to talk about his heart surgery, would say: "Well, you know, it's scheduled for Friday and I'm really scared out of my wits about it. But for the past eight years, I haven't been able to do anything. I haven't been able to play golf, I've been so short of breath, and my surgeon tells me that if I survive the surgery and the postoperative period, I'll be as good as new in six weeks and be able to play golf six weeks from Friday. Hey, that's the first of September. I've got my tee time all arranged, and I'm going to be out there at eight o'clock in the morning and the dew is going to be still on the grass. I've got every hole mapped out in my mind."

Now, in the high-risk group there might be a woman who, when asked to talk about her surgery, would say: "Well, what about it?" And the psychiatrist would prompt: "Why are you having it, why do you need it?" And she would respond: "My doctor told me to."

"Are you looking forward to what you'll be able to do after your surgery?"

"I haven't thought about it."

"You've been so short of breath you haven't been able to go shopping for the past eight years. Aren't you looking forward to going shopping again?"

"Oh good gracious no. I'd be too afraid to drive after all these years."

Taking just the extremes, what this study found—if my memory serves me correctly—was that forty percent of the patients in the high-risk group died, and two percent of the people in the low-risk group died. Same heart disease, same heart surgeons, same heart surgery, and yet a twentyfold difference in mortality rate, which could be predicted before the surgery.

Another study with startling results was conducted by David Siegel, a psychiatrist at Stanford University, who studied two groups of women with metastatic cancer. The first group was given standard medical care; the second group also received standard medical care, but in addition was required to undergo psychotherapy. Not surprisingly, the second group complained of less anxiety, less depression, and less pain. But the astounding thing is that after all but three of the women in the study died, Siegel realized that those in therapy had lived twice as long as those in the other group.

"MIRACLE" CURES

Doctors have known for centuries that there are occasional, very rare cases of what are known as spontaneous remissions of cancer. You've heard of instances where doctors operate on a person and say, "We opened him up and he was just riddled with cancer and there was nothing we could do. The cancer was inoperable. All we could do was close him up. At most he's got six months to live." But then

five, ten years later, that person is still alive without a trace of cancer.

You might think that physicians would be absolutely fascinated by such rare cases, and would have thoroughly studied and investigated them. They haven't. For years doctors have insisted that such a thing was impossible, and it is only in the last fifteen years that studies have been instituted. It is still too early for all the results to be statistically significant—that is, totally up to scientific standards—but there are indications that one of the similarities in all those rare cases is a tendency on the part of the patients to make very profound changes in their lives. Once told they have a year to live, they seem to say to themselves, "I'm darned if I want to live out my days still working for IBM. What I want to do is refinish furniture. That's what I've always wanted to do." Or, "If I've only got a year to live, I'm darned if I want to live it with this fuddy-duddy old husband of mine." So after they make such decisions and such changes in their lives, their cancer goes away.

This phenomenon intrigued some researchers at UCLA, who decided to see if maybe a life change could be induced via therapy. But their problem was finding patients who were willing to try it. Typically, a psychiatrist would go to someone who had been diagnosed as having inoperable cancer and say, "We have some reason to believe that if you're willing to enter psychotherapy and look at your life and make some significant changes, you could prolong your life."

And initially the patient seemed overjoyed. "Oh, doctor, doctor, you're the first person that's given me any hope!"

So the psychiatrist says, "A group of patients like you are meeting with us in room four tomorrow morning at ten. Would you like to come and talk about this?"

"Oh yes, doctor, I'll be there."

But come ten o'clock the next morning, the patient doesn't show up. So the psychiatrist inquires and the patient says, "I'm sorry, it just sort of slipped my mind."

"Are you still interested?"

"Oh yes, doctor."

"We're having another meeting down in room four at three o'clock tomorrow afternoon. Are you free then?"

"Oh yes, I'll be there."

Again the patient doesn't show up. So the psychiatrist tries one more time and finally says, "Perhaps you're not really so keen on this idea of psychotherapy."

And the patient finally admits it. "You know, doc, I have been thinking about it, and I really am too old a dog to learn new tricks."

This isn't necessarily to be condemned. We do become old dogs, and are sometimes too tired to learn new tricks. Doctors are equally guilty of this. I constantly run into extremely well educated physicians who seem to believe that disease has to have only one cause—psychological or physical. It is beyond their comprehension to imagine that a disease, like the trunk of a tree, could have two roots simultaneously, or even more.

The reality is that virtually all diseases are psycho-spiritual-socio-somatic. There are exceptions, of course, like congenital disorders or cerebral palsy, for example. But even in such cases, the *will* to live can significantly prolong life and enhance its quality.

Unfortunately, the reverse is also true. When I was stationed with the armed services on Okinawa, I was asked to treat a nineteen-year-old woman suffering from hyperemesis gravidarum—excessive vomiting in pregnancy. I learned that she had grown up on the East Coast and had a pathological attachment to her mother. At the age of seventeen she had been sent to live with an uncle on the West Coast, and she had started to vomit. She was not pregnant then. She vomited so much that she had to be sent back East, where she remained very happy and healthy until she got pregnant by a soldier who married her and brought her to Okinawa. No sooner had she set foot off the airplane than she started to vomit, and within a very few days she was in the hospital.

I had the right, if my patients were sufficiently ill, to medevac them back home. And I knew that if I sent this patient home, her vomiting would stop immediately. I also knew that it would probably hopelessly entrench this pathology of vomiting every time she was separated from her mother.

In my omnipotence back then, I decided I would not send her home. I told her, "You've got to grow up and learn how to live separate from your mother." And she got better enough to be discharged from the hospital. But then she got worse and came back in. She was vomiting again, and I told her again that I was not going to send her home. Again she got better enough to be discharged. Two days later in her apartment, however, she suddenly dropped dead. She was nineteen years old and four months pregnant. They did an autopsy and never found out why she died. I deeply regretted my own decision, of course. But it is my belief that, for whatever reason, sometime in her life she had made a decision to be a child. I wouldn't let her be a child, so, rather than assume responsibility, she died.

SOMATIC AND PSYCHOSOMATIC DISORDERS

When I was in medical school, we referred to conditions like schizophrenia, manic-depressive disease, and alcoholism as "functional" disorders. By that word "functional" we hedged our bet and acknowledged that maybe one day researchers would discover some very subtle neuroanatomic defect or some kind of biological problem. But we really believed that these disorders were all psychological. And as psychiatrists we had the psychology of them all mapped out.

In the last thirty years, however, we have learned that there are profound biological roots to all of these psychiatric disorders, and more. In fact, one of the problems that we're facing today is that psychiatrists have become so enamored of biochemistry that we're in danger of forgetting all of the

old psychological wisdom, some of which is still very true. Conditions like schizophrenia are not *just* somatic disorders. They are also psycho-spiritual-socio-somatic disorders. And the same applies to diseases like cancer. All have multifaceted causes—somatic and psychosomatic.

The psychosomatic component to our suffering has been recognized in our language for centuries. There's something that psychiatrists refer to as "organ language," which reflects a kind of psychosomatic wisdom. For example: "He gives me a pain in the neck," or, "I've got butterflies in my stomach," or, "My heart is breaking." Any number of people go to emergency rooms late at night with chest pain—with or without heart attacks—just after they have undergone some kind of heartbreak.

Disorders of the spine are disorders of courage. And again, this is reflected in our language. We say, "He's got a yellow streak up his spine," or, "He's spineless," or, "Boy, she's really got backbone," or, "She's got lots of spine." I have suffered from back problems for most of my life, specifically a condition called spondylosis, which has been particularly severe in my neck. To look at an X ray of my neck, you would think I was two hundred years old. When I was first diagnosed with this condition, I asked neurosurgeons and orthopedic surgeons, "What causes my neck to look so old?" And they would say, "Well, probably when you were a kid you broke your neck."

I have never broken my neck. But when I told them that, all they could say was, "In that case we really don't know what caused your spondylosis." I was very glad of that answer, because few doctors are willing to go so far as to say, "I don't know."

Actually, I do know a good deal about what caused my spondylosis. I found out some thirteen years ago when, because my condition was driving me crazy with pain as well as paralyzing one of my arms, I underwent lengthy and serious neurosurgery. I said to myself at that time, "Scotty, you know,

if you don't want to undergo this very expensive, life-threatening surgery every couple of years—and eventually, to take care of the problem they're going to have to cut off your neck—maybe you might look at whether there's any role you are playing in this disorder. Is there any way that you are feeding into this?"

As soon as I was willing to ask that question, I immediately realized there was. I realized that for most of my life I'd been walking on the cutting edge of my profession, and I'd always been fearful of generating hostility. I had run into some hostility, although never as much as I anticipated, so my fear had a basis. But I had been going through life with my head and neck hunched down like a football player about ready to buck into the defensive line of the Pittsburgh Steelers. Try holding your head and neck that way for thirty years, and you too will know something about what causes spondylosis.

Of course, nothing is simple. There are multiple causes for most diseases. Although not to the same degree as I have, it so happens that my father, my mother, and my brother have suffered from an unusual amount of neck spondylosis, even though they were never renowned for "sticking their necks out." So there's obviously a biological—genetic or hereditary—component to my condition. Remember my contention that virtually all disorders are not only psychosomatic but psycho-spiritual-socio-somatic.

I'm not breaking new ground here. Much has been written about the relationship between body and mind. So many are becoming aware of the psychosomatic component of disease that some people these days feel guilty when they get sick. It is, of course, unnecessary to go around feeling guilty every time you get a cold or the flu. But it does behoove you, if you have a serious or a chronic illness, to take a look at yourself and ask whether you may be playing some role in your illness.

But if you do so, for God's sake, be gentle with yourself.

Life in some ways is *meant* to be stressful, and it wears us down. Please remember that sooner or later we all have to *die* from one damn psychosomatic disorder or another.

Again, I do not mean to imply that all terminal cancer is psychosomatic and that a children's cancer ward—with a four-year-old dying from an adrenal carcinoma and a six-year-old dying from a medulloblastoma and an eight-year-old dying from a Wilms' tumor—is nothing more than a repository for childhood suicides. I do not mean to imply that the victims of an airplane crash deliberately came together at the airport in a mass suicide attempt. Or that six million Jews willingly went to their deaths during the Holocaust. But when we consider death simply as an accident, we are ignoring not only the reality of most death but also its mystery.

UNDERSTANDING DEATH

One of the landmarks in our growing awareness of the true nature of death was the publication of the book *On Death and Dying* by Elisabeth Kübler-Ross, M.D. Until that time, death was the sole province of the priest. Doctors were interested in life, and life was for the living. Death was left to the morticians. But Kübler-Ross actually dared to talk to people who were dying, and dared to ask them what they were thinking of, what they were feeling about their impending deaths. She created a veritable revolution. A scant decade later there were courses on death and dying across the country. And the hospice, a place where people could go to die—a whole new institution—was invented or reinvented. It was as if she had caused a dam to burst.

Her work led to other books on the subject, among them *Life after Life* by Raymond Moody and *At the Hour of Death* by Karlis Osis and Erlendur Haraldsson, who wrote of the moment of death and near-death experiences. There is a startling unanimity about what they've found. Raymond Moody,

a scientist and a psychiatrist, reported that most of the people who remember their near-death experience relate a variation on the following sequence. First, they remember looking, as if from the ceiling, at their own bodies lying on a bed, and seeing very exactly what the nurses and doctors are doing to them. The next thing that happens—the only frightening part of the experience—involves going through a dark tunnel of some kind. They are whisked through rapidly, and when they come out of the tunnel, they are confronted by a light, which is perceived as God or sometimes as Jesus. And this being of light requires that they review their lives. In doing so, they tend to realize what a mess their lives were, but the being is extraordinarily loving and forgiving. Then the being directs them to go back, which they do reluctantly but in obedience to the light.

Often people who have had such experiences, according to Moody, were not previously spiritual, but became so afterwards. And invariably they have come to believe in life after death and have a much diminished fear of dying.

Isn't it interesting that when we get up close enough to death, we see that we've got much less to fear from it than we thought? But that might not bring you comfort. You might be saying, "What does it have to do with this life? What possible meaning could there be to this temporary existence of ours?"

If you ask such questions, I suspect it's precisely because you are well aware that your existence is limited, and you are looking for its meaning. But suppose the search for meaning is itself meaningful. Suppose that is part of the game, part of why we're here. Could we be here to search for something? If the answer is yes, then death impels that search.

As I have struggled with the mystery of my death, seeking the meaning of this life, I have found what I am looking for. It is very simple. *We are here to learn.* Everything that happens to us helps our learning. And nothing helps us to learn more than death.

I have also come to conclude that we have been given an

ideal learning environment. I defy you, in your imagination, to come up with a more ideal environment for human learning than life, than this life. It seems to me, in my gloomier moments, a kind of celestial boot camp, replete with obstacle courses which have been, almost fiendishly, designed for our learning. And I think the most fiendishly designed of all obstacles in life is the obstacle of sex. In actuality, death is a consequence of our sexuality.

Organisms at the bottom of the evolutionary scale do not reproduce sexually. They simply clone. They bud, and their genetic material goes on and on and on. They literally never die, unless somebody happens to come along and squish them. They experience no such thing as aging or natural death. Only when you get high enough in the evolutionary scale do you find sexual reproduction, and the moment you do, you find the phenomenon of aging and natural death. There's a price to everything.

We learn best when we have a deadline. What a wonderful word! In my practice of psychotherapy, I often employed a particularly potent and useful technique working with groups. When the members of a group seemed to be acting as if they had all the time in the world, I would come in one day and say, "Okay, guys, this group has only got six months more to live. I'm ending this group in six months. You've had it in six months." It was amazing how quickly people who had been sitting around on their duffs doing absolutely nothing could move once they were given a deadline.

In individual therapy as well, a deadline can be equally potent. The termination of a beloved relationship between a patient and a therapist can sometimes be used to symbolize the whole issue of death and give the patient an opportunity —that most people would never otherwise encounter—to work through death.

STAGES OF DEATH AND GROWTH

Elisabeth Kübler-Ross found that people who were dying went through certain stages—and they occur in this order:

- denial
- anger
- bargaining
- depression
- acceptance

The first stage is denial. They deny. They say, "The lab must have gotten my tests mixed up with somebody else's. It can't be me, it can't be happening to me." But that doesn't work for very long. So they get angry. They get angry at the doctors, angry at the nurses, angry at the hospital, angry at their relatives, angry at God.

When anger doesn't get them anywhere, then they start to bargain. They say, "Maybe if I go back to church and start praying again, my cancer will go away." Or, "Maybe if I start being nicer to my children for a change, my kidneys will improve." And when that doesn't get results, they begin to realize the jig is up, and they're really going to die. At that point, they become depressed.

If they can hang in there and do what we therapists call "the work of depression," then they can emerge at the other end of their depression and enter the fifth stage, of acceptance. This is a stage of great spiritual calm and tranquillity, and even light. People who have accepted death have a light in them. It's almost as if they had already died and were resurrected in some psychospiritual sense. It's a beautiful thing to see.

It is, however, not very common. Most people do not die in this beautiful fifth stage of acceptance. They die still denying, still angry, still bargaining, or still depressed. The reason is that the work of depression is so painful and difficult that when they hit it they usually retreat back into denial or anger or bargaining.

Although Kübler-Ross didn't recognize it at the time, the most fascinating thing about this is that we go through exactly the same stages in exactly the same order any time we make any significant step in our psychological or spiritual growth. Any time we make any giant step forward through the desert, any time we make any significant improvement in ourselves, we go through this process of denial, anger, bargaining, depression, and acceptance.

Let's imagine, for example, that there is a serious flaw in my personality, and that my friends start criticizing me for the manifestations of this flaw. What's my first reaction? I say, "She must have just gotten out of the wrong side of bed this morning." Or, "He must really be angry at his wife. Doesn't have anything to do with me." Denial.

If they keep on criticizing me, then I say: "What gives them the right to stick their noses in my business? They don't know what it's like to be in my shoes. Why don't they mind their own damn business!" I may even tell them that. Anger.

But if they love me enough to keep on criticizing me, then I begin to think: "Gee, I really haven't told them lately what a good job they're doing." And I go around giving them lots of pats on the back, smiling at them a lot, hoping that this will shut them up. Bargaining.

But if they truly do love me enough to keep on criticizing, then maybe I get to the point where I think, "Could they be right? Could there possibly be something wrong with the great Scott Peck?" And if I answer yes, then that's depressing. But if I can hang in there with that depressing notion—that maybe there really is something wrong with me—and start to wonder what it might be, if I contemplate it and analyze it and isolate it, and identify it, then I can go about the process of killing it and purifying myself of it. Having done—fully completed—the *work* of depression, I will then emerge at the other end as a new man, a resurrected human being, a better person.

LEARNING TO DIE

None of this is really new. In *The Road Less Traveled* I quoted Seneca as saying, almost two thousand years ago, "Throughout the whole of life, one must continue to learn how to live, and what will amaze you even more, throughout life one must learn to die." Learning how to live and learning how to die go together. In order to learn how to live, we have to come to terms with our death, because our death reminds us of the limit of our existence. Thus we become conscious of the brevity of our time in order to make full use of our time.

Don Juan, the old Mexican Indian guru in the books by Carlos Castaneda, referred to death as an ally. In Don Juan's parlance, allies were fearsome powers that had to be wrestled with before they could be tamed. And so it is with death. We have to wrestle with it, struggle with the mystery of death, before we can tame it sufficiently to put it on our left shoulder, as Don Juan did. And sitting there, we can continually, day in and day out, benefit from its wise counsel.

"Ally" signifies a friend, but, at least in the Western cultures, we are not accustomed to looking at death as a friend. In the Eastern cultures, in Hindu and Buddhist religions, death is supposedly more welcome than in ours. Indeed, in reincarnation theory—to which both those religions subscribe—the whole reward, the whole goal is death. The idea is that we keep being recycled—reborn and reborn and reborn—until we have learned what it is we are on earth to learn. Then and only then can we get off the wheel of rebirth and finally die for good.

Whether you subscribe to it or not, note that in reincarnation theory the purpose of life is also to learn. Actually, there is no evidence that Hindus or Buddhists are any less afraid of death than the rest of us. It is *normal* to be afraid of dying. Dying is a going into the unknown, and to a degree it is very healthy to be fearful of entering the unknown. What is not healthy is to try to ignore it.

One of the most frequent criticisms I hear from my atheist friends is that religion is a crutch for old people as they face the mystery, the terror of their death. I think they are correct that a mature religion begins in a struggle with the mystery of death. But I think they are incorrect that it is a crutch, as if it would somehow be braver to face a godless existence without afterlife and without meaning. I think that by acknowledging and facing up to the importance of death, the people who become religious may actually be the more courageous. Atheists, in my opinion, tend to deny the importance of death, proclaiming it to be nothing more than a cessation of the heartbeat, and immediately turn away. It is a kind of avoidance. They do not want to get close enough to death to look beneath the surface.

Mind you, the majority of churchgoers do not have any more taste for struggling with the mystery of their death than do atheists. Most churchgoers practice superficial, inherited, hand-me-down kinds of religion, which—like hand-me-down clothes—may keep them warm but are still just trappings. This is the reason for the saying "God has no grandchildren." We cannot relate to God through our parents. We have to establish a direct relationship with God. We cannot let someone else—our ministers, our leaders, or our parents—struggle with the mystery of our death. There are certain parts of the spiritual journey through life which must be done in solitude, and one of those is struggling with the mystery of death. You cannot let anyone else take up that struggle for you.

So, many churchgoers avoid the issue of death like the plague. Most Christian denominations have even taken Jesus off the cross. If you ask them why, they say that they want to emphasize the Resurrection over the Crucifixion. But sometimes I can't help but wonder if they simply don't want to see all that blood and gore and the reality of that death in front of them to remind them of their own.

FEAR OF DEATH AND NARCISSISM

But why are we are so often excessively afraid of death?

It is primarily because of our narcissism. Narcissism is an extraordinary, complex phenomenon. Some of it is necessary as the psychological side of our survival instinct, but most of it past childhood is self-destructive. Unbridled narcissism is the principal precursor of psychospiritual illness. The healthy spiritual life consists in a progressive growing out of narcissism. And while the failure to grow out of it is extremely common, it is also extremely destructive.

When psychiatrists talk about injuries to pride, we call them narcissistic injuries. And on any scale of narcissistic injuries, death is the ultimate. We suffer little narcissistic injuries all the time: a classmate calls us stupid, for example; we're the last to be chosen for someone's volleyball team; colleges turn us down; employers criticize us; we get fired; our children reject us. As a result of these narcissistic injuries, either we become embittered or we grow. But death is the big one. Nothing threatens our narcissistic attachment to ourselves and our self-conceit more than our impending obliteration. So it is utterly natural that we should fear death.

There are two ways to deal with that fear: the common way and the smart way. The common way is to put it out of our mind, limit our awareness of it, try not to think about it. That tends to work fine when we're young. But the longer we put it off, the closer it gets. And after a while everything begins to become a reminder of death—the graduation of a child, the illness of a friend, the creak in a joint. In other words, the common way is not very smart. In fact, the more we put off facing our death, the more frightening our old age is going to be.

The smart way is to face death as early as possible. And in doing so, we can realize something really rather simple. And that is, insofar as we can overcome our narcissism—and

we can probably never do this totally—we can overcome our fear of death.

For people who succeed at this, the prospect of death becomes a magnificent stimulus for their psychological and spiritual growth. "Since I'm going to die anyway," they think, "what's the point of preserving this attachment I have to my silly old self?" And so they set forth on a journey toward selflessness.

It is not an easy journey. The tentacles of our narcissism are subtle and penetrating and have to be hacked away day after day, week after week, month after month, year after year, decade after decade. Forty years after first recognizing my own narcissism, I am still hacking away.

It is not an easy journey, but what a worthwhile journey it is. Because the further we proceed in diminishing our narcissism, our self-centeredness and sense of self-importance, the more we discover ourselves becoming not only less fearful of death, but also less fearful of life. And we become more loving. No longer burdened by the need to protect ourselves, we are able to lift our eyes off ourselves and to truly recognize others. And we begin to experience a sustained, underlying kind of happiness that we've never experienced before as we become progressively more self-forgetful and hence more able to remember God.

This is the central message of all the great religions: Learn how to die. Again and again they tell us that the path away from narcissism is the path toward meaning. Buddhists and Hindus speak of this in terms of the necessity for self-detachment, and, indeed, for them even the notion of the self is an illusion. Jesus spoke of it in similar terms: "Whosoever will save his life [that is, whosoever will hold on to his narcissism] will lose it. And whosoever will lose his life for my sake will find it."

CHAPTER FOUR

The Taste for Mystery

For many years now I have had a mentor. I have never met him, because he comes to me from a sweet little Hasidic story. He was a rabbi who lived in a small Russian town at the turn of the century. And after twenty years of pondering the very deepest religious questions and spiritual issues in life, he finally came to the conclusion that when he got right down to rock bottom, he just didn't know.

Shortly after reaching that conclusion, he was walking across the village square on his way to the synagogue to pray. The cossack, or local czarist cop of this little town, was in a bad mood that morning and thought he would take it out on the rabbi. So he yelled, "Hey, Rabbi, where the hell do you think you're going?"

The rabbi answered, "I don't know."

This infuriated the cossack even more. "What do you mean you don't know where you're going?" he exclaimed in outrage. "Every morning at eleven o'clock you have crossed this village square on the way to the synagogue to pray, and here it is eleven o'clock in the morning and you're going in the direction of the synagogue and you try to tell me you don't know where you're going. You're trying to make some kind of fool out of me and I'll teach you not to do that."

So the cossack grabbed the rabbi and took him off to the local jail. And just as he was about to throw him into the cell, the rabbi turned to him and commented, "You see, you just don't know."

So I just don't know. No one does. We dwell in a profoundly mysterious universe. In the words of Thomas Edison, "We don't even begin to understand one percent about ninety-nine percent of anything."

Unfortunately, very few people realize this. Most of us think we know lots of things. We know our address and our telephone number and our Social Security number. We know how to find the way when we drive to work, and we know how to find our way back. We know that our car has something called an internal combustion engine that makes it work, and that when we turn the key in the ignition that engine will presumably start. We know that the sun rose this morning, and that it will set this evening, and that it will rise again tomorrow. So what is so mysterious?

This is the way I used to feel. When I was in medical school, I used to bemoan the fact that no more frontiers were left in medicine. All of the big diseases had been discovered and mapped out and it seemed clear that I was never going to become a Jonas Salk working late into the night making some great new discovery for the benefit of mankind.

Oh, there were a few things we realized we didn't know. A couple of months into our freshman year we students attended a presentation put on by the chairman of the department of neurology. Using a poor nearly naked man as a demonstration model in front of an amphitheater full of students, he proceeded with brilliant neuroanatomic precision to show us how this man was suffering from a lesion in his cerebellum, and another one in the upper end of his spinal cord and another down in the lower end. It was very impressive. But at the conclusion, one of my classmates raised his hand and said, "Sir, why does this man have these lesions? What's wrong with him?" And the chairman of the department of

neurology puffed out his chest and declared, "This patient is suffering from idiopathic neuropathy." We all went running back to our rooms and our textbooks to look up that term and learn that idiopathic meant "of unknown cause." Idiopathic neuropathy meant nothing more than disease of the nervous system of unknown cause.

So we came to recognize there were still a few rare idiopathic neuropathies and idiopathic hemolytic anemias, and idiopathic theses and idiopathic thats we didn't quite understand yet. But all the large things were known. During my years in medical school, I often had questions, but my professors always had answers. I never once heard a professor in medical school say, "I don't know." I didn't always understand the answers, but I assumed it was my fault and it was clear that I was never—with my little brain—going to make a great medical discovery.

But about a decade after leaving medical school, I did make a great medical discovery. I discovered that we know hardly anything about medicine. I discovered it because instead of asking, "What do we know?" I began to ask, "What don't we know?" As soon as I began to ask, "What don't we know?" all of those frontiers which I thought were closed opened up. And I realized that we live in a world of frontiers.

Let me give you an example. One of those very well mapped out diseases is meningococcal meningitis, a rather uncommon but nevertheless well-known disease which afflicts perhaps one person in every fifty thousand each winter. Were you to ask any physician what causes meningococcal meningitis, she or he will tell you, "Why, the meningococcus, of course." On a certain level this is correct, because if you autopsy people who die from this dreadful disease—and about fifty percent do, while another twenty-five percent are permanently maimed—and you open their skulls, you will see that the membranes covering the brain, or the meninges, are covered with pus. Then, if you look at the pus under the microscope, you will see zillions of little bugs swimming

around. And if you culture them out on the right medium, what do you find? The meningococcus, sure enough.

There is only one problem with this. Had I this past winter cultured the throats of the inhabitants of my little hometown of New Preston, Connecticut—or had I cultured the inhabitants of any northern city, such as Flint, Michigan—I would have discovered this bug in about eighty-five percent of the throats I examined. And yet no one in New Preston contracted, much less died from, meningococcal meningitis last winter, or for generations in the past, or is likely to for generations to come.

How and why is it that this bug, this bacterium which is virtually ubiquitous, can intermittently exist in 49,999 people without harm and yet can get into the brain—often of a previously healthy young person—and cause a fatal infection in but one?

The answer is: We don't know.

The same is true of virtually every disease in the book. Let's take an unfortunately more common one, another well-known disease—cancer of the lung. We all know that smoking causes cancer of the lung. Yet there are certain people whose lips never touched tobacco and who get lung cancer and die. And there are certain people, like my grandfather, who smoked up a storm for most of his ninety-two years and never got lung cancer. So obviously, there is something in addition to smoking that is involved in the causation of cancer of the lung. And what is that something? The answer is, once again: We usually don't know.

This applies not only to virtually all diseases but also to their treatment. When I was in practice, occasionally patients for whom I prescribed certain medications would ask me, "Dr. Peck, how does it work?" And I would tell them that it alters the catecholamine balance in the limbic system of their brains. And that would shut them up. But exactly how does a certain chemical alter the catecholamine balance in the limbic system of the brain in such a way as to make a depressed

person feel less depressed, or a schizophrenic think more clearly? The answer is—you guessed it—we don't know.

You may have caught on some time ago that doctors don't know much. But other people know things, don't they? I mean, medicine may be something of an art, but the hard sciences—physics, say—have all the laws pinned down.

Modern physics in many ways began with Isaac Newton, and when the apple fell on his head, he not only discovered gravity but actually developed a mathematical formula for it. So now everybody knows that two bodies attract each other with a force that is directly proportional to the product of their masses and inversely proportional to the square of the distance between them. That seems very cut-and-dried.

But why? Why do two bodies attract each other? Why should there be this force at all? What does it consist of? And the answer is: We don't know. Newton's mathematical formula simply describes the phenomenon, but why that phenomenon should exist in the first place or how it operates, we don't know. In this great age of technology, we don't even understand what it is that keeps our feet on the ground. So we haven't gotten so far with hard sciences, either.

But surely *somebody* must know something. I mentioned mathematics as very cut-and-dried. Mathematicians must know the truth. We all learned, back in school, that great truth that two parallel lines never meet. But then, along about my senior year in college, I was walking down the quad one day and I heard someone mention something about Riemannian geometry, and I found out that Bernhard Riemann was a German mathematician who, back in the middle of the nineteenth century, asked himself, "What if two parallel lines do meet?" And on the assumption that two parallel lines do meet, and a couple of other alterations that he made in Euclid's theorems, he developed a totally different geometry. This might seem like no more than an intellectual exercise or form of play, sort of like trying to figure out how many angels can dance on the head of a pin, were it not for the fact that

much of Albert Einstein's work, including that which led to the development of the atomic bomb (via the theory of relativity)—which, as we all know, works—was based not on Euclidean geometry but on Riemannian geometry.

My mathematician friends tell me that the number of potential geometries is infinite. Since Riemann's day, we have developed some six additional working geometries, so we now have a total of eight different working geometries. Which is the real one? We don't know.

PSYCHOLOGY AS ALCHEMY

Not having gotten too far with the hard sciences, let me retreat to my own "soft" science of psychology. Some have compared psychology to alchemy. Back in the days of alchemy—when scientists, such as they were, were trying to change base metals to gold—all that was known about the world was that it consisted of four "elements": earth, air, fire, and water. Since then, we have discovered the periodic table of elements and we know that there are more than a hundred fundamental elements—things like hydrogen and oxygen and carbon, and so on. But psychology still seems as if it is back in the dark ages of alchemy.

For instance, the women's liberation movement is based on certain assumptions about the nonanatomical differences or similarities between men and women. What are those nonanatomical differences and similarities? How many of them are cultural or social, and how many are biological? We don't know. Here at the end of the twentieth century, we know how to blow ourselves off the face of the earth, but we don't even begin to understand what sexuality is all about.

Or take the human trait of curiosity, very much related to this subject of mystery. Are all people born equally curious, or are people born with different curiosity levels? Is curiosity something that comes to us genetically, or is it something that we learn as we grow up in our culture? Something that is

drummed into us or drummed out of us? We don't know. Once again, the dawn of a scientific body of knowledge about this most important of human traits has not yet arrived.

Knowing so little, then why is it that we humans go around thinking that we know the score, when actually we don't know beans? There are two reasons. It is because we are scared and because we are lazy.

It is scary to think that we really don't know what we're doing or where we're going, and that we are intellectual infants stumbling around in the dark. It's so much more comfortable, therefore, to live in an illusion that we know much more than we actually do.

We also live in an illusion because we are lazy. Were we to wake to the reality of our terrible ignorance, we would either have to think of ourselves as being profoundly stupid or, at the very least, let ourselves in for a lifetime of effortful learning. Since most people don't like to think of themselves as stupid or let themselves in for a lifetime of effortful anything, it's just so much more comfortable to live in this nice illusion that we know much more than we actually do.

The only problem with this is that it is an *illusion*. It is not real! You might remember in *The Road Less Traveled*, I defined mental health as a process of ongoing dedication to reality at all costs. And "at all costs" means no matter how uncomfortable the reality makes us.

Now, in our pain-avoiding culture mental health is not always encouraged. When someone suffers an emotional setback, we say, "Oh, poor Joe, he's been disillusioned." What we ought to say is, "*Lucky* Joe, he's been disillusioned." But instead we say, "Oh, poor fellow, now he sees things the way they really are, the poor guy." As if being made aware of reality is a bad thing. In the same way, when people come to terms, in therapy, with the fact that they were molested or abandoned as children, we can't say, "Oh, poor person," because this pain they experience is ultimately health-producing.

Of course, there are exceptions to every rule, and I am a

great champion of what psychologists call "healthy illusions." For example, a physician who has a heart attack is probably twice as likely to die in the intensive care unit as someone who is not a physician. The reason is that he knows all the things that can go wrong, whereas someone else will say, "Oh, I just had a heart attack!" So sometimes illusion can be health-producing.

Yet by and large, I think it's good for us to be disillusioned. Generally, the more we are adjusted to reality, the better our lives work. But we can live in a world of reality only if we have a taste for mystery. For the reality of the situation is that our knowledge is like a little raft bobbing up and down in the sea of our ignorance, in an ocean of mystery. And people in that situation are going to be out of luck if they don't like the water. And the only way they are going to be in luck is if they love mystery, if they love to dive in it and swim in it and splash and drink it and taste it. Then they are really going to be in luck.

CURIOSITY AND APATHY

One of the things that tend to characterize the least mentally healthy, the least mature among us is their lack of a taste for mystery, or their relative lack of curiosity. What bothers me the most when I visit a psychiatric hospital is not the insanity, not the rage or the fear or the anger or the depression, but the apathy. Sometimes it is drug-induced, but a terrible apathy often characterizes the mentally disordered.

What happens with healthy people when it begins to snow? They go to the window, look out, and say, "Hey, it's starting to snow," or, "Wow, it's really coming down heavy now," or, "Ah, it's a real blizzard out." But in a psychiatric hospital when someone says, "Hey, it's starting to snow," the patients usually respond, "Don't interrupt our card game." Or they don't want to interrupt their delusions. And they don't

get up and go to the window, and they don't look out to see the mystery of the snow.

Another form that mental illness can take is when people are so unable to tolerate mystery that they may make up explanations for things that are really unexplainable. For instance, a few years ago I received a very sad eight-page letter that was quite well organized on the first page, but happened to offhandedly mention that the writer had a son with Hodgkin's disease. Then as the letter went on, the man's writing began to become considerably more disorganized. He wrote, "Of course you know, Dr. Peck, do you not, the wisdom of the ancients that we all of us have an ethereal double that goes around with us, and that there is an ionization factor that goes on between our regular bodies, our material bodies, and our ethereal doubles and disease is the result of this ionization factor?"

I did not know that. It is a possible and occasionally held esoteric theory, but it is not one for which we yet have the slightest body of evidence. So this man had in a sense found an explanation for his son's Hodgkin's disease. Perhaps it gave him some comfort in removing him from the mystery of that. But his certainty was delusional.

Conversely, one of the things that characterize the most mentally healthy among us is their great taste for mystery and their profound curiosity. They are curious about everything: about quasars and lasers and schizophrenics and praying mantises and stars. Everything turns them on. Most of us, however, fall somewhere in between total mental health and utter insanity, and for most of us, our taste for mystery lies dormant.

When I was in practice, I used to tell my patients that they were hiring me as a guide through inner space. They were hiring me not because I had ever been through their inner space before, but simply because I knew a little something about the rules for exploring inner space. In the practice of psychotherapy, everyone's inner space is different. It's a

different journey each time. That's what makes it so interesting to me.

In order to explore inner space, one has to be an explorer. And to be an explorer, one has to have a taste for mystery. For Lewis and Clark, it was the mystery of what lay on the other side of the Appalachians. For astronauts it is the mystery of outer space. For patients in psychotherapy it is primarily the internal mystery of themselves. If in the course of therapy the patient's curiosity about the mystery of his early childhood was awakened, and if he began to explore forgotten memories and the influence of some experiences and events upon his life, and also the mystery of his genes and his temperament, and his heritage, and culture, and his dreams and what those dreams might mean, then therapy would go far. On the other hand, if in the course of therapy the patient's taste for the mystery of his heritage or his genes or his childhood or his dreams was not awakened, then there was no way that his journey of exploration could proceed very far.

I referred to "awakening" of the patient's taste for mystery because I believe—although we do not yet have any scientific body of knowledge to support it—that the taste for mystery is something that at least in some people can be developed, like, for example, the taste for whiskey. Except that it is an infinitely preferable taste to develop, because the more you drink in mystery, the greater the supply becomes. And no matter how much you drink, there is absolutely no hangover and it is all for free. There is no incise tax, there is no excise tax. It is the one addiction that I can heartily recommend to you.

MYSTERY AND THE SPIRITUAL JOURNEY

Living in the real world is not only the goal of mental health. It is also the goal of the spiritual journey. What is that spiritual journey, after all, but a quest to find the *real* meaning of life? Hopefully we are searching for the *real* God.

One of the confusing things about religion is that people go into it for different reasons. There are some who are attracted to religion in order to approach mystery, while there are others who are attracted to religion in order to escape from mystery.

It is not my intent to knock those people who use religion to escape from mystery. Because there are people who, at a particular point of their psychospiritual development (like alcoholics newly converted to AA, or criminals newly converted to a moral life), *need* some very clear-cut, dogmatic kinds of faiths and beliefs and principles by which to live. Nonetheless, it is my intent to tell you that the fully mature spiritual person is not so much a clinger to dogma as an explorer, every bit as much as any scientist, and that there is no such thing as a complete faith. Reality, like God, is something we can only approach.

> In our endeavor to understand reality we are somewhat like a man trying to understand the mechanism of a closed watch. He sees the face and the moving hands, even hears its ticking, but he has no way of opening the case. If he is ingenious he may form some picture of a mechanism which could be responsible for all the things he observes, but he may never be quite sure his picture is the only one which could explain his observations. He will never be able to compare his picture with the real mechanism and he cannot even imagine the possibility of the meaning of such a comparison.

Those words came from the pen of Albert Einstein, a man who most people would say knew more than anyone else on earth—in fact, his name has become synonymous with genius. And yet he wrote that we can observe and theorize but we can never know. Reality is something we can only approach.

One of the things that some religious people are guilty of is thinking they have God in their back pocket. But a fully mature person knows better. Reality, like God, is not something we can tie up in a nice neat intellectual little package and put in our briefcase and possess. Reality, like God, is not ours to possess. Reality, like God, possesses us.

The spiritual journey is a quest for truth as much as science is a quest for truth. The fully mature person must be a truth seeker every bit as much as the scientist is a truth seeker, and perhaps even more. Because just as some people may go into religion in order to escape from mystery, so some people will go into science in order to escape from mystery.

We all know or have heard of scientists who spend a lifetime on a study of cytochrome oxygenase in homogenate of pigeon prostate tissue at pH 3.7 to pH 3.9 and that is the extent of their interest in the universe. They have carved out a little area for themselves, and have read more papers on the subject than anybody else, so their knowledge of their area is unimpeachable, and they feel safe. But to really seek the truth, one cannot carve out a safe niche and hole up in it. One must blunder out there into the unknown, the mysterious.

In my practice, my patients would sometimes say to me, not in a psychotic way but in an ordinary existential way, "Gee, Dr. Peck, I'm so confused," and I would say, "That's wonderful!" And they would say, "What do you mean? It's awful." And I would say, "No, no, it means that you're blessed." And they would say, "What? It feels terrible. How can I be blessed?"

And I would say, "You know, when Jesus gave His big sermon, the first words out of His mouth were: 'Blessed are the poor in spirit.' " There are a number of ways to translate "poor in spirit," but on an intellectual level, the best translation is "confused." Blessed are the confused. If you ask why Jesus might have said that, then I must point out to you that confusion leads to a search for clarification and with that search comes a great deal of learning.

The people of the fifteenth century, for example, did not go to bed one night in 1492 thinking that the earth was flat only to wake up the next morning knowing that it was round. They went through a whole period of confusion and exploration when they didn't know which end was up. And for an old idea to die and a new and better idea to take its place, we have to go through such periods of confusion.

It is uncomfortable, sometimes painful to be in such periods. Nonetheless it is blessed because when we are in them, despite our feeling poor in spirit, we are searching for new and better ways. We are open to the new, we are looking, we are growing. And so it is that Jesus said, "Blessed are the confused." Virtually all of the evil in this world is committed by people who are absolutely certain they know what they're doing. It is not committed by people who think of themselves as confused. It is not committed by the poor in spirit.

In *The Road Less Traveled*, I said that the path to holiness lies in questioning everything. Seek, and you shall find enough pieces of truth to be able to start fitting them together. You will never be able to complete the puzzle. But you will be able to fit together enough pieces to begin to get glimpses of the big picture and to see that it is very beautiful indeed.

If our whole lives are embedded in mystery and we really don't know where we are going—if we are intellectual infants stumbling around in the dark—then how is it that we survive? I know of only two ways to answer that question. One is to conclude that Scott Peck and Albert Einstein are wrong, and that we know much more than they say we do. The other is to conclude that somehow we are *protected*. And that, of course, is what I have come to conclude. Now how in God's name that protection works, I have no idea except that it somehow *is* in God's name.

In my office I have the figures of seven different angels hanging around in various states of disrobement. The reason

they are there is not because I have ever seen a humanoid creature with wings. But when I come to contemplate the mechanics of this protection, the mechanics of grace—how God can seemingly, literally number the hairs on our heads (which in my case is becoming less and less of a responsibility for Him these days)—I can only imagine Him having armies and legions of angels at His command.

I believe that some of these angels truly do come in human form. Phyllis Theroux wrote a collection of sparkling spiritual essays entitled *Nightlights: Bedtime Stories for Parents in the Dark.* In one of them she recounts how she once had taken a civil service exam and, typical of such examinations, there were four or five questions that were obviously designed to weed out the crazies or paranoids. She said that she could remember only one, and it asked, "Do you think you are a special agent of God?"

For a while, she recounted, she felt paralyzed, thinking of all the civil service benefits that might hang upon her answer to that question. Finally, she concluded that discretion was the better part of valor, and she picked up her pencil and lied and wrote, "No."

So I suspect that there are some special agents around, protecting us as we stumble along on our dark and mysterious journey. I particularly like to think so around the time of Halloween, that most mysterious of Christian and pre-Christian celebrations. It is then I am most likely to be reminded of that famous but anonymous seventeenth-century Scottish prayer which goes:

> From ghoulies and ghosties
> and long-leggedy beasties
> and things that go bump in the night,
> may the good Lord deliver us.

Let me paraphrase this prayer for our late-twentieth-century circumstances:

From the ghoulies of our un-understood feelings and misunderstood hostilities,
From the ghosties of our outworn ideas to which we cling and the illusions of our wisdom and competence,
From the long-leggedy beasties of our ignorance and prejudices and self-satisfaction,
And from all the things that we don't even know enough about to be afraid of that exist in the mysterious night beyond our limited sight,
May the good Lord deliver us—you, me, and the whole of our struggling infant humanity.

PART TWO

The Next Step: Knowing Your Self

CHAPTER FIVE

Self-Love versus Self-Esteem

Humility is a true knowledge of oneself as one is.

That is a paraphrase from a book written by an anonymous fourteenth-century monk, called *Cloud of Unknowing*. It is a profound statement, and an essential one to grasp on the search for self-knowledge.

For instance, were I to say to you that I am a lousy writer, that actually would not be humility. While not the greatest, the truth of the matter is that as people go, I am a relatively good writer. So such a statement would be what I have come to call "pseudo-humility." On the other hand, were I to tell you I was a good golfer, that would be the height of arrogance, for the fact is, I am a mediocre one at best. Genuine humility is always *realistic*.

It's critical for us to be realistic, to have a true knowledge of ourselves as we are, and to be able to recognize both the good parts and the bad parts of ourselves. Further, there is a distinction between self-love and self-esteem, in my opinion. And the difference between self-love (which I propose is a good thing) and self-esteem (which I propose can be a questionable thing) is often confused, because we really do not have accurate words for the phenomenon I am going to dis-

cuss here. I hope that eventually the problem will be somewhat solved by developing new words, but for the moment we're stuck with the old ones.

First, what do I mean by self-love?

Back when I worked as a psychiatrist in the army, the military was interested in what made successful people click, and so a dozen such people from different branches of the services were gathered together for study. They were men and women in their late thirties or early forties who had all been markedly successful. They had been promoted ahead of their contemporaries, yet they also seemed to be popular. Those who had families seemed to be enjoying a happy family life; their children were doing well in school and were well adjusted. These people seemed to have a golden touch.

They were studied in various dimensions, sometimes as a group, sometimes individually. As a part of the study they were asked to write down on a piece of paper—and they did not have the chance to consult with one another about this issue—the three most important things in their life, in order of priority.

There were two phenomena that were quite remarkable about the way the group handled this task. One was the seriousness with which they took it. The first to return his answer sheet took well over forty minutes, and a number of the people took more than an hour, even though they knew that most of the group had finished. The other thing that was remarkable was that, while the second and third items on their lists ranged all over the map, all twelve had written exactly the same answer for number one: "Myself." Not "Love." Not "God." Not "My family." But "Myself."

And that, I suggest, was an expression of mature self-love. Self-love implies the care, respect, and responsibility for and the knowledge of the self. Without loving one's self one cannot love others. But do not confuse self-love with self-centeredness. These successful men and women were loving spouses and parents and caring supervisors.

Now, what is self-esteem?

About eight or nine years after my experience with the armed forces study group, I had occasion to get close to a person of the lie—and as you might recall, I define people of the lie as essentially being evil. Such people are hard to get close to, but I got close enough to this man to ask him, "What is the single most important thing in your life?"

And what do you think his answer was? "My self-esteem."

Notice how close the answers are. The twelve successful people had written, "Myself," and he said, "My self-esteem."

I believe his answer was correct in terms of the way people of the lie function. Their self-esteem *is* the single most important thing in their lives. They will do anything to preserve and maintain their self-esteem at all times and at all costs. If there is anything that threatens their self-esteem, if there is any evidence around them of their own imperfection or something that might cause them to feel bad about themselves, rather than using that evidence and those bad feelings to make some kind of correction, they will go about trying to exterminate the evidence. And this is where their evil behavior arises. Because it is necessary for them to preserve their self-esteem at all costs.

There is a difference between insisting that we regard ourselves as important (which is self-love) and insisting that we always feel good about ourselves (which is synonymous with constantly preserving our self-esteem).

Understanding and making this distinction is crucial to our self-knowledge. In order to be good, healthy people, we have to pay the price of setting aside our self-esteem once in a while, and so not always feel good about ourselves. But we should always love ourselves and value ourselves, even if we shouldn't always esteem ourselves.

THE ADVANTAGES OF GUILT

The tool that helps us not feel good about ourselves when a self-correction is necessary is called existential guilt. We

need a certain amount of guilt—a certain amount of contrition—in order to exist. Without guilt we lack an essential self-correcting kind of mechanism. If we go around thinking that we're okay all the time, then we cannot, of course, correct those parts of us that are not okay.

Most people are familiar with the book *I'm Okay, You're Okay* by Thomas Harris. It is a very good book, but I really don't like the title very much. Because what happens if you're not okay? What happens if you wake up every night at two a.m. drenched in sweat dreaming of drowning, and then you're so filled with dread that you can't get back to sleep until six a.m., and that goes on not only night after night but week after week, month after month. Is it still all right to think that you're okay?

What happens if you can't go into a store without having a panic attack? Is it all right to think that you're okay then? What happens if you're driving your children to drugs or into serious trouble and you're not even conscious of it? Is it all right to think that you're okay?

I believe that Alcoholics Anonymous has a much better way of putting it. They have a saying "I'm not okay, and you're not okay, but that's okay."

Indeed, when I was still in the practice of psychotherapy, I used to have a certain investment in people thinking they were not okay—financial and otherwise. Because people who think they are okay do not come to psychotherapy. It is only people who think they are not okay who come, who have the humility to seek help so that they might get a head start on the journey of self-knowledge.

I cite myself as an example. About a year before I actually went into psychotherapy, I had decided that this would be a good thing for me to do. I was then a psychiatrist-in-training in the armed forces and I knew a therapist who was on the faculty of my hospital who seemed like a hip guy and would be obligated to see me for free. But when I brought up the idea to him, he asked me why I wanted to do it. So I told him,

"Well, I've got a little bit of anxiety over here and a little bit of anxiety over there. It would be a useful educational experience and it would look good on my curriculum vitae." He said, "You're not ready yet," and refused to treat me.

I stormed out of his office, furious at him, but of course, he was quite right. I was not ready. I was going in feeling that I was okay. But I became ready just about a year later, to the day.

I will tell you exactly what happened on that day, but first let me tell you that, while at the time I didn't identify it as such, I was suffering from what could be called an authority problem. For the preceding twenty years, wherever I had worked or studied, there was always some son of a bitch in charge of me whose guts I absolutely hated. Always an older man. A different man each place, but wherever I went, he was there. And I thought that the problem was always that man's fault, and that it didn't have anything to do with me.

In the army at that particular time, my bête noire was the commanding general of the hospital, a gentleman I will call by the name of Smith. I hated General Smith's guts. And perhaps because I did, General Smith wasn't so kindly disposed toward me either. He must have felt the vibrations.

The day I went into therapy began with a case presentation conference, during which I had to play a tape of an interview I had conducted with a patient. My peers and one of my supervisors listened to it, and when it was over they proceeded to rake me over the coals for the clumsy, immature way I had conducted it. So the day didn't start out very well. But I was still able to maintain my self-esteem by telling myself that this was just a standard gauntlet which psychiatry residents and any psychotherapy students have to go through. They always take you to pieces, and it really didn't mean that I was inadequate or wrong in any way, shape, or form. Still, it didn't feel very good.

Then I had a little free time, and I thought I would use it to get a haircut. Now, I did not think I needed a haircut, but

this was the army, and I knew that General Smith would think I needed a haircut. So, having already been criticized by my peers and my supervisor, I went off to get the haircut I didn't want.

On my way to the barbershop, I passed by the post office and decided to check my box to see if by any chance I had some mail. I did. To my dismay, I found a traffic ticket. I had gotten that ticket some two months before when I drove through a stop sign on post on my way to play tennis with the post commander, a colonel by the name of Connor—a good guy in my mind. The only problem was that when you got a ticket from the MPs on post, a copy of it always went to your commanding officer—in this case, General Smith.

Since I was already on General Smith's blacklist, I wasn't very keen about his getting something else on me, and so when I finally arrived to play tennis with Colonel Connor, in my best manipulative fashion—I was not above that sort of thing back then—I had said, "I'm sorry I'm late, sir, but I got held up by one of *your* MPs going through a stop sign trying to get here on time." He picked up on it and said, "Don't worry about it. I'll take care of it." Sure enough, the next morning, the provost marshal, or head cop of the post, called me and said, "Dr. Peck, you know that ticket that you got yesterday? Well, I just wanted to let you know that it's been lost in the mail, and next time drive more carefully." And I said, "Thank you very much, sir."

About six weeks later, however, the provost marshal was relieved of duty so summarily that he didn't even have time to clean out his desk. And when they went to clean it out, they found a whole stack of fixed tickets, which they then proceeded to redistribute. So now, having been raked over the coals by my peers and my supervisor, and on my way to get a haircut I didn't want, I found the ticket I thought had been fixed but hadn't. Feeling worse and worse, I went on to the barbershop.

About three-quarters of the way through my haircut, who

should come in to get his hair cut? You guessed it. General Smith. And even though he might have wanted to, not even a general can bump someone out of a barber chair in the middle of a haircut, so he had to sit and wait his turn. And just to show you what bad shape I was in, all I could think of was: "Should I say hello to the SOB or shouldn't I? Should I or shouldn't I?" Over and over again. "Should I or shouldn't I?"

Sometimes people ask me, "When is the time to go into psychotherapy?" I say, "When you're stuck." I was stuck.

Finally, I decided to behave with great noblesse oblige and savoir faire. When my haircut was finished, I got out of the chair, and walking past him, I said, "Good morning, General Smith," then left the barbershop. Whereupon the barber came running out into the corridor saying, "Doctor, doctor, you no pay for your haircut!" So I had to come back into the barbershop, and at that point I was so nervous I dropped all my change on the floor, right at General Smith's feet. There I was, kneeling in front of him, and he was sitting literally above me, laughing at my predicament.

When I finally got out of there, I was trembling all over, and I said to myself, "Peck, you're not okay. You need help!"

THE GRACE OF BREAKING MOMENTS

That was a very painful moment—the kind of painful moment I have come to call a "breaking moment." As breaking moments go, it was really rather gentle, and that has tended to be the pattern of my life. I think God knows that I can't stand much pain.

But even though it was a very painful moment, a breaking moment, it was also one of my finest moments. Because within the hour, my still-shaking fingers were trembling their way through the Yellow Pages looking for a psychotherapist, with a genuine willingness and intent to work on myself. And

painful though it was, it was the beginning of a very large growth step, a giant step forward through the desert toward salvation, toward healing for me.

Such breaking is actually symbolized in the services of the Christian churches when, at the central moment of the Communion ritual, the priest holds a piece of bread high over the altar and breaks it. A moment of breaking. And one of the things that people signify when they celebrate this ritual—whether or not they know they are doing this, and often they don't—is their own willingness to be broken. This would make Christianity seem like a very strange religion indeed—a religion of a group of people who are actually willing or want to be broken—were it not for the fact that we know it is precisely through these kinds of breakings that we are opened up, and that we make our large steps forward.

We need these moments of breaking, when we come to realize that we are not okay, that we do not have it all together, that we are not perfect, that we are not without sin. Moments of guilt, moments of contrition, moments when we are lacking in self-esteem, moments when we are bearing the trial of being displeasing to ourselves, are essential to our growth.

But even during these moments, we also need to value and love ourselves. Not only is it possible to love ourselves and realize that we are imperfect, but it's possible to do this at the same time. Indeed, often part of our loving ourselves is the realization that there is something about us that we need to work on.

VALUABLE CARGO

About sixteen years ago, I had a patient, a seventeen-year-old boy, an emancipated minor, who had been on his own since the age of fourteen. He had had atrocious parenting. I told him during one session, "Jack, your biggest problem is that you don't love yourself, that you don't value yourself."

That same night I had to drive down from Connecticut to New York in the midst of a terrible rainstorm. Sheets of rain were sweeping across the highway and the visibility was so poor that I couldn't even see the side of the road or the yellow line. I had to keep my attention absolutely glued on the road, even though I was very tired. If I'd lost my concentration for even a second, I would have gone off the road. And the only way I was able to make that ninety-mile trip in that terrible storm was to keep saying to myself, over and over again, "This little Volkswagen is carrying extremely valuable cargo. It is extremely important that this valuable cargo get to New York safely." And so it did.

Three days later, back in Connecticut, I saw my young patient and learned that in the same rainstorm, not nearly as tired as I was and on a much shorter journey, he had driven his car off the road. Fortunately, he hadn't been seriously hurt. He had done this not because he was covertly suicidal —although the lack of self-love can merge into suicidality— but simply because he was not able to say to himself that *his* little Volkswagen was carrying extremely valuable cargo.

Let me give you another example. Shortly after *The Road Less Traveled* was published, I began treating a woman who had to travel from central New Jersey to where I live, a three-hour trip each way. She came to see me because she had read the book and liked it. She was a woman who had spent all of her life in the Christian church; she had been raised in the church and had even married a clergyman. We worked together once a week for the first year, and we got absolutely nowhere—made no progress at all. And then one day she opened the session by saying, "You know, driving up here this morning, I suddenly realized that what is most important is the development of my own soul." I broke out in a roar of joyful laughter at the fact that she had finally gotten it, but also of ironic laughter at the fact that I had assumed that this woman—who had come because she liked *The Road Less Traveled,* who was willing to make a six-hour round trip once a week to see me, and who had spent the entirety of her life

in the church—already knew that what was most important was the development of her own soul. But she didn't, and I suspect that most Christians do not. Once she realized it, however, her progress in therapy was like lightning.

THE WORK OF PREPARATION

So it is terribly important that we love ourselves. Indeed, so important that I would even like to be biblical about it. Some years ago I was leading a retreat in Chicago at a huge Catholic center. The retreat was to conclude on Sunday afternoon with a formal Mass in the center's ornate church. Before the retreat began, the monk who was organizing it had asked me if I would like to give the sermon or homily at that Mass. And in a moment of unwitting stupidity and arrogance, I had said, "Oh, sure," having temporarily forgotten that in the Catholic church you cannot give a sermon on just any subject. You have to give it according to the "propers," or assigned readings for the particular day, and usually the assigned Gospel reading.

But I remembered shortly, and when I had some quiet time while the retreatants were in small groups, I picked up the Bible and found the assigned Gospel reading for that particular Sunday. It was the parable of the five wise and the five foolish virgins. I was horrified. I had never liked that parable. I had never *understood* it.

The parable tells of how ten virgins were hanging around waiting for the Bridegroom—Christ or God—to appear. On the chance that He might appear in the middle of the night and they might have to go out into the darkness to meet Him, five of the virgins had their lamps filled with oil, while the other five hadn't quite gotten around to it yet. Anyway, sure enough, in the middle of the night there was a knock on the door, and it was the servant announcing, "The Bridegroom's coming, the Bridegroom's coming. Come out into the night and meet the Bridegroom."

The five wise virgins immediately lit their lamps and started out the door, whereupon the five foolish virgins said to them, "Please share a little bit of your oil with us. We want to meet the Bridegroom too. Not all of your oil, not half, just a tiny bit of it." But the five wise virgins refused and proceeded out the door.

When they got to see the Bridegroom, what I had imagined He might say was, "You mean, miserable, nasty, stingy virgins! Why wouldn't you share at least a little bit of your oil with those poor, less fortunate virgins?" But that's not what He said. He said, in effect, "Oh, you wise, wonderful, beautiful virgins, I love you, and we are going to romp in the metaphorical hay for eternity. And as far as those foolish virgins go, they can gnash their teeth and rot in Hell forever."

The parable struck me as totally un-Christian. What on earth is Christianity about if it isn't about sharing? But I had to give a sermon on the parable, and that meant I had to think about it. Sometimes it is quite remarkable what can happen when we think. It didn't take me long to realize that the oil in this parable was a symbol for preparation, and that what Jesus was saying to us—realist that He was—was that we cannot share our preparation. You cannot do others' homework for them. Or if you do their homework, you cannot earn their degree for them, which is the symbol of their preparation. So we cannot give away our preparation. The only thing we can do—and it is often very difficult—is to try as best we can to impart to others a motive for them to prepare themselves. And I know of no way of doing that other than attempting to teach them how important they are, how beautiful and desirable they are in the eyes of God.

There is nothing that holds us back more from mental health, more from health as a society, and more from God than the sense that we all have of our unimportance, our unloveliness and undesirability. I am often amazed at how nimportant we consider ourselves to be. A decade ago I was a dinner party where the other guests were talking about a ous film producer and how he had left his mark on history.

Suddenly I blurted out, "We all leave our mark on history." And that stopped the dinner table conversation dead, as if I had said something grossly obscene.

In some ways, we do not like to think of ourselves as being important. To do so would be to place responsibility upon ourselves. We like to think that the people in the Kremlin are important. The congressmen and senators in Washington are important. And if we think of ourselves as ordinary and unimportant, we can't be responsible for history, can we? But whether we like it or not, we *are* that important and, for better or for worse, consciously or unconsciously, we will leave our mark on history. As the expression goes, "If not you, then who? And if not now, when?"

We all have this unrealistic sense of our unimportance, of our unloveliness and undesirability. About six years ago I went to Dallas to address a scientific congress. No sooner had I picked up my key at the reception desk of the hotel than, on my way to my room, I was accosted by a young man who said, "You're Dr. Peck, aren't you? My roommate wanted to come to this conference but was unable to. But he told me that if I happened to see you I should tell you that God forgives you."

It seemed a most bizarre thing to say. But after I had settled into my room, I got to thinking about it, and I realized that there was a part of me that still felt as if I were fifteen years old, covered with pimples, utterly unlovely and inadequate and certainly no one that any scientific congress would find worth listening to. But that part of me was not a manifestation of genuine humility. It was unhealthy and unrealistic. It was in need of healing. It needed to be given up, to be forgiven and cleansed.

So, I repeat, there is nothing that holds us back more from mental health, from health as a society, and from God than the sense we all have of our own unimportance, unloveliness, and undesirability. The reality is that God is the Bridegroom and that what He is saying to us is, "Come to bed with me."

But we are likely to respond, "No, no, no, I'm too fat."

And when God says, "You don't understand. I love you, I want you. You are beautiful. Come to bed with me," we are likely to continue to shrink away, proclaiming that we are too old or too young, too unimportant or too ugly, and not worthy.

Let us prepare ourselves. Let us do so by relearning how important we are, how beautiful we are, and how we are desired beyond our wildest imaginings. And let us, as best we can, go out into the world to teach others how important they are, how beautiful they are, and how they too are desired beyond their wildest imaginings.

CHAPTER SIX

Mythology and Human Nature

To most people, a myth is something that is untrue. But one of the advances we have made in psychiatry and psychology over the past sixty years or so—thanks largely to the work of Carl Jung and more recently to people like Joseph Campbell—is to discover that a myth is myth precisely because it is true.

Myths are stories that are found in every culture. Often they are fleshed out in slightly different ways in different cultures, but nonetheless the reason you find that same myth in culture after culture, age after age, is precisely because it embodies some great truth—virtually always about human nature. And because they have much to teach us about human nature, myths can be extremely useful for understanding ourselves.

LEGENDS

Many of the greatest archaeologists were considered in their early days to be crazy because they believed in legends or tales from the past that other people thought were not true.

Perhaps the best example is that of Heinrich Schliemann. As a boy, growing up in the 1830s, he worked as an apprentice in a grocery. An elderly man used to come to eat his lunch there, and while in his cups, he would reel off verse after verse of Homer's *Iliad.* Listening to him, young Heinrich became absolutely enchanted by the story of Troy. And he vowed that when he grew up, he was going to find Troy.

When he told that to people, they said, "Oh, don't be silly. Homer's *Iliad* is just a myth. There's no such place as Troy. It's a mythical place." Nonetheless, Heinrich believed that Troy was real, and he went into business in order to make enough money to fund his search. By the time he was thirty-six, he was a very wealthy man. That was when he retired from business and went off to look for Troy. And sure enough, after about a decade, he found it, on the western shores of Turkey, proving with that and later discoveries that the stories told in the *Iliad* were not mere myths, but had a basis in fact.

Another example of such an archaeologist is Edward Thompson. At the turn of the century, Thompson heard an old Mayan legend about a well used for the drowning of virgins—who had possibly first been loaded down with gold jewelry so they would sink—as part of a sacrifice to the god of rain, who supposedly lived at the bottom of the well. And he decided he was going to find that well, even though people said, "It's just a silly legend. There's no such well. It never really existed."

Thompson went to Mexico, where he learned about a great ruined Mayan city, deep in the Yucatán jungle, called Chichén Itzá, which means "the Mouth of the Well." He bought a plantation near the ruins and soon discovered that there were two huge wells or cenotes in the area. After analyzing the ruins he guessed that the larger one, about sixty yards in diameter, might be his quarry. He then went back home to Boston, frantically raised money from all his friends, bought dredging equipment and deep-sea diving apparatus, and even learned how to dive himself.

His dredging efforts proved futile; year after year, all he and his laborers dug up was basket upon basket of mud: no gold, no bones. Just as his money was running out, after about five years of effort, he dove down himself out of desperation and found the first bones. In fact, he discovered an entire cache of archaeological remains, including a lot of gold jewelry. He recouped his borrowed fortune and his self-respect. He had proved that the legend of virgins bedecked with jewelry and thrown into a well was in fact a true story after all.

I myself did not believe in the legend of Atlantis, the island civilization said to have sunk beneath the sea. But in 1978 my father and mother took my wife and me and our three children, and my brother, his wife, and their three children on a family reunion to Greece. As part of our trip we rented a boat and sailed around a group of Greek islands known as the Cyclades. The southernmost of those islands has two names —Thera, which is its Greek name, and Santorini, an Italian name—because the Italians conquered the islands in the thirteenth century. As we were sailing toward Santorini or Thera, my father read in a guidebook that there were some people who thought that this island might be Atlantis.

I laughed at the notion. But I began to choke back my laughter as we went through what looked like a gulf between two islands and immediately saw that we had obviously sailed right into the crater of a gigantic volcano about twenty miles in diameter. As we later explored a distant part of the island rim, we learned that there, one evening in 1967, a farmer had been plowing a field with his mule while his wife and children and a neighbor's wife were standing at the edge of the field gossiping. Suddenly the farmer vanished. They didn't know what had happened to him. They ran to where they had last seen him and heard some muffled cries. There was a great hole in the ground, and they realized that he had fallen into it. Not just any hole, mind you—he had fallen into a city. It was the city of Akrotiri, buried beneath volcanic ash. As it began to be excavated, the archaeologists were introduced to

an entire civilization different from any civilizations that had ever been discovered before. It dated to the Bronze Age and was a kind of blending of Greek and African cultures. It was the earliest place in the world ever to have picture windows. The discoveries there were so exciting that by the time we visited Greece a decade later, an entire new wing had already been added to the museum in Athens to house the art and other findings of Akrotiri.

So I have become a believer; I have been to Atlantis.

MYTHS AND FAIRY TALES

There is a difference between a legend and a myth. Legends are tales of the past which may or may not be true. The legend of Troy is true, the legend of the Sacred Well of Chichén Itzá is true. And I think the legend of Atlantis is true. True or not, in and of themselves legends like that of the well at Chichén Itzá do not necessarily have much to teach us about ourselves. But Homer's *Iliad* is not only a true legend; it is also a myth. Woven into this story of Troy are all kinds of meanings about human nature, and that is what distinguishes a myth from a mere legend.

There is also a distinction between a fairy tale and a myth. Santa Claus is just a fairy tale, an imaginary figure who has been around for only a couple of hundred years, and is known to only about one fifth of the globe. Dragons, on the other hand, are a myth. Long before anyone ever cooked up Santa Claus, Christian monks were illuminating dragons on the margins of the manuscripts they were painstakingly copying in their European monasteries. And so were Taoist monks in China, Buddhist monks in Japan, Hindus in India, and Muslims in Arabia.

Why dragons? Why are these mythical creatures so extraordinarily international and ecumenical?

The answer is: They are human-being symbols.

They are snakes with wings. Worms that can fly. And that's us. So, reptilelike, we slink close to the ground, mired in the mud of our sinful proclivities and narrow-minded cultural prejudices. And yet like birds—or angels—we have the capacity to soar in the heavens and transcend those same sinful proclivities and narrow-minded cultural prejudices.

One of the reasons for the popularity of dragons, I think, is that they are the simplest of myths. But even so, they are not simplistic. They are multidimensional, two-sided creatures, representing a paradox. And this is one of the reasons that myths exist—to capture the multidimensional, often paradoxical aspects of human nature.

Because myths are paradoxical and multidimensional, you cannot get into trouble believing in them. However, ordinary fairy tales tend to be one-dimensional and simplistic. And you can get into a lot of trouble believing in simplistic, one-dimensional fairy tales, just as simplistic thinking about anything in our lives can get us into trouble. Simplistic thinking afflicts all of us. We want things black and white. We want things to be either one thing or another, when, in fact, every aspect of our lives is at least two things simultaneously, if not half a dozen things.

For example, when I lecture, certain Christians in the audience sometimes ask me, "Dr. Peck, should homosexuals be ordained as priests?" They ask this question as if homosexuality were just this or just that, when, as far as I can ascertain from my limited psychiatric experience, there are some people who are homosexual by virtue of having grown up in extremely dysfunctional families (and therefore have a condition theoretically treatable, albeit only with difficulty), and there are other people who are homosexual, I am convinced, genetically, and whom God created homosexual. And then there are all kinds of mixtures in between, people who are homosexual as a result of both biological and psychological determinants. So when we regard homosexuality as just this or just that, we do violence to the subtlety and complexity of God's

creation. The answer to the question "Should homosexuals be ordained?" is the same as to the question "Should heterosexuals be ordained?" It depends on the homosexual. It depends on the heterosexual.

THE MYTH OF RESPONSIBILITY

Myths are a wonderful source of learning about the paradoxical, multidimensional, complex aspects of human nature. You might recall that in *The Road Less Traveled,* I mentioned the myth of Orestes, the son of Clytemnestra and Agamemnon. According to Homer, Clytemnestra took a lover and together they murdered Agamemnon. This put Orestes in what might be called a bit of a bind. The greatest obligation a young Greek boy had was to avenge his father's murder. Yet it was his mother who was responsible in this case. And the worst thing a Greek boy could possibly do was to murder his mother.

Orestes murdered his mother and her lover, thus avenging his father's death. But then he had to pay the price and was cursed by the gods with what were called the Furies, three harpies who continually surrounded him, cackling in his ear, giving him hallucinations, driving him to madness. For years and years, Orestes went around the world atoning for what he had done, while the Furies pursued him. Finally he asked the gods to relieve him of their curse. So a trial was held at which the god Apollo, who was Orestes' defense attorney, argued that the whole fiasco was the fault of the gods. Because Orestes hadn't really had any choice in the matter, consequently he should not be blamed for what he had done.

Whereupon Orestes stood up and countered Apollo. "It was I, not the gods, who murdered my mother," he said. "It was I who did this."

Never before had any human being assumed such total responsibility for his behavior, when he could have blamed it

on the gods. Hearing this, the gods deliberated and decided to lift the curse from Orestes. The Furies were transformed into the Eumenides, which means literally "Bearers of grace." Instead of being cackling, nasty, negative voices, they became voices of wisdom.

This myth represents the transformation of mental illness into extraordinary health. And the truth that the price of such a marvelous transformation is accepting the responsibility for ourselves and our behavior.

THE MYTH OF OMNIPOTENCE

Another revealing myth I spoke of in *The Different Drum* is that of Icarus. Icarus and his father sought to escape from prison by building wings of feathers and wax for themselves. When Icarus took flight, he wanted to keep flying to reach the sun. But of course, as soon as he even began to get near the sun, the heat melted his self-made wings and he plummeted to his destruction.

One of the meanings of this myth is the folly of attempting to assume godlike powers. The sun is often a symbol for God. Another meaning of the myth, I think therefore, is that we cannot get to God under our own power. We can get to God only with God pulling us up. And we can get into trouble, we can plummet to our destruction, if we think otherwise.

This is one of the problems people encounter when they discover "spiritual growth," and first fully realize they are on a spiritual journey. They start to think that they can direct it. They think if they go off to a monastery for a weekend retreat or take some classes in Zen meditation, or take up some Sufi dancing, or attend an EST workshop, then they'll reach nirvana. Unfortunately, that is not the way it works. It works only when God is doing the directing. And people can get into a certain kind of trouble—like Icarus—if they think they can do it on their own.

If you think you can plan your spiritual growth, it ain't going to happen. I don't mean to discount workshops or other forms of self-inquiry—they can be valuable. Do what you feel called to do, but also be prepared to accept that you don't necessarily know what you're going to learn. Be willing to be surprised by forces beyond your control, and realize that a major learning on the journey is the art of surrender.

THE MYTHS IN THE BIBLE

What is the Bible? Is it literal truth? Is it a collection of myths? Is it merely some outdated rules? What is it? And what relevance does it have in our lives?

I'm reminded of a woman who said to me, "I had great trouble dealing with the Bible as long as I thought of it as a book of orthodoxy. But then I suddenly realized one day that it is a book of paradoxy, and ever since then I have absolutely loved it."

Indeed the Bible is a collection of paradoxical stories, and as befits a collection of paradoxes, it is itself paradoxical—it is not just one thing. It is a mixture of legend, some of which is true and some of which is not true. It is a mixture of very accurate history and not so accurate history. It is a mixture of outdated rules and some pretty good rules. It is a mixture of myth and metaphor.

How are we to interpret the Bible? Although they place such importance on it, the fundamentalists, in my experience, strangely misuse the Bible. Actually, the term "fundamentalists" is a misnomer. The more proper term is "inerrantists," those who believe that the Bible is not only the divinely inspired word of God but the actual transcribed, unaltered word of God, and that it is subject to only one kind of literal interpretation, namely theirs. Such thinking, to my mind, only impoverishes the Bible.

I once heard Wayne Oates, one of the two founders of

the pastoral counseling movement, speaking of this problem in terms of a young man who had gouged out one of his eyes because Jesus said, "If your eye offend you, pluck it out." And Wayne said, "You know, I'm a good old Southern Baptist boy, and I dearly love my Lord Jesus, but I sure as hell wish He had never said that."

The problem isn't with what Jesus said. The problem is that this young man took what He said literally. Jesus, of course, was speaking metaphorically. He did not mean for you to cut off your arm or gouge out your eye. What He meant was that if there is something in your way, something that stands between you and mental health or spiritual growth, you should get rid of it. Don't sit around complaining about it.

So the Bible is not always meant to be interpreted literally. A great deal of it is metaphor and myth, subject to a variety of complex, and often paradoxical, interpretations.

THE MYTH OF GOOD AND EVIL

Among the most complicated and multidimensional is Genesis 3, the myth of Adam and Eve in the Garden of Eden. Myths, like dreams, can work by what Freud called condensation. A single dream can have condensed into it not just one but two or three different meanings. This certainly applies to the myth of the Garden of Eden. It is an extraordinary story that contains not just one profound truth, not two, not three, but more than a dozen profound truths to teach us about human nature.

Although the fundamentalists—the inerrantists and creationists—may not like it, one of the things that the Eden myth teaches us about is evolution. This doesn't mean that God didn't have a hand in evolution; indeed, I think that He/She very much did. Specifically, Genesis 3 is a myth about how we human beings evolved into consciousness. I have already spoken in the first chapter of some of the conse-

quences of this evolution, so pointedly elucidated through this great story: our shyness, our self-consciousness, our sense of separation from nature, and our need to continue evolving into ever greater consciousness. Now let me note that with consciousness comes the awareness of good and evil.

So another thing this wonderfully rich story teaches us is about the power of choice. Until we ate the apple from the Tree of the Knowledge of Good and Evil, we didn't have real choice. We did not have free will until that moment described in Genesis 3 when we became conscious, and having become conscious, we were faced with the choice of going after the truth or going after the lie. Thus the Eden story also has a great deal to do with the whole genesis of good and evil. You can't have evil unless you have choice. When God allowed us free will, He inevitably allowed the entrance of evil into the world.

It so happens that another, even earlier myth, Genesis 1, also has something to say about evolution as well as good and evil. It tells how God first created the firmament, and then the land and the waters, and then the plants and the animals. It is the same sequence as that suggested by geology and paleontology. As far as scientists can determine, that is the sequence of evolution, even though we can't say it all happened in seven days.

A whole new meaning to Genesis 1 occurred to me when I remembered that God first created light and He looked at it and saw that it was good. So He created the land and saw that it was good. And so He separated the land and the water and saw that *that* was good too, so He went on to create the plants and the animals. And when He saw that they too were good, He then created human beings. Thus, I think the impulse to do good has something to do with what creativity is all about.

Similarly, the impulse to do evil is destructive rather than creative. The choice between good and evil, creativity and destruction, is our own. And ultimately, we must take that responsibility and accept its consequences.

THE MYTH OF THE HERO

Joseph Campbell has done much to teach us about the truth that resides in myths. One of the great myths of the world which Campbell has been particularly effective in elucidating is called "The Myth of the Birth of the Hero," from his book *The Quest of the Hero.* As is typical of myths, this one appears in slightly different variations in different cultures, but nonetheless its bare bones are the same. There is always a sun god and a moon goddess who mate, and they produce a child who is always a boy. (Perhaps we can alter this little piece of the story as time goes by.) In growing up, the boy goes through a period of great struggle and turmoil and pain, from which he emerges as a hero.

What does this myth mean? First, let me explain what a hero is. A hero is defined as the person who can solve a problem or problems that other people can't. Let's say, for example, there is a king who has a wonderful country, or it would be wonderful if it weren't for this mean, miserable, nasty dragon that's making everybody's life difficult. So the king decides that whoever can slay the dragon will get the hand of the beautiful Princess Esmerelda in marriage. Word travels throughout the land, and one by one the bravest Harvard- and Yale-educated knights of the realm come out to do battle with the dragon, and one by one they get eaten. The situation becomes truly dire and all seems lost, when out of the woods of the Bronx there comes a young Jewish man educated at NYU who has a certain kind of smarts. He figures out how to slay the dragon and does. The king isn't necessarily terribly happy about having a Jewish son-in-law; nonetheless he is true to his word. So the young man marries the beautiful Princess Esmerelda, and they live happily ever after in a wonderful country.

This young man, therefore, is the hero because he solved the problem that others couldn't: in this case, how to slay the

dragon. But how did he come by such smarts? Remember that the true hero, according to the myth, must be the offspring of the sun god and the moon goddess. Thus this myth is also about masculinity and femininity, because, typically, the sun god and the moon goddess symbolize masculinity and femininity.

We have long been fascinated by the masculine/feminine dichotomy, in legend and in life. For example, a very popular area of inquiry these days is the relationship of the right brain and the left brain to different kinds of thinking. As that would apply to the "myth of the birth of the hero," the sun god stands for masculinity, for light and reason and rational scientific knowledge—namely, analytic left-brain kind of thinking. And the moon goddess stands for femininity, for darkness and feeling and intuition—namely, the right-brain kind of thinking. Having mated, these two have produced a child that has *both* the sun god and the moon goddess in him—or her. So then, this is a myth about what we call *androgyny.*

The obvious conclusion is that we can become heroes only if we learn how to use both our femininity and our masculinity—our left brain and our right brain. This is something that very few people ever learn to do. Instead, most of us, as we are growing up, learn to emphasize our masculinity at the expense of our femininity, or to elevate our femininity at the expense of our masculinity. Or we may learn how to approach certain kinds of problems in a masculine, left-brained sort of way, and certain other kinds of problems in a feminine, right-brained sort of way. But very seldom do we learn how to approach the same problem with *both* our right brain and our left brain.

This integration of our masculinity and our femininity is achieved very painfully. It is the struggle that the child goes through in the myth in the course of his or her growing up. But if we can go through this struggle of integration and learn how to approach the same problem with both our right brain and our left brain simultaneously, with both our masculinity

and our femininity, then we too can be heroes. We too will be able to solve problems that the world has not yet been able to solve—a world that is desperately in need of heroes and solutions.

THE CHOICE OF INTERPRETATION

Let me return to the matter of the Bible and emphasize how often we have a choice of how to interpret its stories. We can always interpret them literally. Take, for instance, the story of Lot's wife, also in Genesis. When God destroyed the sinful cities of Sodom and Gomorrah, He permitted Lot and his wife to flee on the condition that they not look back. But Lot's wife did look back and she was instantly turned into a pillar of salt. Taken literally, this is simply a story of the kind of punishment we will receive and what can happen to us if we disobey God.

Over the past hundred years there has developed a new school of "scientific" biblical interpretation. It proposes "rational" explanations for the miraculous happenings described in the Bible—like the parting of the Red Sea—suggesting, for instance, that there are places where the Red Sea is very shallow and when the conjunction of the tides is just right once every hundred years or so, it can actually be waded across. This school has also had its hand in the story of Lot's wife. So the story is footnoted in the New Oxford Bible with the comment that it is an "old tradition to account for bizarre salt formations in the area such as may be seen today on Jebel Usdun."

But this supposedly scientific explanation somehow left me feeling cold. So I got to thinking more about it and wondering why God had not wanted Lot or his wife to look back. What is wrong with looking back? Then I got to thinking about people who spend much of their lives looking back—in regret —and what can happen to them when they become obsessed

with the past. And it dawned on me that such people become essentially pickled, as if they had turned into a living pillar of salt. With this metaphorical interpretation, I began to see in the story of Lot's wife deep meaning and a profound statement about human nature.

I sometimes tell people that one of the great blessings of my life was an almost total absence of religious education, because I had nothing to overcome. I say "almost" because I did go to Sunday school for one day. For some reason, when I was eight and my brother was twelve, my parents decided that we needed a religious education. So they packed us off to Sunday school, and I can remember the day very well, because I had to color a picture of Abraham sacrificing Isaac. Perhaps I was a bit of a psychiatrist even back then, because I quickly concluded that God must be crazy for wanting Abraham to kill his son, and that Abraham must have been crazy for even thinking about doing it. And above all, Isaac must have been crazy for just lying there in my coloring book with this beatific expression on his face, waiting to be sliced open.

As it turned out, my brother refused to go back, and with his twelve-year-old power, he was able to make that stick. So I rode his twelve-year-old coattails out of Sunday school, and that was the extent of my religious education. And I still do not think the story of Abraham and Isaac is appropriate for eight-year-olds, because—if you subscribe to Jean Piaget's stages of mental development—children of that age tend to think concretely or literally and have not yet developed much capacity for interpretation. But just as there can be the wrong age for a story, so can there also be a right age and a correct time for interpretation.

Now that I am in late middle age, the story of Abraham sacrificing Isaac has profound meaning for me. I believe it is a most important story for all of us with children who are adolescent or older. Interpreted metaphorically, this wonderful story—or myth—teaches us that the time comes when we have to give up our children. Yes, they were gifts to us and

given unto our keeping—but not forever. Holding on to them beyond a certain point can be extremely destructive to them, and ourselves as well. We need to learn how to return the gift and entrust our children to God. They no longer belong to us. They are God's children now.

CHAPTER SEVEN

Spirituality and Human Nature

People sometimes ask me the most impossible questions —for example, "Dr. Peck, what is human nature?" And because my parents raised me to be an obliging child, I try to come up with answers to such impossible questions, and the first answer I give is: "Human nature is to go to the bathroom in your pants."

It really is. That is exactly the way each one of us started out, doing what came naturally and letting go whenever we felt like it. But then what happened along about the time we were two years old or so, our mother or possibly our father—although usually it is our mother who gets the message across—came to us and said, "Hey, you're a nice kid and I like you a lot, but I'd kind of appreciate it if you would clean up your act."

Initially, such a request makes absolutely no sense whatsoever to the child. What makes sense is to do what comes naturally and let go whenever one feels like it. Moreover, the result is always interesting and different each time. Sometimes it comes in a form that you can write on the walls with, and sometimes it's in hard little balls you can toss out of the crib and watch bounce on the floor. But it makes absolutely no

sense to do what is profoundly *unnatural,* which is to keep a tight fanny and somehow manage to get to the bathroom just in time to see this beautiful stuff flushed away and put to no useful purpose.

However, if there is a good relationship between the child and its mother, and the mother is patient and not too demanding or too controlling—and unfortunately, these circumstances often are not met, which is why psychiatrists are so into toilet training—but if these circumstances are met, the child says to itself: "You know, Mommy is a nice old gal and she's been awful good to me these last couple of years, and I'd like to do something to pay her back. I'd like to give her some kind of gift of my appreciation. But I'm just a puny, helpless two-year-old, so what could I possibly have to give her that she might want or need—except this one crazy thing?"

So the child—as a gift to its mother—starts doing the unnatural and keeping that tight fanny and going to the toilet. But look what happens here over the next few years. Something absolutely marvelous. By the time the child reaches the age of four or five, if in a moment of stress or fatigue it forgets and has an accident, it feels *unnatural* about the messy business whereas it has come to feel utterly *natural* about going to the toilet. In this brief span of time, as a gift of love to its mother, the child has changed its nature.

INSTINCT AND HUMAN NATURE

So the other response I most commonly make when people ask me, "Dr. Peck, what is human nature?" is to say there is no such thing. And that, above all else, is our glory as human beings.

What distinguishes us humans most from other creatures is not our opposing thumb, or our wonderful larynx which is capable of speech, or our huge cerebral cortex, but it is our dramatic relative lack of instincts or preformed, preset inher-

ited patterns of behavior, which give other creatures a much more fixed nature than we have.

I live in Connecticut on the shores of a large lake and to that lake, every March when the ice melts, there comes a flock of gulls, and every December when the lake freezes over, the gulls depart, presumably for parts south. I never used to know where they went, but some friends have recently told me that it's Florence, Alabama.

Whether there are migratory gulls or not, scientists who have studied migratory birds have come to realize that they are actually able to navigate by the stars. They have built into them—through heredity—complex patterns of celestial navigation which enable them to land in Florence, Alabama, right on the dot every time. The only problem is that there is no particular freedom about it. The gulls can't say, "I think this winter I'd like to spend in Bermuda or the Bahamas or Barbados." It's either Florence, Alabama, or nothing.

What distinguishes us humans beings, on the other hand, is the extraordinary freedom and variability of our behaviors. Given the wherewithal, we can go to the Bahamas or Bermuda or Barbados. Or we can do something totally unnatural and, in the middle of winter, go north to Stowe, Vermont, or to the mountains of Colorado and slide down icy hills on little slats of wood or fiberglass. This extraordinary freedom to do the different and often seemingly unnatural is the most salient feature of our human nature.

Nowhere was this better described than in *The Sword in the Stone* by T. H. White. To paraphrase and condense a tale from this wonderful book, it was back in the very early days, when all of the earth's creatures were still in embryonic form. God called all the little embryos together one afternoon and said, "I'm going to give each of you whatever three things you want. So come up here one by one and ask for whatever three things you want and I will give them to you."

So the first little embryo came up and said, "God, I'd like to have hands and feet in the shape of spades so I can dig

myself a safe home underneath the ground, and I'd like to have a thick, furry coat to keep me warm in the winter, and I would like to have some sharp front teeth so I can chew on the grasses."

And God said, "Fine, go and be a woodchuck."

Then the next little embryo came up and said, "God, what I like is the water, and I'd like to have a flexible body so I can swim around in it. I'd also like to breathe underwater with some kind of gills, and I'd like a system that will keep me warm no matter what the temperature of the water is."

And God said, "Fine, go be a fish."

God went through all the little embryos until there was just one left, which seemed to be a particularly shy little embryo—perhaps for the same biblical reasons I've already discussed. It was so shy that God had to motion it forward and ask, "All right, last little embryo, what three things would you like?" And it said, "Well, I don't want to seem pre-presumptuous or anything. It's not that I'm not . . . ah . . . grateful, because I am. But . . . but I was wondering if maybe . . . if it was all right with You . . . I could stay just the way I am—an embryo. Maybe sometime later when I'm smart enough to know the three things I really want, I can ask You for them then. . . . Or maybe . . . if You want me to become a certain something, you can give me the three things that You think I need."

And God smiled and said, "Ah, you are *human*. And because you have chosen to remain a perpetual embryo, I will give you dominion over all of the other creatures."

Of course, most of us throw our embryohood away. As we get older, we become set in our ways, fixed in our nature. Watching my parents and other people as they entered their fifties and sixties, it invariably seemed to me when I was young that they became less interested in new things, more and more convinced of the rightness of their own opinions and worldviews.

Indeed, that was the way I thought it had to be, until I

reached twenty. During the summer of that year, I went to live with the noted author John Marquand, who was sixty-five at the time, and he blew my mind. I found that this sixty-five-year-old man was interested in everything, including me, and no sixty-five-year-old had ever been seriously interested in unimportant little twenty-year-old me before. He and I used to argue late into the night most evenings, and I could actually win some of those arguments. I could actually change Mr. Marquand's mind. In fact, by the end of the summer, I would see Mr. Marquand changing his mind about three or four times a week. I realized that this man, rather than having grown old mentally, had grown younger, and was more open and more flexible than most children or adolescents.

It was at that point, for the first time, I realized that we do not have to grow old mentally. We do have to grow old physically. All of us will eventually become decrepit and die, but most of us do not have to stop growing mentally. So it is that—while we may usually toss it away—this capacity for ongoing change and transformation is the most salient feature of our human nature.

THE STAGES OF SPIRITUAL GROWTH

Our unique human capacity for change and transformation is reflected in our human spirituality. Throughout the ages, deep-thinking people looking at themselves have come to discern that we are not all at the same place spiritually or religiously. There are different stages of spiritual growth or religious development. The person best known today for writing on the subject is Professor James Fowler at the Candler School of Theology at Emory University, author of, among others, a book called *Stages of Faith*.

Fowler describes six stages of spiritual growth, which I have refined into four, but we are saying essentially the same thing. His work is much more scholarly than mine, filled with

academic references to the works of other stage theorists such as Piaget, Erikson, and Kohlberg. I arrived at my own understanding of these stages not out of book learning but through experience—in particular, several of what I've come to call "noncomputing" experiences. The first of these occurred about the time I was fifteen when I decided to visit some of the Christian churches in my area. To some extent I was interested in checking out what this Christianity business was all about, but primarily I was interested in checking out the girls.

The first church I decided to visit was just a few blocks down the street, and it had the most famous preacher of the day, a man whose Sunday sermons were broadcast over every radio wavelength in the land. At the age of fifteen, I had no trouble spotting him as a phony. However, I also went up the street in the opposite direction to another church which also had a well-known preacher, although not nearly as famous as the first. His name was George Buttrick, and at the age of fifteen, I had absolutely no trouble spotting him as a holy man, a true man of God.

My poor fifteen-year-old brain didn't quite know what to make of this. Here was the most famous Christian preacher of the day, and as far as I could see at fifteen, I was already well ahead of him in my spiritual growth. But then, in the same Christian church, there was another preacher who was obviously light-years ahead of me. It didn't seem to make any sense, didn't seem to compute, which is one of the reasons I turned my back on the Christian church for the next twenty-five years or so.

Another one of those noncomputing experiences occurred more gradually later in my life. After I had been practicing psychotherapy for some years, a strange pattern began to emerge. If religious people came to see me because they were in pain and trouble and difficulty, and they really got involved in therapy, then—more often than not—they would leave therapy as questioners, doubters, skeptics, agnostics,

possibly even atheists. But if atheists or agnostics or skeptics came to me in pain, trouble, and difficulty and they really got involved in therapy, then—more often than not—they would leave therapy having become deeply religious or spiritually concerned people.

This pattern just made no sense, did not compute. Same therapist, same therapy, successful yet utterly opposite results. I couldn't figure this out, until it slowly began to dawn on me that we are not all *at the same place* spiritually and that there are these different stages. We must look at them with caution and flexibility, however, because God has this rather peculiar way of interfering with my categories sometimes, and people do not always fall quite as neatly into my psychospiritual pigeonholes as I might like them to do.

At the beginning—the bottom, if you wish—is Stage One, which I label "chaotic/antisocial." This stage probably encompasses about twenty percent of the population, including those whom I call people of the lie. In general, this is a stage of absent spirituality and the people at this stage are utterly unprincipled. I call it antisocial because while they are capable of *pretending* to be loving, actually all of their relationships with their fellow human beings are self-serving and covertly, if not overtly, manipulative. Chaotic because, being unprincipled, they have no mechanism that might govern them other than their own will. Since the unharnessed will can go this way one day and that way the next, their being is consequently chaotic. Because it is, the people in this stage will frequently be found in trouble or difficulty, and often in jails or hospitals or out on the street. Some of them, however, may actually be quite self-disciplined, from time to time, in the service of their ambition and may rise to positions of considerable prestige and power. They may even become presidents or famous preachers.

The people in Stage One may occasionally get in touch with the chaos of their own being. And when they do, it is perhaps the single most painful experience a human can have.

Generally, they just ride it out, but if this painful experience continues, they may kill themselves, and I think that some unexplained suicides may fall into this category. Or occasionally, they may convert to Stage Two. Such conversions are usually—I say usually because there are always exceptions—very sudden and dramatic. It is as if God literally reaches down and grabs that soul and yanks it up in a quantum leap. Something astonishing happens to that person and it is usually totally unconscious. If it could be made conscious, I think it would be as if that person said to himself or herself, "I am willing to do anything—*anything*—in order to liberate myself from this chaos, even submit myself to an institution for my governance."

And so it is that they convert to Stage Two, which I have labeled "formal/institutional." I label it institutional because people in it are dependent upon an institution for their governance. For some the institution may be a prison. In such places, in my experience, there is always a prisoner who, when the new psychiatrist comes in to work in the prison, gathers a group of fellow inmates together for a group therapy session, who is the warden's right-hand man, yet who somehow manages never to get a shiv stuck between his ribs. He is a model prisoner and a model citizen. Because he is so well adjusted in the institution, he is always paroled at the first possible opportunity. Immediately he becomes a walking crime wave, and within a week of his parole, he is rearrested and put right back behind bars, where once again he becomes a model citizen with the walls of the institution around him to organize his being.

For others the institution may be the military. This is a profoundly positive role the military plays in our and other societies. There are tens of thousands of people who would lead chaotic lives were it not for the rather paternalistic and in some ways maternalistic structuring of the military.

For still others, the institution to which they submit themselves for their governance may be a highly organized business corporation. But for most people, it is the church.

Indeed, the majority of churchgoers fall into Stage Two, the formal/institutional stage. Although there are gradations and nothing is absolutely cut-and-dried within these stages, certain things tend to characterize people's religious behavior in Stage Two. As mentioned, they are dependent on the institution of the church for their governance, and I call it formal because they are very attached to the forms of the religion.

Stage Two people become very, very upset if someone starts changing forms or rituals, altering their liturgy or introducing new hymns. For example, in the Episcopal church, in the mid-seventies, it was decided that there might be some alternative ways to say the same things on different Sundays, and many people were so up in arms that a full-blown schism resulted. Another example: In the 1960s, the Vatican II Council of the Roman Catholic hierarchy led to profound changes in that church, and thirty years later Pope John Paul II still seems to be in the process of trying to undo those changes. And it's not just Episcopalians and Catholics. This kind of turmoil goes on in every denomination of every religion in the world. And it's no wonder that people in Stage Two become so upset when the forms of their religion are changed, because it's precisely those forms that they depend upon to some extent for their liberation from chaos.

Another thing that tends to characterize people's religious behavior in this stage is that their vision of God is almost entirely that of an external being. They have very little understanding of that half of God which lives inside each of us—what theologians term immanent—the dwelling divinity within the human spirit. They almost totally think of God as up there, out there. They generally envision God along the masculine model, and while they believe Him to be a loving being, they also ascribe to Him a certain kind of punitive power which He is not afraid to use on appropriate occasions. It is a vision of God as a giant benevolent cop in the sky. And in many ways, this is exactly the kind of God that people in Stage Two need.

Let's say that two people who are firmly rooted in Stage

Two meet and marry and have children. They raise their children in a stable home because stability tends to be of great value to people in Stage Two. They treat their children with dignity and importance because the church says that children are important and should be treated with dignity. And while their love may be a little bit legalistic or unimaginative at times, nonetheless they are loving because the church tells them to be loving and teaches them a little something about how to be loving.

What happens to a child raised in such a stable, loving home and treated with dignity and importance? That child will absorb his parents' religious principles—be they Christian, Buddhist, Muslim, or Jewish—like mother's milk. By the time the child reaches adolescence, these principles will have become virtually engraved on his heart, or "internalized," to use the psychiatric term. But once this happens, they will have become principled, self-governing human beings who no longer need to depend upon an institution for their governance. It is at this time, which in healthy human development is usually at adolescence, that they start saying, "Who needs these silly myths and superstitions and this fuddy-duddy old institution?" They will then begin—often to their parents' utterly unnecessary horror and chagrin —to fall away from the church, having become doubters or agnostics or atheists. At this point they have begun to convert to Stage Three, which I call "skeptic/individual."

Again speaking generally, people in Stage Three are ahead of people in Stage Two in their spirituality, although they are not religious in the ordinary sense of the word. They are not the least bit antisocial. Often they are deeply involved in society. They are the kinds of people who tend to make up the backbone of organizations like Physicians for Social Responsibility or the ecology movement. They make committed and loving parents. Frequently they are scientists, and certainly scientific-minded. Invariably they are truth seekers. And if they seek truth deeply enough, and widely enough, as

I've suggested, they do begin to find what they are looking for, and get to fit enough pieces of truth to catch glimpses of the big picture and see that it is not only very beautiful, but that it strangely resembles many of those primitive myths and superstitions their Stage Two parents or grandparents believed in. And it is at this point that they begin to convert to Stage Four, which I call "mystical/communal."

I use the word "mystical" to describe this stage even though it is a word that is hard to define and one that has been given a pejorative connotation in our culture and is usually misdefined. But certain things can be said about mystics. They are people who have seen a kind of cohesion beneath the surface of things. Throughout the ages, mystics have seen connections between men and women, between humans and other creatures, between people walking the earth and those who aren't even here. Seeing that kind of interconnectedness beneath the surface, mystics of all cultures and religions have spoken of things in terms of unity and community. They also have always spoken in terms of paradox.

Mystical has as its root the word *mystery*. Mystics are people who love mystery. They love to solve mysteries, and yet at the same time, they know the more they solve, the more mystery they are going to encounter. But they are very comfortable living in a world of mystery whereas people in Stage Two are most uncomfortable when things aren't cut-and-dried.

These principles hold true not only for Christianity and not only in the United States but in all nations, cultures, and religions. Indeed, one of the things that characterize all of the world's great religions is that they seem to have a capacity to speak to people in both Stage Two and Stage Four as if the very teachings of a given religion have two different translations. To take an example from Judaism, Psalm 111 ends with "The fear of the Lord is the beginning of wisdom." At Stage Two this is translated to mean, "When you start fearing that big cop in the sky, you really wise up." That's true. At Stage

Four it is translated to mean, "The awe of God shows you the way to enlightenment." And that's also true.

"Jesus is my Savior" is a favorite statement among Christians and provides another example. Among Stage Two people, that tends to be translated to mean that Jesus is a kind of fairy godmother who can rescue me whenever I get in trouble as long as I can remember to call upon His name. And that's true; He will do exactly that. Whereas in Stage Four, people read it to mean that Jesus, through His life and death, taught me the way that I myself must follow for my salvation. And that is also true.

As I noted, this quality of dual translation holds true not just for Christianity and Judaism but also for Islam, Taoism, Buddhism, and Hinduism. Indeed, I think it is what makes them great religions. They all give room for both the Stage Two and the Stage Four believers.

ANTAGONISM AND FAITH

The greatest problem of these different stages—and the biggest reason it is so important to understand them—is the sense of threat that exists between people at such different points on the spiritual journey.

To some extent, we all may be threatened by the people still in the stage we have just left, because we may not yet be sure or secure in our new identity. But for the most part the threat goes the other way, and we particularly tend to be threatened by people in the stages ahead of us.

People in Stage One will often tend to appear like cool cats—seemingly nothing bothers them very much. But if you are able to penetrate that facade, you find they are terrified of virtually everything and everyone.

People in Stage Two are not particularly threatened by the Stage One people: the sinners. They *love* the sinners, seeing them as fertile ground for their ministrations. But they

www.thomascranelibrary.
org

Title: Further along the
road less traveled : the
Author: Peck, M. Scott
(Morgan Scott), 1936-2005
Item ID: 31641008282968
Date due: 7/8/2023,23:59

Title: Making habits,
breaking habits : why we
do things
Author: Dean, Jeremy,
1974-
Item ID: 31641005328640
Date due: 7/8/2023,23:59

Title: 5000 B.C. and other
philosophical fantasies
Author: Smullyan, Raymond
M.
Item ID: 31641000436745
Date due: 7/8/2023,23:59

tend to be threatened by the skeptic individualists of Stage Three, and more than anything, by the Stage Four people, who seem to believe in the same things they believe in and yet believe them with a kind of freedom they find absolutely terrifying.

Stage Three people, the skeptics, are not particularly threatened by the unprincipled people of Stage One, or by the Stage Two people, whom they simply toss off as superstitious idiots. But once again, they tend to be threatened by the Stage Four people, who seem to be scientific-minded like them and know how to write good footnotes, yet still somehow believe in this crazy God business. And if you mentioned the word "conversion" to the Stage Three people, they would see a vision of a missionary arm-twisting a heathen and they would go through the roof.

I have used the word "conversion" rather freely to describe the transition from one stage of spirituality to the next. It is, however, a markedly different experience in each case. Conversions from Stage One to Stage Two are usually very sudden, very dramatic. Conversions from Stage Three to Stage Four, on the other hand, tend to be gradual. For example, I was in the company of Paul Vitz, the author of *Psychology as Religion,* when he was asked when he had become a Christian. He scratched his head and said, "Well, it was along about somewhere between '72 and '76." Compare that to the Stage Two man who says, "It was eight p.m. on the night of the seventeenth of August!" Obviously, a different sort of phenomenon is going on here.

I have also spoken of Stage Three people—the skeptics and doubters—as being spiritually ahead of the vast majority of churchgoers of Stage Two. These people have also undergone a "conversion"—that is, a conversion to skepticism and doubt, which is something equivalent to what the Bible calls a "circumcision of the heart." They are ahead of the Stage Two man who acknowledges Jesus to be his Lord and Savior at exactly eight p.m. on the night of the seventeenth of Au-

gust, but may yet have to undergo a conversion to peace or to justice. Conversion is not a onetime thing. Like any kind of spiritual growth, it is a continuing process. I expect and hope to continue to be converted until the day I die.

APPEARANCES CAN BE DECEIVING

I'd like us to be reminded at this point how God can interfere with my categories, and how we need to be both cautious and flexible when we make diagnoses of where our fellow humans—and we ourselves—fall in this spectrum of spiritual growth. There are quite a number of people who superficially appear to be in one stage when, in fact, they are someplace else entirely. For example, there are people who attend church and who, to the naked eye, appear to be in Stage Two, but who inwardly are dissatisfied with their religion and are skeptical of it and have become scientific-minded. This is so common that entire congregations have been created which are only faintly religious. A lot of Methodist and Presbyterian ministers in wealthy suburban communities don't talk to their congregations about God on Sunday mornings, but about psychology. God forbid they should talk about God. It would be too threatening. Then again, there are people who talk about God but are not the least bit religious or spiritual. These are people who may appear to be in Stage Four, who can wear Stage Four veneer—like certain cult leaders—but who, in fact, are Stage One criminals.

Similarly, not all scientists are Stage Three people. They too know how to write good footnotes, but only in an extremely narrow area of research where they have the scientific doctrine down so pat that they feel very safe while ignoring all the mystery of the world. Such scientists are really Stage Two people.

There are also people whom psychiatrists refer to as bor-

derline personalities. One of the things that characterize them is that they seem to have a foot in Stage One and a foot in Stage Two, and a hand in Stage Three, and a finger in Stage Four. They're all over the place. They lack coherency, and that, in a sense, is why we call them borderline: they don't have much in the way of borders or boundaries.

Furthermore, there are people who might begin to enter a more advanced stage, then slip backwards. We actually have a name for the person who slips back from Stage Two to Stage One—"backslider." Typically, he might be a man who ran around drinking and gambling and chasing after women and leading a dissolute life, until one day he bumped into some fundamentalist folk who had a chat with him and he was saved. For the next couple of years, he leads a sober, God-fearing, righteous life and then he vanishes one day, and nobody knows where he is until six months later when he is discovered back in the gutter or gambling house. His church friends talk with him and he is saved again and does pretty well for another couple of years, until he backslides once more.

There are also people bouncing back and forth between Stage Two and Stage Three. An example of such a person might be a churchgoer who says, "Of course I still believe in God. I mean, look how beautiful nature is—those hills turning green and the white clouds flying and the flowers blooming. Obviously, no human intelligence could have created such beauty, so there *must* have been a divine intelligence that set all this in motion millions and millions of years ago. But you know, it's just as beautiful out on the golf course as it is in church on Sunday morning and I can worship my God out on the golf course just as well."

So this man chooses the golf course over church. And all is well, until his business undergoes a mild reversal and he says, "Oh my God, I haven't been going to church! I haven't been praying!" He goes back to church and starts praying very hard, until after a couple of years there is an upturn in the

economy—for all I know perhaps because he's been praying so hard—and he begins to drift back onto his Stage Three golf course.

Then there are people bouncing between Stage Three and Stage Four. I had a friend like that named Theodore. By day Theodore had an absolutely brilliant scientific mind with a precisely honed rational capacity, and was probably just about the dullest human being I ever had to listen to. But occasionally in the evening Theodore would have a little bit to drink or he would smoke a little bit of pot and all of a sudden he would start talking about life and death and meaning and glory. He would become so spirit-filled that I would sit at his feet enthralled. But the next morning he would come in to see me and say, "I don't know what got into me last night. I was talking about the craziest things. I've got to stop drinking or smoking pot." I do not mean to bless the use of drugs but simply to indicate that in his particular case, they seemed to loosen him up enough to flow in the direction in which he was being called, but from which, in the cold clear light of day, he would retreat in abject terror right back into his accustomed Stage Three rationality.

HUMAN DEVELOPMENT AND SPIRITUAL GROWTH

While it is possible when we are not yet firmly rooted to backslide, it is not possible for us to skip over any of the stages of spiritual development, any more than it is possible to skip over any of the purely psychological stages of normal human development. And in fact, these two patterns of growth follow a similar progression. For example, children up until the age of five or so are pretty much Stage One creatures. They haven't yet internalized the difference between right and wrong, and they will lie, cheat, steal, and manipulate with abandon. It's hardly remarkable that many of them grow up to be adult liars, cheats, thieves, and manipulators. In fact,

it's harder to explain how so many of them grow up to be honest, decent, law-abiding folk.

From about the age of five to twelve, children tend to be Stage Two creatures. They may be mischievous, but they're not seriously rebellious. Basically, they think that the way Mommy and Daddy want things to be done is the way things ought to be done. They are great imitators and followers. But with adolescence, all hell breaks loose. Everything that Mommy and Daddy say—which always used to be like the word of God—is now subject to rebuttal and rejection. This is the stage of individual questioning and of skepticism. And Stage Four cannot begin until adolescence has been worked through.

If none of the stages can be skipped over, movement through certain stages can proceed more swiftly for some people than for others. For instance, I have a friend who was raised in a Stage Two Irish Catholic home, and when he was fifteen, just as he was entering his adolescent rebellion period, his father's company transferred the family to Amsterdam. There my friend was sent to a Dutch Jesuit school. The Dutch Jesuits are very sophisticated people. Indeed, one of Pope John Paul II's enduring problems has been to figure out how to excommunicate all of Holland, because the entire country leans remarkably toward a Stage Four culture. So my friend fell into the hands of these sophisticated and accepting Jesuits, who encouraged his doubt, and led him in his doubting. When he came back from Amsterdam at the age of nineteen, he was already in early Stage Four.

While it is possible to move quickly through the stages, it is also quite possible to get stuck. Years ago when I was a consultant to a convent, I interviewed their postulants before they were clothed as novices, the first very formal process of determining whether one is really cut out to be a monk or nun. I remember one such postulant in particular, a woman in her mid-forties, whom I was asked to interview because the novice mistress was concerned about her; while she was an

ideal postulant, the other postulants and novices just didn't like her that much.

As I was interviewing this woman, it hit me that it was not like having a forty-five-year-old woman in my office. Her carriage and manner were more like those of a slightly silly eight-year-old girl. When I asked her about her spirituality, what I heard didn't sound original. It sounded like some good little girl reeling off her well-learned catechism. Being a psychiatrist, after a while I said, of course, "Tell me about your childhood."

And she said, "Oh, I just had a wonderful, wonderfully happy childhood." This naturally made me suspicious immediately, because no one has had a wonderful, happy childhood. So I said, "Go on, what was so wonderful about it?" She then told me that she had a sister who was just a year older than she was, and that they were very close and used to play all the time. The sister had invented a ghost called Oogle, and one time she and her sister were in the bathtub together and her sister exclaimed, "Watch out! Oogle is coming!" So she ducked underneath the water to get away from Oogle, and her mother beat her. I asked her why and she said, "Because I got my hair wet."

Then I learned that her mother had gotten multiple sclerosis when this postulant was twelve, and died when she was eighteen. How can you have an adolescent rebellion against a woman who not only would beat you for getting your hair wet but also has a fatal illness at the time when you ordinarily begin your adolescence, and dies before you're old enough to sort it out? If you can't have an adolescent rebellion, you will likely become fixated in Stage Two. That is what had happened to this woman.

CHECK YOUR DUNGEON

Another important thing to know about the stages of spiritual growth is that no matter how far we develop, all of us

retain vestiges of earlier stages, just as we retain our vestigial appendix. There is a Stage One segment lurking down in the dungeon of my personality—Scott Peck, the criminal—although I don't intend to let him get out. Indeed, it is only because I recognize his existence that I can add another cinder block to his cell every week or so. Nonetheless, it is a very comfortable cell. It's got wall-to-wall carpeting and a color TV, and sometimes in the evening when I'm in need of certain kinds of street smarts, I may go down to that dungeon and talk with him, keeping well to the other side of the bars.

Similarly, there is a Stage Two segment to my personality—the Scott Peck who also in times of stress or strain would very much like to have a big brother or big daddy around to give him some clear-cut, black-and-white answers to life's difficult and ambiguous dilemmas, who will take over the responsibility by providing me with formulas to tell me exactly what I should do. Sometimes I keep him on bread and water.

And similarly, there is a Stage Three Scott Peck, who in certain other times of stress tends to regress and is tempted to lean on his scientific side as opposed to relying on his spiritual side. I used to tell people that if I was ever invited to address the American Psychiatric Association—of which the chances were like a snowball's in Hell—I would probably just talk about controlled studies and not say anything about this immeasurable spirit business. But the truth of the matter is that I *was* invited to speak to the American Psychiatric Association and I generally managed to throw the Stage Three Scott Peck right into the dungeon along with the Stage One Scott Peck.

Make no mistake about it. We all retain within us, no matter how far we develop, vestiges of earlier stages of our spirituality. So if you are feeling smug right now, having convinced yourself you are safely walking the righteous path of Stage Four, check your dungeon. Conversely, if you're feeling either superior or inferior, it might be helpful to realize that we all also contain within us traces—the lurking potential—

of the more advanced stages. As Oscar Wilde once put it, "Every saint has a past and every sinner a future."

There is another reason for some humility in this matter. The first time I ever talked about these stages was at a seminar with Paul Vitz, whom I have already mentioned as one of the nation's authorities on the integration of psychology and religion. During the period he had for rebuttal after I had spoken, Paul said, "I was very interested in hearing about Dr. Peck's stages. I think there is a great deal of validity to them. Indeed, I think that I will be using them myself in my own practice of psychotherapy. But I would like all of you to remember that what Scotty calls Stage Four is the beginning."

CHAPTER EIGHT

Addiction: The Sacred Disease

I must confess that I am an addict. In particular, I am almost hopelessly addicted to nicotine. I write and lecture all about self-discipline, yet I don't have enough of it myself to stop smoking.

Having put that admission behind me, let me point out that drug and alcohol abuse and addiction are multifaceted, multidimensional problems. While I am going to consider here only the psychological and spiritual aspects of addiction, I am well aware that there are profound biological and sociological roots as well. Alcoholism is a genetic, inherited disorder. We know that now. But that doesn't mean that because you have a gene for alcoholism you will become an alcoholic, or that once you become one you have to continue drinking. It does mean, simply, that there are biological roots to this disorder.

Similarly, although not yet as well studied, it seems to me that there are obviously biological determinants to the kinds of drugs one might prefer, and become addicted to. For example, while not quite addicted, I happen to be partial to alcohol and other sedative drugs, all of which are called central nervous system depressants. In other words, I like down-

ers. I don't give a fig for uppers. But I know people who could kill for uppers and don't care in the least about downers. There are also sociological determinants to addiction. Drug abuse is most severe in places of sociological hopelessness, where people have no better way to feel good about themselves than getting high.

One way of looking at addictions is to see them as forms of idolatry. For the alcoholic the bottle becomes an idol. And idolatry comes in many different forms, some of which we're quite accustomed to recognize. So there are nondrug addictions, such as addictions to gambling or sex. The idolatry of money is another. Idolatry also comes in forms we are not accustomed to recognize as readily. One is the idolatry of family. Whenever it becomes more important to do or say what will keep the family matriarch or patriarch happy than it is to do or say what God wants you to do or say, we have fallen prey to the idolatry of family. Family togetherness has become an idol, and often a most oppressive one.

To put things in perspective, therefore, it is important for us to keep in mind that there are innumerable kinds of idolatries or addictions, many of which can be far more dangerous than the addiction to drugs. The addiction to power. The addition to security. In some ways, drug and alcohol addictions may be among the least destructive of addictions or idolatries in terms of their overall cost to society.

With that by way of introduction, let us now restrict ourselves to the consideration of the problem of drug addiction alone. I think that people who become slaves to alcohol and other drugs are people who want, who yearn, to go back to Eden—who want to reach Paradise, reach Heaven, reach home—more than most. They are desperate to regain that lost warm, fuzzy sense of oneness with the rest of nature we used to have in the Garden of Eden which I spoke about in the first chapter. So it is that Kurt Vonnegut's son, Mark, in writing about his own mental illness and drug abuse, entitled his book *The Eden Express.* But of course, one cannot go

back to Eden. One can only go forward through the painful desert. The only way to reach home is the hard way. But addicts, who have a terribly powerful yearning to go home, are going the wrong way—back instead of forward.

There are two ways of looking at this yearning to go home. One is to look at it as a regressive kind of phenomenon, a yearning not only to go back to Eden but to crawl back into the womb. The other way to look at it is as a potentially progressive kind of phenomenon; that in this yearning to go home, addicts are people who have a more powerful calling than most to the spirit, to God, but they simply have the directions of the journey mixed up.

JUNG AND AA

Few people know that Carl Jung—who did more than anyone else to marry psychology with spirituality—actually played an indirect role in the founding of Alcoholics Anonymous. Jung had a patient back in the 1920s, an alcoholic man who after about a year of therapy had made no progress. Finally Jung threw up his hands and said to him, "Listen, you're just wasting your money with me. I don't know how to help you. I can't help you." And the man asked, "Is there no hope for me then? Nothing you can suggest?" And Jung said, "The only thing I can suggest is that you might seek a religious conversion. I have heard reports of a few people who underwent religious conversions and stopped drinking. It makes a kind of sense to me."

The man took Jung at his word and went out seeking a religious conversion. Seek and you shall find? Well, he found it. After about six years, he underwent a religious conversion and stopped drinking.

Shortly after it happened, he bumped into one of his old drinking buddies, a man by the name of Ebby, and Ebby said, "Hey, have a drink." But he said, "No, I don't drink anymore."

Ebby was astonished. “What do you mean, you don’t drink anymore? You’re a hopeless alcoholic, just like me.” So the man explained that Jung had told him to seek a religious conversion, and that he had stopped drinking.

Ebby thought that might be a good idea. So he went out looking for a religious conversion. It took him about two years. And he too stopped drinking for a significant period.

Not long after that, Ebby dropped in one night to see his old drinking buddy Bill W. Bill W. said, “Hey, Ebby, have a drink.” But Ebby said, “No, I don’t drink anymore.” Now it was Bill W.’s turn to be astonished, “What do you mean, you don’t drink anymore? You’re a hopeless alcoholic, just like me.” So Ebby recounted how he had met this patient of Jung’s who had undergone a religious conversion and stopped drinking, and how he had done the same thing.

Bill W. thought that was a good idea. So he too went out looking for a religious conversion. It took him a couple of weeks, and shortly thereafter he started the first AA meeting in Akron, Ohio.

About twenty years later, once it had really gotten off the ground, Bill W. wrote to Jung to tell him about the role he had inadvertently played in the founding of AA. And Jung wrote back to him an absolutely fascinating letter. He said he was terribly glad that Bill W. had written to him; he was glad to know that his patient had done well; he was glad to know the role he had inadvertently played. But he also said he was particularly glad because, while there were not many people that he, Jung, could talk to about such things, it had occurred to him that it was perhaps no accident that we traditionally referred to alcoholic drinks as spirits, and that perhaps alcoholics were people who had a greater thirst for the spirit than others, and that perhaps alcoholism was a spiritual disorder, or better yet, a spiritual condition.

Thus, there are two ways to look at this yearning that addicts have to go home, and both are true. It would be wrong to totally disregard the regressive aspects of addiction, but nonetheless, in working with people, I have found that the

greatest payoff generally comes in emphasizing the positive. So in dealing with addicts, the greatest payoff comes from emphasizing not the regressive aspects of the disorder but rather the progressive ones—the yearning for the spirit and for God.

A PROGRAM OF CONVERSION

When I was in psychiatry training, back some thirty years ago, psychiatrists already knew that Alcoholics Anonymous had a much better track record in working with alcoholics than we psychiatrists had. But we dismissed it as nothing more than a substitute for the neighborhood bar. We believed that alcoholics had what we called "oral personality disorders," and that rather than opening their mouths to drink, they would get together at AA meetings and yap a lot and drink a lot of coffee and smoke a lot of cigarettes, and in that way they would satisfy their "oral" needs. That was the reason, we psychiatrists smugly said, that AA worked.

I am ashamed to tell you that the majority of psychiatrists, including those who are training right now, continue to believe that the reason AA works is because it is a substitute addiction. I do not want to say that there is no element of this. "Substitute addiction" is perhaps one half of one percent of the reason AA works so well. But the real reason AA works is because of "the program." And there are at least three reasons why the program works.

The first reason is that the twelve steps of AA are the only existing program for religious conversion, although AA people call it "spiritual" conversion, because they do not want in any way to imply that AA is an organized religion. It is not. However, the very core of the twelve-step program is the concept of higher power, and the program actually teaches people *why* they should go forward through the desert—namely, toward God "as we understand Him."

Because it is the only program for conversion, AA might

be looked upon as the most successful "church" in this country today. Any other denomination would envy its extraordinary, phenomenal growth. AA people are incredibly smart. They're so smart that they don't even bother about budgets and buildings. In fact, they use existing church buildings for their meetings. This is one of the positive roles the institutional church plays today—it hosts AA meetings.

About a year ago I was speaking in a modest-sized church in a Connecticut town, and during the break time I looked at the bulletin board and saw that that church hosted some fourteen AA meetings each week, along with four Al-Anon meetings and two Overeaters Anonymous meetings.

So, while AA people will use church buildings for meetings, they are not affiliated with organized religion. They will also soft-pedal even the "spiritual" aspect of the program in order to attract new members who are threatened by it. And lots of people are threatened by it. People simply don't like to be converted very much. They resist it. Consequently, AA is a very tough program.

To give you an idea of how tough it is, an alcoholic executive came to see me about a dozen years ago because "AA wasn't working." By that he meant that for the past six months he had been going to AA meetings every other night, and on alternate nights he had been continuing to get blind drunk. He said he didn't know why AA wasn't working, because he understood all about the twelve steps.

When he told me that, I said with some surprise, "As far as I understand the twelve steps, they are a rather profound body of spiritual wisdom, and it usually takes people at least three years to even *begin* to be able to comprehend them."

He then acknowledged that maybe there was something to what I was saying, because certainly he didn't understand anything about all this higher power stuff. But he was sure that he understood at least the first step.

And I said, "Oh, what's that?"

"I've come to admit that I'm powerless over alcohol."

So I prodded him on. "What does that mean?"

"That means I've got this kind of biochemical defect in my brain such that whenever I take a drink, the alcohol takes over and I lose my willpower. So I can't take that first drink."

"Why are you still drinking, then?"

He fell silent and looked confused.

And I said, "You know, maybe the first step means not only that you are powerless over alcohol after you've taken that first drink, but that you're powerless over alcohol even before you've taken that first drink."

He shook his head vehemently. "That's not true. It's up to me whether or not I take that first drink."

"That's what you say, but it's hardly how you're behaving, is it?"

But he kept insisting, "It's still all up to me."

So I said, "Well, have it your way, then."

This executive had not yet undergone the surrender required of the very first of the twelve steps, much less the remaining eleven.

A PSYCHOLOGICAL PROGRAM

The second reason AA works is that it is a psychological program. It teaches people not only *why* to go forward through the desert toward God but also a great deal about *how* to go forward through the desert. It teaches this in two primary ways.

One is through the use of aphorisms and proverbs. I have already mentioned a few of them, "Act as if," and "I'm not okay and you're not okay, but that's okay." But there are many others—all marvelous gems: "The only person you can change is yourself." Or "One day at a time."

I will tell you a personal story of why I am so convinced that proverbs are important. I had the kind of grandfather every boy ought to have. He was not a particularly smart man,

and his speech was seldom more than a series of clichés. He would say to me, "Don't cross your bridges until you've come to them," or, "Don't put all your eggs in one basket." Not all were admonishments; some were consoling, like, "It's often better to be a big fish in a little pond than a little fish in a big pond," or, "All work and no play makes Jack a dull boy."

He was not above repeating himself, however. If I heard "All that glitters is not gold" once, I must have heard it a thousand times. But he loved me. And from the time I was about eight or nine years old until the time I was thirteen, once a month I used to travel across Manhattan Island to spend a weekend with my grandparents. The ritual of those weekends never varied. I would arrive there on Saturday morning in time for my grandmother to serve me lunch, and then after lunch—this was before the days of TV—my grandfather would take me to a double-feature movie and sit with me through it. Then we would go home for dinner, and after dinner, my grandfather would take me to a second double feature. On Sunday morning the movie theaters were closed in deference to God, but Sunday afternoon he would take me to a third double feature before sending me home. And that was love.

It was on the walks with my grandfather, back and forth to the double features, that I was able not only to hear but to digest and absorb his proverbs, and their wisdom has stood me in very good stead over the years. As he himself might have put it, "A spoonful of sugar helps the medicine go down."

Years later when I was practicing psychiatry, a fifteen-year-old boy came to see me, referred from his local prep school because of poor grades. And as I talked to him, he struck me as not being terribly bright. I thought that maybe the reason he had poor grades was because he was stupid. We psychiatrists have a way of assessing intelligence as part of what we call a "mental status exam," and one of the parts of that exam is to ask people to interpret proverbs. So I asked him, "Why do people say, 'People who live in glass houses shouldn't throw stones?' "

He immediately answered, "If you live in a glass house and you throw stones, your house is going to break."

"But most people don't really live in real glass houses. How would you apply that saying to relationships between people?"

"I don't know."

I tried again. "Why do people say, 'Don't cry over spilt milk'?"

And he said, "If I spilled some milk, I'd get the cat in to lick it up."

That seemed somewhat imaginative, but didn't explain why it was a common expression. Finally, because intelligence was such a critical issue, I referred him to a psychologist for tests that are much more accurate in assessing intelligence, and I specifically referred him to an elderly woman particularly famous in the testing field. I was surprised when her report came back demonstrating that this boy had a full-scale IQ of 105. Not great, and low for that prep school, which might have explained something about his poor grades, but still above average. I would have assessed his IQ at about 85, and because of the discrepancy, I called her and said that I couldn't believe his IQ was 105, that I was sure it had to be much lower since he did so badly on proverbs. "Oh, we don't worry about that," she said. "None of the young people these days know any of the old proverbs anymore."

I've often thought that it would be saving if we could develop some program of mental health education in our public schools, but I know we wouldn't get away with it. People would object to it. There is an anti–mental health movement in this country consisting of people who are frightened by the influences of secular humanism and psychology movements in our lives. They are horrified that someone would think that it is good for children to talk back to their parents, and they consider that this kind of thinking has to be the work of the devil. But even they couldn't possibly object to a program in our schools to teach the old proverbs to our children, could they? So I hope someone will start instituting such a program.

I also hope it will be done soon. For, as my grandfather would have said, "A stitch in time saves nine."

LAY PSYCHOTHERAPY

AA uses proverbs very effectively and it also has another effective mechanism: a system of sponsors. When you join AA or another twelve-step program, after a while you may choose a sponsor, who is really a lay psychotherapist.

If you feel you need psychotherapy but you can't afford it, then one thing you could do is to pretend you're an alcoholic, go to AA, and get yourself a sponsor. There are actually some people who do that. I'm not into pretense, so that isn't what I would really recommend. Instead, I would suggest that you pretend you've got an alcoholic relative and go to Al-Anon and get yourself a sponsor. Actually, you don't have to pretend. Undoubtedly somewhere in your family you do have an alcoholic relative.

I don't mean to imply that sponsors in the twelve-step programs are the exact equivalent of paid-for, professional psychotherapists. In some ways they're not as good. The reason I know as much as I do about AA is because I have had patients who came to me after spending years in the program, feeling that maybe I had a little something extra I could give them as a psychiatrist that they couldn't get from their sponsors. In the process of trying to give them that little extra boost, I learned a great deal from them.

There is something of a tradition in the twelve-step programs that it is really okay to outgrow your sponsor. And, in this respect, I believe the sponsor system superior to traditional therapy. It's considered normal to go to your sponsor and say, "Look, I'm really grateful for the help you've given me for the past three years, but I think at this point I'm ready for a more sophisticated sponsor." And the sponsor is likely to say, "I couldn't agree with you more, and I'm delighted that

I've been able to help you and that you've come this far." There are not that many psychiatrists who would take as kindly to their patients' outgrowing them.

A COMMUNITY PROGRAM

Thus, AA works because it is a program of spiritual conversion, teaching people *why* they must go forward through the desert—namely, toward God. And it works because it is a psychological program, teaching people a great deal about *how* to go forward through the desert, and it does so through proverbs and sponsors. There is a third reason: AA works because it teaches people that they do not have to go forward through the desert alone. It is a *community* program.

For the past several years, since I gave up practicing psychiatry, I have been working with others on the development of the Foundation for Community Encouragement. My book *The Different Drum* was all about that effort. In it I pointed out that community develops naturally only in response to crisis. So it is that strangers in the waiting room of an intensive care unit will rapidly come to share with each other their deepest fears and joys, because their relatives lie across the hall on the critical list. Or within a few hours of an earthquake, like the one in 1985 in Mexico City, where over four thousand people were killed, normally self-centered, wealthy adolescents will be working hand in hand with poor laborers in around-the-clock sacrificial love.

The only problem is that as soon as the crisis passes, so does the community. As a result, there are millions of people who are mourning their lost crises. I can guarantee you that this Saturday night, if not this Thursday night, there will be tens of thousands of old men in VFW and American Legion clubs drinking themselves silly, mourning the days of World War II. They remember those days with such fondness because even though they were cold and wet and in

danger, they experienced a depth of community and meaning in their lives that they have never quite been able to recapture since.

THE BLESSING OF ALCOHOLISM

Alcoholics in AA have a great blessing and a great genius.

The blessing is the blessing of alcoholism. It is a blessing because it is a disease which visibly breaks people. Alcoholics are not any *more* broken than people who are not alcoholics. We all have our griefs and our terrors; we may not be conscious of them, but we all have them. We are all broken people, but alcoholics can't hide it anymore, whereas the rest of us can hide behind our masks of composure. We are not able to talk with each other about the things that are most important to us, about the way our hearts are breaking. So the great blessing of alcoholism is the nature of the disease. It puts people into visible crisis, and as a result they get into community—an AA group.

The great genius of alcoholics in AA is that they refer to themselves as recovering alcoholics. They do not refer to themselves as recovered alcoholics, or ex-alcoholics, but recovering alcoholics. And by using that word "recovering" they are constantly reminding themselves that the process of recovery is ongoing, the crisis is ongoing. And because the crisis is ongoing, the community is ongoing.

One of the worst problems I have in my work with the Foundation for Community Encouragement is trying to explain to people what it is about. The only people who get it right away are those in the twelve-step programs, because to them I can say that the Foundation for Community Encouragement tries to teach people how to get into community without having to be an alcoholic first, without having to have a crisis first. Or better yet, it is trying to teach people that they are—we all are—already in crisis.

MEETING CRISES EARLY

In our pain-avoiding culture, we have a very strange attitude toward mental health. We Americans think that what characterizes the mentally healthy is an absence of crises. *That is not what characterizes mental health!* What characterizes mental health is the ability to meet our crises early.

The word "crisis" has become quite fashionable these days; we are all talking about the midlife crisis, for example. But long before we ever coined that term, we spoke about the midlife crisis in women. It was menopause. Many women, when they reached their fifties and their period stopped, tended to fall apart. But curiously, it didn't happen to *all* women, and I can tell you why.

A mentally healthy woman does not face a big midlife menopausal crisis at fifty-six, because she has handled many small crises along the way. At age twenty-six, for example, she wakes up one morning and looks in the mirror and sees that she's got the beginning of crow's feet at the corner of her eyes. That's when she's apt to think to herself, "You know, I'm not really sure that a Hollywood talent scout is going to come around after all." And ten years later when she's thirty-six and her youngest child goes off to kindergarten, she thinks, "You know, maybe I'm going to have to do a little more with my life than focus it on my children." When such a woman reaches her fifties and her period stops, she will sail right through it. Other than a few hot flashes, she will have absolutely no trouble because psychologically she met her menopause twenty years before.

The woman who gets into trouble, on the other hand, is the one who holds on to the fantasy that a Hollywood talent scout is going to come around, and who doesn't develop any interests outside the home. When fifty hits, which is the time her period stops, and which is also the time no amount of makeup can hide the wrinkles any longer, and which is also

the time her children leave home—leaving her with not only an empty nest but an empty life—it is no wonder that she falls apart.

I do not want to stereotype either women or menopause here, because midlife crisis is just as common and just as severe in men. I know. Not long ago, I went through my *third* midlife crisis. I was more depressed than I've been at any time since the age of fifteen, and it hurt. I just want to make the point clearly that what characterizes mental health in both men and women is not measured by how well we can avoid crises, but how early we can meet a crisis and can get on to the next one—and perhaps how many crises we can cram into a lifetime.

There is a rare, devastating form of psychological disorder afflicting perhaps one percent of the population which impels them to lead lives of compulsive theatricality. They have to have excitement all the time. But the far more devastating psychological disorder which afflicts at least ninety-five percent of us Americans is that we fail to live our lives with a sufficient sense of drama and to wake up to the critical nature of our lives on a daily basis.

Herein lies one of the virtues of being a "religious" person. Other people simply have ups and downs in their lives, whereas we religious folk get to have "spiritual crises." It is much more dignified to have a spiritual crisis than a depression. In fact, it is quite possible that you will get over your depression more quickly if you recognize it to be a spiritual crisis, which very often it is. One of the things that I deeply believe we need to do in our culture is to start dignifying crises, including certain types of depression and all types of existential suffering. It is only through such suffering and crisis that we grow.

AA people, because they are always recovering, live with ongoing crisis. And they cope with ongoing crisis because they help each other. That is what community is.

I am able to tell you what community is, but I cannot tell

you how it feels. Jesus had a similar problem. He had stumbled on this thing He called the Kingdom, and got very excited about it. But when He tried to describe it to people, their eyelids drooped and they would yawn. So He made up parables to explain Himself better. He would say: "Look, it's like a man who has found a pearl of great price." Or, "It's like a man who had a vineyard and needed some workers." Or, "It's like a man who had a prodigal son." By and large they still didn't understand what He was talking about.

Two thousand years later, even though His parables have become the most famous of literature, people still don't understand what He was talking about. Most Christians don't really understand what is meant by the Kingdom. I think it is no accident that Jesus had the same kind of difficulty talking about the Kingdom that we have talking about community. Because I think the Kingdom is the closest analogue there is to community.

You have heard Jesus quoted as saying that "the Kingdom is within you," but actually that is not what He said. Jesus was speaking Aramaic and the Gospels were written in Greek and then translated into every language known to man. So there were bound to be mistakes, and there have been thousands of books written trying to get at the correct translations and the actual words of Jesus.

One of the ways that scholars have found to test the accuracy of a Gospel passage is to see if it is possible to translate the Greek back into Aramaic. Most scholars now agree that Jesus did not say "the Kingdom is within you." He said "the Kingdom is among you." And I believe that the best way we find the Kingdom is among us in community.

In his book *The Scent of Love,* Keith Miller writes about this very thing in terms of the first followers of Jesus. It has been said that the early Christians were such phenomenally successful evangelists because the Holy Spirit came down and gave them various gifts—of charisma and of tongues—so that they could speak all languages, and thus Christianity spread

like crazy. But Miller suggests that that wasn't the major reason.

What really happened was that, through Jesus, the disciples and early followers had discovered the secret of community. Someone would be walking down a back alley in Ephesus or Corinth and see people sitting together talking about the strangest things that didn't make any sense at all: something about a man and an execution on a tree and visitations. But there was a quality about the way these people talked to each other, cried together, laughed together, touched each other, the way they interacted with each other, so oddly compelling that strangers passing by would be drawn to them. It was as if the scent of love had drifted down the alley and could draw people like bees to a flower. And people started to say, "I don't understand this yet, but I want in."

We've done community-building workshops in the most sterile of hotel rooms, and desk clerks and barmaids would come by and say, "I don't know what you're doing here, but I get off at three—can I join you?" So I have an idea how it might have worked.

Thus I believe the greatest positive event of the twentieth century occurred in Akron, Ohio, on June 10, 1935, when Bill W. and Dr. Bob convened the first AA meeting. It was not only the beginning of the self-help movement and the beginning of the integration of science and spirituality at a grass-roots level, but also the beginning of the community movement.

That is the other reason why I think of addiction as the sacred disease. When my AA friends and I get together, we often come to conclude that, very probably, God deliberately created the disorder of alcoholism in order to create alcoholics, in order that these alcoholics might create AA, and thereby spearhead the community movement which is going to be the salvation not only of alcoholics and addicts but of us all.

PART THREE

The Ultimate Step: In Search of a Personal God

CHAPTER NINE

The Role of Religion in Spiritual Growth

I am very cautious about my use of "religious" words. I often talk about spirituality rather than religiosity, for example, or about higher power instead of God. I am cautious because these words may have negative connotations. One of the great sins of organized religion is that it has tended to corrupt some very holy words. And when people encounter these words, they associate them with the hypocrisy of organized religion and can no longer see or hear their real meaning.

Many of us have been harmed by religion. And when I talked about the necessity of forgiving your parents for the sins they committed in your childhood, I should have also said that it is equally important to forgive your church for the sins it may have committed in your childhood. Forgiving does not mean going back. I am not telling you to go back to the church of your childhood, any more than I would tell you to move back home with your parents. But your spiritual growth demands that you forgive nevertheless. Without such forgiveness you cannot begin to separate the true teachings of that church from its hypocrisy. And you need the true teachings.

A book called *Oneness: Great Principles Shared by All*

Religions carries the following quotation from the Dalai Lama on its cover.

> Every major religion of the world has similar ideas of love, the same goal of benefitting humanity through spiritual practice, and the same effect of making their followers into better human beings.

Inside, you find that the founders of every major religion in the world—among them Jesus, Buddha, Krishna, Confucius, and Muhammad—have all taught the notion of loving one's neighbor. Wherever you might choose to anchor your spirituality—be it in Christianity, Judaism, Hinduism, Taoism, Buddhism, or Islam—you will have to accept these basic truths. Because you need these basic truths as signposts on your own spiritual journey. Which religion that should be I cannot tell you, because each of us is unique.

INDIVIDUAL UNIQUENESS

I am constantly impressed by how different people are. I am impressed with the different gifts they possess. I have no idea whether God creates the uniqueness in their souls before they're born, or whether it is in their genes. I do know that it starts from the word go.

My two daughters were clearly different beings by the time Lily and I brought them home from the hospital. Had we just had a boy and a girl, we might have said, "They're different because of their sex." But having two of the same sex really brought it home dramatically that we had, right from birth, two very different beings.

People are born different, and among the problems they have to solve is how to deal with their own uniqueness, their own differences, and come to terms with that in relation to

other people. Being different, we each have our own special vocation, our own special calling. We each have a will, the mysterious freedom of choice which operates within certain biological limitations and the confines of one's particular gifts. The one thing I regret in *The Road Less Traveled* is that I made the journey sound like a template clearer than it actually is. As I reread that book, I am amazed by the depth of truth that was given to me, but a bit dismayed by a certain glibness I no longer seem to have. I did not take into account all the variety that exists out there.

There's great benefit in variety. This variety of people is part of what makes community and it is necessary to make up a whole. We need variety to be whole. There is also a great variety of roads that we can take. Because each of us is unique, we have our own choices to make. And if we ask again and again and again, the answer will come to us, and we will choose the right road.

Gandhi said, "Religions are different roads converging upon the same point. What does it matter that we take different roads as long as we reach the same goal?" And we are all struggling along the rocky, thorny road of the desert to reach God.

God, unlike some organized religions, does not discriminate. As long as you reach out to Her, She will go the better part of the way to meet you. There are an infinite number of roads to reach God. People can come to God through alcoholism, they can come to God through Zen Buddhism, as I did, and they can come to God through the multiple "New Thought" Christian churches even though they are distinctly heretical. For all I know, they can come to God through Shirley MacLaine. People are at various stages of readiness, and when they're ready, virtually anything can speak to them.

A minister was shaking hands with the congregation of his Protestant church after the service, and at the end of the line there was a man whom he had seen only occasionally in church. The man came up and said, "Reverend, Reverend,

what you said today in your sermon was exactly what I needed to hear. Thank you very, very much. It was so helpful to me. It revolutionized my life. Thank you, thank you."

The minister, quite pleased, said, "I'm glad I said something that was helpful to you, but I'm curious—what in particular was it?"

And the man answered, "Well, you may remember, you began your sermon by saying that you wanted to talk to us about two things this morning, and then in the middle you said, 'That completes this *first part* of what I wanted to tell you and now it's time I moved on to the *second part* of my sermon.' And at that moment I realized I had come to the end of the first part of my life, and it was high time that I got on to the second part. Thank you, Reverend, thank you, very much."

MY ROAD TO GOD

I came to God through Zen Buddhism, but that was just the first stretch of the road. The road I have chosen for myself, after twenty years of dabbling with Zen, is Christianity. But I doubt that I could have made that choice without Zen. To accept Christianity one must be prepared to accept paradox, and Zen Buddhism—which a lot of people say shouldn't even be considered a religion but a philosophy—is the ideal training school for paradox. Without that training, I don't think there is any way I could have been prepared to swallow the literally God-awful paradoxes of Christian doctrine.

I became a Christian several years after *The Road Less Traveled* was published—and remember, the very first sentence in that book is the great Buddhist truth "Life is difficult" —although subconsciously I had been tending in that direction for quite some time, and *The Road Less Traveled* is full of Christian concepts. An important man said to me, "Scotty, it was so clever of you the way you disguised your Christianity

in *The Road Less Traveled* in order to get the Christian message across to people." And I replied honestly, "Well, I didn't disguise my Christianity. I wasn't a Christian."

The Road Less Traveled can be looked at as very much a statement of where I was at that time in my journey. And in some ways I have come a great distance since then, and in some ways I have come a very short way. Much of what I have done since it was published has been a kind of working out of concepts that are in that book.

One of the inner events of my journey occurred around age thirty when I read C. S. Lewis's *The Screwtape Letters,* a novel composed of letters of advice from Screwtape, a senior demon, to his nephew, Wormwood, whose task is to undermine the spiritual life of a young man. At one point, Screwtape advises Wormwood to make sure that the man, now a young Christian due to their combined bungling, "regards his time as his time." This sentence, at first, made no sense to me. I read it three times. I wondered whether there might not be some typographical error. How else could anybody think of his time except as his own? Then it dawned on me that the possibility existed of my time belonging to a power higher than myself. For a good while it was a most discomfiting notion, and still today I am continuing to learn to submit my time to God's ownership. Submission is always a matter of degree, but it is teachable, just as C. S. Lewis taught it to me. It wasn't until a dozen years later, however, that I actually submitted to being baptized a Christian.

One of the reasons I very gradually gravitated toward Christianity is that I came to believe that Christian doctrine has the most correct understanding of the nature of sin. It is a paradoxical, multidimensional understanding, and the first side of the paradox is that Christianity holds that we are all sinners. We cannot not sin. There are a number of possible definitions of sin, but the most common is simply missing the mark, failing to hit the bull's-eye every time. And there's no way we can hit the bull's-eye every time. Sometimes we're

going to be just a little careless. No matter how good we are, sometimes we're going to be a little tired or overconfident and not exert or extend ourselves quite enough. We cannot hit the bull's-eye every time; we cannot be perfect.

Christianity allows for that. In fact, the one prerequisite for membership in the true Christian church is that you be a sinner. If you do not think you are a sinner, you are not a candidate for the church. But the other side of the paradox is that Christianity holds that if you confess or acknowledge your sin with contrition, then it is wiped out. The word "contrition" is very important here, and what is required is feeling bad, suffering over what you have done. If you acknowledge your sin with contrition, then the slate is wiped clean. It is as if the sin never existed. You can start over again, fresh and clean every time.

There is a very sweet story about this concept. A little Filipino girl said she talked to Jesus, and people in her village began to get excited about that. Then word got around to some of the neighboring villages, and other people began to get excited about it. Finally, word reached the bishop's palace in Manila, and the bishop became somewhat concerned, because, after all, you can't have any unauthorized saints walking around in the Catholic church. So he appointed a monsignor to investigate this case.

The little girl was brought to the bishop's palace for a series of psychotheological diagnostic interviews. At the end of the third interview, the monsignor threw up his hands and said, "I just don't know, I don't know what to make of this. I don't know whether you're for real or not. But there is one acid test. The next time you talk to Jesus, I want you to ask Him what I confessed to at my last confession. Would you do that?" The little girl said she would. She went away and came back for her interview the next week, and with barely disguised eagerness the monsignor asked, "So, my dear, did you talk to Jesus again this past week?"

She said, "Yes, Father, I did."

"And when you talked to Jesus this past week, did you remember to ask Him what I confessed to at my last confession?"

"Yes, Father, I did."

"Well? When you asked Jesus what I confessed to at my last confession, what did Jesus say?"

And the little girl answered, "Jesus said, 'I've forgotten.' "

There are two possible interpretations to this story. One is that that girl was one smart little psychopath. But the more likely is that she really did talk to Jesus, because what she was expressing is pure, thoroughbred Christian doctrine. Once our sins are confessed with contrition, they are forgotten: they no longer exist in the mind of God.

THE REALITY OF JESUS

When people ask me whether I've been "born again," I say, "Well, maybe so. But if so, it was a very prolonged labor and difficult delivery." There were all kinds of milestones on that journey, but perhaps the most important was reading the Gospels for the first time at the age of forty. It was after I had written the first draft of *The Road Less Traveled.* I'm one of those people who tend to do their writing first and their research afterwards, so having quoted Jesus a couple of times, it seemed incumbent upon me to check out the references.

It was a very graceful time for me to come to the Gospels. Had you asked me a dozen years before whether Jesus was real, I would have said that there was more than enough evidence to indicate there was a historical Jesus, obviously a pretty wise chap who was executed in the manner of the day for speaking out a bit too much, and then, for some reason or another, people began to build a religion around him. That's what I would have replied, and I would have left His reality at that. I knew, you see, that the Gospel writers were not contemporaries of Jesus, that they were writing thirty or more

years after His death, that what they wrote were obviously second- or third- or even fourth-hand accounts, and with my education in this age of enlightenment, I simply assumed that they were all into PR and embellishment.

But when I did finally come to read the Gospels, I did so with a dozen years of experience of trying in my own small way to be a teacher or healer, so I knew a little something about teaching and healing and what it's like to be a teacher and healer. With this experiential knowledge under my belt, I was absolutely thunderstruck by the extraordinary *reality* of the man I found in the Gospels. I discovered a man who was almost continually frustrated. His frustration leaps out of virtually every page: "What do I have to say to you? How many times do I have to say it? What do I have to do to get through to you?" I also discovered a man who was frequently sad and sometimes depressed, frequently anxious and scared. A man who was prejudiced on one occasion, although He was able to overcome that prejudice and transcend it in healing love. A man who was terribly, terribly lonely, yet often desperately needed to be alone. I discovered a man so incredibly real that no one could have made Him up.

It occurred to me then that if the Gospel writers had been into PR and embellishment, as I had assumed, they would have created the kind of Jesus three quarters of Christians still seem to be trying to create—what Lily refers to as "the wimpy Jesus." He is portrayed with a sweet, unending smile on His face, patting little children on the head, just strolling the earth with this unflappable, unshakable equanimity, because with His mellow-yellow Christ consciousness, He's got peace of mind. But the Jesus of the Gospels—who some suggest is the best-kept secret of Christianity—did not have much "peace of mind," as we ordinarily think of peace of mind in the world's terms, and insofar as we can be His followers, perhaps we won't either. Perhaps that's not the point.

So that's when I began to suspect that, rather than being public relations specialists, the Gospel writers were accurate

reporters, generally going to great pains to record as accurately as possible the events and sayings in the life of a man they themselves hardly began to understand, but in whom they knew that Heaven and earth had met. And that's when I began to fall in love with Jesus.

It is as if most Christians haven't read the Gospels, and most Christian clergy are not even able to preach the real truth of the Gospels, because if they did, their congregations would flee out the door.

I don't want to imply that the Gospels are totally accurate. Some things obviously seem to have been added. Others seem to me to be obviously missing. Jesus' sense of humor, for instance, and His sexuality. The latter may have been left out on purpose because Jesus' sexuality seems to me rather ambiguous. He appears to have been very fond of Mary Magdalene, who might have been a prostitute, and He is frequently pictured in an intimate pose with the Apostle John, who is referred to as "the one whom Jesus loved." I believe that Jesus was an androgynous figure; that is, not without sex, or unisexed, but whole. What does survive, however, shows Jesus to be really human, and a divine genius.

THE GENIUS OF JESUS

Lily and I used to belong to a little country club on the coast of Maine where we went every year or so for a few days in the summer. We were there just as *The Road Less Traveled* was being published, and in my narcissism I took pains to let it drop within the first twenty-four hours at the club that I was having a book published—that I was not only a psychiatrist but also an author. Shortly, I came to regret my narcissism, because the second night we were there, one of the other guests, who was quite a well-known litigation lawyer, approached me at cocktail hour and said, "I hear you've written a book. What's it about?"

I answered, "Well, it's a kind of integration of psychology and religion."

"Fine, fine, but what does it say?" he asked, with some of the abrasiveness that makes such specialists so good at their work.

"It says a whole bunch of things, and I'm not sure you want to sit here for an hour while I try to tell you all the things it says," I lamely replied.

He said, "You're right, I don't. I want you to tell me in one or two succinct sentences what it says."

And I said, "Well, if I could do that, I wouldn't have had to write a book."

"Nonsense," he persisted. "We've got an expression in the law that anything worth saying can be said well in one or two succinct sentences."

The best I could do was to comment, "I guess that you'd really not find it worth hearing, then," and awkwardly slink away.

One example of the genius of Jesus was that when confronted with this same type of situation, He handled himself infinitely more gracefully. He was in some equivalent of a "happy hour" when out of the small crowd there stepped forth —you guessed it—a lawyer. The man said to him in effect, "Well now, come on, Jesus, what is it that You are trying to say? I don't want a whole sermon on the mount or anything like that. Just tell me what Your message is in one or two succinct sentences. What are You trying to say?" And Jesus obliged him: two sentences so succinct they can be rolled into one. Jesus said, "Love the Lord your God with all your heart, and with all your soul and with all your might. And love your neighbor as yourself."

That is a statement of what a Christian is—or should be. Unfortunately, most people don't understand the passion behind those words. To love God with all your heart and soul and might is to abandon yourself to Him. Abandoning yourself to God is a long and tough process, and I have come to

discover many years after I became a Christian that I have not yet completed it.

After I had read the Gospels and *The Road Less Traveled* had been accepted for publication, I decided I deserved a vacation. I didn't want to do anything with the family, but I didn't want to travel alone and just sit on the beach someplace. Then I got this crazy idea to go on a retreat—that would be something different! So I went off for two weeks to a convent.

I had a number of agendas for this retreat. One was to try to stop smoking, which I succeeded in doing for that time alone. But my largest agenda item was to decide what to do if by some dim chance *The Road Less Traveled* made me famous. If that happened, should I give up my privacy and go out on the lecture circuit, or should I retire into the woods like J. D. Salinger and immediately get an unlisted phone number? I didn't know which way I wanted to go. And I didn't know which way God wanted me to go. So, at the top of my agenda was the hope that in the quietness of the retreat and the holiness of the atmosphere, I might get a revelation from God about how I should deal with this dilemma.

I thought I would do my best to help God out by paying attention to my dreams, since I believe that dreams can serve a certain revelatory function. So I started writing down my dreams, but they were mostly very simple images of bridges or gates, and they didn't tell me anything I didn't already know—namely, that I was at a point of transition in my life.

But I had one dream that was far more complex. In this dream, I was an onlooker in a distinctly middle-class home. In this home there was a seventeen-year-old boy who was the kind of son that every mother and father would love to have. He was president of the senior class in high school, he was going to be valedictorian at graduation time, he was captain of the high school football team, he was good-looking, he worked hard after school at a part-time job, and if all that wasn't enough, he had a girlfriend who was sweet and de-

mure. Moreover, the boy had his driver's license, and was an unusually responsible, mature driver for his age. Only his father wouldn't let him drive. Instead, the father insisted on driving this boy wherever he had to go—football practice, job, dates, proms. And to add insult to injury, the father insisted that the boy pay him five dollars a week out of his hard-earned after-school earnings for the privilege of being driven around, which he was quite capable of doing himself. I awoke from this dream with a sense of absolute fury and outrage at what an autocratic creep the father was.

I didn't know what to make of the dream. It didn't seem to make any sense at all. But three days after I had written it down, when I was rereading what I had written, I noticed that I had capitalized the *F* in "Father." So I said to myself, "You don't happen to suppose that the father in this dream is God the Father, do you? And if that's the case, you don't suppose that you might be that seventeen-year-old boy?" And then I finally realized that I had gotten a revelation. God was saying to me, "Hey, Scotty, you just pay your dues and leave the driving to me."

It is interesting that I had always thought of God as being the ultimate good guy. Yet in my dream I had cast Him in the role of autocratic, overcontrolling villain, or at least I was responding to Him as such with fury and outrage and hatred. The problem, of course, was that this wasn't the revelation I had hoped for. It wasn't what I wanted to hear. I wanted some little bit of advice from God such as one might get from his agent or accountant, which I would be free to accept or reject. I didn't want a *big* revelation, particularly not one where God said, "I'm going to do the driving after this."

Sixteen years later I'm still trying to live up to this revelation, to abandon myself to God by learning the surrender that welcomes His or Her being in the driver's seat of my still-adolescent life.

BAPTISM AS DEATH

Another thing that happened on that two-week retreat was that I began to toy with the notion of becoming a Christian. It was not a very pleasant notion. To act on it, I felt, would require a kind of death on several levels. For one, there was this old business of me being in the driver's seat of *my* time. It seemed to me that if I were to become a Christian my time would no longer belong to me, that it would have to belong to Christ/God and to the mystical "Body of Christ." My ownership of my time would have to die, and that very much felt like having to die myself.

No one likes to die, and so I dragged my feet as long as I could. I used every rationalization in the book to avoid being baptized. The best was that I couldn't decide whether I wanted to be baptized as an Eastern Orthodox, or Roman Catholic, or Episcopalian, or Presbyterian or Lutheran or Methodist or Baptist. Since this complex, intellectual denominational decision was obviously going to take at least thirty years of research, I didn't have to get on with it. But then it hit me that I didn't have to choose a denomination, that, in fact, baptism is not a denominational celebration. So when I was finally drowned March 9, 1980, it was by a North Carolina Methodist minister at the chapel of a New York Episcopal convent in a deliberately nondenominational party. And I have very jealously guarded my nondenominational status ever since. For one thing, it is good for business. But the more compelling reason is that, on a certain deep level, I don't believe in denominations. I do believe there should be different flavors of worship for different folk, but the idea of one denomination denying Communion to another—or to any individual at all—is anathema to me. As far as I am concerned, I feel free to walk into a Christian church of whatever denomination because I belong there.

SINS OF THE CHURCH

I would not have become a Christian or have been baptized at the age of forty-three if I thought that Christianity was a second-best religion, or that one religion was just as good as another. On the intellectual level, the reason I became a Christian is that I gradually came to believe that, on the whole, Christian doctrine approaches the reality of God and reality in general more closely than the other great religions. This doesn't mean that there isn't a great deal to be learned from the other religions. There's an enormous amount to be learned, and it is the responsibility of any educated Christian to garner as much of the wisdom of other religious traditions as she or he possibly can.

Perhaps the greatest sin of the Christian church has been that particular brand of arrogance, or narcissism, that impels so many Christians to feel they have got God all sewn up and put in their back pocket. Those who think that they've got the whole truth and nothing but the truth, and that those other poor slobs who believe differently are necessarily not saved, as far as I'm concerned have a very small God. They don't realize the truth that God is bigger than their own theology. As I've said, God is not ours to possess, but we are His or Hers to be possessed by. And there is nothing that does more than this narrow-minded narcissism to de-evangelize Christianity.

When I became a Christian, I knew that in identifying myself as such I would have to take upon myself, in one way or another, the burden of the sins of the Christian church, of which arrogance is only one. Another of the burdens of those sins is having to atone for such atrocities as the virulent anti-Semitism of the church throughout the ages and more recently the church's failure to stop the Holocaust. I am convinced that had the Christian churches—as they should have—declared Nazism to be incompatible with Christianity, labeled it worse than heresy and threatened all Nazis with

excommunication, the course of history would have been very different.

Still another one of the burdens of those sins is to be misunderstood. As soon as I mention Jesus or Christianity, many people take offense either because they are of a different religion or because of the experience they have had with the hypocrisy of the church. One of those people was my own wife, who, as the daughter of a Chinese Conservative Baptist minister, was raised in a home where faith and love were preached, but where fear and hate were the order of the day. So there I was, beginning to get excited about all these "new" concepts which I associated with positive meanings, and to Lily they represented red flags of hypocrisy. It was a very painful time for us until gradually I learned to become much less "preachy" and she learned that there are different levels of Christianity, as in all religions, and I wasn't on the same level that her parents had been.

So I knew full well before I was baptized that if I spoke out about my beliefs, there were many who would dislike me and tune me out by virtue of their often understandable prejudice. But one of the things that Jesus taught is that life is not a popularity contest. Still, another way in which my baptism was a death for me was the very act of publicly declaring myself a Christian and thereby assuming this small burden of prejudice.

In bearing it I have found some consolation in a magazine originally called *The Wittenberg Door* and now renamed simply *The Door.* It is a magazine of Christian humor—which some might think is a contradiction in terms. It's put out by a group of evangelicals who are deeply offended by the sins of the church and its oh-so-common blasphemy and distortion of decent evangelism. They deal with that by poking fun at it. Each issue features the "Green Weenie Award" given to the most tasteless example of Christianity. One month it was the Bible Belt—a belt made out of snakeskin that had a miniature Bible attached to it. They feature songs like:

Drop kick me Jesus
through the goal posts of life,
Straight over, end over end,
through those righteous uprights.

So I am tuned out by many Stage Two Christians, some of whom have even picketed my lectures, calling me "the anti-Christ." I am also tuned out by a few New Agers as being too conservative. I never thought I would be a middle-of-the-road anything, and here I've found myself a middle-of-the-road Christian. And as bad as that might sound, it is good, I've decided. It is not fence-sitting. It is a path of tension. An important doctrine of Buddhism is called the Middle Path, which stands for the embracing of opposites. Buddha himself, after following two paths of extremes—one of study and one of asceticism—chose the middle path. It was after he had almost starved himself to death that he sat under the tree and became enlightened. The Chinese like to portray him as fat, because fatness means prosperity in the Chinese culture. Occasionally you might run across a skinny, wasted Buddha, but generally he is depicted as neither fat nor skinny, but as middle-of-the-road.

LIFE AFTER DEATH

While I continue to make use of what I have learned from Buddhism, there are aspects of Buddhism—like reincarnation—that I am an agnostic about. That means I don't disbelieve it and I don't believe it; I just don't know.

On the one hand, there is a psychiatrist, Dr. Ian Stevenson, who has been investigating reincarnation in his spare time for years. The last time I heard about his work, which was a decade or so ago, he completely debunked hypnotic regression to past lives, but had discovered some seven cases

which he simply could not explain except through the concept of reincarnation. If someone as rigorous as Dr. Stevenson believes in reincarnation, then it is something I have to take seriously. On the other hand, I am extremely leery of any doctrine that can be used to explain everything. And the idea of reincarnation can be used—or misused—to explain everything.

William James in his *Varieties of Religious Experience* brought up the notion of "old souls," which I do not discount. He said that there are certain people who seem to be born with the knowledge to live life as if they had lived before. I have known children who seem to be capable of extraordinary flashes of wisdom, and I wrote my children's book, *The Friendly Snowflake*, "for young people with old souls and older people with young souls."

While open to the possibility of reincarnation, I perhaps would be more passionate about it were there not an alternative way of dealing with the issue, which has come to appeal to me much more deeply—namely, the traditional Christian belief in life after death with its concepts of Heaven, Hell, and Purgatory. Although Purgatory is primarily a Roman Catholic notion, the psychiatrist in me takes to it with ease. I imagine Purgatory as a very elegant, well-appointed psychiatric hospital with the most modern and highly developed techniques for making learning as gentle and painless as possible under divine supervision.

On the other hand, I find distasteful the traditional idea of Christianity which preaches the resurrection of the body. Frankly, I see my body as more of a limitation than a virtue, and I will be glad to be free of it rather than having to continue to cart it around. I prefer to believe that souls can exist independently from bodies. I think it is possible for souls to exist independently of bodies and even to be developed independently of bodies. Certainly all the literature describing near-death experiences tends to support this view.

HELL

My view of Hell is also not so traditionally Christian, although I am mainly indebted for it to C. S. Lewis, the greatest Christian writer of this century. His novel *The Great Divorce* is a story about a group of people in Hell—which he depicts as a miserable, gray British Midlands city—who manage to get on a bus which takes them to Heaven. Heaven is very bright and cheerful, a delightful place. They are greeted with great hospitality and warmth by their friends and relatives. But by the end of the day, all except one of the people have gotten back onto the bus, and it is still left a bit unclear about that one. All but one choose to go back to Hell!

Why? Lewis uses many examples. Taking the liberty of condensing some of them in a composite, I cite this as typical of what happens to all of them. Let's say one of the people on the bus is a man who is welcomed by his nephew. He is surprised to find his nephew in Heaven, because he thought the young man had never amounted to much on earth. But the nephew is very welcoming and Heaven is bright and cheerful. The man says, "This seems a nice enough sort of place and I might want to stay here. Now, as you know, I was a professor of history at Columbia University. Do you have universities here?"

The nephew says, "Yes, Uncle, of course."

"I assume that I would get tenure."

"But of course you'd get tenure. Everybody in Heaven has tenure."

The uncle is astonished. "How is it possible for everyone to get tenure? Don't you distinguish between the competent and the incompetent?"

The nephew says, "Everybody is competent here, Uncle."

That doesn't sit well with the uncle, but he continues to interrogate his nephew. "As you know, I was chairman of the department, and I assume I would be chairman here."

"I'm sorry, but we don't have chairmen. It doesn't work that way. Everyone is responsible, so we work by consensus and just don't seem to need chairpeople anymore."

That's when the uncle sputters, "If you think I am going to join some kind of half-baked organization that doesn't distinguish between the competent and the riffraff, you've got another think coming." So he boards the bus and goes back to Hell.

My vision of Hell is distinctly like that of Lewis. The gates of Hell are wide open. People can walk right out of Hell, and the reason they are in Hell is that they choose not to. I know that is not traditionally Christian, but there are many ways that I deviate from traditional Christianity. I simply cannot accept the view of Hell in which God punishes people without hope and destroys souls without a chance for redemption. He/She wouldn't go to the trouble of creating souls, with all their complexity, just to fry them in the end.

GOD AS AN EFFICIENCY EXPERT

People often ask me to name the most influential book I've ever read, and I wish I could say that it was Plato or Aristotle or Thomas Aquinas. But, in fact, the book that has perhaps had the greatest influence on me was *Cheaper by the Dozen* by Frank Gilbreth, which I ran across when I was about ten or eleven. It is the true story of a couple who have twelve children, and because the parents are, in fact, efficiency experts, they run their large family with extreme efficiency. It was the first time I had ever encountered the concept of an efficiency expert, and I thought, "Wow, that would be a neat thing to become when I grow up!" In some ways I like to think that is what I have become—as a psychotherapist trying to help people live their lives more efficiently, and then as a lecturer and writer trying to help them live their lives more efficiently, and very much in my work with community trying to help groups behave more efficiently.

As an efficiency expert—if I am that—I admire other people who are good at it, and so I am in *awe* of God's efficiency. For example, in 1982, I took a much reduced fee to do a lecture and workshop at a Mormon conference in Salt Lake City because I thought it would be a marvelous opportunity to learn more about Mormonism. At the last moment, I asked our older daughter, who was twenty then, whether she would like to go along with me to Salt Lake City, and she said she would. It proved to be a very healing time in our relationship. We made several good friends out there, I got all that I had hoped in terms of learning about Mormonism, and my engagement was very successful.

About three days after I returned to Connecticut, I got a phone call from a woman who wanted an appointment. She came in a few days later, and it turned out that she was a Mormon. She told me that she had been very nurtured in some ways by the Mormon church, but felt very oppressed by it in other ways, and was conflicted by that. I don't think there was any way I could have understood her as deeply as I did, nor empathized with her dilemmas, had I not just been to that conference. Now, there are not many Mormons in rural northwestern Connecticut, and it so happens that in ten years of busy practice there, this was the first such patient who had ever crossed my threshold, and I asked, "God, did You send me out to Salt Lake City simply to prepare me to work with this woman?" Then I thought of all the other beneficial things that had been accomplished on that trip, and the efficiency of God amazed me. Not a wasted motion!

Lily and I have a beautiful flower garden which we have relished tending over the years. Flower gardens do not just happen. To develop a really fine flower garden takes an enormous amount of money and time and love and care. It would be inconceivable for me to take a bulldozer or a flamethrower and just devastate the garden that we have poured so much energy and care into. That's my feeling about life after death. Knowing God's efficiency, it makes no sense to me that She/

He should put so much energy into developing souls just to obliterate them, to waste them. There must be something more.

HEAVEN

I have spoken about Hell and Purgatory. What about Heaven?

Some people are referring to me these days as a "lay theologian," by which I think they mean someone who talks about God but hasn't read anything. But one thing that real theologians are now universally well agreed upon is that God loves variety. In variety, She/He delights. Sit in a meadow on a lazy summer afternoon and look about you. Without even moving, you will be able to see dozens of different species of plants. Hundreds of different kinds of insects will be buzzing around in the air. And if you had microscopic vision, you could look into the soil and see whole societies and cultures of viruses and bacteria intermingling. What variety!

Or look at the human race. Over the years I have come not only to be more and more impressed by the extraordinary variety of human beings but also to depend upon it. We are male and female, straight and gay, white, yellow, red, and black, old and young, Jewish and Christian and Muslim and Hindu, and what a dreary world it would be if we were all middle-aged Episcopalians.

Because God so loves variety, the one thing I can surmise with any assurance about Heaven is that it does not conform to the stereotypical notion of identical cherubs with standard-issue halos and harps sitting around on fluffy clouds. Perhaps the most commonly quoted sentence at funerals is: "In my Father's house there are many mansions." When I was a child, I used to think that this was simply an expression of the magnificence of size alone. I thought it to mean that God's house—or Heaven—was so magnificently huge that it could

contain within it a large number of smaller mansions. But now I interpret it as a statement of variety, and I suspect that when we get to Heaven, we will indeed find many mansions there, some of which will be Colonials, some will be ranch-type, some stucco, and some wood, some will have swimming pools, some will be built on cliffs and others in valleys. In my Father's house there will be many mansions!

Beyond this, I don't know. All this business of Heaven, Hell, and Purgatory is what is called "speculative theology." The best we can do is to speculate. We won't know until we have been freed from our bodies by death.

Speaking of knowing, my primary identity—before that of a religious person—is that of a scientist. We scientists are what are called empiricists. Empiricism holds that the best—not the only, but the best—route to knowledge is through experience. So what do we scientists do but conduct experiments—or controlled experiences—from which we can learn and eventually know? Thus it has been through the experiences of my life—my experiences of grace—that I have come to what little knowledge I have about God.

In this regard, I am very much like Carl Jung, another scientist. Toward the end of his life he submitted himself to a film interview. After many rather prosaic questions, the interviewer finally said, "Dr. Jung, a lot of your writing has a religious flavor. Do you believe in God?"

Old Jung puffed on his pipe. "Believe in God?" he mused out loud. "Well, we use the word 'believe' when we think that something is true but we don't yet have a substantial body of evidence to support it. No. I don't believe in God. I *know* there's a God."

CHAPTER TEN

Matter and Spirit

There is a hunger these days, a gnawing dissatisfaction with the answers provided by materialism and scientific progress, a craving for an inner life . . . Increasingly, Americans are looking for solutions that speak to the spirit as well as the psyche.

These lofty words did not come from the latest inspirational best-seller. They came from a December 7, 1992, issue of *U.S. News & World Report.* The magazine devoted five of its pages to trying to explain why Carl Jung has suddenly become so appealing, more than thirty years after his death, and concluded that Jung provides a perfect marriage between psychology and spirituality, between religion and science.

The Road Less Traveled was once described as "Jung translated for the masses," and its popularity obviously has a great deal to do with the fact that it was published at the right time, just when this "gnawing dissatisfaction" was beginning to be felt. Its popularity surprised me, because I wasn't saying anything new. I was repeating things that Carl Jung and William James and others had said long before me. Then I realized that although I wasn't saying anything new, people had

not listened before. Now they were ready to pay attention. I realized that people had changed.

Soon after its publication, *The Road Less Traveled* seemed to have great appeal to people living in the Bible Belt, and at first the vast majority of requests for me to lecture came from that area. This was astonishing to me since I am not a fundamentalist. But then it dawned on me that the people who wanted to hear me speak might live in the Bible Belt but did not share the fundamentalist mentality. There were a great many people out there who had preserved their passion for God and spirituality but were fed up to the gills with a simplistic black-and-white religious faith that claims to have all the answers and doesn't deal with mystery. They were yearning for some fresh air. They needed some way to bridge the gulf between a purely materialistic science and a rigid, doctrinaire theology.

To understand why that gulf existed, we have to go back in time before there was such a thing as psychology. We need to examine the history of the relationship between religion and science.

Some twenty-five hundred years ago, the original relationship between religion and science was one of integration. And this integration had a name—philosophy. So early philosophers like Plato and Aristotle, and later ones like Thomas Aquinas, were men of scientific bent. They thought in terms of evidence and they questioned premises, but they also were totally convinced that God was an essential reality.

But in the sixteenth century things began to go sour, and they hit bottom in 1633 when Galileo was summoned before the Inquisition. The results of that event were decidedly unpleasant. They were unpleasant for Galileo, who was forced to recant his beliefs in Copernican theory—that the planets revolve around the sun—and then was placed under house arrest for the remainder of his life. However, in short order, things got even more unpleasant for the church.

To describe what happened next, let me indulge in a fantasy. Imagine that the year is 1705 and we are in London,

England, privileged to be witnesses to a secret meeting in the private offices of Queen Anne herself. To this meeting, traveling in secret all the way from Rome, has come Pope Clement XI. And responding to a summons from his queen has come, from his laboratories at the Royal Society of London for Improving Natural Knowledge, none other than Isaac Newton.

The Queen begins the meeting by saying: "As you know, I have God-given responsibility for the political order and stability of our civilization. I am grateful to His Holiness for recently sending me a secret message which suggested an action that might be taken to help me fulfill, by God's grace, those responsibilities. Since it was at your initiation that this meeting came to pass, Your Holiness, perhaps you would be so kind as to convey to Mr. Newton the sense of your message."

"Thank you, Your Majesty," says the Pope. "As you know, Mr. Newton, the Galileo affair has been of considerable embarrassment to the church for some years now. All I did was to propose to your queen that it is high time that there should be some healing in the conflict between science and religion."

"Such would certainly be in the best interest of the state," says the Queen.

Newton is quick to respond that the means and aims of science as they have developed over the past century have become quite different from those of religion. "The age of the armchair philosopher is past," he says. "I do not see how we can turn back the clock or that we should attempt to do so."

"Oh, I quite agree, Mr. Newton," says the Pope. "A true reunification is not possible, but surely there could be some reconciliation at least, a rapprochement of sorts, between the scientific and the religious communities."

"But what do you want me to do?" asks Newton.

"A deal, Isaac," says the Queen. "The time has come to make a deal."

"An agreement, Mr. Newton," says the Pope. "As the

representative of the Holy See, I am empowered to make an agreement whereby the church would no longer harass any genuine member of the scientific establishment, as long as the scientific establishment agrees, in turn, to keep its scientific nose out of religious matters."

"What we are proposing, Isaac," says the Queen, "is a mutual respect for each other's territories, through a stable balance of power and a cooperative relationship in which everyone's back can be scratched. This is an accord with already existing boundaries. The aim of your society—which, I might add, currently thrives under my auspices and protection—is, as its title suggests, to improve *natural* knowledge. Now, natural knowledge is quite different from *supernatural* knowledge, which I'm sure you will agree is quite properly the province of the church."

"Just as politics is quite properly the domain of the politician," says the Pope. "Surely the scientific quest for natural knowledge should not be sullied by the vagaries of vulgar politics. Should science stand above political concerns as well as aside from religious matters, I can even foresee the possibility of support for science in the form of government subsidies for scientific departments within the universities as well as for the increasingly complex equipment coming to be required for scientific investigation."

"Quite possibly," says the Queen. "Should you be willing to support the idea of pure science along the lines we have been considering, Isaac, well then, the church would be able to create an image of the pure scientist as a public hero."

"Which would surely pave the way," says the Pope, "for public tax moneys to be made available for scientific investigation, properly restricted to natural phenomena."

Newton sits for a lengthy moment in obviously thoughtful silence. Finally he says, "Well, the advantages of the arrangement do seem rather compelling."

The Queen smiles. "As president of the Royal Society, Isaac, you are the most influential scientist in Christendom.

If you can support the development of the ideal of pure science we have been describing, I have no doubt that a giant step will have been taken to ensure the stability of Christian civilization for centuries to come. But of course, it all must be done rather quietly. This is a subtle sort of business. It is a matter of vision. I see no need for us to mention this meeting to anyone. It should all be done without any fanfare. I know that I can count on your cooperation."

"I'll see what I can do, Your Majesty," says Newton.

"Oh, thank you, Isaac," says the Queen. "And by the way, since I know that you can keep secrets, I see no harm in telling you now that I have been seriously considering you for knighthood before the year is out."

THE UNWRITTEN CONTRACT

So ends my fantasy. Of course, no such meeting took place. But just such an unwritten social contract dividing up the territory between government, science, and religion was developed toward the end of the seventeenth and the beginning of the eighteenth centuries. It was not consciously developed. It was an almost unconscious response to the needs of the day. Nonetheless, this unwritten social contract has done more than anything else to determine the nature of our science and our religion ever since.

Indeed, it might be looked upon as one of the great intellectual happenings of humankind. All manner of good came from it: the Inquisition faded away, religious folk stopped burning witches, the coffers of the church remained full for several centuries, slavery was abolished, democracy was established without anarchy, and, perhaps because it did restrict itself to natural phenomena, science thrived, giving birth to a technological revolution beyond anybody's wildest expectations, even to the point of paving the way for the development of a planetary culture.

The problem is that this unwritten social contract no longer works. Indeed, at this point in time, it is becoming downright diabolic. You may know that the word *diabolic* comes from the Greek *diaballein,* which means "to throw apart or to separate, to compartmentalize." It is the opposite of *symbolic,* which comes from the word *symballein,* meaning "to throw together, to unify." This unwritten social contract is tearing us apart.

THE EVIL OF COMPARTMENTALIZATION

When I was working for the armed services in 1970–71, I used to wander the halls of the Pentagon, talking to people about the Vietnam War. I could get away with this kind of thing because I was in uniform. I would go to people and ask about the war, and they would say, "Well, yes, Dr. Peck, we understand your concerns. Yes, we do. But you see, we're the ordnance branch here, and we are only responsible for seeing to it that the napalm is manufactured and sent to Vietnam on time. We really don't have anything to do with the war. The war is the responsibility of the policy branch. Go down the hall and talk to the people in policy."

So I would go down the hall and talk to people in policy, and they would say, "Yes, Dr. Peck, we understand your concerns. Yes, we do. But here in the policy branch, we simply execute policy, we don't really make policy. Policy is made at the White House." Thus, it appeared that the whole Pentagon had absolutely nothing to do with the Vietnam War.

This same kind of compartmentalization can happen in any large organization. It can happen in businesses and in other areas of government, it can happen in hospitals and universities, it can happen in churches. When any institution becomes so large and compartmentalized, with departments and subdepartments, then the conscience of the institution will often become so fragmented and diluted as to be virtually nonexistent, and the organization becomes inherently evil.

The same kind of compartmentalization can occur within individuals as well. Human beings have a remarkable capacity to take things that are related to each other and stick them in separate airtight compartments so they don't rub up against each other and cause them much pain. We're all familiar with the man who goes to church on Sunday morning, believing that he loves God and God's creation and his fellow human beings, but who, on Monday morning, has no trouble with his company's policy of dumping toxic wastes in the local stream. He can do this because he has religion in one compartment and his business in another. He is what we have come to know as a "Sunday morning Christian." It is a very comfortable way to operate, but integrity it is not.

The word *integrity* comes from the same root as *integrate.* It means to achieve wholeness, which is the opposite of compartmentalize. Compartmentalization is easy. Integrity is painful. But without it there can be no wholeness. Integrity requires that we be fully open to the conflicting forces and ideas and stresses in life.

ABORTION AND INTEGRITY

The issue of abortion is one such conflict. I've been torn apart trying to resolve this issue with integrity. It seems to me that arbitrarily assigning a moment to when life begins—whether in the first trimester or the second trimester—is just a way of evading the issue. Obviously life begins at conception, and obviously any interruption of that life involves the killing of a human being. I also believe that a simple policy of abortion on demand can tend to diminish what Albert Schweitzer called our "reverence for life."

On the other hand, there is the life of the woman to consider. And the father. And the society. The lives of many women would have been seriously damaged had they carried a child to term, even if they intended to give that child up for adoption—and not every child is adoptable. Or lives would

have been damaged if they carried a child to term and then tried to parent it while not being capable of parenting a child. So I don't have the answer to abortion, except to say that any simplistic, one-dimensional answer like "Thou shall not abort" simply isn't going to cut it.

My rule of thumb whenever I am faced with a proposed social solution is to bear in mind the question "What is missing?" And if you ask what is missing in a law that proclaims "Thou shall not abort," the answer you get is responsibility. Responsibility is missing. The lawmakers take the responsibility away from the mother or parents of the unborn child by simply declaring: "You must bear that child." But where do they place that responsibility? The answer is nowhere. They certainly do not want the responsibility themselves for the child once it is born. Therefore, a law that proclaims "Thou shall not abort" is a law without compassion and integrity.

I actually look forward to the day when we might be able to say "Thou shall not abort" *with* compassion and integrity. But the only way we can do that is within community, where it becomes a community decision whether there should or shouldn't be an abortion. If there should, then the community takes upon itself some of the guilt around the decision. But if it decides that there shouldn't be an abortion, then the community assumes some responsibility for the financial and psychological welfare not only of that child but also of its parents. Of course, we don't even begin to have enough community in this country either to fit the bill or to foot the bill. Until such time as we do, a simplistic policy against abortion would be atavistic and would achieve nothing except to return us to where we were forty years ago when the poor had coat hangers and the rich their trips to Sweden.

So, if you want to think with integrity—as long as you're willing to bear the pain involved—all you need do is to remember to ask this single question: "What is missing?" But it is not always comfortable, because sooner or later you will come to the realization that, on a certain level, each of us needs to be responsible for *everything.*

WHAT IS MISSING?

I first learned to look for what is missing during the Korean War. I was fourteen years old then, and I used to enjoy running out every morning to get *The New York Times.* One day I'd read that thirty-seven MIGs were shot down—a great triumph for the American air force, which suffered no casualties whatsoever. The next day I would be happy again to read that forty-one MIGs were shot down, and all American planes returned to home base. And the next day forty-three MIGs were shot down, and only one American plane was lost. The next day, thirty-nine MIGs were shot down, and all American planes were safe, and then forty-three MIGs were shot down, and only one American plane was slightly damaged. While I grieved over the rare loss of a plane or pilot, I rejoiced at these statistics, which, the same *Times* explained, were the result of the superior manufacture of the American planes and the shoddy work of the Russian plane builders. The *Times* also said that our American pilots were much better trained than the poor starving Chinese or North Korean pilots who had inferior reflexes.

The same *New York Times* also referred to China and Russia as underdeveloped countries. And year after year, as these statistics went on, I began to wonder how industrially underdeveloped countries could manufacture all those MIGs, shoddily made as they were, just to be shot down. After a while it dawned on me that something was *missing.* Ever since then I've never quite been able to believe everything I read in *The New York Times.*

I learned the lesson again in medical school when Lily and I read *Atlas Shrugged* by Ayn Rand, a book that so compellingly puts forth a philosophy of rugged individualism and unrestrained self-interest that I was tempted to convert to being a right-wing Republican. But something vaguely bothered me about it, and it wasn't until ten days or so after I finished reading it that I realized that in this panoramic novel

of almost twelve hundred pages there are virtually no children. Children were missing. Of course, that's exactly where Rand's philosophy of unrestrained self-interest and rugged individualism begins to break down—with children and people in our society who need other people.

And all of these lessons came together in my psychiatry training when I learned that what the patient says is not as important as what the patient doesn't say. If you have patients who talk freely about the present and the future but never about the past, you can bet your bottom dollar that they have some problem, something that's unintegrated from their past. Or if they talk freely about the past and the future but not about the present, again the problem is most likely to be the present—often a problem with vulnerability and the "here and now." Or if they talk about the past and the present but don't talk about the future, you can guess there's a problem with the future—a problem with hope or faith.

COMPARTMENTALIZATION IN PSYCHIATRY

When the patient's problem is one of hope and faith—and in many other circumstances—psychotherapy fails if it is compartmentalized rather than integrated, or if it does not deal with the question of values. When I was in psychiatric training, we were taught that, following the model of pure science, psychotherapy should be a value-free kind of endeavor. The therapist must stay clear of all issues involving values, and be careful not to impose his or her values upon a patient. To do so would be to step into the dreaded realm of countertransference, and therapy would be contaminated and no longer pure.

My otherwise brilliant psychiatry residency chief lectured all of us students that a good therapist should, by the second or third session with a patient, tell him or her, "I am not here to judge you." Having committed that to heart, when I began

to see outpatients for lengthy psychotherapy I told the first dozen I saw that I was not there to judge them. It was a lot of nonsense. The reason that entering therapy is such a courageous act is precisely because patients know that nothing will be accomplished unless they submit themselves to judgment.

The fact of the matter is that there has never been such a thing as value-free psychotherapy. It's simply that psychotherapists have been unconscious of their own value system, and the predominant value system with which they've been operating is called secular humanism. It is a value system which puts the emphasis on earthly problems and dismisses otherworldly concerns. In many ways it is a very good value system, and many of those who attack it would be well advised to become more like the secular humanists whom they condemn.

Let me give you a couple of examples of the values of secular humanism. Freud, an atheist, defined mental health in terms of *lieben* and *arbeiten,* which mean "love" and "work." Loving well is a value of secular humanism, as is working productively. Another example: About fifteen years ago, I was seeing an extremely depressed woman, and talking with her was like pulling teeth. The first year of our work together, she would come in for her appointment and say, "Well, I'm more depressed this week." And I would ask, "Well, why do you think that is?" And she would immediately answer, "I don't know." Sometimes she would come in and say, "I'm less depressed this week." And I would inquire, "Well, why do you think that is?" And she would instantly reply, "I don't know."

Finally I said, "Listen, I've asked you to think about something, and you answer 'I don't know' in one thousandth of a millisecond. There's no way you could have done what I've asked you to do—namely, to think. Before we get any further, the first thing you're going to need to learn how to do is to think." Thinking is a value of secular humanism.

The value system of secular humanism is sufficient for

the treatment of perhaps sixty percent of psychiatric patients. However, it is insufficient for the treatment of approximately forty percent. And that is why, for example, AA has been much more effective than psychiatry in treating alcoholics, who, generally speaking, fall into this forty percent. This is partly because, as we have discussed, AA addresses the spiritual needs of these people—something that traditional psychotherapy, with its secular humanist values, does not address.

Spiritual/religious ideas and concepts are necessary in the treatment of many people, and not only addicts and alcoholics. Those suffering from phobias are often another case in point. In my own practice, everyone who has come to me with a specific phobia about a certain street, or cats, or planes, has also turned out—as I got to know them better—not to be very keen on interstates, or dogs, or trains. And I would come to find out that, in fact, they were phobic about life. They had what I would call phobic personalities.

Over the years, in working with a few of these patients, I was struck by the fact that their views of the world had two significant features in common. One, they regarded the world as being a very dangerous place, and two, they felt themselves all alone in this dangerous world in which it was up to them to survive solely by their own wits. Feeling this way, they would tend, through their phobias, to limit the scope of their activity, to narrow the world down to a space over which they could have complete control and hence where they could feel safe.

About fifteen years ago, for example, I was working with a woman among whose many phobias was the fear of the water and of swimming. She had children who were five and seven—the swimming age—so this phobia bothered her especially. She was afraid to go swimming with them. After we had been working for about a year, she came in one day and told me what a wonderful weekend she had had, and that on Sunday she had gone to a pool party, where she had a grand

time swimming around with the kids in the pool. Nothing of extraordinary psychodynamic significance had happened as far as I knew, so I scratched my head and I said, "I thought you were phobic about swimming." And she said, "Well, I am, but I'm not phobic about swimming pools." That puzzled me. "What makes swimming pools different?" I asked. And she said, "Oh, in swimming pools, the water is clear." So I learned she wasn't phobic about swimming but just about lakes, rivers, and oceans, into which she could only go up to her ankles or knees. Beyond that she was unable to see her toes. And then God knows what might happen to them! She had lost control of her toes.

After a while I realized that there was no way to treat such people effectively without trying to *convert* them to a more benign worldview: a view of the world either as less dangerous than they thought or at least as a place in which they were not all alone, but had some kind of protection in the form of God's grace.

I believe that the *judicious* use of religious concepts can also enhance or speed up psychotherapy in many of the remaining cases that are susceptible to the traditional approach. Such concepts can be used both to confront and to console. For example, when people need to stop feeling sorry for themselves, I might remind them that Jesus taught us to carry our crosses joyfully. But others who are particularly conscientious may need permission to feel sorry for themselves every once in a while. To such a patient, I would say that while Jesus taught us to carry our crosses joyfully, He didn't expect us to carry them joyfully twenty-four hours a day. Anyone who can do that has got some kind of brain damage. "What was Jesus feeling when he climbed Mount Golgotha with three hundred pounds on his back?" I would ask them to imagine. He was feeling sorry for Himself. So I would point out to these patients that they're entitled to take five minutes twice a day to feel sorry for themselves.

Another example I have made frequent use of is that of

Saint Thérèse of Lisieux, who said: "If you are willing to serenely bear the trial of being displeasing to yourself, then you will be for Jesus a pleasant place of shelter." If I was working with someone who was suffering from realistic guilt—let's say a Vietnam veteran having nightmares because he had killed innocent children in wartime—then I might say to him, "Let's celebrate the fact that you're going through this guilt and that you are truly displeased with yourself, because now you are for Jesus a pleasant place of shelter." And I could console him with that.

On the other hand, if I was working with a man who had a Christian identity but was not experiencing existential guilt—who was notably self-righteous and self-satisfied—I would likely confront him by asking, "Gee, what do you think Saint Thérèse meant by 'the trial of being displeasing to yourself'?"

These words from Saint Thérèse I have found particularly useful in understanding patients with depressive personalities, who are real experts at being displeasing to themselves. They would say to me, "Dr. Peck, I'm such a useless human being. I've never done anything worthwhile in my life. I know back in the service I was a three-star admiral, but that was just a fluke. I don't know why you'd want to see somebody like me. I'm no good to my wife, I'm no good to my children, I'm no good to anybody. Oh God, it must be hard for you to keep seeing a wretch like me week after week."

Saint Thérèse, who died at the age of twenty-four, was a smart woman who chose her words carefully. Remember, she said, "If you are willing to *serenely* bear the trial of being displeasing to yourself . . . " The problem with depressives is that they're not particularly serene about it. And indeed, such excessive breast-beating was labeled by the Catholic church centuries ago as the sin of "excessive scrupulosity," and correctly diagnosed as a perverted form of the sin of pride. What these people are really saying is, "I know God forgives me but I'll be the judge." If you scratch through their pseudo-humil-

ity, you frequently come to a core of arrogance and narcissism.

Many articles have appeared in professional journals recently about something called the cognitive theory of depression. Psychiatrists have figured out that depressed people do not cognate the same way as nondepressed people. By cognition they mean not just thought but all that goes into thinking, including perception. Specifically, depressed people selectively perceive the negative in the world, both inside and outside, and they fail to perceive the positive.

For many years Lily fought a heroic battle against depression, which she ultimately won, but before she won it, we used to go out in the backyard of our house on a May morning and I would look around and think to myself, "Isn't it wonderful that spring is here and the grass is turning green and the trees are in bud, and how fortunate we are to live in this lovely old Colonial house! It needs some painting, but we'll get around to it next year and thank God we've got the money for it." But Lily would be standing next to me saying, "When is Fritz going to come and mow the lawn? And look, somebody left the clippers out all night and look at this house—it's a mess." Two people standing within the same few square feet but perceiving totally different worlds.

So psychiatrists have figured out that in treating depressives it's often necessary to teach them how to cognate differently. To stop selectively perceiving the negative, these people need to be taught to perceive the positive. But the psychiatrists who are just now catching on to this might be a little bit embarrassed to realize that their new "cognitive therapy" is no different from Norman Vincent Peale's *The Power of Positive Thinking,* a book written decades ago. Actually, the most succinct words ever spoken about depression were spoken in the twelfth century by Jalālu'l-Dīn Rūmī, a Muslim mystic, who, in my opinion, was the smartest person who ever lived, next to Jesus. He said, "Your depression is connected to your insolence and refusal to praise." And by insolence, he was refer-

ring to narcissism or that kind of perverted pride which underlies depression.

DEPRESSION AND FANTASY

In my work with depressed people, I have frequently encountered what I call the Prince or Princess. The first time I had this experience, my patient was a woman. She had made good progress in dealing with her depression, thanks to her work with another psychiatrist, and came to me because she felt she had a little further to go. After we had been working for nearly a year, she was talking one day about a very complex problem with her children. The stakes seemed high and it was most unclear what she should do about it. In the midst of evaluating the problem, she exclaimed, "God, I'll be glad when therapy is over!" I said, "Why did you just say that?" And she said, "I'll be glad when therapy is over and I no longer have to agonize over these problems!"

I smelled a fantasy—that psychotherapy would take away not only all present but future pain—and this is a fantasy that is common in the Prince or Princess.

To explain how people can come to hold such a fantasy, I have to give a little background on child psychology. Infants during the first year of life, as best we can discern, come to learn what we call their ego boundaries. Before they learn this, they don't really recognize the difference between their hand and Mommy's hand, for example; they think that because they have a stomachache, Mommy has a stomachache, and the world has a stomachache. By the second year they learn their physical boundaries, although not yet the boundaries of their power, so they generally still go around thinking they are the center of the universe, with their parents and siblings and dogs and cats merely minions of their private royal army.

Then during the terrible twos, Mommy and Daddy start

saying, "No. No, Johnny, you can't do that. No. No, you can't do that, either. No, no, you can't do that, either. No. No. We love you very much, Johnny, and you're very important, but no, you can't do that. You're not the boss." Thus, in the course of a year, the child is psychologically demoted from a four-star general to a private. It is no wonder that it's a time of depression and tantrums, which is what the terrible twos are.

Nonetheless, if parents can be gentle with the child and support it as much as possible through this difficult period, by the time it leaves the terrible twos, it will have taken its first giant step out of narcissism. Unfortunately, this is not always the way it happens. Sometimes the parents are not gentle and do not support the child in this necessarily humiliating time, but instead aggravate the humiliation.

The woman who had the fantasy that she would no longer have to agonize about problems when psychotherapy was over had been raised in a home that was strict, to say the least. While she could not remember her terrible twos, she could remember the time when she was three or four and was subjected to a particular ritual whenever she did something wrong. She would be told to go and take down a switch that hung on the wall, carry it to her father, and present it to him. Then she would have to pull down her panties, hold up her skirt, bend over, and stand there while she was beaten until she had cried loudly and long enough that he stopped. Then she would have to pull up her panties and take the switch from her father and replace it on the wall. Then she would go to her mother to be consoled, and when she had been consoled sufficiently and had stopped crying, her mother would say, "Now get down on your knees and pray out loud to God for forgiveness." So she would get down on her knees and pray out loud for God's forgiveness, and when her prayers were judged by her mother to be sufficient in length, the mother would say, "Now you can get up and go over to your earthly father and ask him for his forgiveness." So she would

go to her father, and if her petitions were sufficient, he would grant her his forgiveness, and the ritual would be over until the next time she did something wrong.

How do children survive that kind of treatment? The way they survive is not by giving up their infantile omnipotence and narcissism but by holding on to them. The mechanism for this is so specific that we psychiatrists have a name for it; it is called the "family romance." What such children do (and indeed, this is what my patient could remember doing) is to tell themselves, "These people who say they are my parents really aren't my parents. In reality I am the daughter of the King and Queen, a child of royal blood, a Princess, and someday I will be recognized for who I am. Then I will come into my own."

This is a very consoling fantasy to get children through such humiliation, except that as they grow significantly into adulthood—and by then the fantasy is much more subconscious—nobody has come to take them to the King and Queen, nobody has recognized them for who they feel they really are. So they become depressed. And what can lie at the base of the cognitive difficulty of depressives is this core fantasy that bad things shouldn't happen to them. Of course they selectively perceive the negative when they believe they should be exempted from it—and fail to perceive the positive which they feel should be their royal right.

There's a psychiatrist in Brazil named Norberto Keppe who suggests that the most common human mental illness is what he calls theomania: the delusion that we human beings can be God. Theomania is very much like the Prince or Princess fantasy although infinitely more ordinary. For example, a decade or so ago, I was working with a man who had a very deeply entrenched Christian identity. He had been a professional Christian youth worker in his twenties and was now a middle-aged businessman I'll call Joe Jones. At the time he came to see me, he was in league with a couple of unscrupulous people who were financing his business venture, and

there was an enormous amount of pressure on him to sell out, to lie—specifically, to go to a hardware show with a product and pretend he had a patent, which he did not, in order to sell it. Had I been in his position, I would have been anxious myself, but this man was in unrelenting panic. Trying to console him one day, I said, "Joe, all that you can do is the best that you can do." And that is when he snapped, "The best that I can do isn't good enough for Joe Jones!"

It seemed a strange statement to make, so I asked, "What do you mean?" And he said, "It's not only necessary that I do the best job I can do, but it's also necessary that this business not fail."

I said, "Listen, Joe, for all you know, the best thing that could happen to you in the long run would be for this business to fail. And for all we know, God wants this business to fail. Look, we are all of us actors in a wonderfully complex celestial drama, and the best we can hope for is to get little glimpses of what the drama is all about and how we might best play our roles. What I hear you saying, Joe, is that not only do you want to be the best actor you can be in this drama, but you also want to be the scriptwriter."

Joe is Everyman. We all go around suffering from theomania, the illusion that we can be the scriptwriter in the drama of our lives, and we become furious, depressed, or terrified when things don't go as we would have written the script or wanted them to go. In fact, many of us are never able to adjust to the reality that life is larger than something that is just our show. In this failure to adjust, we fail to learn. But for real learning and growing, we have to come to terms with the fact that, as someone once put it, "life is what happens when you've planned something else." Thank God!

CHAPTER ELEVEN

New Age: Symboline or Diaboline?

In the escalating search for road signs on the journey through the desert, many people have found themselves needing "religion," but unable to stomach what much of "organized religion" passes off as religion. This has led to the popularity of various cults and to an interest in Eastern philosophies evidenced by the popularity of such books as *The Tao of Pooh* and *The Te of Piglet, The Tibetan Book of the Dead,* and even *Am I a Hindu?*

Although the interest in Eastern philosophy has been around for a long time, it has recently been popularized by what has come to be known as the New Age movement. A great many people today are confused by the movement and I am frequently asked whether I consider it a force for the good or not. To answer that question, let me pose another: Is the New Age movement a force for integration or for separation?

I have two hobbies. One is collecting Freudian slips, and the other collecting light bulb jokes. And my two favorite light bulb jokes are, of course, religious light bulb jokes. The first is: "How many Episcopalians does it take to change a light bulb? Two. One to mix the martinis and one to call the elec-

trician." The second is: "How many Zen Buddhists does it take to change a light bulb? Two. One to change the light bulb and one not to change the light bulb."

While that might strike you as funny, it is, in fact, a statement of integration and a very succinct way of defining paradox, of which Zen Buddhism has been my best teacher. I highly recommend Zen Buddhism for this very reason, since accepting the many paradoxes of life is essential to mental health.

I cannot stress enough how important thinking paradoxically is to me. I am very much like the professor of philosophy who was asked by one of his students, "Professor, it is said that you believe that the core of all truth is paradox. Is that correct?" And the professor answered, "Yes and no." Thus, to answer the question of whether the New Age movement is a force for integration or for separation, I am also going to answer yes and no.

THE AQUARIAN CONSPIRACY

A lot of people have questioned whether the New Age movement really exists at all. Perhaps it is somewhat mistitled, since the kinds of things that people who are in the New Age movement believe or are interested in have been around forever. But I think that there *is* a genuine New Age movement in that for the past thirty years, more and more people, a very significant portion of the population, have been turning to these beliefs and interests.

But when we call it a movement, I do not mean that it is an organized kind of movement. There have been many Christian fundamentalists who have declared it a satanic conspiracy to undermine Christian doctrine. It is because of this kind of thinking that Marilyn Ferguson, who authored a classic work on the New Age movement, called her book *The Aquarian Conspiracy*—very tongue in cheek, of course. She

made the point very validly that it is not a conspiracy at all. People didn't get together and cook up this kind of thing. Like most important intellectual movements, the New Age movement sprang up spontaneously in response to the needs, pressures, and forces of the day. And thus it might be looked upon more as a revolutionary movement than an evolutionary one.

Like most revolutionary movements, New Age is primarily an upper-middle-class movement; it is not terribly important among the poor or blue-collar workers. And it is an international movement, not only an American or North American phenomenon. It is just as alive in places like Germany and England as it is in the United States.

Finally, and most important, the New Age movement is, in my opinion, a reaction against the institutional sins of Western civilization. Sins tend to be interrelated, and so, even though I may discuss them singly, keep in mind that they exist in conjunction with one another.

Please also keep in mind that not all institutional sins are "Western." Institutional sexism is even more entrenched in the East than in the West. But, among other things, the New Age movement is a reaction against the sexism found in industry, in the church, in government, and as such it is a movement toward feminism.

A more "Western" sin is the emptiness of spirit and the arrogance, narcissism, and blasphemy of the Christian church. The New Age movement, consequently, is a movement away from Western religions to Eastern religions, to Buddhism, to Zen, to Taoism, to Hinduism, to Native American religions, or to the more feminist religions of the Mother Goddess and Wicca. And because organized religion has been very intolerant of beliefs other than its own, the New Age movement has tended to incorporate an extraordinary hodgepodge of ideas, including many esoteric notions ranging from astrology to astral projection to ethereal bodies. The list is almost endless.

The New Age movement is also a reaction against the

sins of science, or at least science as it has been translated into technology, and those sins too are very real. Modern science has led us into a kind of excessive specialization which, in turn, tends to lead to a technological inhumanity. Anyone who has been hospitalized, getting the best of modern medical technology, is likely to have experienced some of this inhumanity in the name of "care" or "treatment." So, in reacting against technology, the New Age movement has tended away from Western medicine to, once again, Eastern medicine, to such things as acupuncture and chakras, to healing rituals of the Native Americans, to shamanism. Moving away from the specialization of Western medicine and technology, it has also paved the way for some very good holistic medicine and health through exercise. It has reintroduced herbal medicine and the idea of caring for the sick at home, and the hospice movement may be considered one of its very beneficial spin-offs.

And lastly, the New Age movement is a reaction against the sins of capitalism, against the sins of imperialism and exploitation of the environment and of people. Again terribly real sins. So it is a movement away from exploitation and toward pacifism, toward the tolerance of diversity, and toward an ecological consciousness and balance with nature.

If anything characterizes the New Age movement, it is its openness to new ideas and new ways of doing things. And all that is wonderful. The problem—and it is the only problem, as far as I'm concerned, but it is *huge*—is what psychiatrists call reaction formation. Unfortunately, when you react against something that is sinful, you will often go to the other extreme, and you can get into as much trouble as you were in before. You can jump from the frying pan into the fire, or, as I often put it, throw out the baby with the bathwater.

Let me give you an example from my own history of what reaction formation can mean. My father was a judge and was in the habit of going on judicial tirades from time to time. Quite frequently, he would inappropriately bawl out desk

clerks or hapless waiters. I can remember standing around at age twelve in restaurants or hotels, squirming with embarrassment as my father went on for fifteen or twenty minutes because some poor fellow had committed the most minor error. And I can remember vowing to myself that when I grew up, I was never going to make an ass out of myself like my father.

So when I did grow up, I never got angry in public. But as the years went on, I developed high blood pressure and my acquaintances started telling me that I was cold and distant and aloof and unfeeling. Finally, after I got into therapy, I realized that I had thrown the baby out with the bathwater—that in reacting against my father's inappropriate rages in public, I had cleansed myself, expurgated myself of all public anger. In fact, what I needed to get rid of was not *all* anger in public but simply *inappropriate* anger in public. Sometimes it is appropriate and necessary to get angry in public. But I had gone too far to the other extreme, and it took me some effort to relearn how to be angry, appropriately, in public. And it was only then that people started seeing me as less aloof and my blood pressure started to come down.

Unfortunately, the New Age movement has also gone to extremes. For instance, in reacting against male sexism, it has created a brand of radical feminism that can be not only distinctly unpleasant and unsettling but also rude and uncivil and even silly at times. I have spoken to audiences that comprised primarily radical feminists and it was difficult going indeed, even though I always go to some pains to use nonsexist language and to combat sexism.

Another example: In reacting against Judeo-Christian tradition the New Age movement has created a considerable amount of what I call spiritual confusion. In every large city in the United States you will find one or more organizations that I have come to call spiritual supermarkets. They put on various kinds of programs about virtually everything from Sufi dancing to the I Ching to Dionysian celebrations. You'll see everything there except Judaism or Christianity. And some

people have been confused by this mixture, while others have used it as an excuse to run away from responsibility.

A few years after *The Road Less Traveled* was published, a man who was a kind of aging hippie came to see me. He was in his early forties, had a beard, long hair, a knapsack on his back, and he had hitchhiked to my home in Connecticut. He said he needed spiritual direction. He was at loose ends in his life and didn't know quite what he wanted to do. There was this Zen monastery in Vermont he was thinking of going to. On the other hand, there was a New Age commune out in Oregon that appealed to him. But then again there was this voice that said, "You ought to pay some attention to Christianity," which he hadn't done since he had run away from the Catholic church of his parents as soon as he could, at the age of sixteen. Anyway, what did I think he ought to do?

"Well," I said, "you'll have to tell me more about yourself before I can offer an opinion." So he proceeded to tell me that he had been married twice. He had two children by his first marriage and one by his second marriage, and he hadn't seen the children of the first marriage for over a dozen years, and hadn't seen the child from the second marriage for six years. When I asked why, he said, "It was a lot of hassle at the time of the divorces, and I figured it would really be better for the kids if I dropped out of the picture. But anyway, what shall I do about this spiritual groping?"

In answer, I told him that I had become a Christian since I wrote *The Road Less Traveled* and that I had done so in part because I had gradually come to believe in the meaningfulness of Christian doctrine. I explained that at the core of that doctrine there is the strange concept of sacrifice. I didn't think it meant that we need to sacrifice ourselves masochistically at every turn. But while I really didn't know yet what it means to be a Christian, I said, "At the very least what it means is that whenever there is a decision to be made, an alternative shouldn't be discarded simply because it *is* sacrificial."

When I said that, the man literally started to twitch and I

thought he was going to have an epileptic seizure. I asked him what was the matter, and he said, "What you're doing is serious spiritual surgery on me." And I had to say, "I'm sorry it hurts."

He claimed that it was good for him. He wanted to come and see me again and he made an appointment. But then he called up two days later to cancel it. I suspect that rather than attempting to reestablish a relationship with his children, he opted for the New Age commune in Oregon.

THE WRONG SIN

It is my own particular belief that Christian doctrine, on the whole, approaches reality more closely than do the other great religions, although I also believe that on occasion the others may come a bit closer. In any case, there is a great deal of good in Christian thought that should not be dismissed. In my opinion, the New Age movement has been reacting against the wrong sin. The sin of Christianity has not been the sin of doctrine. It has been the sin of practice—a failure to integrate its behavior with its theology. As G. K. Chesterton put it, the greatest problem with Christianity is not that it has been tried and found wanting, but that it has hardly been tried at all.

The New Age movement, however, has reacted not only against the way Christians have behaved but against Christian theology as well, which the sinful Christian behavior does not embody. And in so doing New Agers have often thrown the baby out with the bathwater. Of course, not all of them dismiss Christianity. Some embrace it, but in the process of marrying it with Eastern religions, they not infrequently end up with something that is an unfortunate hybrid.

In moving away from Judeo-Christian theology to Eastern religions, New Agers also seem to have a tendency to advertise those religions as leading to the greater spiritual advancement. Stage Two people in every religion claim that

their beliefs are the only true beliefs, and the reality is that at our own community-building workshops, we suffer at least as much from New Age fundamentalists as we do from Old Age ones. While as a whole it is characterized by openness to new ideas, there are many people in the New Age movement who are fundamentalists or inerrantists and are no more advanced than Christians of the same ilk. Some are what I call "herbal fundamentalists." They insist not only that there be herbal tea present, but that everybody at the workshop ought to drink it.

This I would not call tolerance. On the other hand, there are people in the movement who get into what I call tolerance in the extreme, which can result in a kind of inappropriate individualism. In one community-building workshop, we were screening a possible future workshop leader who said, "In community anything is appropriate." We had to teach him that in community not everything is appropriate. People cannot be in community who think it is appropriate to hit others or to verbally abuse them or champion a hidden agenda.

This excessive tolerance can also be seen in the real inability of many "liberals" to work together. Before Lily and I started the Foundation for Community Encouragement, we first considered a foundation that would work to unify the five hundred different peace organizations in this country. But gradually, as I played that scenario out in my mind, it became clear that any foundation we might start for that purpose would simply become the five hundred and first peace organization. Because even the peace organizations haven't yet learned how to work together, the task we eventually decided to invest our time and money in—community building—had to come first.

THE ISSUE OF EVIL

One area where Christian theology and the New Age movement tend to part company radically concerns the issue of evil. Christian doctrine holds that evil is real. Eastern reli-

gions do not consider it to be real. They consider it to be illusion or false knowledge, what they call maya.

I do not claim there is nothing to this view. There is no doubt in my mind that by thinking of evil we can create it. If we read the demonic into everything with which we disagree —as many Stage Two religious folk are prone to do—then we will cause fragmentation and hostility rather than healing. Through the New Age movement, however, the simplistic idea has spread that if we could just change our thinking, we would realize there's no such thing as evil in the world. It would all just go away, vanish. But the reality is that there really are people out there who like to maim, to torture, and to crush other people. There are people who want war because they profit from war. And you can get into serious trouble if you believe that there aren't. Because sooner or later you will be accosted with real evil, and dealing with it will not be as easy as some New Age books imply.

The one New Age book that has attracted the most attention, and the one I am most often asked about, is *A Course in Miracles.* It is a very good book, filled with a lot of first-rate psychiatric wisdom. But *A Course in Miracles* also denies the reality of evil, saying that evil is unreal, a kind of figment of our imagination. This is not all that far from the truth, because evil does have a great deal to do with unreality. In fact, in my book *People of the Lie,* I defined Satan as "a real spirit of unreality." So evil does have a great deal to do with unreality—that is, with lies and untruth. But that doesn't mean that it in itself doesn't exist.

While *A Course in Miracles* purports to be Christian, it distorts Christian doctrine. It is not all the truth; rather, it is a half-truth, and in failing to deal with the problem of evil, it leaves out a major part of the picture. It runs with only one side of the "paradox" of evil.

The denial of evil is such a characteristic pitfall of the New Age movement that it has given rise to the one New Age joke I know. It was quite properly told to me by a New Age

woman herself, who recounted how three clergy were sitting down in Hell: a Catholic priest, a Jewish rabbi, and a New Age minister. They begin to talk about what they are doing down there and the Catholic priest confesses, "Back on earth I used to be called a whiskey priest. I just loved my booze too much, and that's why I'm here in Hell. How about you, Rabbi, what are you in here for?" And the rabbi says, "I have to confess that I had this thing about ham sandwiches. I just couldn't leave them alone." And then the two of them turn to the New Age minister and ask him, "What about you? What are you doing down here in Hell?" And he answers, "This isn't Hell and I'm not the least bit warm."

THE SINS OF TECHNOLOGY

A similar problem has occurred in the New Age reaction against technology. It has tended to throw out scientific rigor. The scientific method, as I have explained, is only a collection of procedures and conventions that we have developed over the centuries in order to combat our very human tendency to want to deceive ourselves, and we have developed such procedures in the interest of something higher than our immediate intellectual or emotional comfort. Thus, the scientific method is a principled, highly disciplined kind of behavior, and represents a very holy pursuit after truth.

But in reacting against the sins of Western civilization, New Age has tended to throw out the scientific method. It is another example of throwing out the baby with the bathwater. The sin of technology is not the scientific method but the way that science has been translated by industry and government into technology.

The New Age movement in its reaction formation tends to exhibit a certain lack of "scientific" discernment, in matters of both theology and science. A friend of mine refers to California, the heart of the New Age movement, as Mars' Hill. It

is a reference to what Saint Paul said in Athens when he went to Greece to preach. Paul was often an abrasive man, but he could also be a bit of a smoothie. And so when he reached the top of Mars' Hill, he began by saying he could see that the Athenians were a very spiritual people because, climbing up the hill, he had seen statues of a thousand different gods. And only a very spiritual people could have a thousand different gods.

This same lack of discernment among New Agers can lead to a lot of pretty flaky stuff. Some in California would be well advised to imitate those from Missouri, the "Show Me" state. The expression "I'm from Missouri" refers to an often healthy and discerning skepticism. I believe that before you undertake any adventure, and certainly any spiritual journey, you've got to know something about how to discern what is healthy and what is dangerous.

Golf is a great metaphor for this lesson. Playing a game of golf is an adventure, and in that sense it is fun. It can be more fun if you take risks and try new things, but there comes a point when the more chances you take, the worse golf you are going to play. Sometimes it is necessary to play it safe.

For example, the pin is often placed on the part of the green that is likely to cause golfers the most trouble; there is a steep cliff on one side, a sand trap in front, and maybe another steep cliff right in the back. A pro would probably go straight for the pin, but the pro is one in ten thousand golfers. And out of ten thousand golfers, probably nine thousand would be downright stupid to go for the pin. I think the rule for playing good golf is not to go for the pin, but to analyze the hole and work within your limitations. That is the rule, except on those rare occasions when you have a feeling you can beat the rule. Your intuition says go for it, and that is exactly what you should do. Take the risk.

This applies to one's spiritual life as well. But the New Age movement tends to encourage always going for the pin, adventuring without discernment, which has gotten people

into trouble. That is why some have quipped that Shirley MacLaine should more aptly have titled her distinctly New Age autobiography not *Out on a Limb* but *Out on a Broken Limb.*

HERESY

Until about fifteen years ago, I believed heresy was a totally arcane subject that properly belonged back in the Middle Ages, along with the Inquisition, and had no relevance to our modern world. But then I began working in the hospital with a seriously disturbed "New Age" woman who had been involved with a whole variety of cults. By virtue of the intensity of her spiritual confusion, there was a priest who was serving me as a consultant on the case. Because the matter of religion was involved, I asked her one day, "Tell me about Jesus."

She proceeded to draw a cross on a piece of paper with circles in all quadrants, saying, "There are three Jesuses up here on the top part of the cross, and three down here on the bottom, and three on this arm, and three on that arm."

Sometimes it is necessary to be a bit confrontational. "Cut out that stuff," I ordered, and then asked, "How did He die?"

"He was crucified," she answered.

Something—perhaps the fact that she did everything she could to avoid pain—propelled me to inquire, "Did it hurt?"

"Oh no," she responded.

"What do you mean, it didn't hurt?" I persisted. "How could it not have hurt?"

"Oh," she replied happily, "He was just so highly developed in His Christ consciousness that He was able to project Himself into His astral body and take off from there."

This seemed to me a wacky sort of answer, but I couldn't make any more of it than that until that night when, because

it was so strange, I recounted it to my priest consultant, and he immediately said, "Oh, that's Docetism."

"What on earth is Docetism?" I inquired.

"It was one of the very early church heresies," he explained to me. "The Docetists were a group of early Christians who believed that Jesus was totally divine and His humanity was simply an appearance."

It is important to understand here that Christian heresy is something that only Christians can be guilty of. There are other kinds of heresies we shall address shortly. But Christian heresy is something that is put forth in the name of Christian doctrine but that seriously undermines what the doctrine is all about. It is not difficult to see, then, why Docetism is a heresy. If Jesus was totally divine and His humanity simply an appearance, then His suffering on the cross—as my patient believed—was nothing more than a divine charade, and this whole business of sacrifice that lies at the center of Christian doctrine is nothing but a celestial sham by which so many have been taken in.

Heresy most commonly arises when we run with just one side of a paradox. It is also Christian heresy to believe the opposite of Docetism: namely, that Jesus was totally human, and that His divinity was nothing more than appearance. For if we believe that Jesus was simply another rather wise, "self-actualized," but otherwise perfectly ordinary mortal man, then we must conclude that God did not "come down to live and die as one of us."

So what we are left with at the center of Christian doctrine—whether one cares to believe it or not—is a paradox: that Jesus was paradoxically both human and divine—not fifty percent one and fifty percent the other but, as the doctrine states, "fully human and fully divine."

Since that time I have come to realize that most of the old Christian heresies are alive and well in all manner of places. There are, for instance, two schools of theology called Immanence and Transcendence. Immanence focuses upon

the indwelling divinity within human beings, the God of the Holy Spirit or what Quakers call "the inner light." Transcendence, on the other hand, focuses upon the divinity external to us humans: our Father who art in Heaven, or the big cop up in the sky. Both of these foci are necessary. Whenever people run solely with one or the other, they can get into trouble.

If we believe that God resides totally inside of us, then every thought or feeling that we have can assume the status of revelation. This has been a problem with some of the New Age denominations that are referred to as "New Thought" churches. If we believe the opposite, however, and think that God resides totally up there and out there, then we have the problem of how on earth God ever communicates with us mere mortals except through weird prophets like Moses and Jesus, whose words and deeds are then interpreted to us by a priestly class. This can lead to what I sometimes call "the heresy of orthodoxy" and such things as the Inquisition, where the Inquisitors were, of course, far worse heretics than anyone they were torturing or burning in the name of heresy —if for no other reason than the fact that they were killing the indwelling divinity of their victims. Indeed, an exclusive focus on transcendence is a heresy that some ultratraditional, right-wing Catholics or fundamentalists still fall into.

So what we are left with, once again, is another paradox: that God resides both inside of us in His or Her still, small voice and, simultaneously, outside of us in all of His or Her transcendent, magnificent otherness.

Let me give a final example of two different styles of thinking that are also quite prevalent in these modern days. About fifteen hundred years ago there was a workaholic Irish monk by the name of Pelagius, who taught his followers that salvation was achieved by doing lots of good works. That has since come to be known as the heresy of Pelagianism because it can get us into various kinds of difficulty. It can lead us not only to become workaholics ourselves but also to conclude

that salvation is purely something that we earn, and that the grace of God has nothing to do with it. This can further encourage us to a certain kind of unwarranted pride in our "own" achievements.

Around three hundred years ago in Europe there was a group of Christians who believed the opposite: namely, that salvation was the result of grace alone. They became known as the Quietists, because they sat around quietly waiting for grace to happen. Because this is not the kind of doctrine that would encourage the sorts of social activism Jesus urged us toward, Quietism is also considered a heresy. So, once again, we are pushed to conclude that salvation is the result of some paradoxical mixture of both grace and good works for which we do not have—nor will we ever—any mathematical formula.

NON-CHRISTIAN HERESIES

Other religions can have heresies and may even share them with Christianity. For instance, the struggle over the paradox of grace and good works has been just as much a problem for Muslims as it has for Christians. In fact, the best advice I know on the subject came from Muhammad, who said, "Trust in God, but tie your camel first."

There is also such a thing as secular heresy. The ethic of rugged individualism is the best example. This ethic holds that we are called to become individuals. And that is partly true. Carl Jung said the whole goal of psychospiritual growth was individuation, the ability to be separate from our own parents and to think for ourselves. We are called to become independent and stand on our own two feet, to become captains of our ship, if not necessarily masters of our own destiny. We are called to those things. But rugged individualism rejects the whole other side of the coin, which Jung also talked about. We're called to come to terms with our limitations, our bro-

kenness, our inevitable mutual interdependence. As do other kinds of heresies, rugged individualism neglects that whole other side of the paradox.

This leads to terrible pain—people sitting next to each other in the same pew, hiding behind their masks of composure, pretending they've got it all together, because we're told we ought to have it all together. But in fact, nobody's got it all together, and as a result of the ethic of rugged individualism huge numbers feel that they're not able to talk to each other about the things that are most important to them. It is so isolating, being in our little airtight compartments.

To escape heresy, we must accept paradox. Thinking with integrity is paradoxical thinking. And it is not only necessary that we think with integrity, it's also necessary that we act with integrity. Behaving with integrity is "praxis," a term that was popularized initially by Marxists, and since then has been picked up by liberation theologists. Praxis refers to the integration of your practice with your belief system. As Gandhi said: "What is faith worth if it is not translated into action?" Obviously, we have to integrate our behavior with our theology in order to become people of integrity. Too often that is not done, whatever the religious belief.

HERESY IS ALIVE AND WELL IN MODERN CHRISTIANITY

I do not wish to lay the blame for heresy on New Age churches, because in fact heresies prevail in formal, traditional Christian churches. One more evident than any other I call pseudo-Docetism. Christians guilty of this heresy have had enough religious training to know the paradoxical reality of Jesus being both human and divine, but put ninety-nine percent of their money on His divinity, and only one percent on His humanity. This leads to the excuse that we can't really be expected to behave like Jesus because it places us way down

here, ninety-nine percent human, and Him way up there, beyond identification or imitation.

Here is an example of how bad this has become. Not long ago I participated in a conference of Christian therapists and counselors, where the speaker, Harvey Cox, a Baptist theologian, told the Gospel story of Jesus being called to resuscitate the daughter of a wealthy Roman. As Jesus is going to the Roman's house, a woman who has been hemorrhaging for years reaches out from the crowd and touches His robe. He feels her touch and turns around and asks, "Who touched me?" The woman comes forward and begs Him to cure her and He does, and then goes on to the house of the Roman whose daughter had died.

After telling the story, Cox asked this audience of six hundred mostly Christian professionals whom they identified with. When he asked who identified with the bleeding woman, about a hundred raised their hands. When he asked who identified with the anxious Roman father, more of the rest raised their hands. When he asked who identified with the curious crowd, most raised their hands. But when he asked who identified with Jesus, only six people raised their hands.

Something is very wrong here. Of six hundred more or less professional Christians, only one out of a hundred identified with Jesus. Maybe more actually did but were afraid to raise their hands lest that seem arrogant. But again something is wrong with our concept of Christianity if it seems arrogant to identify with Jesus. That is exactly what we are supposed to do! We're supposed to identify with Jesus, act like Jesus, be like Jesus. That is what Christianity is supposed to be about—the imitation of Christ.

Another brand of heresy has to do with the Christian interpretation of blasphemy, which is the violation of the Second Commandment, "Thou shalt not take the name of the Lord thy God in vain." Most Christians I meet as I go around the country erroneously interpret this to mean that you shouldn't swear or use dirty language. But that is not what

blasphemy is about. Blasphemy is just the opposite. It is using sweet religious language to cloak irreligious behavior.

I once attended a conference where the great Sufi, Idries Shah, was lecturing. And after he had lectured twice over the course of two days, he finally said, "You know that I have been talking to you for four hours now, and I have not yet once used the words 'God' or 'love.' We Sufis do not use these words lightly. They are *sacred.*"

Unfortunately, these words are not sacred to many Christians. I spent a weekend with a born-again couple in South Carolina whose every other sentence was God did this and God did that, and God would do this and God would do that, interspersed with nasty gossip about who was sleeping with whom and who wasn't going to church and whose children had gone sour. When I finally got out of there after three days, I thought if I'd heard God did this and God did that one more time, I would have puked! Their sin was even graver to me than petty gossip because I felt all their "God talk" was blasphemous—the use of "the name of the Lord" in such a way as to trivialize God.

I do not think that the order of the Ten Commandments is accidental. Violation of the First—idolatry—tends to be at the root of all sin. But violation of the Second—blasphemy—is the sin of sins, the lie of lies. It is the pretense of piety accompanied by a total lack of praxis: the ultimate lack of integrity, the refusal even to attempt to integrate one's behavior with one's theology.

COMMUNITY VERSUS CULT

So there are many traps for traditional Christians as well as for New Agers. One open to both is the phenomenon of cults. I do not, in any way, object to people wanting to live together in community. That is a holy calling as far as I am concerned. But there is a big difference between a community

and a cult. Community draws people in by its interconnectedness; community applies no pressure for people to stay; community glories in the extraordinary differences of its members. Cults, on the other hand, are characterized by the brainwashing of their members, by a tremendous pressure to join and not leave, and by a certain sameness of the people in them.

To help make the distinction, I have identified ten characteristics of what makes a cult:

1. Idolatry of a single charismatic leader

The Reverend Sun Myung Moon, acclaimed by Moonies as "The Lord of the Second Advent," is an obvious, overtly religious example of such idolatry. So were Jim Jones and David Koresh, charismatic men who led their followers to disaster and death. There are many "gurus" who encourage adoration of themselves.

2. A revered inner circle

Not even the most ambitious charismatic leader can single-handedly manage an organization beyond a certain size. He or she needs trusted disciples. Generally, all large cults have an inner circle of members who are revered by others almost as much as is the leader. They are held in awe; they are feared; they are envied; they are gossiped about. This revered inner circle is not an utterly distinctive feature of cults; it exists to a greater or lesser degree in any large organization, government, business corporation, university, or church. The question is the degree of reverence or awe and hence the potential for the abuse of power.

3. Secrecy of management

One of the distinguishing features of cults is the great secrecy with which these inner circles operate. Again, this secrecy is characteristic of a great many nonreligious organizations. Think of the executive branch of our government and its obsession with secret documents and security classifications. Think of the industrial secrets of our business corpora-

tions. Think of the boardrooms, the smoke-filled rooms, the seemingly casual breakfast meetings that *really* count. But cult leaders do not maintain even the pretense of accountability for their actions.

4. Financial evasiveness

Some years ago, Lily and I had the opportunity to spend the better part of a day with the top leadership of a New Age peace organization. One of the many disheartening things about that day, which led us to conclude that the organization was a cult, was the group's evasiveness concerning its finances. Why the secrecy? we wondered. The organization was nonprofit, and presumably its finances were a matter of public record and could be investigated by anyone who wanted to take the trouble. I could only assume that the secrecy characteristic of cult leadership was so habitual that it unnecessarily contaminated this most important, public area. It was not the only way in which this organization seemed evasive to us; it was just the most surprising. In any case, financial evasiveness, for whatever reason, does seem to be a characteristic of many cults.

5. Dependency

Perhaps the major reason cults are justifiably feared is that their authoritarian leadership nurtures the dependency of the followers. Rather than encouraging their followers to become a group of all leaders, cults tend to discourage the capacity of their members to think for themselves. This used to be a problem in the Catholic church. Now it can be a problem of flocking to the East for our spiritual answers. It is actually a tradition of Hinduism for its gurus to teach their disciples to look upon them as gods.

6. Conformity

This, to me, is the saddest feature of cults. The leaders of the peace organization I mentioned earlier struck me with their sameness. They varied in age from thirty to seventy; they were men and women; some were dressed formally, others informally. Yet I have never sat in a meeting in the military

or government or anywhere else with twenty people who seemed so oppressively the same.

7. Special language

It is natural for any group of people who work closely and intensively with each other to develop a special internal language—that is, a set of words that have a special meaning to them often incomprehensible to people outside the organization. The more closely the organization moves toward being a cult, the more special this internal language tends to become. Ultimately, it is like a secret language, known only to initiates, and quite untranslatable. For instance, I receive mail from a variety of New Age organizations attempting to enlist my interest. They might succeed if I could take them seriously, but I have a hard time connecting with phrases like "resonating core groups" or "reevolutionizing." Such groups have become so imbued with their special language that they have lost the capacity to communicate effectively with the outside world.

8. Dogmatic doctrine

One cult used to be fond of saying that they were in the process of "developing" their theology and that they wanted to enlist the aid of outsiders, such as myself, in this development. I think it was largely a ploy. As far as I could assess the situation, their theology was already quite developed and most of its doctrines had long since become doctrinaire.

9. Heresy

All organizations exist in relationship to God, consciously or unconsciously, whether they like it or not. In the case of a business corporation, it is usually a relationship of at least passive denial of God. In the case of a satanic cult, it is a relationship of active, vehement denial. The relationship between cults and God is virtually always out of kilter and heretical.

10. God in captivity

In their skewed relationship to God and their satisfaction with dogmatism, cults—one way or another—feel they have

God all sewn up. They have captured God. But the reality is that God is not ours to possess, we are His/Hers to be possessed by, individually and collectively.

If you are trying to evaluate a particular organization, let me point out that to be a cult, a group does not have to satisfy all ten criteria. If it meets three or four, I would be suspicious. It is also important to realize that cults are a dime a dozen and that a great many businesses are cults. I believe that IBM used to be something of a cult, exerting tremendous pressure on its employees to dress the same, look the same, and behave the same.

It has been pointed out to me that the Catholic church fits most of the above criteria. However, I do not believe that the American Catholic church is a cult. It may have been a cult before the Vatican II Council in the 1960s, but Vatican II totally revolutionized Catholicism in this country. In a cult the authority system is totally accepted and never challenged. The authority system in the American Catholic church is now being challenged every day of the week and twice on Sunday. The women's movement in the Catholic church is one of the most active in any Christian church today. There is a great deal of turmoil, but also a great deal of variety in how individual churches practice their faith, ranging from very conservative to very liberal. And this is why I joke that the current, very conservative pope is doing his best to annul Vatican II.

The credit for the incredible transformation of the Catholic church in recent years goes, of course, to Pope John XXIII, who was originally elected as only an interim pope. At the time of his election, the College of Cardinals had a hell of a time agreeing on a suitable candidate, and finally, as a compromise, they decided to elect one of the oldest and most inoffensive of men. John, in his seventies, was overweight and seemed like a sweet old man who wouldn't last long or do much. Within a year of being elected, however, he had initiated Vatican II, and when asked why such a council was

necessary, he threw open one of the ancient windows in the Vatican and exclaimed, "Fresh air! Fresh air!"

NEW AGE AS A SYMBOLINE FORCE

Fresh air is what the New Age movement at its best is about. And while I have so far focused on the "diaboline" aspects of the New Age movement, I firmly believe that the sins New Age is reacting against are very real sins, and that they should be reacted against. The virtues of the New Age movement are absolutely enormous, if the problem of reaction formation can be avoided. In its "symboline" aspects—and that is precisely the right word—New Age is a movement in the direction of integration and integrity, and you see the results. You see it in holistic medicine, which integrates different kinds and aspects of medicine rather than being excessively specialized. You see it in the ecology movement, which integrates the contributions of all living things to the cycle of life. You see it in a much more global kind of thinking than the old mind-set we were once used to.

For example, some years ago, before the Berlin Wall fell, I had the good fortune to meet in an intimate group for three days with two Soviet citizens, one of whom was a high-ranking member of the Central Committee of the Communist Party, who had come here to try and convince us in America that *glasnost* was a real phenomenon. At that point most Americans thought it was some kind of propaganda trick the Russians had cooked up. But through meeting with them in community, I became convinced that it was real.

Shortly after that, I was at a conference where Jack Anderson, the famous Washington columnist, was speaking. Anderson is a man who has done a lot of good things in his life, but he still had an old mind-set. During the question-and-answer period, he was asked about *glasnost,* and he said, knowing the facts, that *glasnost* was a very real phenomenon.

He commented quite accurately that there was a lot of opposition to it in the Soviet Union, particularly from an organization made up largely of older people who were profoundly anti-Semitic and who were fighting against *glasnost.* There was also a great deal of resistance to it, he commented, within the very strong and entrenched Soviet bureaucracy. And then Anderson said, "Thank God the Russians have an even worse bureaucracy than we do."

This is what I mean by the old mind-set—when we actually thank God that other people are worse off than we. I thank God that this old competitive mind-set has, indeed, begun to change. And in a paradigm shift—which is another popular term in the New Age movement—we do need a kind of *glasnost* in America, an openness of our own. We need to move away from competition and compartmentalization toward greater integration in all aspects of our social and spiritual lives.

REVOLUTION OR REFORM

Having answered the question "Is the New Age movement symboline or diaboline?" with a yes and no, I am still left pondering its future. Is it going to be a revolution or a reformation? If it swings to the side of revolution, I think it is going to fail and be dangerous. If, on the other hand, it can keep to a path of reformation, then I think it will become a very holy thing, because we are in great need of reform.

Reformation is more difficult than revolution. It's often easier just to do something different than to hang in there and bring about reform. And the sins of the Old Age that the New Age movement has tackled are not easy to reform. Take medicine, for example. I very much believe in holistic medicine, but it is not cheap medicine. In fact, good holistic medicine is much more expensive than our typically specialized assembly-line kind of medicine. There are also a lot of New Age fads

associated with it, and a lot of charlatans making heaps of money pretending to be practitioners of holistic medicine.

I ponder sometimes whether FCE—the Foundation for Community Encouragement which Lily and I helped start in 1984—is a New Age organization. In some ways it is. One of our clearly stated values, for instance, is "Openness to new ideas." On the same list of values, however, is another that reads: "Valid data"—a value of very traditional science and business practice. We must wage an ongoing, paradoxical struggle to keep such values integrated.

Integrity is not easy. It is always painful. And it is much more difficult to behave with integrity than without it. Since integrity is never painless, reformation is much more difficult than revolution. Whether the New Age movement is going to be saving or damning will come down to whether it is a movement of revolution or of reformation—whether it can motivate the people attracted to its new ideas to do the painful work and practice the discipline required not to throw the baby out with the bathwater, to integrate the best of the new with the best of the old.

CHAPTER TWELVE

Sexuality and Spirituality

The notion that there is a relationship between sexuality and spirituality is shocking to some people—at least to those who have never read the Song of Solomon in the Bible, which begins "Let him kiss me with the kisses of his mouth . . ." This Song of Songs, as it is more properly titled, is an exquisite, erotic duet between God and His or Her people. There is, however, a particular brand of religion that identifies sex and sexuality with the devil, who supposedly tempts us with lust and the sinful pleasures of the flesh. In that context the only possible relationship there can be between sexuality and spirituality is one of war, in which one side must win out over the other. But my own view is that insofar as there is conflict between sexuality and spirituality, it is more in the nature of a lovers' quarrel or a sibling rivalry, both of which to some extent can be outgrown.

If we begin by asking what sexuality is, right away we run into a scientific stone wall. Here at the end of the twentieth century, we know how to blow ourselves off the face of the earth, but we can't even begin, from a scientific point of view, to understand what the nonanatomical differences or similarities are between men and women. I'm afraid that mythology

once again has much more to tell us about the nature of sexuality than does our science.

One of the basic themes in mythology is fear on the part of the gods that human beings are becoming like them, and the myth of sexuality is a variant of this same theme. This myth tells us that, at the beginning, human beings were androgynous, unified creatures. But as such, they were rapidly gaining in power and were about to encroach upon the gods. So the gods split human beings into halves—male and female. And as half creatures, we were no longer capable of competing with the gods. Yet we were also left feeling incomplete, yearning for our lost wholeness, forever searching for our other half, hoping that in the moment of sexual union with our other half we might reexperience the lost bliss of our near godlike totality.

So, at least according to the myth, our sexuality arises out of a sense of incompleteness and is manifested by an urge toward wholeness and a yearning for the godhead. But what is our spirituality if not the same thing? What is our spirituality if not something that arises out of a sense of incompleteness and is manifested by an urge toward wholeness and a yearning for the godhead?

Sexuality and spirituality are not, of course, exactly the same thing. They are not identical twins, but they are kissing cousins, and they arise out of the same kind of ground, not only in myth but in actual human experience.

The fact is that sex is the closest that many people ever come to a spiritual experience. Indeed, it is because it is a spiritual experience of sorts that so many chase after it with a repetitive, desperate kind of abandon. Often, whether they know it or not, they are searching for God. It is no accident that even atheists and agnostics will, at the moment of orgasm, routinely cry out, "Oh God!"

ORGASM AS A MYSTICAL EXPERIENCE

The great psychologist Abraham Maslow one day decided, instead of studying sick people, to study particularly healthy people—the one in ten thousand who seemed to have gotten most of it together, who seemed to have fulfilled their potential, become most fully human. These he called "self-actualized people." (Personally, I would prefer the term "co-actualized.") Studying them, he discerned some thirteen things they had in common. And one of them was that they routinely experienced orgasm as a spiritual, even mystical event.

Again, that word "mystical" is more than an analogy. Throughout the ages mystics have spoken of an ego death as a necessary part of the spiritual, mystical journey, or even as the goal, the end of the mystical journey itself. And you may know that the French have traditionally referred to orgasm as *la petite mort,* or "the little death."

The subjective quality of the orgasmic experience is, of course, highly dependent on the quality of the relationship of the partners involved. So, if it is the best possible orgasm you are after, then the best way to achieve it is with someone who is deeply beloved to you. But while a relationship with a beloved other is necessary to bring us to the very highest mystical heights of the orgasmic experience, once we reach those heights we actually lose the awareness of our partner. At that brief peak point of little death, we forget who and where we are. And in a very real sense, I think, this is because we have left this earth and entered God's country.

As Ananda Coomaraswami put it, "At the moment of mutual climax, each as individuals has no more significance to the other than the gates of Heaven for the one within." Or as Joseph Campbell paraphrased it, "When one has lost oneself in the rapture of love, the partner is of no more importance

than the portals of the temple through which one has passed to the altar."

So the sexual experience is potentially religious. Is the religious experience sexual? I don't believe it is an accident that throughout history most of the very best erotic poetry has been written by monks and nuns. You may already be familiar with the famous "Dark Night" poem of Saint John of the Cross:

1. One dark night,
fired with love's urgent longings
—ah, the sheer grace!—
I went out unseen,
my house being now all stilled.

2. In darkness and secure,
by the secret ladder, disguised,
—ah, the sheer grace!—
in darkness and concealment,
my house being now all stilled.

3. On that glad night,
in secret, for no one saw me,
nor did I look at anything,
with no other light or guide
than the one that burned in my heart.

4. This guided me
more surely than the light of noon
to where he was waiting for me,
—him I knew so well—
there in a place where no one appeared.

Note the mixing of the sexes in this next stanza:

5. O guiding night!
O night more lovely than the dawn!

O night that has united
the Lover with his beloved,
transforming the beloved in her Lover.

6. Upon my flowering breast
which I kept wholly for him alone,
there he lay sleeping,
and I caressing him
there in a breeze from the fanning cedars.

7. When the breeze blew from the turret,
as I parted his hair,
it wounded my neck
with its gentle hand,
suspending all my senses.

8. I abandoned and forgot myself,
laying my face on my Beloved;
all things ceased; I went out from myself,
leaving my cares
forgotten among the lilies.

I believe that the final stanza of this poem, which describes the mystical union possible between human beings and God, is also as fine a description of orgasm as anything in literature: "I abandoned and forgot myself . . . all things ceased . . . I went out from myself . . ."

I have learned in my encounters with monks and nuns that the best monk or nun is someone who loves God the most passionately. And in order to love God passionately, one has to be a passionate, sexual person. How is it then that just such people choose chastity or celibacy?

There are two reasons. The first, if you will pardon the pun, is that sex can screw up relationships. As soon as we make a sexual object of another person, there is a profound tendency to use him or her. Although we've got somewhat differing masculine and feminine styles of doing this, we each

have a tendency to use the sex object in our lives in ways that are covertly, if not overtly, manipulative and self-serving.

There have been experiments with noncelibate convents and monasteries, but thus far they have all been failures. Therefore, those who firmly resolve to relate with their fellow human beings in an unfailingly healing fashion usually decide that a highly restrained sexuality, such as celibacy or chastity, is the price they must pay. And often they find the price well worth it.

THE ILLUSION OF ROMANTIC LOVE

In *The Road Less Traveled,* I drew a sharp distinction between love (which I defined as concern for the spiritual growth of another) and romantic love (which I have come to understand as a form of narcissism). The whole American ideal of romantic love holds that it ought to be somehow possible for Cinderella to ride off with her prince into the sunset of endless orgasms. It is an illusion. Romantic love is preferable to what preceded it in history—namely, a culture of marriage by arrangement. But nonetheless, anyone who believes that permanent romance in a relationship is a perpetual possibility is doomed to perpetual disappointment. In fact, it is the search for God in human romantic relationships that is, I think, one of the greatest problems we have in this and other cultures.

What we do is to look to our spouse or lover to be a god unto us. We look to our spouse or lover to meet all of our needs, to fulfill us, to bring us a lasting Heaven on earth. And it never works. And among the reasons it never works—whether or not we're aware when we do this—is that we are violating the First Commandment, which says, "I am the Lord thy God, and thou shalt not have any other gods before me."

It is, however, also very natural that we should do this. It

is very natural to want to have a tangible God, one whom we can not only see and touch but also hold and embrace and sleep with and perhaps even possess. So, we keep looking to our spouse or lover to be a god unto us, and in the process, we forget about the true God.

Thus the other reason the profoundly religious so often choose celibacy is that they do not want to be distracted from their love of God. They do not want to fall prey to the idolatry of human romantic love. They know that, as Saint Augustine said, "You made us for Yourself, dear Lord, and we cannot find true rest except in You." And that it is possible, if their number-one relationship is with God, that they may not need to seek another.

THE SEXINESS OF SPIRITUALITY

It is not my intent to make an impassioned plea for celibacy as a necessity for spiritual growth. On the contrary, I celebrate not only sexuality but sex. I like sex and I like other people to have sex.

About a dozen years ago, after many months of working with a rigid, frigid woman in her mid-thirties, I had the opportunity to witness her undergo a sudden and quite profound Christian conversion. And within three weeks of that conversion, she became orgasmic for the first time in her life. Could the timing have been accidental? I doubt it. As a friend of mine once put it, "The sexual and the spiritual parts of our personality lie so close together that it is hardly possible to arouse one without arousing the other." I do not think it an accident that when this woman became able to give herself wholeheartedly to God, in very short order she became able to give herself wholeheartedly to a human partner, praise the Lord!

I have another friend, a priest, who actually uses this phenomenon as a yardstick of conversion. He tells me that if

a conversion occurs in a previously sexually repressed individual and is not accompanied by some kind of sexual awakening or blossoming, then he has reason to doubt the depth of the conversion.

So it is that you hear stories about ministers who become involved with female parishioners. Ministers and other people in similar positions tend to be sitting ducks when such passions are aroused. And I will confess that when I was practicing psychotherapy, any time I got on the same spiritual wavelength with a female patient of mine under the age of ninety, I had to watch my step.

THE UNIVERSAL PROBLEM

Sex is a problem for everyone. Sex is a problem for children, sex is a problem for adolescents, sex is a problem for young adults, sex is a problem for middle-aged adults, sex is a problem for elderly adults. Sex is a problem for celibates, sex is a problem for married people, sex is a problem for single people, sex is a problem for straight people, sex is a problem for gay people. Sex is a problem for bricklayers and plumbers, sex is a problem for dentists and lawyers, sex is a problem for surgeons and therapists and psychiatrists. And sex is a problem for Scott Peck.

In my vision of this world as a kind of celestial boot camp—replete with obstacles that have been almost fiendishly designed for our learning—of all the obstacles that God designed for our learning, I think the one that He or She most fiendishly designed is sex. God built into us a feeling that we can solve the problem of sex and be forever sexually fulfilled, that we can get over the obstacle. Indeed, for a couple of weeks or a couple of months, or maybe even for a couple of years, if we are lucky, we may feel that we have solved the problem of sex. But then, of course, we change or our partners change, or the whole ball game changes, and once again

we are left trying to scramble over that obstacle with this built-in feeling that we can get over it, when actually we never can.

However, in the process of trying to get over it, we learn a great deal about vulnerability and intimacy and love and how to whittle away at our narcissism. Some of us even get to graduate from boot camp. And if you involve God in the process, the chances of success improve, and to do that you don't have to be a monk or a nun.

I have come up with my own definitions of celibacy and chastity. I arrived at these definitions thinking about the times when I was "on the make." That is the appropriate expression, because what I was trying to do was to make sex happen. I would have it all plotted out. I would take the woman who was the object of my desire out to dinner at a nice restaurant, and then to a movie, and then back to my apartment, where I would have tapes and records all picked out, and then we would go to bed. That's how I was going to make it happen. But contrary to my best-laid plans, I usually couldn't make it happen, and occasionally when I did, it wasn't a particularly great experience.

Some of the most glorious sexual experiences I ever had, however, were the ones that not only seemed just to happen but also seemed to be orchestrated by angels off in the wings —specifically, not by me. So I got to thinking that chastity maybe should be defined as a three-way relationship between two human beings and God, in which God is allowed to call the shots.

If you were to define chastity in that way, then there are a number of implications. One is that chastity is much harder than celibacy, which I define simply as the decision to refrain from sexual activity, at least for a period of time. Another is that chastity is filled with traps because it's extraordinarily easy for us to convince ourselves that God wants us to do what we are doing. Still another implication is that it is possible for premarital or extramarital sex to be quite chaste. And con-

versely, that it is possible for marital sex to be profoundly unchaste.

When I was practicing psychotherapy, I sometimes suggested to married couples whose sex had gotten perfunctory that they might want to experiment with periods of chastity. Chastity and celibacy are two valid options for at least some people. And I think I would have made that suggestion even if I were a secular psychiatrist and not a religious one, because of several experiences I have had.

One was a number of years ago. I was working with a young woman, a Ph.D. schooled at the best universities, and among her many symptoms was a compulsive need to engage in sexual relationships which she neither desired nor enjoyed. We went through all the usual Freudian psychodynamics trying to get to the root of this symptom without any success, until one day I asked her, "You don't happen to believe, do you, that a very active sex life is a necessary part of mental health?" And she said, "Well of course. I mean, isn't that the way it is?"

The poor woman felt that she had to compulsively engage in sexual relationships which she neither desired nor enjoyed simply to maintain an image of herself as mentally healthy. What an extraordinary relief it was for her when, after she had abstained from sex for three weeks, I gave her a certificate of mental health.

I have seen the same phenomenon among elderly couples. In the past dozen years or so, there has been a whole spate of articles in the psychiatric and psychological literature saying that it is really pretty normal for elderly people to have sexual relationships. However, as with any kind of change in outlook, I'm always worried a little bit about the pendulum swinging too far. I am concerned that now that we professionals have so graciously given the elderly permission to have sex, we may start telling them they should have it whether they like it or not—in order to stay young, or something.

In the course of my career, I have run into two elderly

couples who were deeply in love with each other, yet in both instances each partner confessed to me individually, in private, that he or she had lost sexual interest in the other, or in anyone else for that matter. They were continuing to have a sexual relationship, however, because each felt that the other partner wanted it. So I got the two of them together, brought this out in the open, and suggested, "Since neither of you wants sex, why don't you stop?" It was like a veritable revelation to them. They had never considered that it was all right to stop.

I am reminded of that famous passage from Ecclesiastes which begins, "To every thing there is a season, and a time to every purpose under the heaven," and goes on to say, "A time to embrace, and a time to refrain from embracing." This is profound secular as well as spiritual wisdom. Sex is a great gift, but that doesn't necessarily mean that it is a gift to be picked up by all people at all times in all seasons.

GOD AND SEX

In any discussion of sex, the notion of a sexual relationship between human beings and God is likely to be the most controversial and shocking. While I think that almost everyone would accept that the most passionate relationships we can have with God are romantic ones, they would question whether sex or sexuality is actually involved. Most people would maintain that the erotic poetry of the Bible or of people like Saint John of the Cross is no more than a poetic metaphor for a passionate spirituality. At most they might agree with Alan Jones, who said that sexual love is a robust symbol of a yet more robust love. I think there is some truth in this. But I do not think it is the whole truth.

Shocking as it may seem, I think there *is* a genuine sexual element in the relationship between human beings and God. What this means, if I am correct, is not only that we human

beings are sexual creatures, but also that God is in fact a sexual being. That is hardly what I have always believed. When I was in college, my favorite quote was one from Voltaire: "If God created us in His own image, we have certainly returned the compliment." Nothing seemed more absurd to me than imagining God in anthropomorphic terms, as an old man with a long white beard or a being with genitalia. It seemed to me that God must be infinitely different and infinitely more than we can possibly imagine Him or Her to be. And so He or She is.

However, in the years since college, I have also come to realize that the very deepest means we have to even begin to comprehend something about the nature of God is through a projection onto Him or Her of the very best of our human nature. And that God—among other things and above all other things—is *humane*. He represents humanity at its best, which has something to do with what is meant by God creating us in His own image.

GOD AS A SEDUCER

I believe that God not only created us in His own image but continues to do so. And I am indebted to the Episcopal theologian and author Robert Capon for pointing out the obvious logic that since God created us in His own image, and since we are sexual creatures, it might only stand to reason that God is a sexual being.

One reason that this syllogism makes sense to me, in addition to its logic, is that I myself have experienced God as a seducer. Substitute another word in your mind, like "lover" or "wooer," if you will, but obviously God has succeeded in seducing me, although more often than not I have run away from Him like a frightened, reluctant virgin. Once again, in Capon's words, this sexy God's love for us is profoundly seductive—"He is a God who is continually on the make."

God could have made sex as secular as breathing or eating. But instead He brushed it with a spiritual flavor, and He did this very deliberately, I think, in order to give us a taste for Him. Because above all else, He wants to lure us to Him. This notion of God not only as a sexual being but as a particularly seductive one is perhaps somewhat supportive of our traditional masculine image of Him. Certainly He does behave with an aggressiveness in the hunt that we have typically associated with males. I think that this association itself is sexist and I have met a few good huntresses in my time. But in any case, as Francis Thompson's famous poem "The Hound of Heaven" suggests, He chases after us with a vigor that is matched only by the vigor with which we may flee from Him. And when we are finally caught, we may experience our conversion, as I suggested in *The Road Less Traveled,* not necessarily as an "Oh joy!" phenomenon, but often as an "Oh shit!" phenomenon. Because we have been trapped. Because we have been brought to bay. Because we have finally and irrevocably been caught.

That's what it's all about. Not that He is male, not that She is female—He/She is both and more—but that He is after us, that He wants us, that He loves us beyond belief, and that He intends to have us, no matter how fast and far we flee. And our individual struggle is only over how long we are going to stick with our prudish little hang-ups and our narcissistic little reticences before we finally and willingly open ourselves in surrender to Him. As John Donne did when he wrote his Holy Sonnet XIV:

> Batter my heart, three person'd God . . .
> Take me to you, imprison me, for I,
> Except you enthrall me, never shall be free,
> Nor ever chaste, except you ravish me.

EPILOGUE

Psychiatry's Predicament*

All of us are agents of history, playing out our roles, shifting or failing to shift according to its tides. And at this moment in history, many feel the need for a shift in American psychiatry. Over the past twenty-five years, American psychiatry has increasingly run with the "medical model" —namely, a model which places far greater emphasis on the distinctly materialistic and biological aspects of psychiatric disease than on other aspects. It is in no way my intent to disparage the profound biochemical advances that have been made over the past forty years in the treatment and understanding of mental illness, or to discourage future progress in this area. Nonetheless, along with many, I am concerned that psychiatry, in its recent enamoredness with biochemistry, may be in grave danger of losing all its old psychological and social wisdom, as well as of failing to gain any new wisdom on these fronts.

It is not an idle concern. In 1987, a colleague and I ex-

* *Adapted from an address as Distinguished Psychiatrist Lecturer to the American Psychiatric Association on May 4, 1992, in Washington, D.C.*

amined a candidate for certification by the American Board of Psychiatry and Neurology. He was a highly intelligent man in his late thirties who possessed at least as much compassion as the other candidates. However, when asked by my colleague to give a psychodynamic formulation of the case in question, he replied, "I don't do psychodynamics." A certain shift or correction might seem to be in order.

Indeed, I believe we need to explore the possibility of an even greater shift. Although perhaps recently underestimated, the psychodynamic and social aspects of mental illness have held a respected place in the history of American psychiatry. Its spiritual aspects, however, have not. Psychiatry has not only neglected but actively ignored the issue of spirituality.

Contributing to this situation is the fact that the topic of spirituality is so subject to misinterpretation. In part, this is due to a poverty in our language. Throughout the world, there is confusion between the terms "spirituality" and "religion." Many identify the term "religion" with organized religion and a system of dogma and sanctions with which they have often had unfortunate experience. It is a hot-button word. There is even disagreement about the meaning of its Latin root, *religio,* which has been variously translated as "restrain," "reliance," or "connection"—all very different concepts.

The classic turn-of-the-century work by the great American psychologist William James, *The Varieties of Religious Experience,* is mandatory first-year reading for most divinity students and unread by most students of psychiatry. In it, James defined religion as "the attempt to be in harmony with an unseen order of things." He was using "religion" in its sense of "to connect." I will use it here as my definition of spirituality. The attempt to be in harmony with an unseen order does not imply a preference for any one doctrine over another or the necessity for membership in any particular organization.

It is my own faith—call it a theory, if you so choose—that there is indeed an unseen order of things behind the veil

of materialism. And not only is it proper that humans attempt to be in harmony with that order, but also that the unseen order is actually and actively attempting to be in harmony with us. One consequence of this faith is my belief that everyone has a spiritual life, just as they have an unconscious, whether they like it or not. That many ignore, actively deny, or vigorously flee from the unseen order doesn't mean they are not spiritual beings; it only means they are trying to avoid the fact. Others may think of themselves as atheists and deny the existence of God, yet they passionately believe that things like truth, beauty, and social justice are very much a part of an unseen order, and dedicate themselves to such an unseen order with a passion far greater than that of most who regularly attend a church, synagogue, mosque, or temple. Thus, we are all spiritual beings, and I believe that a psychiatry which does not regard humans as spiritual beings may be largely missing the boat.

In discussing the topic of spirituality, I hope I do not strip it of all its power and poetry. For some of us, myself included, the essence of the unseen order is God, and God should not be taken lightly. A Hasidic story passed on to me by Erich Fromm makes the point. It is the story of a good Jewish man —let us call him Mordecai—who prayed one day, "O God, let me know Your true name, even as the angels do." The Lord God heard his prayer and granted it, allowing Mordecai to know His true name. Whereupon Mordecai crept under the bed and yelped in sheer animal terror, "O God, let me forget Your true name." And the Lord God heard that prayer and granted it also. Something of the same point was made by the Apostle Paul when he said, "It is a terrifying thing to fall into the hands of the living God."

I do not pretend to know the true name of God. I see enormous virtue in the wording of the third step of AA and the other twelve-step programs: "Make a decision to turn our will and our lives over to the care of God *as we understand Him.*" I would only alter the phrase to "as we understand Him or Her." Henceforth, I will perhaps be more dispassionate,

but only having made the point that we are touching on holy ground.

Psychiatry has its own power. For instance, during my training in the mid-sixties when psychiatry was more broad-based—more bio-psycho-social—than it is today, I was taught a terribly important principle: "All symptoms are overdetermined." It is a principle which many other physicians, theologians, scholars, and most lay people desperately need to learn. In any case, I believe the failure of American psychiatry to deal with the issue of spirituality is itself a profoundly overdetermined symptom rooted in multiple historical forces and other factors. Five of them seem more important to me than any others.

Far and away the most important and deepest root of our current predicament extends back long before Freud, long before Philippe Pinel and Benjamin Rush and the existence of "modern" psychiatry. Prior to the seventeenth century, the relationship between science and religion was primarily one of integration. That integration was known as philosophy. The early philosophers—men like Plato, Aristotle, and Thomas Aquinas—were of scientific bent, thinking in terms of evidence and questioning premises, but they were also utterly convinced that God, as they understood Him, was the central reality. By the beginning of the seventeenth century, however, things had begun to go sour, coming to a head in 1633 when Galileo was summoned before the Inquisition. In order to deal with the fallout from such events—in order to smooth the waters between science and religion—near the end of the seventeenth century, an unwritten social contract was developed, divvying up the territory between science, religion, and government. Peace was achieved by giving each its own turf. With minor exceptions, government was not supposed to interfere with science or with religion. Religion was not supposed to interfere with government or science. And science was not supposed to interfere with religion or government. All manner of good came from this unwritten contract.

But in the last half of the twentieth century, it is becom-

ing increasingly obsolete, and a new and very different kind of contract is beginning to be drawn in virtually all spheres of human activity. What is going on in psychiatry is only a small part of the big picture. The influence of American psychiatry on human intellectual life during the past ninety years has been far greater than the number of psychiatrists might imply. But if American psychiatry fails to shift with the new tide, it is likely to end up in an intellectual backwater.

Let us consider the roles of science and religion under the old unwritten contract. In the early 1700s, Isaac Newton was president of the Royal Society of London for Improving Natural Knowledge. Under the old contract, then already in place, natural knowledge was distinguished from supernatural knowledge. "Natural knowledge" was the province of science, "supernatural knowledge" was the province of religion, and according to the rules of the old contract, never the twain should meet. One effect of that separation was the emasculation of philosophy. Since natural knowledge became the province of the scientists and supernatural knowledge the province of the theologians, the poor philosophers were left only with what fell through the cracks, which was not much. Philosophy eventually became a relatively arcane and totally elective subject in our colleges. The most visible remnant of its once glorious past is in outmoded titles which have their origin in the Middle Ages. So it is today that a graduate student, after some years of study and research in the field of microbiology, will be awarded for his or her efforts a doctor of philosophy degree, even though she or he may never have taken a single philosophy course.

The separation of science and religion also had a profound effect upon the practice of psychotherapy. I was taught —as virtually all psychiatrists are taught—that psychotherapy should somehow be a scientific form of endeavor. An ideal of "pure science" was held before us, and we were admonished that science should be "value-free." It was nonsense, of course. It is not possible to do anything, much less practice

psychotherapy, without values. All along, we psychotherapists were operating within a value system so close to us that we were not particularly conscious of it. The name that has been given to that value system is secular humanism.

As for religion specifically, the APA has actual guidelines to the effect that a psychiatrist should not inject religion into treatment when it is counter to the patient's belief system, nor should he or she attempt to discredit the patient's belief system. Those sound like "nice" guidelines—and I would hardly advocate their demolition—but they are woefully incomplete. First of all, they are frequently not followed. The guideline against "attempting to discredit the patient's belief system" is generally interpreted to mean that a religious psychiatrist should not impose his or her religion upon a secular humanist patient. But what about the secular humanist psychiatrist who attempts to impose his or her secular humanism upon a religious patient? That imposition is so frequent as to be almost standard, and is made by large numbers of psychiatrists, overtly or covertly, without their even being aware of it.

Let us take the other side of the coin and suppose that a secular humanist psychiatrist is well aware of his own value system and these guidelines, but is dealing with a patient in psychotherapy whose overtly religious belief system comprises either the outer defense or the core of a psychological fixation. Is the psychiatrist prevented then from questioning or confronting such a belief system? What is appropriate? The fact of the matter is that with three hundred years of historical tradition pronouncing that religion is totally out of their domain, and having been trained in this tradition, psychiatrists are ill-equipped indeed to deal with either religious pathology or religious health. No amount of training will ever be sufficient to ensure that the practitioner never founders. The traditional lack of training in the realm of spirituality, however, assures that most well-trained, astute practitioners will often flounder destructively in these matters.

The second most important determinant, to my mind—a

consequence of the first—for American psychiatry's profound neglect of spirituality is the virtually total ignorance on the part of psychiatrists of the stages of spiritual development. I doubt that it is possible for a psychiatrist to complete his or her residency training without significant exposure to stage theory: to Freud's stages of psychosexual development, to Piaget's stages of cognitive development, and Erikson's stages of maturation and their predictable crises. Yet, to my knowledge, in their training psychiatrists receive absolutely no exposure to the stages of spiritual development. Not the only, but the primary reason for this fact is that psychiatry residency training programs have simply not regarded it as their responsibility to teach anything about spirituality. Indeed, in some respects, they have regarded it as their responsibility *not* to teach anything about spirituality. This extraordinary state of affairs is, of course, the result of that unwritten social contract which allocated the study of spirituality to religion or theology, while psychiatry clearly identified itself with the scientific camp, which was constrained to restrict itself to the study of "natural phenomena."

I have described elsewhere my understanding and interpretation of the stages of spiritual development. In brief, they are: Stage One, which I label chaotic/antisocial and which may be thought of as a stage of lawlessness, absent of spirituality;

Stage Two, which I label formal/institutional and which may be thought of as a rigorous adherence to the letter of the law and attachment to the forms of religion;

Stage Three, which I label skeptic/individual and which is a stage of principled behavior, but one characterized by religious doubt or disinterest, albeit accompanied by inquisitiveness about other areas of life;

And finally Stage Four, the most mature of the stages, which I label mystical/communal and which may be thought of as a state of the spirit of the law, as opposed to Stage Two, which tends to be one of the letter of the law.

You may quickly see parallels between these stages of

spiritual development and the psychosexual developmental stages with which psychiatrists are generally familiar—Stage One corresponding in some ways to the first five years of life, Stage Two to the latency period, Stage Three to adolescence and early adulthood, and Stage Four to the last half of life in healthy human development. And like developmental stages, the stages of spiritual development are sequential. They cannot be skipped over, there are people in between stages, and there are gradations within stages.

The diagnosis of the stage into which a particular individual falls needs to be made with some care and discernment. Because a man is a scientist, he may look as if he is in Stage Three, when actually he has a primarily Stage Two spirituality. Another may sell mystical sayings in Stage Four language but actually be a Stage One con artist. Just as there are fixations of psychosexual development, so people may become spiritually fixated in one of these stages, sometimes for some of the same reasons. Finally, let me point out that a small minority may not fit very well into this stage system, but that in itself may be diagnostic. For instance, those we call borderline personalities tend to have a foot in Stage One, a foot in Stage Two, a hand in Stage Three, and a hand in Stage Four—it being no accident that since they are "borderline," they tend to be all over the place.

There are many reasons why an understanding of these stages of spiritual development is critical, but the most important relate to the fact that the vast majority of psychiatrists—including those who are training new psychiatrists—are Stage Three people. As such, on the whole they are more spiritually developed than the majority of churchgoers or those who are identifiably religious. On the other hand, they are less spiritually developed than a minority of the identifiably religious. Ignorance of this reality has profound implications. It predisposes psychiatrists not only to look upon all religion as inferior and pathological, but also to be oblivious to the fact that they themselves may have a spiritual distance to travel.

The third root cause for American psychiatry's neglect of

spirituality is the profound influence of Freud. Whatever the reasons, Freud has had a far more profound influence upon American psychiatry than upon psychiatry anywhere else on the globe, with the possible exceptions of Brazil and Argentina. In his native Austria, for instance, he is a figure of relatively minor significance. In the United States he is, even today—and, I believe, deservedly so—a towering figure.

Freud grew up and came into maturity during the heyday of the unwritten social contract separating science and religion. He was a Stage Three individual who completely identified himself with science and was deeply threatened by the issue of spirituality, so much so as to terminate his relationship with his most beloved disciple, Jung.

In 1962, during my training in psychiatry in medical school, we fourth-year students received a brief series of lectures on the history of psychiatry. An entire lecture was devoted to Freud. In another lecture about lesser figures, our professor stated, "And then there is Carl Jung, who received a certain amount of undeserved attention for reasons that are unclear." End of discussion. At that time, many of Freud's writings could be found in the average local bookstore, and none of Jung's. Today, of course, you are likely to find some of Jung's works in the local bookstore and unlikely to find Freud's.

I believe that Freud was the greater psychiatrist, and while he made more mistakes than Jung, he made so many major contributions to psychiatry that we even take them for granted. And while Jung made fewer mistakes and his work is profoundly significant, his contributions have hardly matched those of Freud. He was the lesser psychiatrist. He was also the more spiritually developed individual. This, incidentally, points up the fact that there is no one-to-one correspondence between the importance of the contributions made by individuals and their stage of spiritual development. In any case, the influence of the Stage Three Freud in the United States has further entrenched the secularism of American psychiatry.

The fourth factor that has predisposed American psychiatry to excessive secularism and neglect of spirituality has been the large number of patients we have all seen who have been hurt by religion or in the name of religion. Such experiences have cemented the already overdetermined antipathy of many psychiatrists to religion. And in their antipathy and predisposition, they have generally failed to realize they are dealing with a biased sample of humanity.

Two biases have been involved. The first is that, as physicians, we tend to see the diseased, the casualties. We see people who have been hurt by rigid, frigid nuns or else by their early Stage Two, destructively dogmatic, fundamentalist Protestant parents. We are less likely to see people such as Babe Ruth and Ethel Waters, who were dramatically rescued or saved from antisocial Stage One childhoods by supposedly rigid, frigid nuns.

The second bias affecting psychiatrists specializing in psychotherapy has been patient self-selection. Many patients have gravitated to Stage Three secular psychotherapists precisely because they themselves have already begun their spiritual journey out of Stage Two and primitive religion into skepticism and individuation.

One of the most important reasons it is so critical to understand the stages of spiritual development is because of the sense of threat that exists between people in different stages, and their inevitable interaction in the therapeutic setting. There is a profound tendency for us human beings to look up to someone who is one step—perhaps a third of a stage—ahead of us as a wise person or guru. On the other hand, if someone is two steps ahead of us, we usually think that he or she is a threat, even evil. That is what happened to Socrates and Jesus. This means that the most spiritually developed people do not necessarily make the best therapists for everyone. Rather, it is Stage Two people and rigid programs that often offer the best therapy for Stage One people. Stage Three people—a role that has been played by secular psychothera-

pists—often serve as the best guides for people moving out of Stage Two. And Stage Four people make the best therapists for those in the further reaches of Stage Three or spiritual directors for those who have already entered Stage Four. In any case, secular therapists have tended to be sought out by those who have already begun to identify Stage Two formulistic religious thinking as a destructive influence in their lives and something they are at least partially ready to outgrow.

The fifth and final determinant of American psychiatry's prevailing antipathy toward spirituality has been the profound distrust and suspicion of psychiatry by many Stage Two religious people. This antipathy has often been unjustified, and is a function not of realistic thinking but of the sense of threat that exists between people in different stages of spiritual development. Many fundamentalist Christians, for example, have ascribed psychiatry—along with evolution and world government—to the devil.

I have had personal experience with the sense of threat that exists among both Stage Two religious people and Stage Three secular people. For over a decade, without any success, I have tried to encourage the development of what I call an Institute for the Scientific Study of Deliverance, defining deliverance as any form of healing in which deities are invoked, and which can range from such extremely common phenomena as prayer healing through deliverance—a form of mini-exorcism routinely practiced by fundamentalist Christians—all the way to full-scale "combative" exorcism. Only once did it look as if I might possibly succeed in this endeavor.

Ten years ago I worked with the chairman of the board of a large psychiatric center. The center consisted of two parts. One was a 120-bed inpatient unit led primarily by Stage Three secular scientific-minded psychiatrists; the other was a large outpatient service led primarily by Stage Two religiously oriented pastoral counselors. In the forty years of the center's existence, these two parts of the organization had been almost armed camps at dramatic odds with each other. The chairman of the board thought that my proposed institute might be

something that could bring these two hostile factions together. He was correct. They came together in opposition to my proposal. The secular psychiatrists said that my operational definitions were too fuzzy, there were too many variables, and the whole field was inherently unresearchable. The religious nurses and pastoral counselors said that everyone knows that prayer works, and you shouldn't tamper with faith. So it was that the first time in forty years that these two armed camps came together was to oppose the scientific study of spiritual phenomena.

American psychiatry is, I believe, currently in a predicament. I call it a predicament because its traditional neglect of the issue of spirituality has led to five broad areas of failure: occasional, devastating misdiagnosis; not infrequent mistreatment; an increasingly poor reputation; inadequate research and theory; and a limitation of psychiatrists' own personal development. Taken further, these failures are so destructive to psychiatry that the predicament can properly be called grave.

In the category of misdiagnosis are the cases in which otherwise competent psychiatrists routinely ignore or distort the spiritual aspects of their patients' lives so as either to totally miss the diagnosis or to make a diagnosis which is harmfully incomplete. To illustrate this area of failure, I offer two clinical vignettes from my personal experience over the past nine years—a period when I have hardly been in practice at all.

The earliest occurred in the winter of 1983, when I had already largely wound down my practice but was still doing some consulting. I was phoned by a man requesting my consultation in the case of his sixty-four-year-old wife, who had been hospitalized for the preceding three years in one of the most prestigious psychiatric hospitals in the nation. From the husband I learned of the very sudden onset of devastating psychosis at the age of sixty in a woman who for the entirety of her life had apparently been mentally completely healthy and, for almost forty years, an ideally functioning, perfectly

stable wife, mother, grandmother, and member of the community. Upon questioning, however, I did spot a red flag.

Three years prior to the sudden onset of psychosis, this woman, who had been a lifelong and active member of the Presbyterian church, had suddenly, without any explanation to her husband or others, left that traditional denomination and joined the Unity church, a far more liberal Christian church (indeed, so liberal that some would consider it to be heretical—a bit of a New Age church). I also learned that she had become extremely close to the younger and very charismatic minister of this new church.

A month later I went to the hospital to see the woman in consultation. I spent half an hour with her personally. She was well kept, polite, and proper. She was oriented times three. She did not appear depressed. In our brief time together, I was not able to arrive at my own diagnosis. The only thing I could say with certainty was that she was both facilely and profoundly evasive about her personal life and, particularly, her spiritual life. Our meeting was so brief because she insisted that it end when I confronted her with her evasiveness.

I spent much time reviewing her records. She had been variously diagnosed as having depression, involutional psychotic depression, bipolar disease manifested by depression, possible schizophrenia, and possible chronic organic brain syndrome. Over the course of her three years in the hospital, she had failed utterly to respond to antidepressants, phenothiazines, and electroshock therapy, or even to respond to or become engaged in psychotherapy. Reluctantly, her psychiatrist acknowledged that they were unsure of what diagnostic category to put her in. There was no mention in her records of a spiritual history, much less her sudden change in denominations three years before the onset of her psychosis. Nor were the psychiatrists then in charge of her case aware of any spiritual history or this particular red flag. I recommended an intensive psychodynamic diagnostic intervention process that

would include spiritual consultation. My recommendation was not acted upon, on the grounds that a lengthier stay in the hospital was unsupportable. The woman was transferred to a nursing home, and my further services were not sought.

I cannot tell you that woman's diagnosis. What I can tell you, however, is that in the course of three years of unbelievably expensive treatment in this most prestigious, traditional psychiatric hospital, a patient's spiritual life had been utterly overlooked and no adequate diagnosis had been formulated. I will go further and state that no adequate diagnosis had even been attempted in a case where the traditional diagnostic rubrics did not seem to fit.

The second case is that of a young man I never saw. He was a patient of a highly competent, secular psychiatrist—Ted, I will call him—who had been a friend of mine in medical school. In 1989, happening to be lecturing in his city, I dined with him and had the opportunity to catch up on the twenty-five years since we had last met. I learned that he had come to specialize in the treatment of multiple-personality disorder. He was particularly excited about a young man he was currently treating, in whom he had, to date, uncovered some fifty-two different personalities, one of which, he commented as an aside, "calls himself Judas—and he's a real bad guy."

I asked Ted whether he ever had the feeling that his patient was "toying" with him. "No," Ted responded. "Why do you ask?" I suggested the possibility that he might have a case of possession on his hands—either one coexisting with multiple-personality disorder or possibly even one for which the MPD was a sham. With his secular orientation, Ted wouldn't even consider my suggestion. I left feeling sad at what seemed to me a significant possibility—if not probability—that my otherwise competent friend was misdiagnosing and hence mistreating his most intensive case at the time. And that he was utterly immune to even my gentlest consultation on the matter.

Misdiagnosis almost inevitably results in mistreatment. But that is hardly the end of it, because mistreatment or inadequate treatment can occur in the face of a correct diagnosis. Indeed, my concern with misdiagnosis is relatively minor. A far greater problem, to my mind, has been the vast amount of mistreatment of patients with a correct primary diagnosis by virtue of psychiatry's neglect of and antipathy for spiritual issues. This kind of mistreatment generally falls into one or more of five categories: failure to listen, denigration of the patient's humanity, failure to encourage healthy spirituality, failure to combat unhealthy spirituality or false theology, and failure to comprehend important aspects of the patient's life.

The single most common complaint I hear from psychotherapy patients about their therapists (they are just as likely to be secular-minded psychologists and social workers as psychiatrists, but psychiatry has tended to call the tune) has been that they did not or would not listen to the spiritual aspects of their lives. When patients talk about such things as a feeling of calling, consideration of entering monastic life or the ministry, mystical experiences, or even simple belief in God, the prevailing tendency of psychotherapists is to simply shut down until the patients are speaking of more mundane matters—or else to actively attempt to divert them to more mundane matters. Many patients have left therapists as a result.

Even more common is that the patient, picking up on the therapist's cues, will enter into a kind of unspoken collusion where both agree to avoid spiritual issues. Typically, patients will tell me, "I really like my therapist. He [or she] is a decent person. I feel he is trying to help me, and indeed, he has been of some help. But you wouldn't believe how threatened he gets whenever I mention the spiritual side of my life. So, since I'm getting some help, I've learned to simply hide that side of my life from him and never mention it. But I sure wish it could be different. I wish I could be wholly myself in his office. Sometimes I think I would be better off with a therapist who is more receptive, but at the moment it doesn't seem

worth the trouble to start all over again. And besides, I'm not that far away from termination. But if I ever go back into therapy, I'm certainly going to look for a more broad-minded therapist."

I have also heard a significant number of stories of therapists who have actively denigrated their patients' spiritual life. This is not to say that a person's spirituality is always healthy and should never be confronted, but my impression of these cases is that the therapist involved was unable to discern between a healthy and an unhealthy spirituality.

Of even deeper concern to me, however, is a more general denigration of the humanity of psychiatric patients. Let me provide an example. I have had the unusual opportunity of seeing one schizophrenic patient roughly twice a year over the course of the past eighteen years. When I first saw her in consultation at a local clinic, she was in her early thirties, suffering from suspiciousness, frequent periods of depression and apathy, fleeting delusions, social isolation, and grave difficulty in sustaining either employment or social relations. Additionally, she demonstrated profound ambivalence, flattening of affect, and extreme social maladeptness. Shortly after I first saw her, she was placed on Social Security disability and has remained on it ever since.

When I left my consulting position at the clinic, she continued to drop by my home twice a year for a free visit of fifteen to thirty minutes. Today, at age fifty, she demonstrates all the signs of moderate, well-entrenched, chronic schizophrenia. The course of her disease over eighteen years has been consistent and stable. From a traditional psychiatric point of view, she has neither deteriorated nor made any progress whatsoever. It would be easy to regard her as a chronic lost cause. However, over the course of those years, she has moved from skepticism to a tentative interest in religion to a deep faith. She now attends Mass at least weekly. Her theology is not in the least bizarre; it is, as best I can ascertain, not only traditional and sound but quite sophisticated. In return for my extremely minor ministrations, she regularly prays for

me. I think I have, by far, the better part of the bargain. Many would regard hers as a wasted sort of life in which there has been no progress. From my point of view, while there has been no improvement in her schizophrenia or growth in her social skills, there has been immense growth in her soul. Something very profound has slowly been happening within her.

When we psychiatrists do not know how to help those with a chronic mental illness such as schizophrenia, we have a tendency to write them off. We also do this with mental retardation and, even more so, with such conditions as senility. Yet I have seen patients who have been correctly diagnosed with Alzheimer's disease who have made considerable spiritual strides in their lives since that diagnosis.

Since psychiatrists are generally unable to distinguish between a healthy and an unhealthy spirituality, they are generally unable to align themselves with a healthy one and support it. A bright spot on the horizon has been the appearance of several recent articles in the professional literature by therapists offering clinical vignettes of how their patients' treatment seemed to be clearly enhanced or speeded up by the encouragement of their seemingly healthy religious activity or spiritual belief system.

Another reason for either misdiagnosis or mistreatment or both through psychiatrists' ignorance of theology and the realm of spirituality is their failure to spot false ideas, false thinking, or, in religious terms, heresies. You may think—as I once did—that heresy is a subject properly belonging back in the days of the Inquisition or the Middle Ages, but I can assure you that heresy is very much alive and well at the end of the twentieth century and adversely affecting millions of individuals as well as society as a whole. Much heresy arises when people run with just one side of a paradox in their thinking. And heresies, being at best half-truths, are essentially lies.

Another effect of misdiagnosis or, more commonly, mistreatment resulting from the avoidance or disparagement of

spirituality has been a significant deterioration in the reputation of psychiatry and psychiatrists. The word is out. Large numbers of people steer clear of the psychotherapy that psychiatrists have to offer because they have heard of psychiatry's antipathy to spirituality. This, in turn, has encouraged the competition. Sometimes competition can be good. It is no accident that pastoral counseling has been one of the most rapidly growing career fields over the course of the past twenty-five years. The first pastoral counseling training program was established in 1948. There are now approximately two hundred such programs. Many of them, as best I can ascertain, are very good. And many pastoral counselors are doing superb work. Indeed, unless a patient has a severe psychiatric disturbance clearly suggesting pharmacotherapy in addition to psychotherapy, I am probably more likely to refer him or her to a pastoral counselor than to a psychiatrist.

But not all competition is healthy. In reaction to psychiatry's failure to deal with spiritual issues over the past decade, there has been an explosive expansion of Christian fundamentalist treatment programs, on the one hand, and what I choose to call New Age fundamentalist practitioners, on the other. I have reason to question the healthiness of this kind of competition from the fringes. But if it is unhealthy competition, it exists largely by traditional psychiatry's default.

Psychiatry's dis-ease with spirituality has also resulted in a significant failure of both research and theory. A tiny amount of research in the area of spirituality and religion has been undertaken at Harvard and a few other places, but it is minuscule compared to the need. And psychiatry is not the only villain involved. As I noted, religion has as much reluctance to subject spirituality to real research as does psychiatry.

It is hardly remarkable that where a dearth of research exists, there is also going to be a stagnation of theory. Perhaps I suffer from being out of the mainstream. From my vantage point, however, as far as I can ascertain, the most significant contributions to personality theory and psychodynamic the-

ory over the past generation have not been made by psychiatrists; they have been made by pastoral counselors, by management consultants and industrial psychologists, and by theologians and poets. Perhaps the most serious aspect of psychiatry's predicament is that by ignoring their own spirituality as individuals—and by being taught by their mentors to so ignore it—psychiatrists themselves are placing severe limitations upon their psychospiritual development.

Fifteen years ago my wife, Lily, and I had the opportunity to consult with a convent as an organization. The consultation was requested because many of the nuns were suffering from disorders which were, quite obviously, psychosomatic, and the community did not know how to deal with the situation. Over and over again, Lily and I kept saying to the twenty or so gathered together in the Mother House, "Look, you are a highly educated group of people, many of you with doctorates, who are specialists in love and healing. If any group of people ought to have the capacity to deal with each other about such issues, you should." But they didn't buy it. Over and over again, they kept rebutting, "But we're not professionals. We're not trained to discern what is physical and what is psychological, what is psychological and what is spiritual." For twenty-four hours we were at an absolute impasse, until a novice suddenly blurted out, "If I hear you correctly, what being a psychotherapist means—and doing psychotherapy—is essentially working on oneself." We exclaimed in return, "You've got it." The consultation was a success.

So I would hold that the essential characteristic of a psychiatrist's development is her, or his, capacity to work on herself. But what to work on? If she does not regard herself as being on a spiritual journey, it seems to me that the work is likely to be merely intellectual and probably arid. On the other hand, if she can accept—embrace—the idea that she is on a spiritual journey, then it is highly likely that such self-work will be rich and rewarding, not only for herself but for her patients. There are enormous ambiguities involved. For in-

stance, she may outgrow her patients. She may even leave the practice of psychiatry for strange new fields. But the overall result, I suggest, is that her journey will be more fruitful both to herself and to those she treats. Conversely, should she deny that she herself has a spiritual life, I suspect that her own development will be narrow and also that of her patients.

Although the predicament of psychiatry is, I believe, grave, the treatment of its condition could be quite simple. I would propose five therapeutic measures. If all of them were undertaken, the problem would be completely taken care of. If even one of them was taken, there would be substantial alleviation of the problem. Three of these proposed five measures would best be implemented within psychiatric residency training and, therefore, the responsibility of such residency-training program directors.

Let me begin with the simplest. I believe that in the first month of their training, all psychiatry residents should be taught to routinely take a spiritual history, just as they are now taught to routinely take a more general history and do a mental status exam.

I made this proposal once to an already spiritually oriented, sixty-year-old man who was chairman of the department of psychiatry at a major university medical center. He asked, "What on earth is a spiritual history?" I explained it was a process of asking the patient rather simple and obvious questions: "What religion were you raised in? What denomination? Are you still in that same religion? The same denomination? If not, what religion do you adhere to, and how did the change come about? Are you an atheist? An agnostic? If you are a believer, what is your notion of God? Does God seem abstract and distant, or does God seem close to you and personal? Has this changed recently? Do you pray? What is your prayer life like? Have you had any spiritual experiences? What were they? What effect did they have upon you? And so on. Six weeks later, the chairman wrote to me saying, "I took my first spiri-

tual history on a patient the other day, and it was amazing what it revealed."

This is such a simple and obvious remedy we must wonder why it wasn't adopted years ago. But again we are confronted with the extraordinary reluctance of psychiatry to relate to spiritual issues. Do these questions seem too intimate? Have psychiatrists thought they would be too threatening to their patients? The fact of the matter is that such questions are not the least bit threatening to patients. They appreciate being asked and like to answer them. I believe the people who have been threatened are the psychiatrists. As well as improving psychiatric diagnosis and psychotherapeutic treatment, it is possible that this simple remedy of routinely taking a spiritual history might make psychiatrists themselves aware that they have their own spiritual life.

My second recommendation would be that during the course of their three years of training—preferably during the first year—psychiatric residents be taught about the different stages of religious growth or spiritual development. Perhaps only one lecture would be required. A simple synopsis of the work of James Fowler would be sufficient reading. Additionally, however, they should be taught some of the factors that might fixate people in immature or self-destructive spiritual stages—factors that are not necessarily different from those that fixate people in more standardly recognized psychosexual stages.

A major effect of such simple training and teaching would be not only to improve the psychiatrist's diagnostic capacity but also to make him aware that spirituality is something that does develop. And that while he may already have come a good way in his own spiritual life, he may still have a way to go. I believe that this training and awareness would contribute enormously to the ongoing maturation of psychotherapists.

My third recommendation is that during the three years of their training, psychiatry residents receive at least one lecture on the nature of heresy, false ideas, and false assump-

tions. I believe the more they familiarize themselves with theology, the more adept they will be at spotting such heresies or lies.

My fourth proposal is a task for the formulators of revisions to *DSM III* (*Diagnostic and Statistical Manual of Mental Disorders III*) or other future manuals. This proposal is in two parts. First, I suggest that there are at least two new diagnoses of mental disorders that need to be seriously considered for incorporation into the *DSM*. One is the diagnostic category of people whom I have labeled as evil, or people of the lie. One man has recently taken up my own work in this regard and devoted his doctoral dissertation to arguing on behalf of a diagnostic category he entitled "virulent personality disorder." I believe his thesis is compelling and the label appropriate. I further believe that serious consideration needs to be given to the diagnosis of possession, with criteria for distinguishing between it and multiple-personality disorder as well as other conditions (with the understanding that it is possible for a patient to suffer from both multiple-personality disorder and possession).

In addition to these new diagnostic categories, I also believe that consideration should be given to establishing a spiritual axis to our diagnoses, an axis along which the patient's stage of spiritual development would be assessed, along with other spiritual factors—ascertained from a discerning spiritual history—that are relevant to his condition and primary diagnosis.

Finally, there is the matter of research. Some research, such as my proposal for an Institute for the Scientific Study of Deliverance, could best be performed under the aegis of a specific, separately funded institute, preferably in conjunction with a university. For instance, among other things, such an institute could serve as an archive and repository for videotapes of exorcisms which students and researchers could see, but only under constraints guaranteeing the confidentiality of such materials. Most research, however, could be done within

existing academic departments of psychiatry, focusing on smaller projects. Were psychiatry to enter into the field of spiritual research, I believe we would witness a most exciting and badly needed renaissance of personality theory.

All these proposals could be quite simple in their implementation. The big question is the *will* to implement them. The treatment of psychiatry's predicament is simple, but is the patient willing? I am convinced the treatment would already have been successfully effected had the patient been willing in the past. Consequently, it seems very clear to me that the kind of treatment I have proposed will be implemented only if psychiatry undergoes a change of attitude toward its own therapy in this regard. Is American psychiatry going to change from a position of disinterest in and resistance to issues of human spirituality to a position of openness and vivacious curiosity?

That question can be answered only by psychiatrists themselves. As such, they are agents of history. American psychiatry has had enormous influence upon the entire intellectual life of our civilization. I do not decry the current medical model as long as it is broad-minded and broadly defined. Over the past generation, however, in running with a medical model that has been remarkably one-dimensional and almost purely materialistic, psychiatrists have increasingly backed themselves into a corner where they are expected to function as mere pill pushers and to leave a deep understanding of the human condition to the theologians and pastoral counselors. Perhaps psychiatry will even decide to get out of the psychotherapy business entirely. Perhaps that would be the proper course. I don't really know. But I do know that psychiatry's influence upon the intellectual life of our civilization is waning.

As a psychiatrist myself, who sees great value in the medical model, who has glimpsed the great beauty of the realm of microscopic anatomy, but who has also personally grown enormously from my frequently blind efforts in the field of

psychotherapy, I hope the members of my profession will undergo the historic attitude change I have proposed. I hope that as they deliberate within the depths of their souls as well as their minds, they will choose the role of change by no longer being embarrassed by their own spirituality and by proclaiming humans to be spiritual beings to whom psychiatry can offer not only biochemical adjustment but also at least some measure of spiritual sustenance.

About the Author

M. Scott Peck, M.D., is a psychiatrist, diagnostician, management consultant, best-selling author, and a founder of the Foundation for Community Encouragement. He lives in northwestern Connecticut.

THOMAS CRANE PUBLIC LIBRARY
3 1641 0082 8296 8

2009

ABOUT THE TYPE

This book was set in Bembo, a typeface based on an old-style Roman face that was used for Cardinal Bembo's tract *De Aetna* in 1495. Bembo was cut by Francisco Griffo in the early sixteenth century. The Lanston Monotype Machine Company of Philadelphia brought the well-proportioned letter forms of Bembo to the United States in the 1930s.

ABOUT THE AUTHOR

Throughout her several careers—as television producer and performing personality, as motion picture and Broadway actress, FANNIE FLAGG has been, first and last, in spirit and in practice, a writer. She began writing for, and later appearing in, *Candid Camera* segments. In films, she acted in *Five Easy Pieces,* with Jack Nicholson; *Stay Hungry;* and, most recently, *Crazy in Alabama,* with Melanie Griffith.

For the theater, she did *Come Back to the Five and Dime, Jimmy Dean, Jimmy Dean,* and played the lead role in *The Best Little Whorehouse in Texas.*

Her first novel, originally published as *Coming Attractions,* later republished as *Daisy Fay and the Miracle Man,* was on the *New York Times* paperback bestseller list for ten weeks, and her second, the beloved *Fried Green Tomatoes at the Whistle Stop Cafe,* was on that list for thirty-six weeks. Produced by Universal as a feature film with Kathy Bates, Jessica Tandy, and a distinguished cast, Flagg's script was nominated for an Academy Award and a Writers Guild of America Award. It won the prized Scripters Award from her peers. She was also nominated for a Grammy for her reading of the audio version. Her third novel, the bestselling *Welcome to the World, Baby Girl!,* was a triumphant success in its hardcover as well as paperback editions, and was named a *New York Times* Notable Book.

She lives in California and in Alabama.